WELCOME TO ST. HELL

LEWIS HANCOX

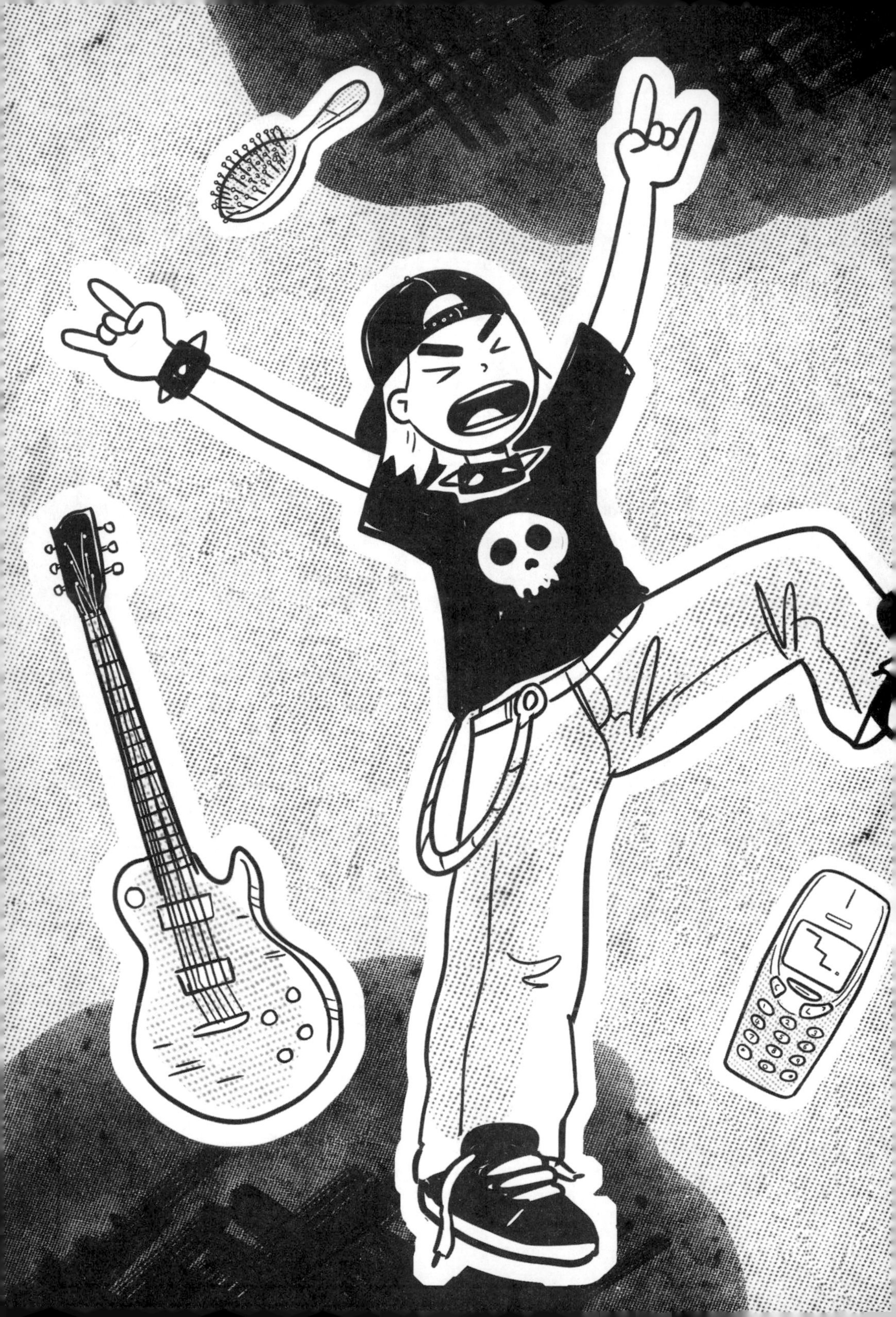

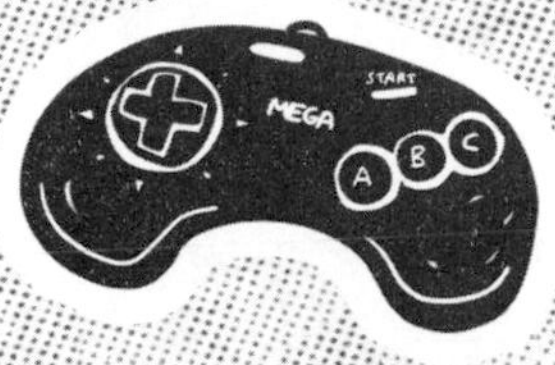
START
MEGA
A
B
C

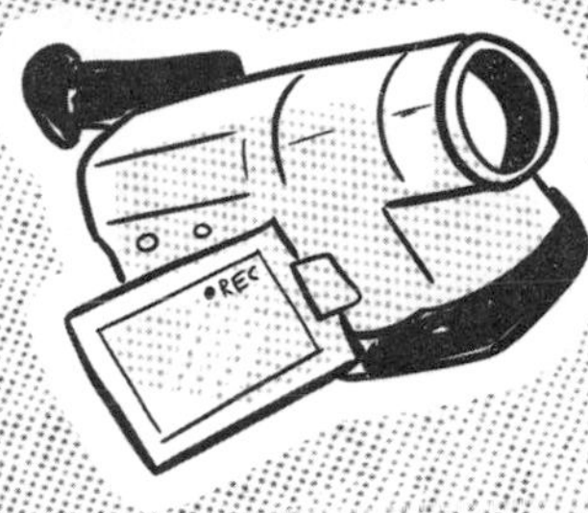
●REC

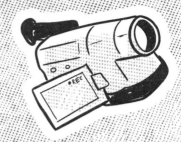

WELCOME TO ST. HELL

LEWIS HANCOX

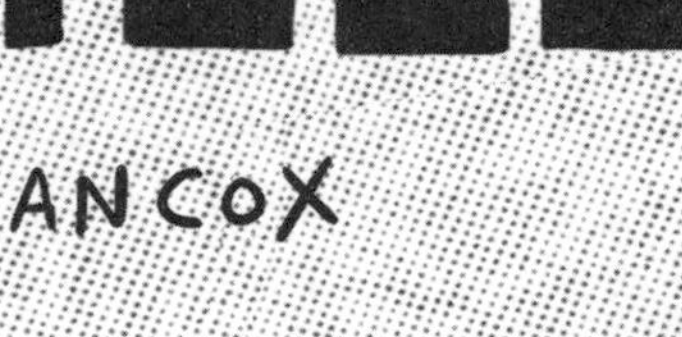

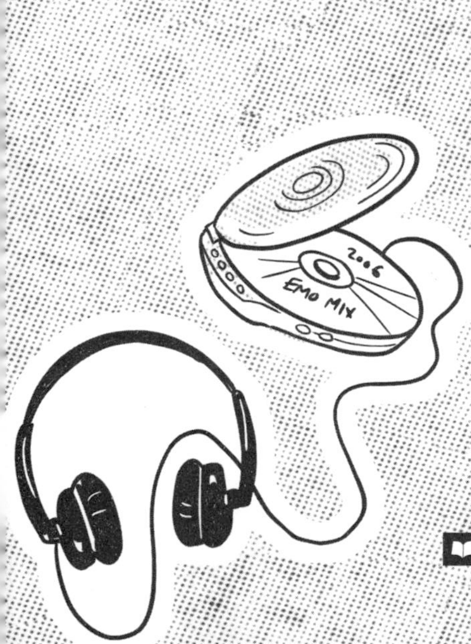
2006
EMO MIX

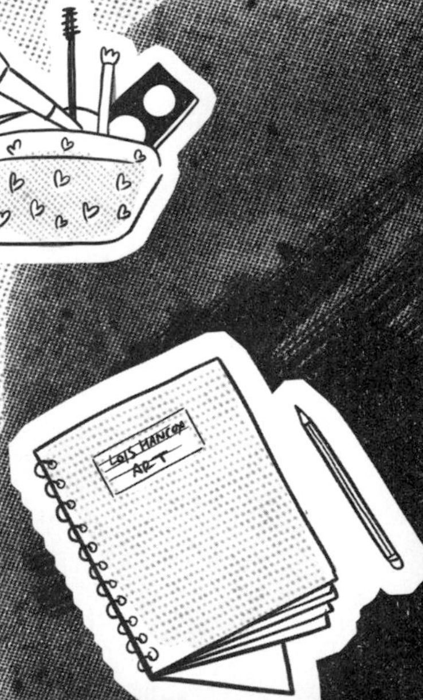
LOIS HANCOX
ART

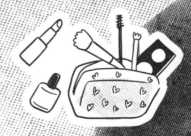

graphix
An Imprint of
SCHOLASTIC

Copyright © 2022 by Lewis Hancox

All rights reserved. Published by Graphix, an imprint of
Scholastic Inc., *Publishers since 1920.* SCHOLASTIC, GRAPHIX,
and associated logos are trademarks and/or registered trademarks
of Scholastic Inc.

Library of Congress Cataloging-in-Publication Data available

ISBN 978-1-338-82444-5 (hardcover)
ISBN 978-1-338-82443-8 (paperback)

10 9 8 7 6 5 4 3 2 1   22 23 24 25 26

Printed in the U.S.A.   40
First edition, June 2022

Edited by David Levithan
Book design by Carina Taylor
Creative Director: Phil Falco
Publisher: David Saylor

TO MY GRANDAD.
FOR EVERY COMIC YOU BOUGHT ME
AS A KID, NOW I HAVE MY OWN!
MISS YOU EVERY DAY, GRAMPS.

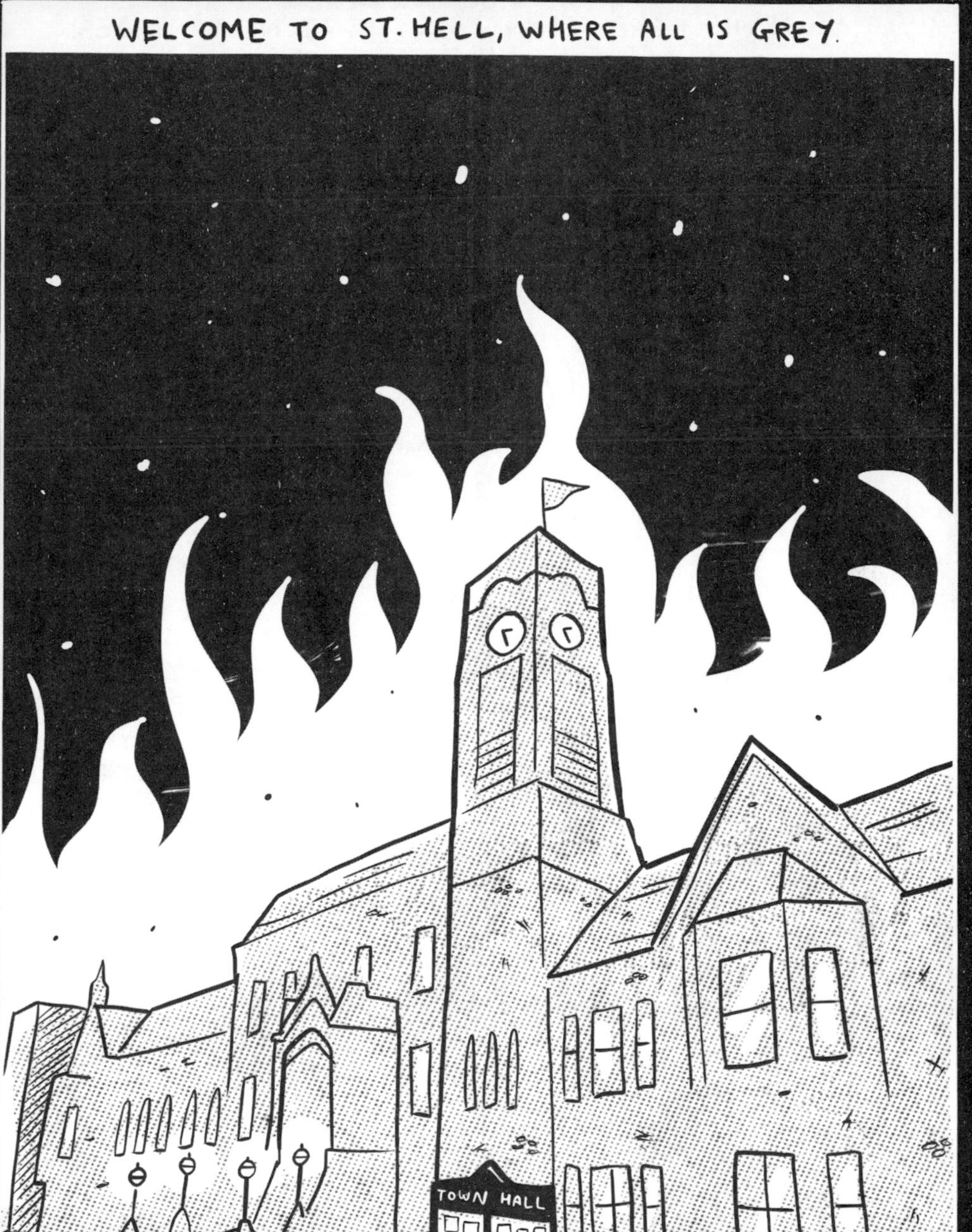
WELCOME TO ST. HELL, WHERE ALL IS GREY.
TOWN HALL

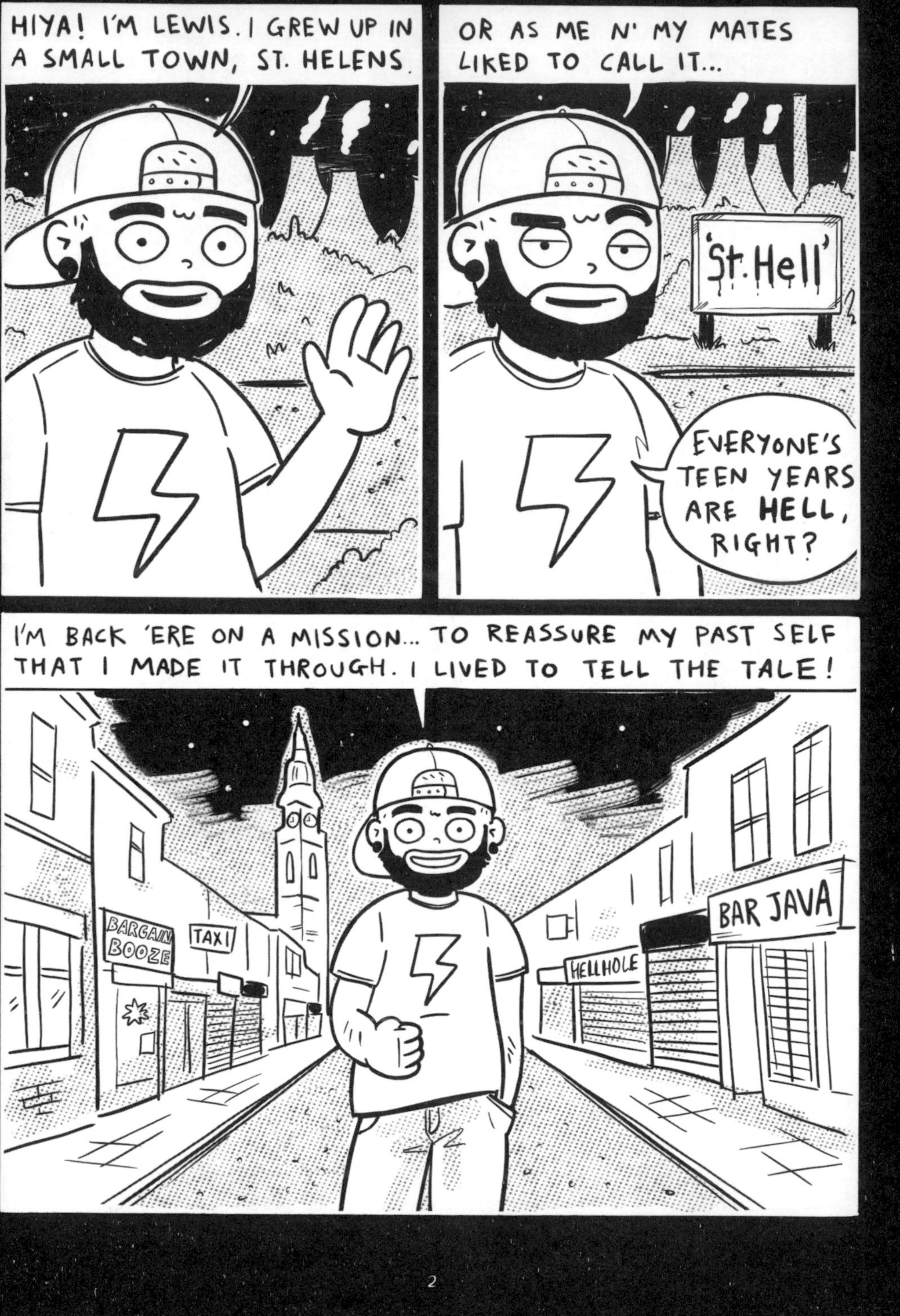
HIYA! I'M LEWIS. I GREW UP IN A SMALL TOWN, ST. HELENS.
OR AS ME N' MY MATES LIKED TO CALL IT...
'St. Hell'
EVERYONE'S TEEN YEARS ARE **HELL**, RIGHT?
I'M BACK 'ERE ON A MISSION... TO REASSURE MY PAST SELF THAT I MADE IT THROUGH. I LIVED TO TELL THE TALE!
BARGAIN BOOZE
TAXI
HELLHOLE
BAR JAVA

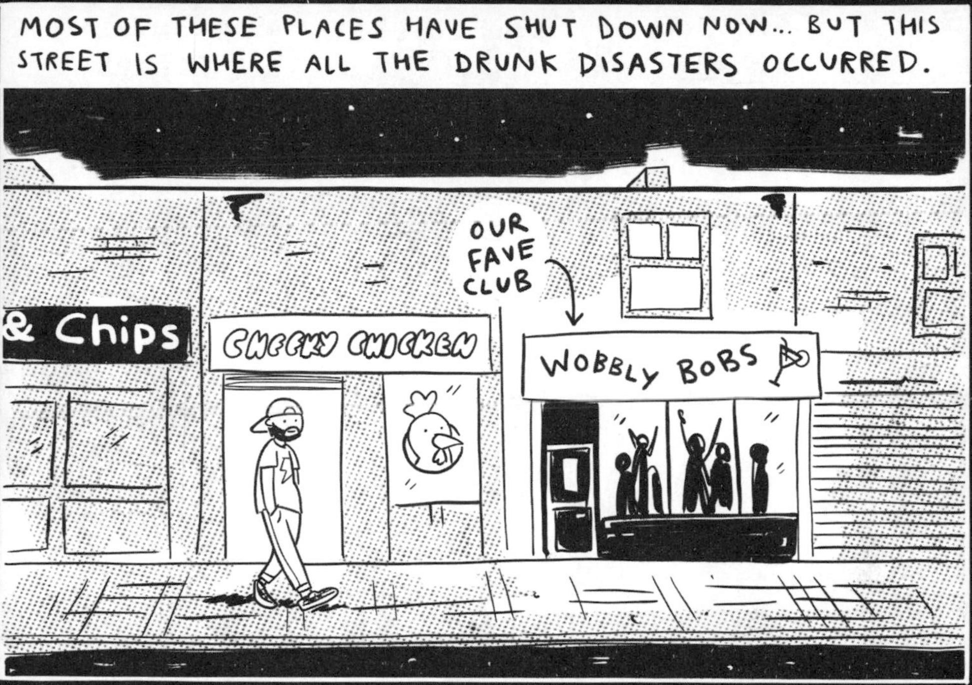
MOST OF THESE PLACES HAVE SHUT DOWN NOW... BUT THIS STREET IS WHERE ALL THE DRUNK DISASTERS OCCURRED.
OUR FAVE CLUB
& Chips
CHEEKY CHICKEN
WOBBLY BOBS

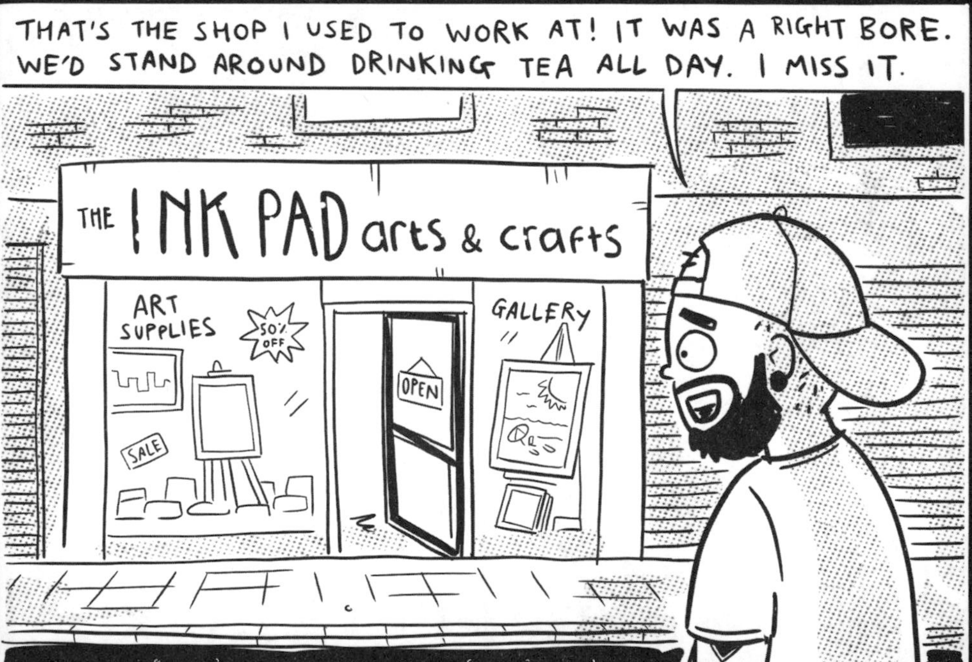
THAT'S THE SHOP I USED TO WORK AT! IT WAS A RIGHT BORE. WE'D STAND AROUND DRINKING TEA ALL DAY. I MISS IT.
THE INK PAD arts & crafts
ART SUPPLIES
50% OFF
SALE
OPEN
GALLERY

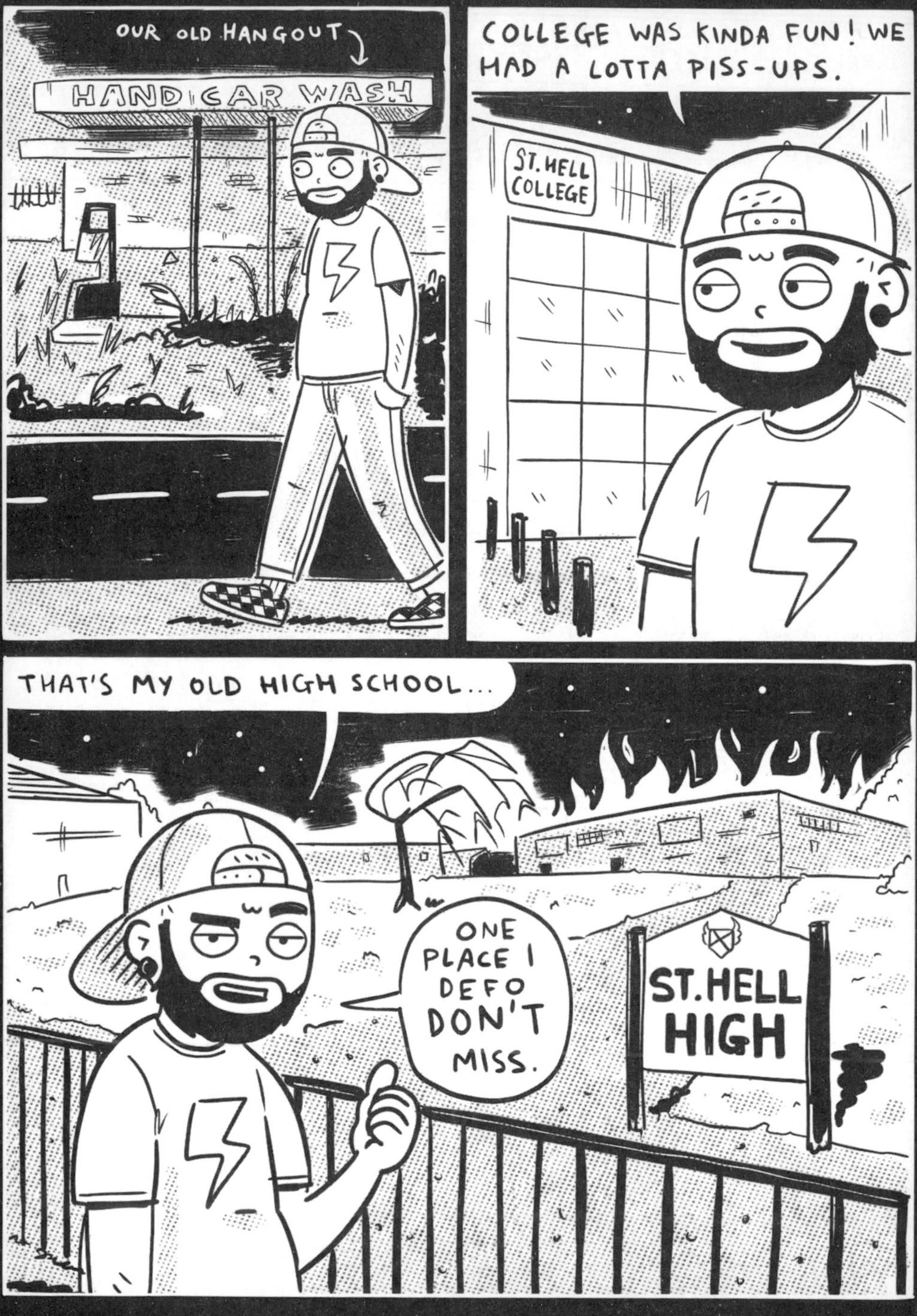
OUR OLD HANGOUT
HAND CAR WASH
COLLEGE WAS KINDA FUN! WE HAD A LOTTA PISS-UPS.
ST. HELL COLLEGE
THAT'S MY OLD HIGH SCHOOL...
ONE PLACE I DEFO DON'T MISS.
ST. HELL HIGH

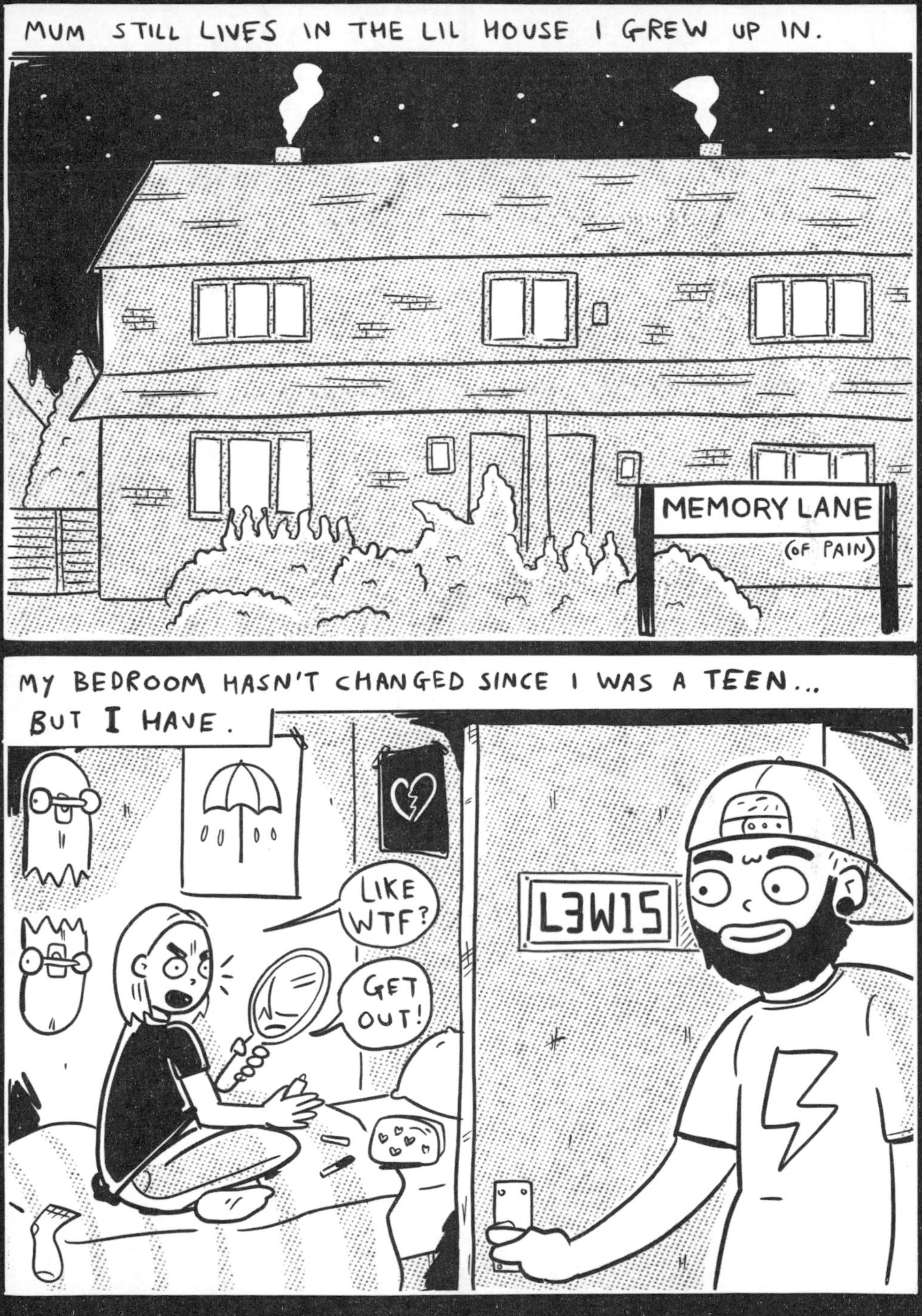
MUM STILL LIVES IN THE LIL HOUSE I GREW UP IN.
MEMORY LANE
(OF PAIN)
MY BEDROOM HASN'T CHANGED SINCE I WAS A TEEN...
BUT I HAVE.
LIKE WTF?
GET OUT!
L3W15

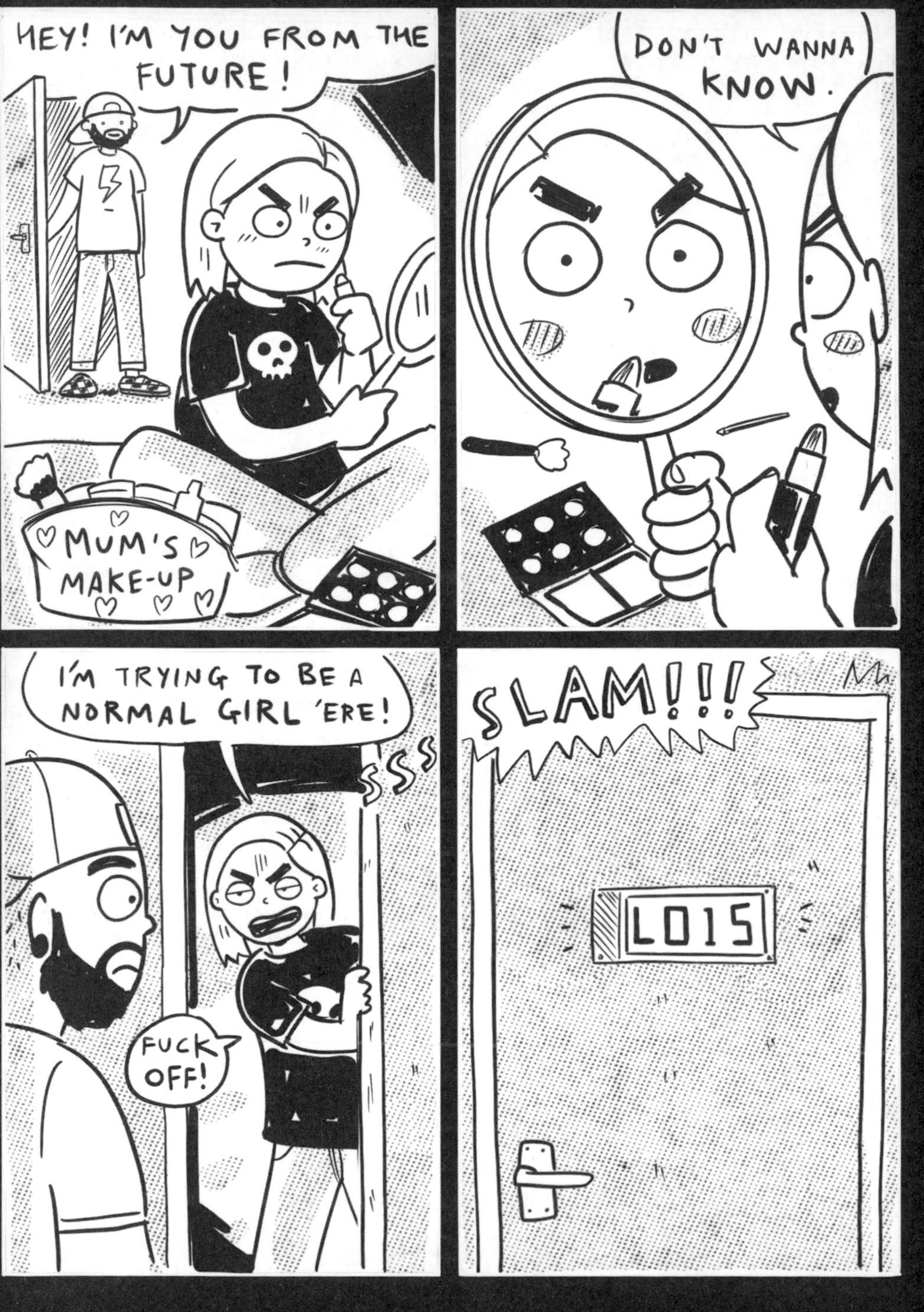

HEY! I'M YOU FROM THE FUTURE!
MUM'S MAKE-UP
DON'T WANNA KNOW.
I'M TRYING TO BE A NORMAL GIRL 'ERE!
SSS
FUCK OFF!
SLAM!!!
LOIS

PART ONE:
BOY PROBLEMS

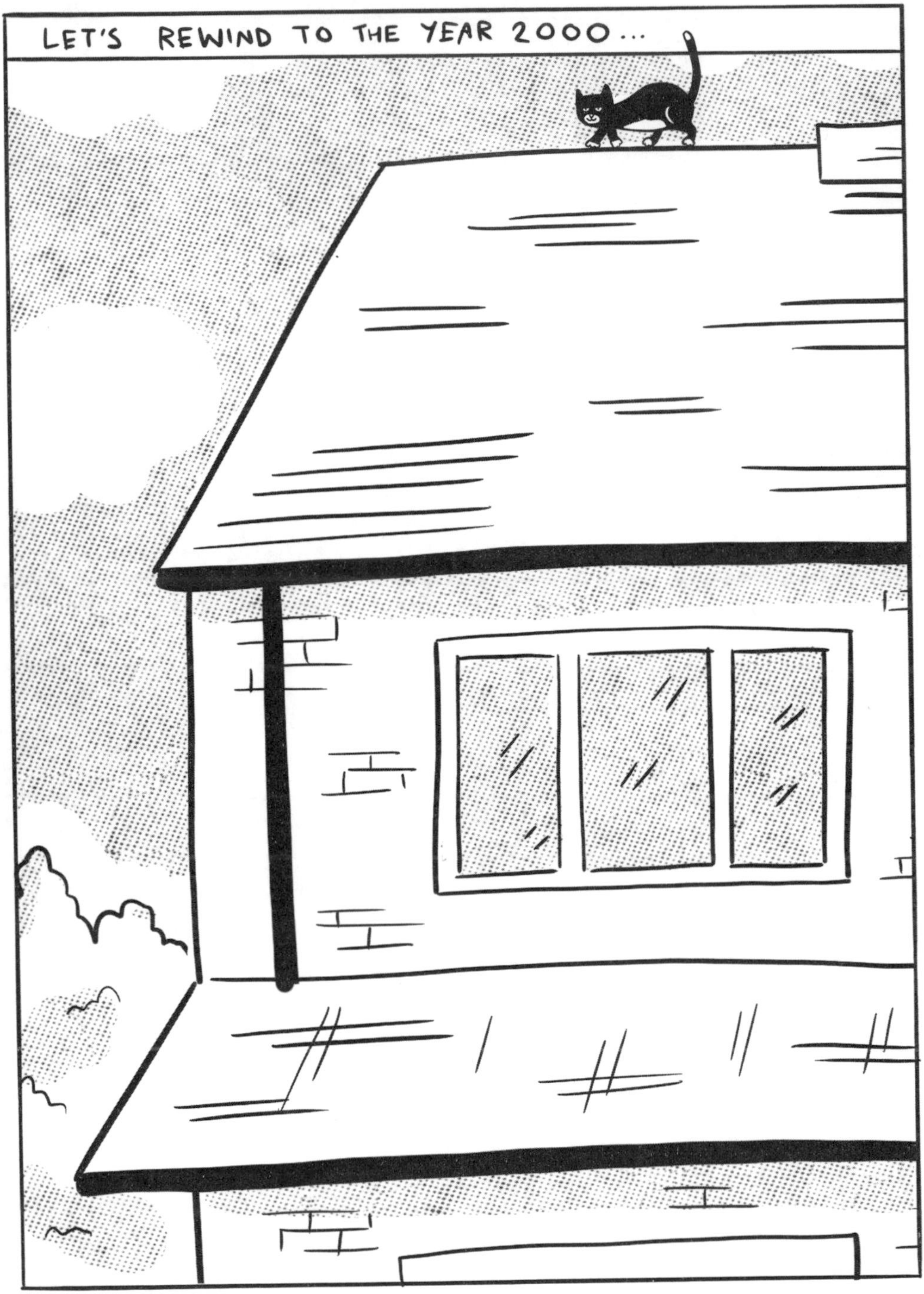
LET'S REWIND TO THE YEAR 2000...

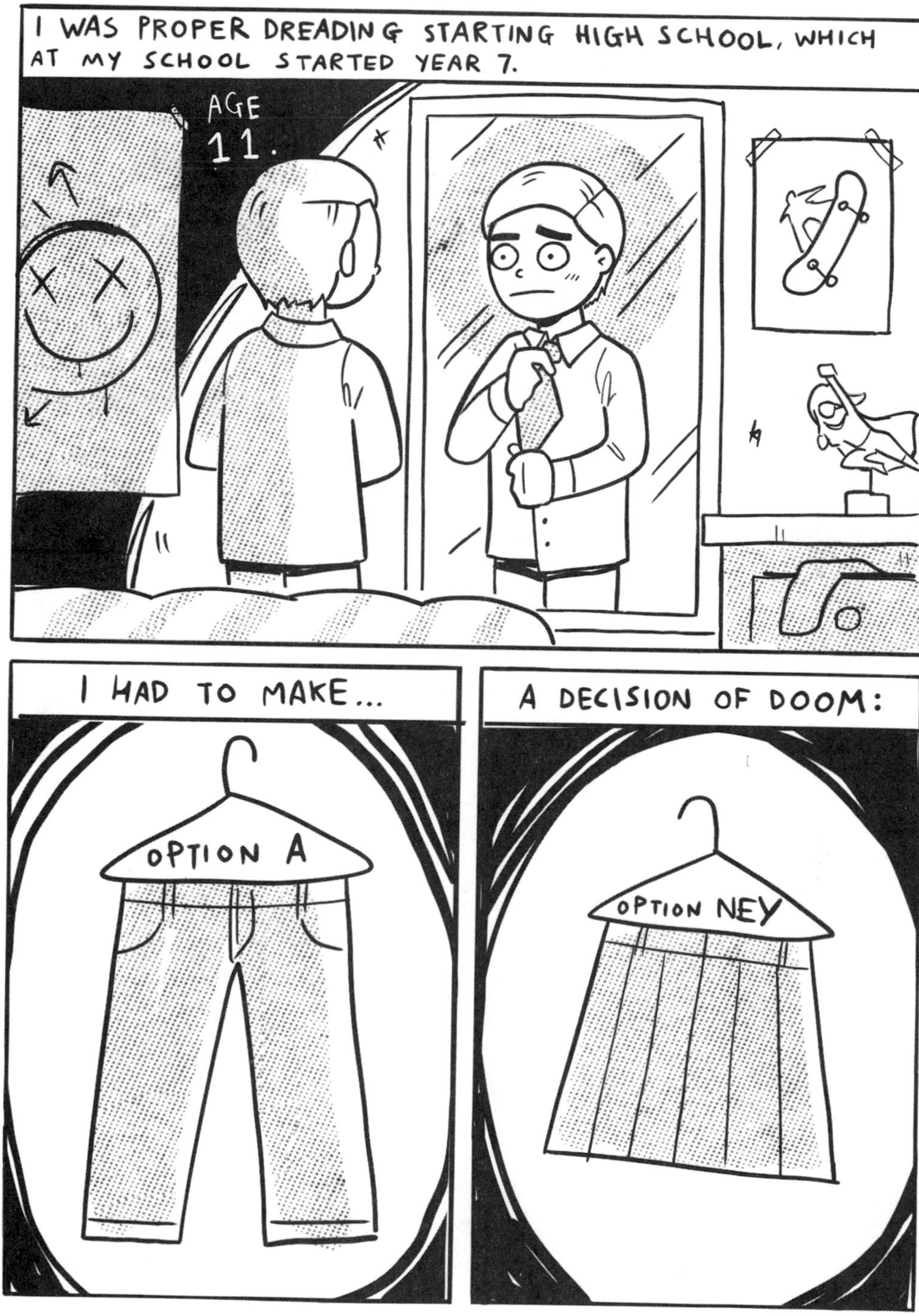
I WAS PROPER DREADING STARTING HIGH SCHOOL, WHICH AT MY SCHOOL STARTED YEAR 7.
AGE 11.
I HAD TO MAKE...
OPTION A
A DECISION OF DOOM:
OPTION NEY

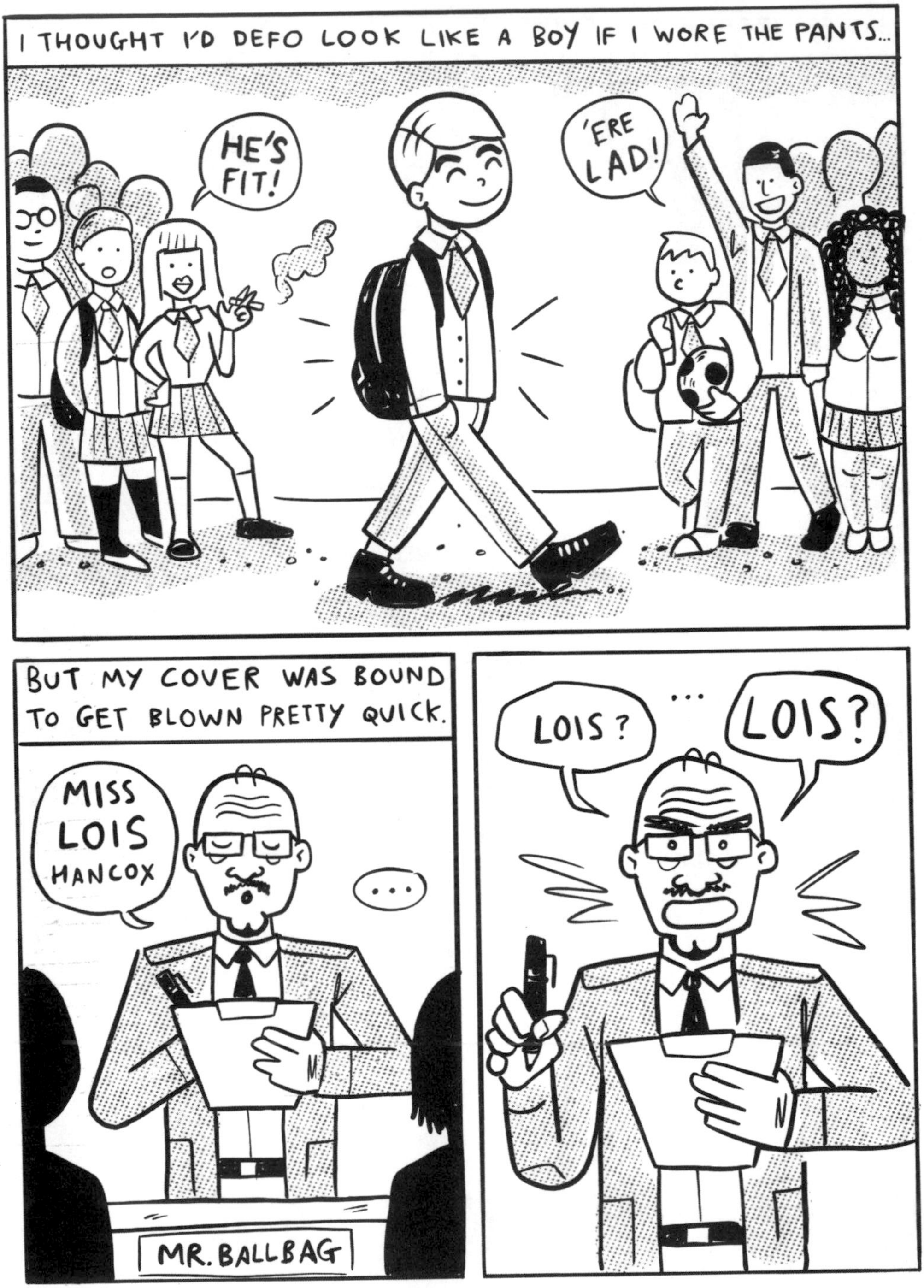
I THOUGHT I'D DEFO LOOK LIKE A BOY IF I WORE THE PANTS...
HE'S FIT!
'ERE LAD!
BUT MY COVER WAS BOUND TO GET BLOWN PRETTY QUICK.
MISS LOIS HANCOX
...
MR. BALLBAG
LOIS?
...
LOIS?

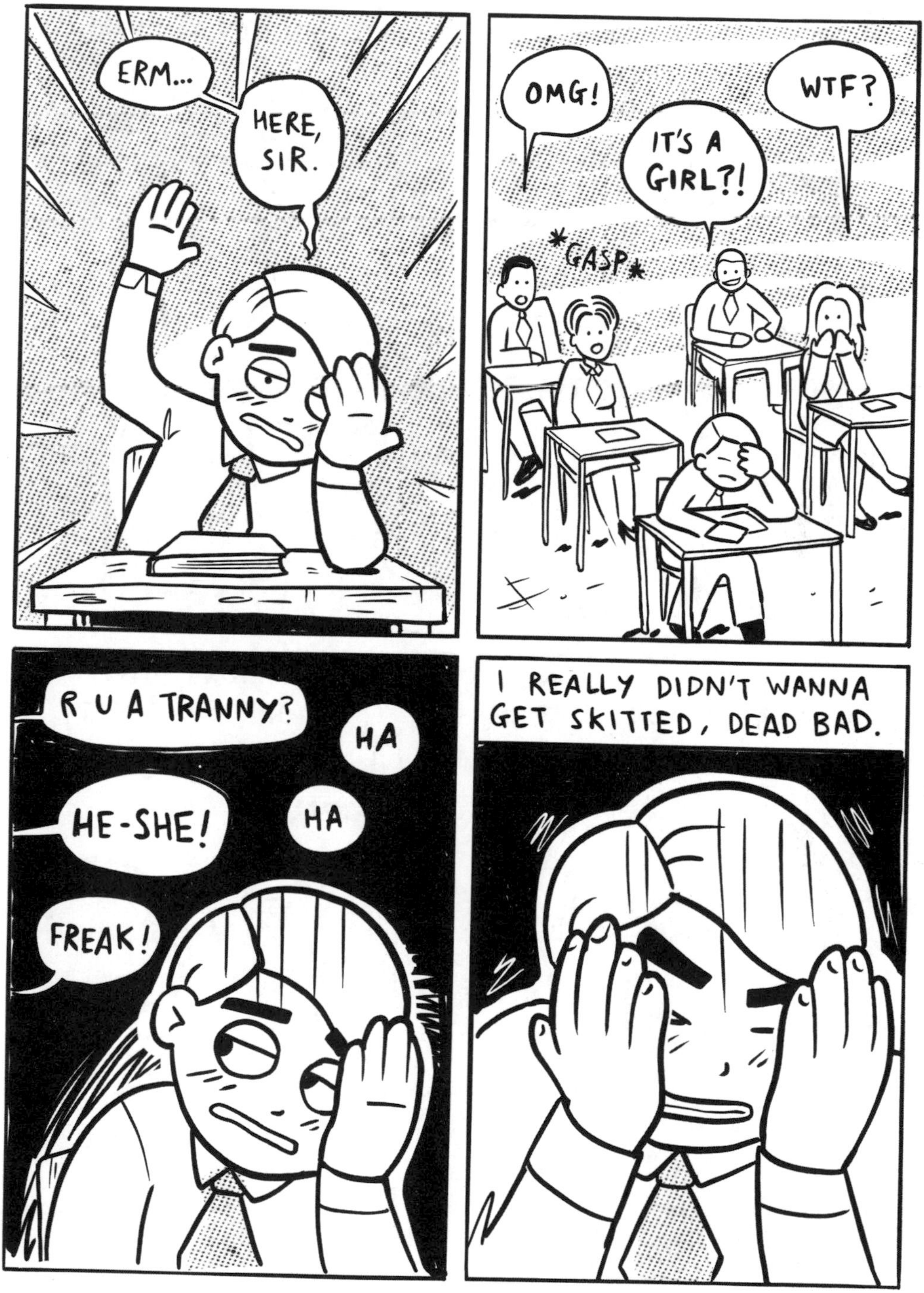
ERM...
HERE, SIR.
OMG!
IT'S A GIRL?!
WTF?
GASP
R U A TRANNY?
HA
HE-SHE!
HA
FREAK!
I REALLY DIDN'T WANNA GET SKITTED, DEAD BAD.

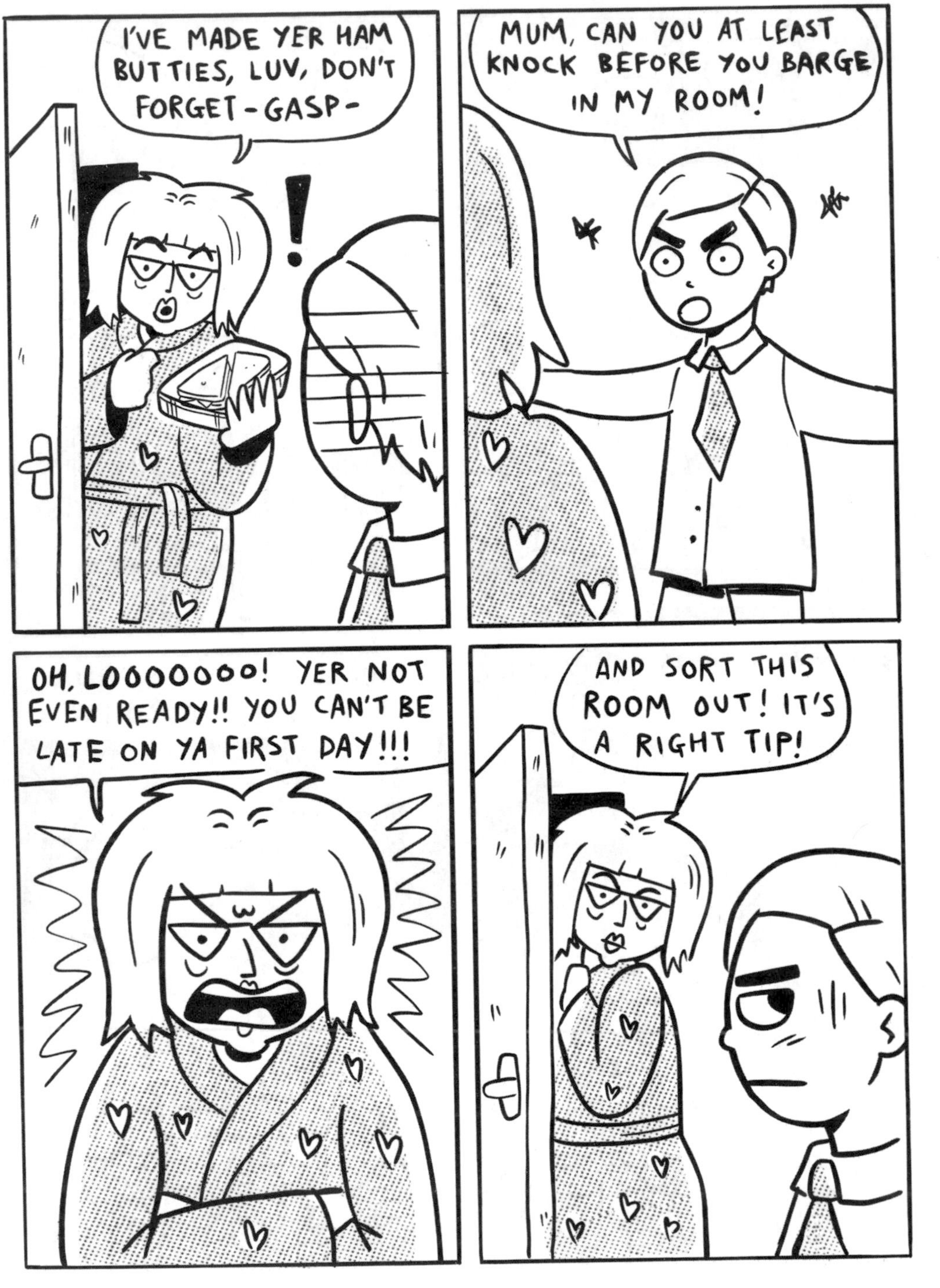
I'VE MADE YER HAM BUTTIES, LUV, DON'T FORGET-GASP-
!
MUM, CAN YOU AT LEAST KNOCK BEFORE YOU BARGE IN MY ROOM!
OH, LOOOOOOO! YER NOT EVEN READY!! YOU CAN'T BE LATE ON YA FIRST DAY!!!
AND SORT THIS ROOM OUT! IT'S A RIGHT TIP!

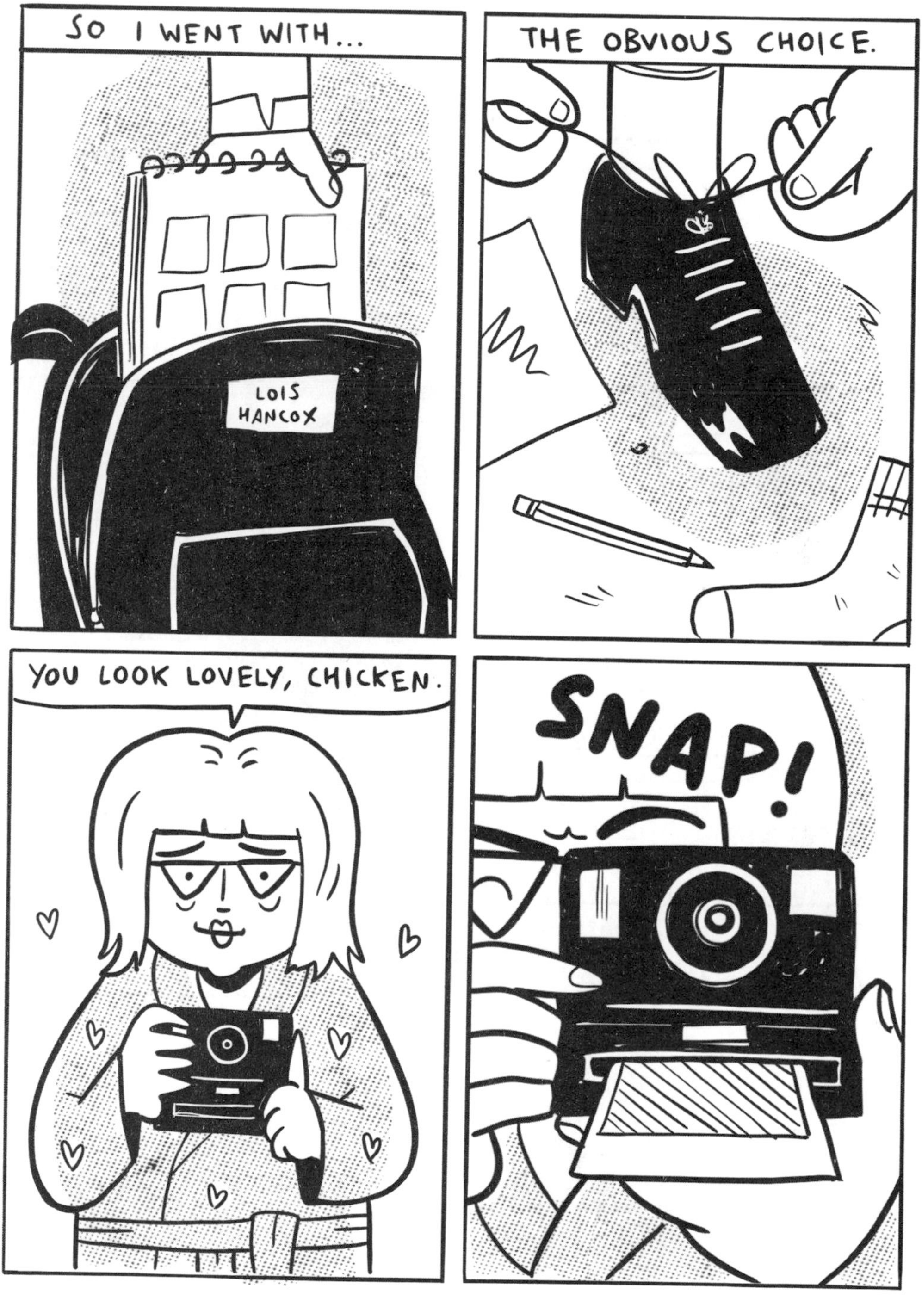
SO I WENT WITH...
LOIS HANCOX
THE OBVIOUS CHOICE.
YOU LOOK LOVELY, CHICKEN.
SNAP!

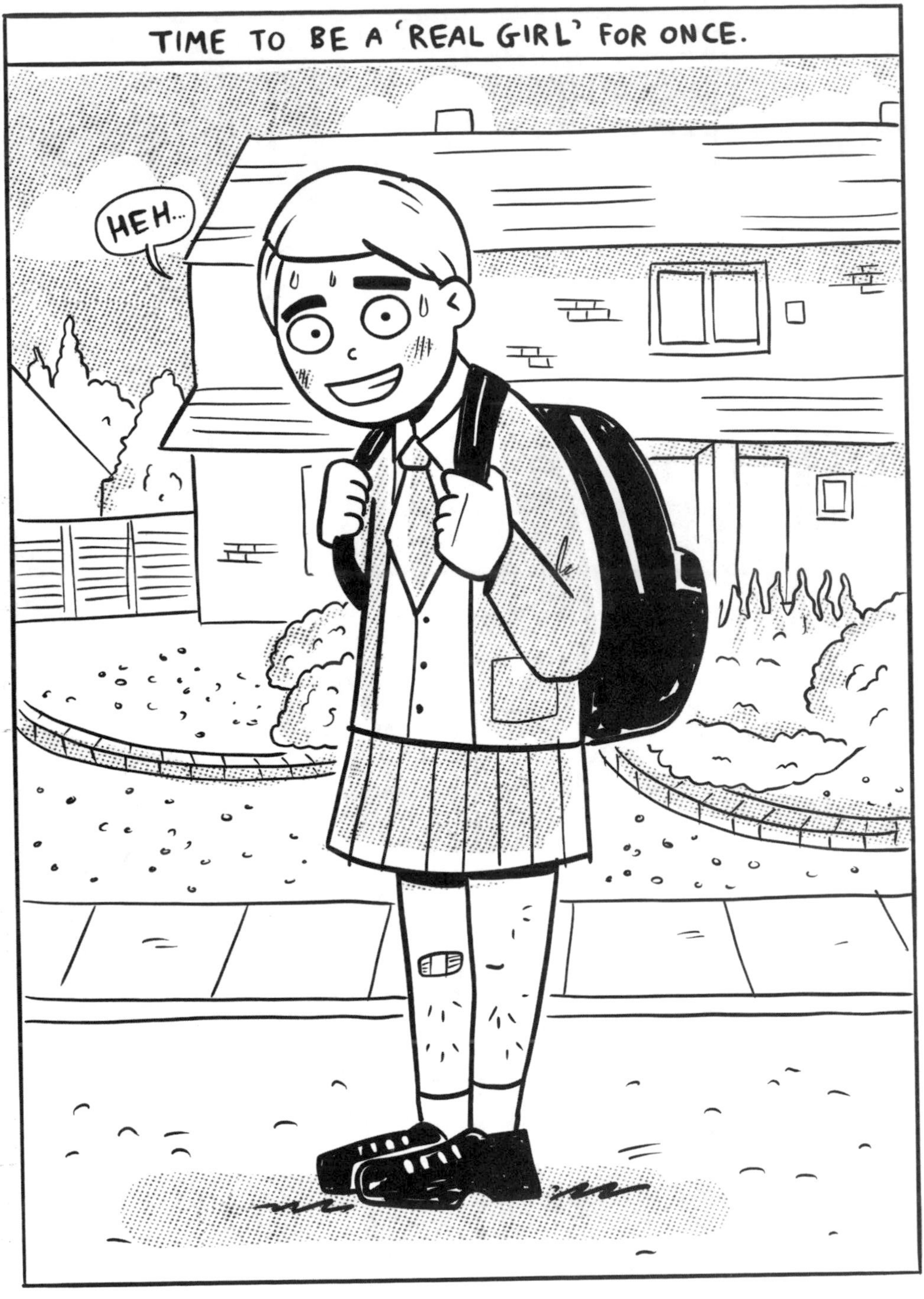
TIME TO BE A 'REAL GIRL' FOR ONCE.
HEH...

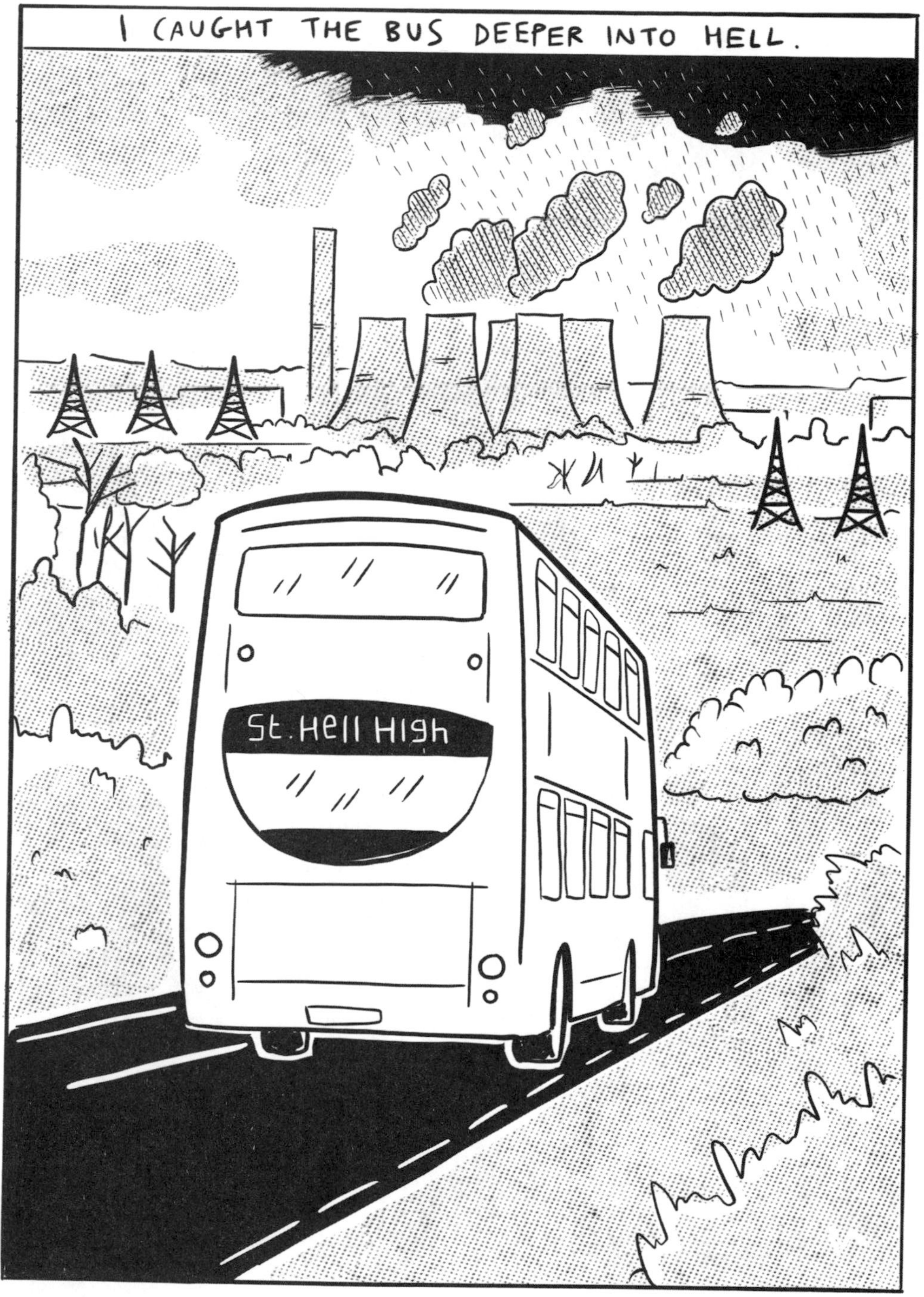
I CAUGHT THE BUS DEEPER INTO HELL.
St. Hell High

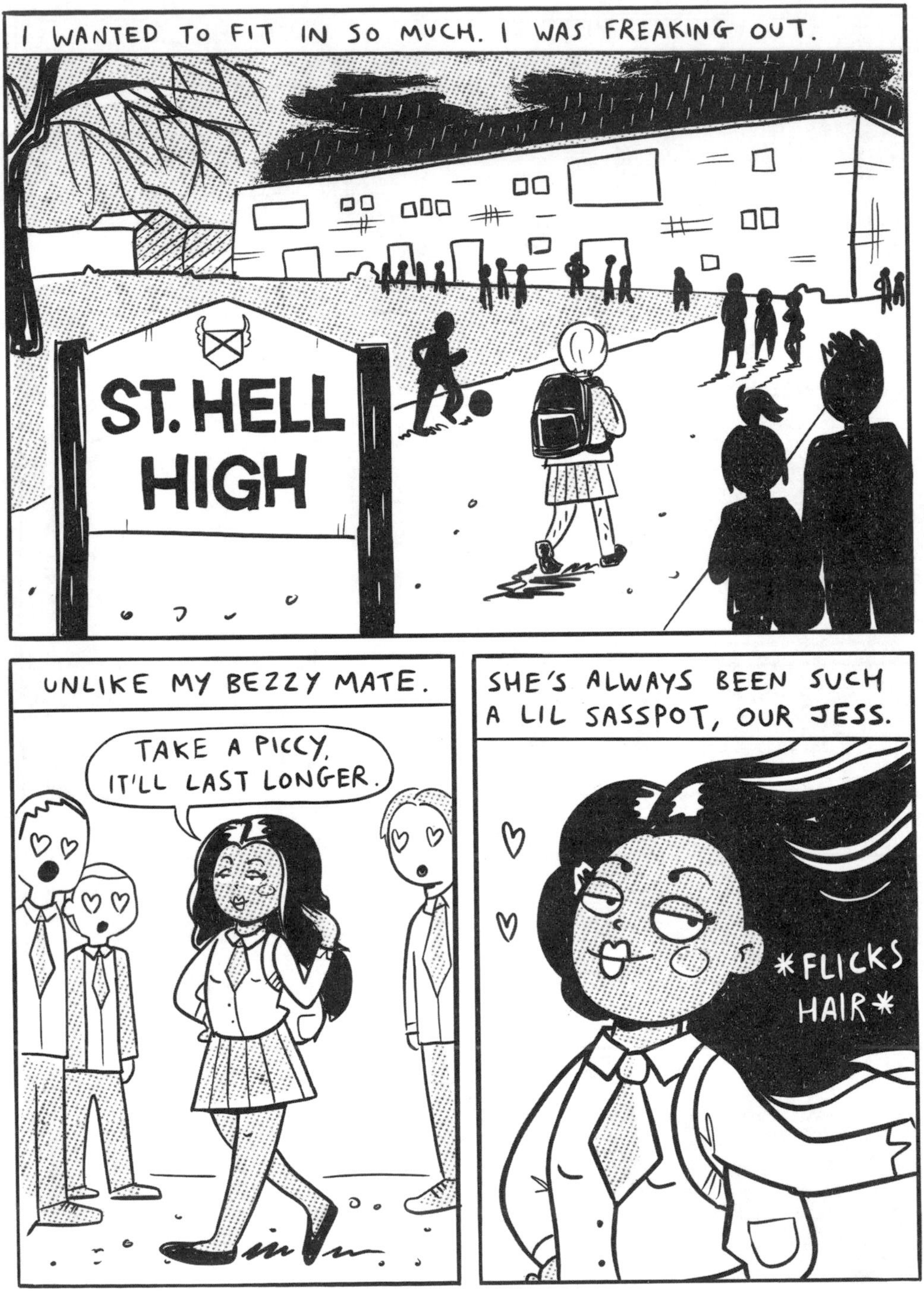
I WANTED TO FIT IN SO MUCH. I WAS FREAKING OUT.
ST. HELL HIGH
UNLIKE MY BEZZY MATE.
TAKE A PICCY, IT'LL LAST LONGER.
SHE'S ALWAYS BEEN SUCH A LIL SASSPOT, OUR JESS.
FLICKS HAIR

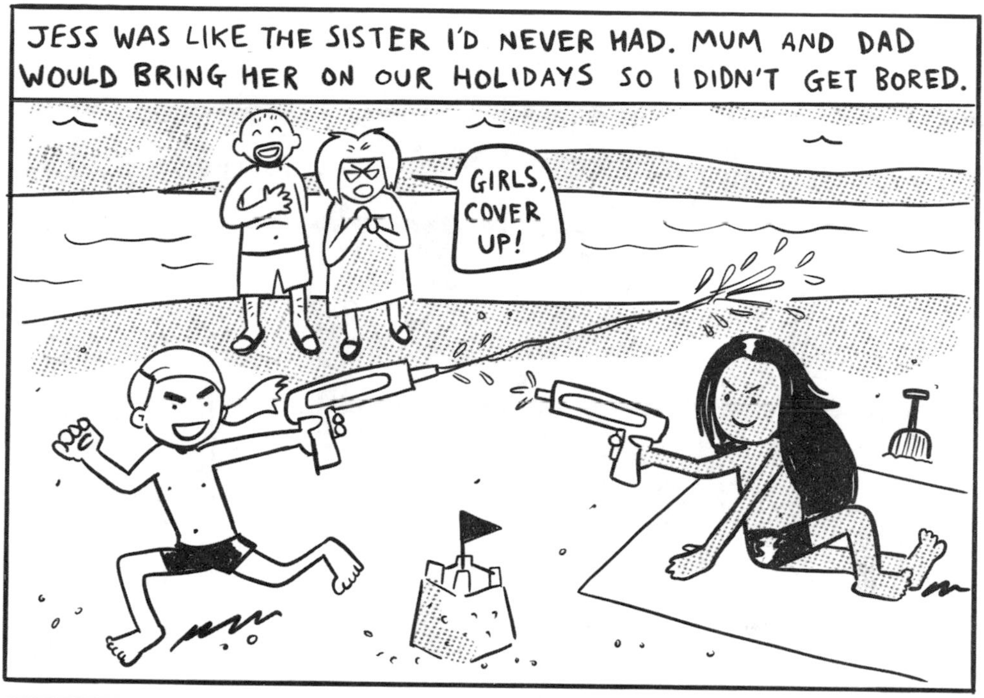
JESS WAS LIKE THE SISTER I'D NEVER HAD. MUM AND DAD WOULD BRING HER ON OUR HOLIDAYS SO I DIDN'T GET BORED.
GIRLS, COVER UP!

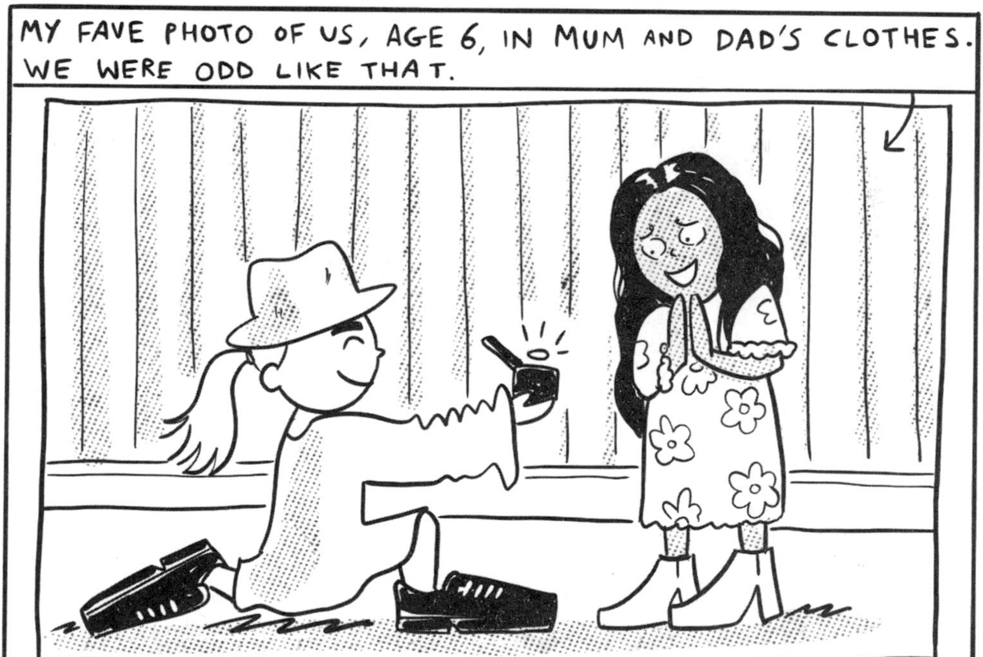
MY FAVE PHOTO OF US, AGE 6, IN MUM AND DAD'S CLOTHES. WE WERE ODD LIKE THAT.

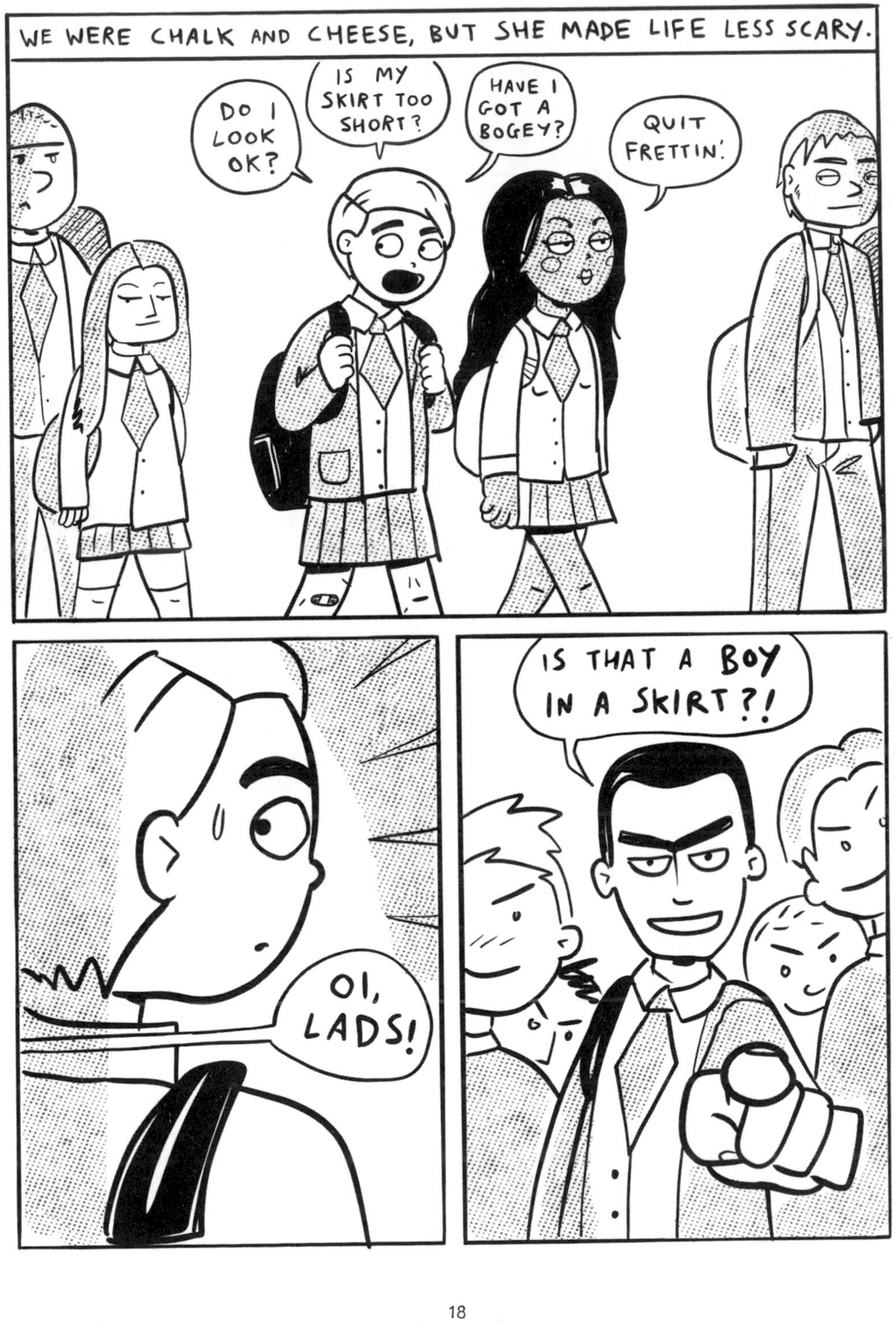
WE WERE CHALK AND CHEESE, BUT SHE MADE LIFE LESS SCARY.
DO I LOOK OK?
IS MY SKIRT TOO SHORT?
HAVE I GOT A BOGEY?
QUIT FRETTIN'.
OI, LADS!
IS THAT A BOY IN A SKIRT?!

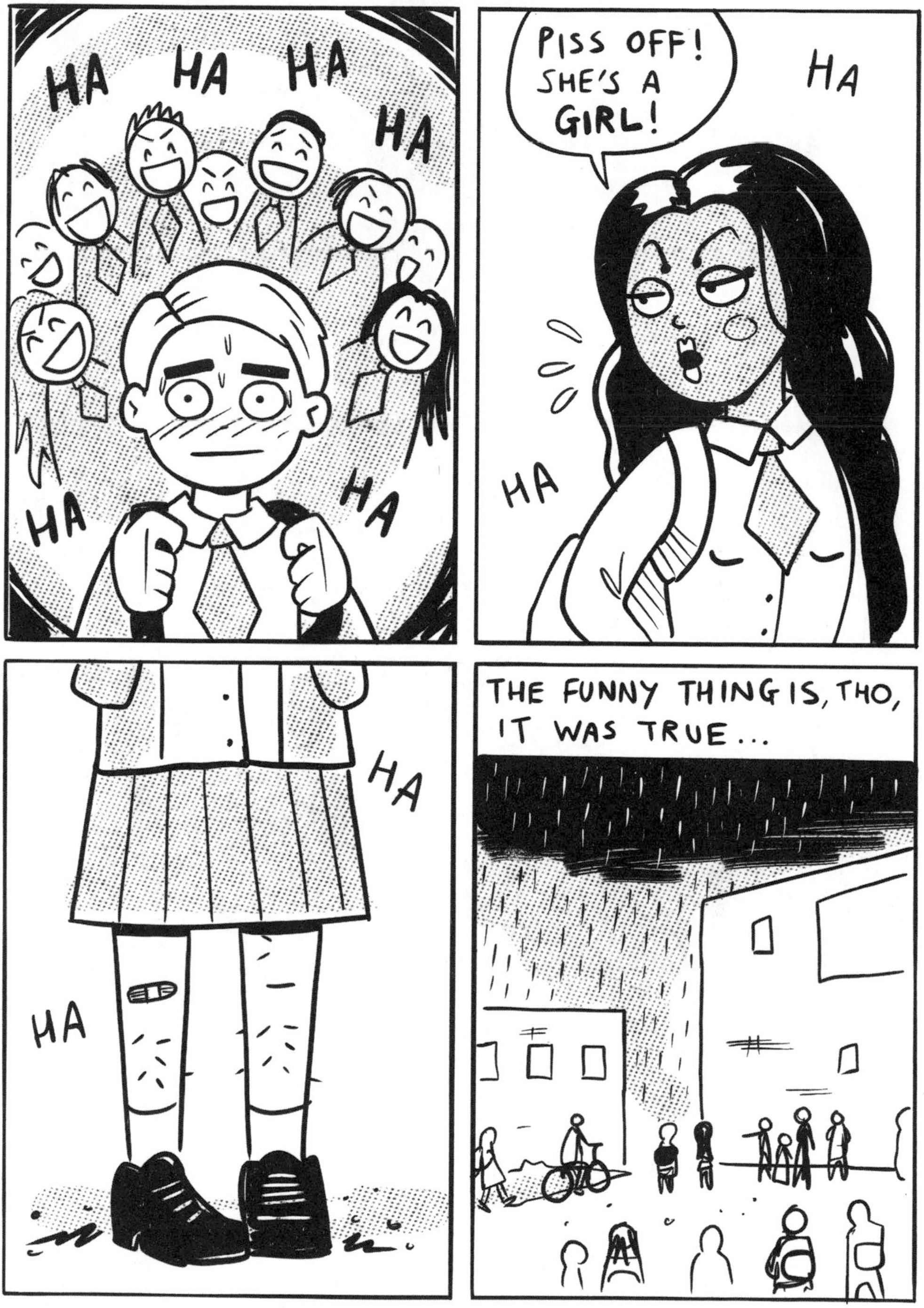
HA HA HA
HA
HA
HA
PISS OFF! SHE'S A GIRL!
HA
HA
HA
HA
THE FUNNY THING IS, THO, IT WAS TRUE...

I WAS A BOY IN A SKIRT.

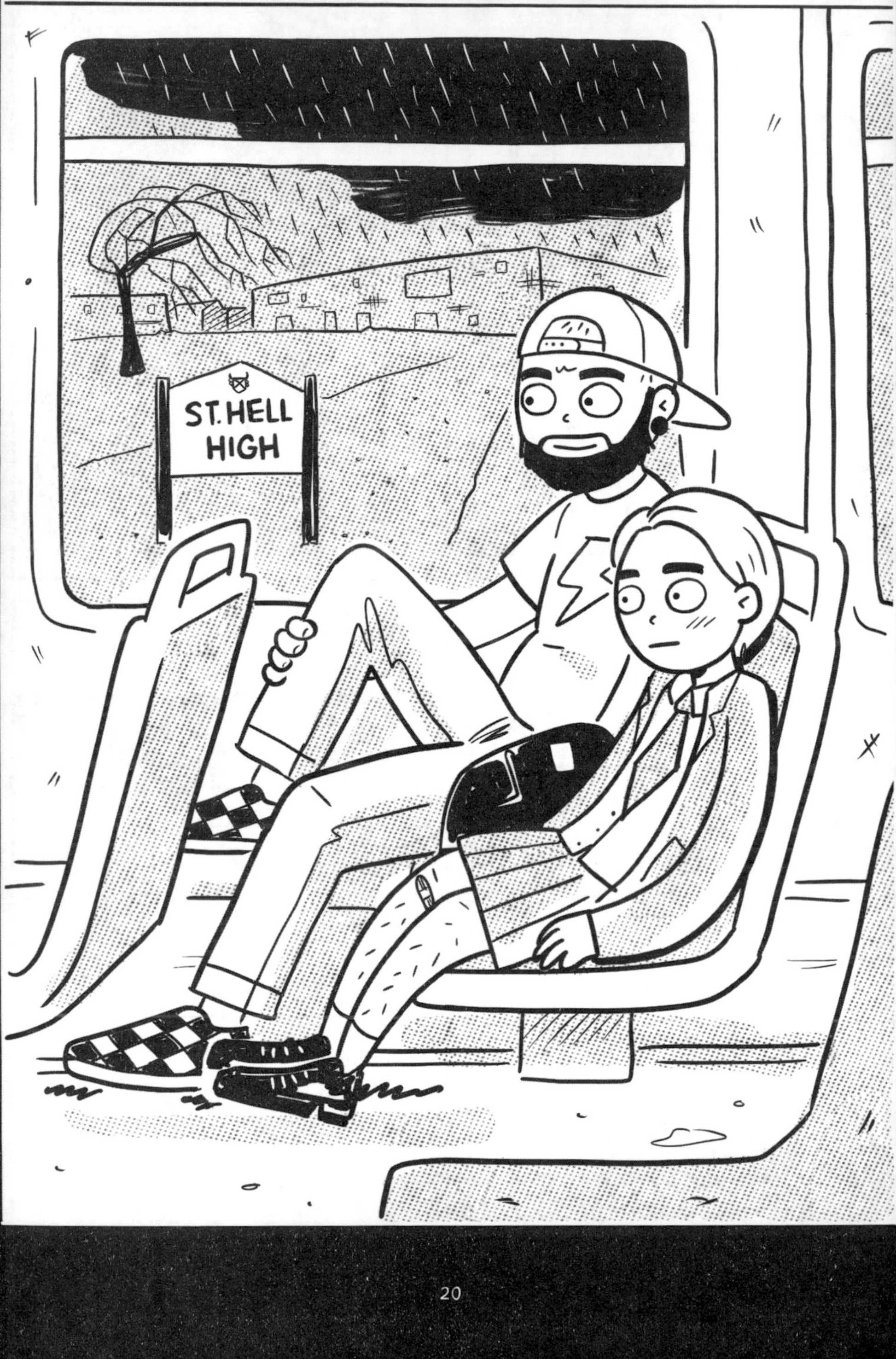
ST. HELL
HIGH

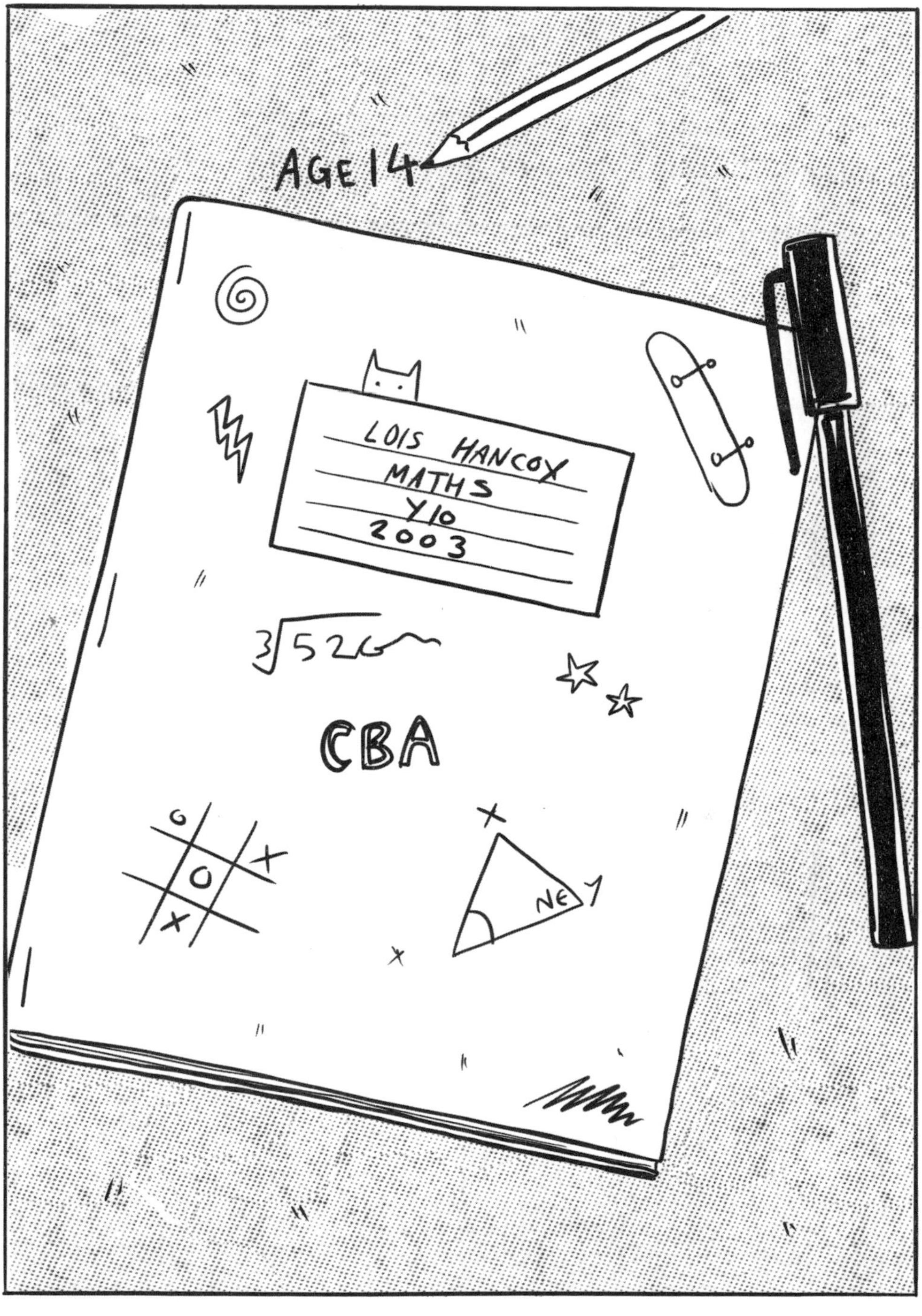

AGE 14
LOIS HANCOX
MATHS
Y10
2003
CBA

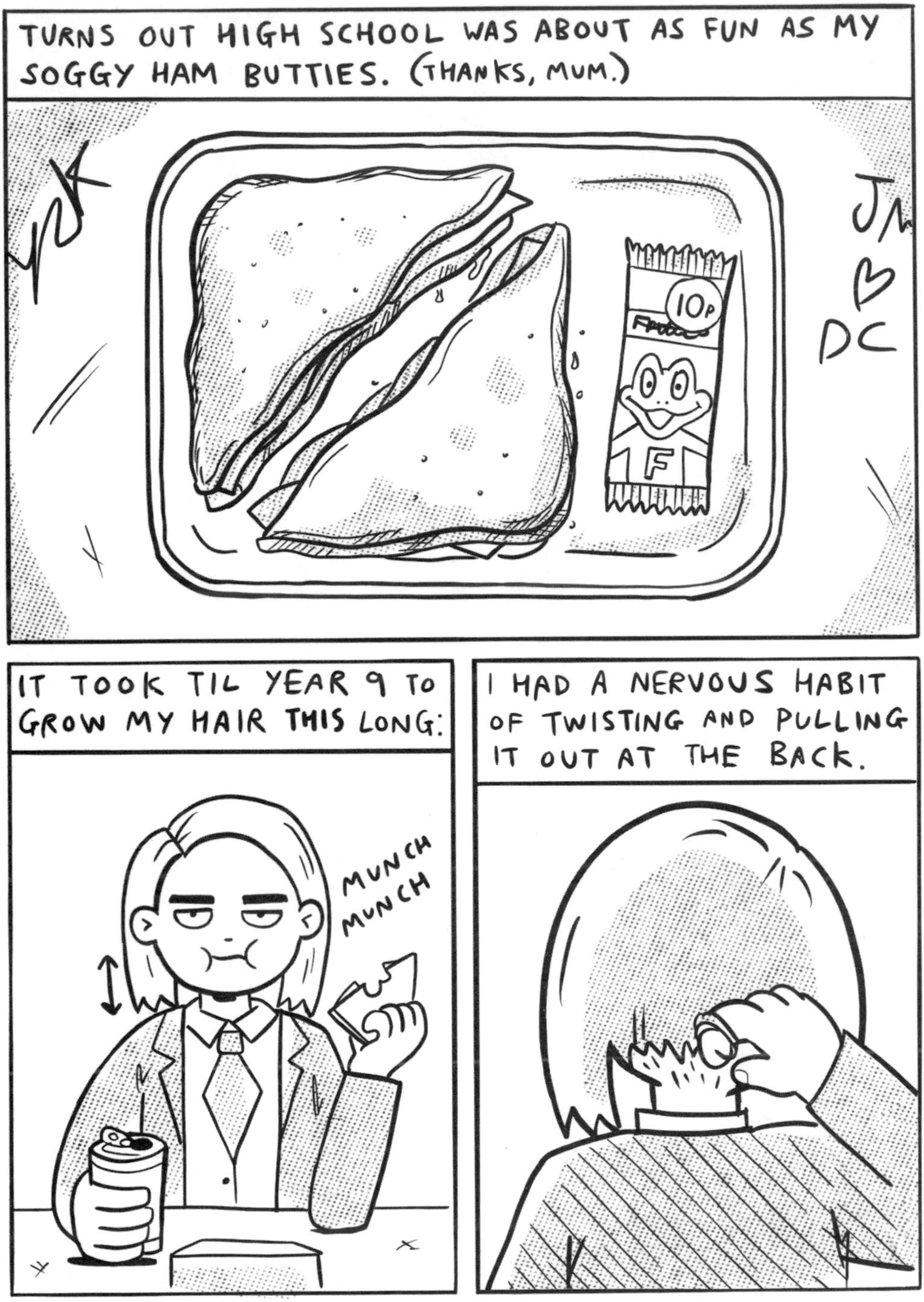
TURNS OUT HIGH SCHOOL WAS ABOUT AS FUN AS MY SOGGY HAM BUTTIES. (THANKS, MUM.)
JM
DC
10p
F
IT TOOK TIL YEAR 9 TO GROW MY HAIR THIS LONG:
MUNCH MUNCH
I HAD A NERVOUS HABIT OF TWISTING AND PULLING IT OUT AT THE BACK.

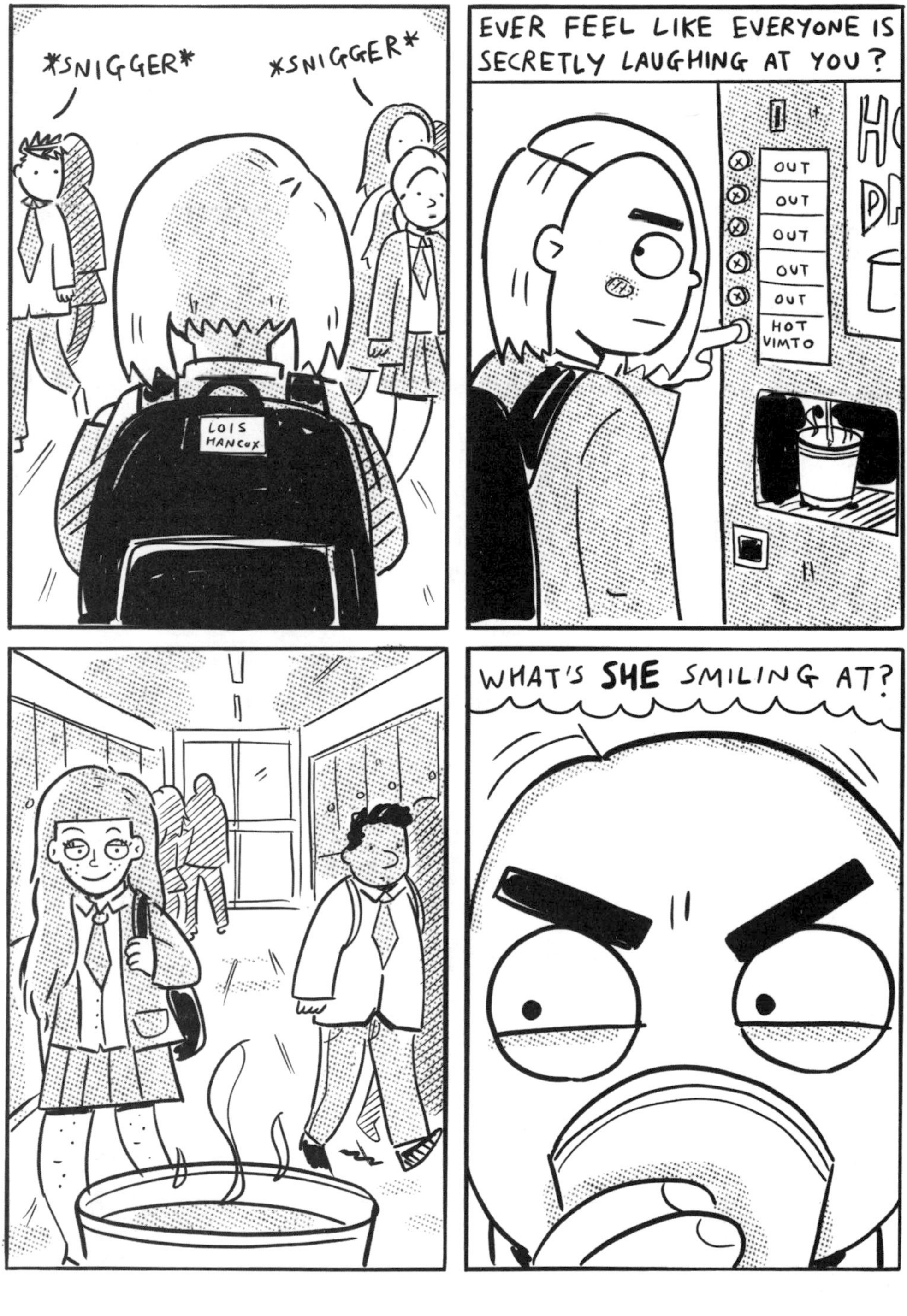
SNIGGER
SNIGGER
LOIS HANCOX
EVER FEEL LIKE EVERYONE IS SECRETLY LAUGHING AT YOU?
OUT
OUT
OUT
OUT
OUT
HOT VIMTO
WHAT'S **SHE** SMILING AT?

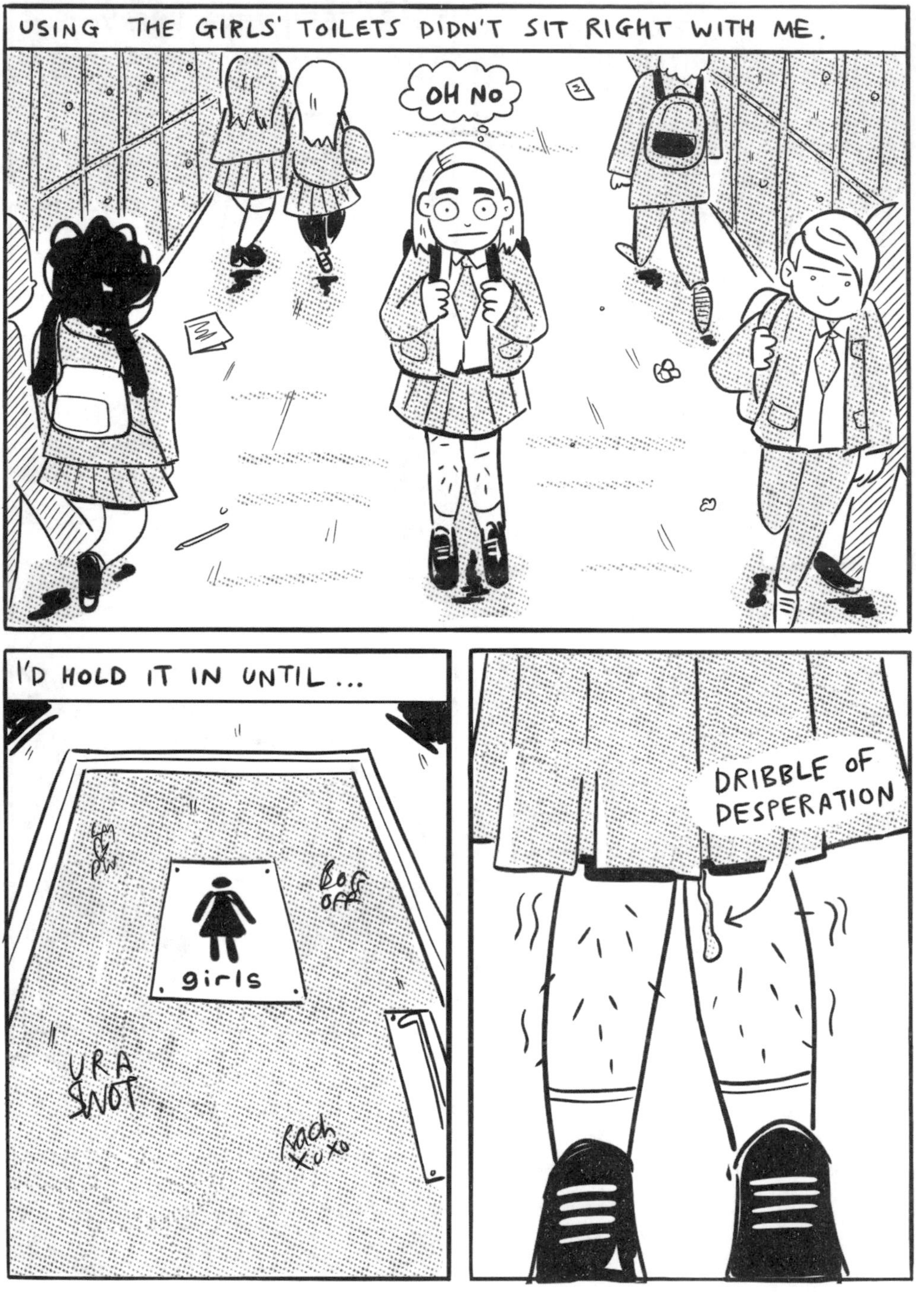

USING THE GIRLS' TOILETS DIDN'T SIT RIGHT WITH ME.
OH NO
I'D HOLD IT IN UNTIL...
girls
BOG OFF
URA SNOT
Rach xoxo
DRIBBLE OF DESPERATION

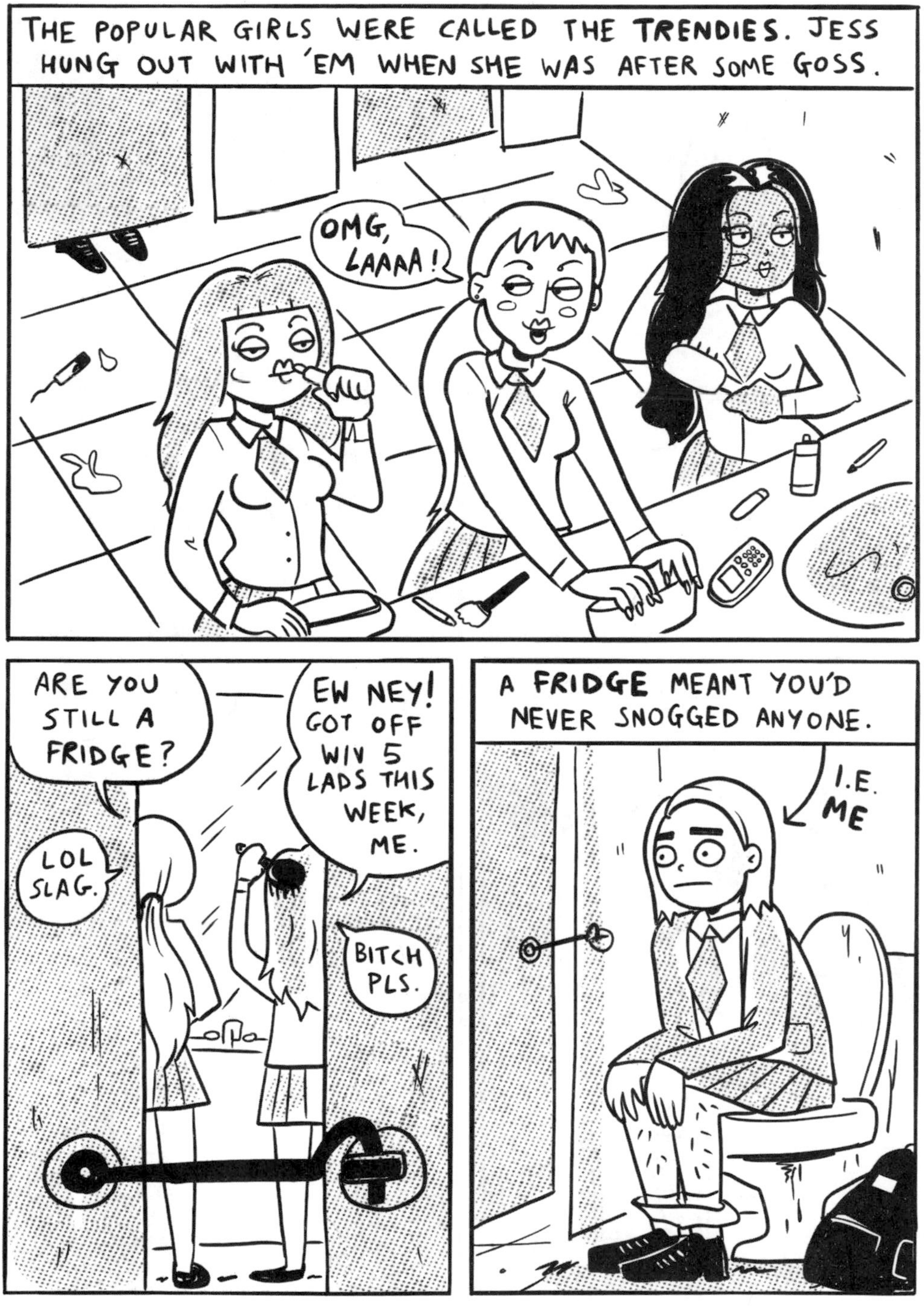
THE POPULAR GIRLS WERE CALLED THE **TRENDIES**. JESS HUNG OUT WITH 'EM WHEN SHE WAS AFTER SOME GOSS.
OMG, LAAAA!
ARE YOU STILL A FRIDGE?
EW NEY! GOT OFF WIV 5 LADS THIS WEEK, ME.
LOL SLAG.
BITCH PLS.
A **FRIDGE** MEANT YOU'D NEVER SNOGGED ANYONE.
I.E. ME

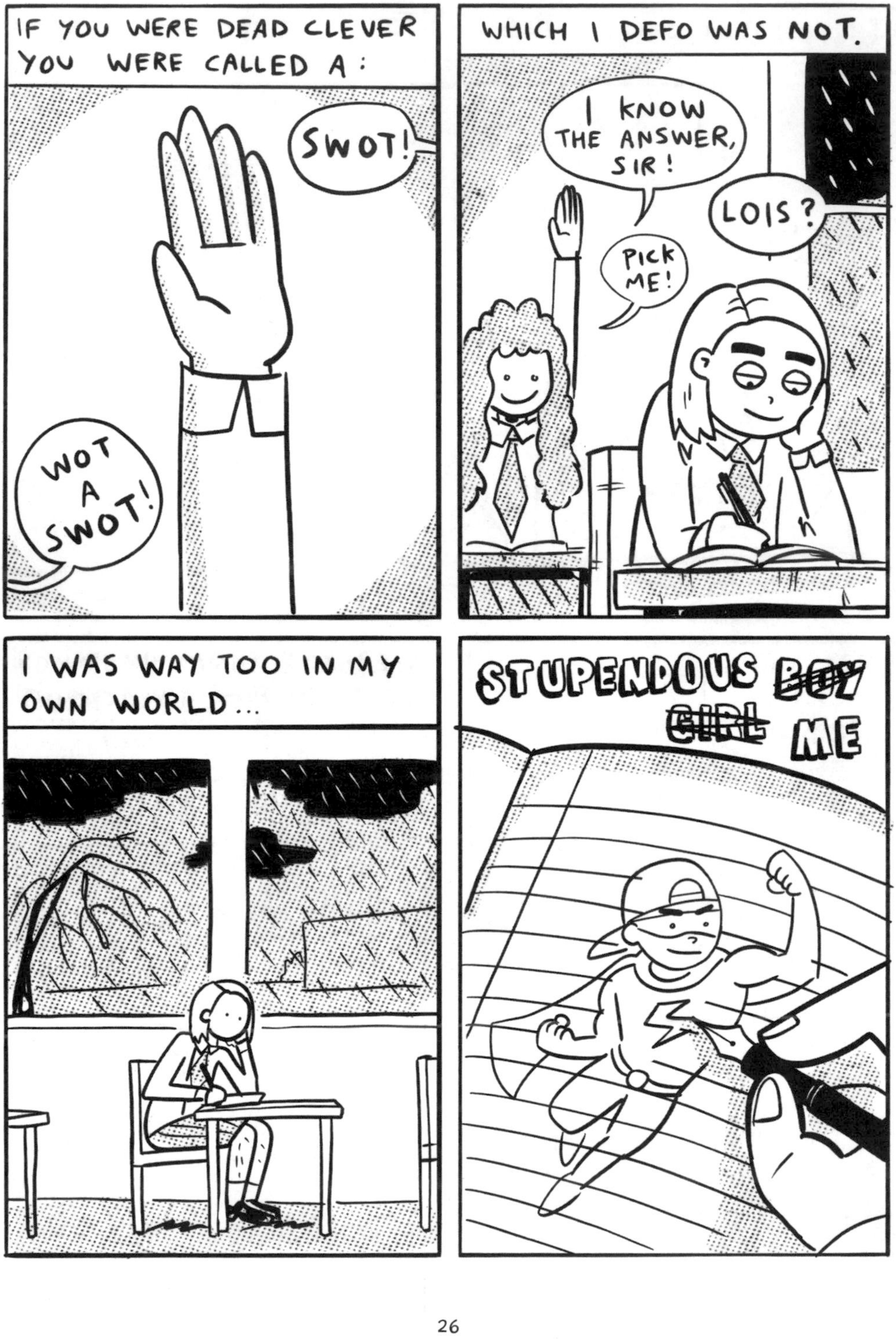
IF YOU WERE DEAD CLEVER YOU WERE CALLED A:
SWOT!
WOT A SWOT!
WHICH I DEFO WAS NOT.
I KNOW THE ANSWER, SIR!
PICK ME!
LOIS?
I WAS WAY TOO IN MY OWN WORLD...
STUPENDOUS ~~BOY~~ ~~GIRL~~ ME

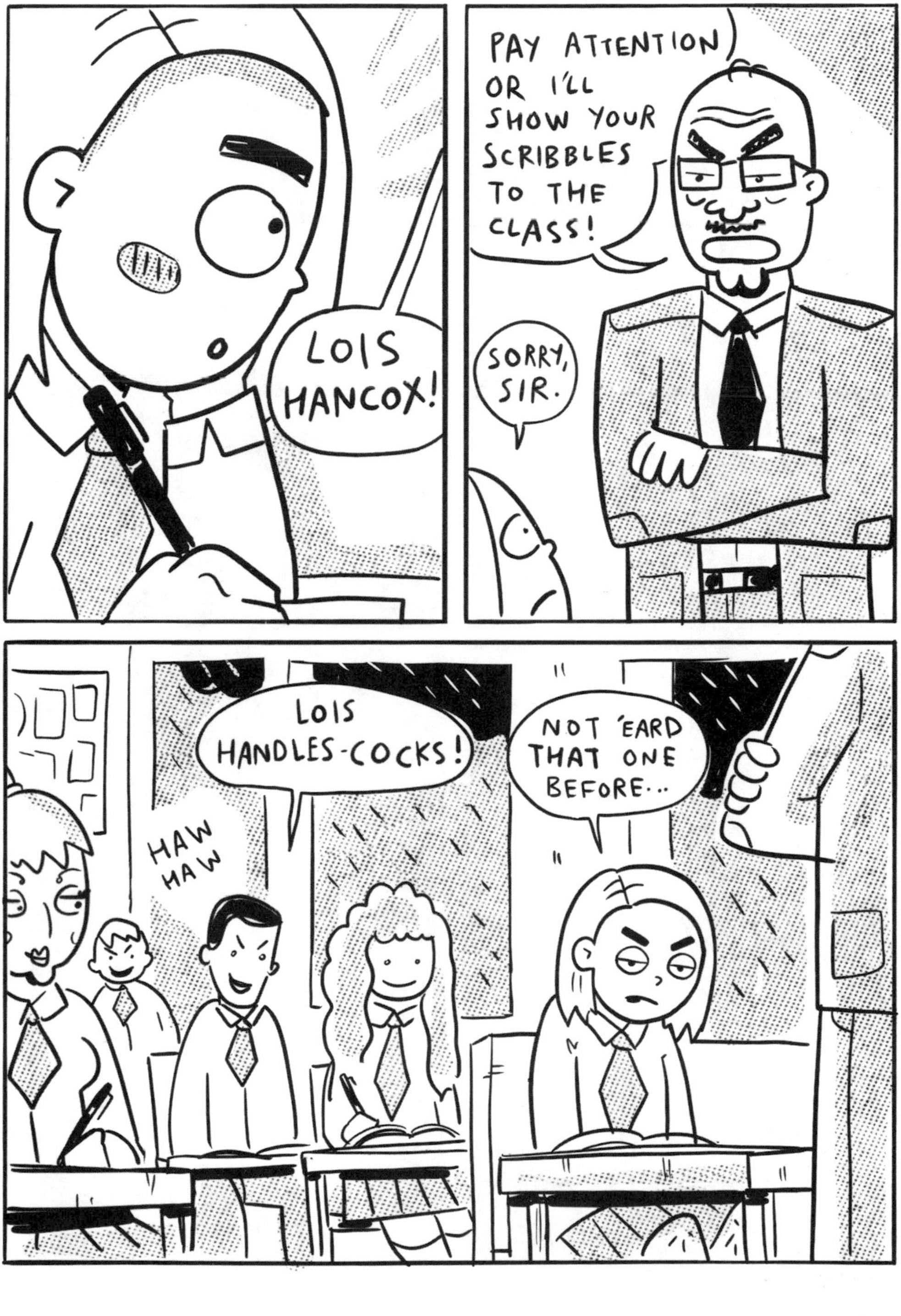
LOIS HANCOX!
PAY ATTENTION OR I'LL SHOW YOUR SCRIBBLES TO THE CLASS!
SORRY, SIR.
HAW HAW
LOIS HANDLES-COCKS!
NOT 'EARD THAT ONE BEFORE...

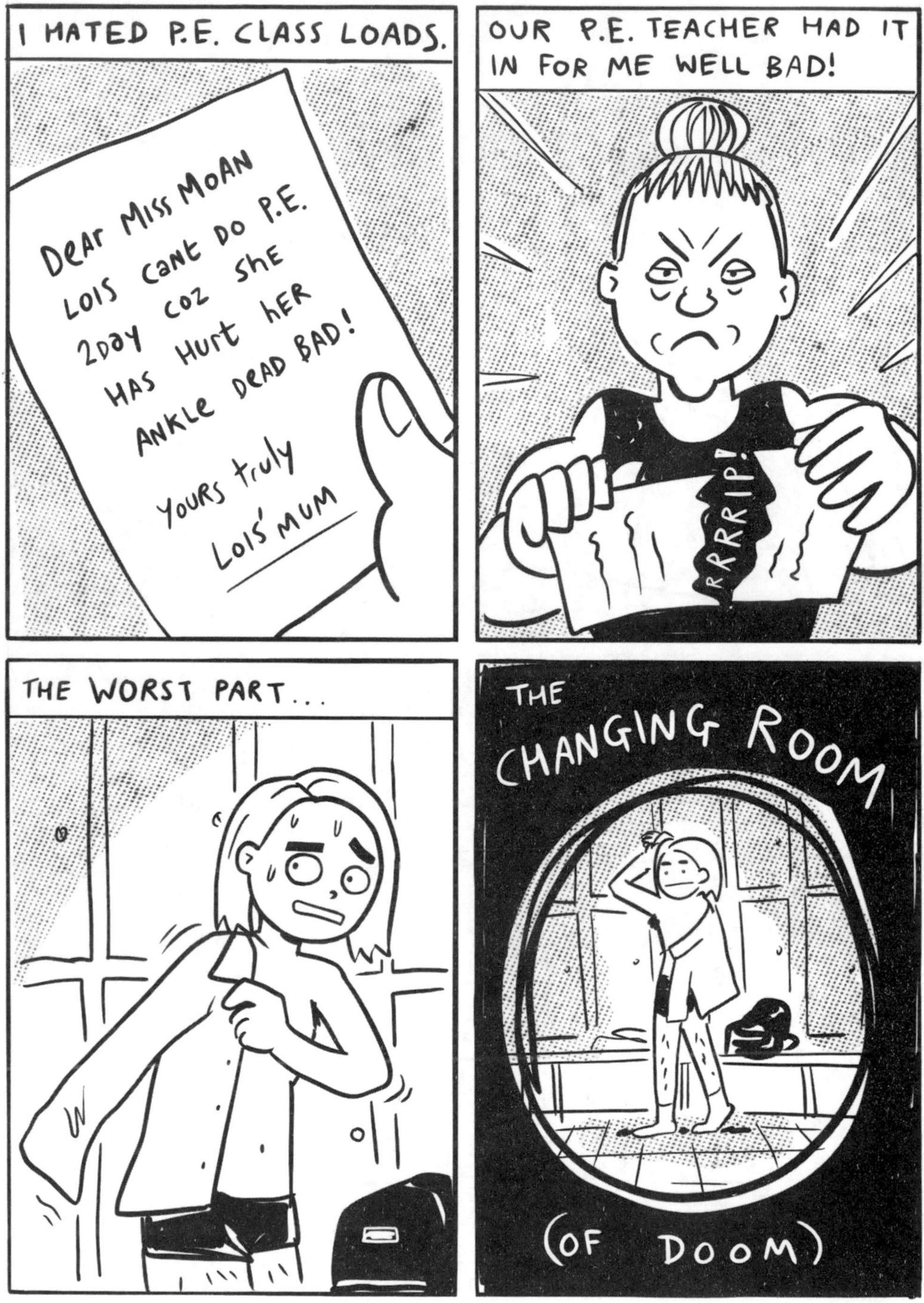
I HATED P.E. CLASS LOADS.
Dear Miss MOAN
LOIS cant do P.E.
2day coz she
HAS Hurt her
ANKLE DEAD BAD!
Yours truly
Lois' MUM
OUR P.E. TEACHER HAD IT IN FOR ME WELL BAD!
RRRRRIP!
THE WORST PART...
THE CHANGING ROOM
(OF DOOM)

I DIDN'T SHAVE LIKE ALL THE OTHER GIRLS...

OR WEAR A BRA...

FUCK! NIP SLIP.

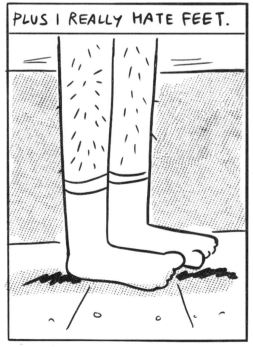

PLUS I REALLY HATE FEET.

WAY TOO MANY TOES ABOUT.

EW

YOUNG LADY!
TIE YOUR HAIR UP!
ERM... I DUNNO HOW, MISS.
ARE YOU THICK?
I'LL TIE IT FOR YOU.
AWW, SHE TRIES TO BE A GUURL.
LOL, BLESS 'ER.

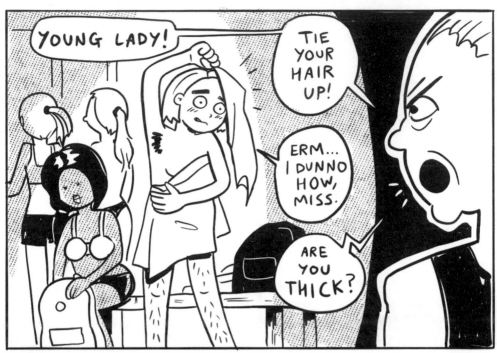

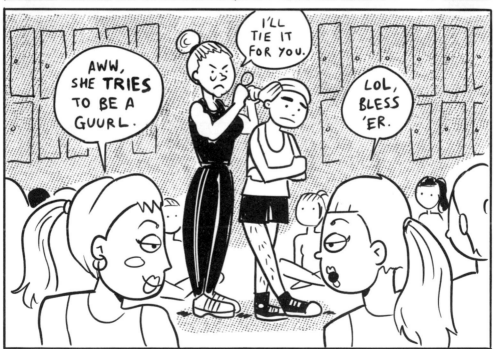

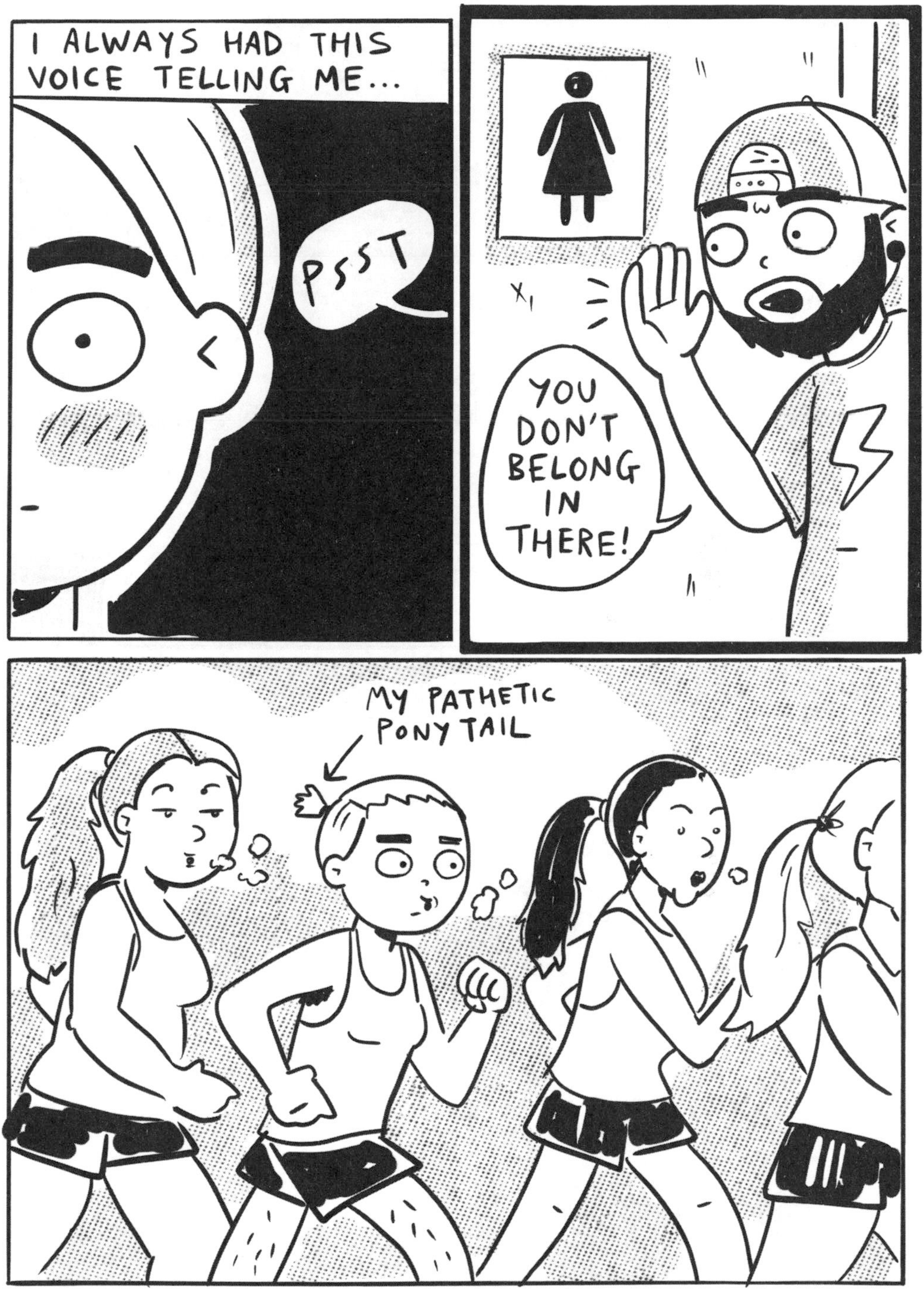
I ALWAYS HAD THIS VOICE TELLING ME...
PSST
YOU DON'T BELONG IN THERE!
MY PATHETIC PONYTAIL

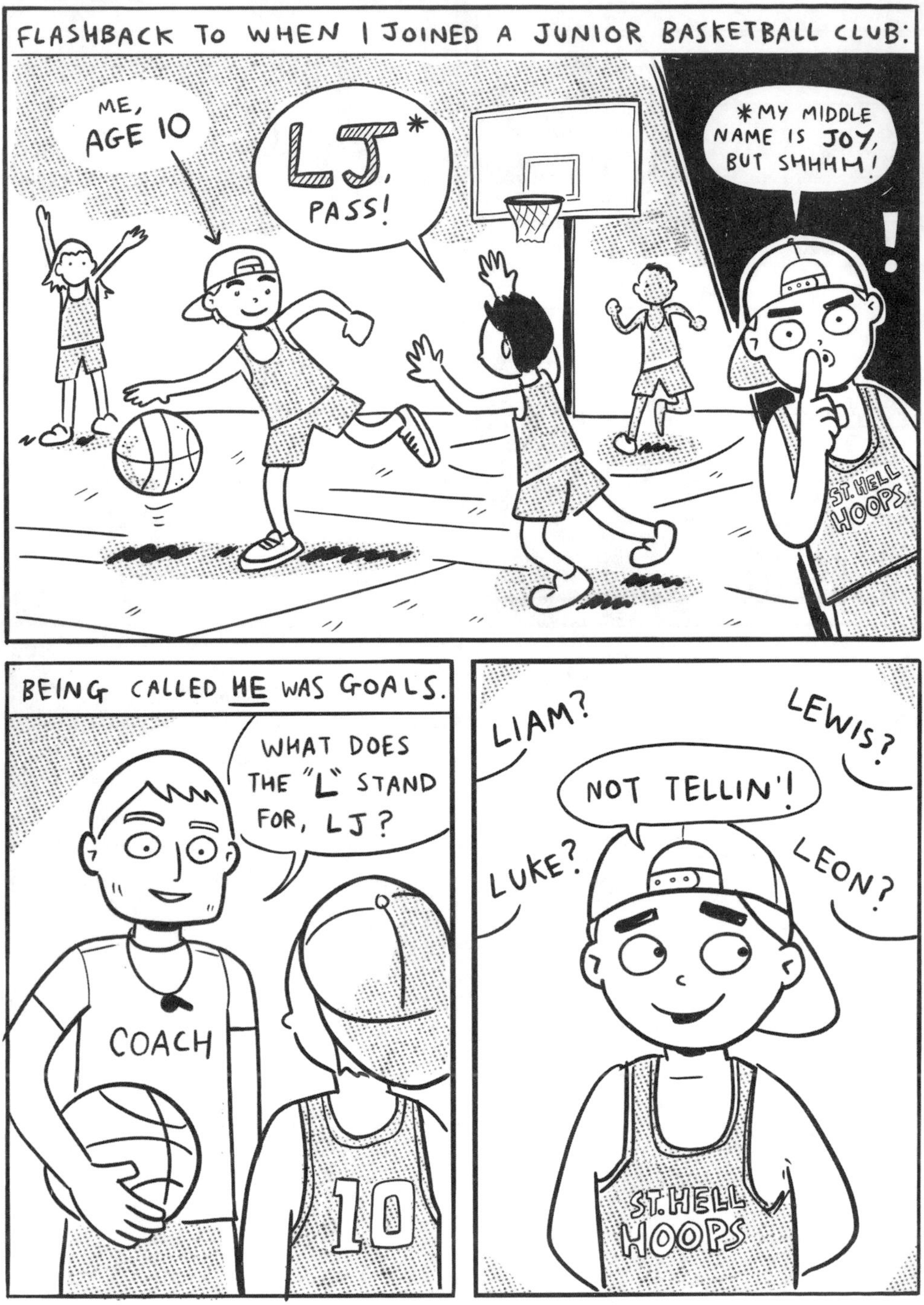
FLASHBACK TO WHEN I JOINED A JUNIOR BASKETBALL CLUB:
ME, AGE 10
LJ,* PASS!
*MY MIDDLE NAME IS JOY, BUT SHHHM!
!
ST. HELL HOOPS
BEING CALLED HE WAS GOALS.
WHAT DOES THE "L" STAND FOR, LJ?
COACH
10
LIAM?
LEWIS?
NOT TELLIN'!
LUKE?
LEON?
ST. HELL HOOPS

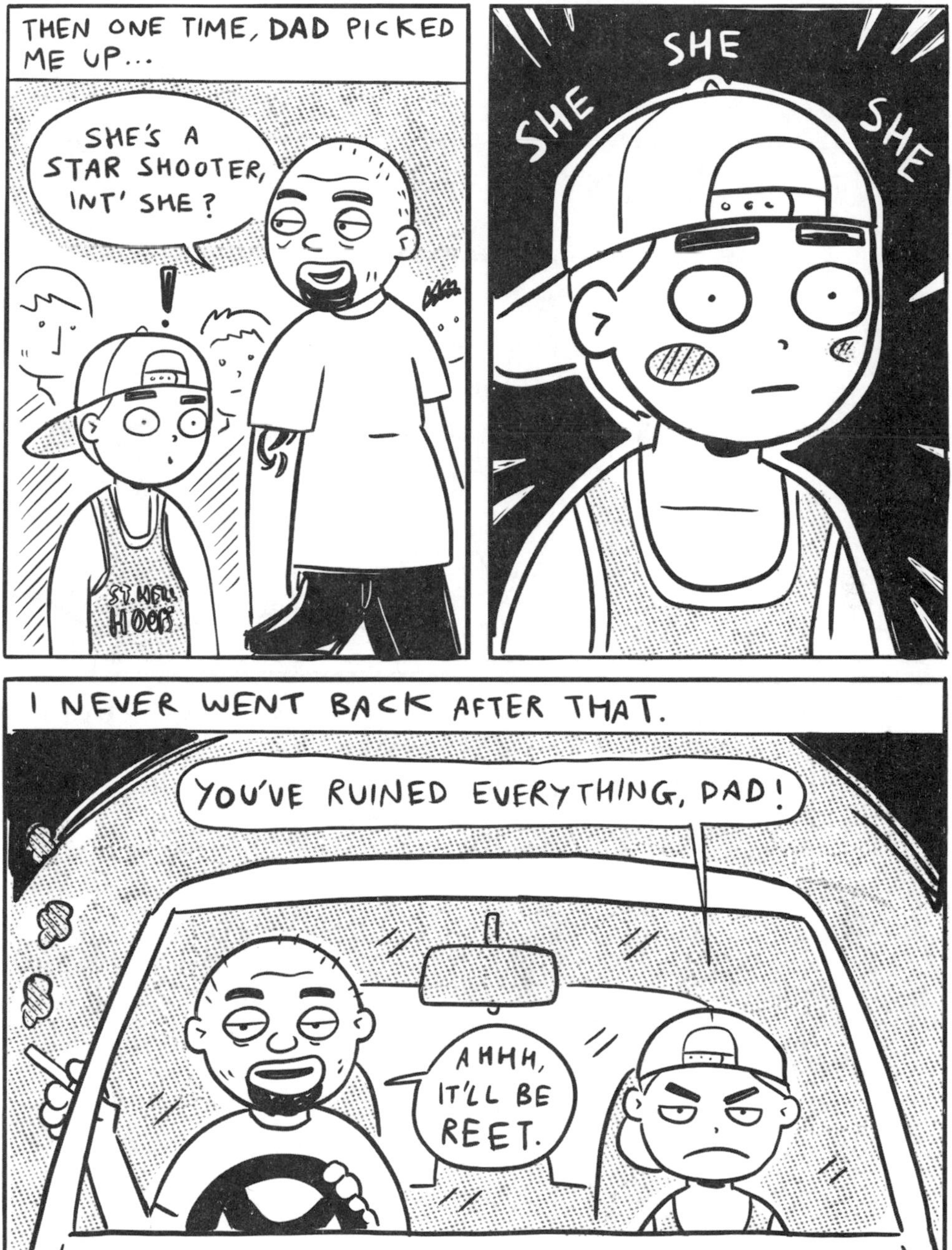
THEN ONE TIME, DAD PICKED ME UP...
SHE'S A STAR SHOOTER, INT' SHE?
!
SHE
SHE
SHE
SHE
I NEVER WENT BACK AFTER THAT.
YOU'VE RUINED EVERYTHING, DAD!
AHHH, IT'LL BE REET.

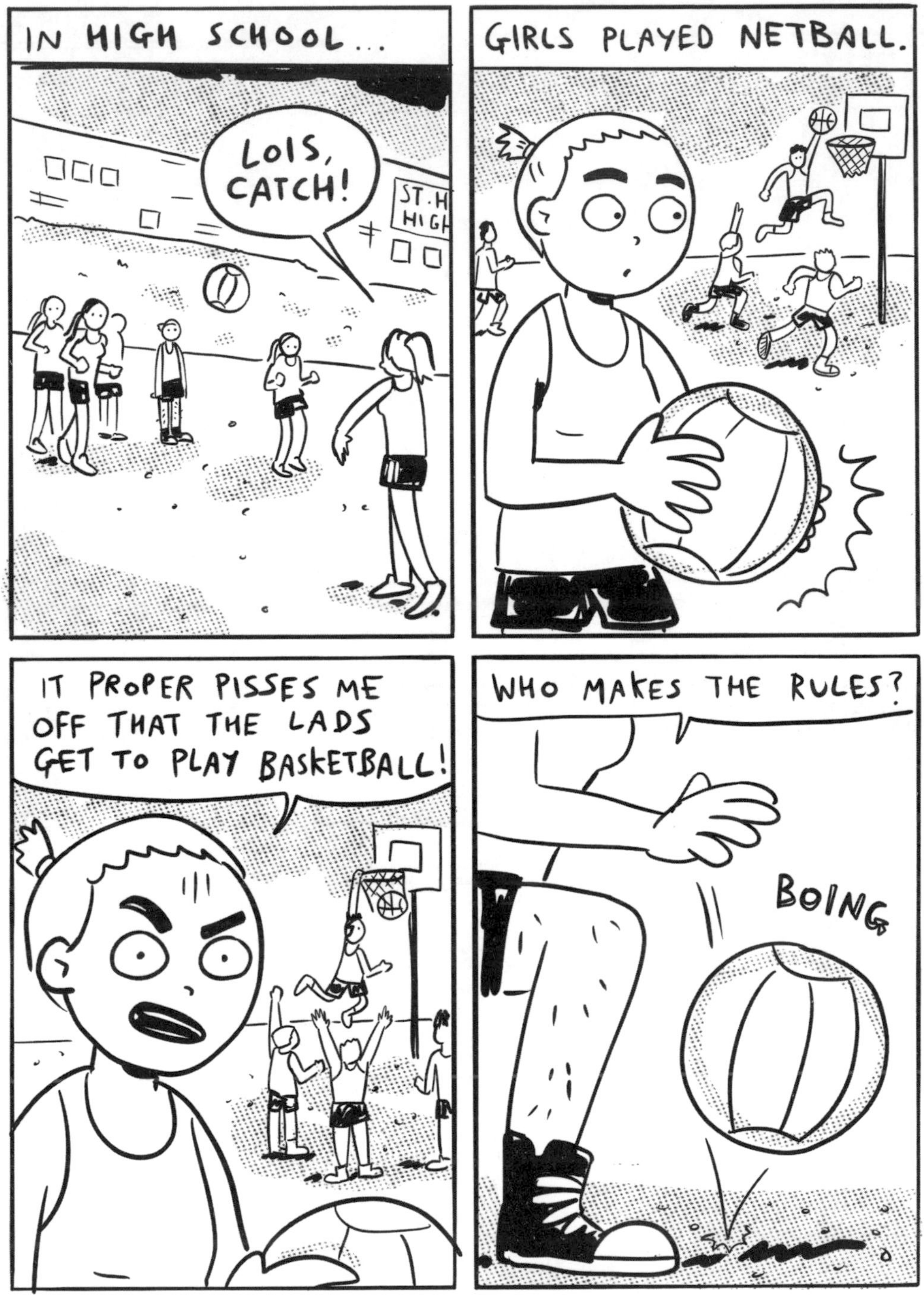
IN HIGH SCHOOL...
LOIS, CATCH!
ST. H HIGH
GIRLS PLAYED NETBALL.
IT PROPER PISSES ME OFF THAT THE LADS GET TO PLAY BASKETBALL!
WHO MAKES THE RULES?
BOING

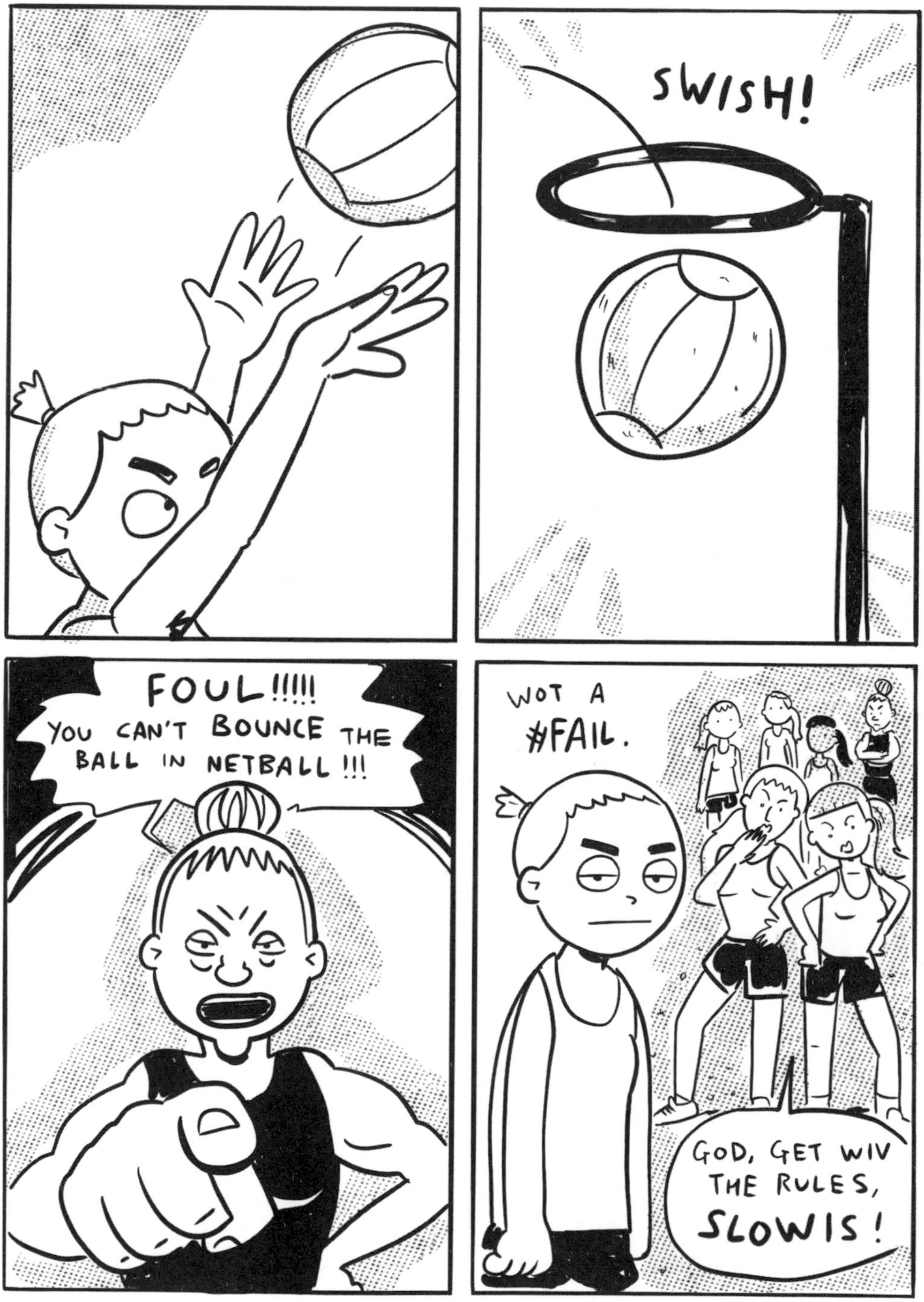
SWISH!
FOUL!!!!!
YOU CAN'T BOUNCE THE BALL IN NETBALL!!!
WOT A #FAIL.
GOD, GET WIV THE RULES, SLOWIS!

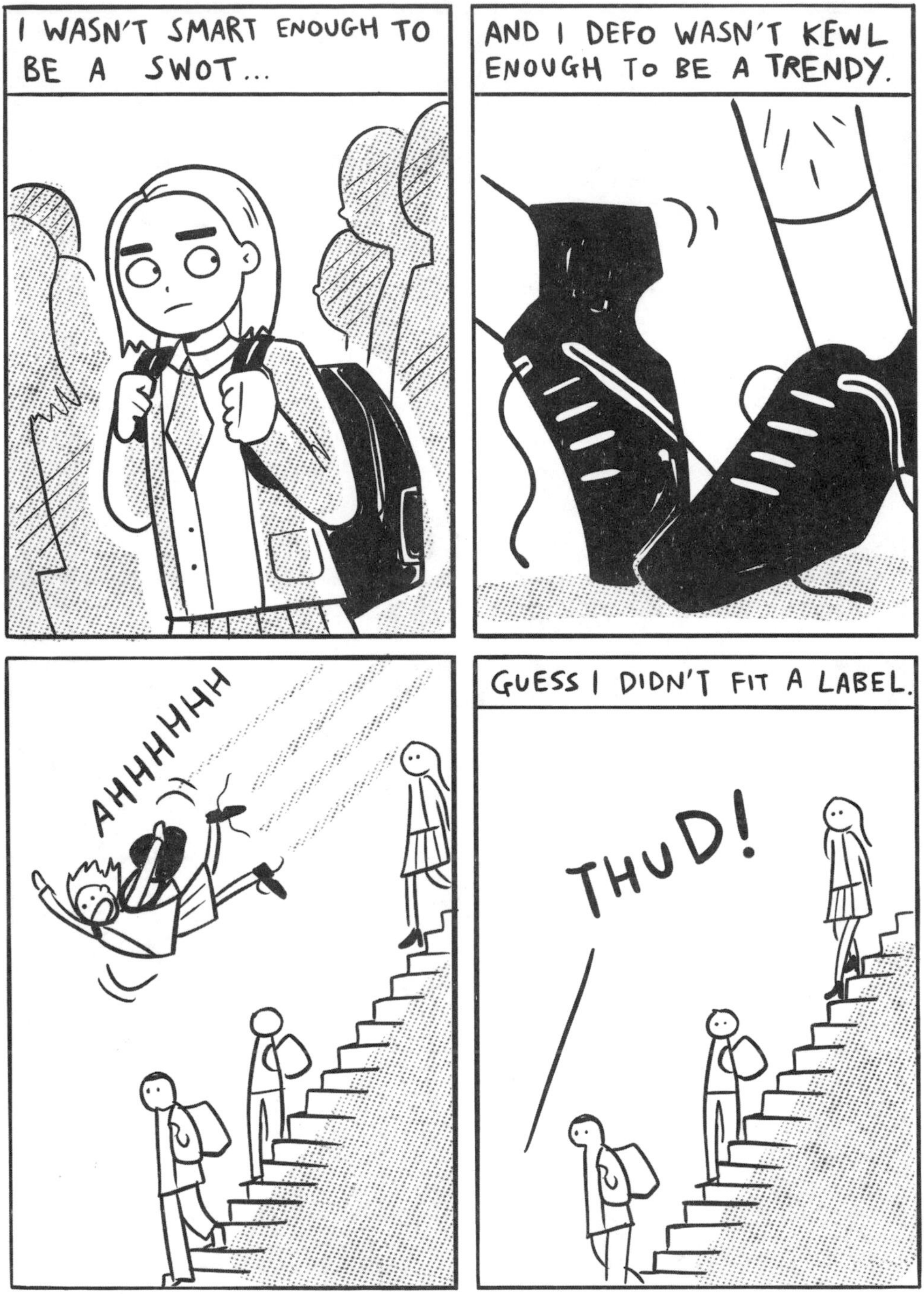
I WASN'T SMART ENOUGH TO BE A SWOT...
AND I DEFO WASN'T KEWL ENOUGH TO BE A TRENDY.
AHHHHHH
GUESS I DIDN'T FIT A LABEL.
THUD!

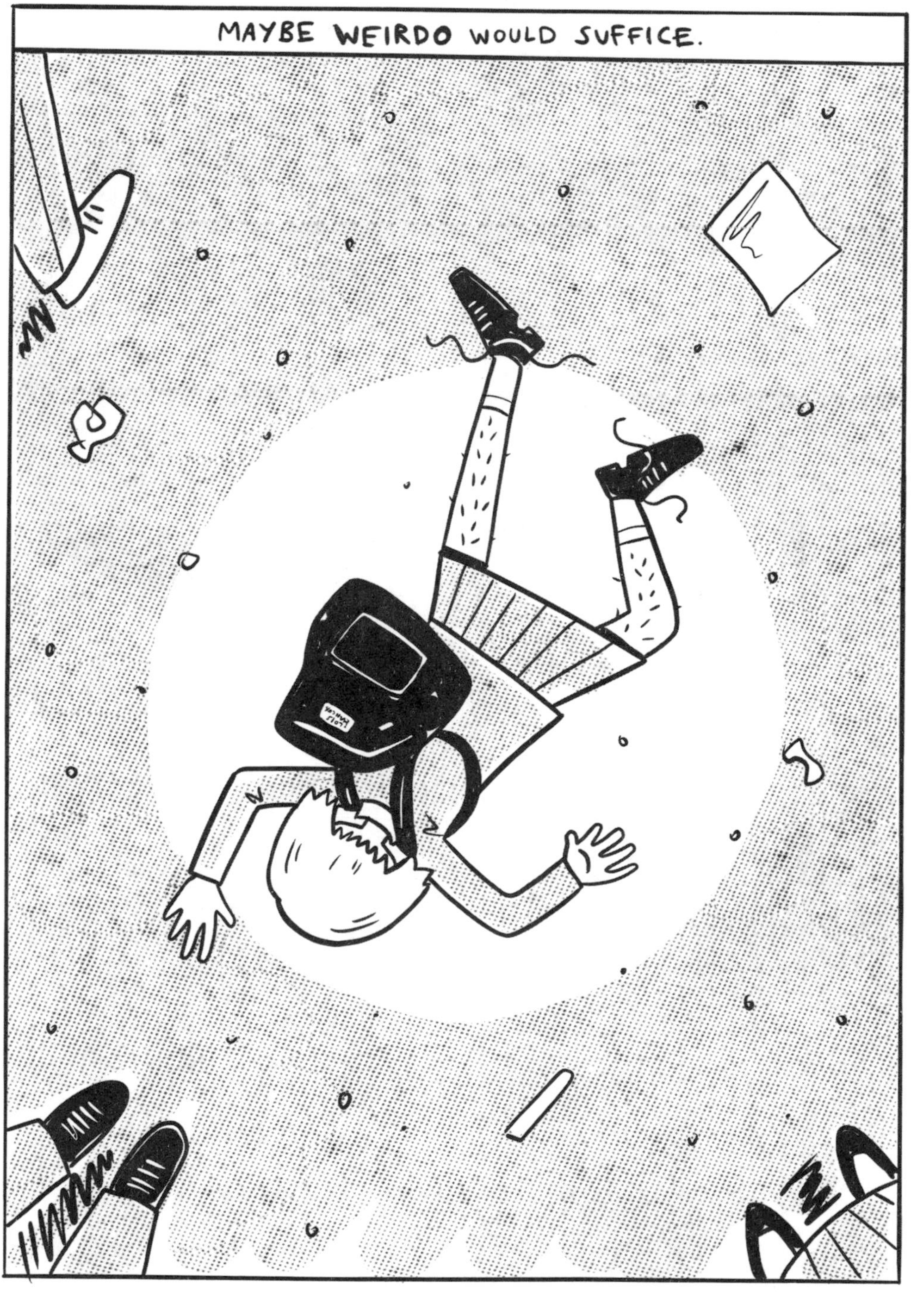
MAYBE WEIRDO WOULD SUFFICE.

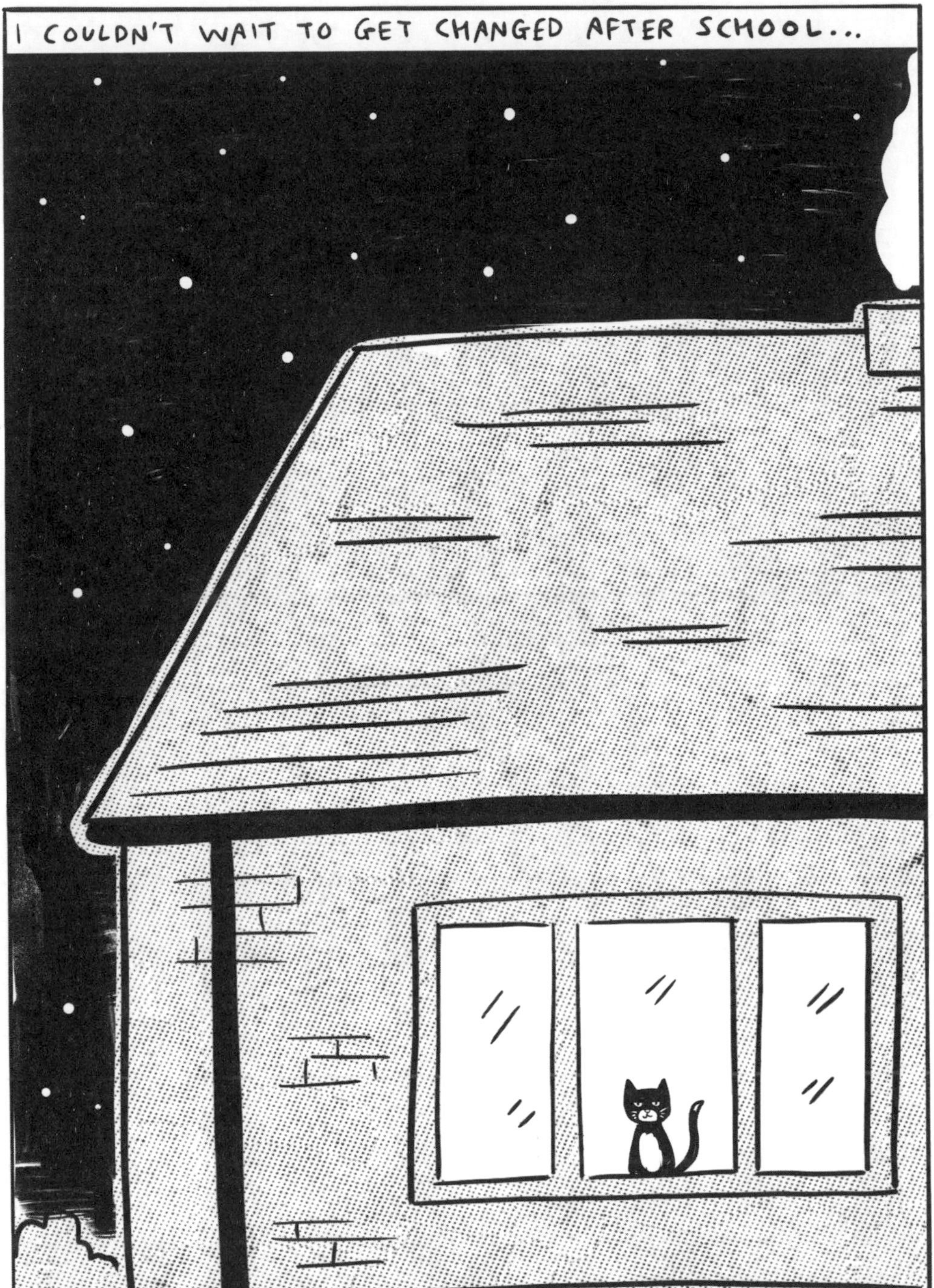
I COULDN'T WAIT TO GET CHANGED AFTER SCHOOL...

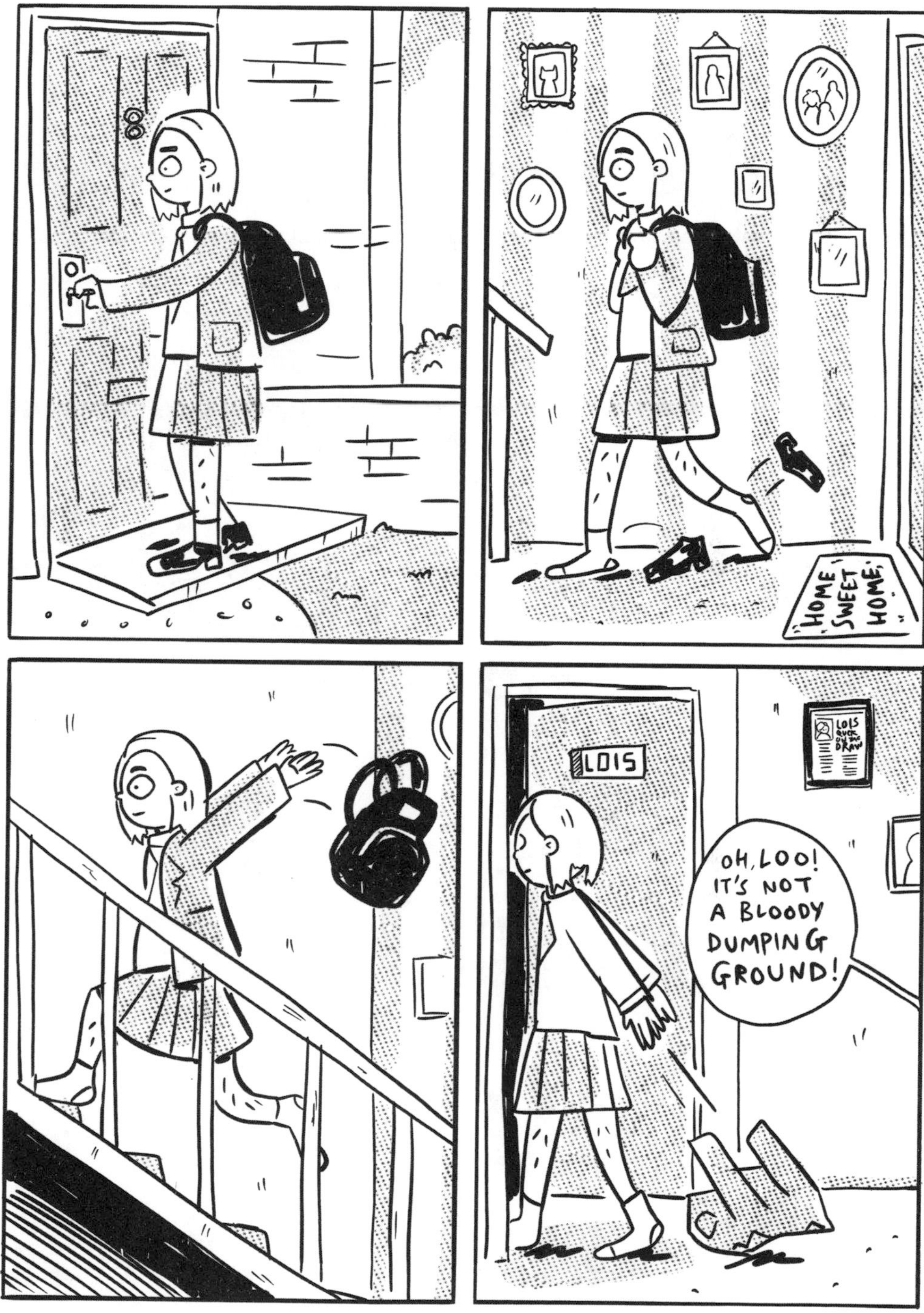
HOME SWEET HOME
LOIS
LOIS QUICK ON THE DRAW
OH, LOO! IT'S NOT A BLOODY DUMPING GROUND!

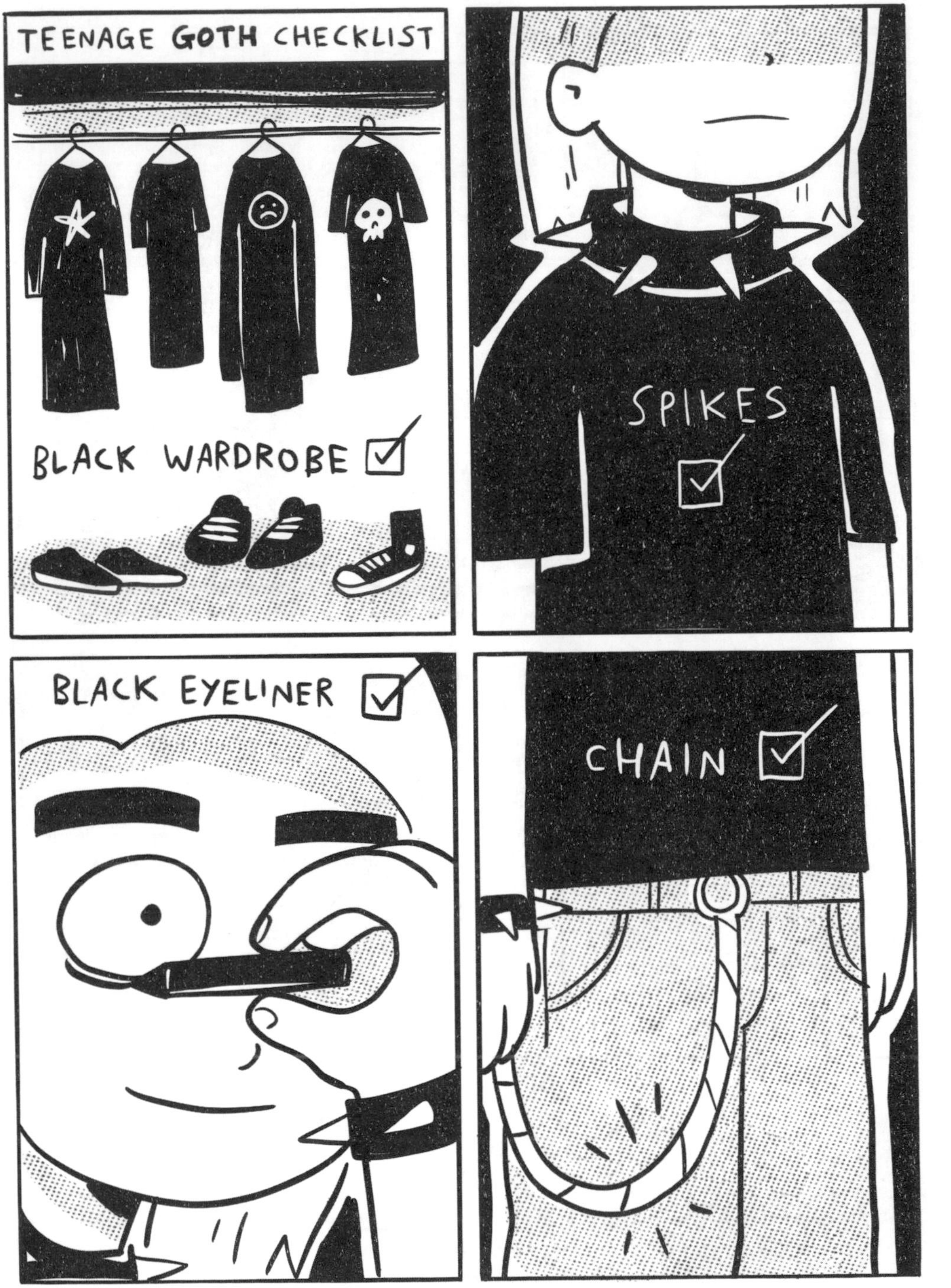
TEENAGE GOTH CHECKLIST
BLACK WARDROBE
SPIKES
BLACK EYELINER
CHAIN

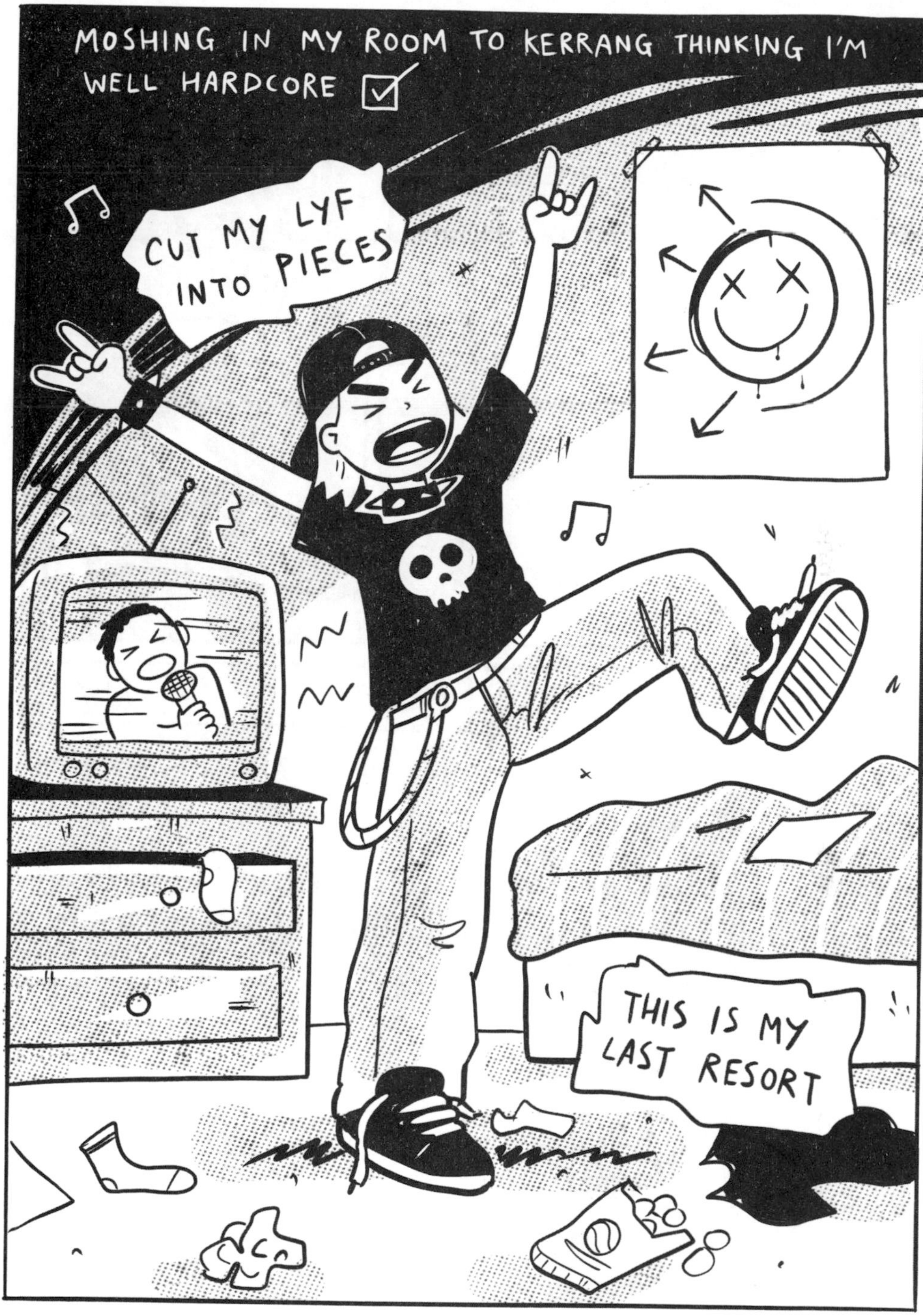
MOSHING IN MY ROOM TO KERRANG THINKING I'M WELL HARDCORE ☑
CUT MY LYF INTO PIECES
THIS IS MY LAST RESORT

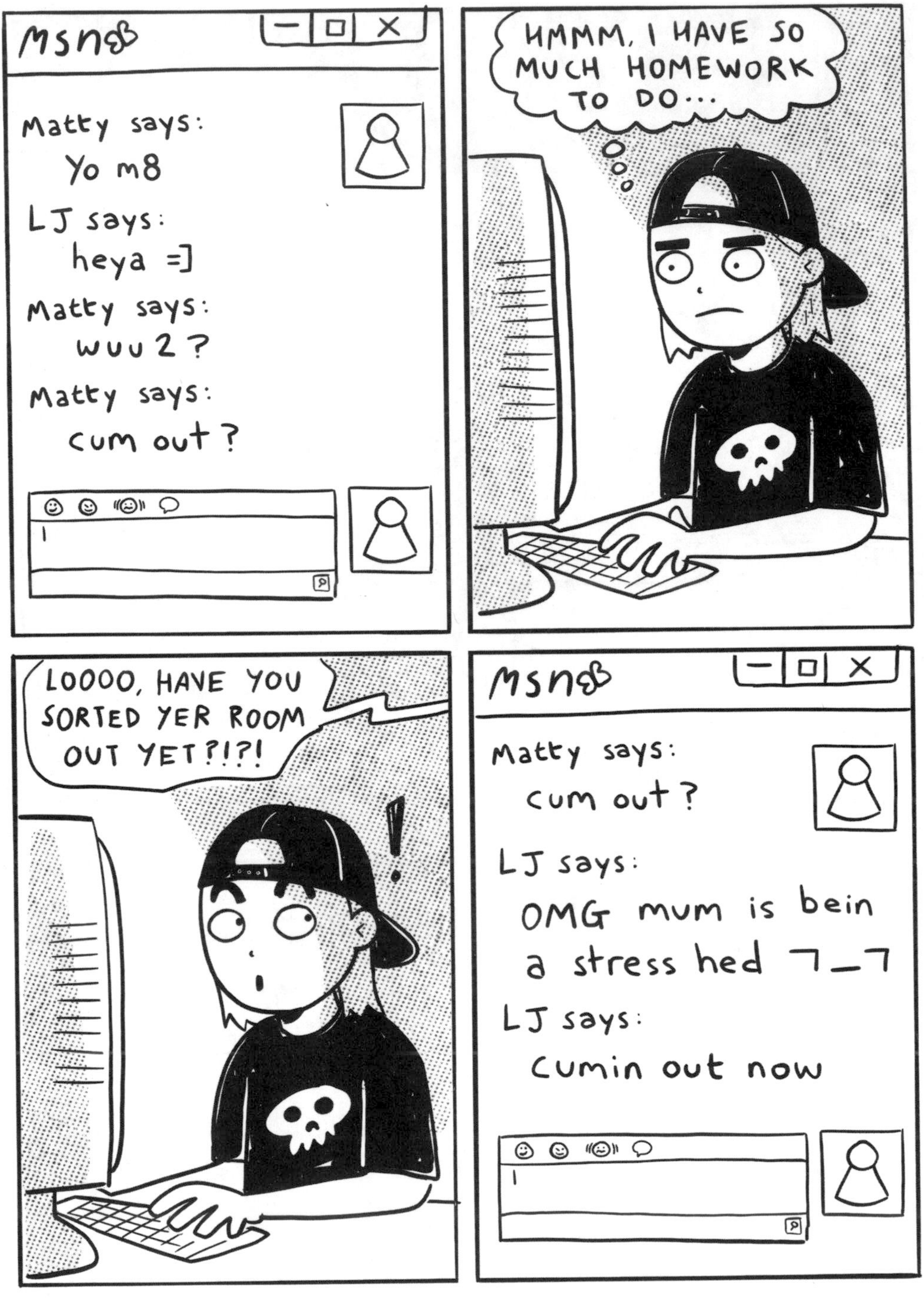
MSN
Matty says:
Yo m8
LJ says:
heya =]
Matty says:
wuu2?
Matty says:
cum out?
HMMM, I HAVE SO MUCH HOMEWORK TO DO...
LOOOO, HAVE YOU SORTED YER ROOM OUT YET?!?!
!
MSN
Matty says:
cum out?
LJ says:
OMG mum is bein a stress hed ¬_¬
LJ says:
cumin out now

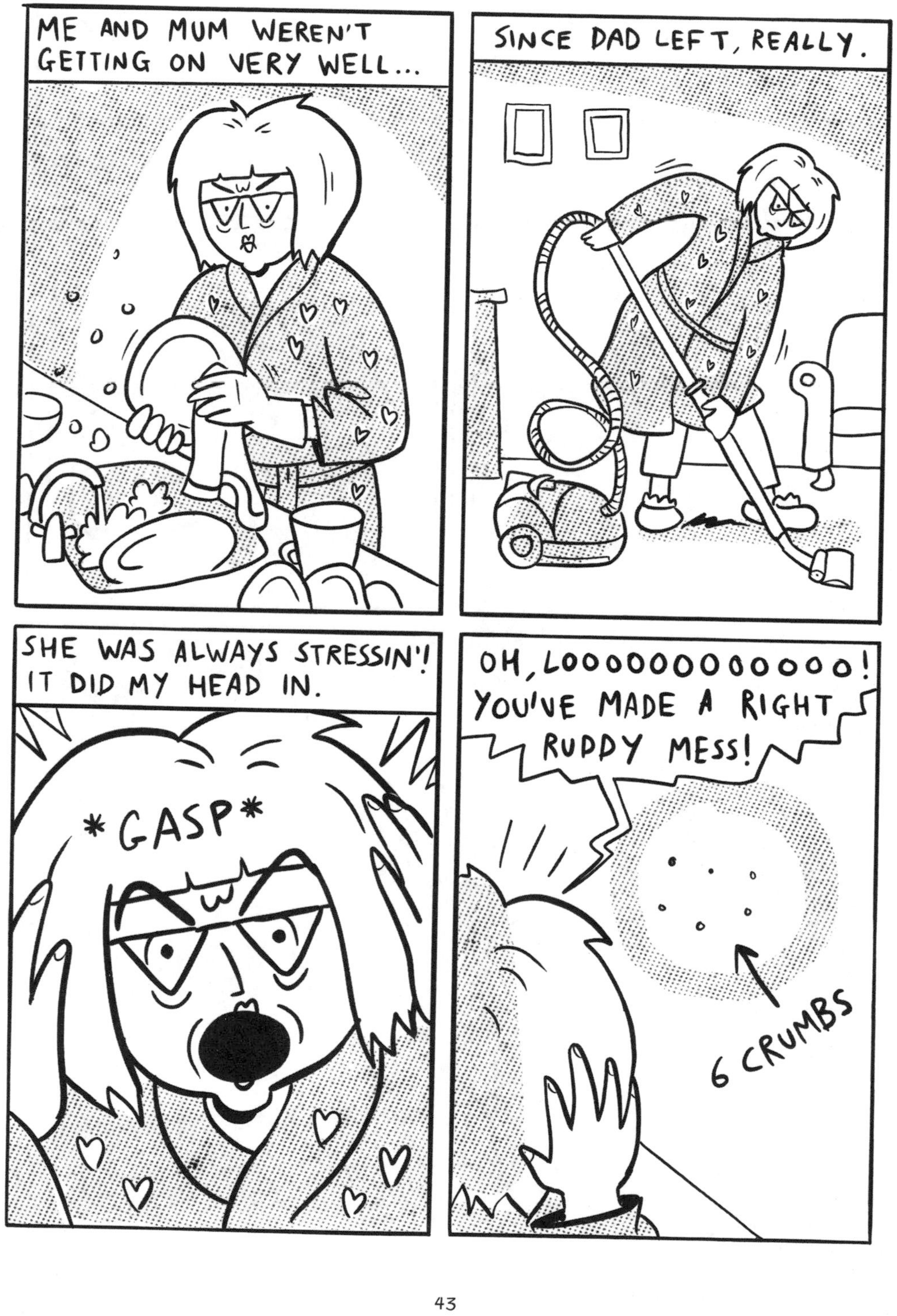
ME AND MUM WEREN'T GETTING ON VERY WELL...
SINCE DAD LEFT, REALLY.
SHE WAS ALWAYS STRESSIN'! IT DID MY HEAD IN.
GASP
OH, LOOOOOOOOOOOOO! YOU'VE MADE A RIGHT RUDDY MESS!
6 CRUMBS

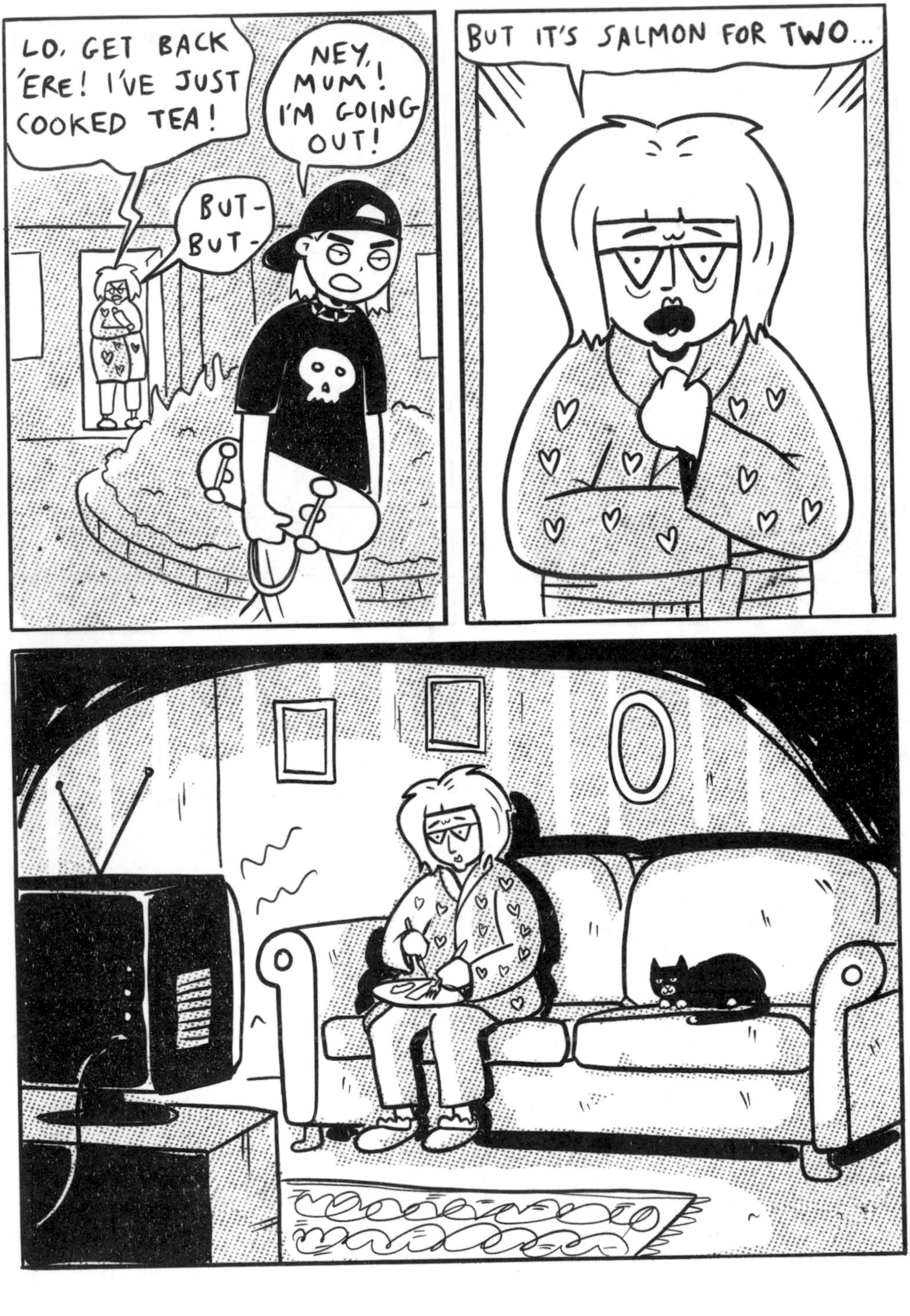
LO, GET BACK 'ERE! I'VE JUST COOKED TEA!
NEY, MUM! I'M GOING OUT!
BUT- BUT-
BUT IT'S SALMON FOR TWO...

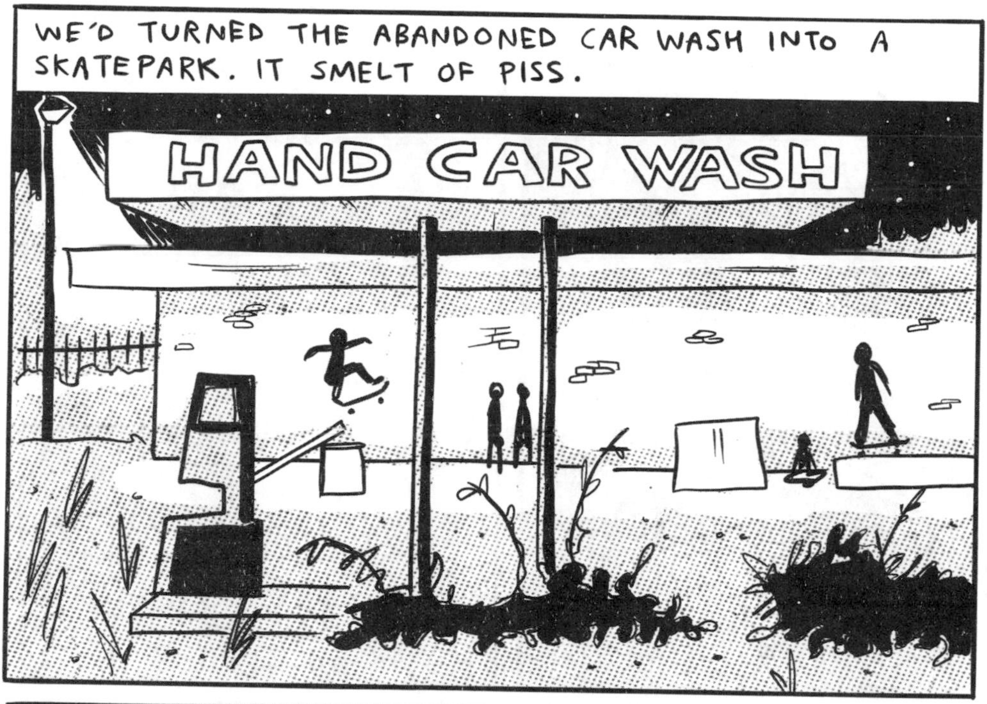
WE'D TURNED THE ABANDONED CAR WASH INTO A SKATEPARK. IT SMELT OF PISS.
HAND CAR WASH

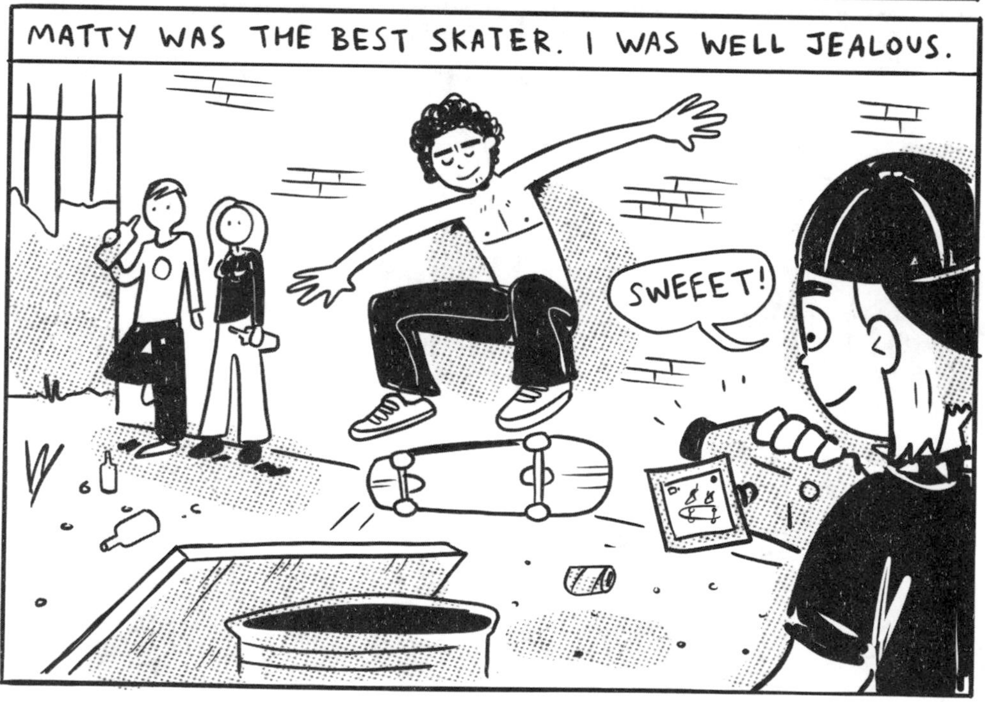
MATTY WAS THE BEST SKATER. I WAS WELL JEALOUS.
SWEEET!

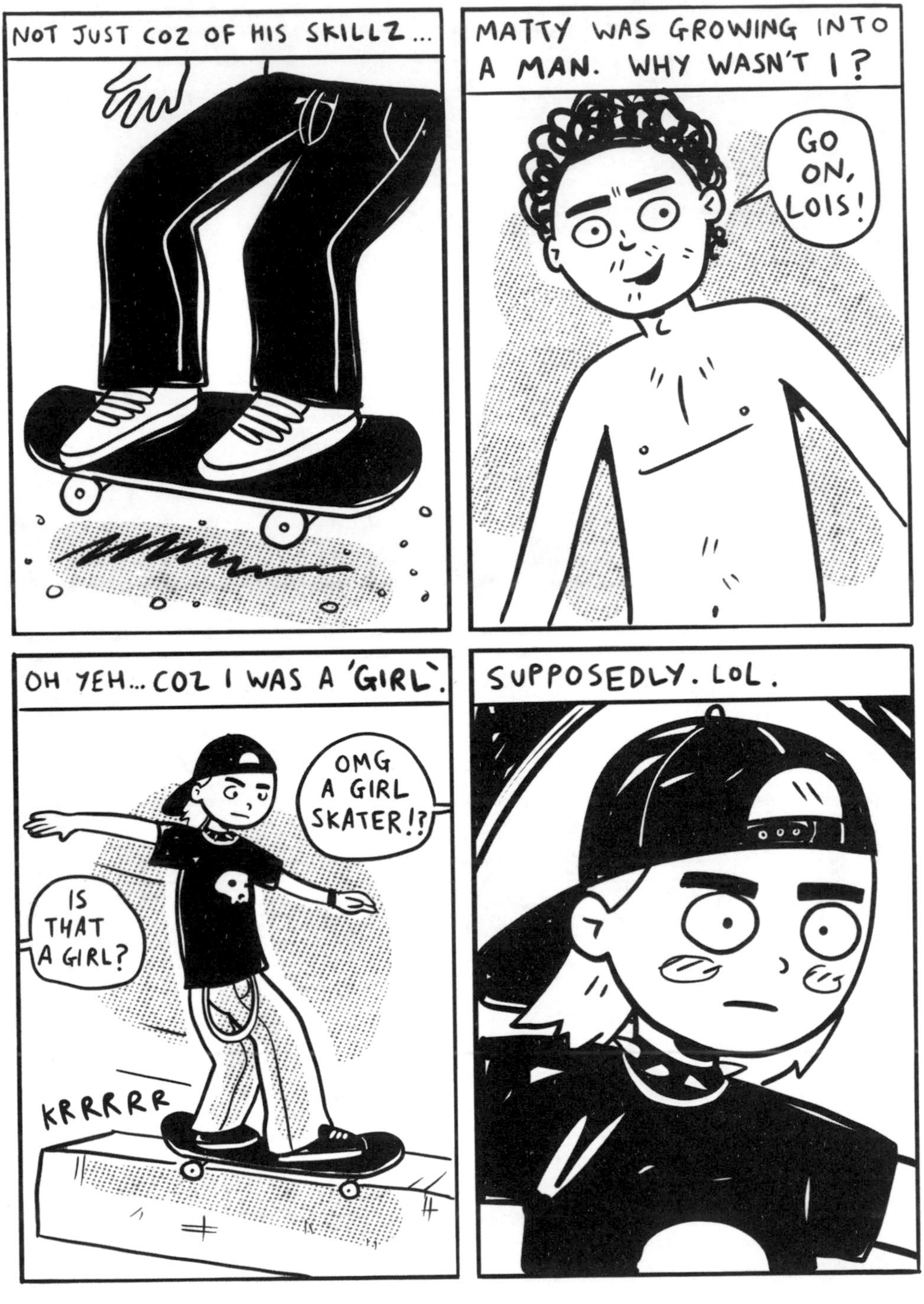
NOT JUST COZ OF HIS SKILLZ...
MATTY WAS GROWING INTO A MAN. WHY WASN'T I?
GO ON, LOIS!
OH YEH... COZ I WAS A 'GIRL'.
OMG A GIRL SKATER!?
IS THAT A GIRL?
KRRRRR
SUPPOSEDLY. LOL.

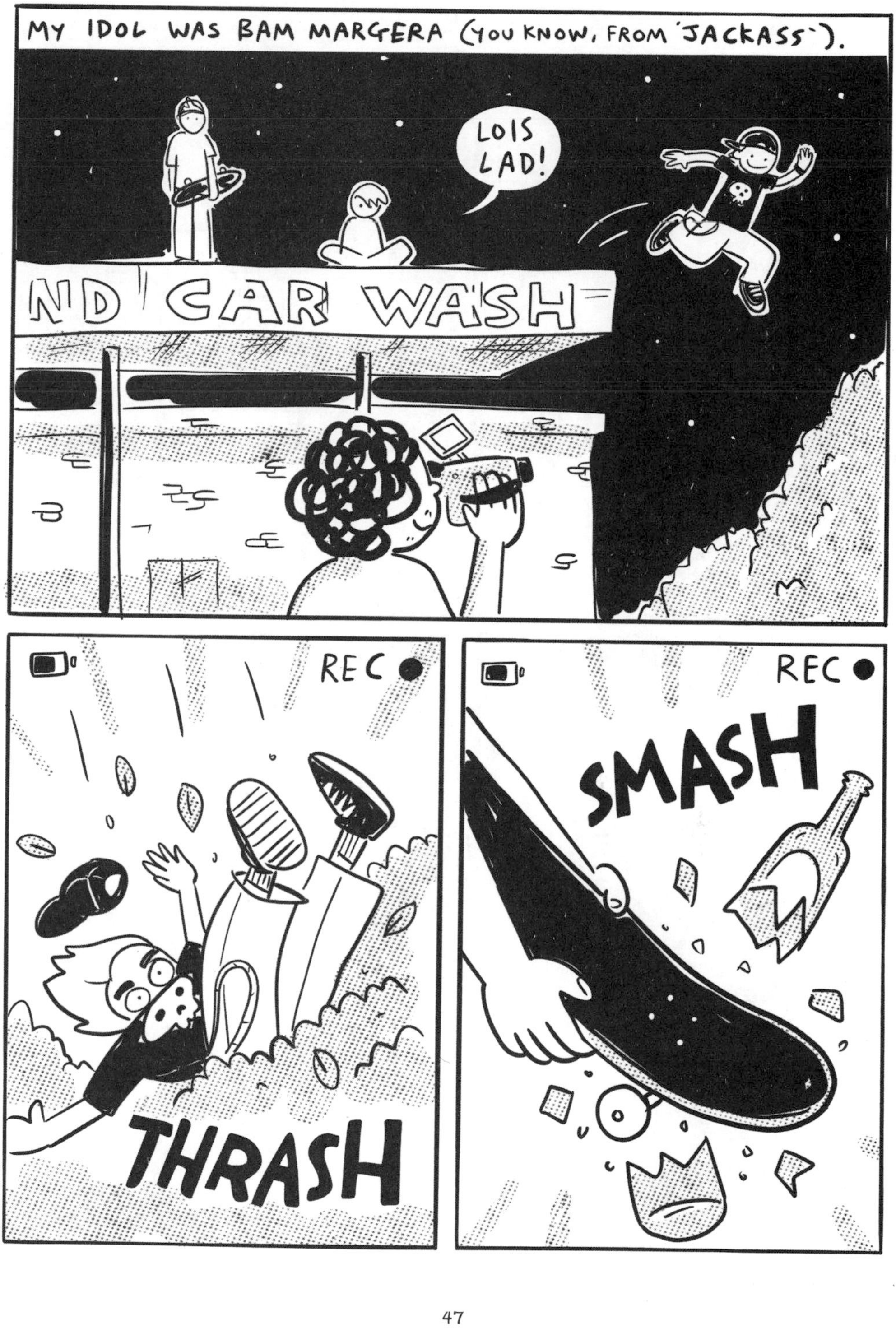
MY IDOL WAS BAM MARGERA (YOU KNOW, FROM 'JACKASS').
LOIS LAD!
ND CAR WASH
REC
THRASH
REC
SMASH

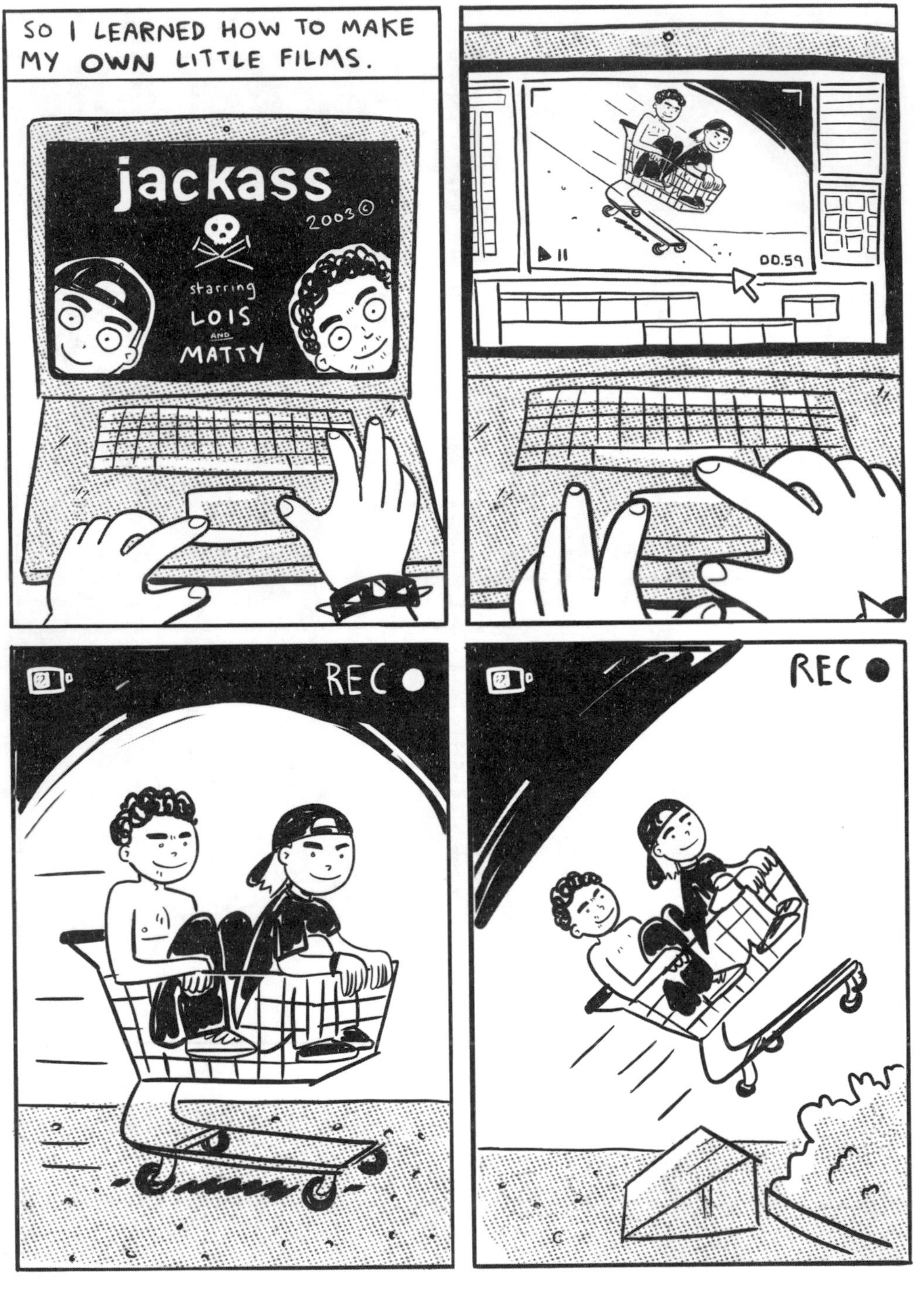
SO I LEARNED HOW TO MAKE MY OWN LITTLE FILMS.
jackass
2003©
starring
LOIS
AND
MATTY
00.59
REC
REC

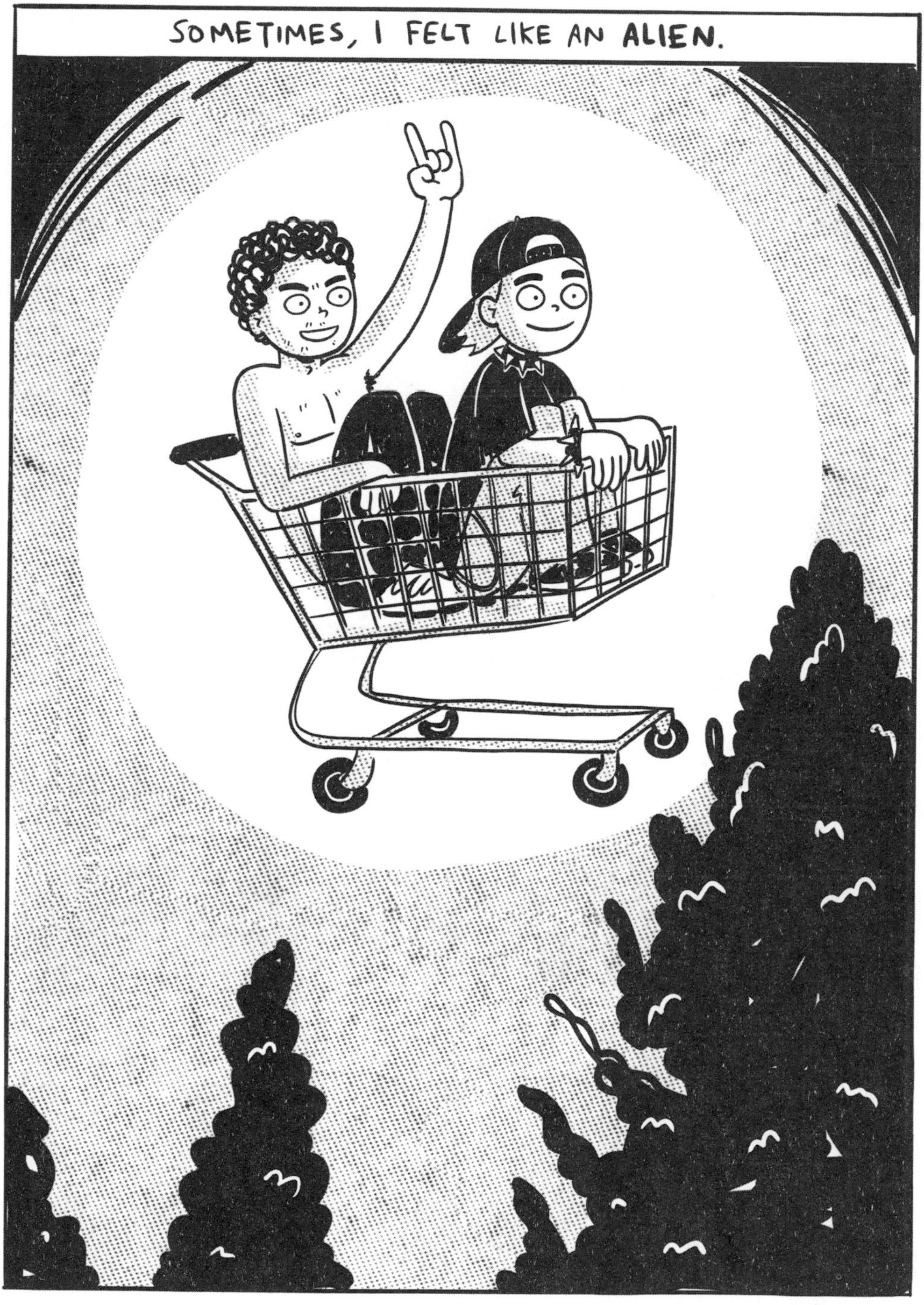
SOMETIMES, I FELT LIKE AN **ALIEN**.

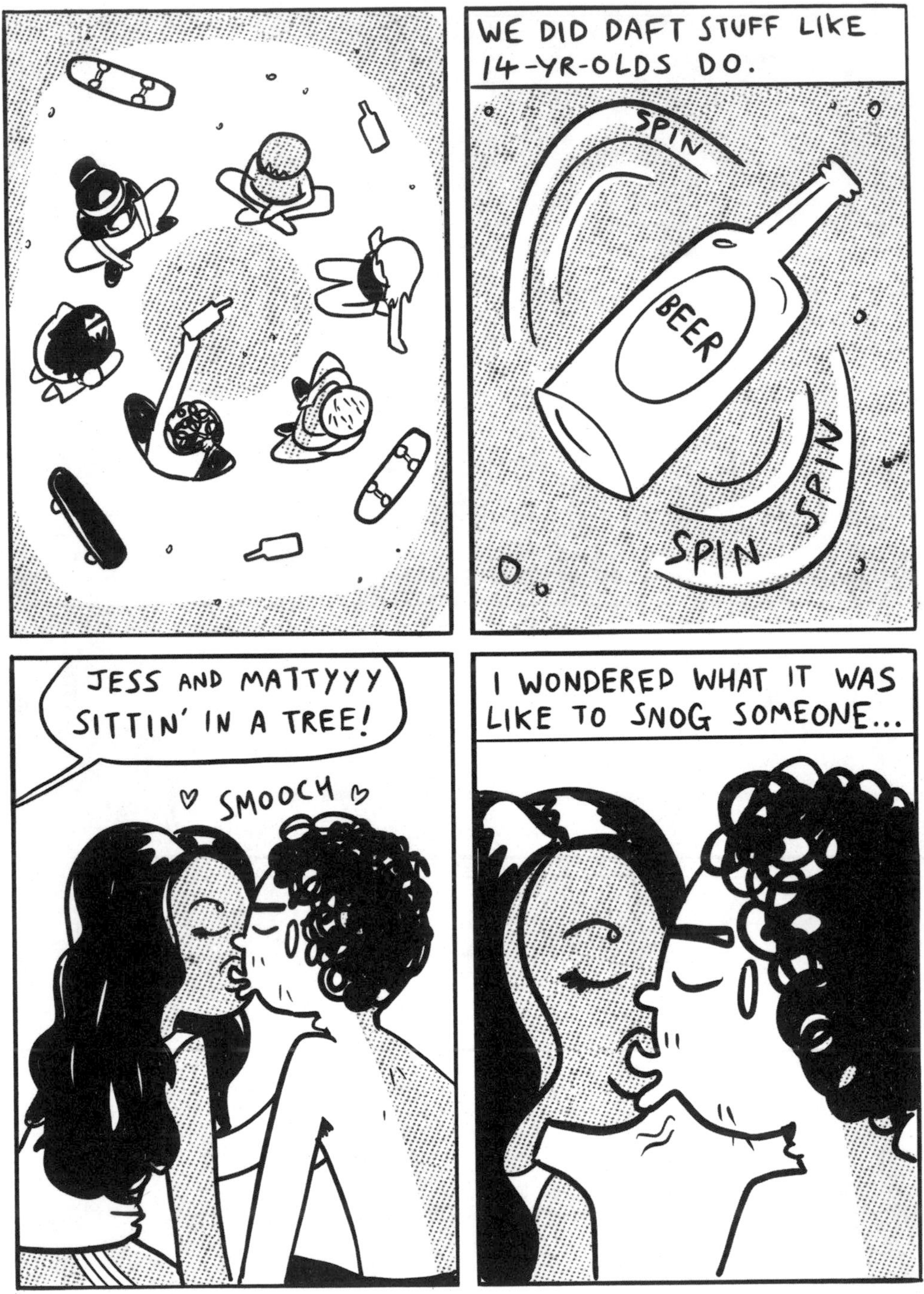

WE DID DAFT STUFF LIKE 14-YR-OLDS DO.
SPIN
BEER
SPIN
SPIN
JESS AND MATTYYY SITTIN' IN A TREE!
SMOOCH
I WONDERED WHAT IT WAS LIKE TO SNOG SOMEONE...

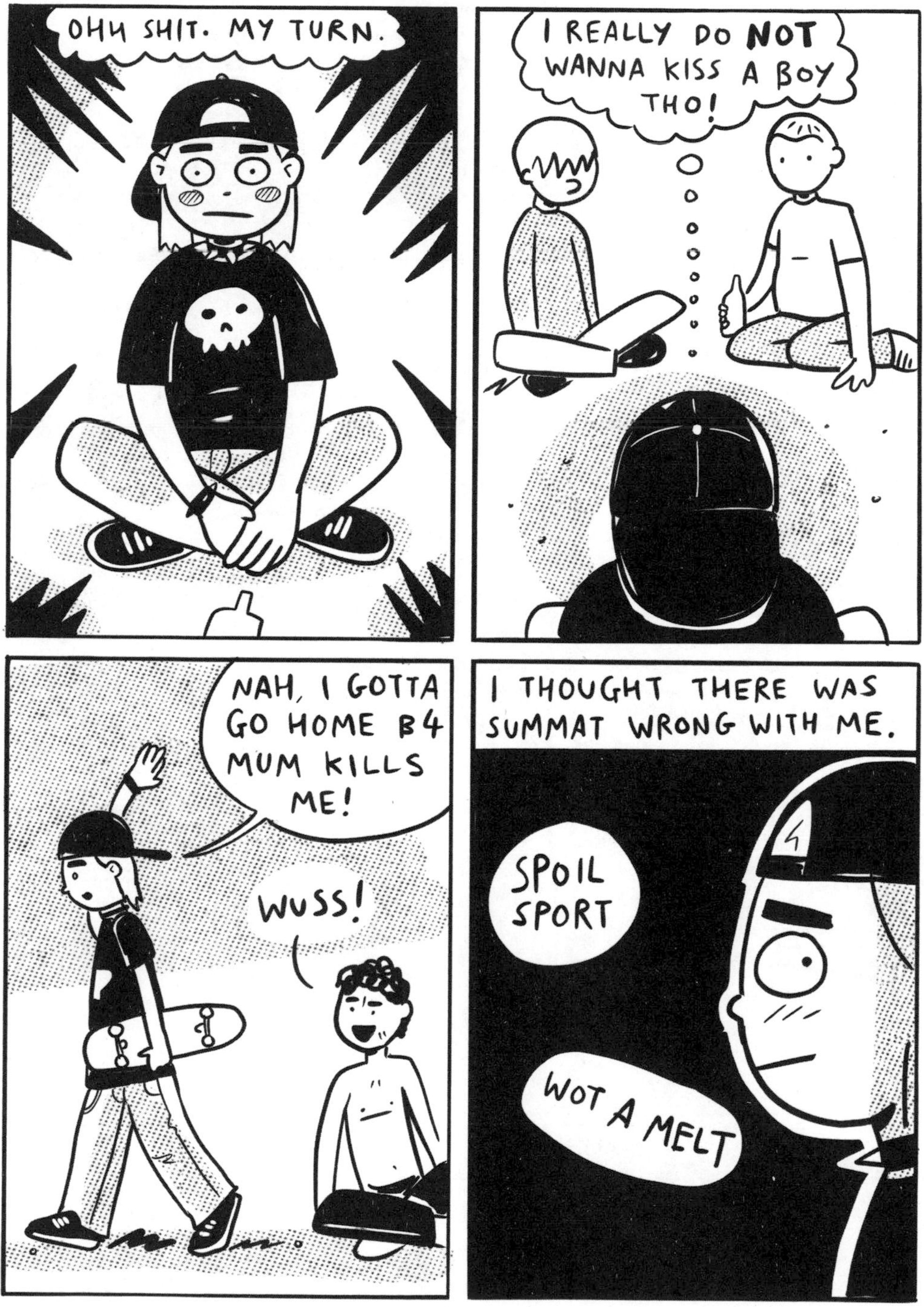
OHH SHIT. MY TURN.
I REALLY DO NOT WANNA KISS A BOY THO!
NAH, I GOTTA GO HOME B4 MUM KILLS ME!
WUSS!
I THOUGHT THERE WAS SUMMAT WRONG WITH ME.
SPOIL SPORT
WOT A MELT

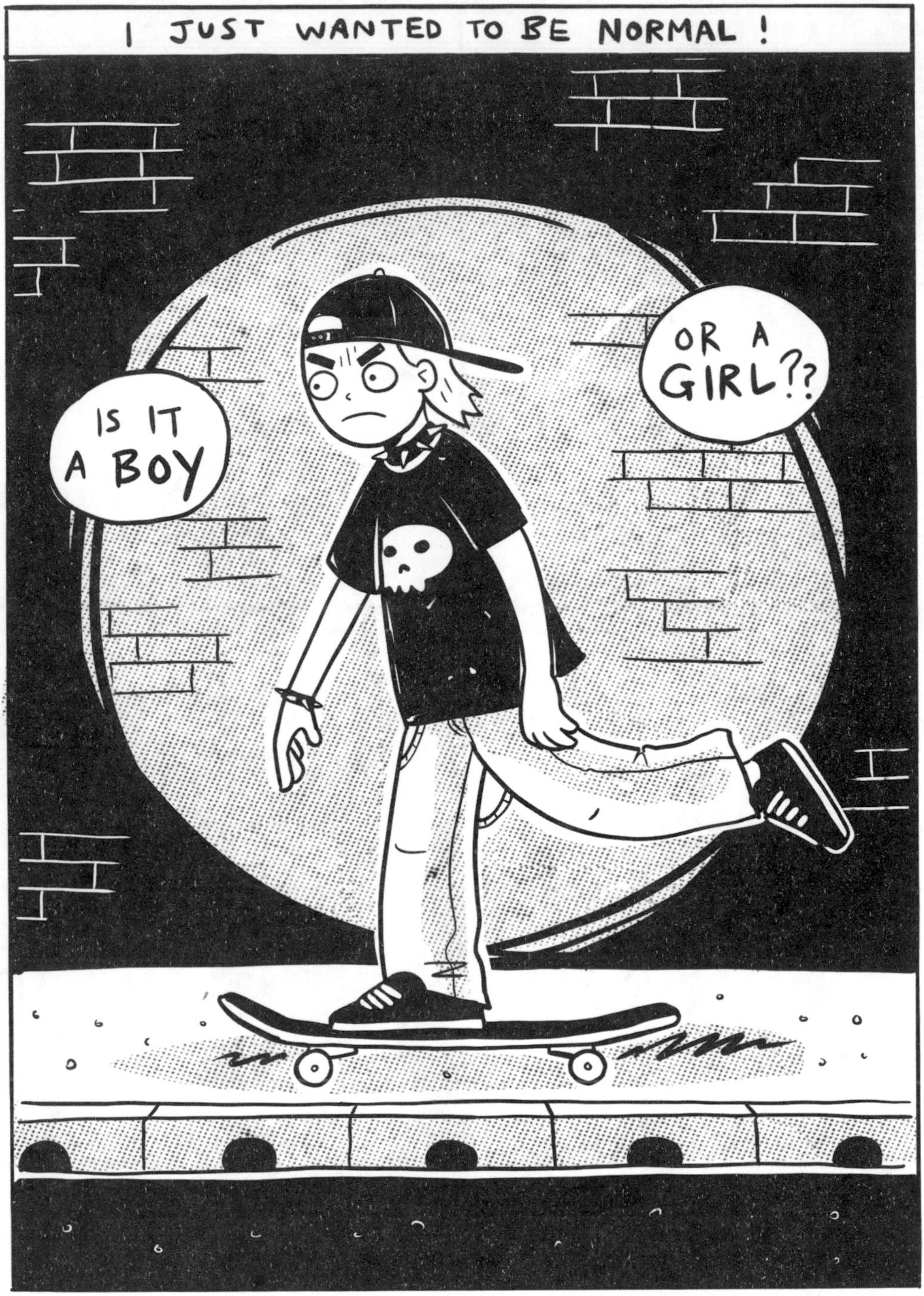
I JUST WANTED TO BE NORMAL!
IS IT A BOY
OR A GIRL??

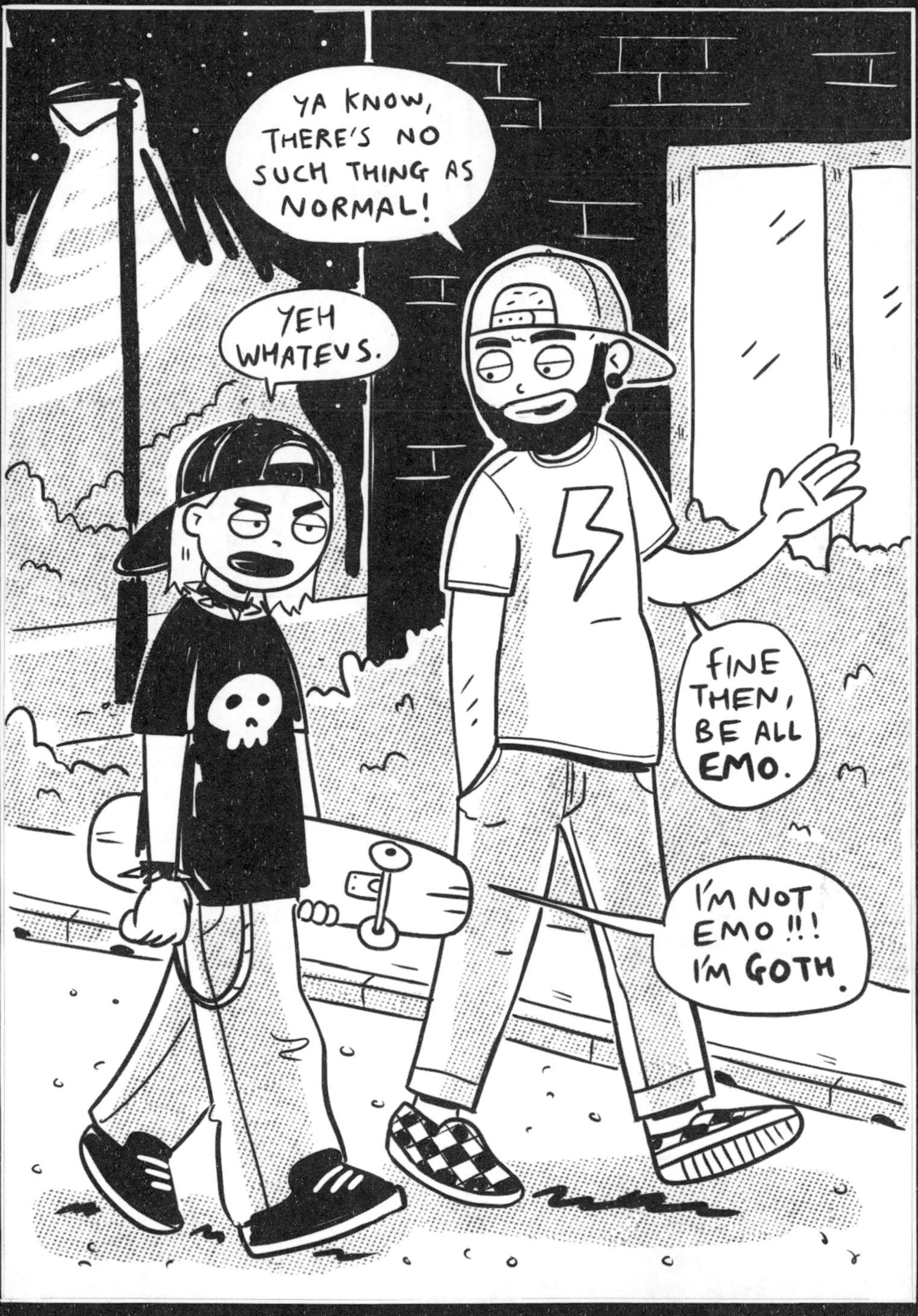
YA KNOW, THERE'S NO SUCH THING AS NORMAL!
YEH WHATEVS.
FINE THEN, BE ALL **EMO**.
I'M NOT EMO!!! I'M **GOTH**.

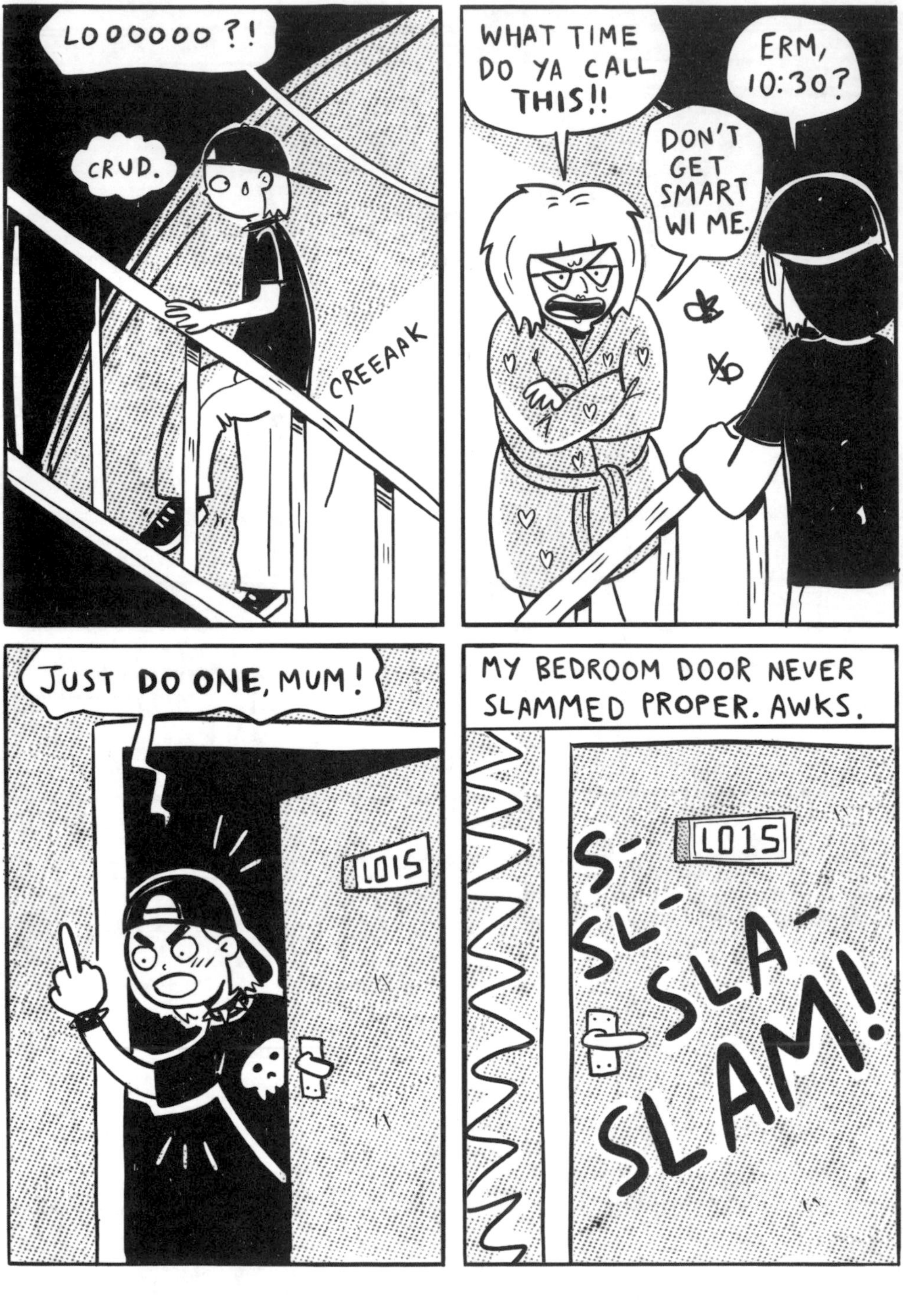
LOOOOOO?!
CRUD.
CREEAAK
WHAT TIME DO YA CALL THIS!!
ERM, 10:30?
DON'T GET SMART WI ME.
JUST DO ONE, MUM!
LOIS
MY BEDROOM DOOR NEVER SLAMMED PROPER. AWKS.
LOIS
S- SL- SLA- SLAM!

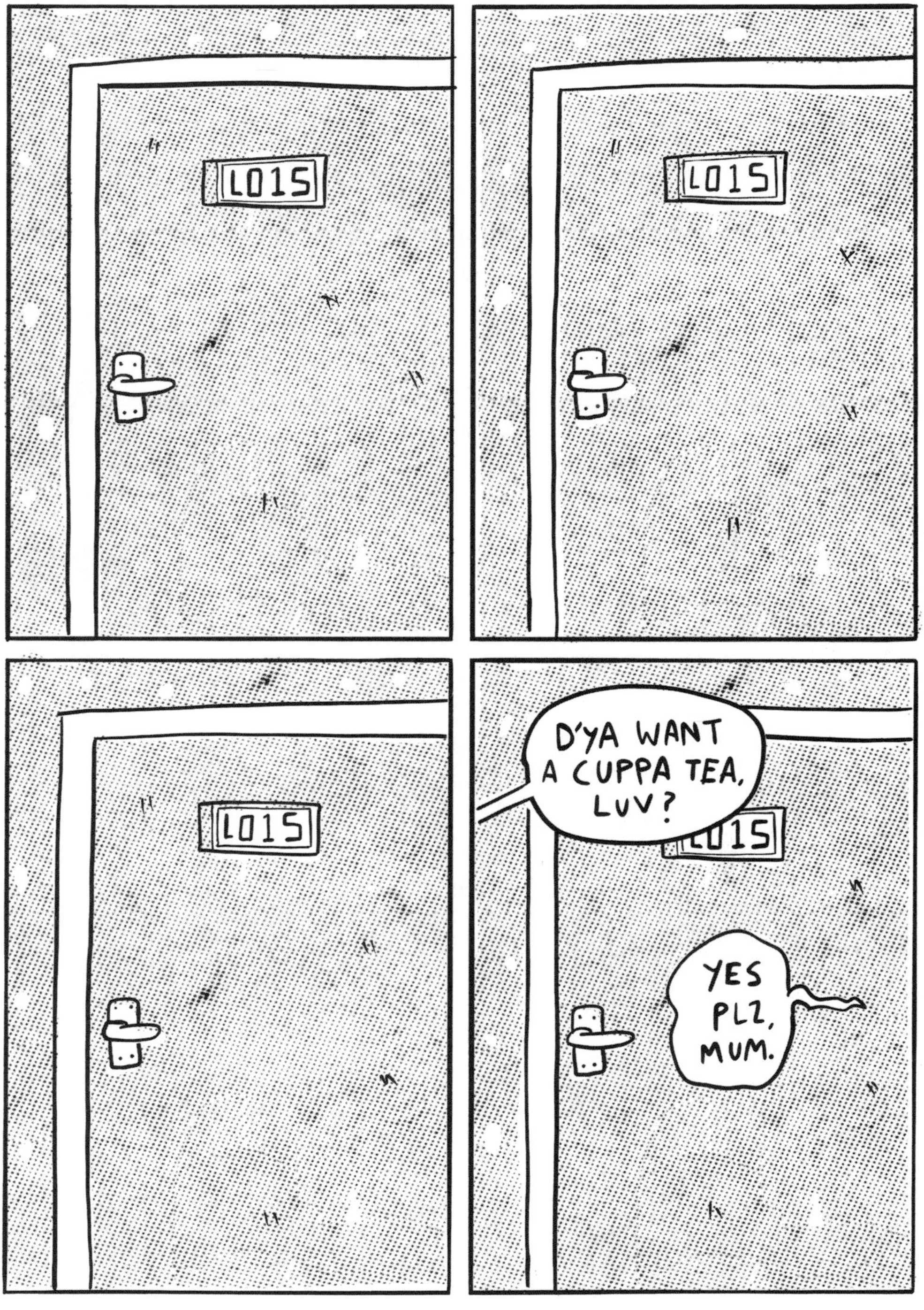
L015
L015
L015
D'YA WANT A CUPPA TEA, LUV?
L015
YES PLZ, MUM.

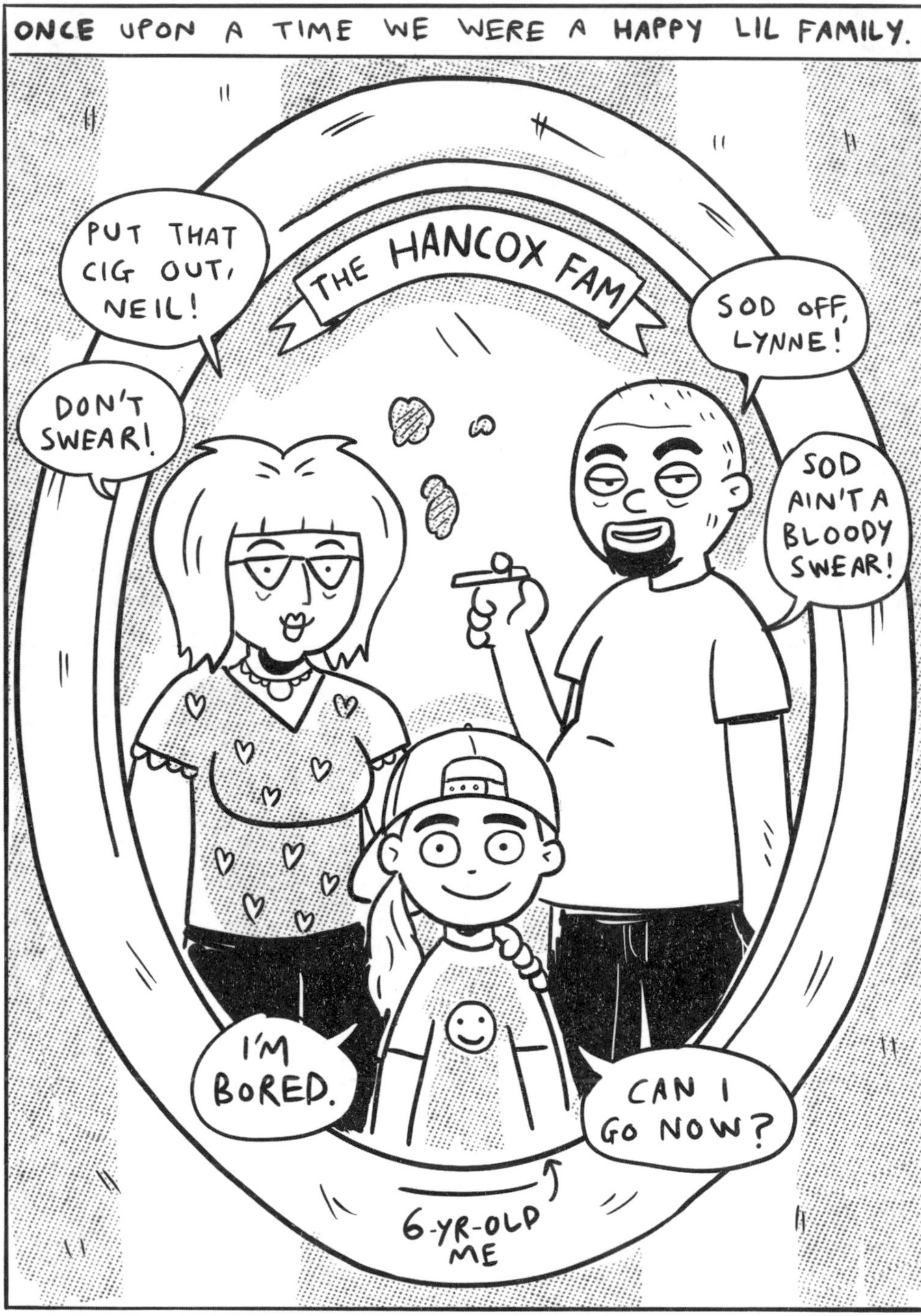
ONCE UPON A TIME WE WERE A HAPPY LIL FAMILY.
THE HANCOX FAM
PUT THAT CIG OUT, NEIL!
SOD OFF, LYNNE!
DON'T SWEAR!
SOD AIN'T A BLOODY SWEAR!
I'M BORED.
CAN I GO NOW?
6-YR-OLD ME

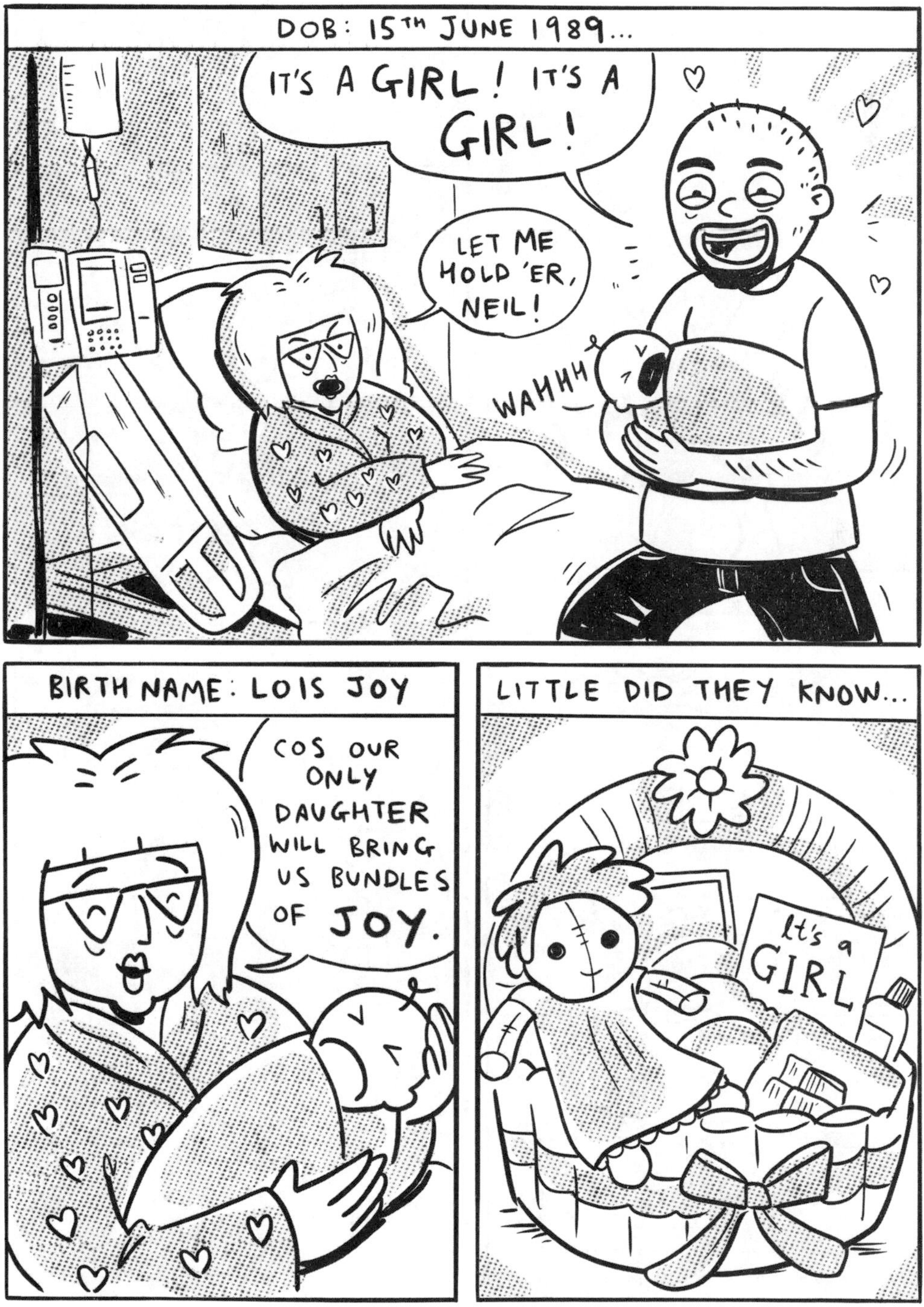
DOB: 15TH JUNE 1989...
IT'S A GIRL! IT'S A GIRL!
LET ME HOLD 'ER, NEIL!
WAHHH
BIRTH NAME: LOIS JOY
COS OUR ONLY DAUGHTER WILL BRING US BUNDLES OF JOY.
LITTLE DID THEY KNOW...
It's a GIRL

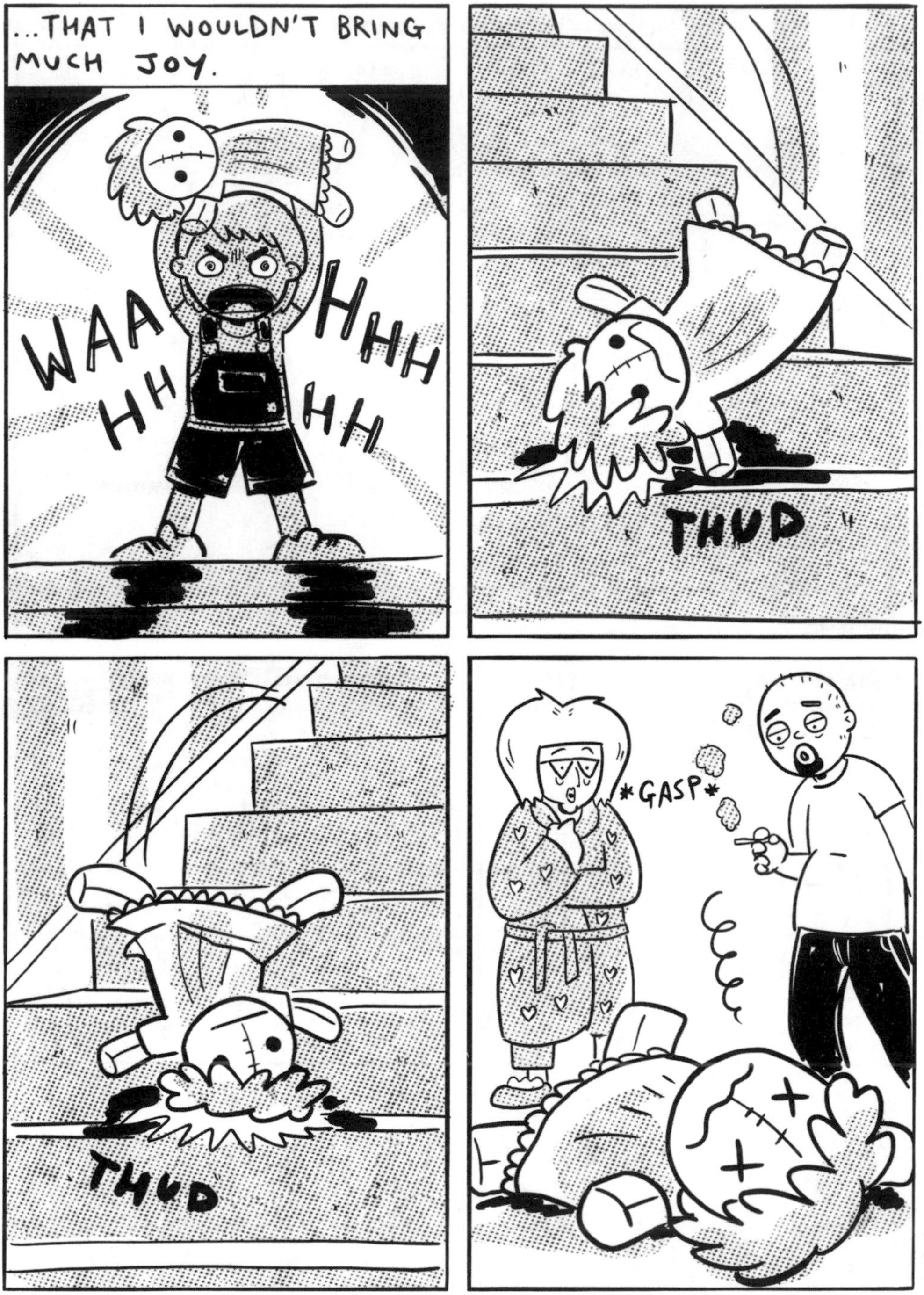
...THAT I WOULDN'T BRING MUCH JOY.
WAAHH HHHHHH
THUD
THUD
GASP

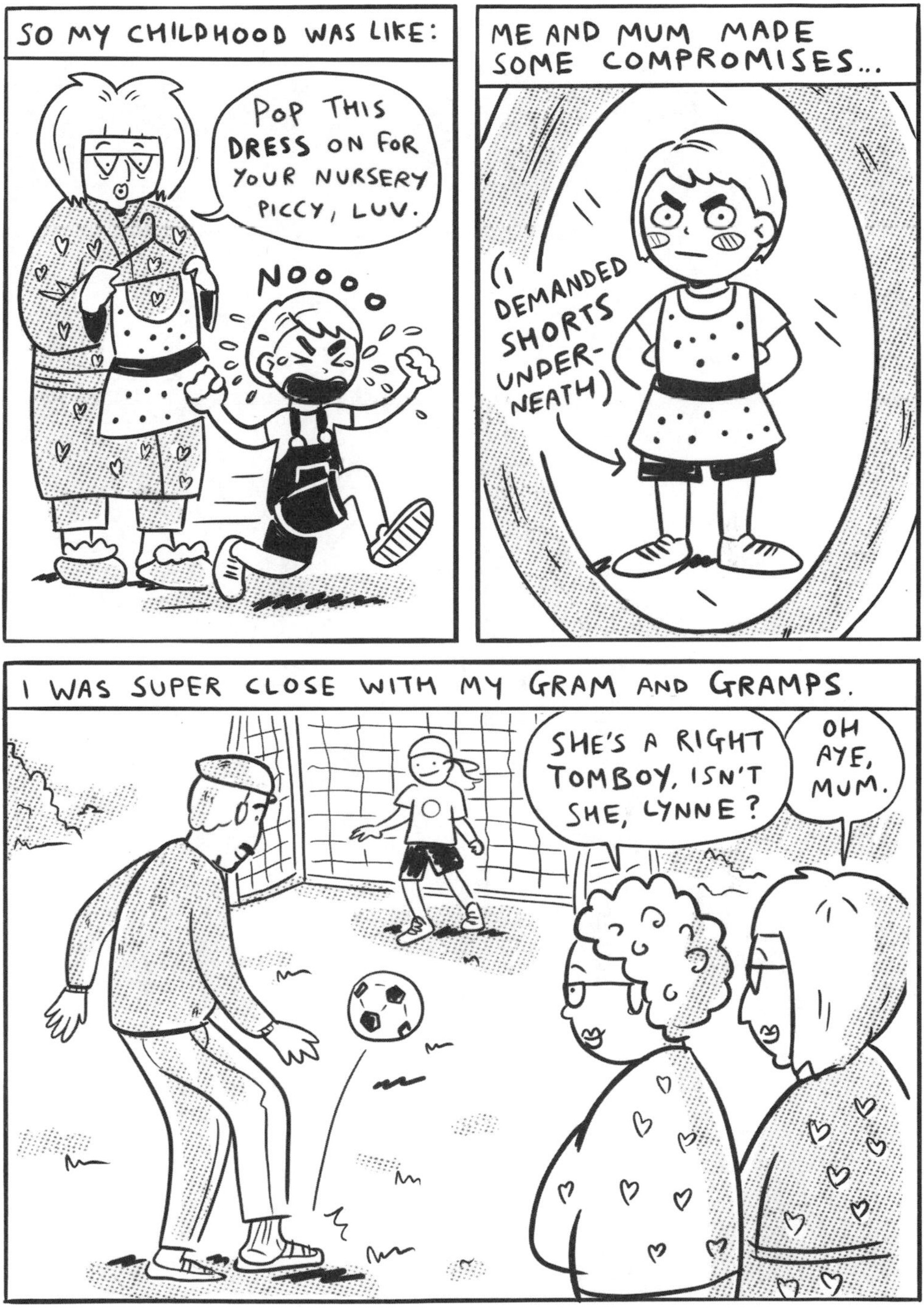
SO MY CHILDHOOD WAS LIKE:
POP THIS DRESS ON FOR YOUR NURSERY PICCY, LUV.
NOOOOO
ME AND MUM MADE SOME COMPROMISES...
(I DEMANDED SHORTS UNDER-NEATH)
I WAS SUPER CLOSE WITH MY GRAM AND GRAMPS.
SHE'S A RIGHT TOMBOY, ISN'T SHE, LYNNE?
OH AYE, MUM.

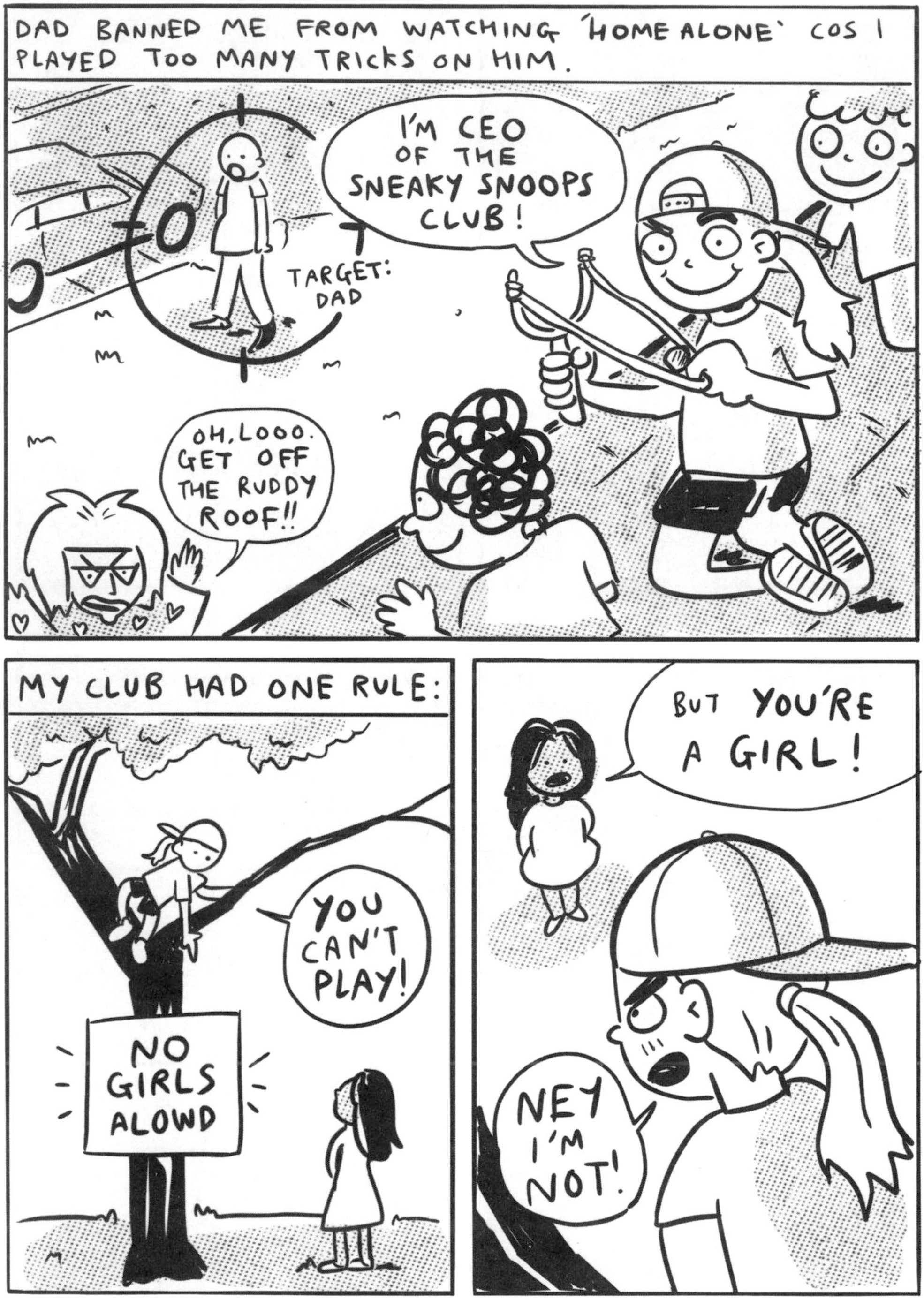
DAD BANNED ME FROM WATCHING 'HOME ALONE' COS I PLAYED TOO MANY TRICKS ON HIM.
I'M CEO OF THE SNEAKY SNOOPS CLUB!
TARGET: DAD
OH, LOOO. GET OFF THE RUDDY ROOF!!
MY CLUB HAD ONE RULE:
YOU CAN'T PLAY!
NO GIRLS ALOWD
BUT YOU'RE A GIRL!
NEY I'M NOT!

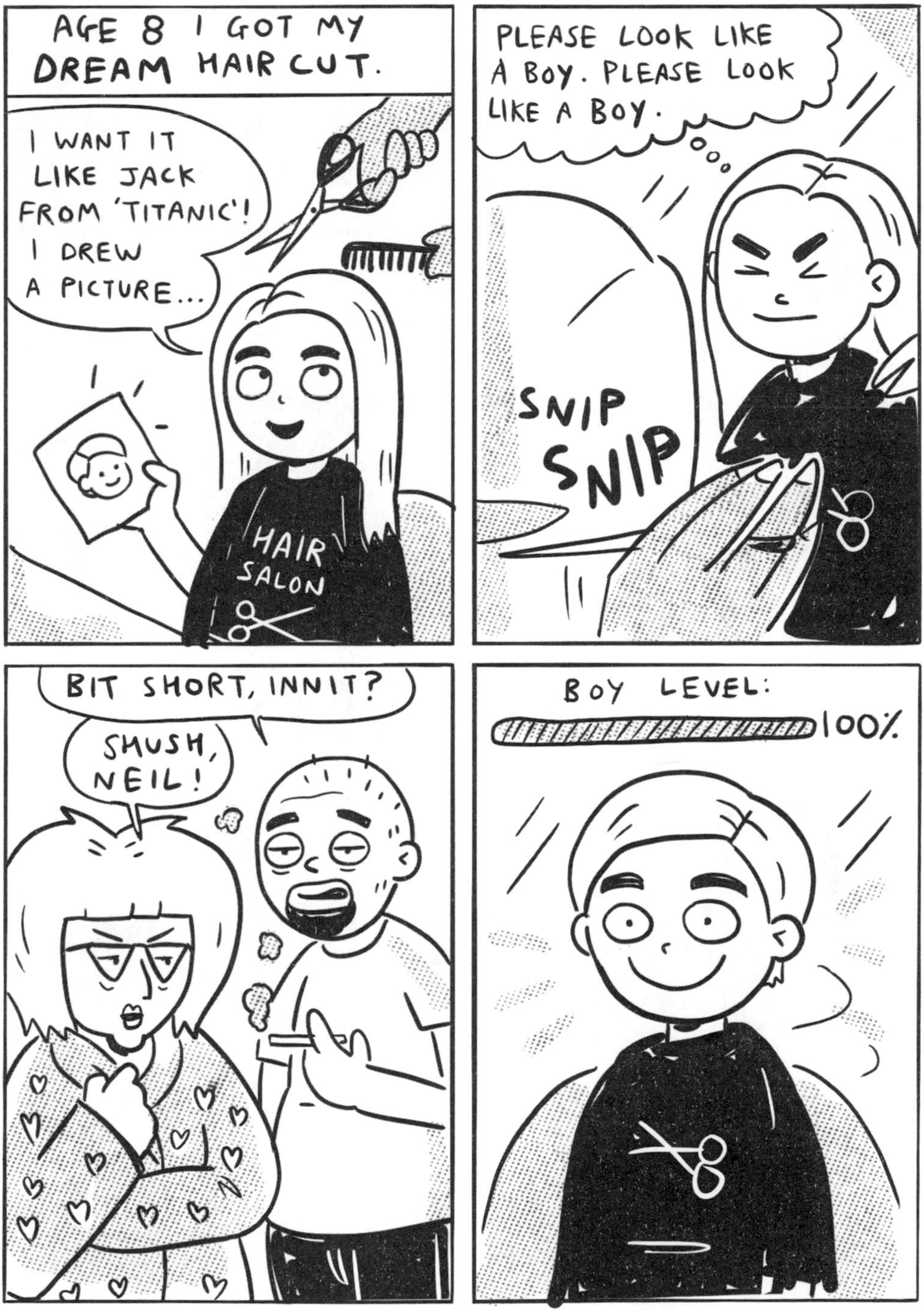
AGE 8 I GOT MY DREAM HAIR CUT.
I WANT IT LIKE JACK FROM 'TITANIC'! I DREW A PICTURE...
HAIR SALON
PLEASE LOOK LIKE A BOY. PLEASE LOOK LIKE A BOY.
SNIP SNIP
BIT SHORT, INNIT?
SHUSH, NEIL!
BOY LEVEL:
100%

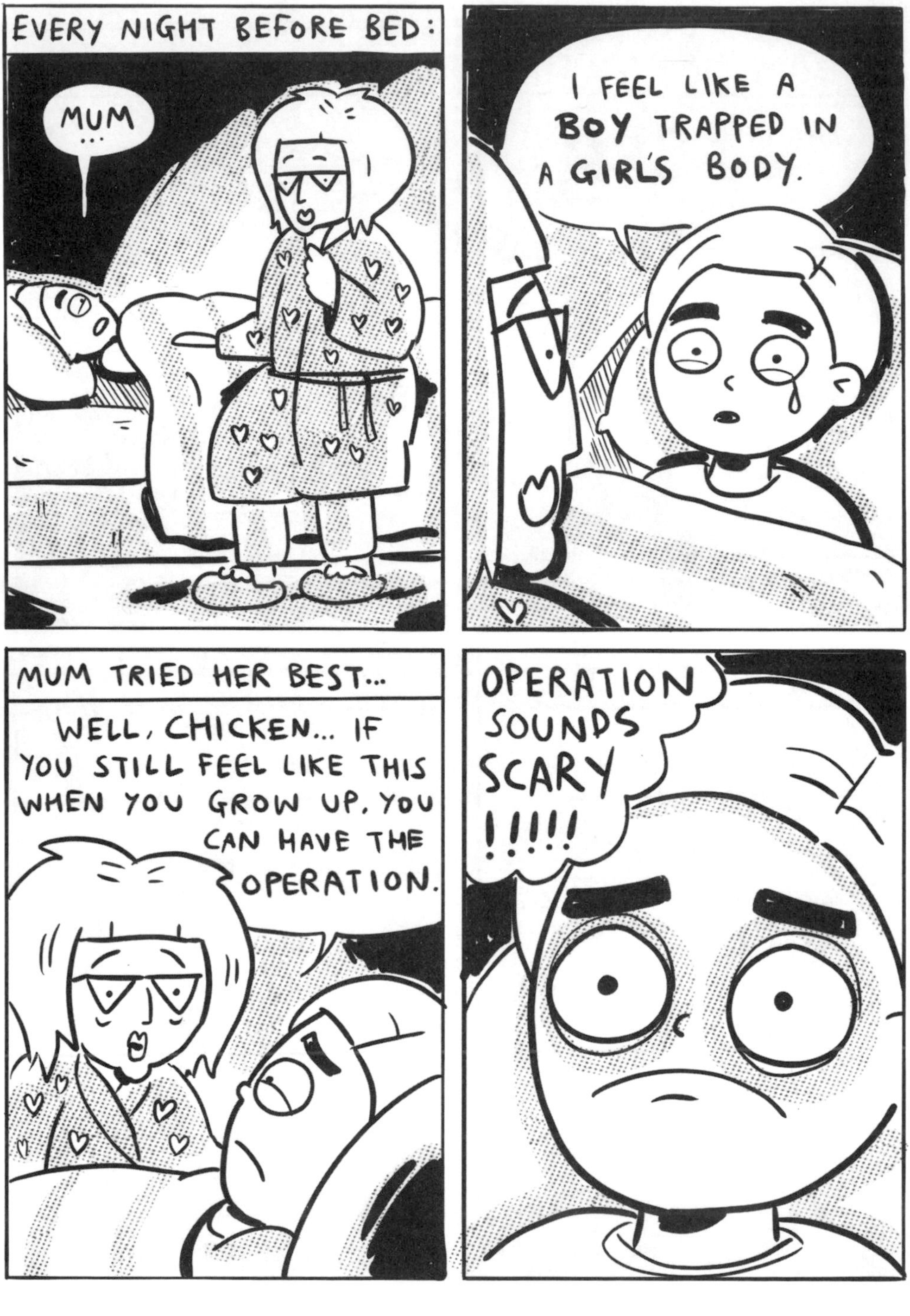
EVERY NIGHT BEFORE BED:
MUM ...
I FEEL LIKE A BOY TRAPPED IN A GIRL'S BODY.
MUM TRIED HER BEST...
WELL, CHICKEN... IF YOU STILL FEEL LIKE THIS WHEN YOU GROW UP, YOU CAN HAVE THE OPERATION.
OPERATION SOUNDS SCARY !!!!!

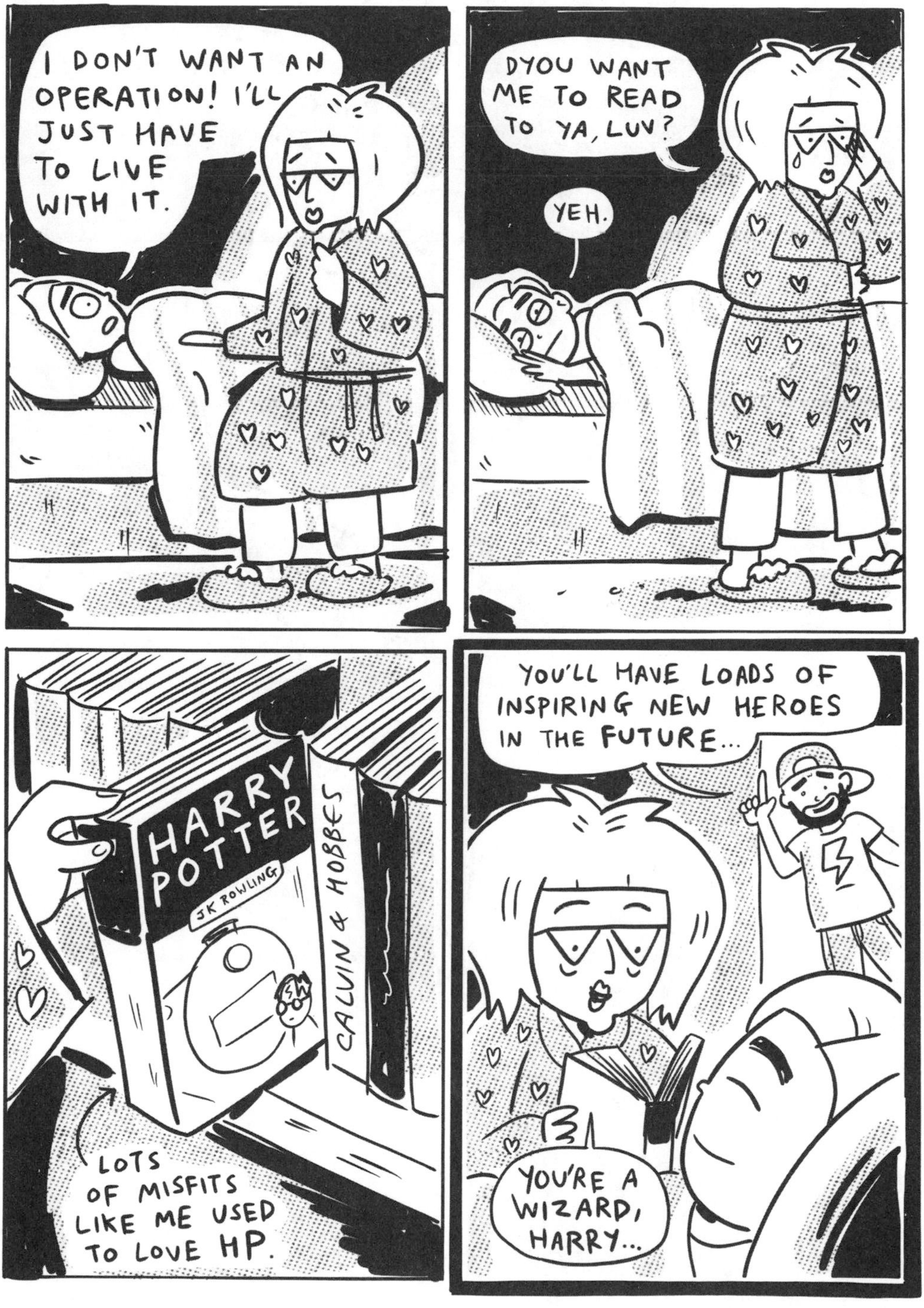
I DON'T WANT AN OPERATION! I'LL JUST HAVE TO LIVE WITH IT.
DYOU WANT ME TO READ TO YA, LUV?
YEH.
HARRY POTTER
JK ROWLING
CALVIN & HOBBES
LOTS OF MISFITS LIKE ME USED TO LOVE HP.
YOU'LL HAVE LOADS OF INSPIRING NEW HEROES IN THE FUTURE...
YOU'RE A WIZARD, HARRY...

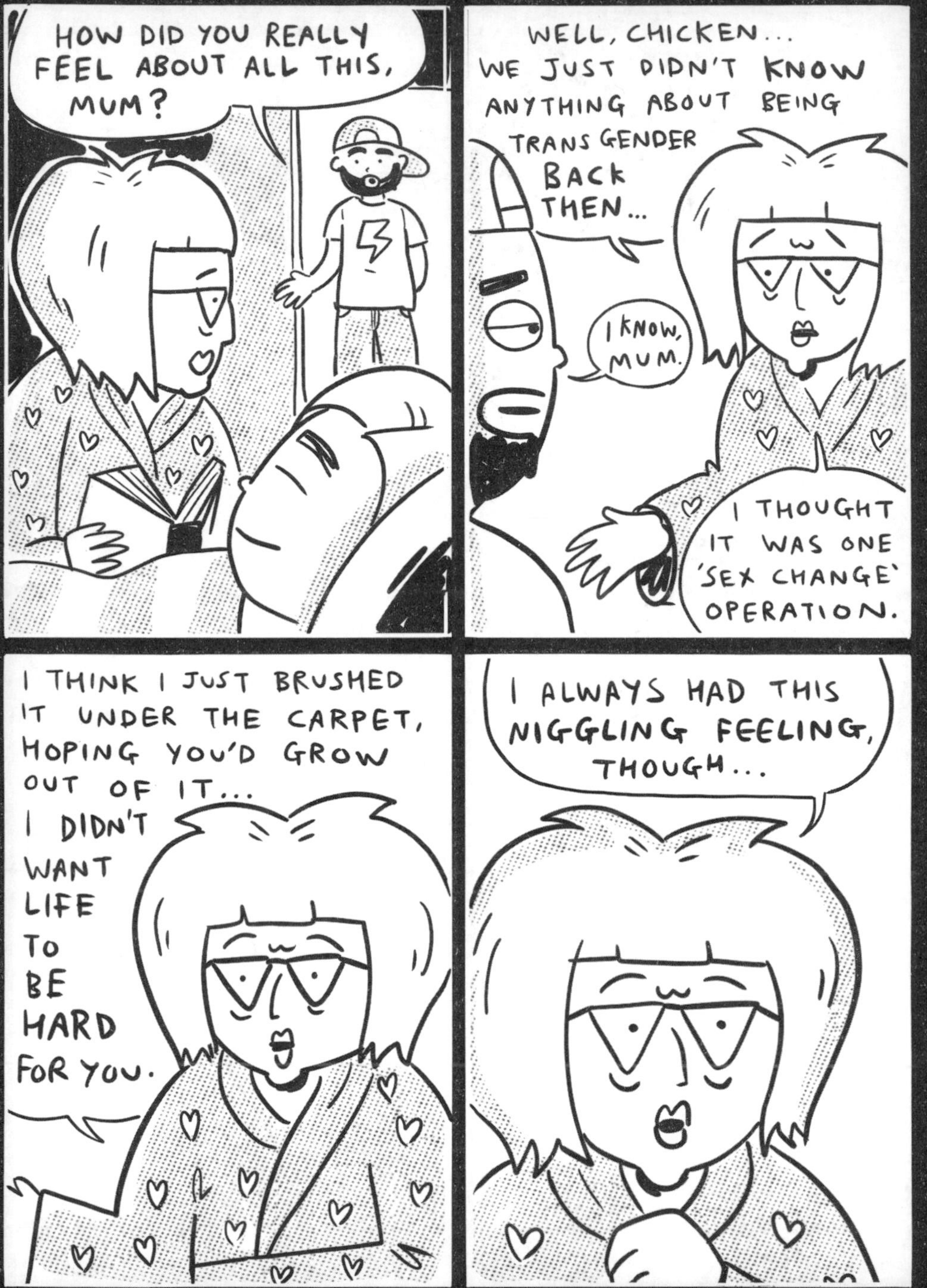
HOW DID YOU REALLY FEEL ABOUT ALL THIS, MUM?
WELL, CHICKEN... WE JUST DIDN'T KNOW ANYTHING ABOUT BEING TRANS GENDER BACK THEN...
I KNOW, MUM.
I THOUGHT IT WAS ONE 'SEX CHANGE' OPERATION.
I THINK I JUST BRUSHED IT UNDER THE CARPET, HOPING YOU'D GROW OUT OF IT... I DIDN'T WANT LIFE TO BE HARD FOR YOU.
I ALWAYS HAD THIS NIGGLING FEELING, THOUGH...

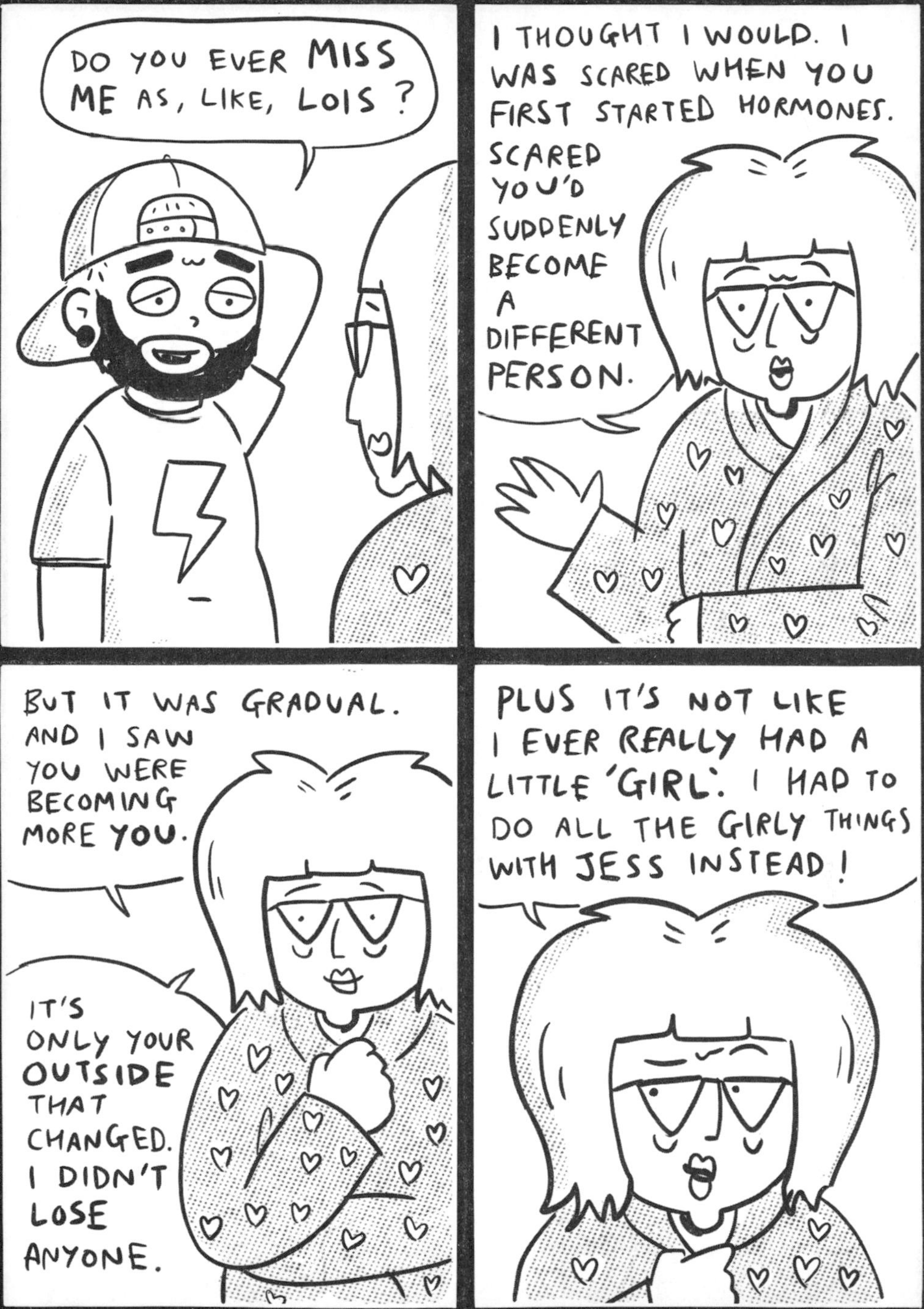
DO YOU EVER MISS ME AS, LIKE, LOIS?
I THOUGHT I WOULD. I WAS SCARED WHEN YOU FIRST STARTED HORMONES.
SCARED YOU'D SUDDENLY BECOME A DIFFERENT PERSON.
BUT IT WAS GRADUAL. AND I SAW YOU WERE BECOMING MORE YOU.
IT'S ONLY YOUR OUTSIDE THAT CHANGED. I DIDN'T LOSE ANYONE.
PLUS IT'S NOT LIKE I EVER REALLY HAD A LITTLE 'GIRL'. I HAD TO DO ALL THE GIRLY THINGS WITH JESS INSTEAD!

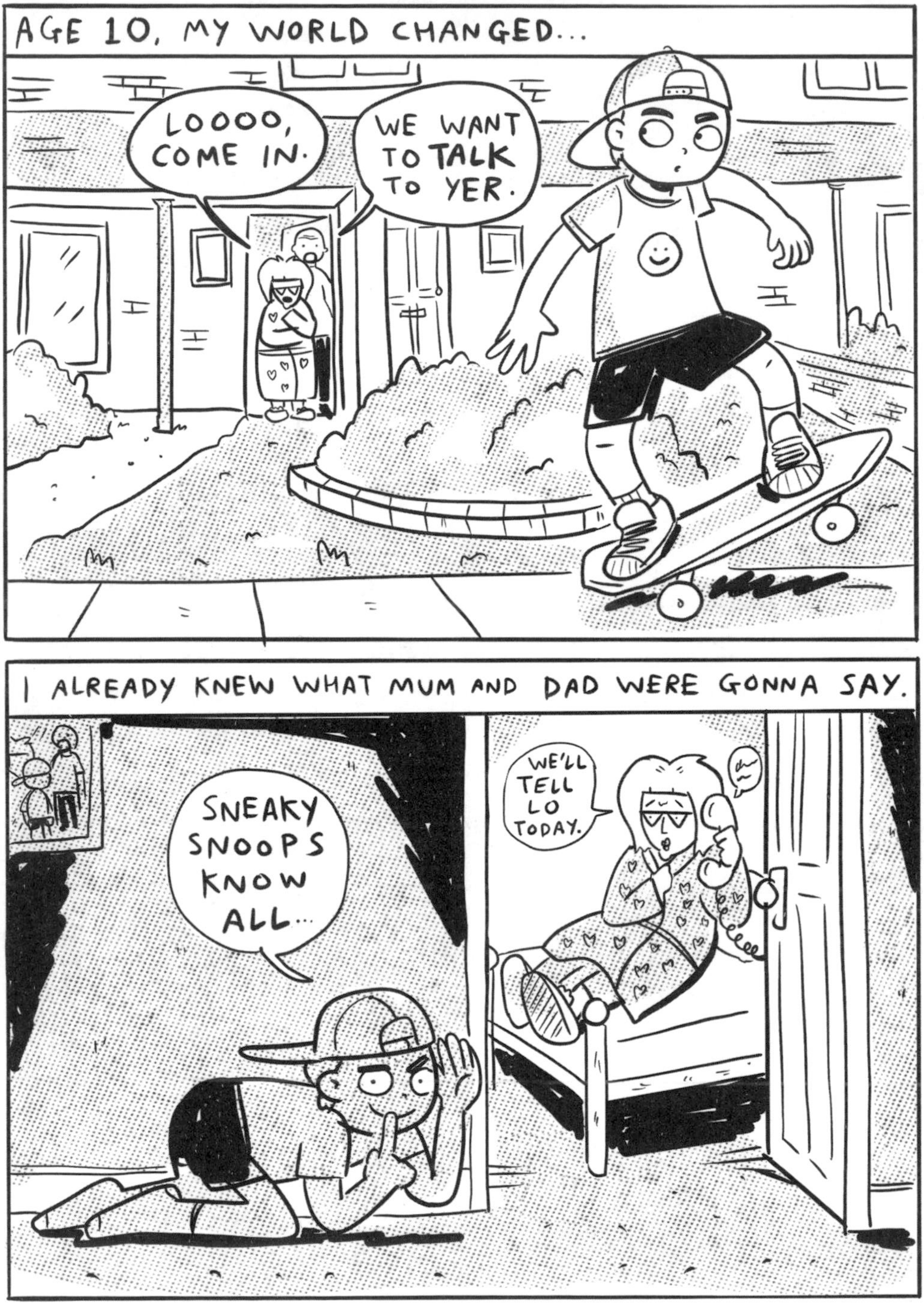
AGE 10, MY WORLD CHANGED...
LOOOO, COME IN.
WE WANT TO TALK TO YER.
I ALREADY KNEW WHAT MUM AND DAD WERE GONNA SAY.
SNEAKY SNOOPS KNOW ALL...
WE'LL TELL LO TODAY.

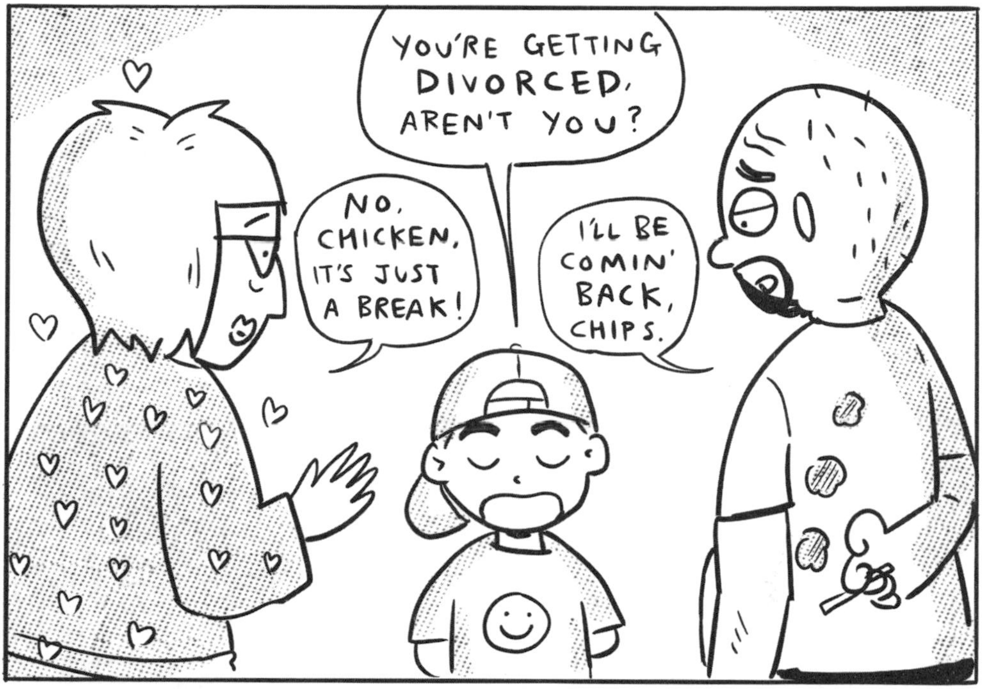
YOU'RE GETTING DIVORCED, AREN'T YOU?
NO, CHICKEN, IT'S JUST A BREAK!
I'LL BE COMIN' BACK, CHIPS.

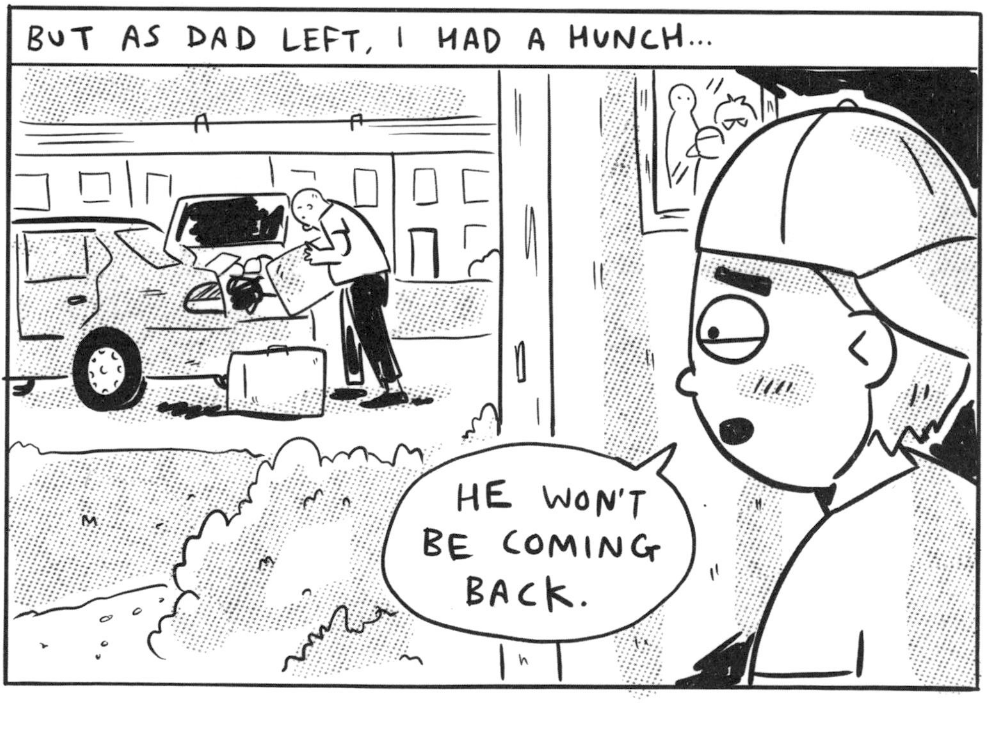
BUT AS DAD LEFT, I HAD A HUNCH...
HE WON'T BE COMING BACK.

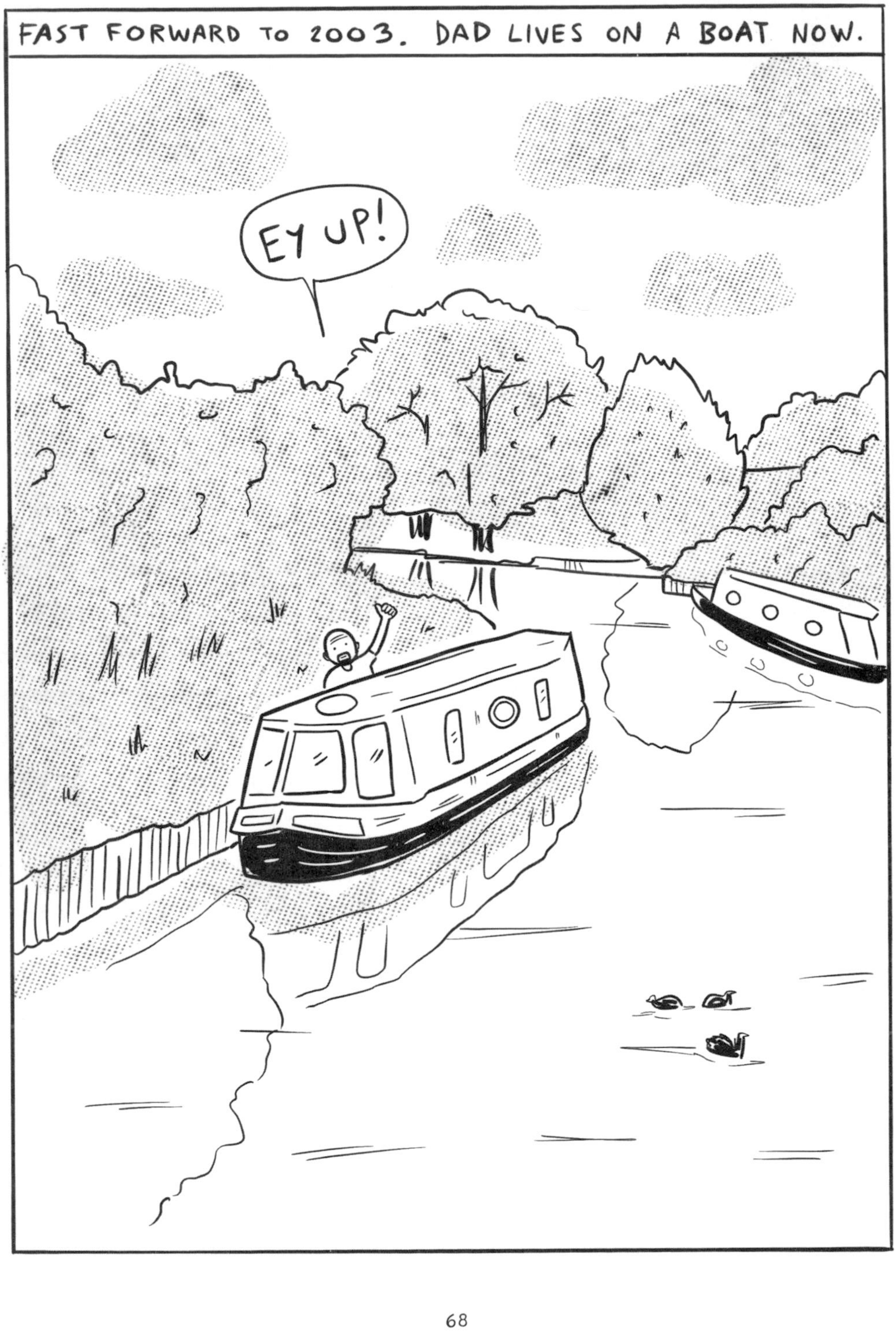
FAST FORWARD TO 2003. DAD LIVES ON A BOAT NOW.
EY UP!

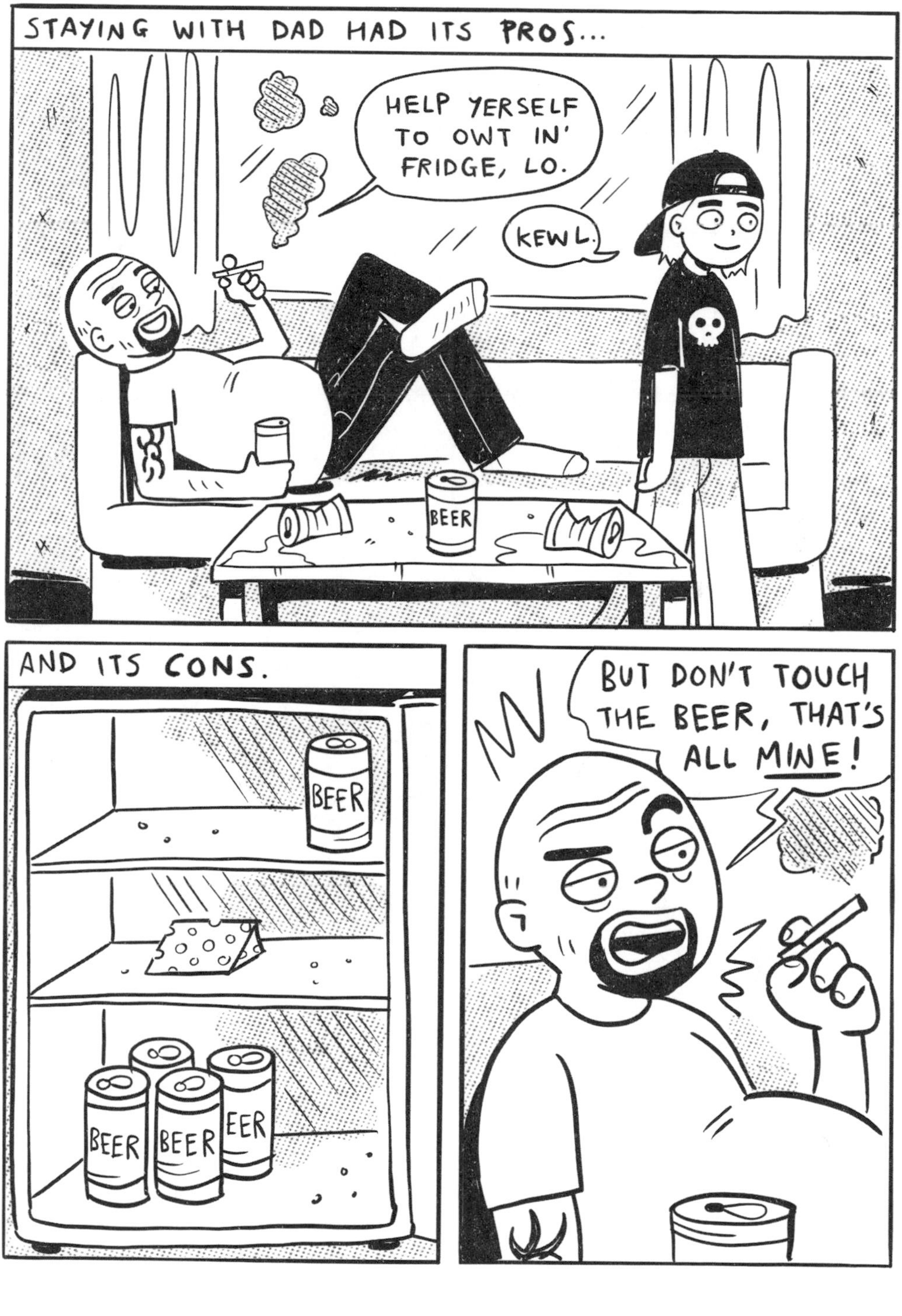
STAYING WITH DAD HAD ITS PROS...
HELP YERSELF TO OWT IN' FRIDGE, LO.
KEWL.
BEER
AND ITS CONS.
BEER
BEER
BEER
EER
BUT DON'T TOUCH THE BEER, THAT'S ALL MINE!

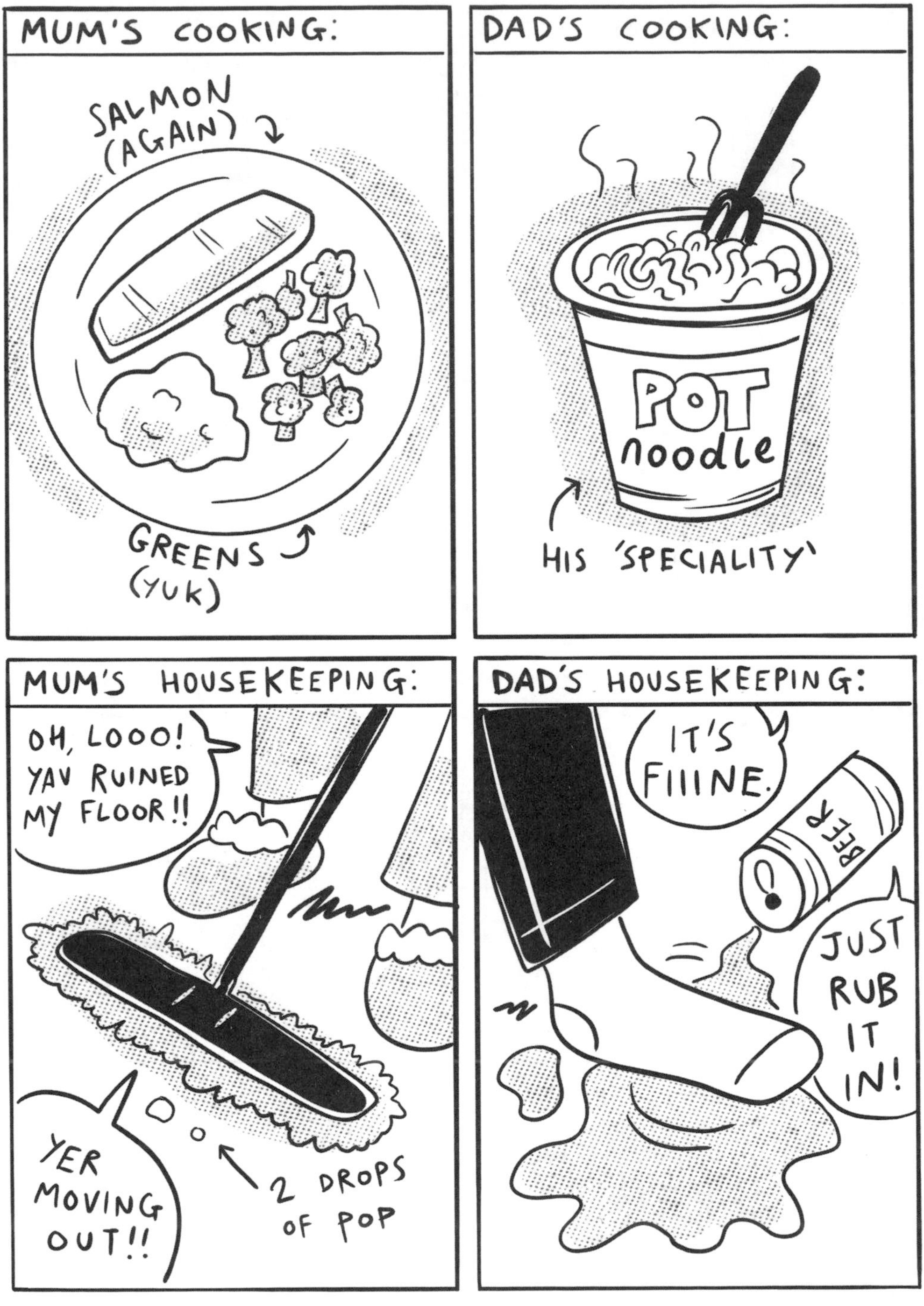
MUM'S COOKING:
SALMON (AGAIN)
GREENS (YUK)
DAD'S COOKING:
POT noodle
HIS 'SPECIALITY'
MUM'S HOUSEKEEPING:
OH, LOOO! YAV RUINED MY FLOOR!!
YER MOVING OUT!!
2 DROPS OF POP
DAD'S HOUSEKEEPING:
IT'S FIIINE.
BEER
JUST RUB IT IN!

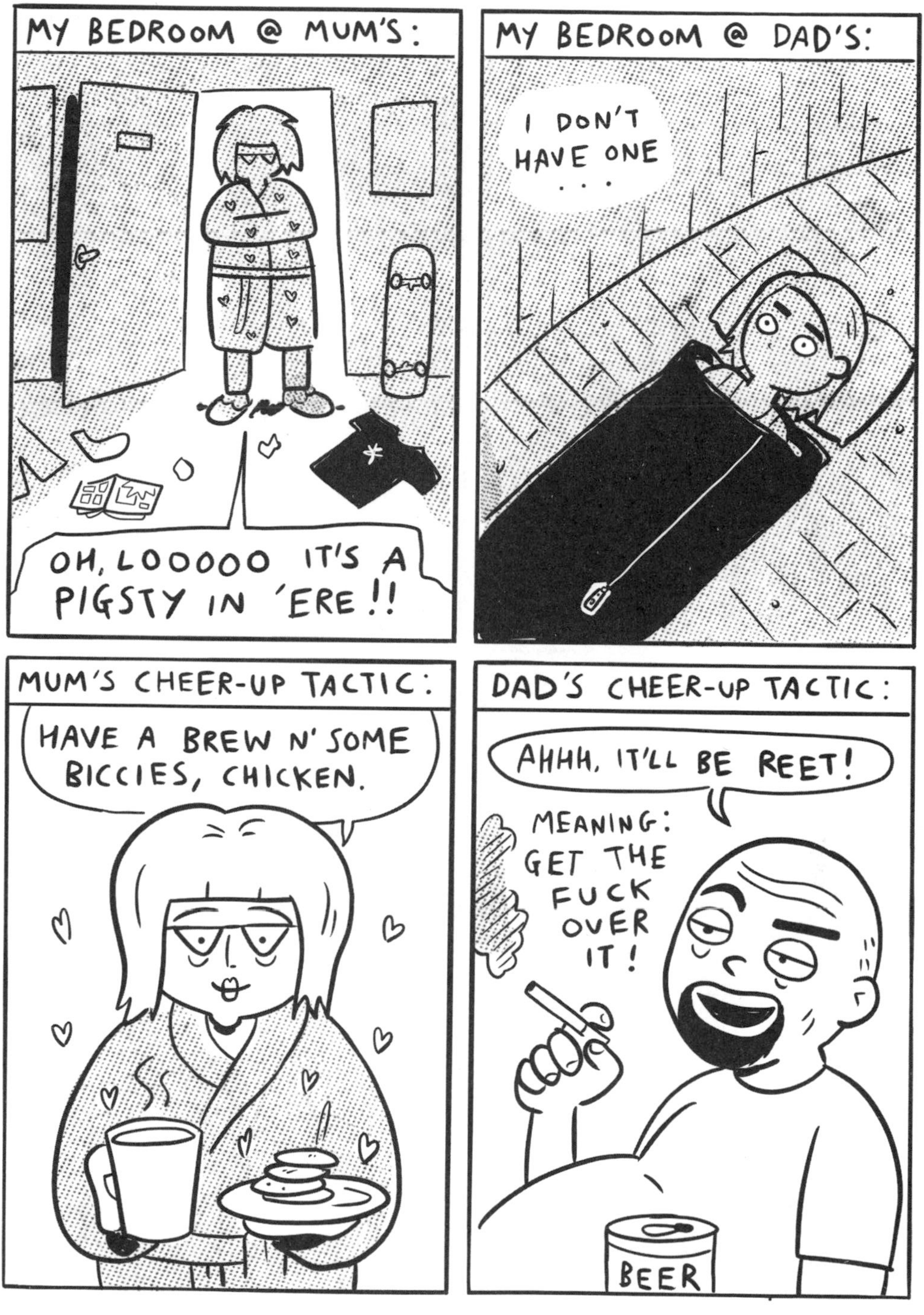
MY BEDROOM @ MUM'S:
OH, LOOOOO IT'S A PIGSTY IN 'ERE!!
MY BEDROOM @ DAD'S:
I DON'T HAVE ONE . . .
MUM'S CHEER-UP TACTIC:
HAVE A BREW N' SOME BICCIES, CHICKEN.
DAD'S CHEER-UP TACTIC:
AHHH, IT'LL BE REET!
MEANING: GET THE FUCK OVER IT!
BEER

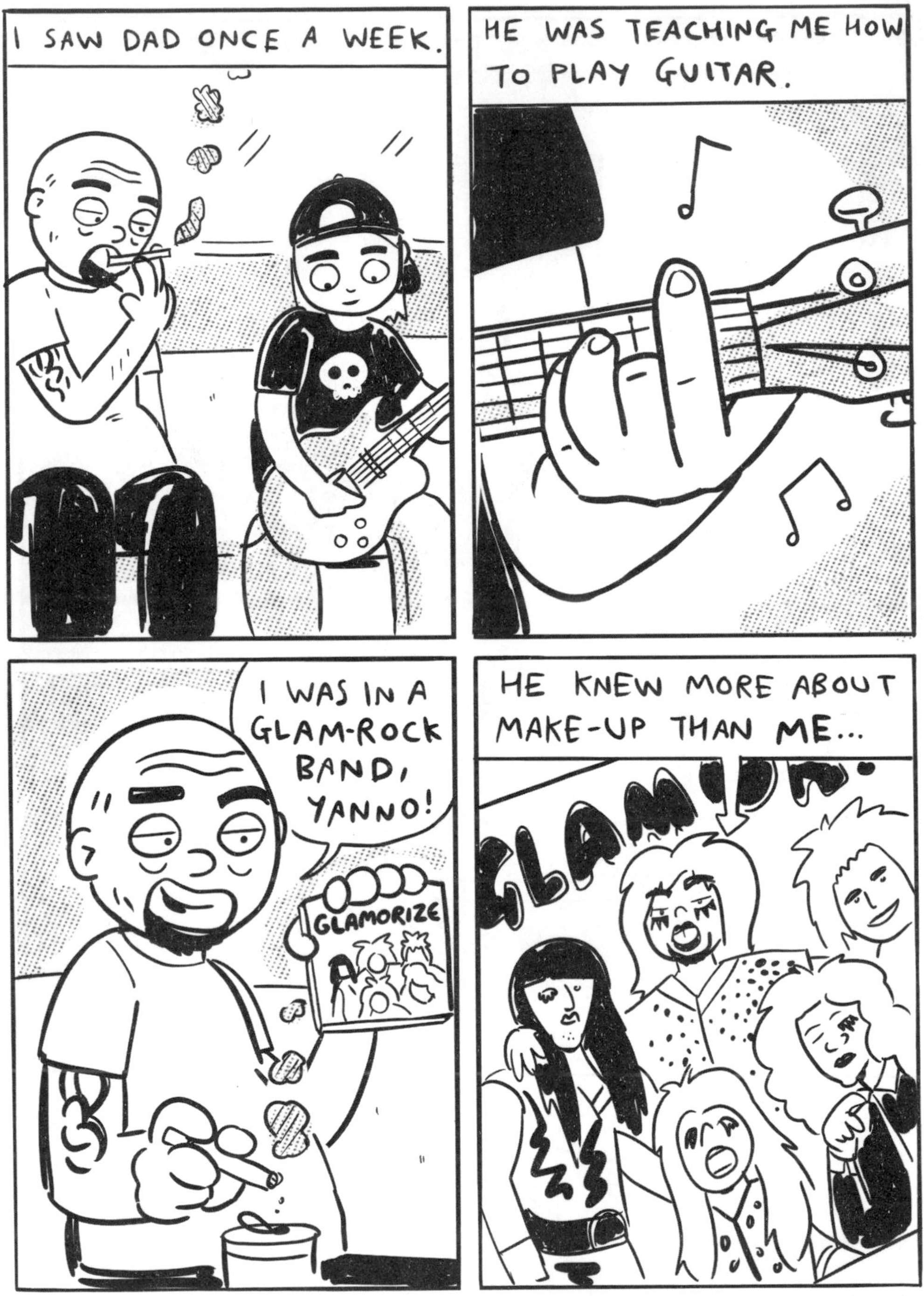
I SAW DAD ONCE A WEEK.
HE WAS TEACHING ME HOW TO PLAY GUITAR.
I WAS IN A GLAM-ROCK BAND, YANNO!
GLAMORIZE
HE KNEW MORE ABOUT MAKE-UP THAN ME...

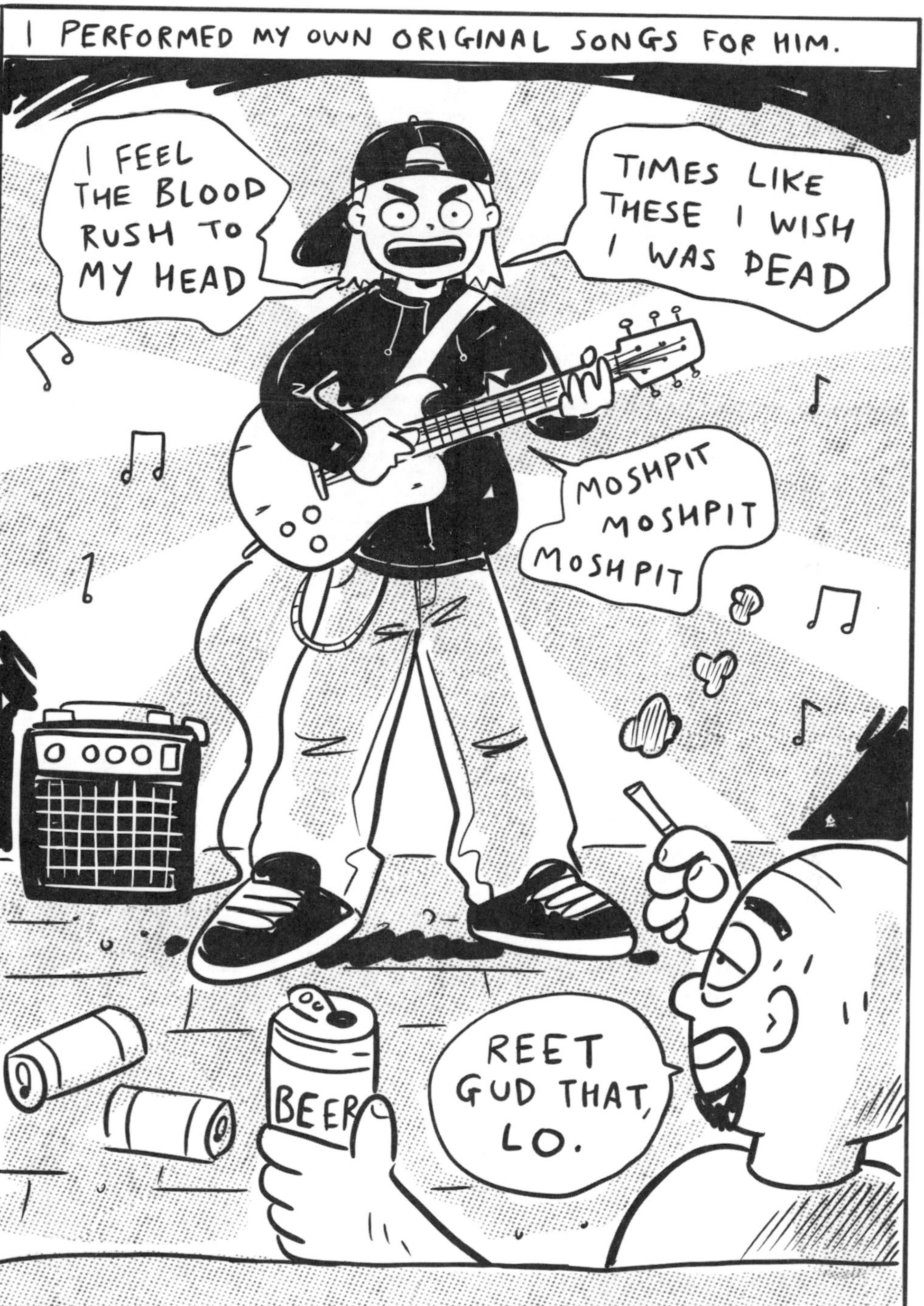
I PERFORMED MY OWN ORIGINAL SONGS FOR HIM.
I FEEL THE BLOOD RUSH TO MY HEAD
TIMES LIKE THESE I WISH I WAS DEAD
MOSHPIT MOSHPIT MOSHPIT
BEER
REET GUD THAT, LO.

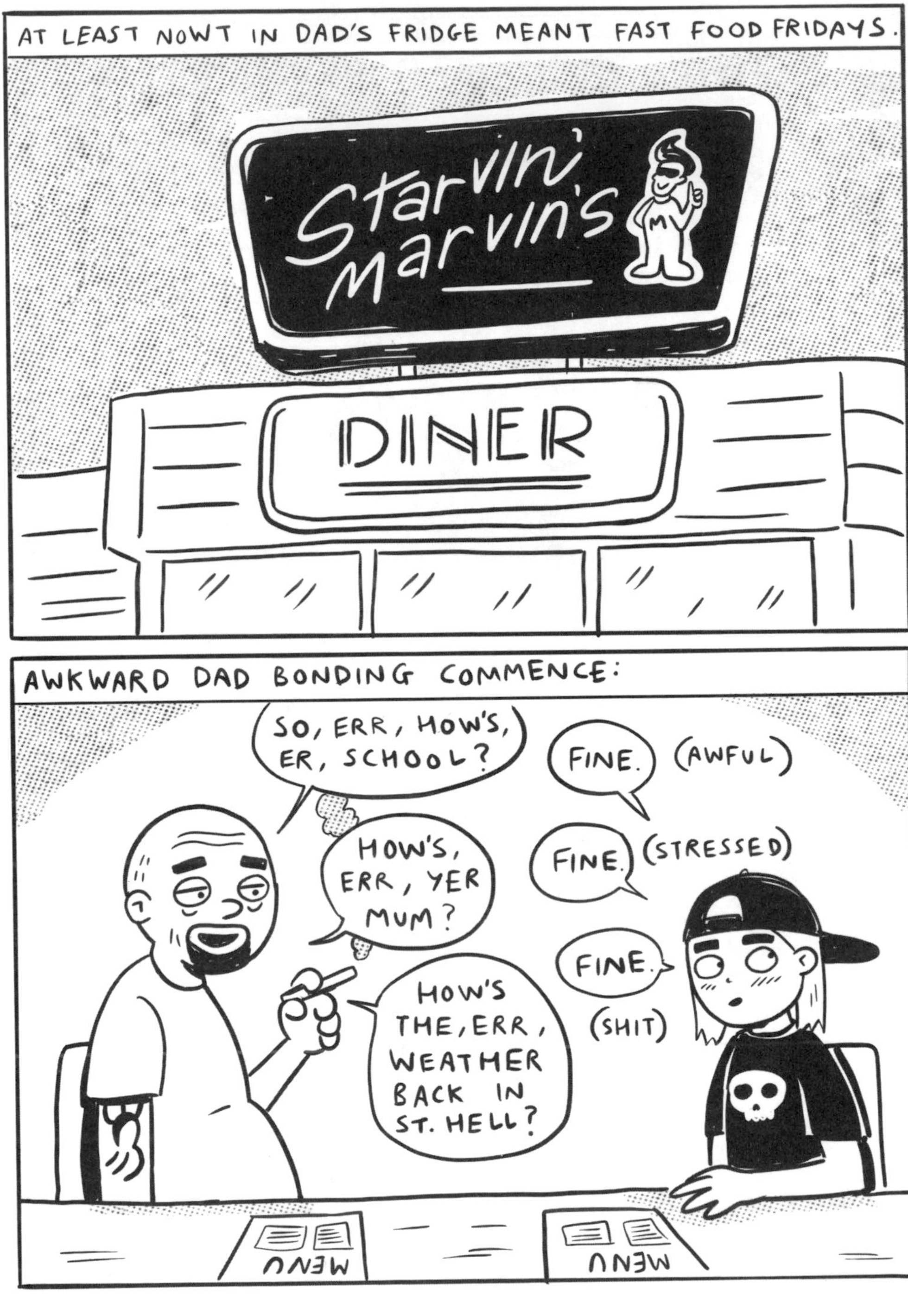
AT LEAST NOWT IN DAD'S FRIDGE MEANT FAST FOOD FRIDAYS.
Starvin' Marvin's
M
DINER
AWKWARD DAD BONDING COMMENCE:
SO, ERR, HOW'S, ER, SCHOOL?
FINE.
(AWFUL)
HOW'S, ERR, YER MUM?
FINE.
(STRESSED)
HOW'S THE, ERR, WEATHER BACK IN ST. HELL?
FINE.
(SHIT)

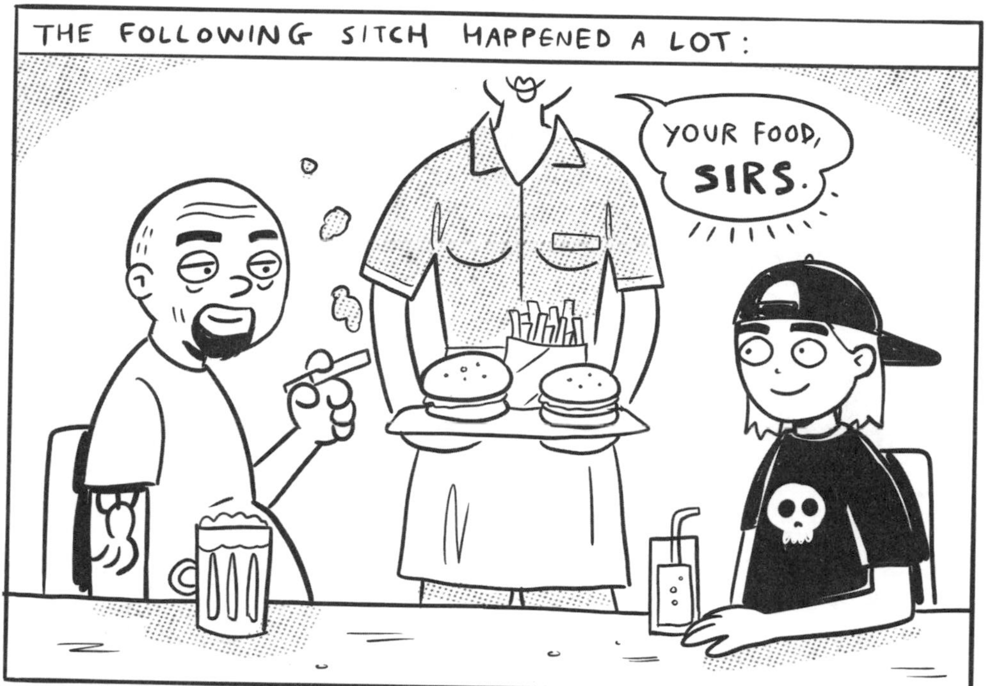
THE FOLLOWING SITCH HAPPENED A LOT:
YOUR FOOD, SIRS.

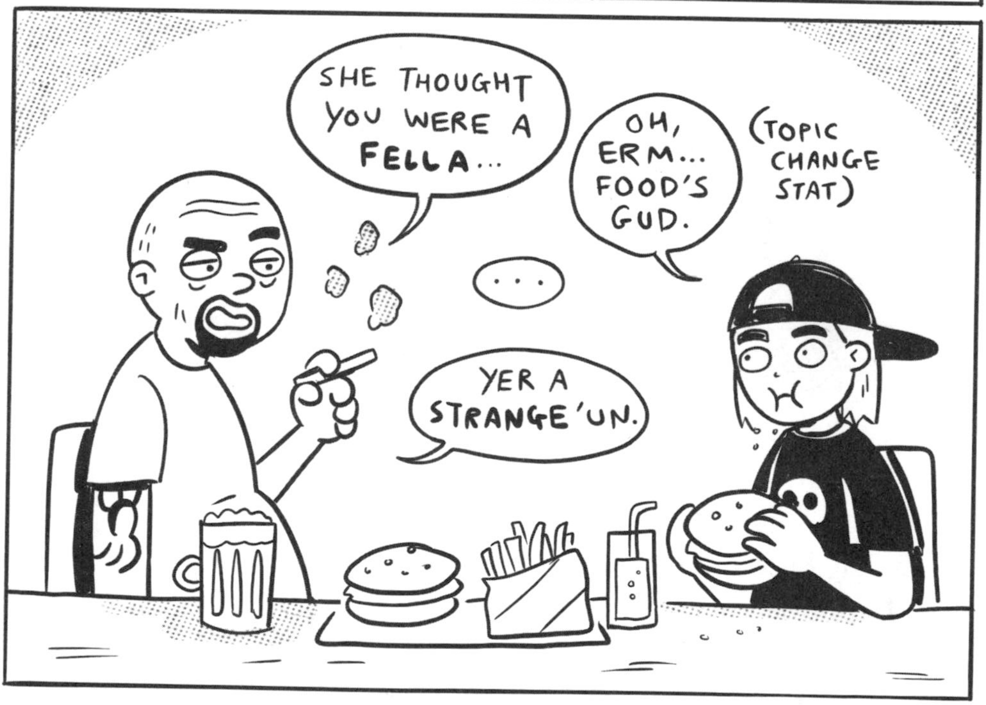
SHE THOUGHT YOU WERE A FELLA...
OH, ERM... FOOD'S GUD.
(TOPIC CHANGE STAT)
...
YER A STRANGE'UN.

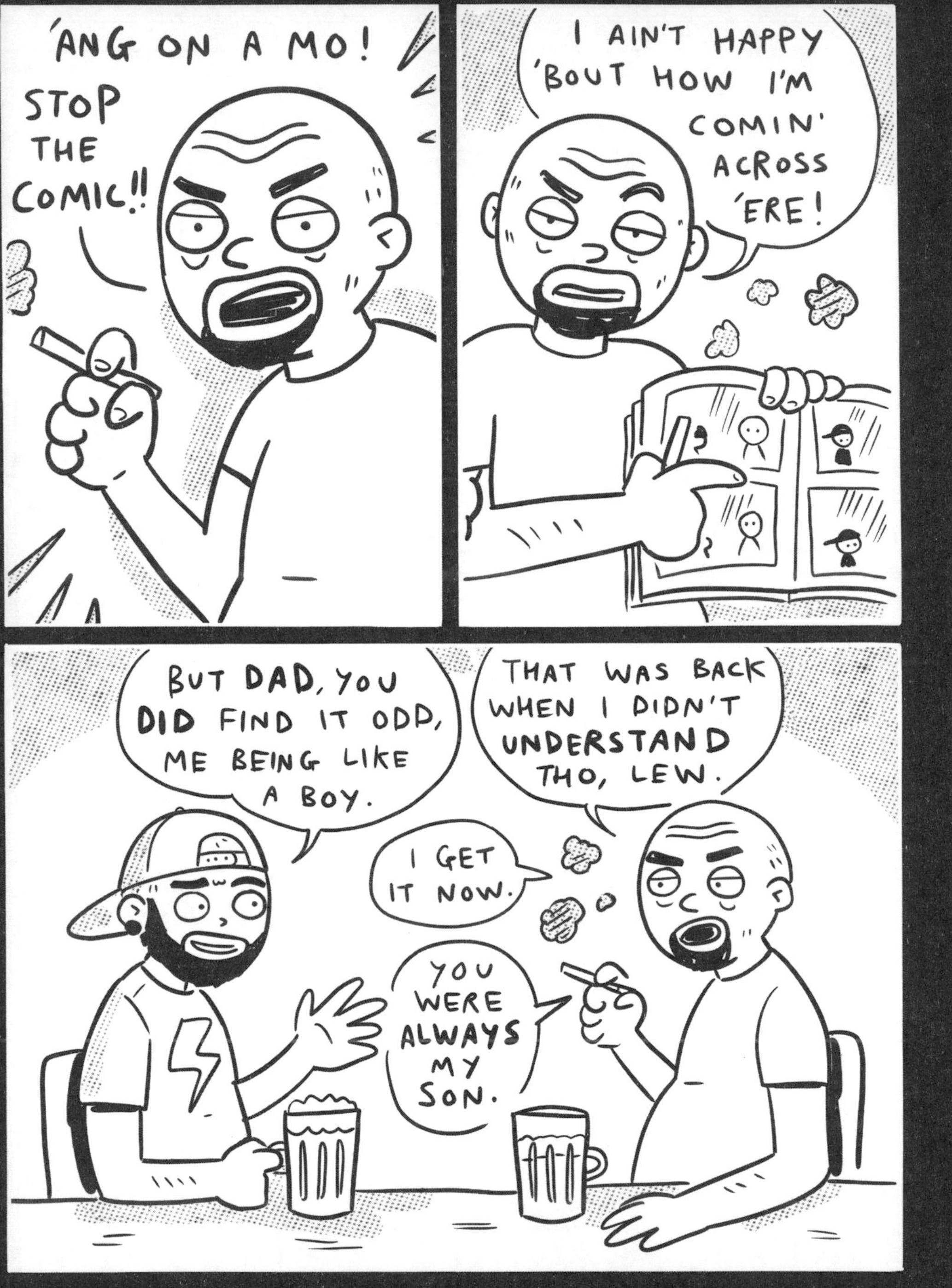
'ANG ON A MO!
STOP THE COMIC!!
I AIN'T HAPPY 'BOUT HOW I'M COMIN' ACROSS 'ERE!
BUT DAD, YOU DID FIND IT ODD, ME BEING LIKE A BOY.
THAT WAS BACK WHEN I DIDN'T UNDERSTAND THO, LEW.
I GET IT NOW.
YOU WERE ALWAYS MY SON.

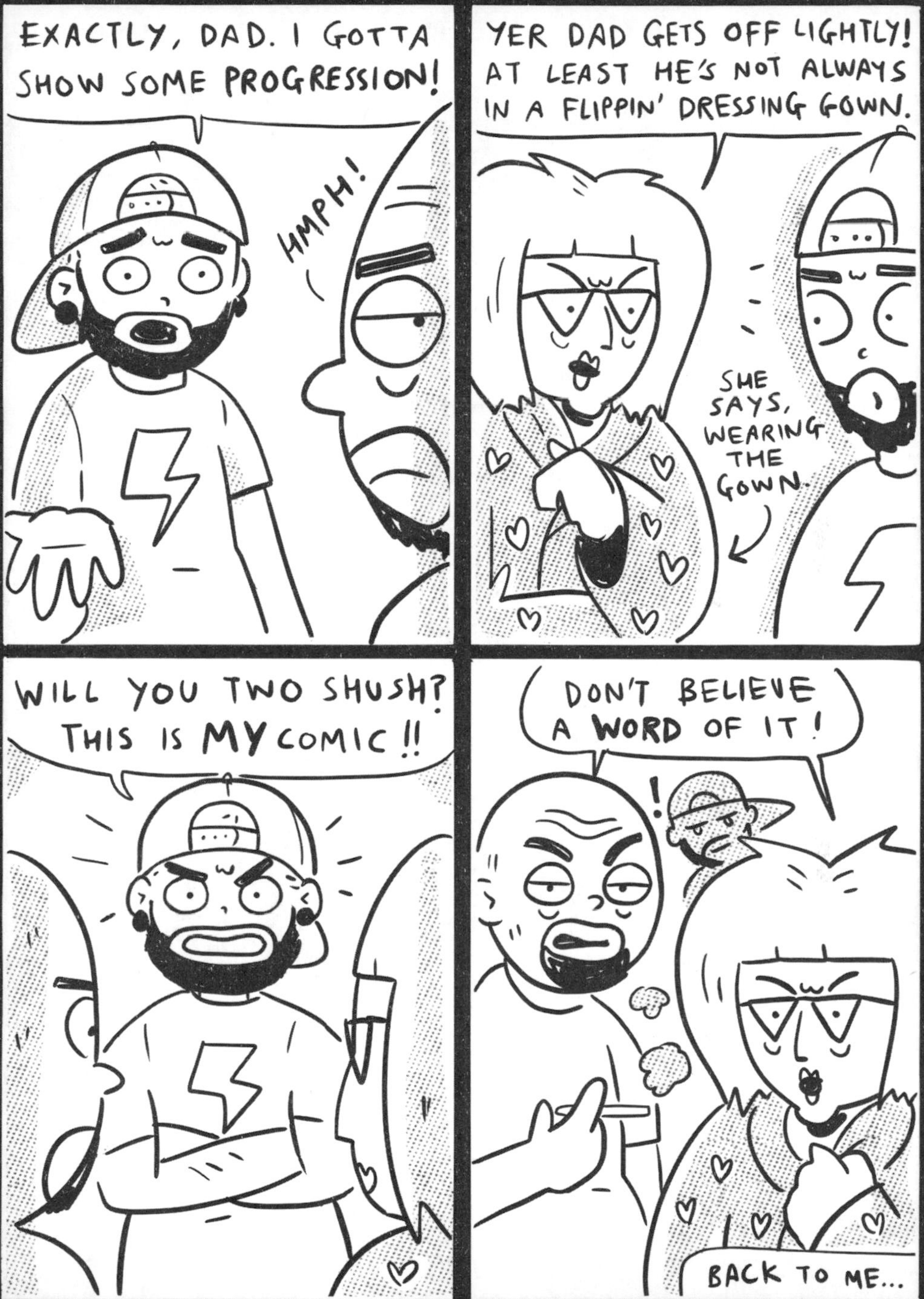
EXACTLY, DAD. I GOTTA SHOW SOME PROGRESSION!
HMPH!
YER DAD GETS OFF LIGHTLY! AT LEAST HE'S NOT ALWAYS IN A FLIPPIN' DRESSING GOWN.
SHE SAYS, WEARING THE GOWN.
WILL YOU TWO SHUSH? THIS IS MY COMIC!!
DON'T BELIEVE A WORD OF IT!
!
BACK TO ME...

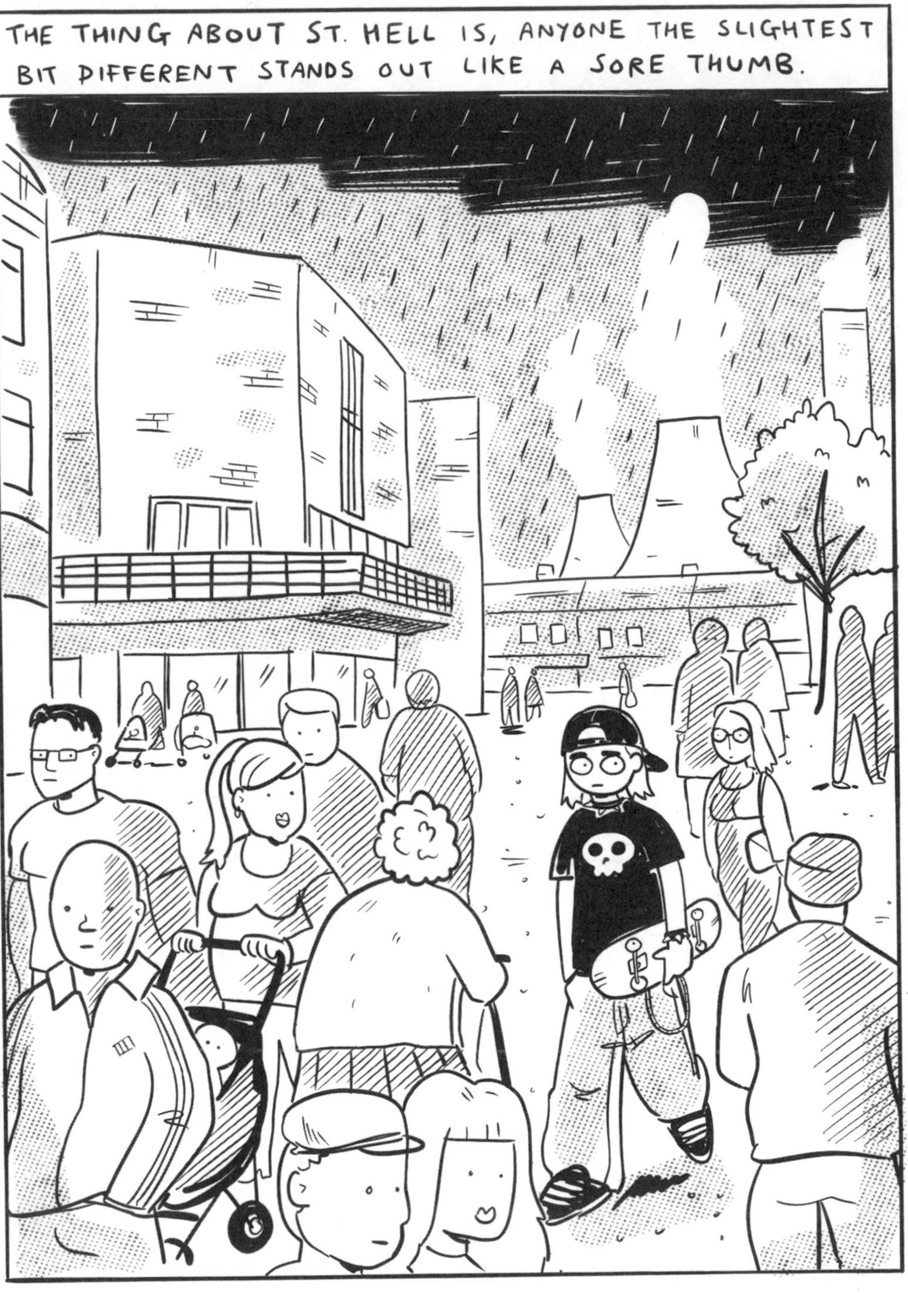
THE THING ABOUT ST. HELL IS, ANYONE THE SLIGHTEST BIT DIFFERENT STANDS OUT LIKE A SORE THUMB.

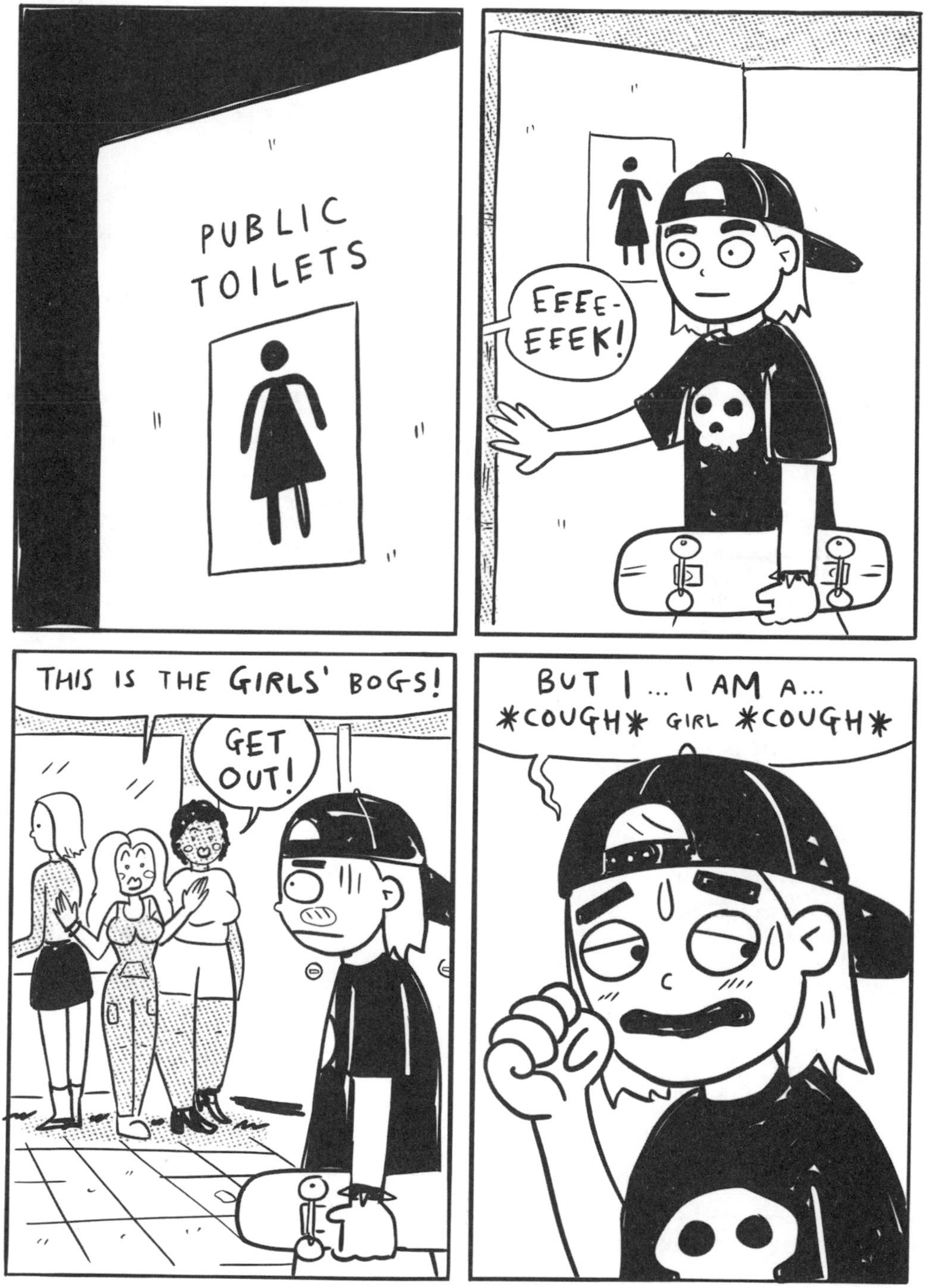
PUBLIC TOILETS
EEEE-EEEK!
THIS IS THE GIRLS' BOGS!
GET OUT!
BUT I ... I AM A...
COUGH GIRL *COUGH*

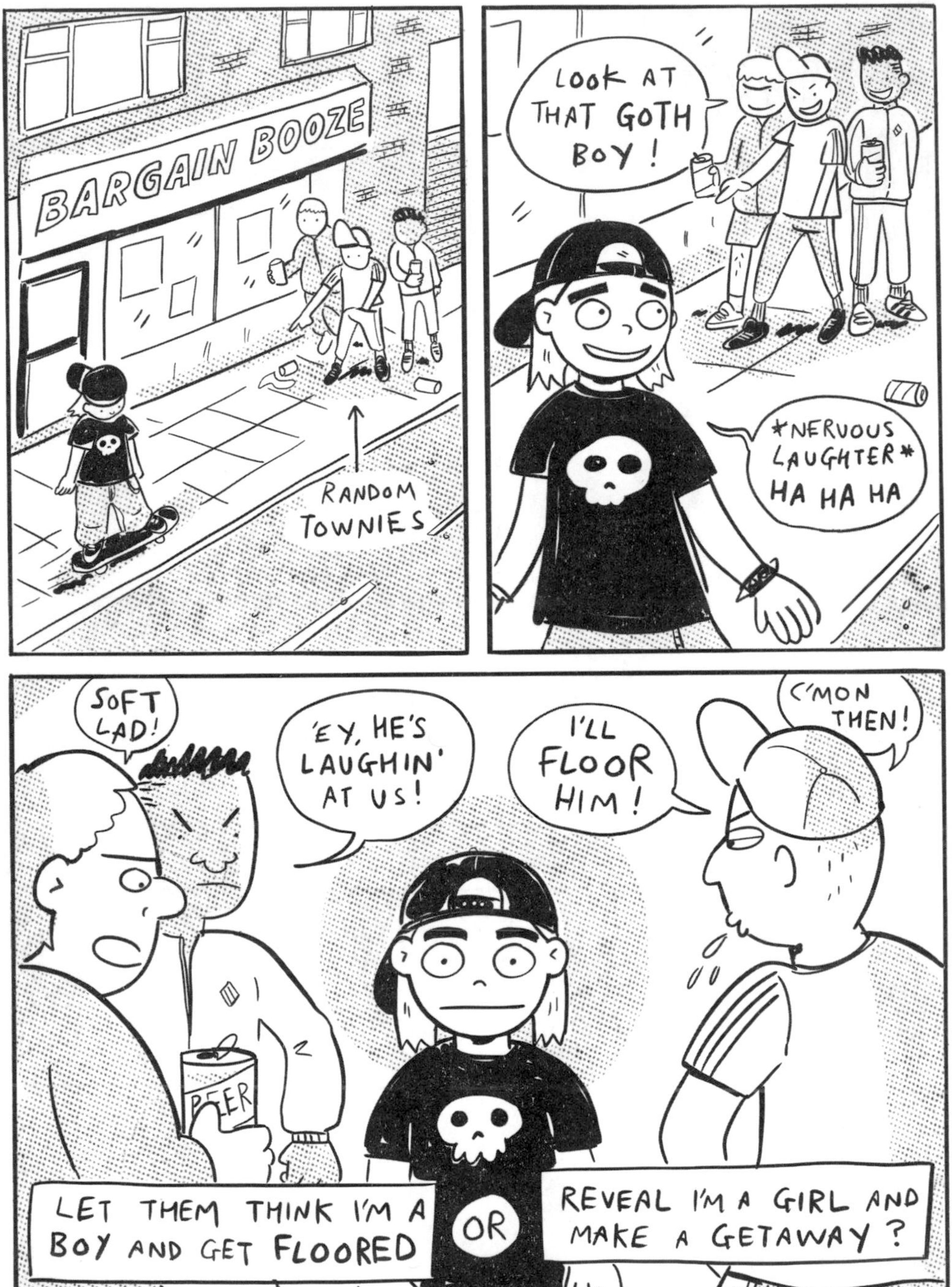
BARGAIN BOOZE
RANDOM TOWNIES
LOOK AT THAT GOTH BOY!
NERVOUS LAUGHTER HA HA HA
SOFT LAD!
'EY, HE'S LAUGHIN' AT US!
I'LL FLOOR HIM!
C'MON THEN!
BEER
LET THEM THINK I'M A BOY AND GET FLOORED
OR
REVEAL I'M A GIRL AND MAKE A GETAWAY?

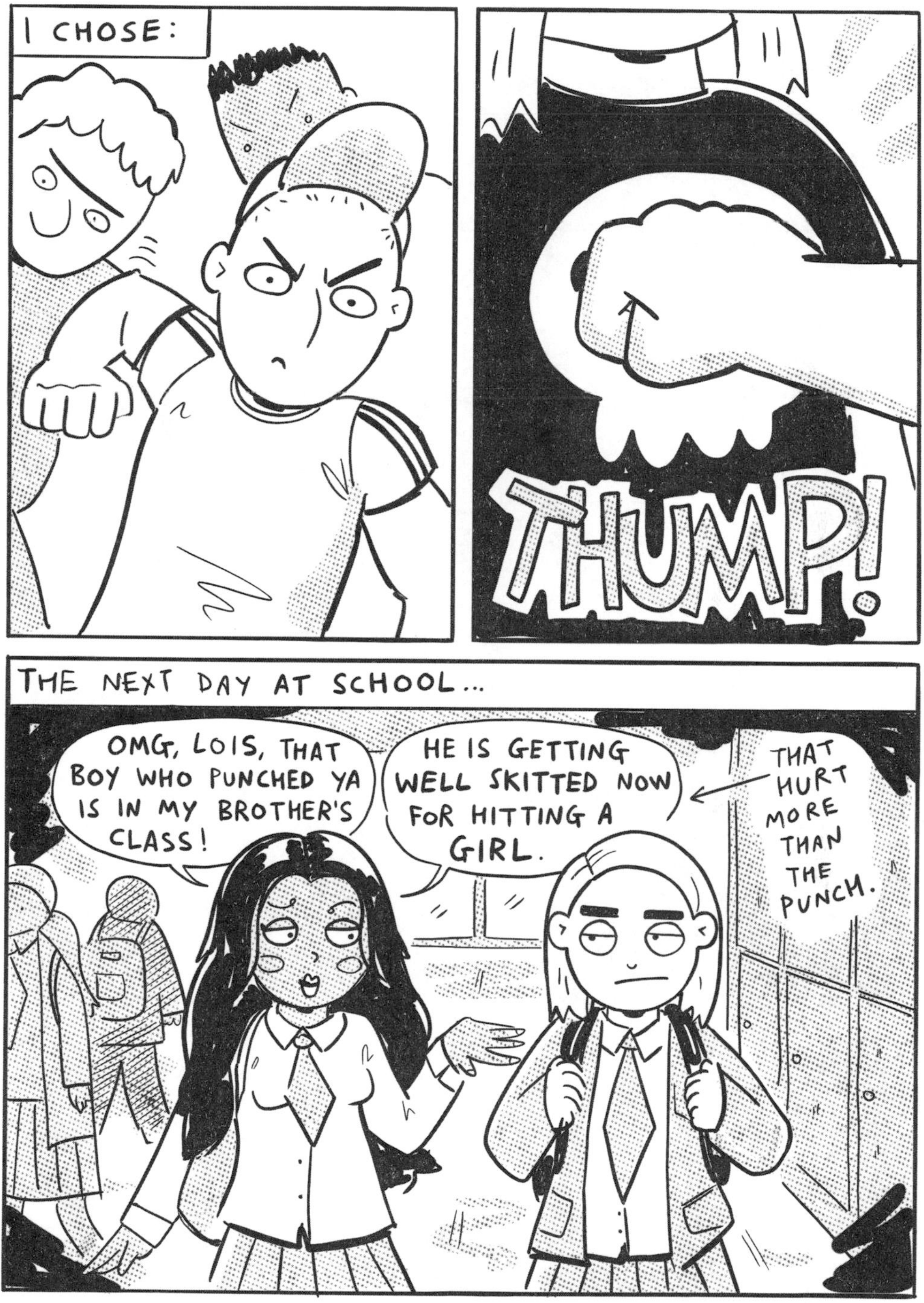
I CHOSE:
THUMP!
THE NEXT DAY AT SCHOOL...
OMG, LOIS, THAT BOY WHO PUNCHED YA IS IN MY BROTHER'S CLASS!
HE IS GETTING WELL SKITTED NOW FOR HITTING A GIRL.
THAT HURT MORE THAN THE PUNCH.

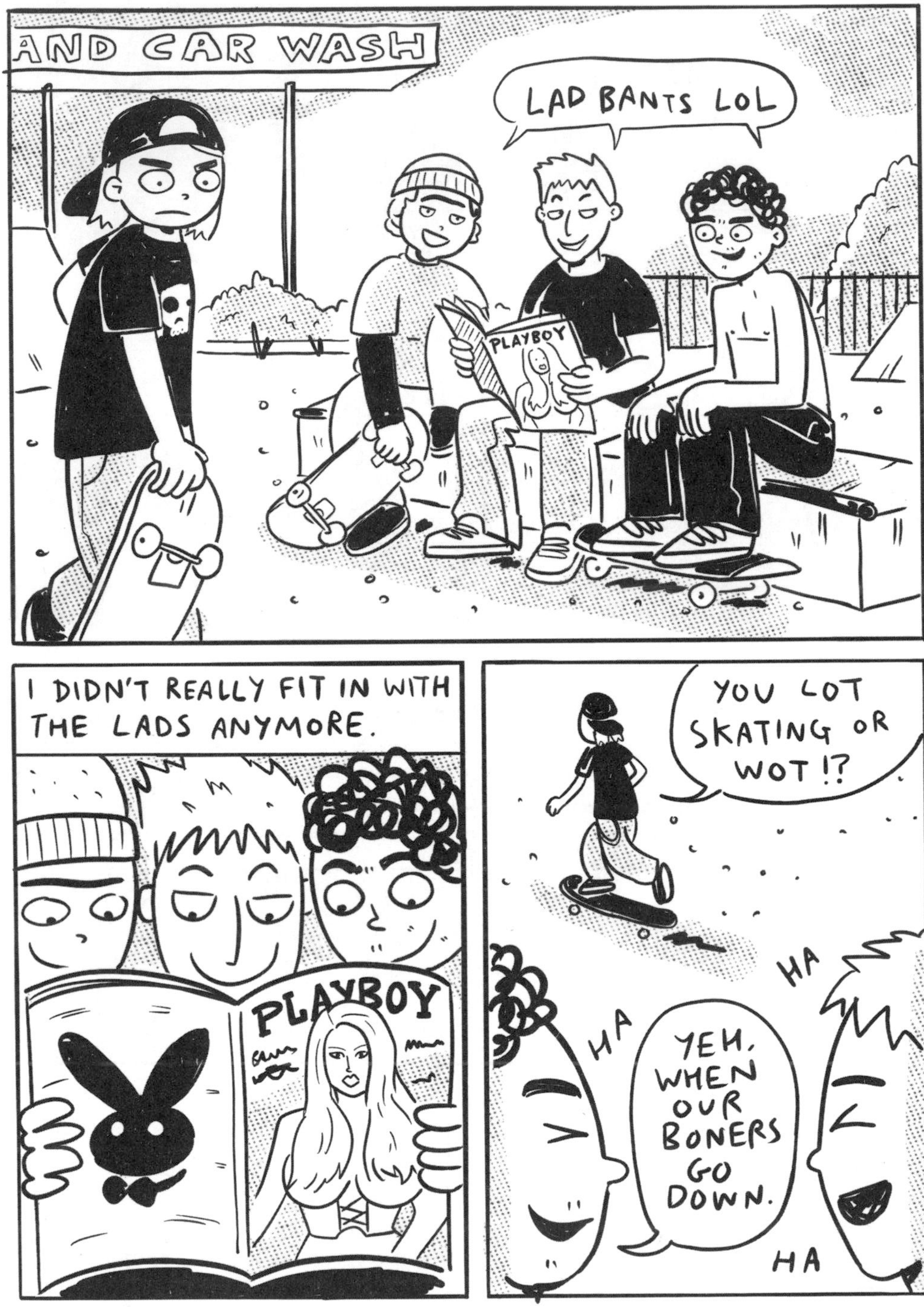
AND CAR WASH
LAD BANTS LOL
PLAYBOY
I DIDN'T REALLY FIT IN WITH THE LADS ANYMORE.
PLAYBOY
YOU LOT SKATING OR WOT!?
HA
HA
YEH, WHEN OUR BONERS GO DOWN.
HA

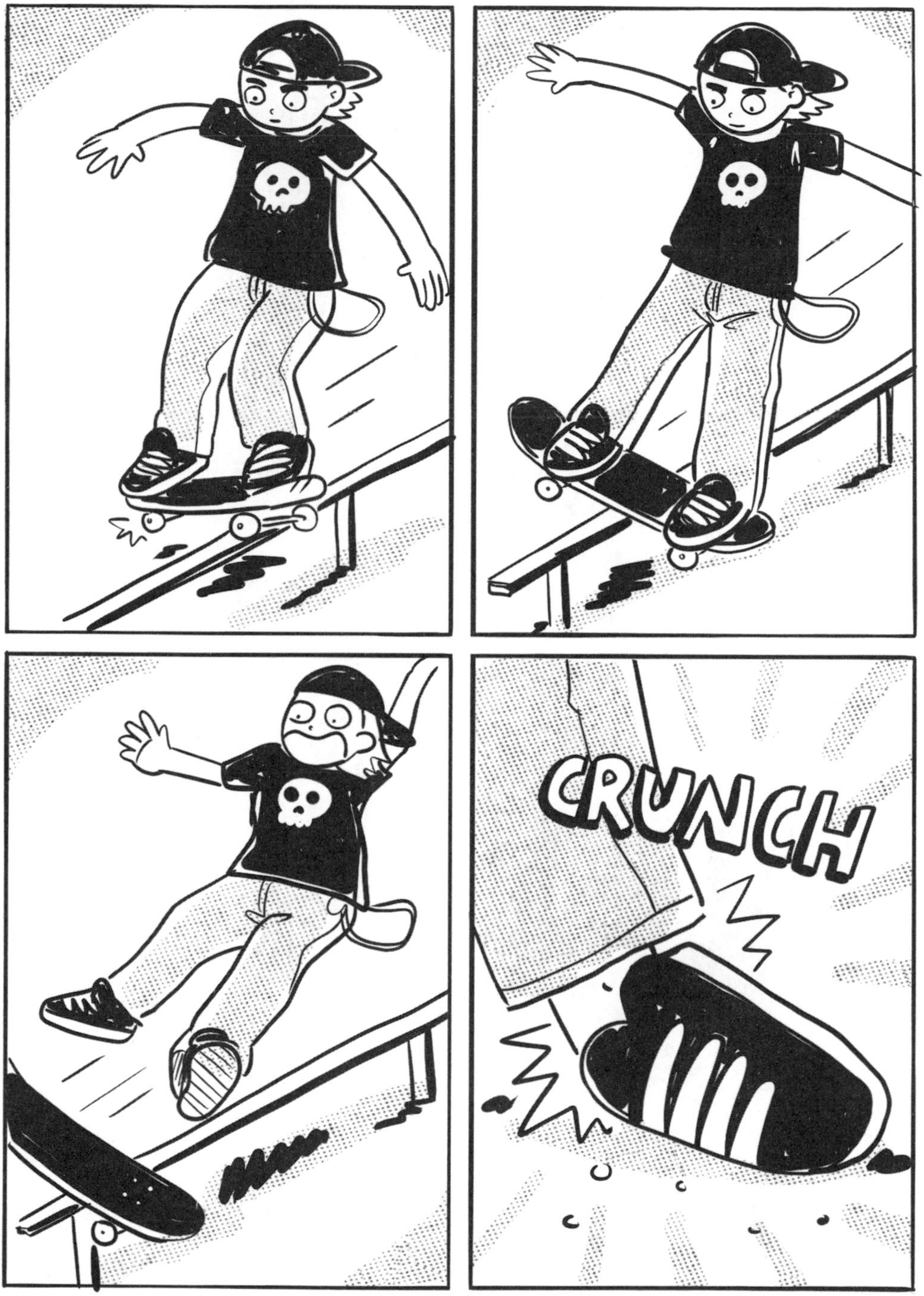
CRUNCH

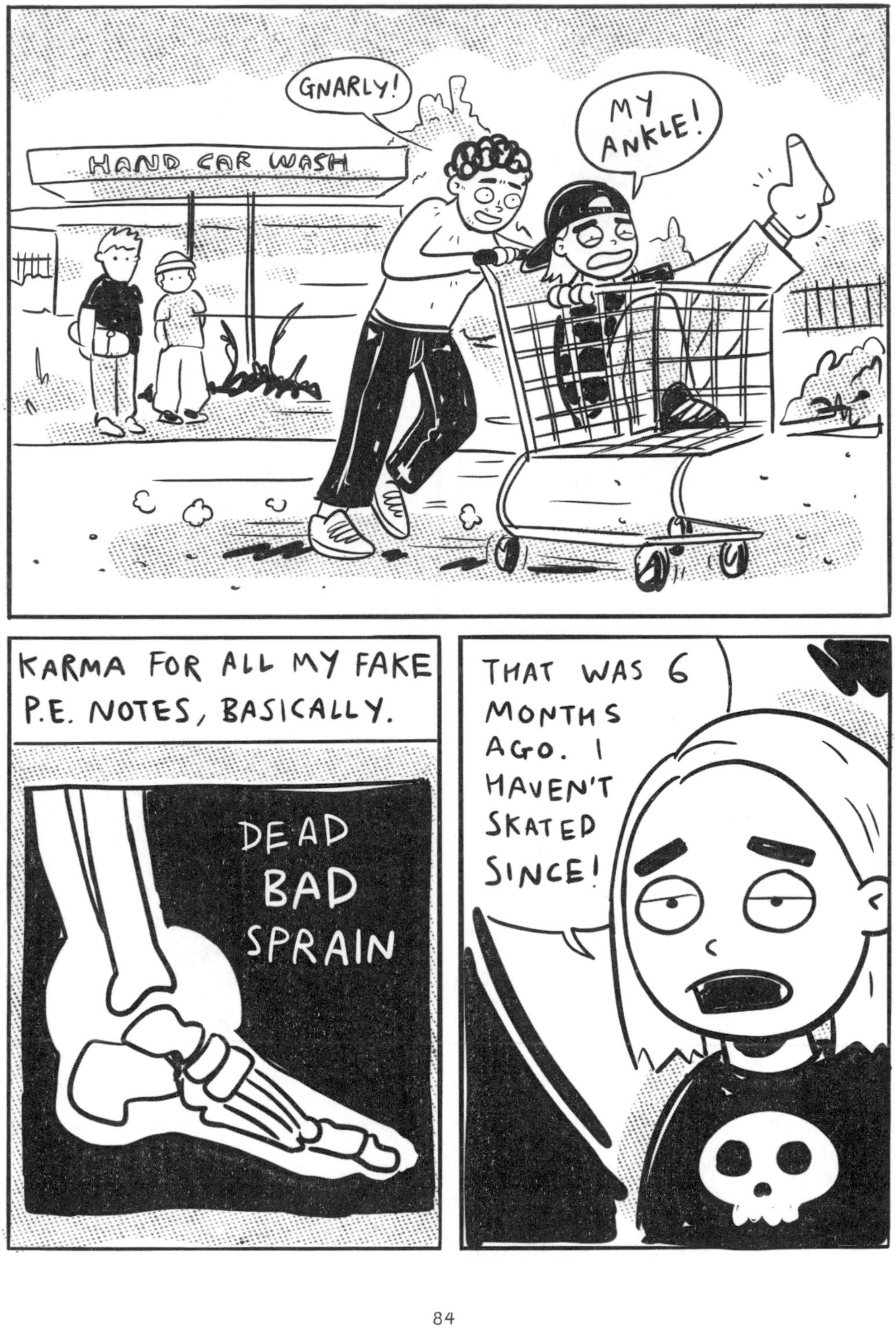
GNARLY!
MY ANKLE!
HAND CAR WASH
KARMA FOR ALL MY FAKE P.E. NOTES, BASICALLY.
DEAD BAD SPRAIN
THAT WAS 6 MONTHS AGO. I HAVEN'T SKATED SINCE!

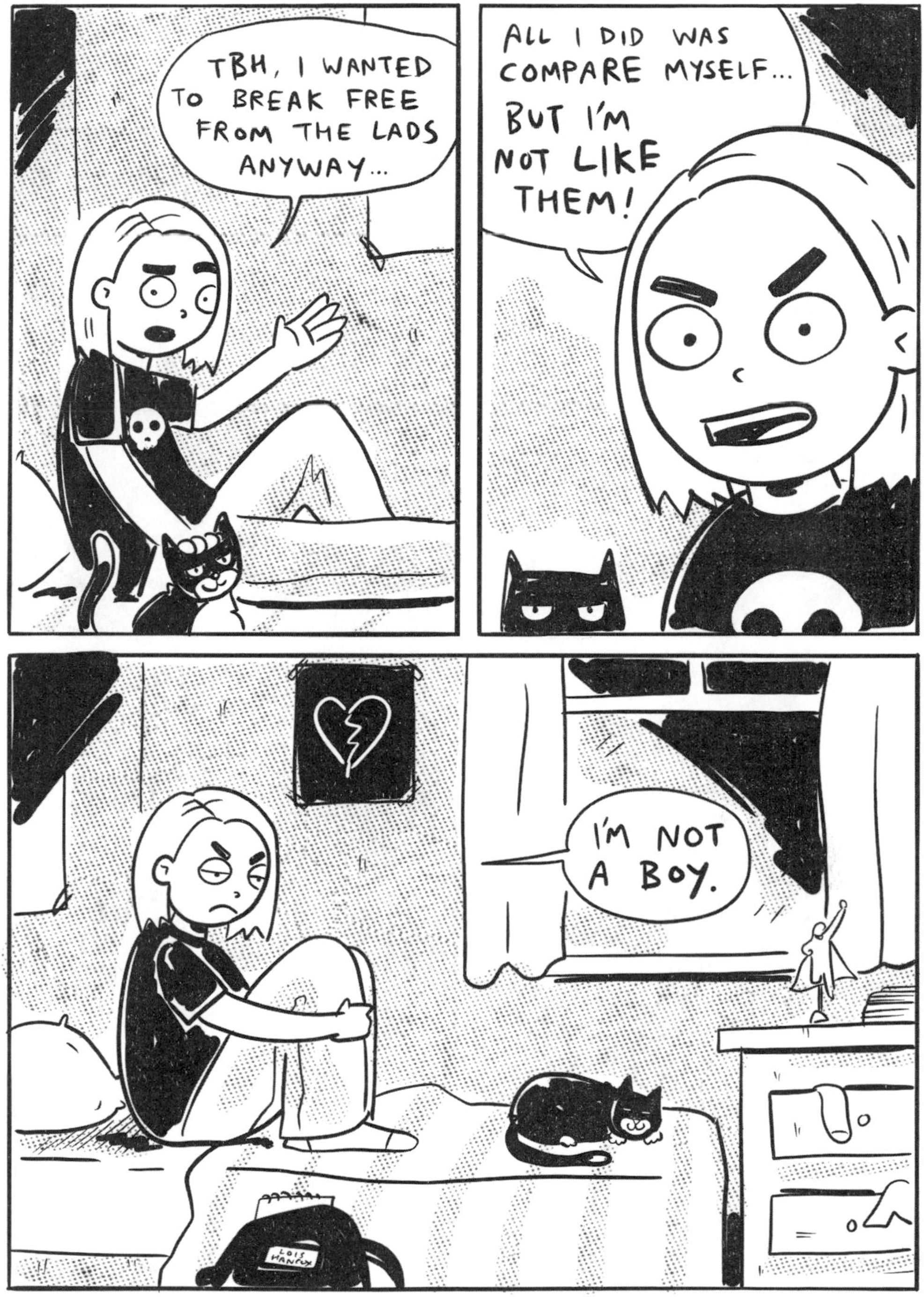
TBH, I WANTED TO BREAK FREE FROM THE LADS ANYWAY...
ALL I DID WAS COMPARE MYSELF...
BUT I'M NOT LIKE THEM!
I'M NOT A BOY.

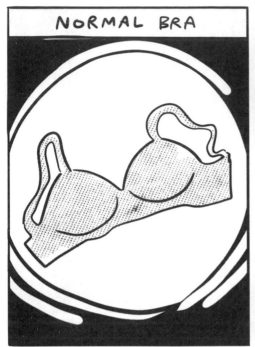

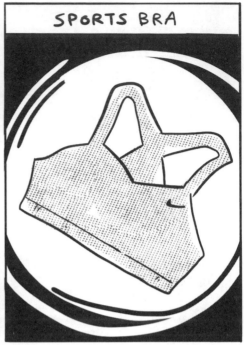

THAT WAS THE QUESTION.

JUST LET ME KNOW IF YOU NEED A BIGGER SIZE, CHICKEN.

GET OUT MY ROOM, MUM!

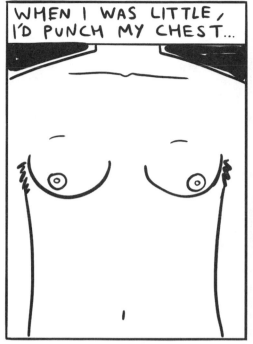

WHEN I WAS LITTLE,
I'D PUNCH MY CHEST...

HOPING NOWT WOULD
GROW THERE.

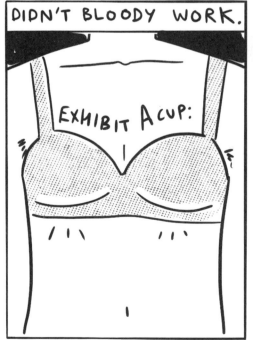

DIDN'T BLOODY WORK.

EXHIBIT A CUP:

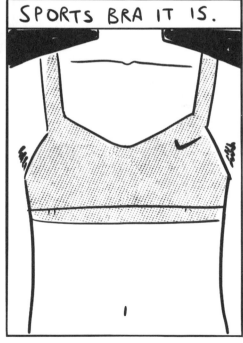

SPORTS BRA IT IS.

87

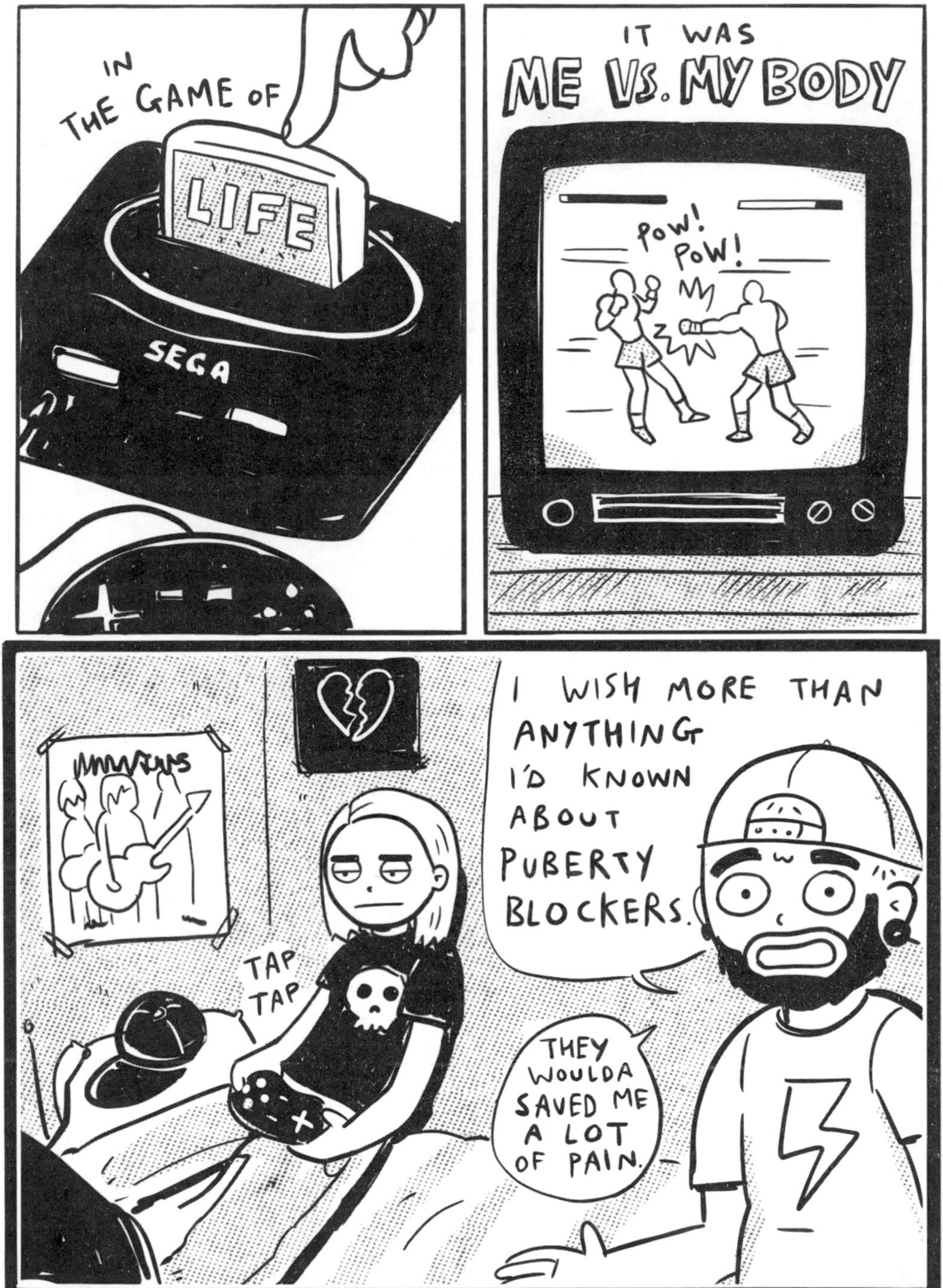

IN THE GAME OF
LIFE
SEGA
IT WAS
ME VS. MY BODY
POW! POW!
I WISH MORE THAN ANYTHING I'D KNOWN ABOUT PUBERTY BLOCKERS.
TAP TAP
THEY WOULDA SAVED ME A LOT OF PAIN.

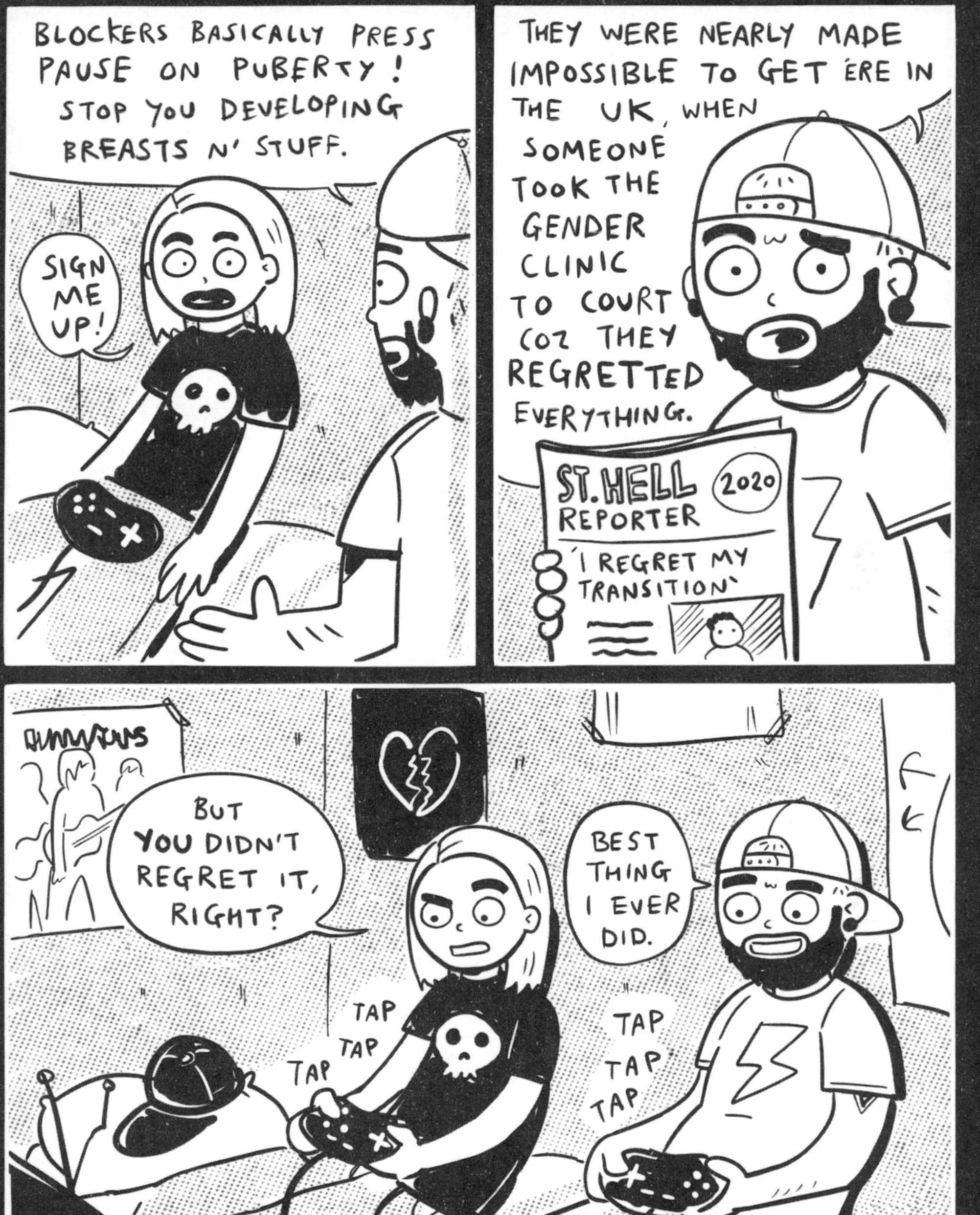

BLOCKERS BASICALLY PRESS PAUSE ON PUBERTY! STOP YOU DEVELOPING BREASTS N' STUFF.
SIGN ME UP!
THEY WERE NEARLY MADE IMPOSSIBLE TO GET 'ERE IN THE UK, WHEN SOMEONE TOOK THE GENDER CLINIC TO COURT COZ THEY REGRETTED EVERYTHING.
ST. HELL REPORTER
2020
'I REGRET MY TRANSITION'
BUT YOU DIDN'T REGRET IT, RIGHT?
BEST THING I EVER DID.
TAP TAP TAP
TAP TAP TAP

2004. AGE 15.
WHAT'S ON MY TIMETABLE TODAY... DOUBLE P.E. - KILL ME NOW.
GAME OVER
MON TUES WEDS THURS FRI
P.E
MATHS
P.E
ART
P.E

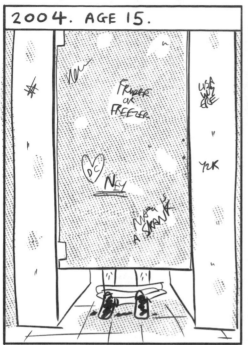

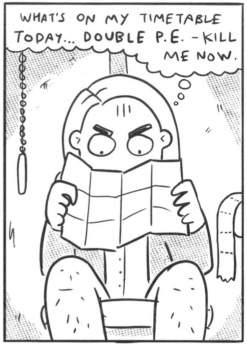

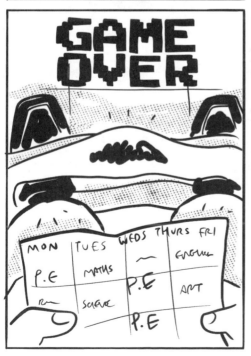

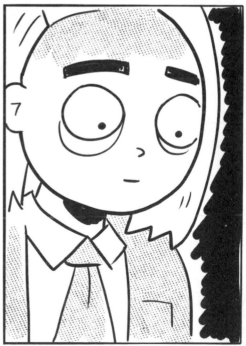

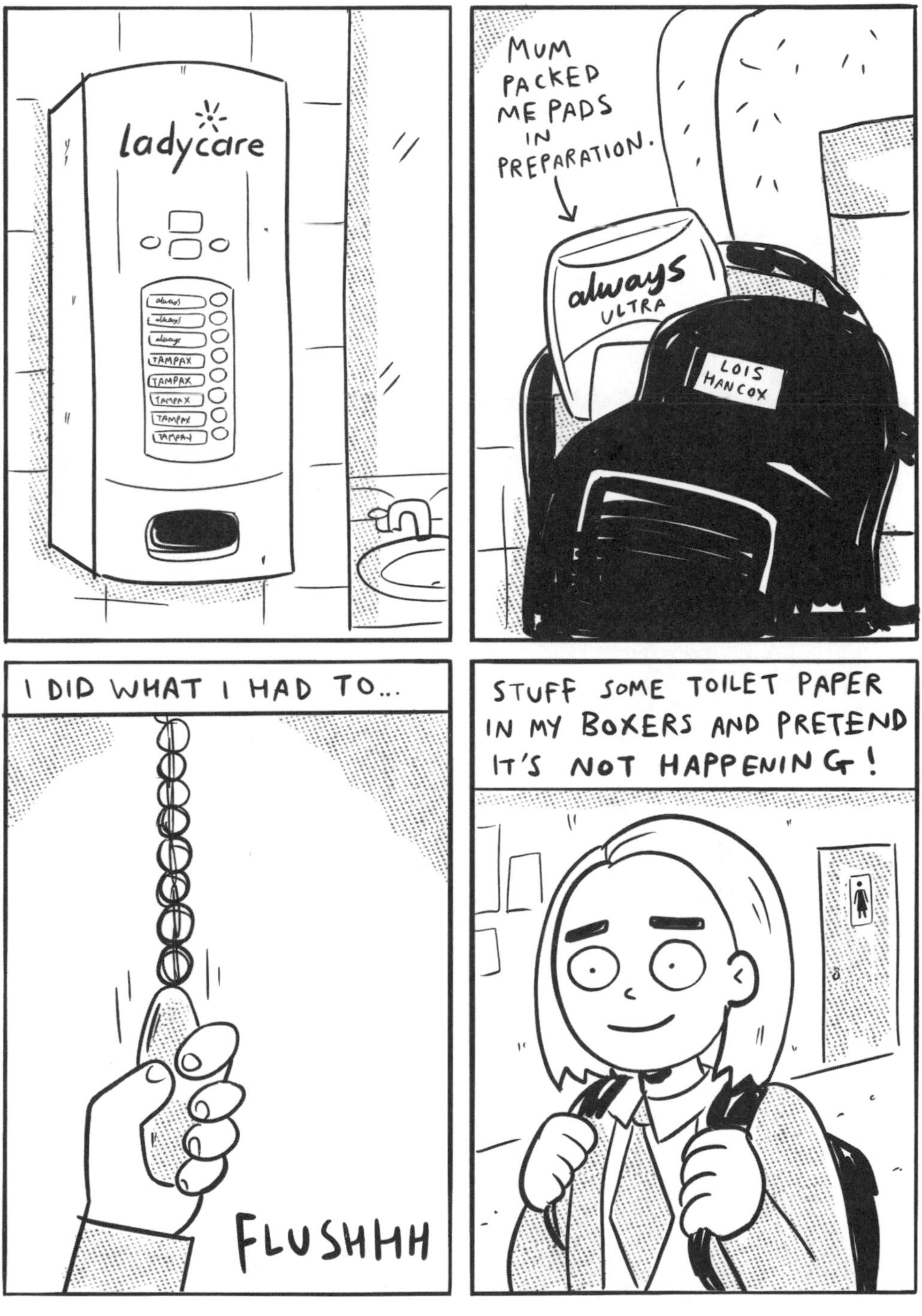
ladycare
always
always
always
TAMPAX
TAMPAX
TAMPAX
TAMPAX
TAMPAX
MUM PACKED ME PADS IN PREPARATION.
always ULTRA
LOIS HANCOX
I DID WHAT I HAD TO...
FLUSHHH
STUFF SOME TOILET PAPER IN MY BOXERS AND PRETEND IT'S NOT HAPPENING!

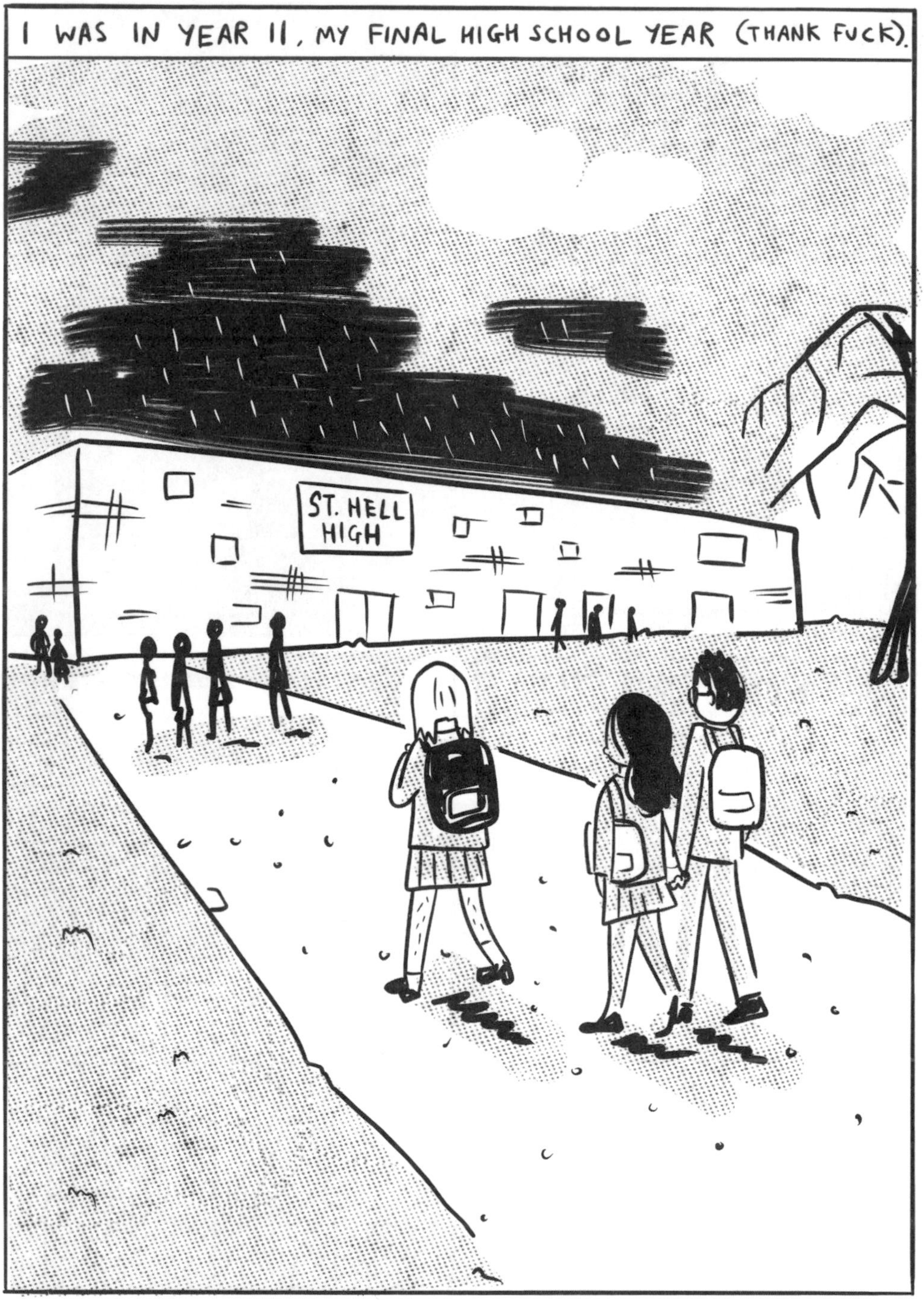
I WAS IN YEAR 11, MY FINAL HIGH SCHOOL YEAR (THANK FUCK).
ST. HELL HIGH

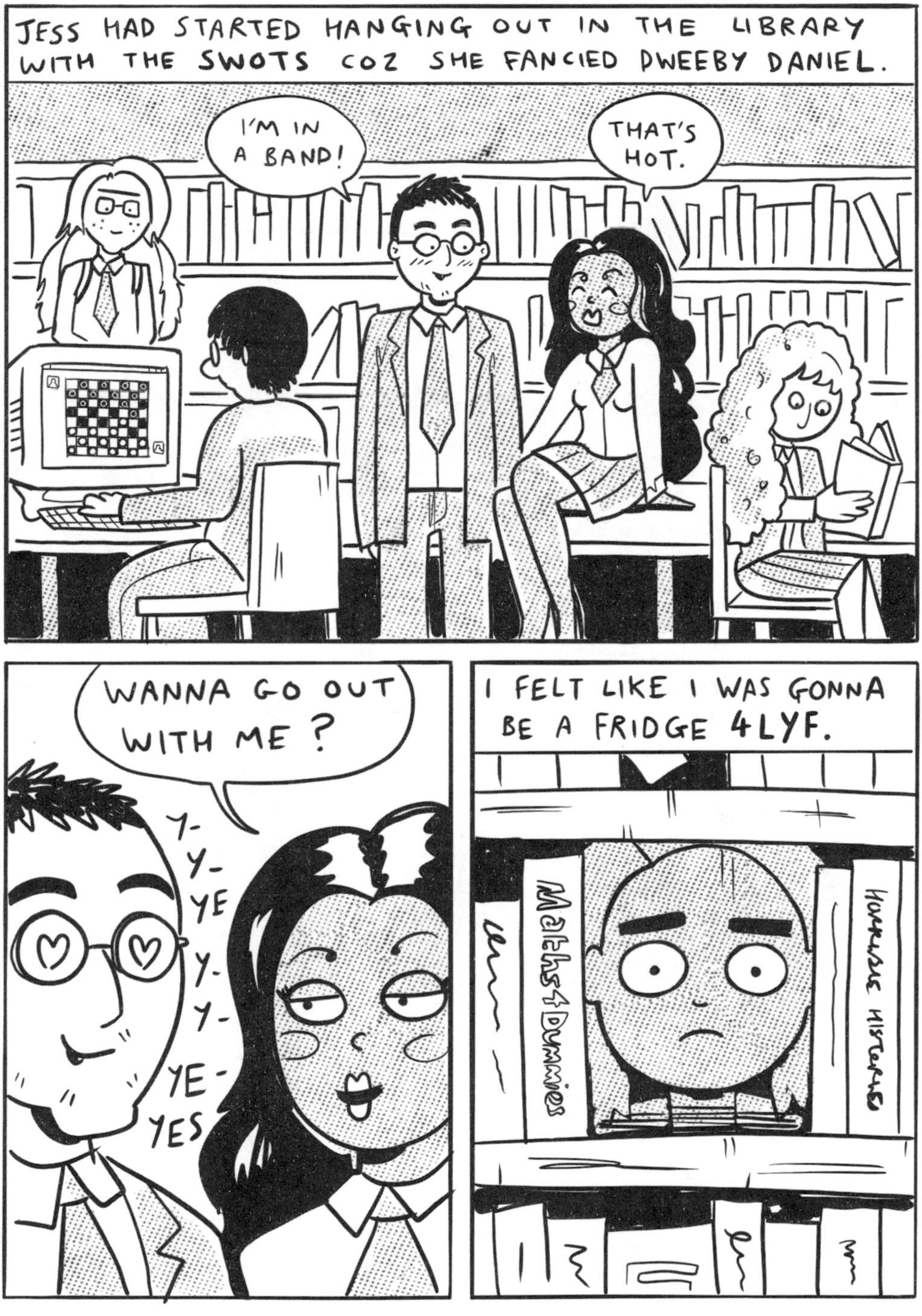
JESS HAD STARTED HANGING OUT IN THE LIBRARY WITH THE SWOTS COZ SHE FANCIED DWEEBY DANIEL.
I'M IN A BAND!
THAT'S HOT.
WANNA GO OUT WITH ME?
Y- Y- YE Y- Y- YE- YES
I FELT LIKE I WAS GONNA BE A FRIDGE 4LYF.
Maths4Dummies

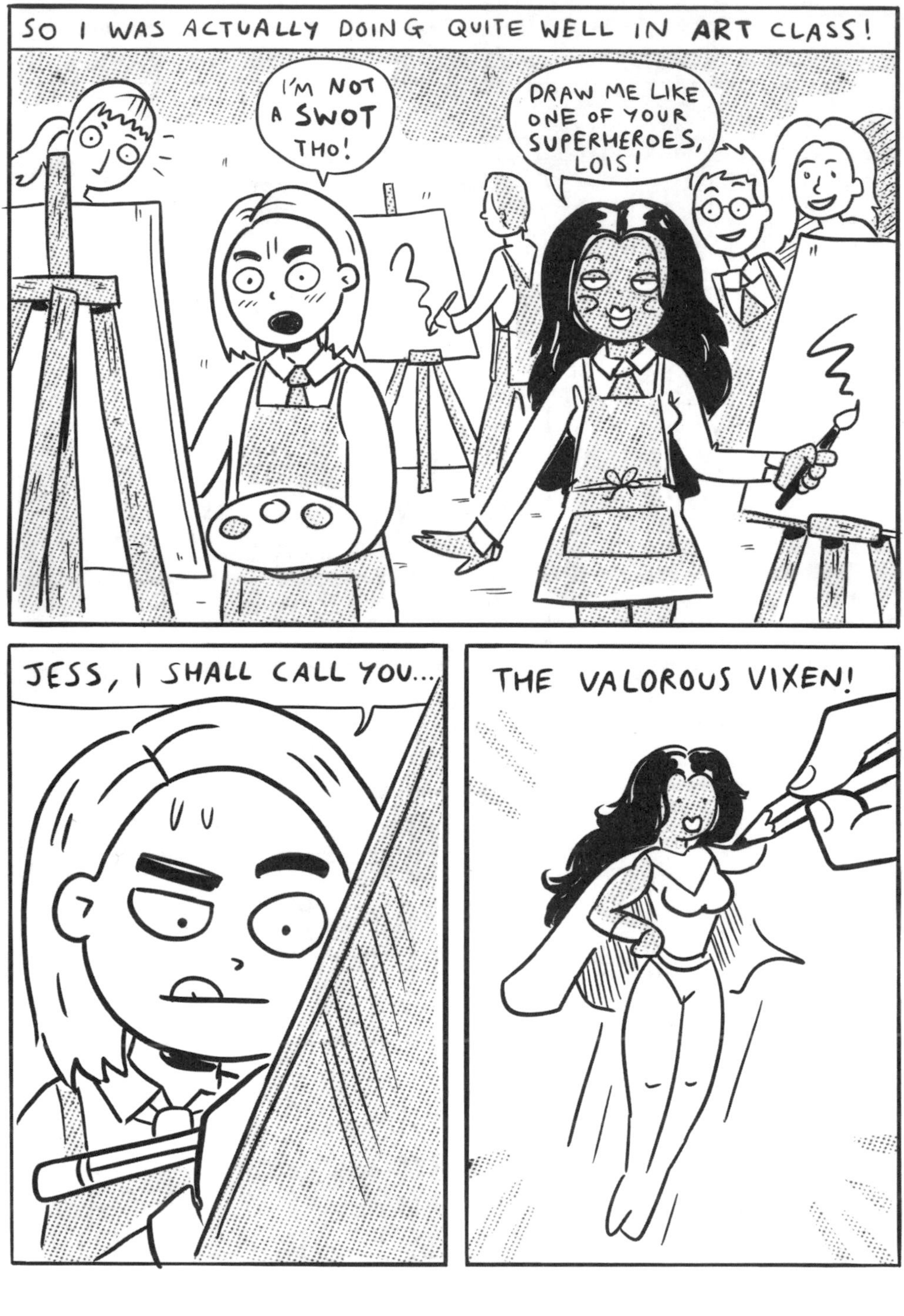
SO I WAS ACTUALLY DOING QUITE WELL IN ART CLASS!
I'M NOT A SWOT THO!
DRAW ME LIKE ONE OF YOUR SUPERHEROES, LOIS!
JESS, I SHALL CALL YOU...
THE VALOROUS VIXEN!

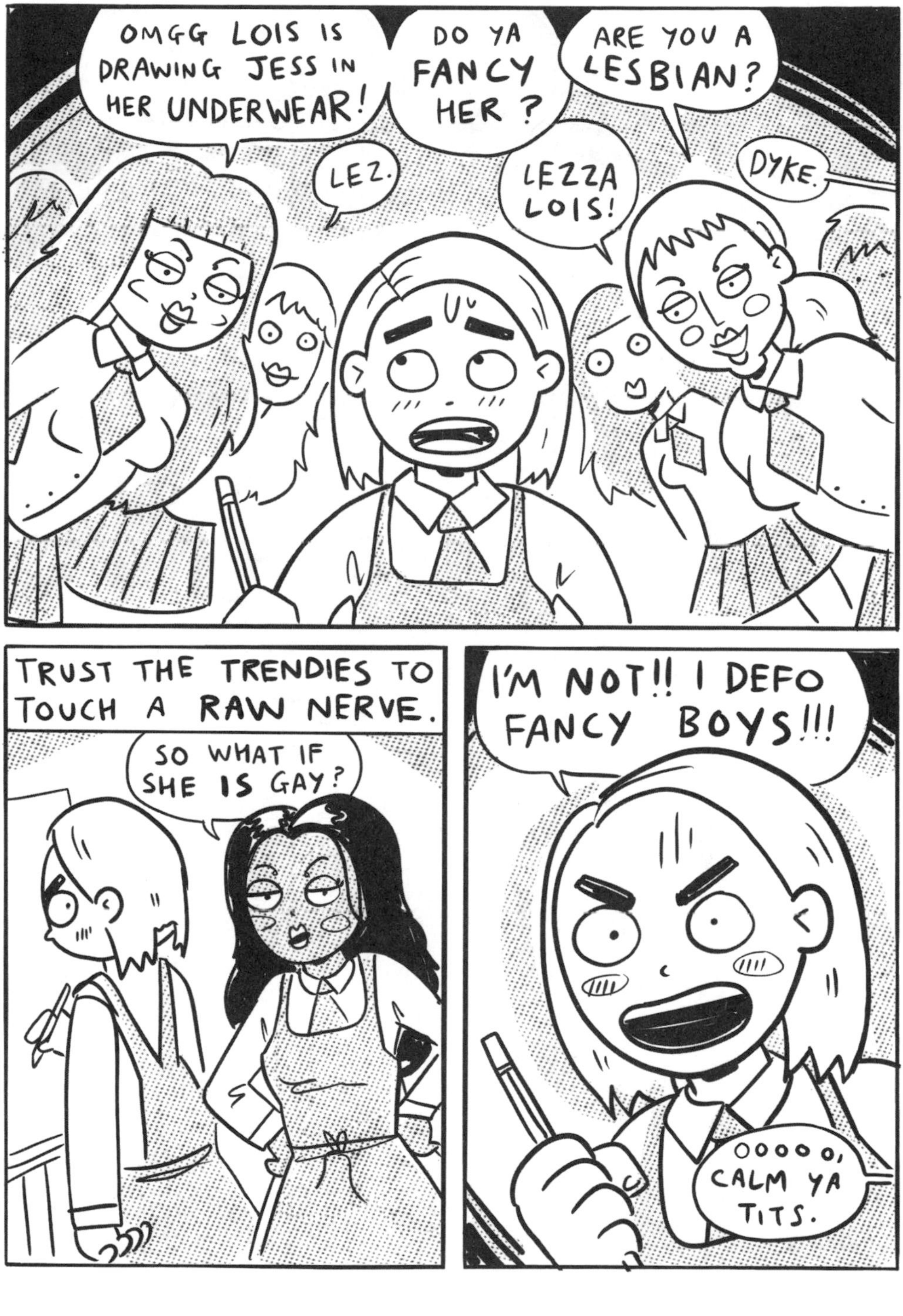

OMGG LOIS IS DRAWING JESS IN HER UNDERWEAR!
DO YA FANCY HER?
ARE YOU A LESBIAN?
LEZ.
LEZZA LOIS!
DYKE.
TRUST THE TRENDIES TO TOUCH A RAW NERVE.
SO WHAT IF SHE IS GAY?
I'M NOT!! I DEFO FANCY BOYS!!!
OOOOO, CALM YA TITS.

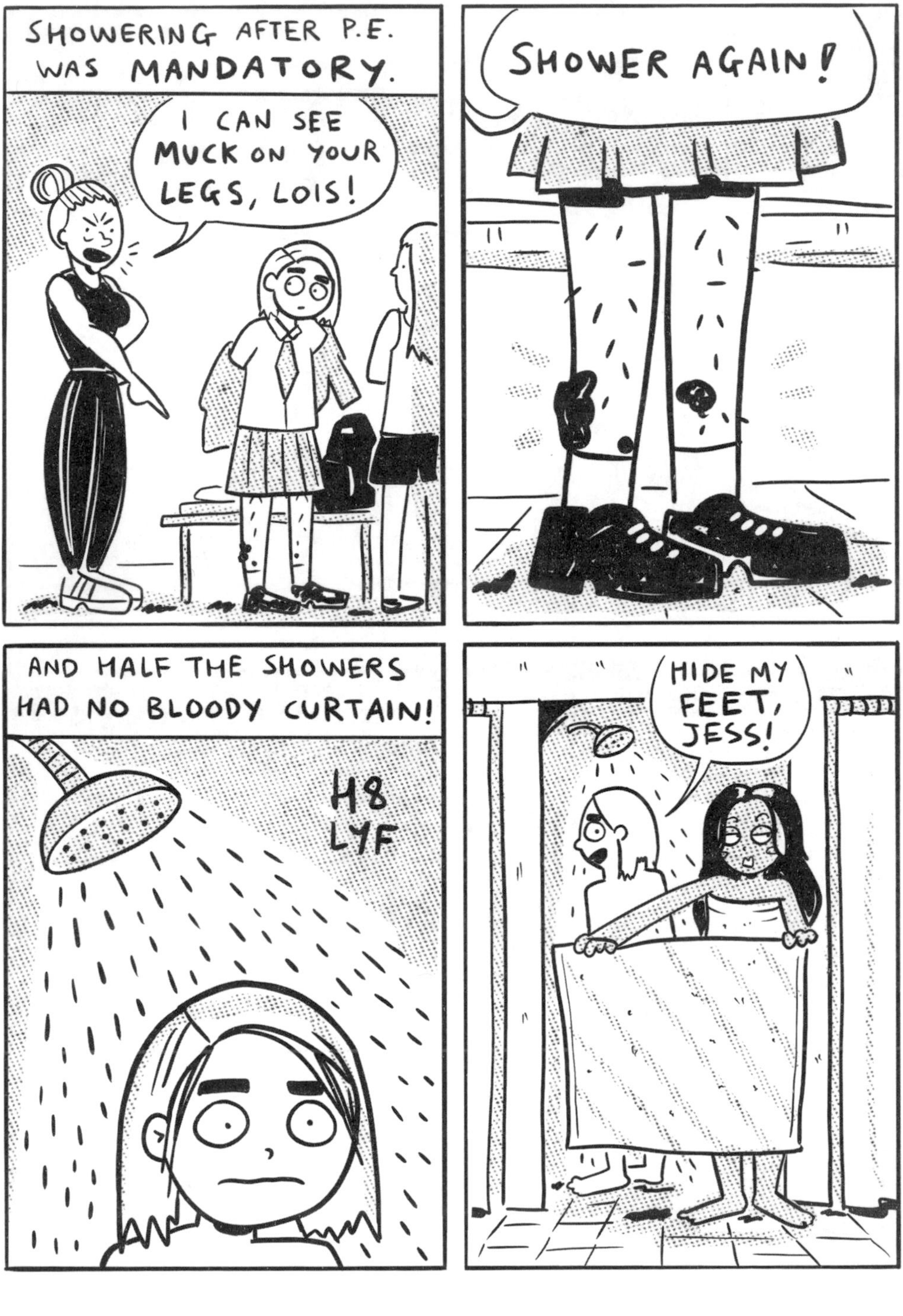

SHOWERING AFTER P.E. WAS MANDATORY.
I CAN SEE MUCK ON YOUR LEGS, LOIS!
SHOWER AGAIN!
AND HALF THE SHOWERS HAD NO BLOODY CURTAIN!
H8 LYF
HIDE MY FEET, JESS!

THERE WAS ONE EXEMPTION.
LISA?
YES, MISS.
PERIOD + P.E. = NO SHOWER
JESSICA ?
YES, MISS.
= ANSWERING THE REGISTER WITH:
LOIS?
NO, MISS.
TEEHEE
LOIS ON THE BLOB!

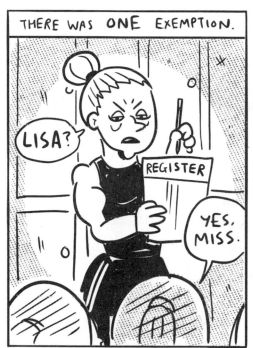

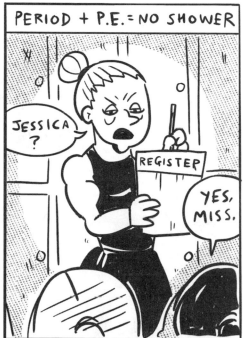

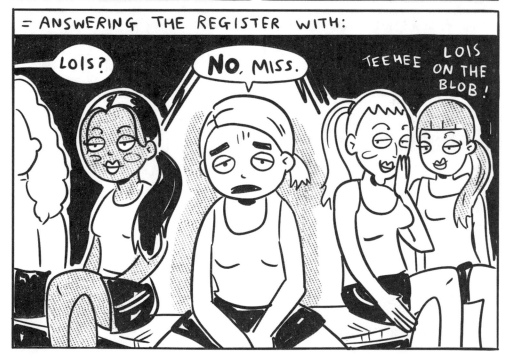

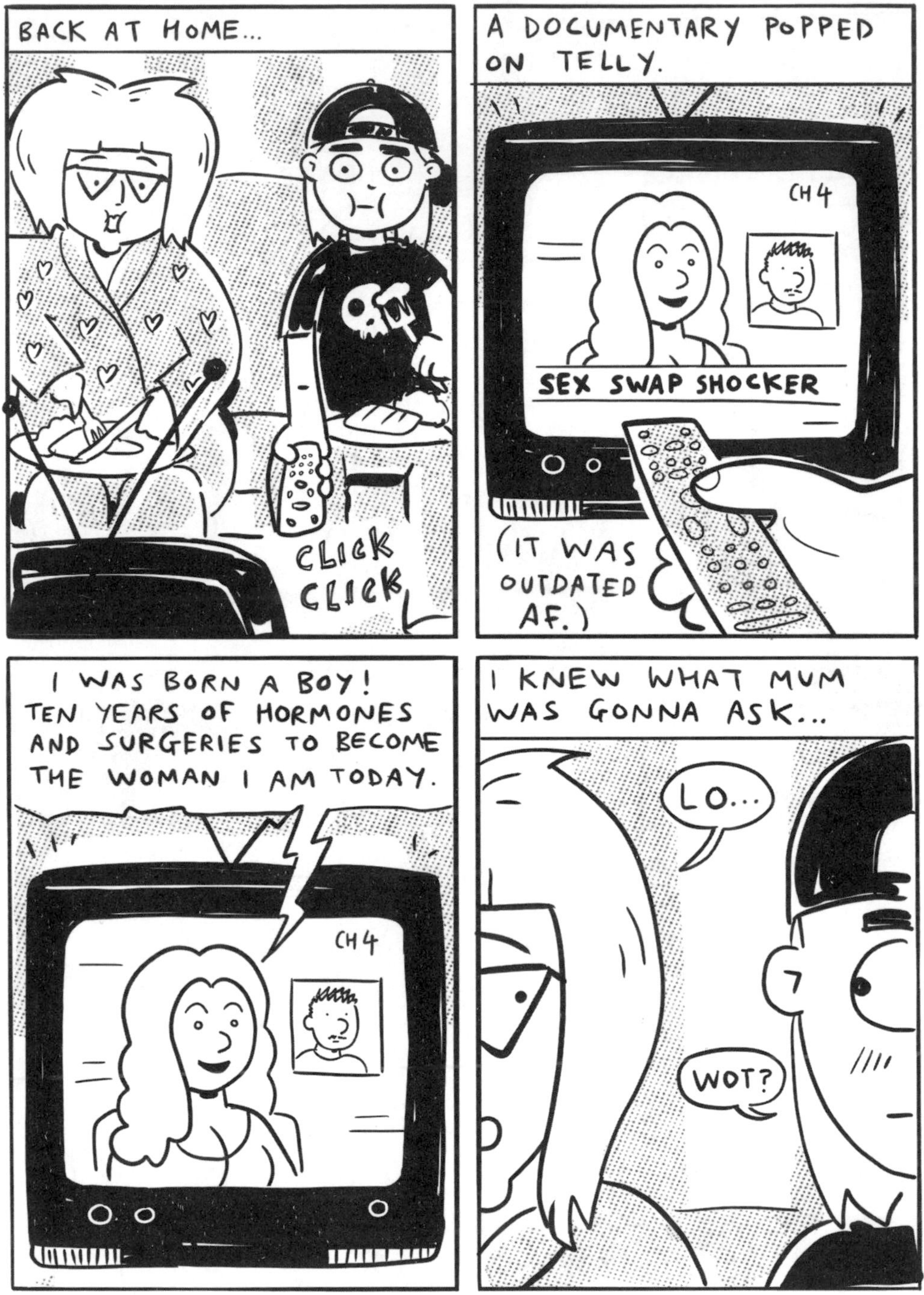
BACK AT HOME...
CLICK CLICK
A DOCUMENTARY POPPED ON TELLY.
CH4
SEX SWAP SHOCKER
(IT WAS OUTDATED AF.)
I WAS BORN A BOY! TEN YEARS OF HORMONES AND SURGERIES TO BECOME THE WOMAN I AM TODAY.
CH4
I KNEW WHAT MUM WAS GONNA ASK...
LO...
WOT?

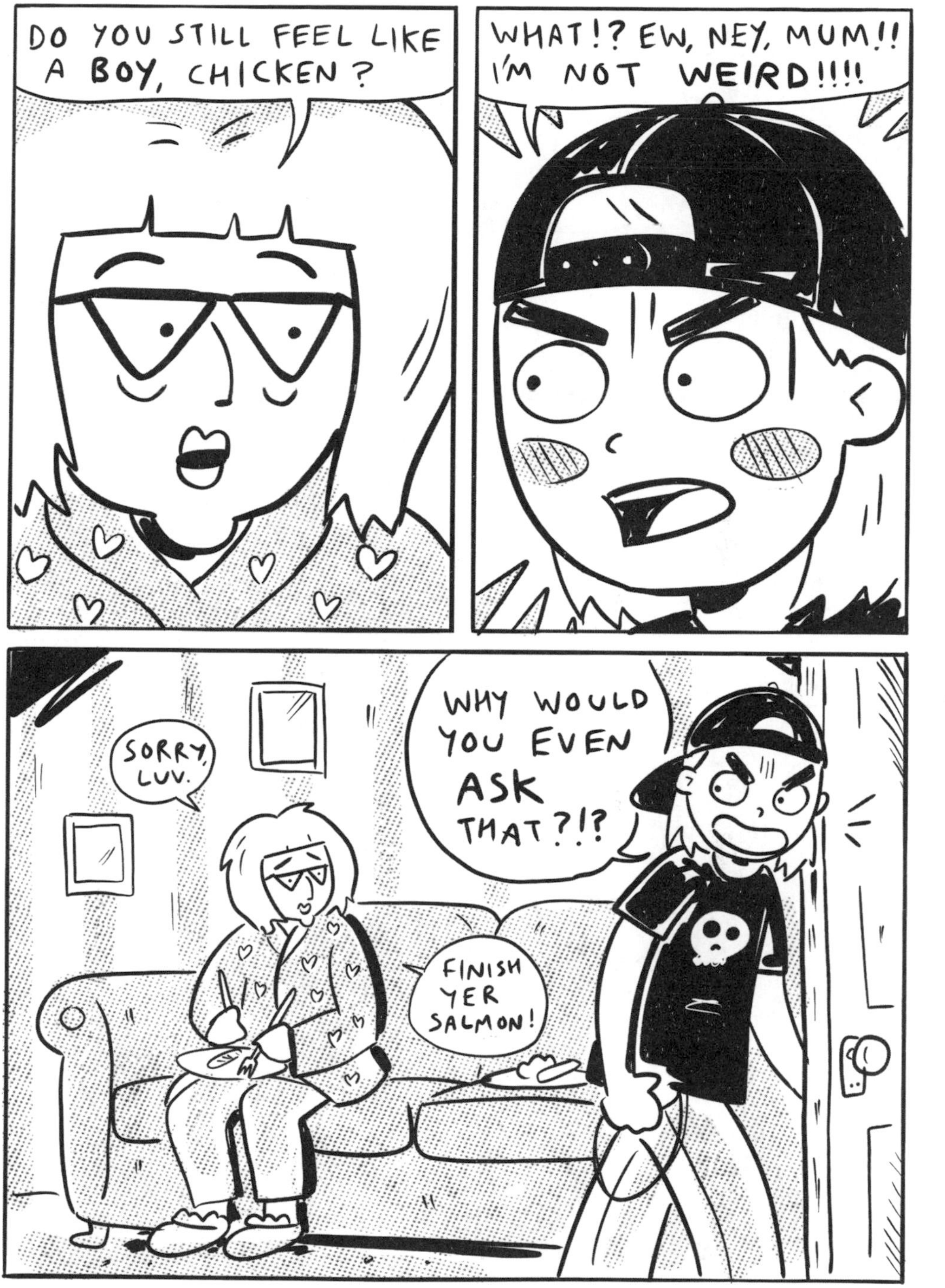
DO YOU STILL FEEL LIKE A BOY, CHICKEN?
WHAT!? EW, NEY, MUM!! I'M NOT WEIRD!!!!
SORRY, LUV.
WHY WOULD YOU EVEN ASK THAT?!?
FINISH YER SALMON!

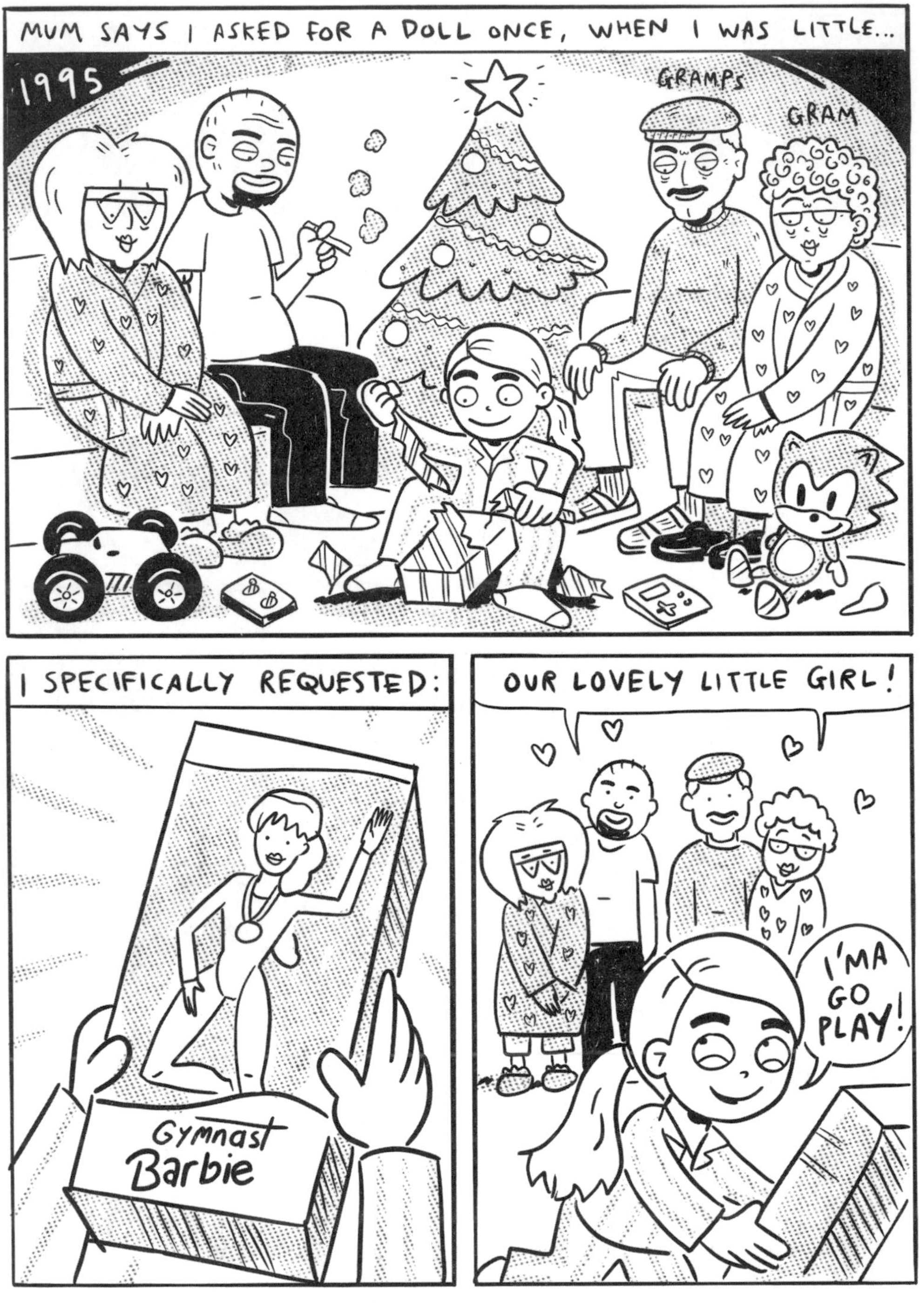
MUM SAYS I ASKED FOR A DOLL ONCE, WHEN I WAS LITTLE...
1995
GRAMPS
GRAM
I SPECIFICALLY REQUESTED:
Gymnast
Barbie
OUR LOVELY LITTLE GIRL!
I'MA GO PLAY!

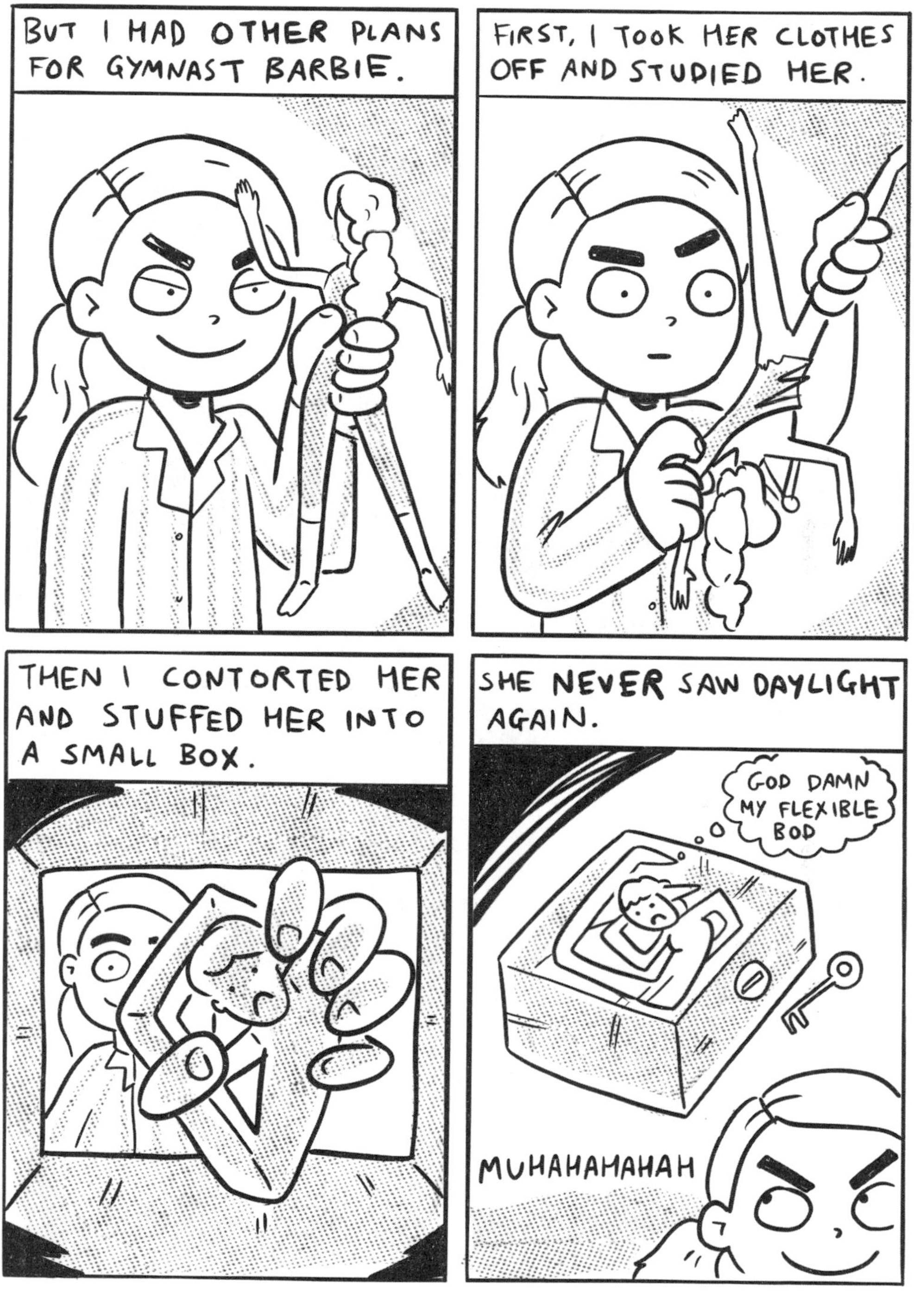
BUT I HAD OTHER PLANS FOR GYMNAST BARBIE.
FIRST, I TOOK HER CLOTHES OFF AND STUDIED HER.
THEN I CONTORTED HER AND STUFFED HER INTO A SMALL BOX.
SHE NEVER SAW DAYLIGHT AGAIN.
GOD DAMN MY FLEXIBLE BOD
MUHAHAHAHAH

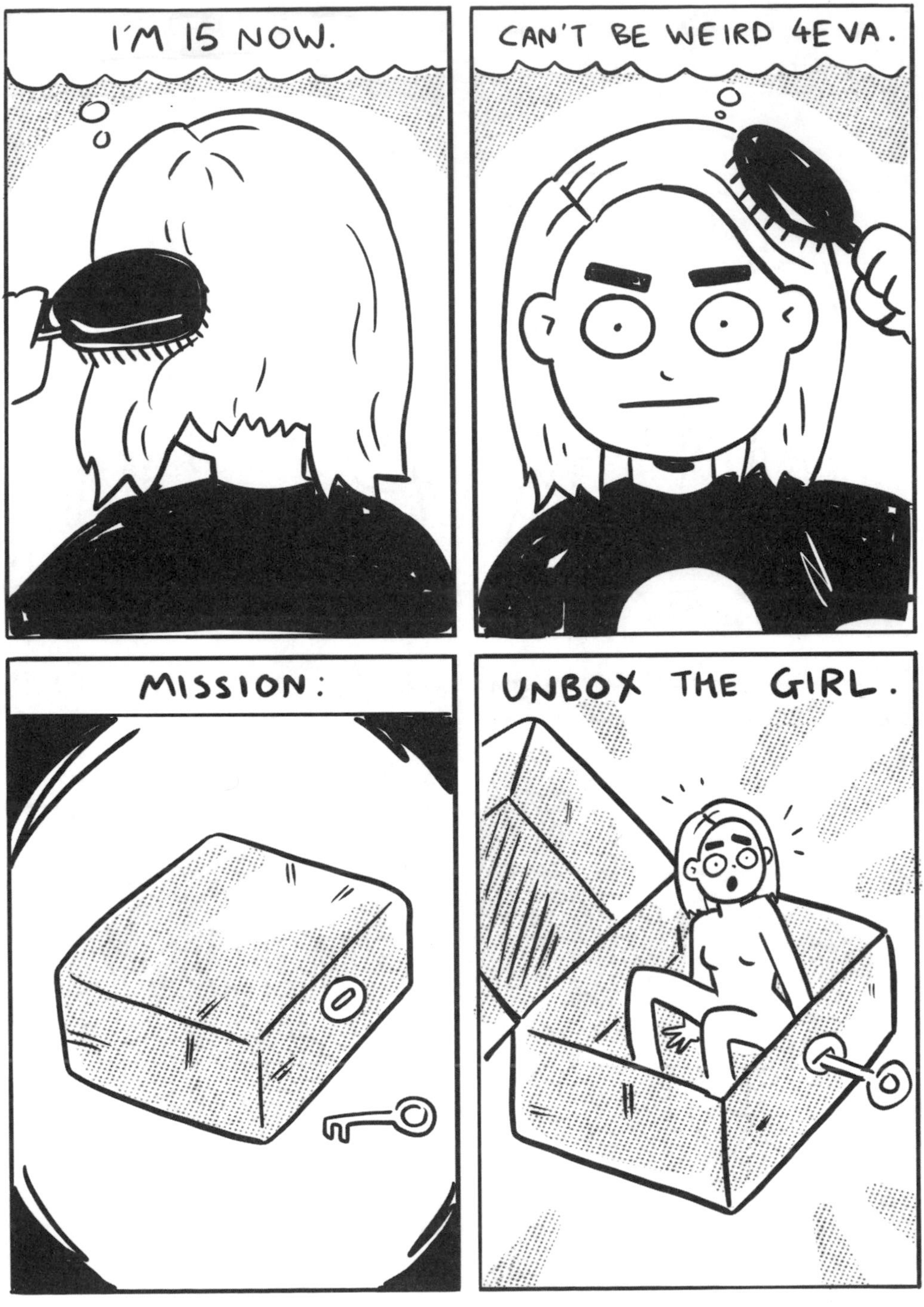
I'M 15 NOW.
CAN'T BE WEIRD 4EVA.
MISSION:
UNBOX THE GIRL.

DO MY RESEARCH
£1.50
COSMO girl!
WHAT BOYS WANT
500 ways to look HOT
DEFO FANCY BOYS
JUSTIN TIMBERLAKE
OW.
OW.
OW.
OW.
SHAVE ME LEGS
LOOKED BLOODY BETTER BEFORE!
REGRET

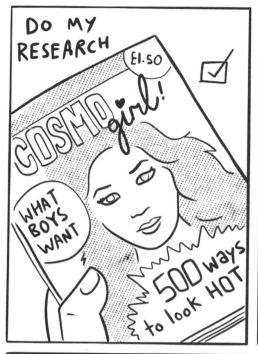

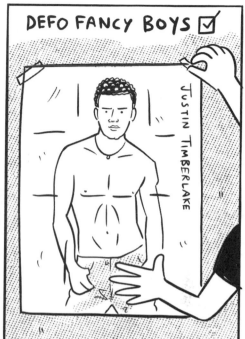

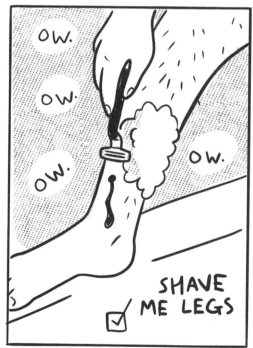

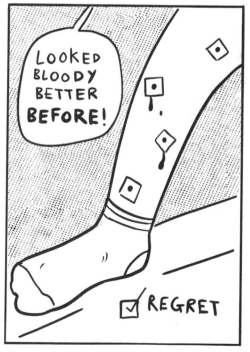

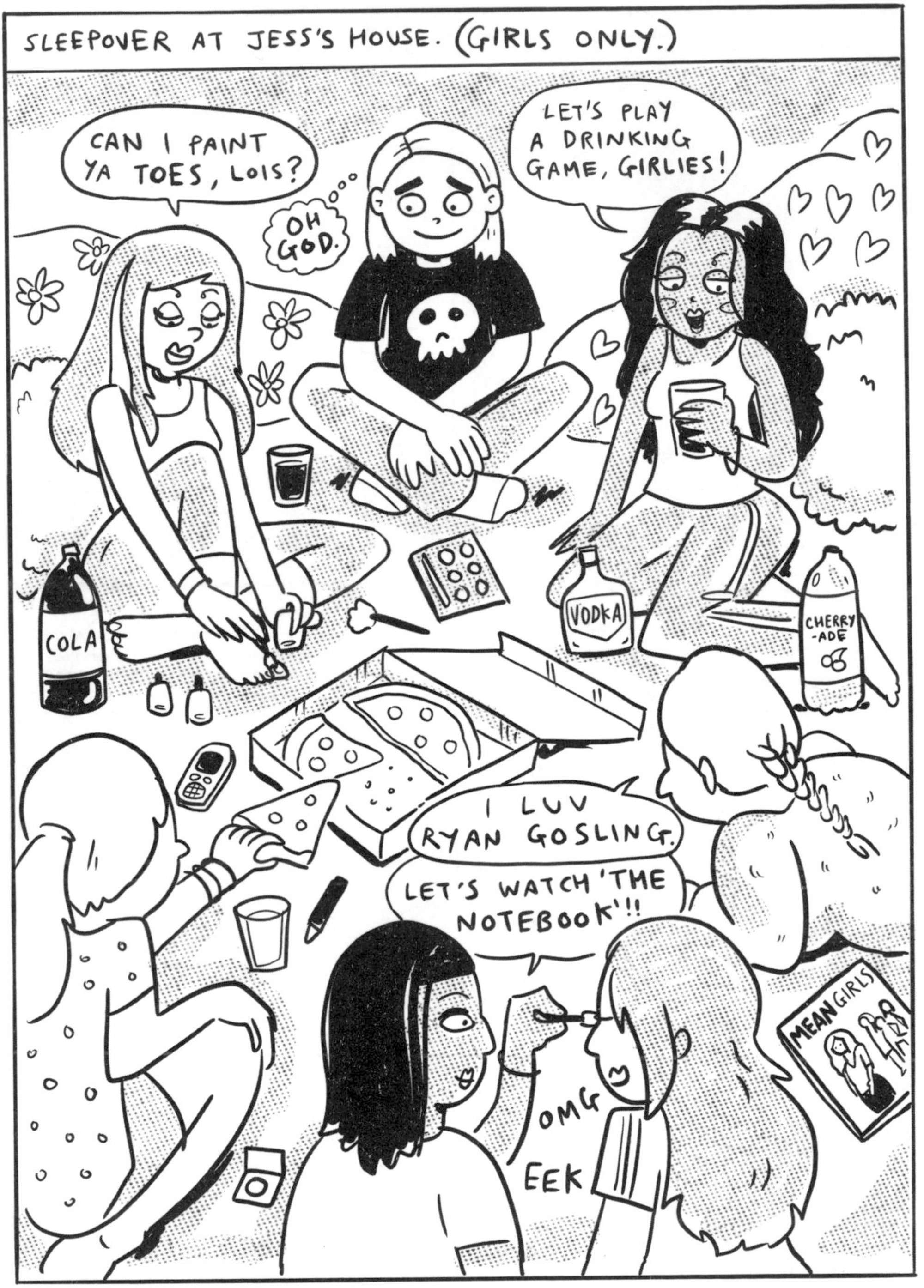
SLEEPOVER AT JESS'S HOUSE. (GIRLS ONLY.)
CAN I PAINT YA TOES, LOIS?
OH GOD.
LET'S PLAY A DRINKING GAME, GIRLIES!
COLA
VODKA
CHERRY-ADE
I LUV RYAN GOSLING.
LET'S WATCH 'THE NOTEBOOK'!!
MEAN GIRLS
OMG
EEK

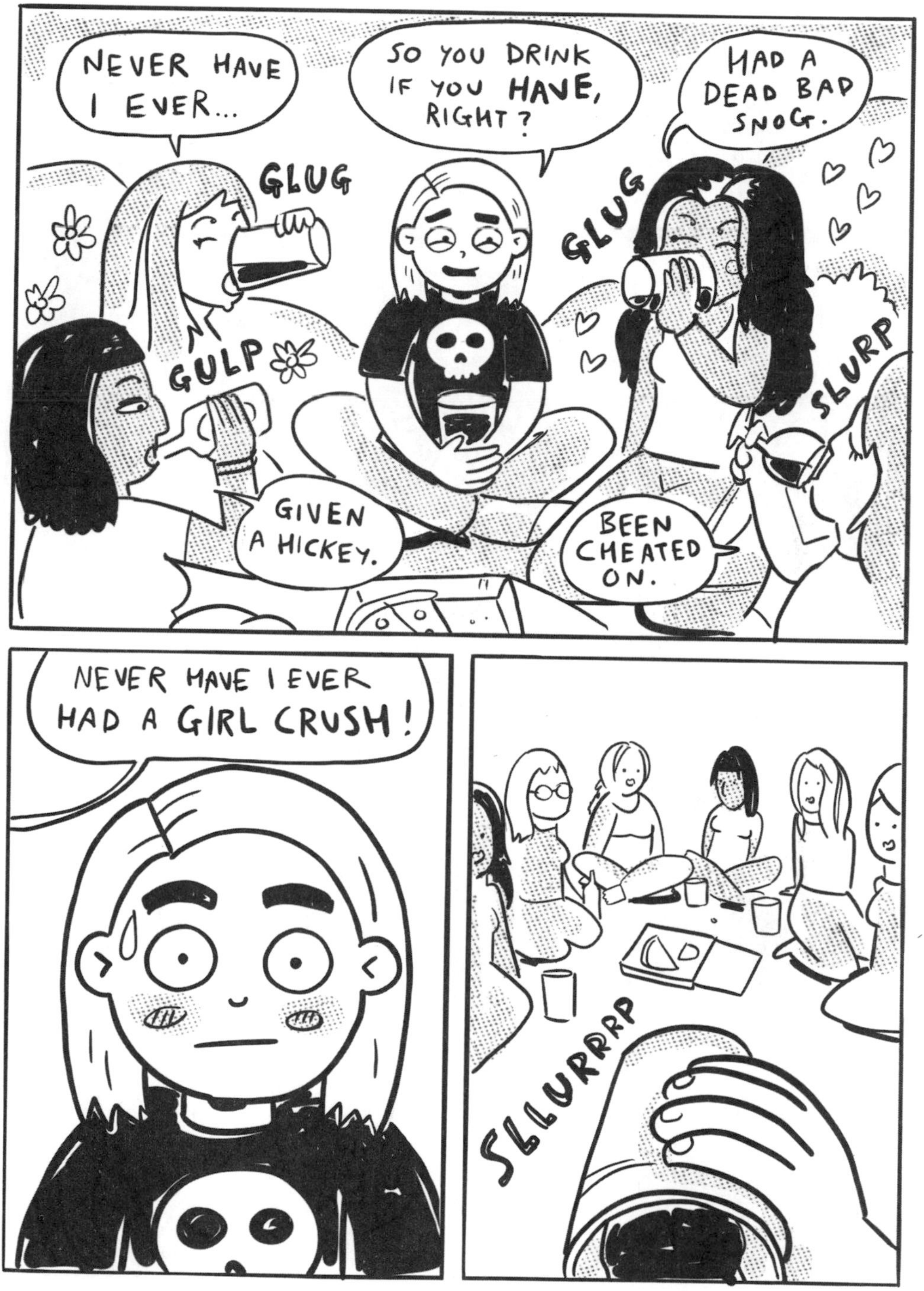
NEVER HAVE I EVER...
SO YOU DRINK IF YOU HAVE, RIGHT?
HAD A DEAD BAD SNOG.
GLUG
GLUG
GULP
SLURP
GIVEN A HICKEY.
BEEN CHEATED ON.
NEVER HAVE I EVER HAD A GIRL CRUSH!
SLLURRRP

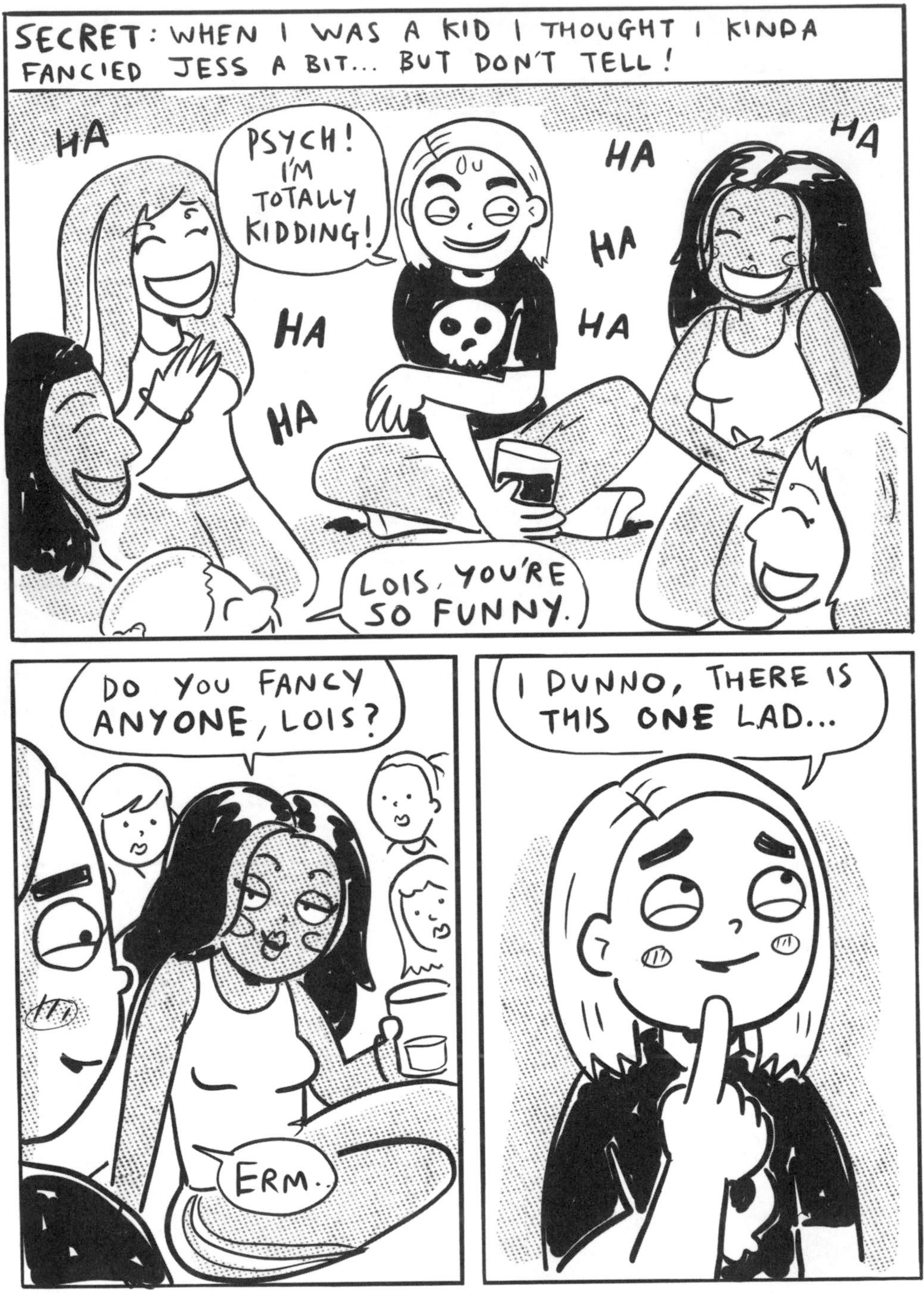
SECRET: WHEN I WAS A KID I THOUGHT I KINDA FANCIED JESS A BIT... BUT DON'T TELL!
HA
PSYCH! I'M TOTALLY KIDDING!
HA
HA
HA
HA
HA
HA
HA
LOIS, YOU'RE SO FUNNY.
DO YOU FANCY ANYONE, LOIS?
ERM..
I DUNNO, THERE IS THIS ONE LAD...

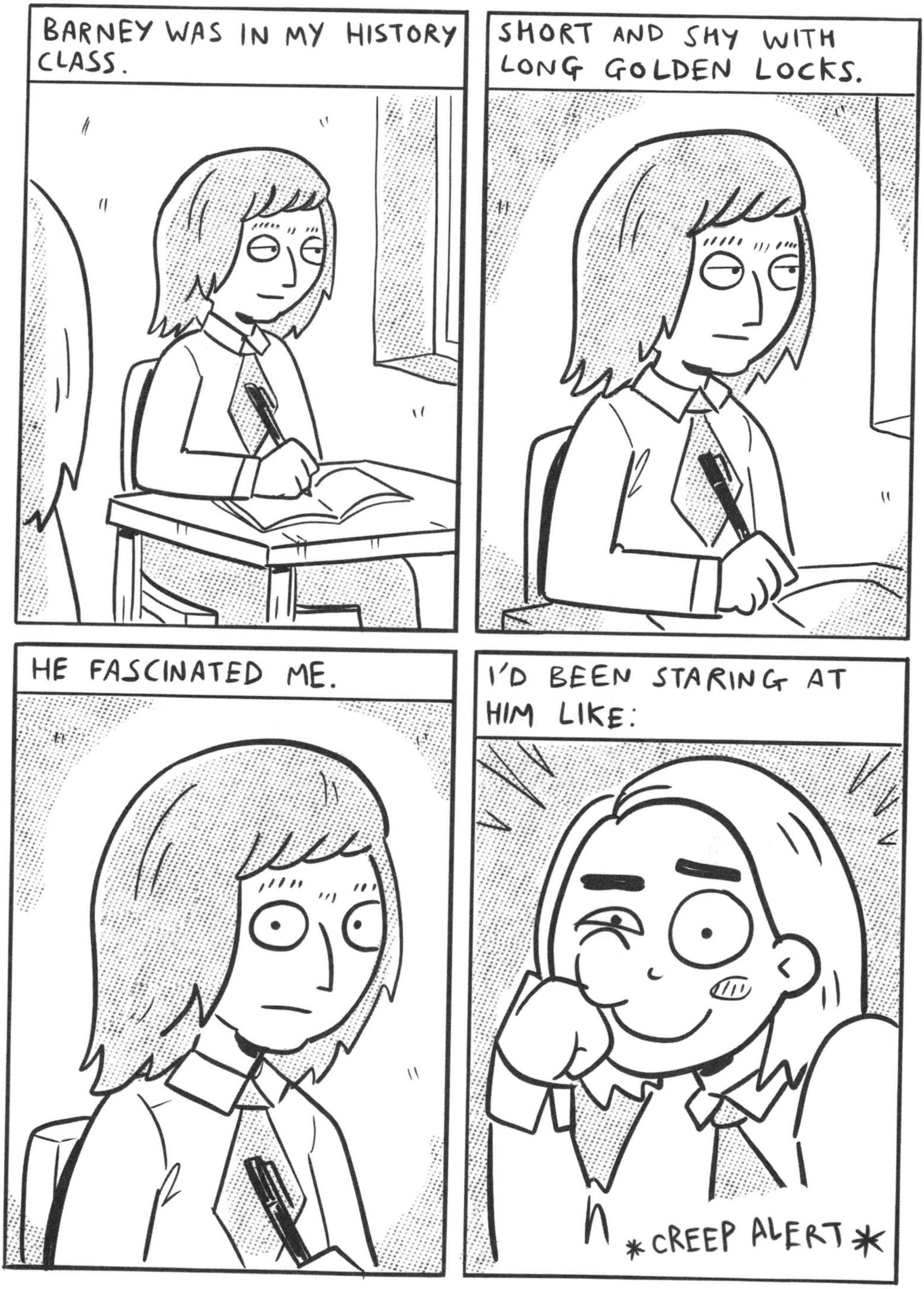
BARNEY WAS IN MY HISTORY CLASS.
SHORT AND SHY WITH LONG GOLDEN LOCKS.
HE FASCINATED ME.
I'D BEEN STARING AT HIM LIKE:
CREEP ALERT

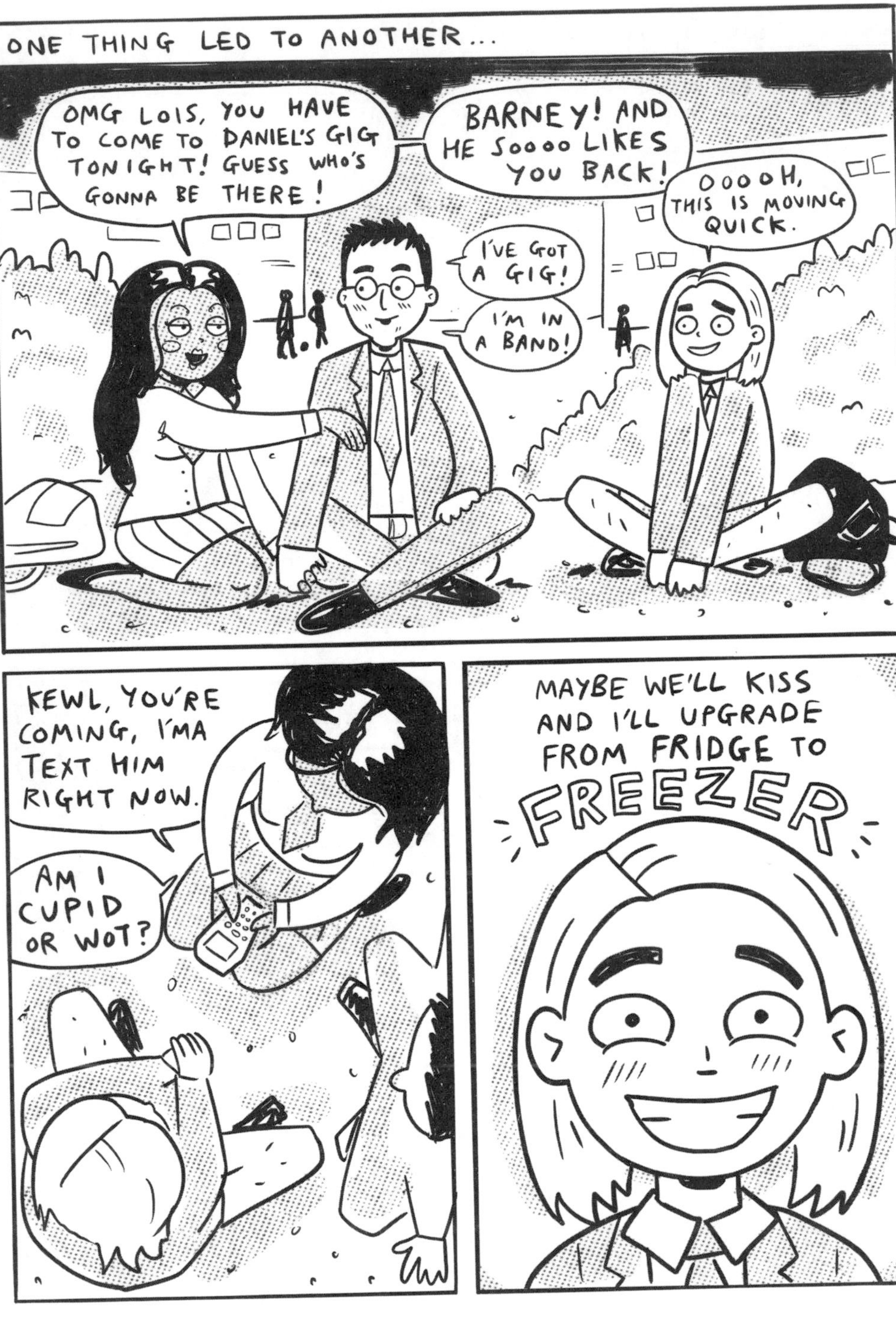
ONE THING LED TO ANOTHER...
OMG LOIS, YOU HAVE TO COME TO DANIEL'S GIG TONIGHT! GUESS WHO'S GONNA BE THERE!
BARNEY! AND HE SOOOO LIKES YOU BACK!
OOOOH, THIS IS MOVING QUICK.
I'VE GOT A GIG!
I'M IN A BAND!
KEWL, YOU'RE COMING, I'MA TEXT HIM RIGHT NOW.
AM I CUPID OR WOT?
MAYBE WE'LL KISS AND I'LL UPGRADE FROM FRIDGE TO
FREEZER

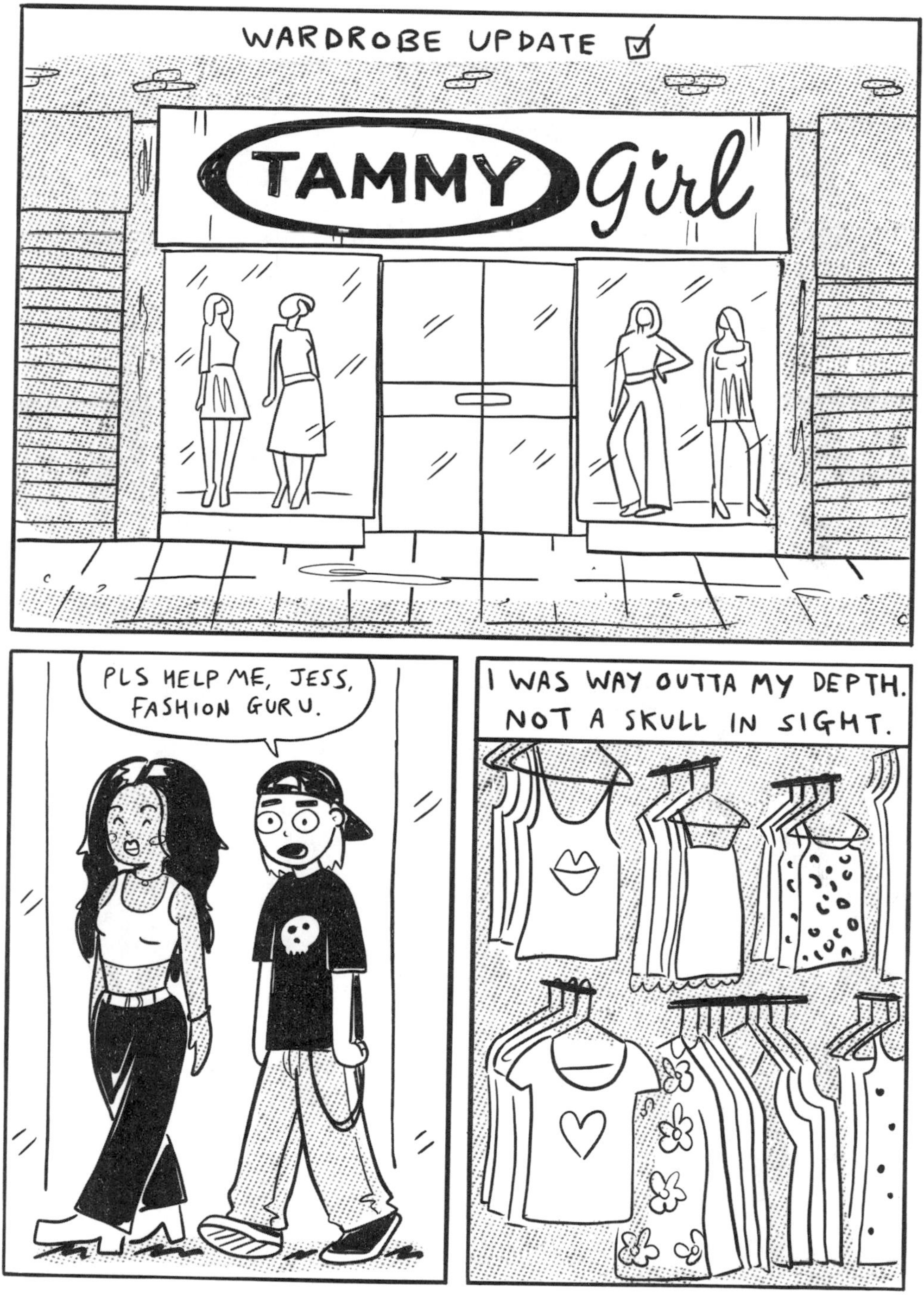
WARDROBE UPDATE ☑
TAMMY girl
PLS HELP ME, JESS, FASHION GURU.
I WAS WAY OUTTA MY DEPTH. NOT A SKULL IN SIGHT.

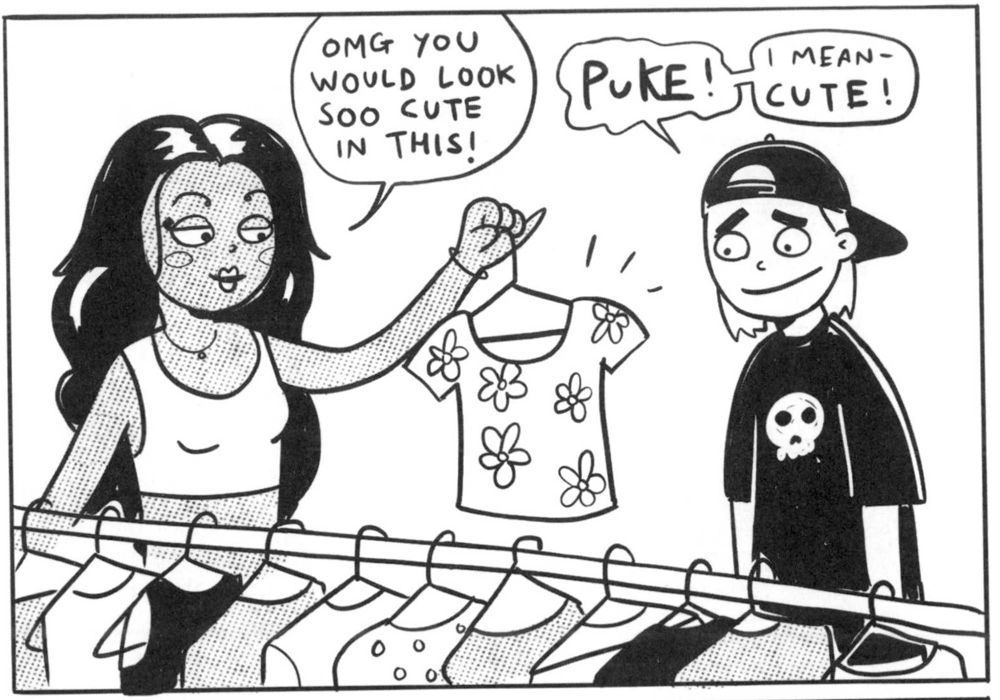
OMG YOU WOULD LOOK SOO CUTE IN THIS!
PUKE!
I MEAN- CUTE!

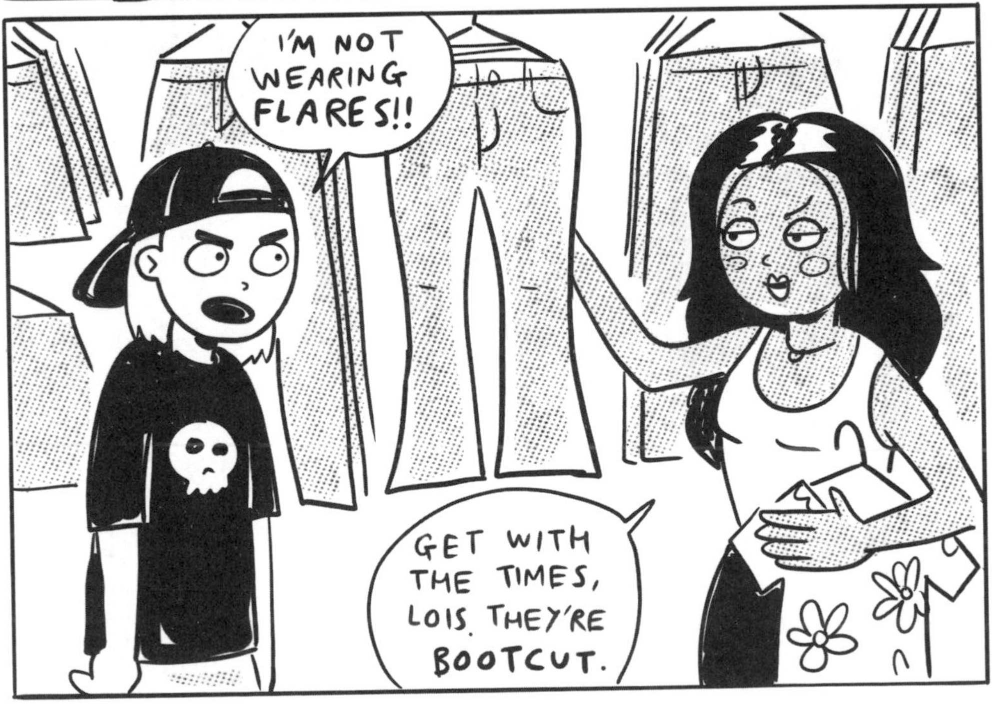
I'M NOT WEARING FLARES!!
GET WITH THE TIMES, LOIS. THEY'RE BOOTCUT.

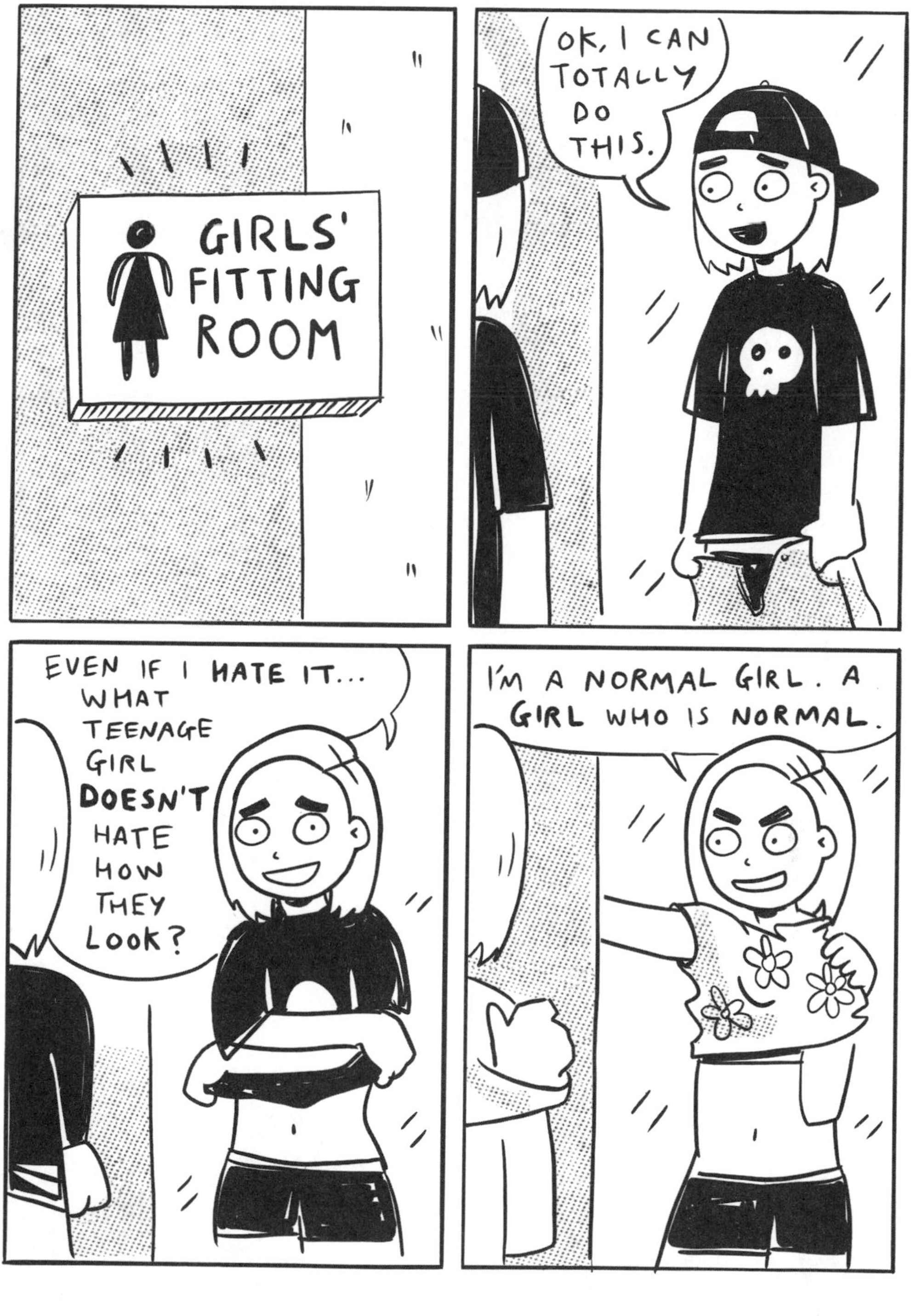
GIRLS' FITTING ROOM
OK, I CAN TOTALLY DO THIS.
EVEN IF I HATE IT... WHAT TEENAGE GIRL DOESN'T HATE HOW THEY LOOK?
I'M A NORMAL GIRL. A GIRL WHO IS NORMAL.

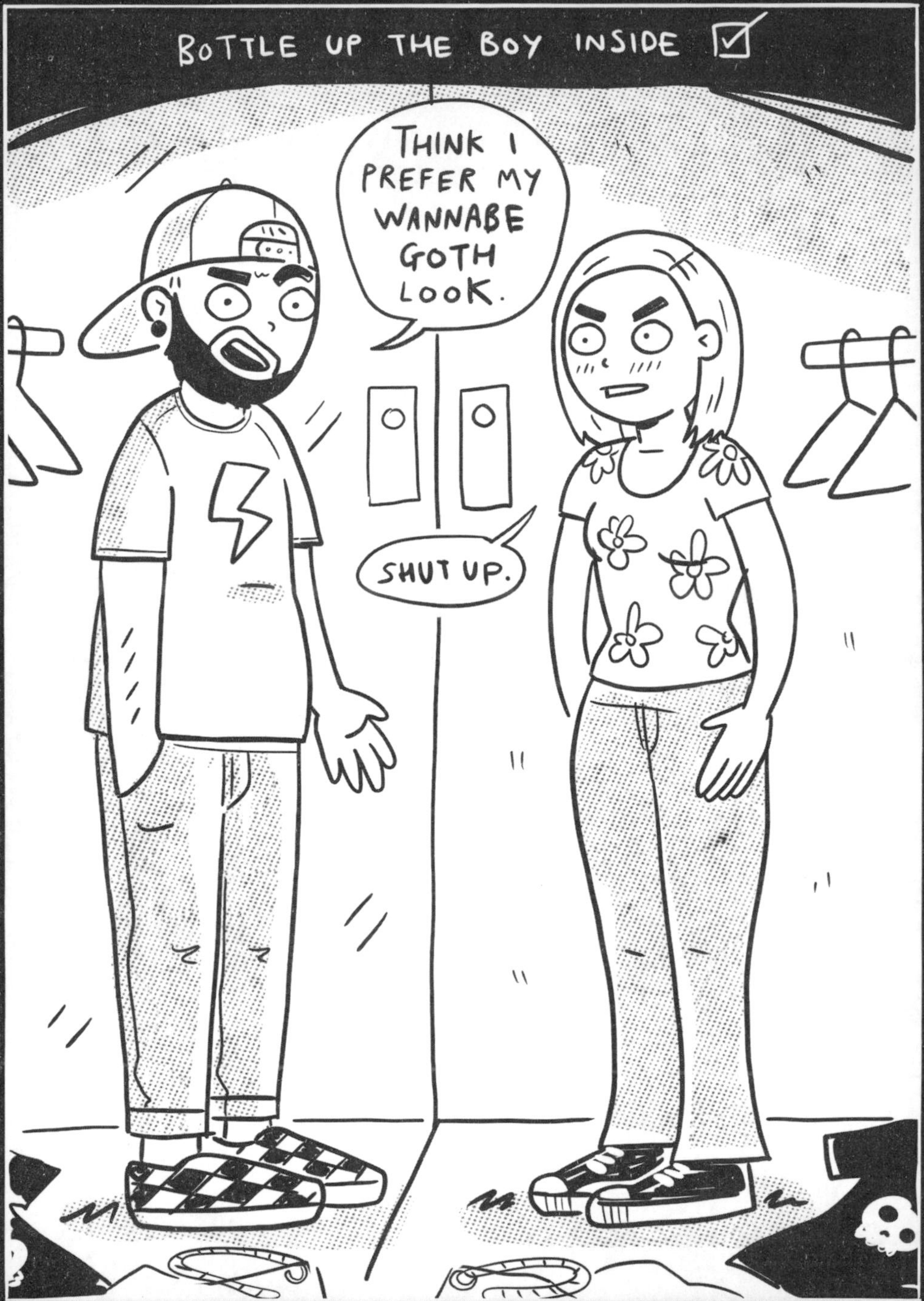
BOTTLE UP THE BOY INSIDE ☑
THINK I PREFER MY WANNABE GOTH LOOK.
SHUT UP.

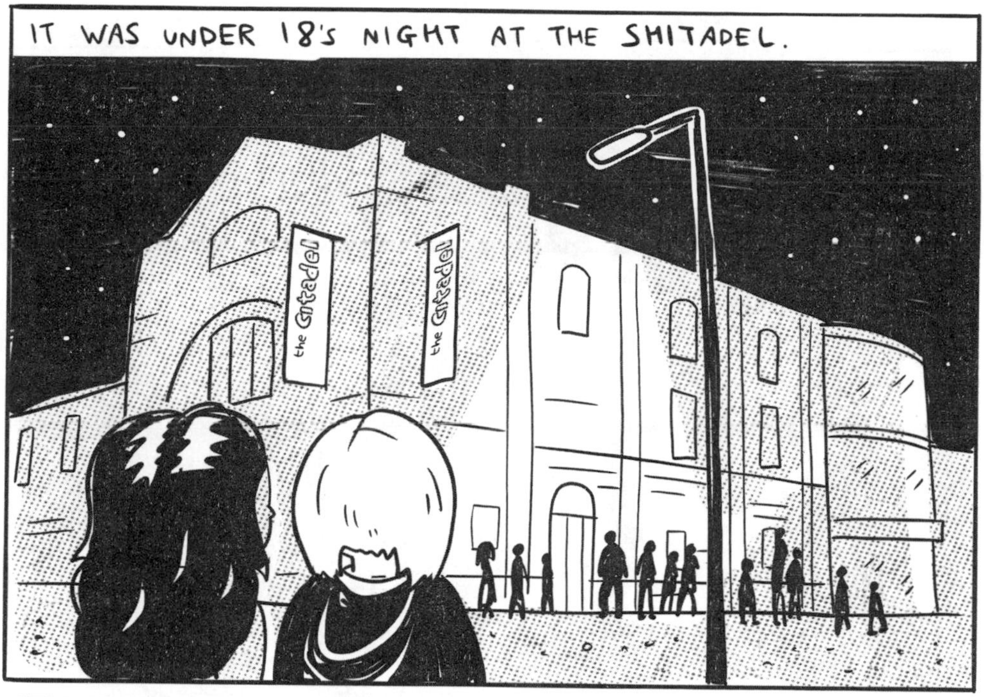
IT WAS UNDER 18'S NIGHT AT THE SHITADEL.
the Shitadel
the Shitadel

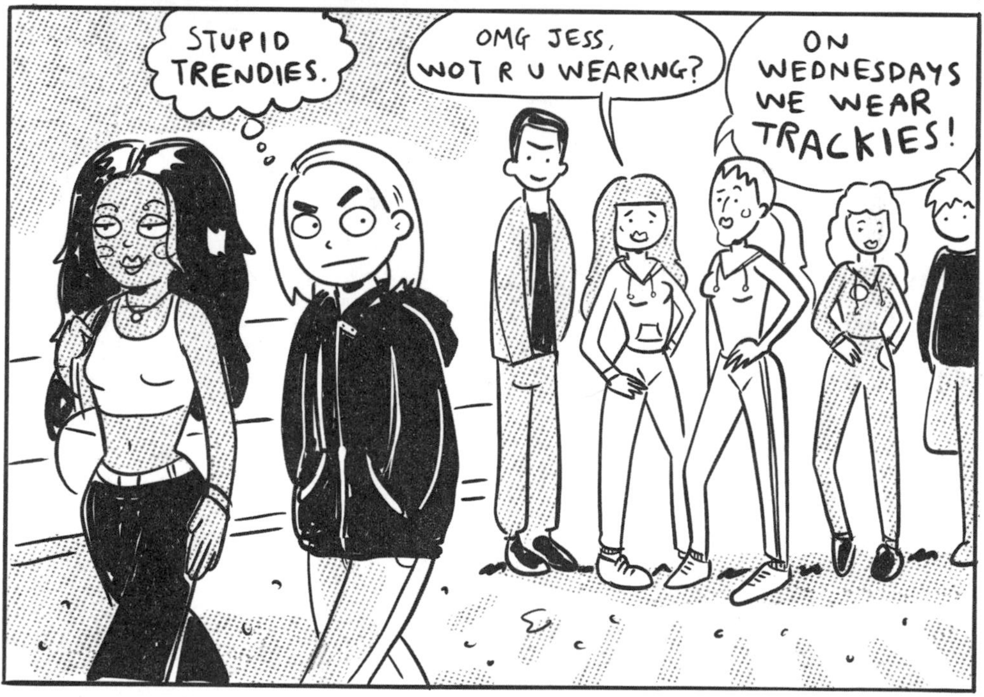
STUPID TRENDIES.
OMG JESS, WOT R U WEARING?
ON WEDNESDAYS WE WEAR TRACKIES!

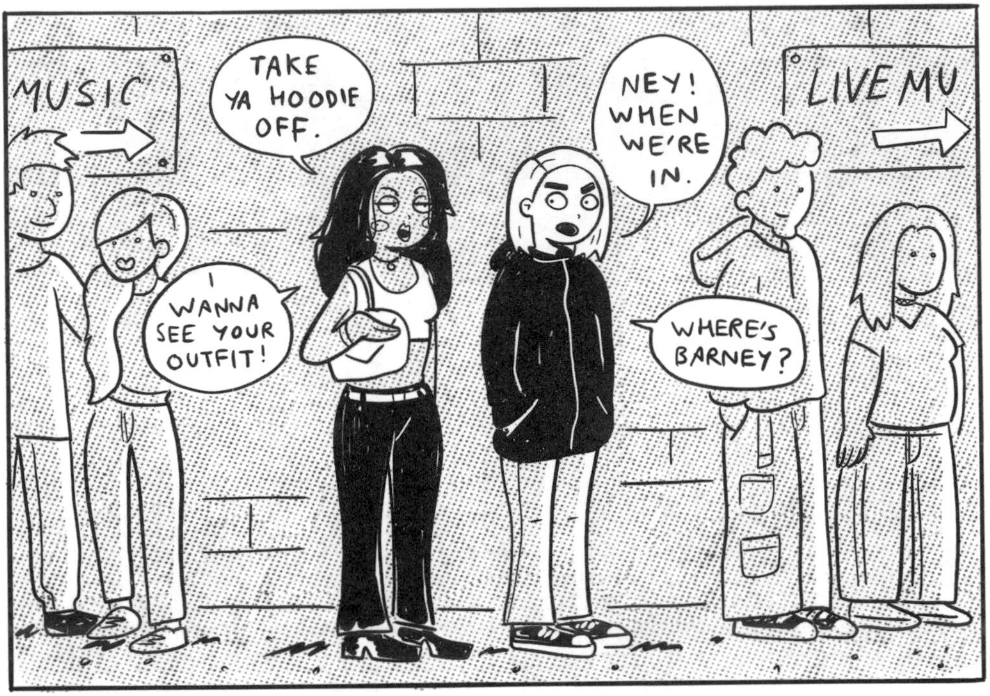
MUSIC
TAKE YA HOODIE OFF.
NEY! WHEN WE'RE IN.
LIVE MU
I WANNA SEE YOUR OUTFIT!
WHERE'S BARNEY?

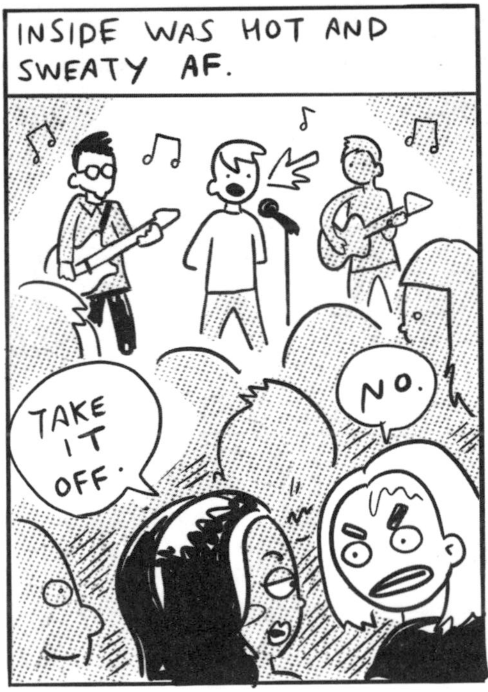
INSIDE WAS HOT AND SWEATY AF.
NO.
TAKE IT OFF.

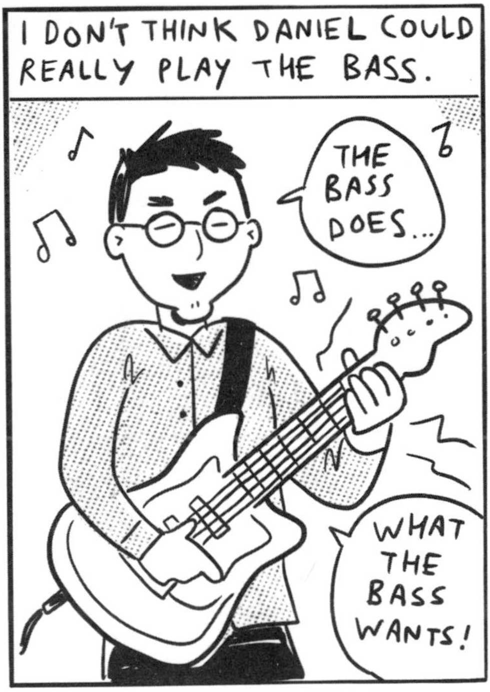
I DON'T THINK DANIEL COULD REALLY PLAY THE BASS.
THE BASS DOES...
WHAT THE BASS WANTS!

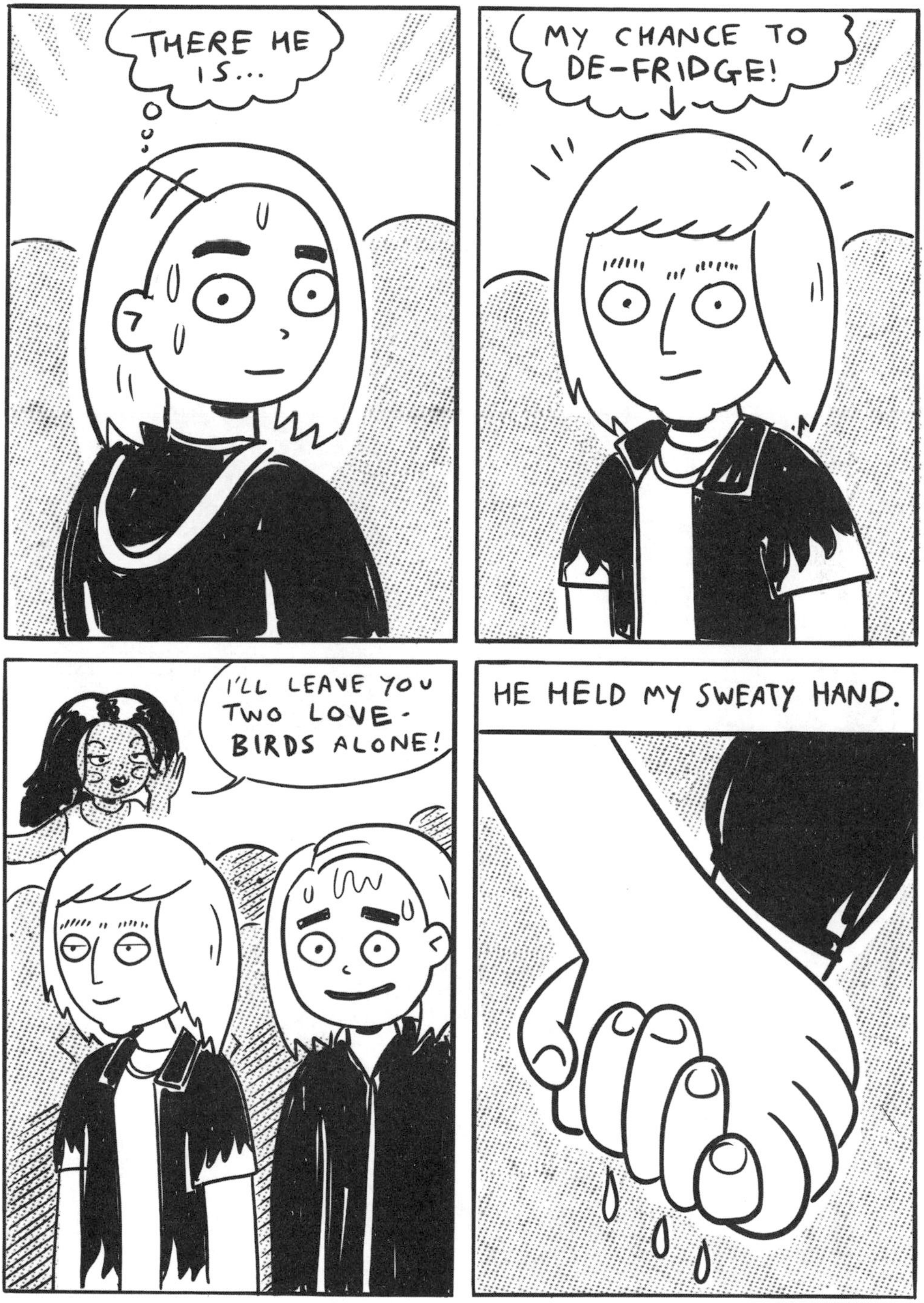
THERE HE IS...
MY CHANCE TO DE-FRIDGE!
I'LL LEAVE YOU TWO LOVE-BIRDS ALONE!
HE HELD MY SWEATY HAND.

I THINK JESS MUSTA TOLD THE TRENDIES SUMMAT:
I'VE TOTES DOLLED LOIS UP...
BUT SHE'S TOO SHY TO SHOW HER BODY OFF!
COZ THEY CAME FOR ME...
MY HOODIE!
LUV YA MAKEOVER, LOIS!
GORGE, BABE!
ZZZZZZIP

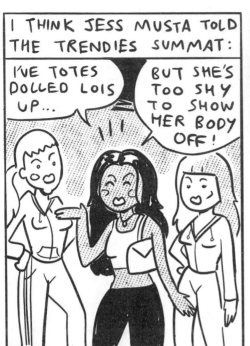

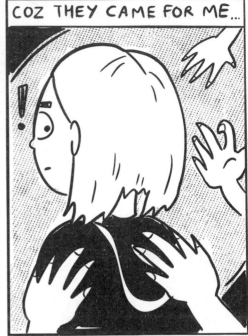

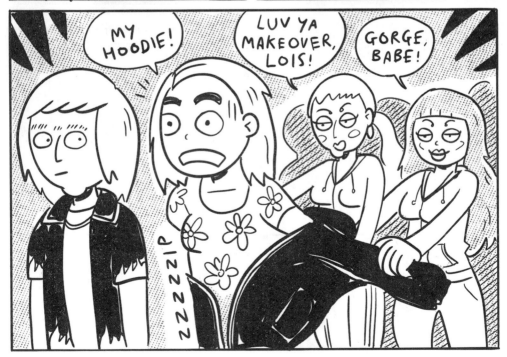

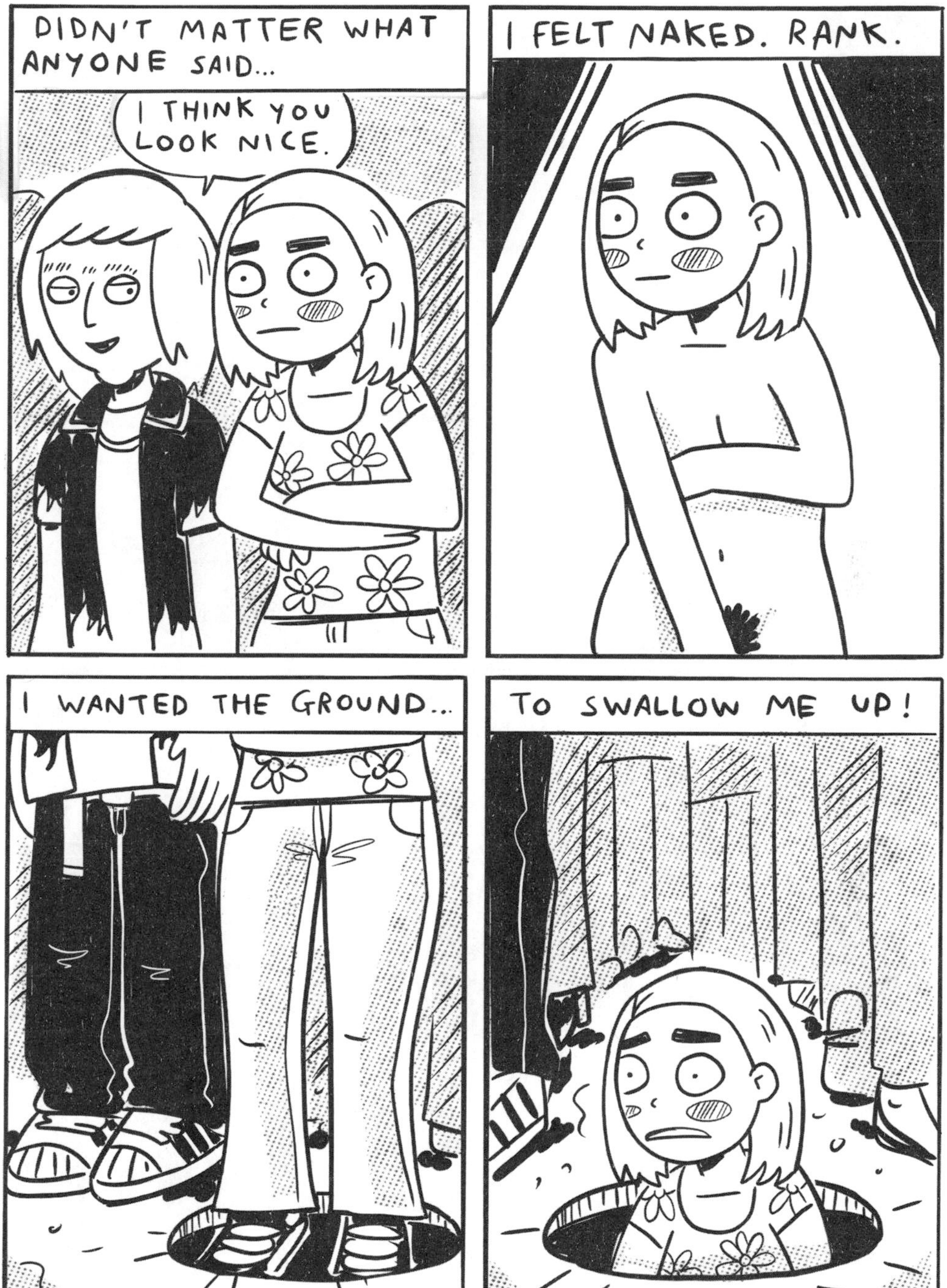
DIDN'T MATTER WHAT ANYONE SAID...
I THINK YOU LOOK NICE.
I FELT NAKED. RANK.
I WANTED THE GROUND...
TO SWALLOW ME UP!

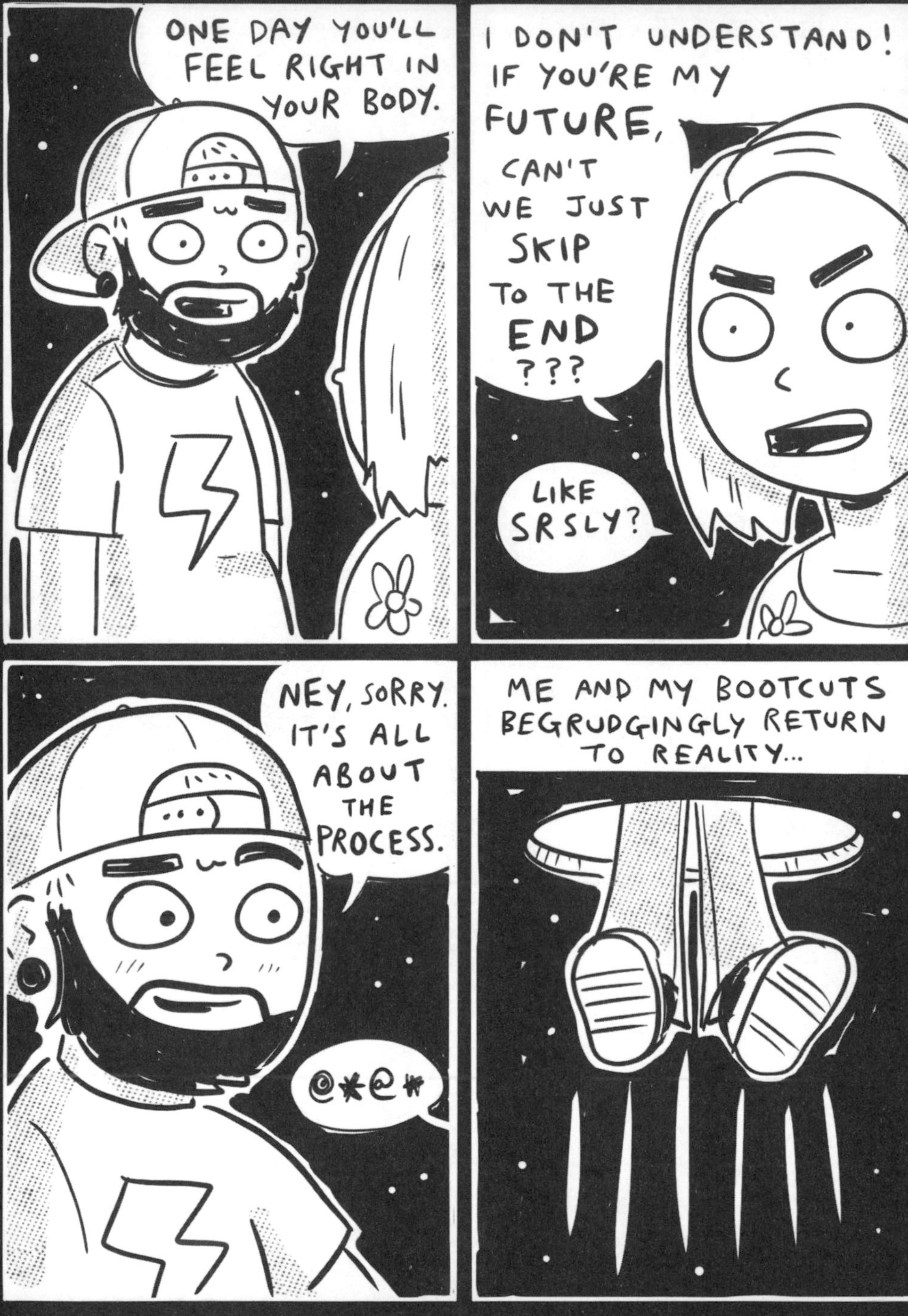
ONE DAY YOU'LL FEEL RIGHT IN YOUR BODY.
I DON'T UNDERSTAND! IF YOU'RE MY FUTURE, CAN'T WE JUST SKIP TO THE END???
LIKE SRSLY?
NEY, SORRY. IT'S ALL ABOUT THE PROCESS.
@*@#
ME AND MY BOOTCUTS BEGRUDGINGLY RETURN TO REALITY...

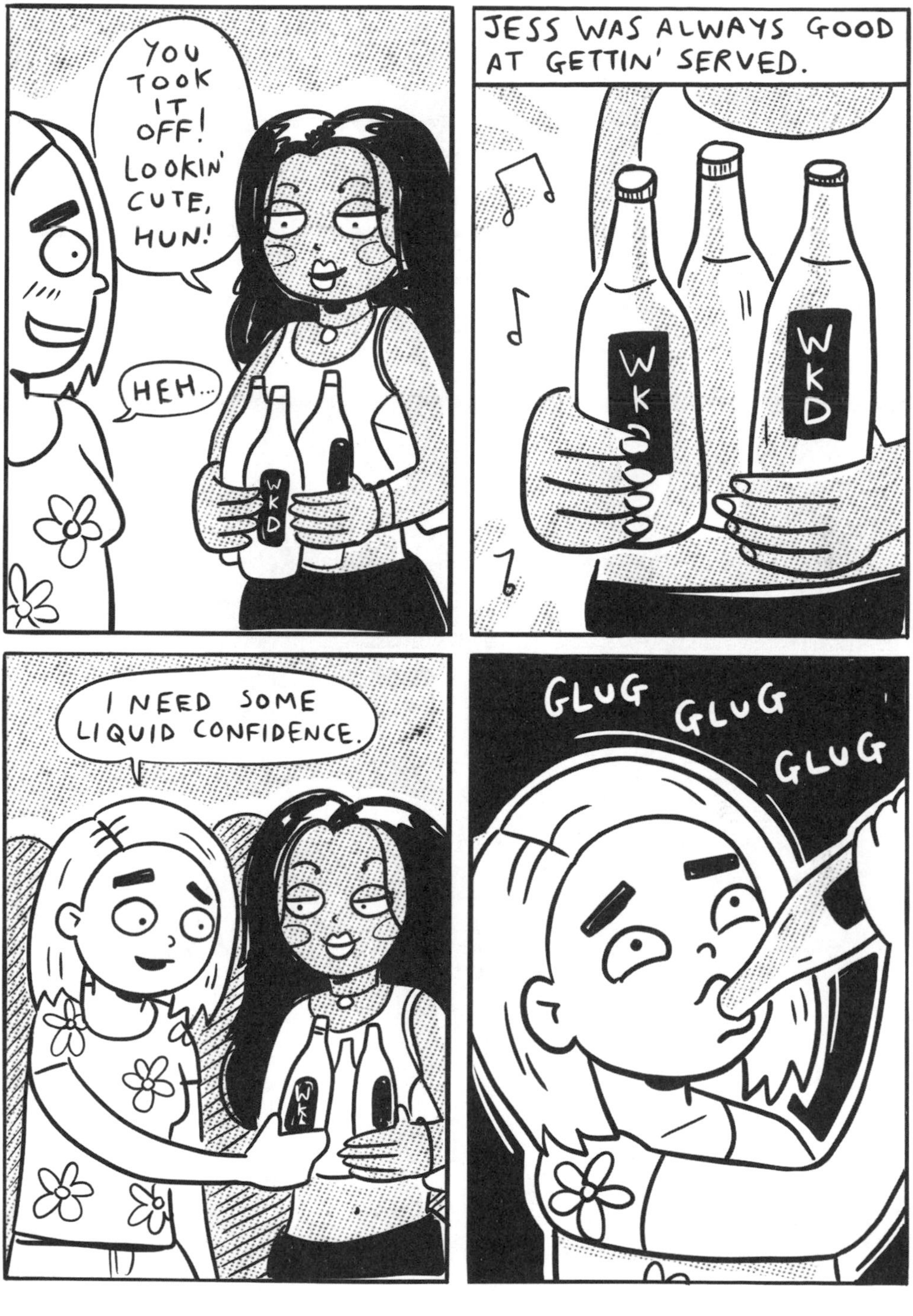
YOU TOOK IT OFF! LOOKIN' CUTE, HUN!
HEH...
WKD
JESS WAS ALWAYS GOOD AT GETTIN' SERVED.
WKD
WKD
I NEED SOME LIQUID CONFIDENCE.
GLUG GLUG GLUG

THE MORE I DRANK...

MY DREAM OF DE-FRIDGING GOT CLOSER.

AND CLOSER...

AND CLOSER...

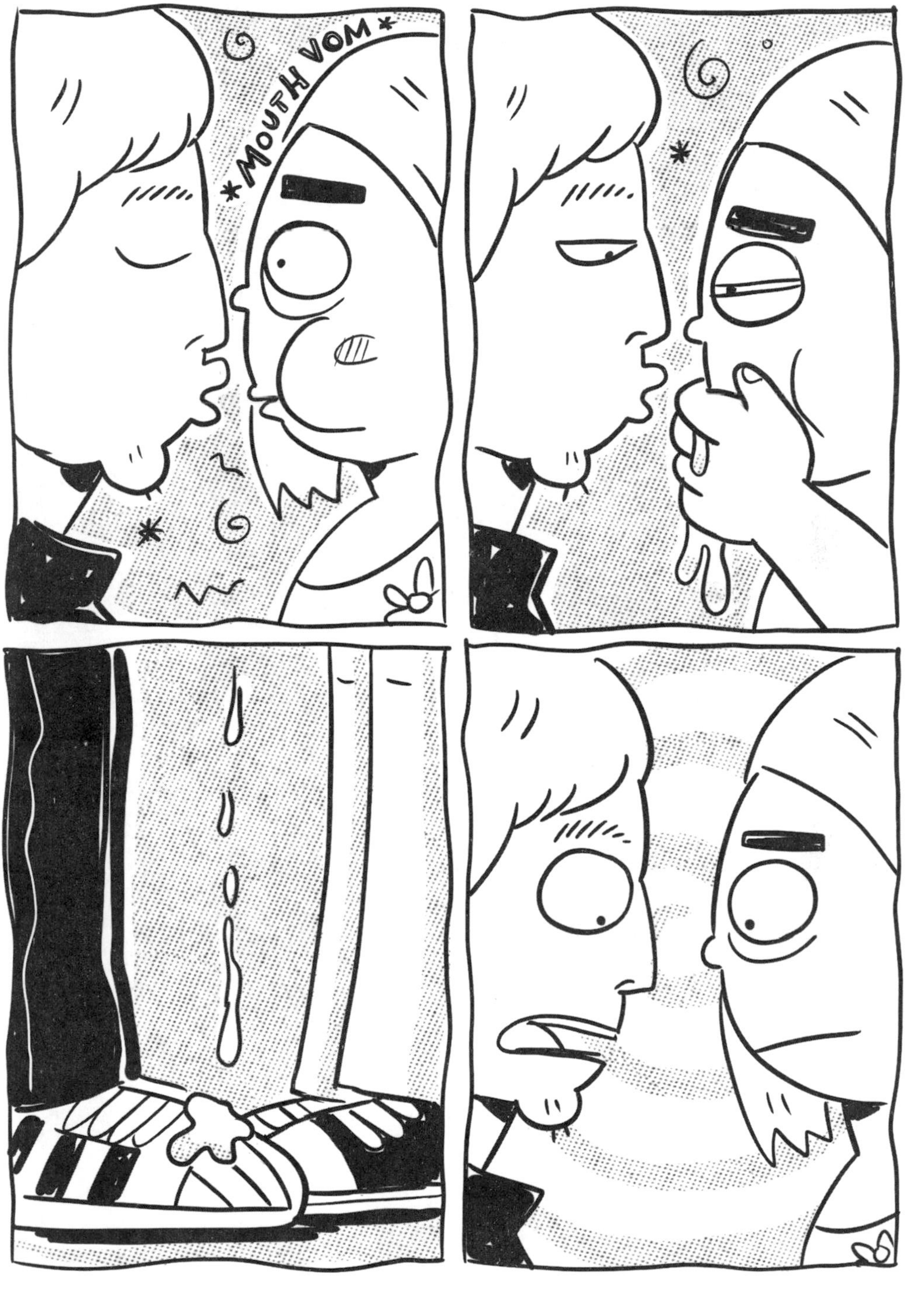
MOUTH VOM

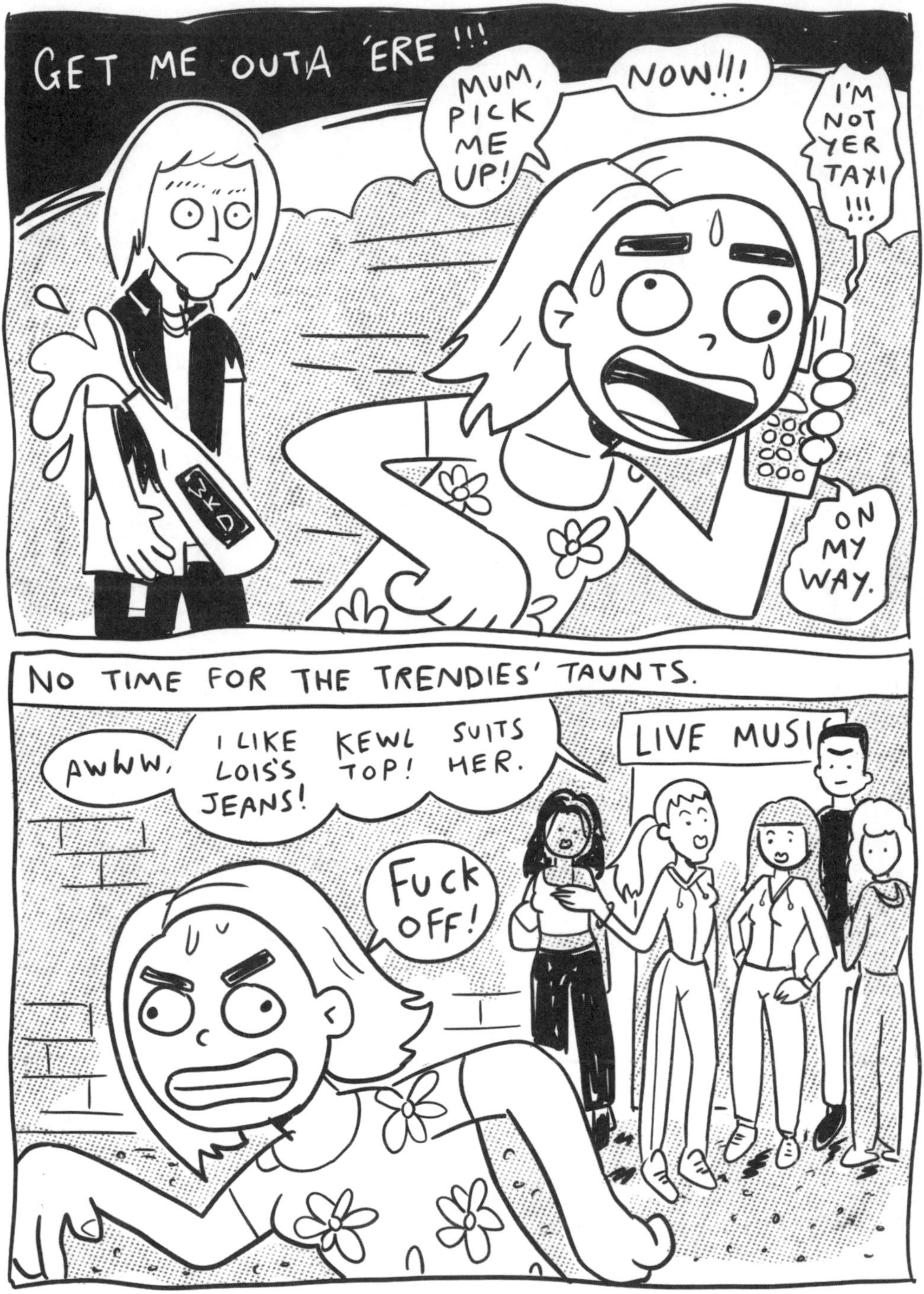
GET ME OUTA 'ERE !!!
MUM, PICK ME UP!
NOW!!!
I'M NOT YER TAXI !!!
ON MY WAY.
WKD
NO TIME FOR THE TRENDIES' TAUNTS.
AWWW, I LIKE LOIS'S JEANS! KEWL TOP! SUITS HER.
LIVE MUSI
FUCK OFF!

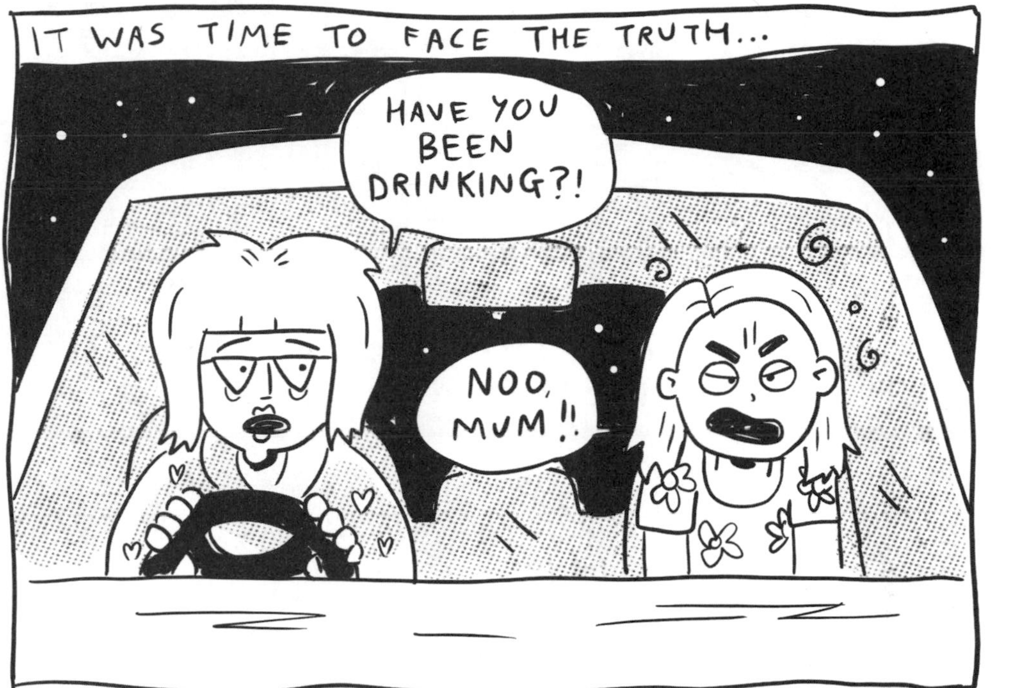
IT WAS TIME TO FACE THE TRUTH...
HAVE YOU BEEN DRINKING?!
NOO, MUM!!

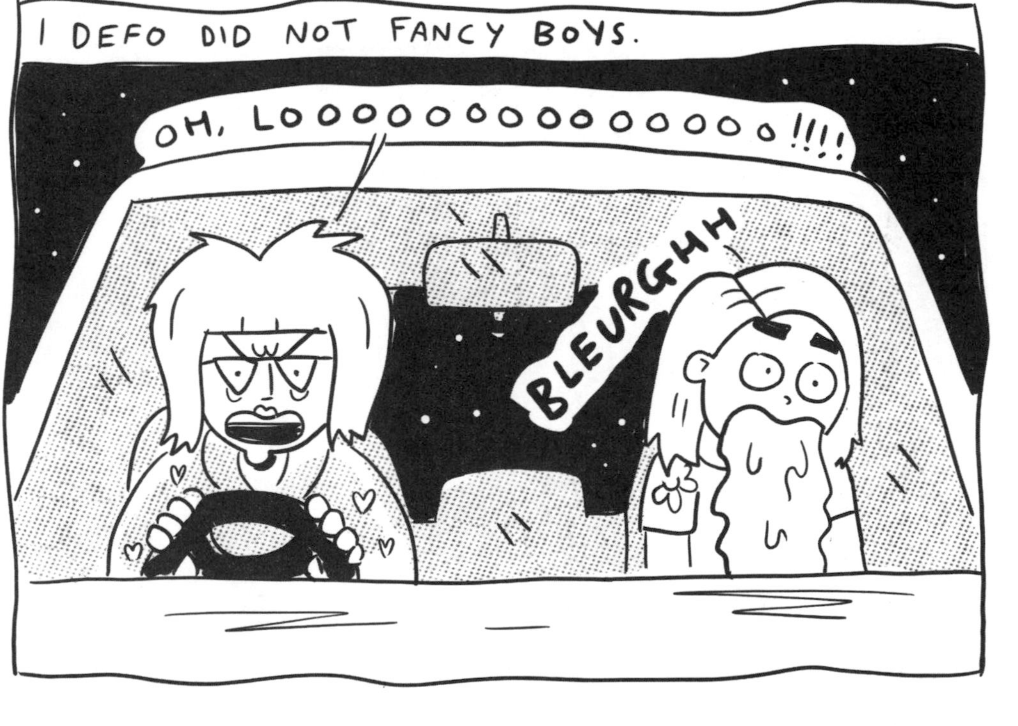
I DEFO DID NOT FANCY BOYS.
OH, LOOOOOOOOOOOOOOOOO!!!!
BLEURGHH

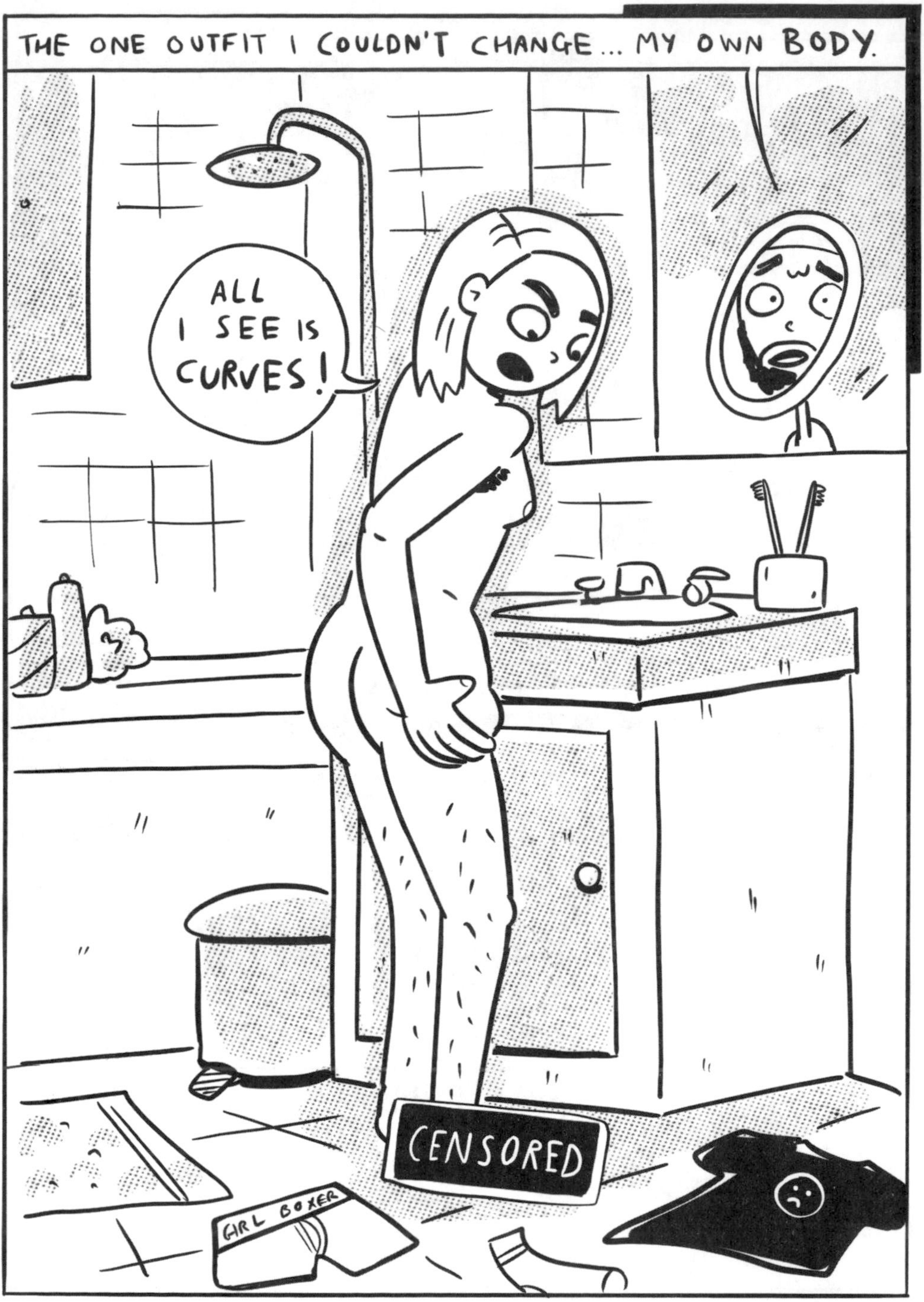
THE ONE OUTFIT I COULDN'T CHANGE... MY OWN BODY.
ALL I SEE IS CURVES!
CENSORED
GIRL BOXER

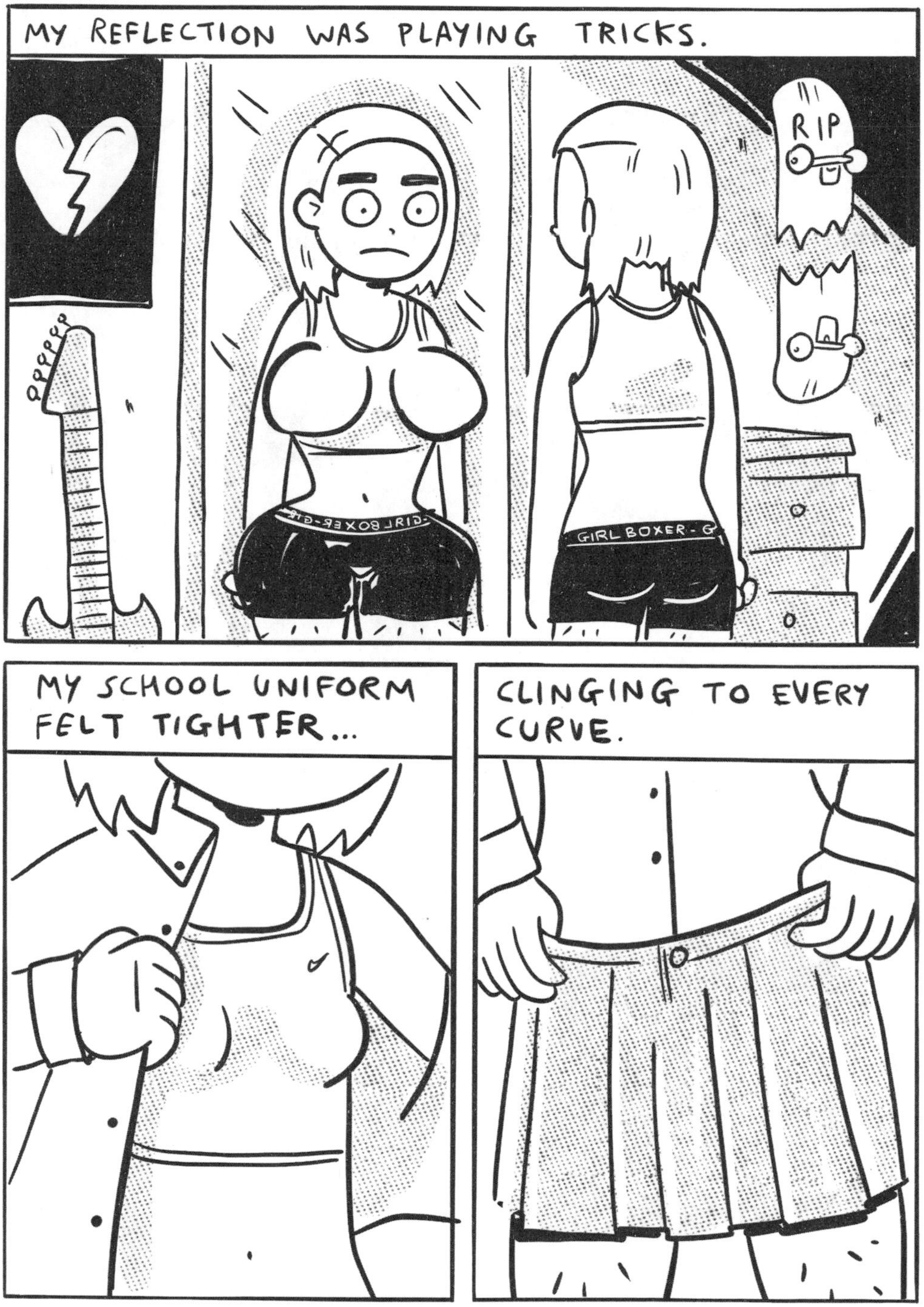
MY REFLECTION WAS PLAYING TRICKS.
RIP
GIRLBOXER-GIR
GIRLBOXER-G
MY SCHOOL UNIFORM FELT TIGHTER...
CLINGING TO EVERY CURVE.

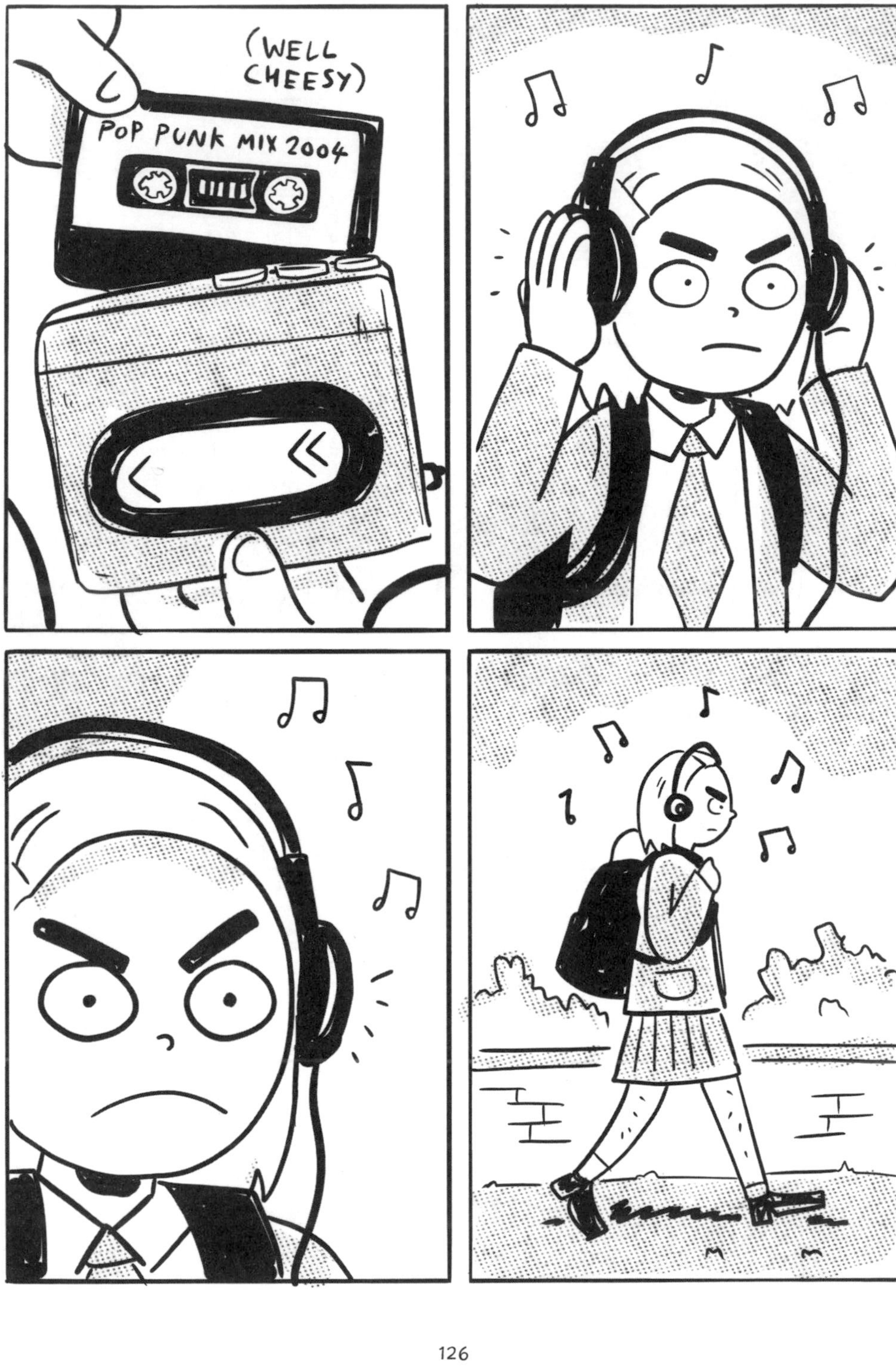
(WELL CHEESY)
POP PUNK MIX 2004

OH, LOOOO! YAV FORGOT YER HAM BUTTIES!
!
DON'T WANT 'EM, MUM.
I'M ON A DIET!

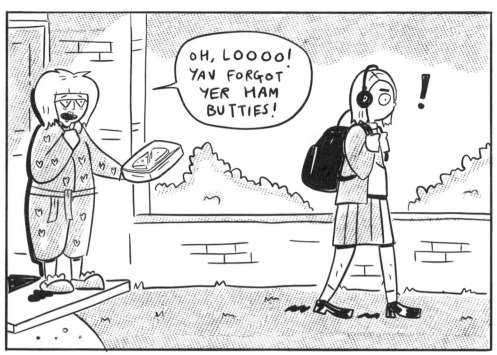

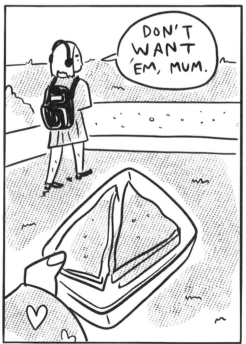

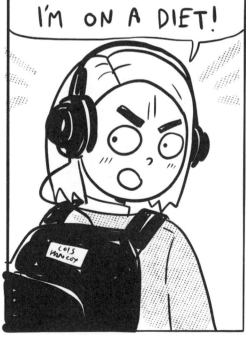

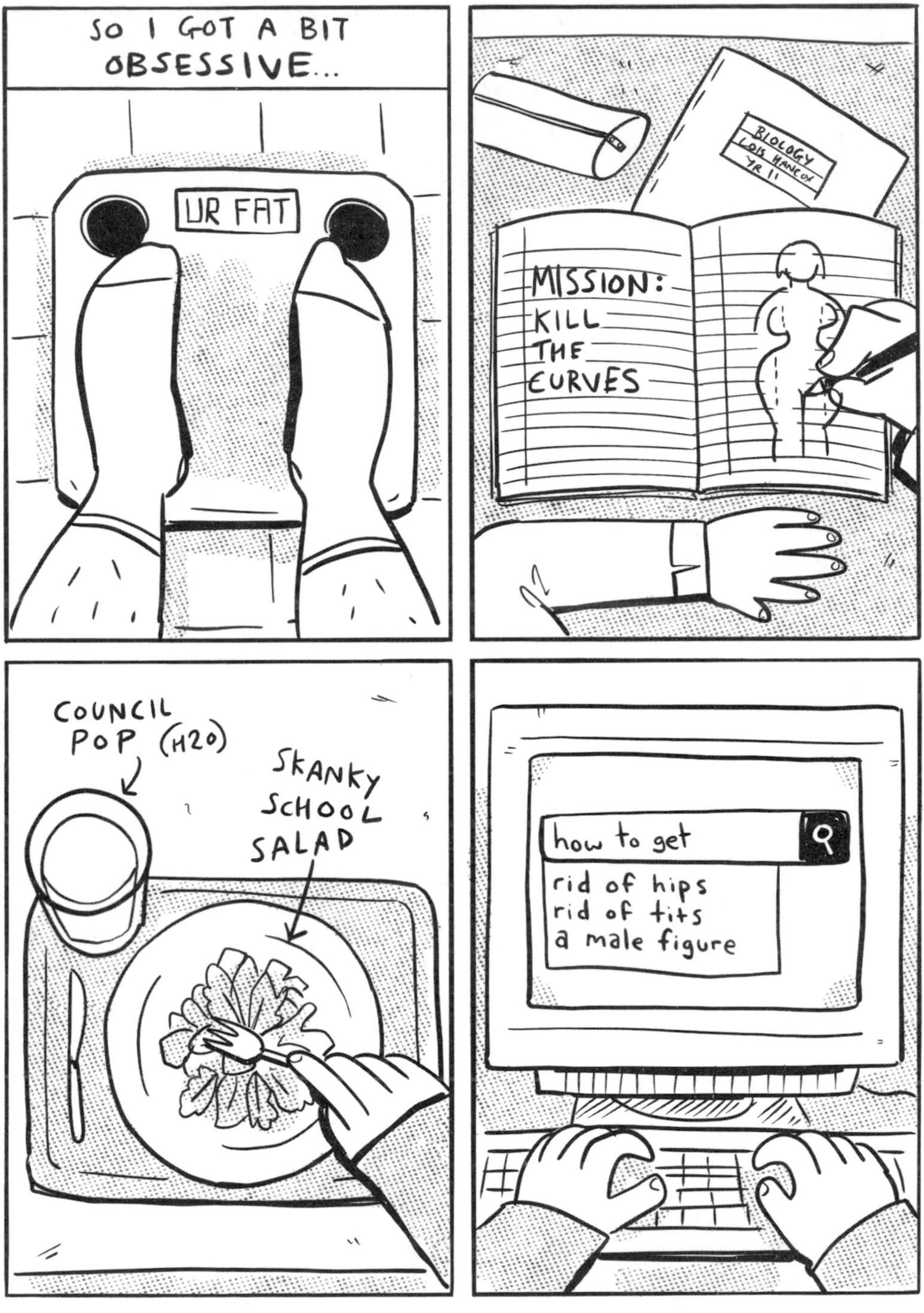
SO I GOT A BIT OBSESSIVE...
UR FAT
BIOLOGY
LOIS HANCOX
YR 11
MISSION:
KILL THE CURVES
COUNCIL POP (H2O)
SKANKY SCHOOL SALAD
how to get
rid of hips
rid of tits
a male figure

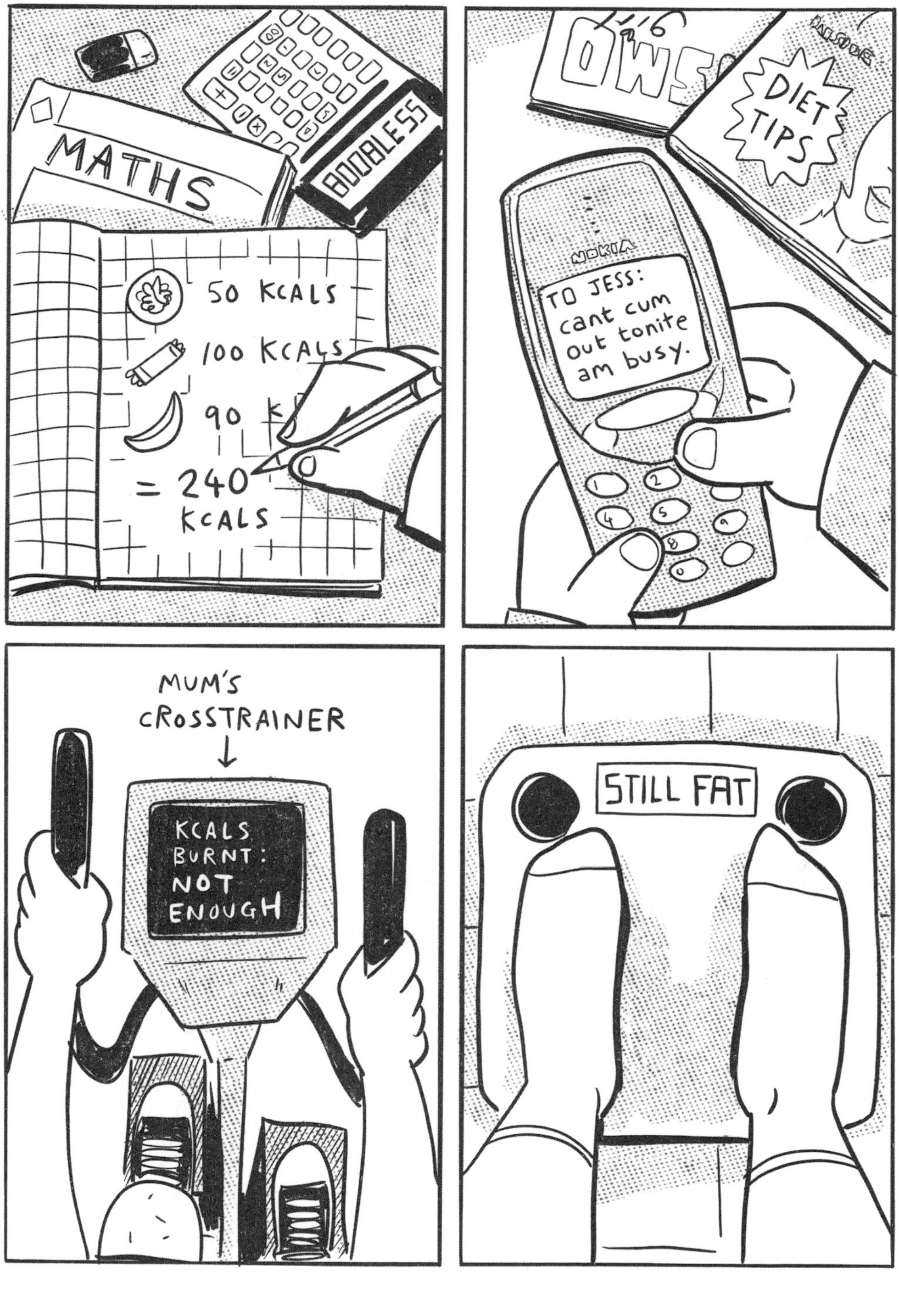
MATHS
BOOBLESS
50 KCALS
100 KCALS
= 240 KCALS
DIET TIPS
NOKIA
TO JESS: cant cum out tonite am busy.
MUM'S CROSSTRAINER
KCALS BURNT: NOT ENOUGH
STILL FAT

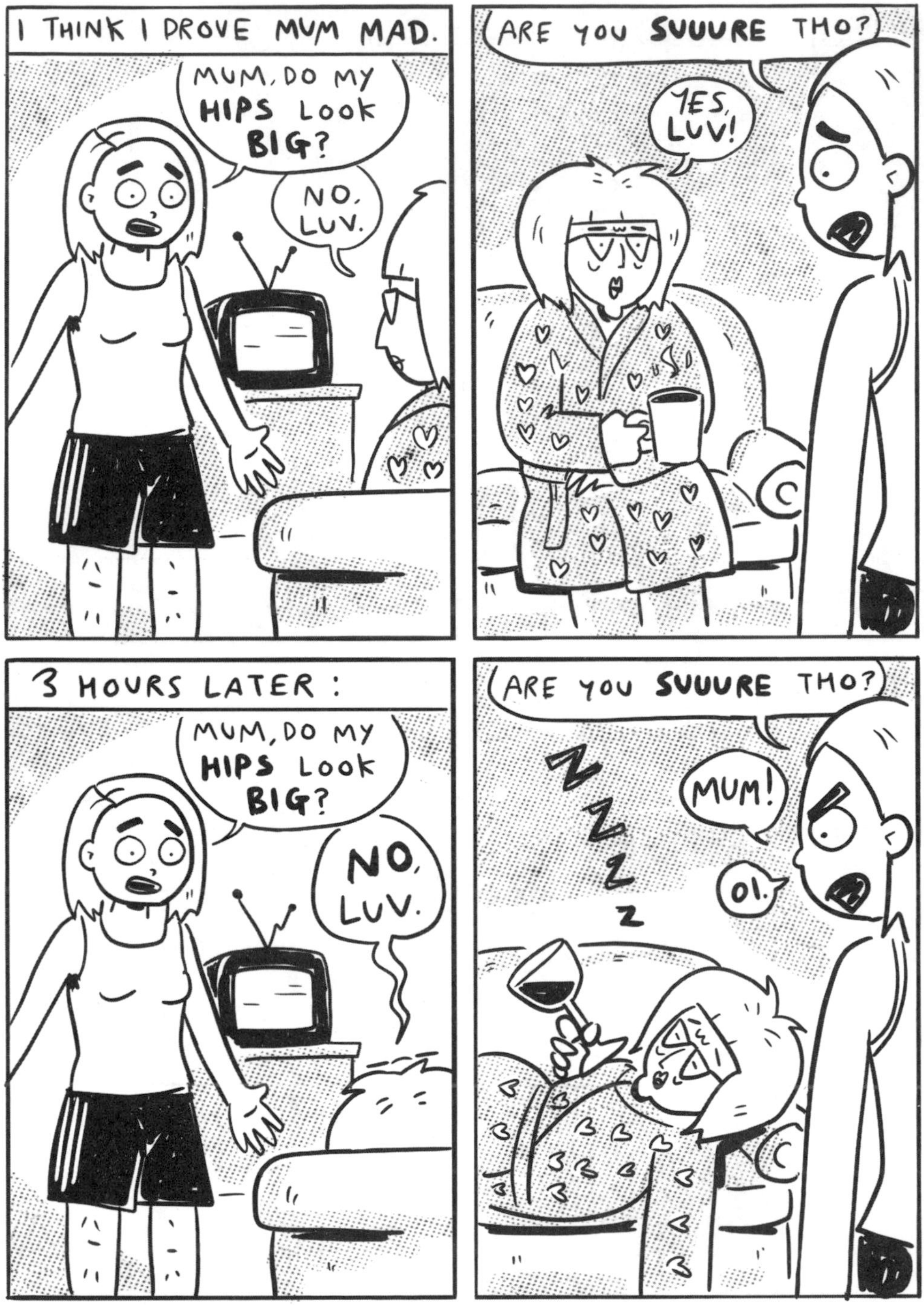
I THINK I DROVE MUM MAD.
MUM, DO MY HIPS LOOK BIG?
NO, LUV.
ARE YOU SUUURE THO?
YES, LUV!
3 HOURS LATER:
MUM, DO MY HIPS LOOK BIG?
NO, LUV.
ARE YOU SUUURE THO?
Z Z Z Z
MUM!
OI.

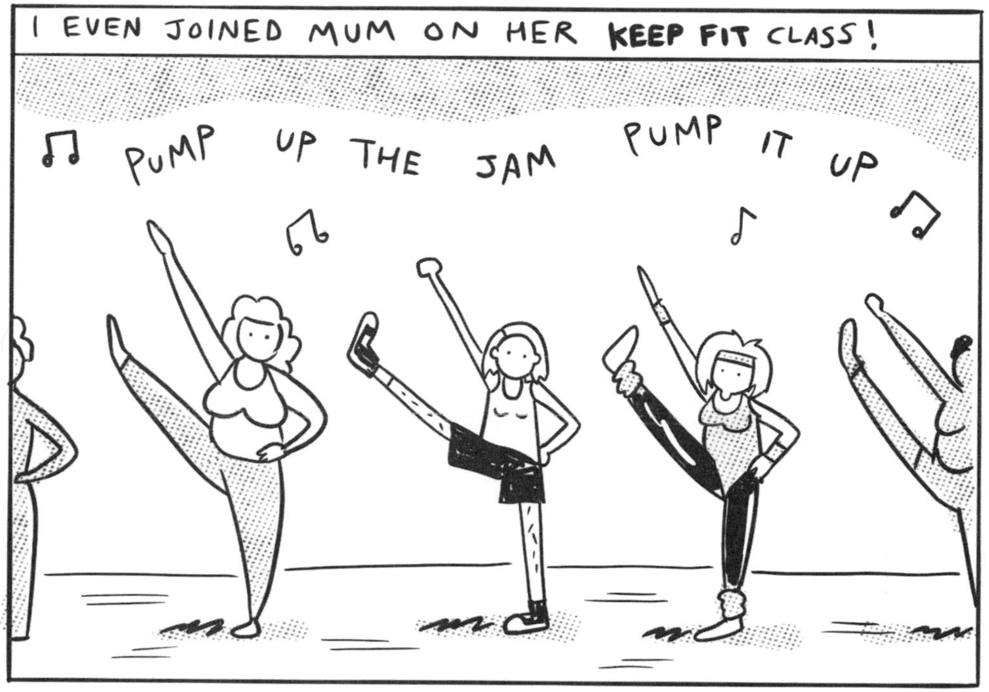
I EVEN JOINED MUM ON HER KEEP FIT CLASS!
PUMP UP THE JAM PUMP IT UP

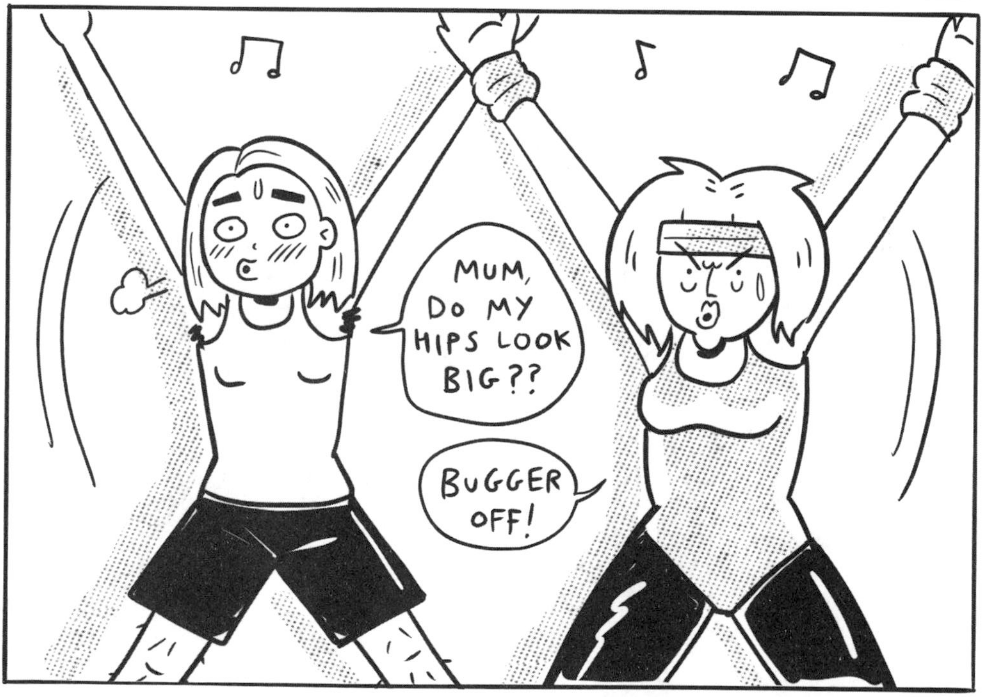
MUM, DO MY HIPS LOOK BIG??
BUGGER OFF!

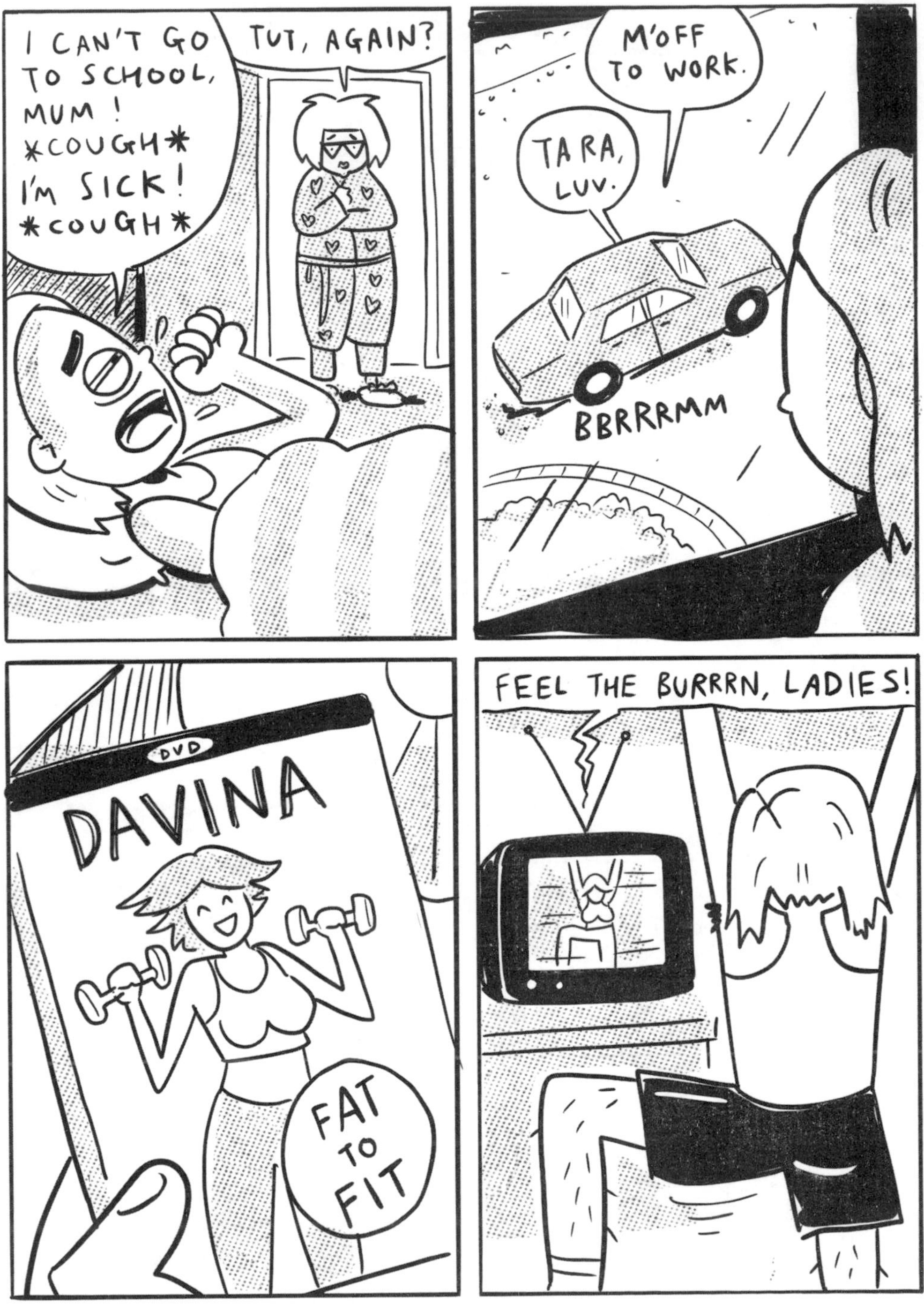
I CAN'T GO TO SCHOOL, MUM! *COUGH* I'M SICK! *COUGH*
TUT, AGAIN?
M'OFF TO WORK.
TARA, LUV.
BBRRRMM
DVD
DAVINA
FAT TO FIT
FEEL THE BURRRN, LADIES!

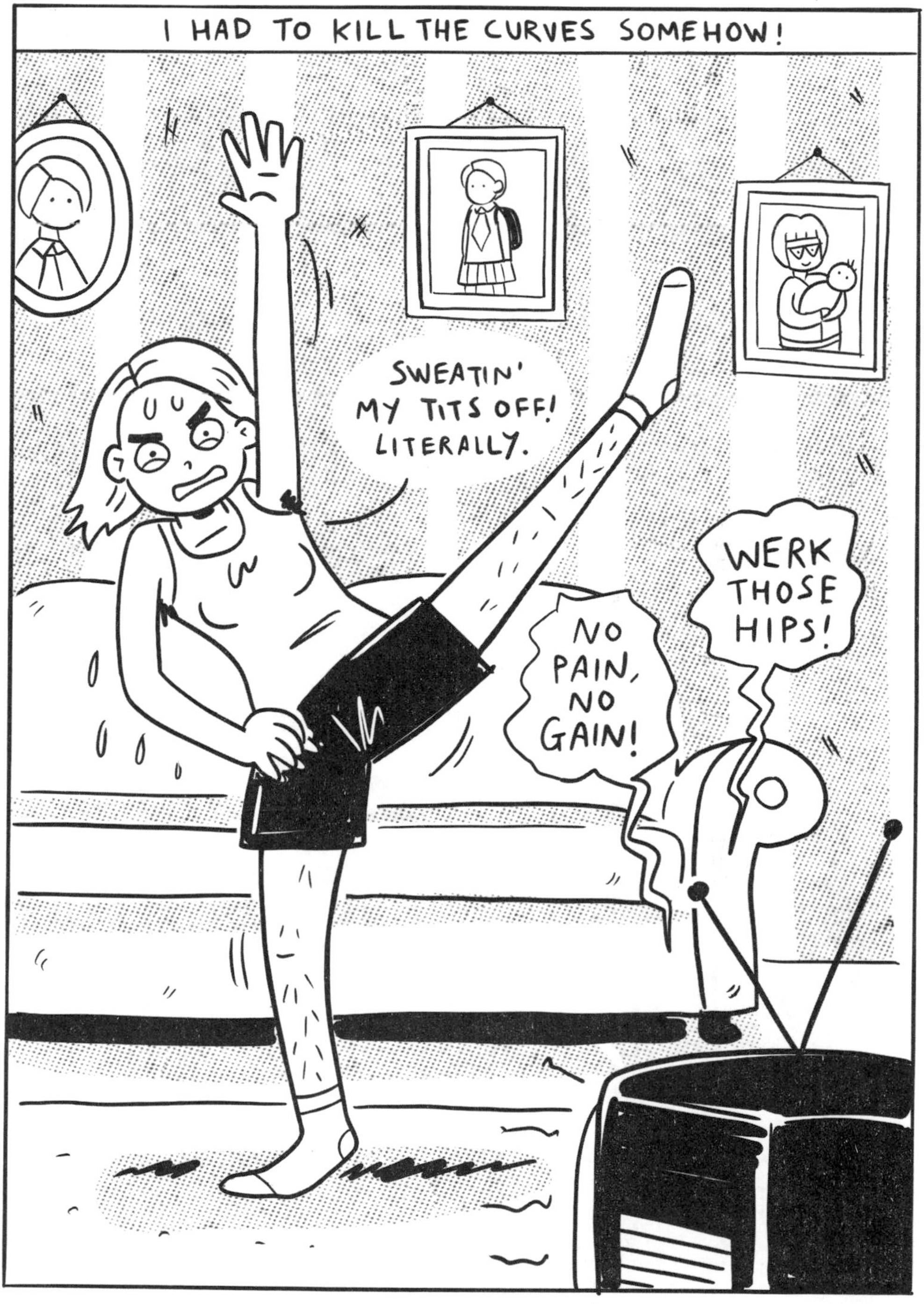
I HAD TO KILL THE CURVES SOMEHOW!
SWEATIN' MY TITS OFF! LITERALLY.
NO PAIN, NO GAIN!
WERK THOSE HIPS!

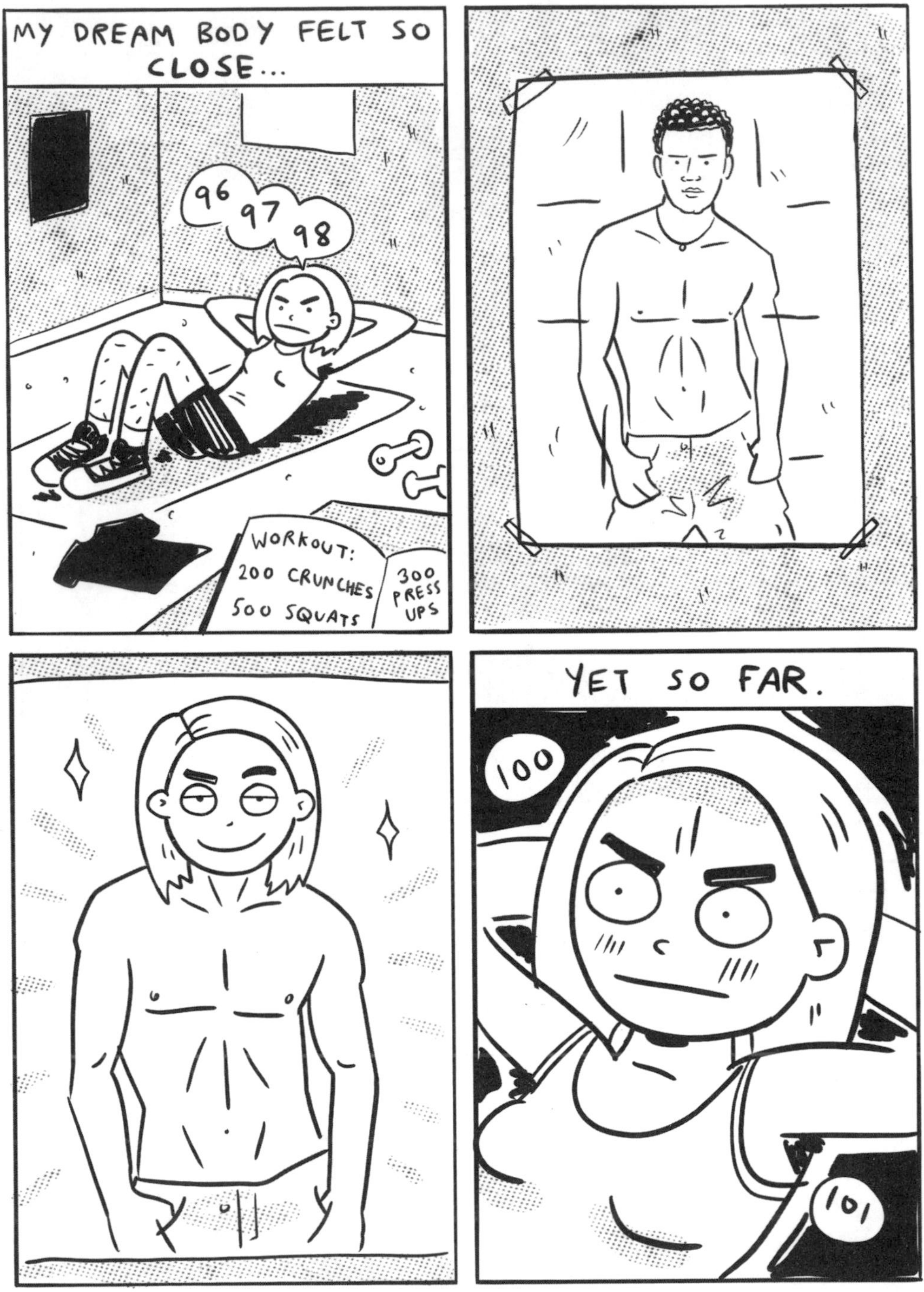
MY DREAM BODY FELT SO CLOSE...
96
97
98
WORKOUT:
200 CRUNCHES
500 SQUATS
300 PRESS UPS
YET SO FAR.
100
101

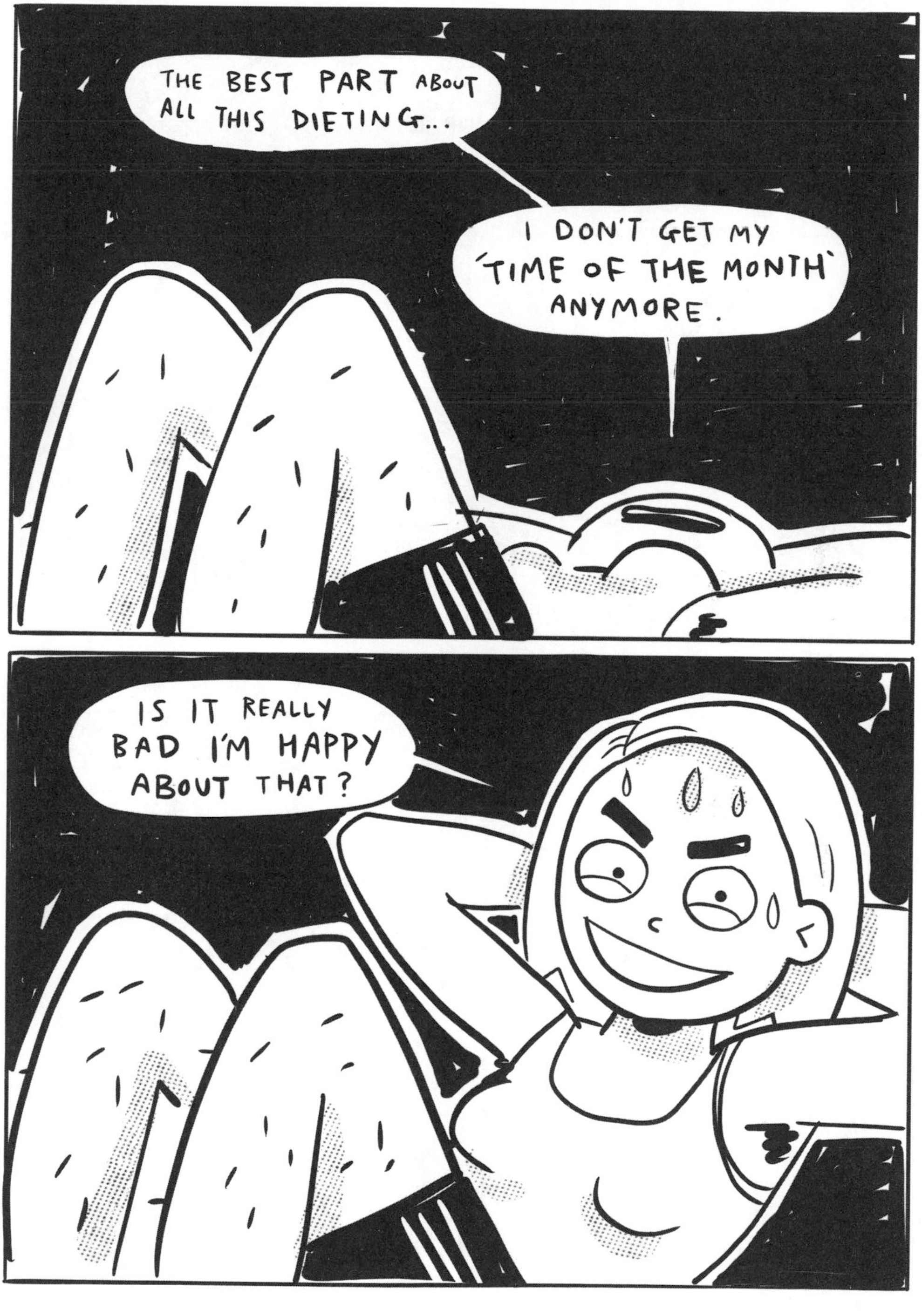
THE BEST PART ABOUT ALL THIS DIETING...
I DON'T GET MY 'TIME OF THE MONTH' ANYMORE.
IS IT REALLY BAD I'M HAPPY ABOUT THAT?

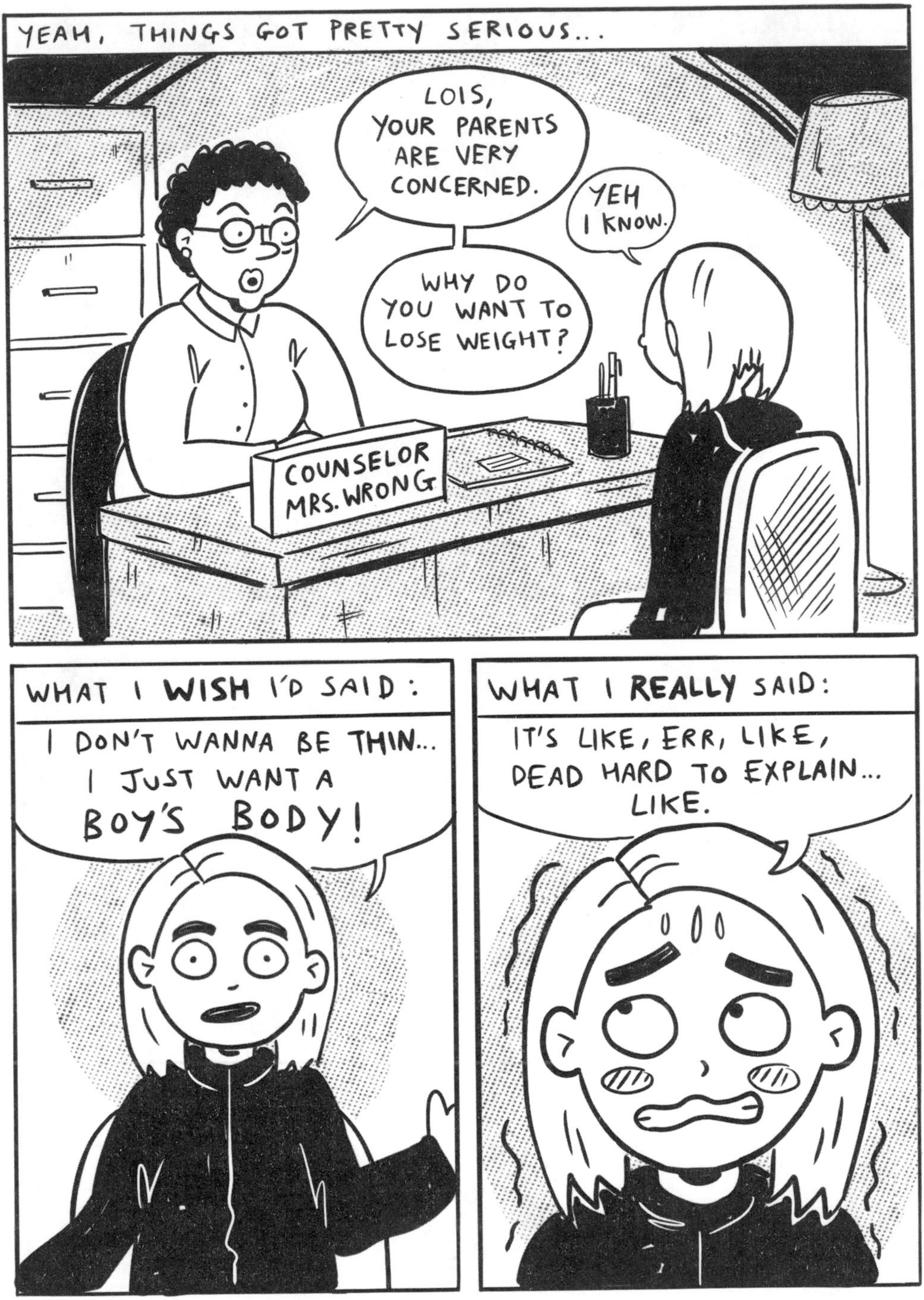
YEAH, THINGS GOT PRETTY SERIOUS...
LOIS, YOUR PARENTS ARE VERY CONCERNED.
WHY DO YOU WANT TO LOSE WEIGHT?
YEH I KNOW.
COUNSELOR MRS. WRONG
WHAT I **WISH** I'D SAID:
I DON'T WANNA BE **THIN**... I JUST WANT A BOY'S BODY!
WHAT I **REALLY** SAID:
IT'S LIKE, ERR, LIKE, DEAD HARD TO EXPLAIN... LIKE.

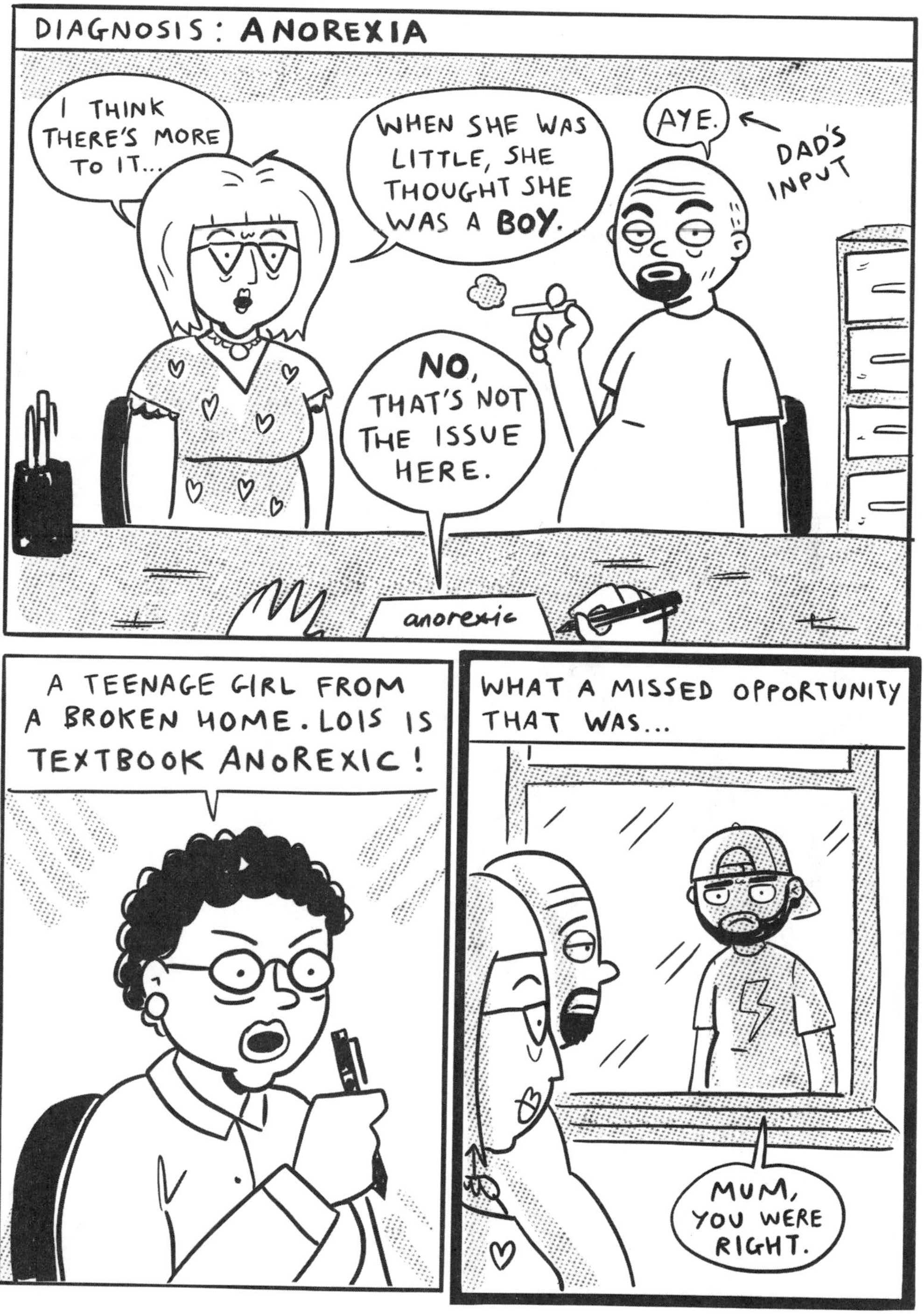
DIAGNOSIS: ANOREXIA
I THINK THERE'S MORE TO IT...
WHEN SHE WAS LITTLE, SHE THOUGHT SHE WAS A BOY...
AYE.
DAD'S INPUT
NO, THAT'S NOT THE ISSUE HERE.
anorexic
A TEENAGE GIRL FROM A BROKEN HOME. LOIS IS TEXTBOOK ANOREXIC!
WHAT A MISSED OPPORTUNITY THAT WAS...
MUM, YOU WERE RIGHT.

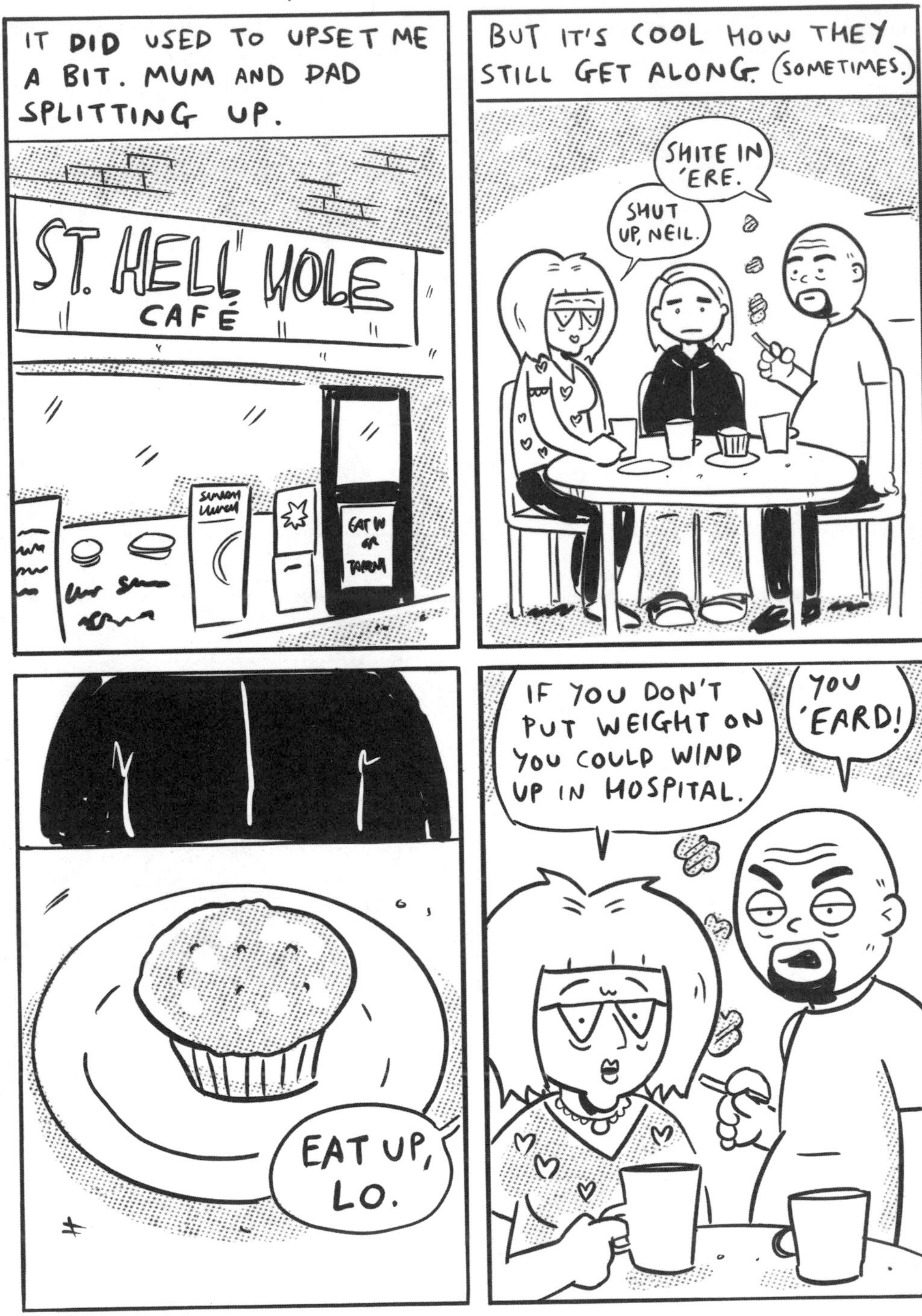
IT DID USED TO UPSET ME A BIT. MUM AND DAD SPLITTING UP.
ST. HELL HOLE CAFÉ
BUT IT'S COOL HOW THEY STILL GET ALONG. (SOMETIMES.)
SHITE IN 'ERE.
SHUT UP, NEIL.
EAT UP, LO.
IF YOU DON'T PUT WEIGHT ON YOU COULD WIND UP IN HOSPITAL.
YOU 'EARD!

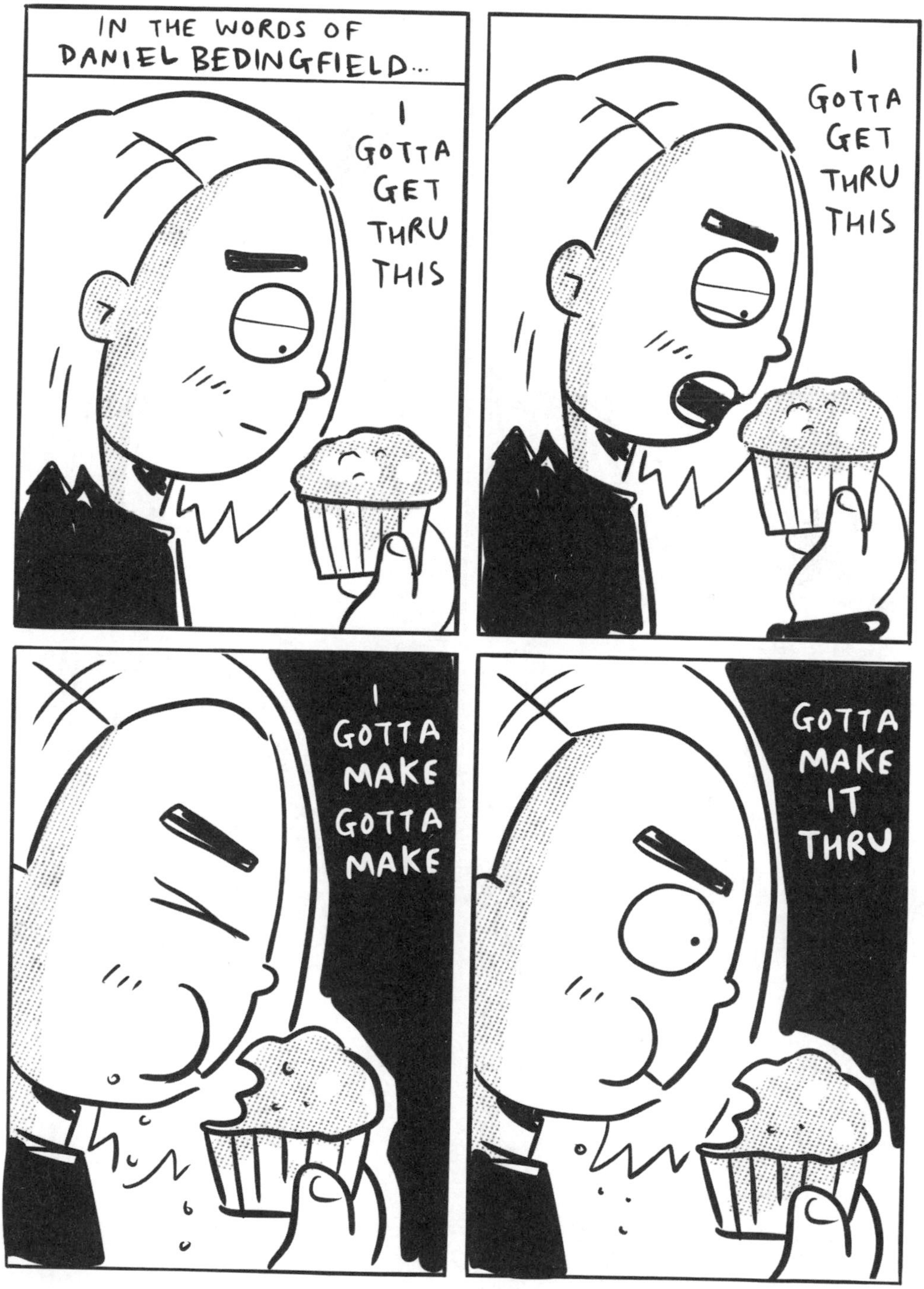
IN THE WORDS OF DANIEL BEDINGFIELD...
I GOTTA GET THRU THIS
I GOTTA GET THRU THIS
I GOTTA MAKE GOTTA MAKE
GOTTA MAKE IT THRU

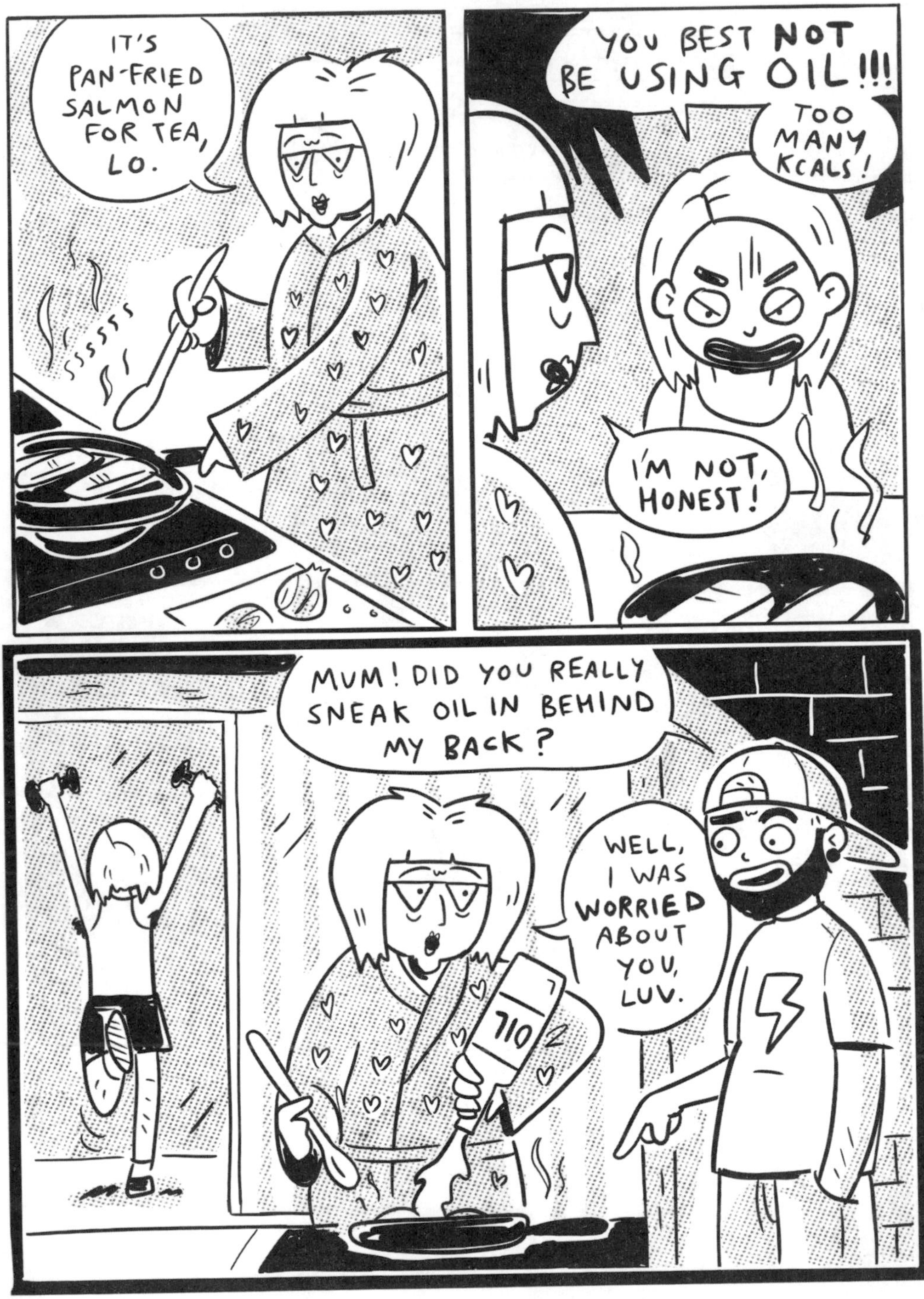
IT'S PAN-FRIED SALMON FOR TEA, LO.
SSSSSS
YOU BEST NOT BE USING OIL!!!
TOO MANY KCALS!
I'M NOT, HONEST!
MUM! DID YOU REALLY SNEAK OIL IN BEHIND MY BACK?
WELL, I WAS WORRIED ABOUT YOU, LUV.
OIL

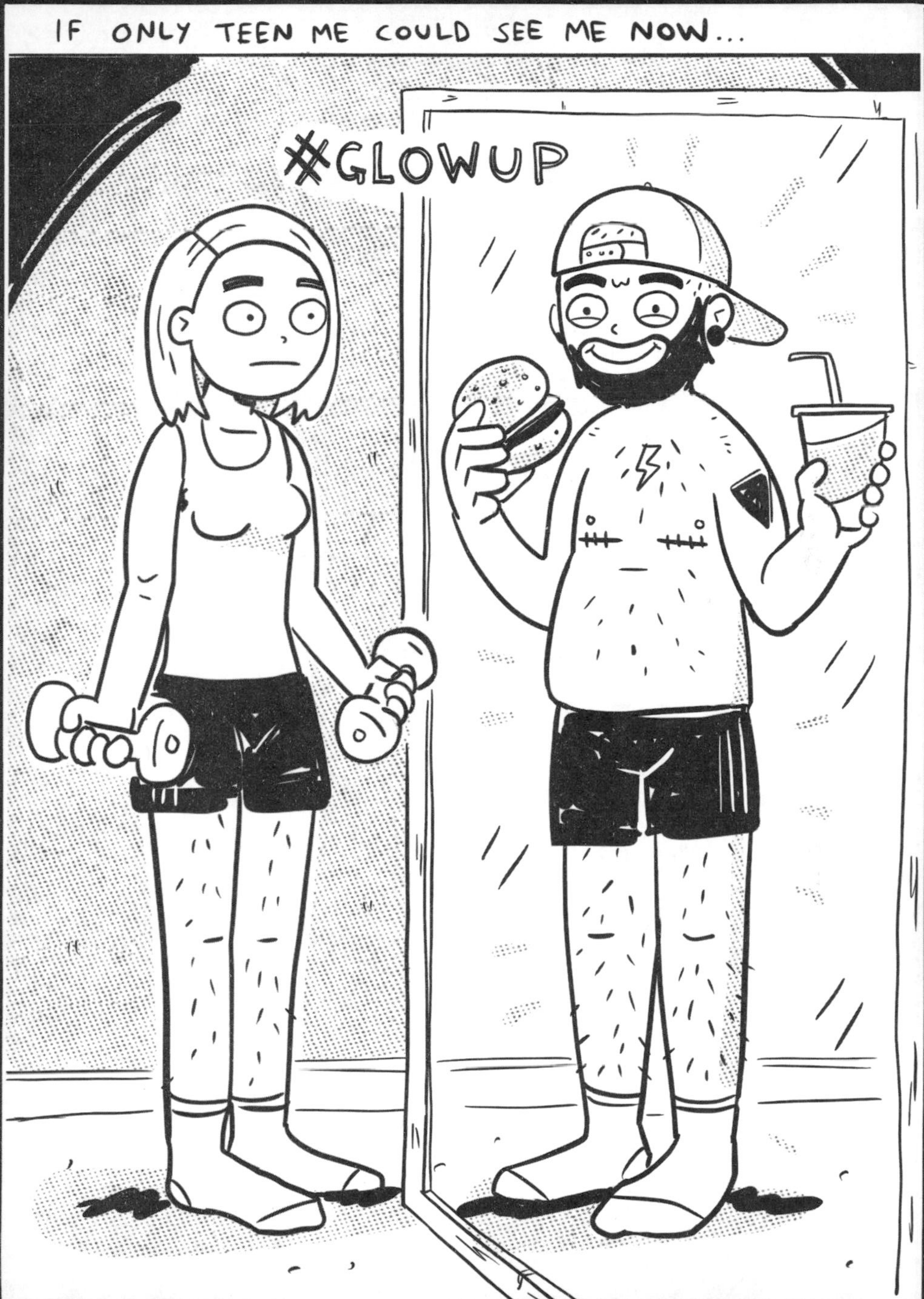
IF ONLY TEEN ME COULD SEE ME NOW...
#GLOWUP

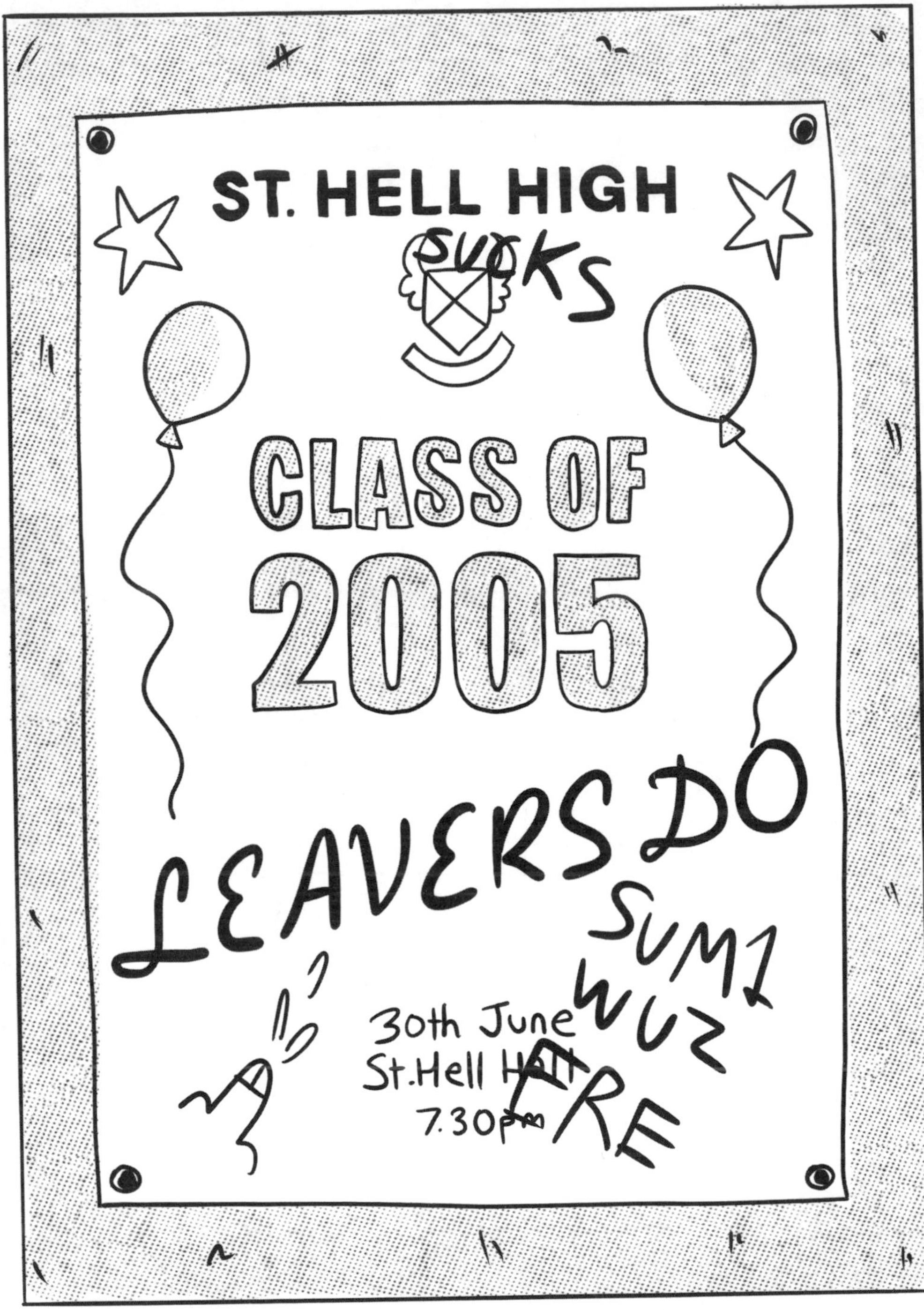
ST. HELL HIGH
SUCKS
CLASS OF 2005
LEAVERS DO
SUM1 WUZ ERE
30th June
St.Hell Hall
7.30pm

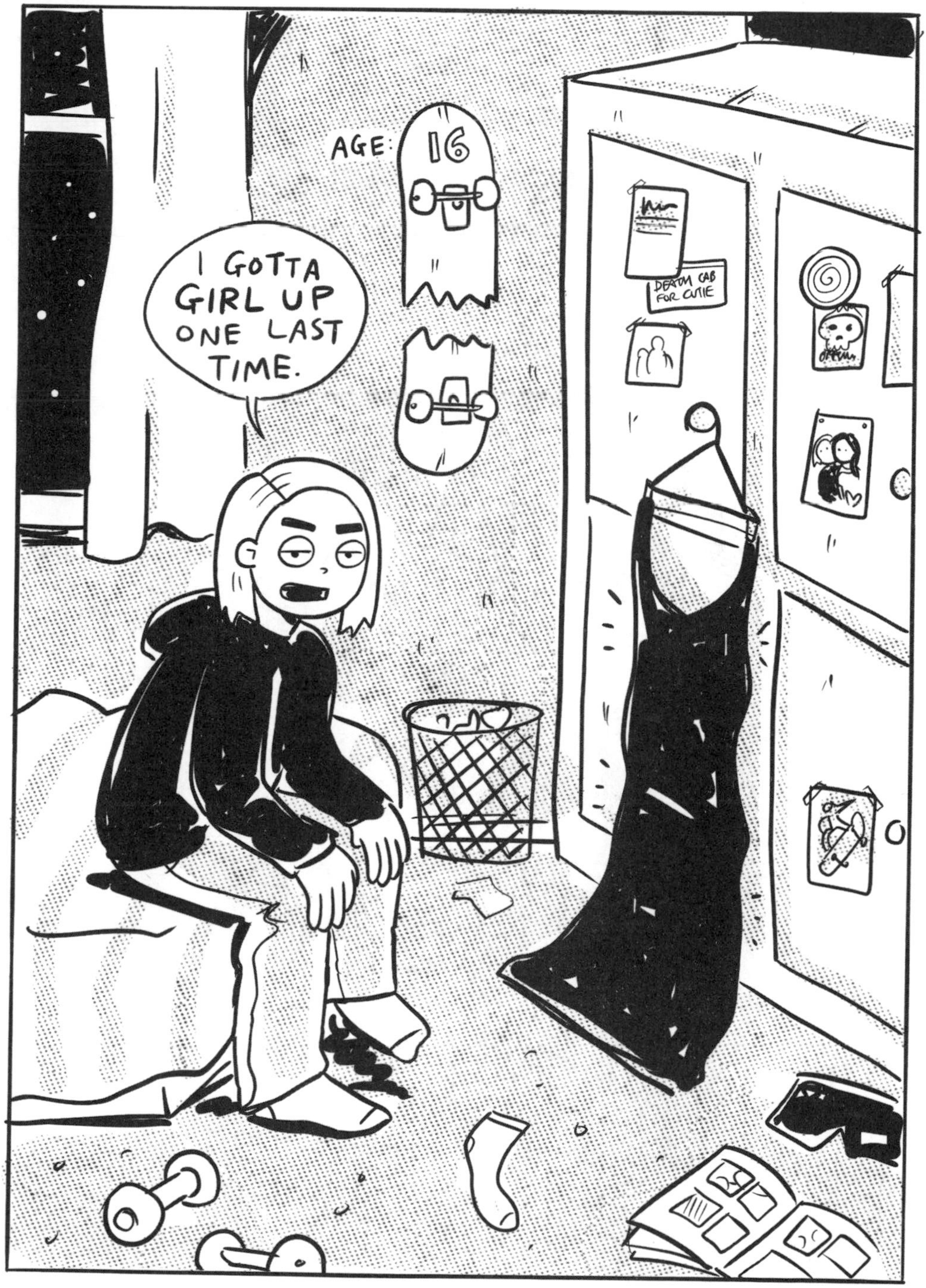
AGE: 16
I GOTTA GIRL UP ONE LAST TIME.
DEATH CAB FOR CUTIE

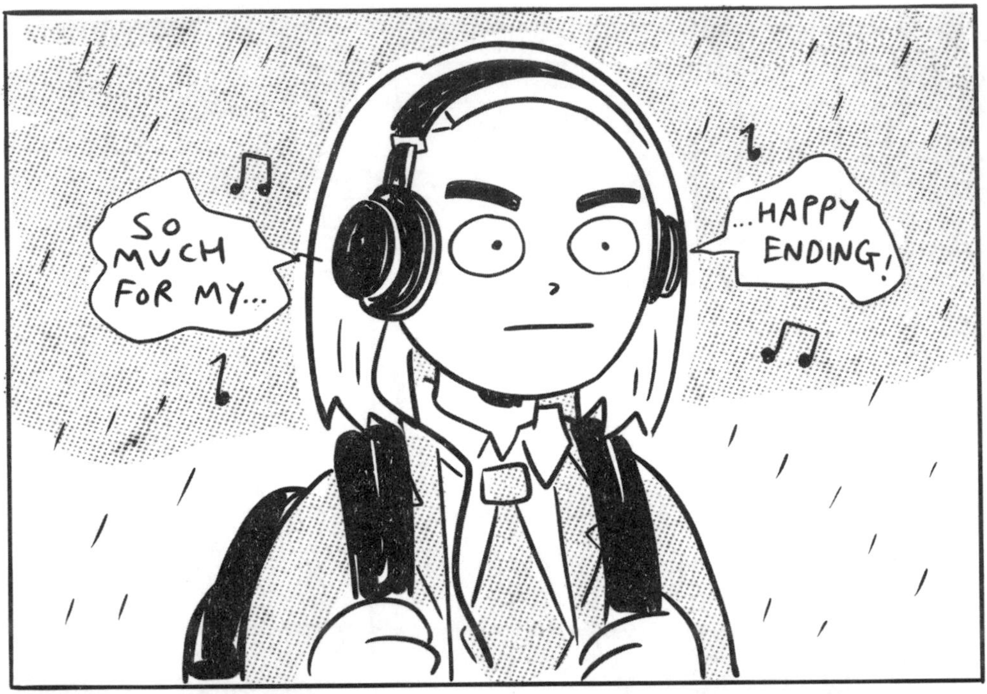
SO MUCH FOR MY...
...HAPPY ENDING!

IF THERE'S **ONE** THING I LEARNED AT HIGH SCHOOL...

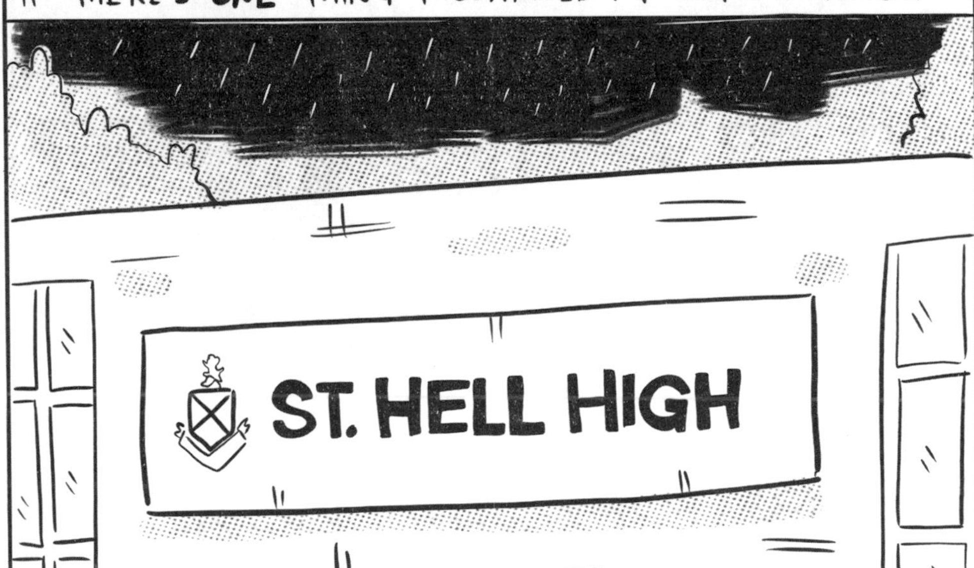
ST. HELL HIGH

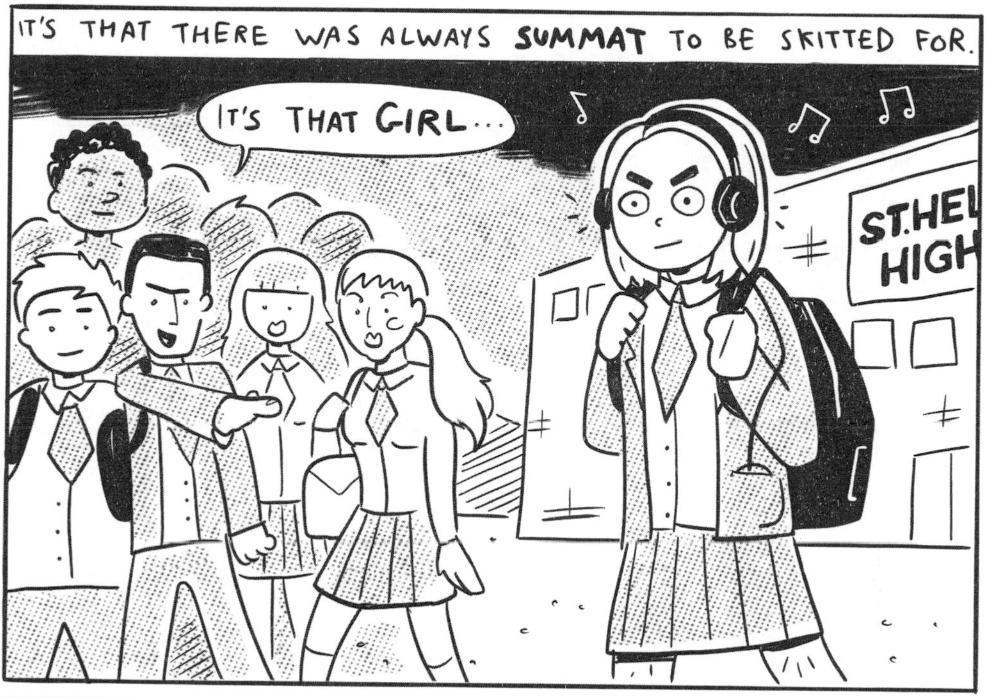
IT'S THAT THERE WAS ALWAYS SUMMAT TO BE SKITTED FOR.
IT'S THAT GIRL...
ST.HEL
HIGH

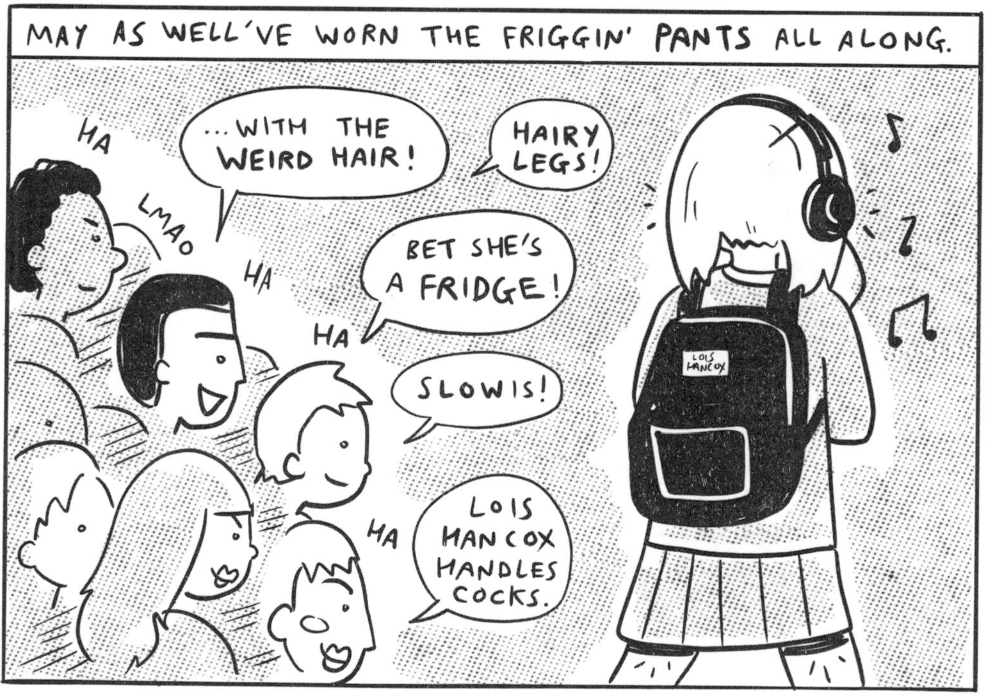
MAY AS WELL'VE WORN THE FRIGGIN' PANTS ALL ALONG.
HA
...WITH THE WEIRD HAIR!
HAIRY LEGS!
LMAO
HA
BET SHE'S A FRIDGE!
HA
SLOWIS!
HA
LOIS HANCOX HANDLES COCKS.
LOIS HANCOX

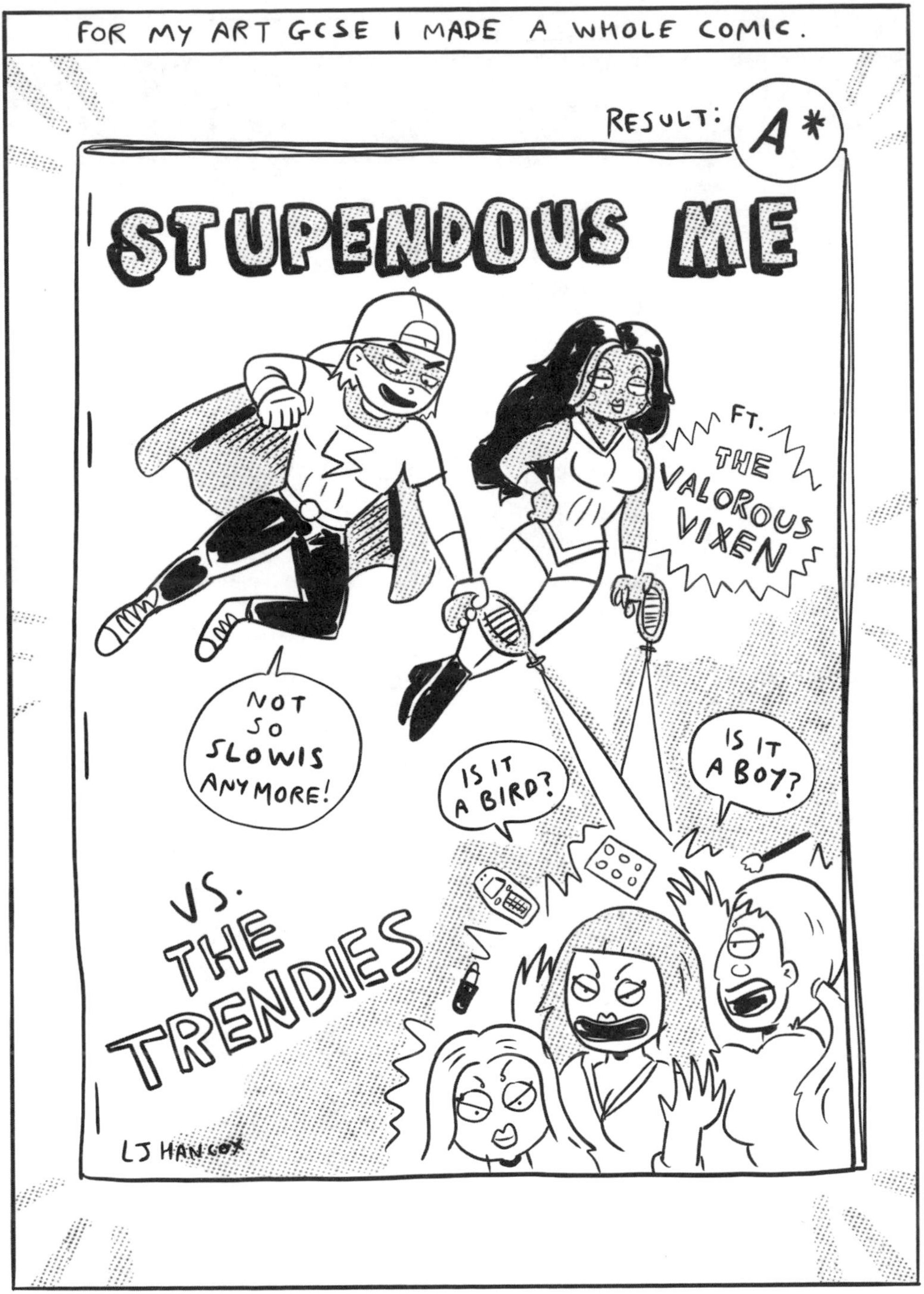
FOR MY ART GCSE I MADE A WHOLE COMIC.
RESULT: A*
STUPENDOUS ME
FT. THE VALOROUS VIXEN
NOT SO SLOWIS ANYMORE!
IS IT A BIRD?
IS IT A BOY?
VS. THE TRENDIES
LJ HANCOX

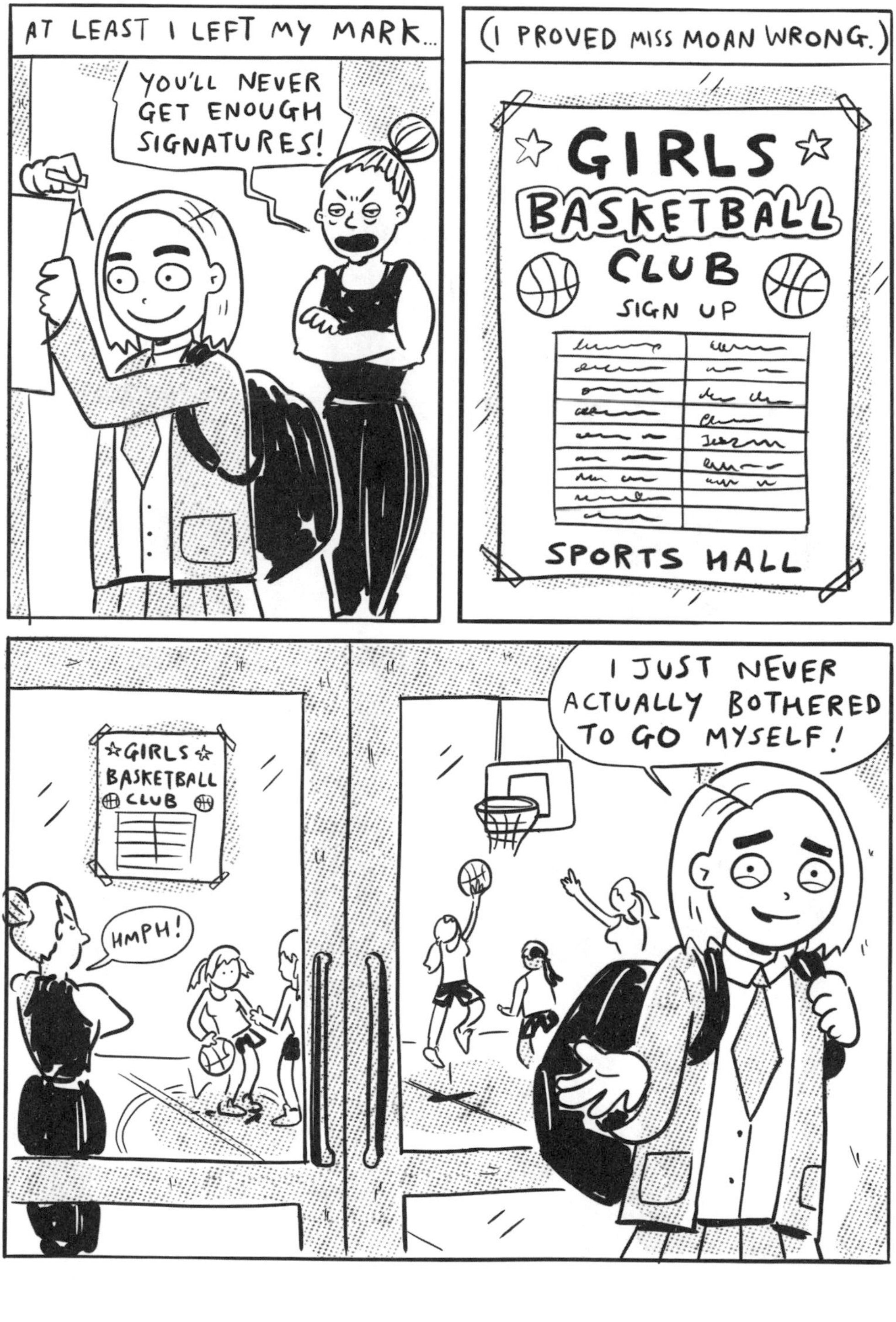
AT LEAST I LEFT MY MARK...
YOU'LL NEVER GET ENOUGH SIGNATURES!
(I PROVED MISS MOAN WRONG.)
GIRLS BASKETBALL CLUB
SIGN UP
SPORTS HALL
GIRLS BASKETBALL CLUB
HMPH!
I JUST NEVER ACTUALLY BOTHERED TO GO MYSELF!

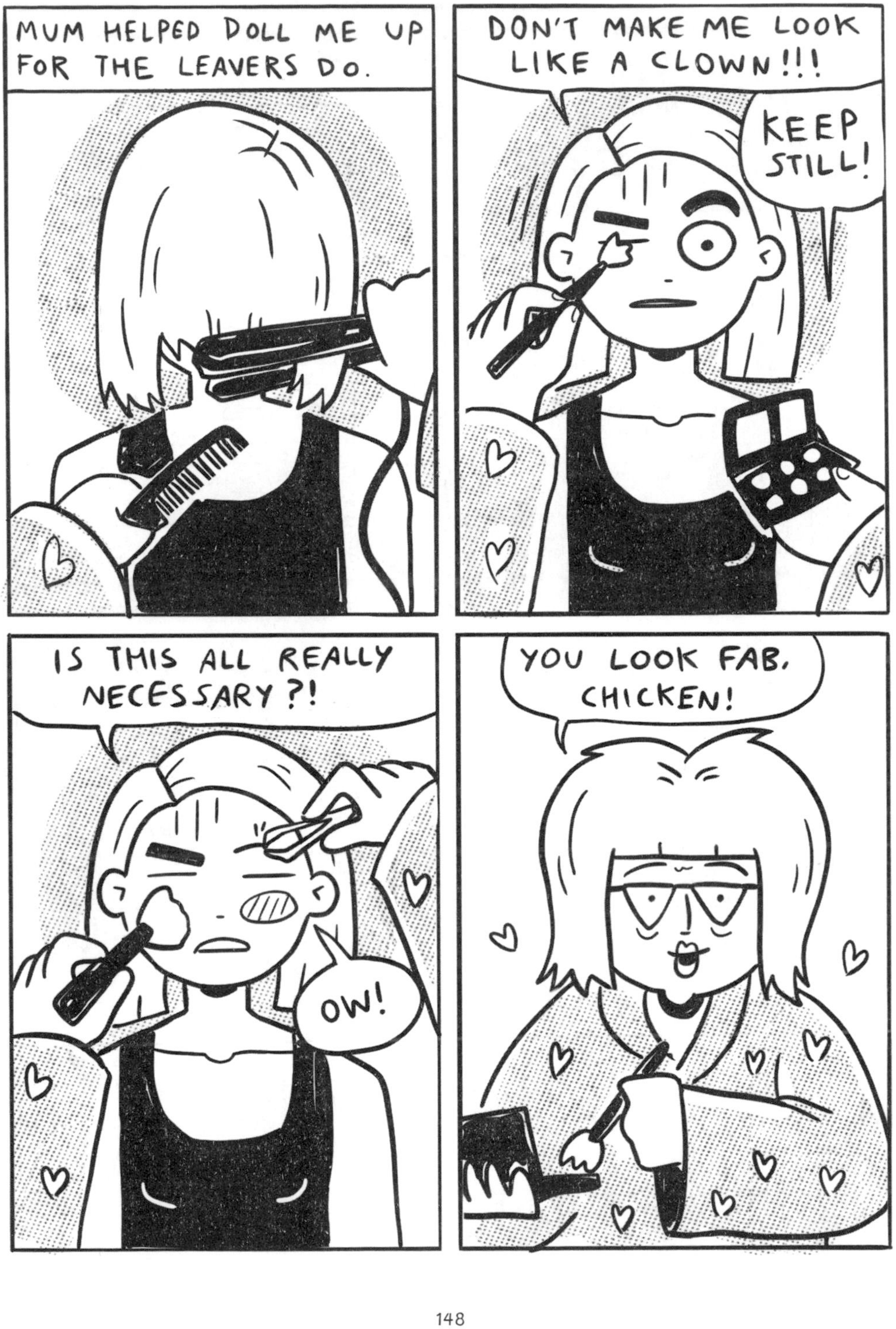
MUM HELPED DOLL ME UP FOR THE LEAVERS DO.
DON'T MAKE ME LOOK LIKE A CLOWN!!!
KEEP STILL!
IS THIS ALL REALLY NECESSARY?!
OW!
YOU LOOK FAB, CHICKEN!

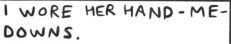

I WORE HER HAND-ME-DOWNS.

THE GROUND IS GETTING CLOSER...

THE GROUND IS GETTING CLOSE-

OH DEAR... WE'LL GO WITH THE FLATS, LUV.

SPLAT

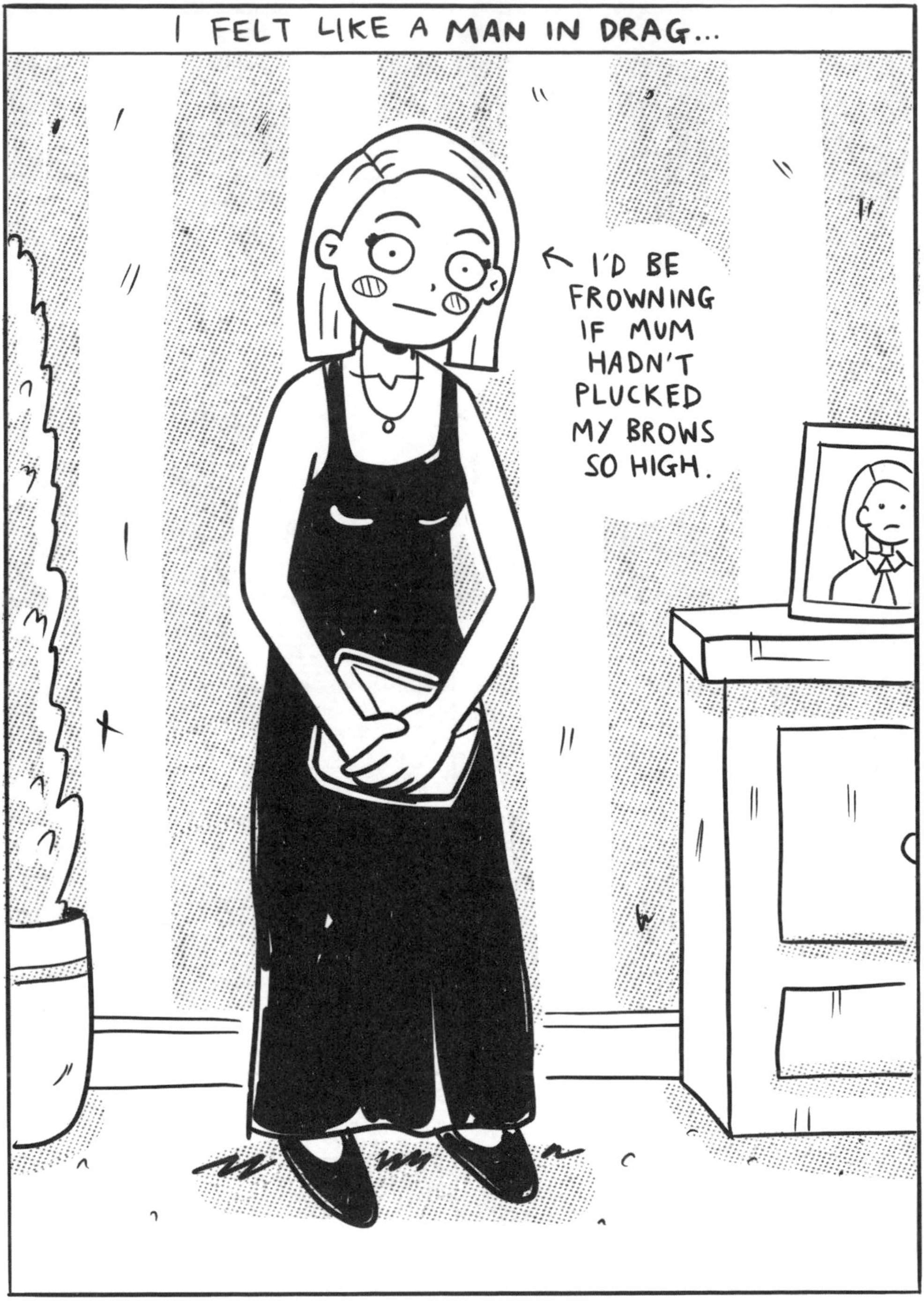
I FELT LIKE A MAN IN DRAG...
I'D BE FROWNING IF MUM HADN'T PLUCKED MY BROWS SO HIGH.

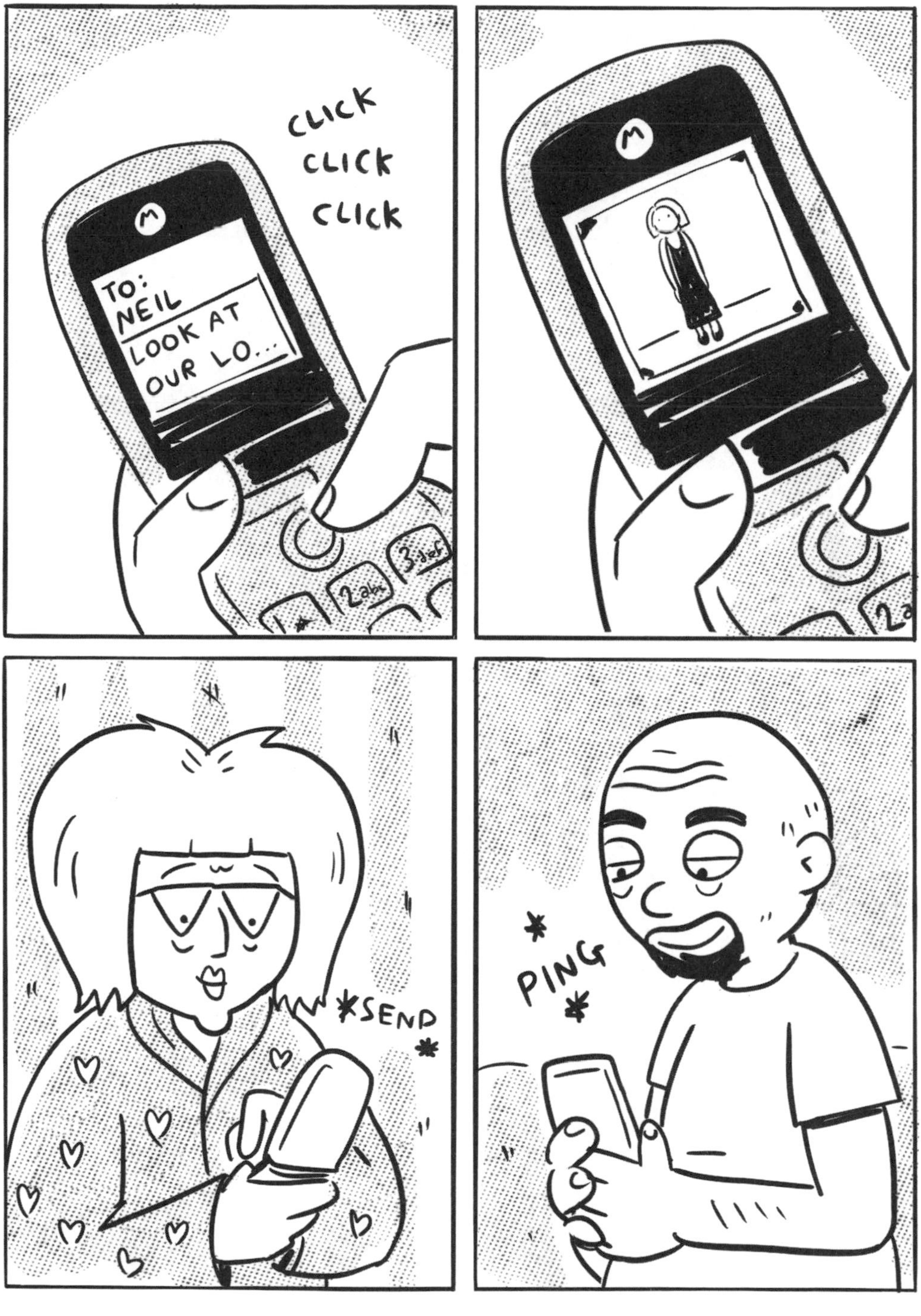
CLICK
CLICK
CLICK
TO:
NEIL
LOOK AT
OUR LO...
SEND
PING

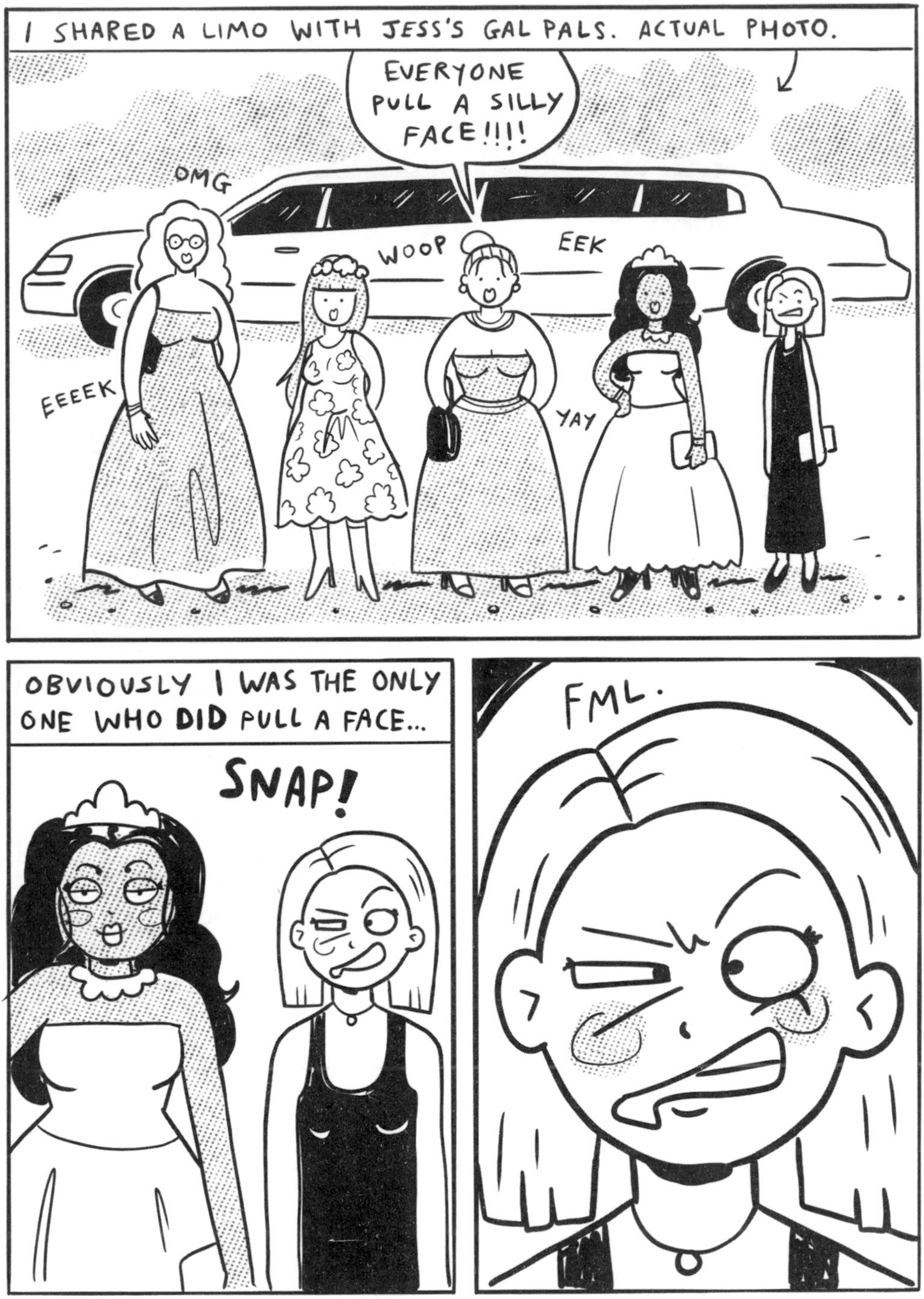
I SHARED A LIMO WITH JESS'S GAL PALS. ACTUAL PHOTO.
EVERYONE PULL A SILLY FACE!!!!
OMG
WOOP
EEK
EEEEK
YAY
OBVIOUSLY I WAS THE ONLY ONE WHO **DID** PULL A FACE...
SNAP!
FML.

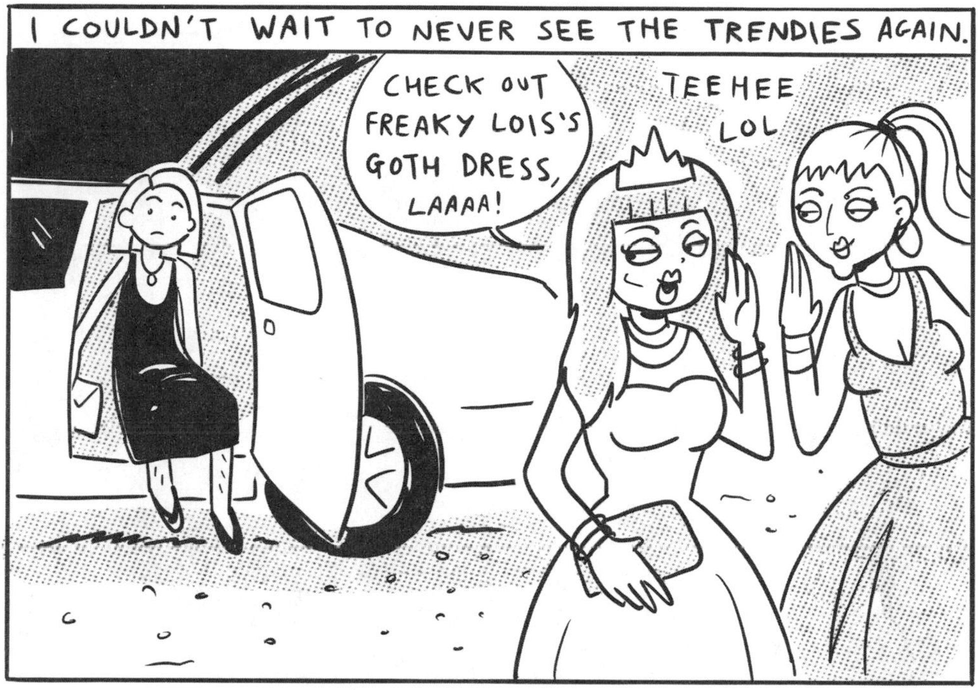
I COULDN'T WAIT TO NEVER SEE THE TRENDIES AGAIN.
CHECK OUT FREAKY LOIS'S GOTH DRESS, LAAAA!
TEEHEE LOL

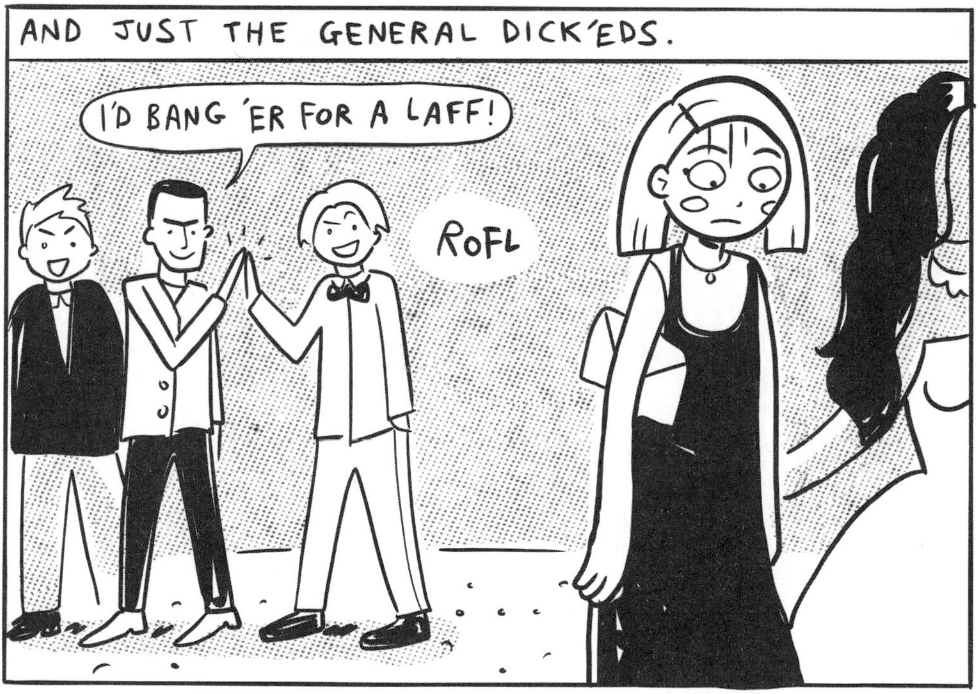
AND JUST THE GENERAL DICK'EDS.
I'D BANG 'ER FOR A LAFF!
ROFL

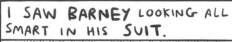I SAW BARNEY LOOKING ALL SMART IN HIS SUIT.

I COULDA LOOKED LIKE THAT.

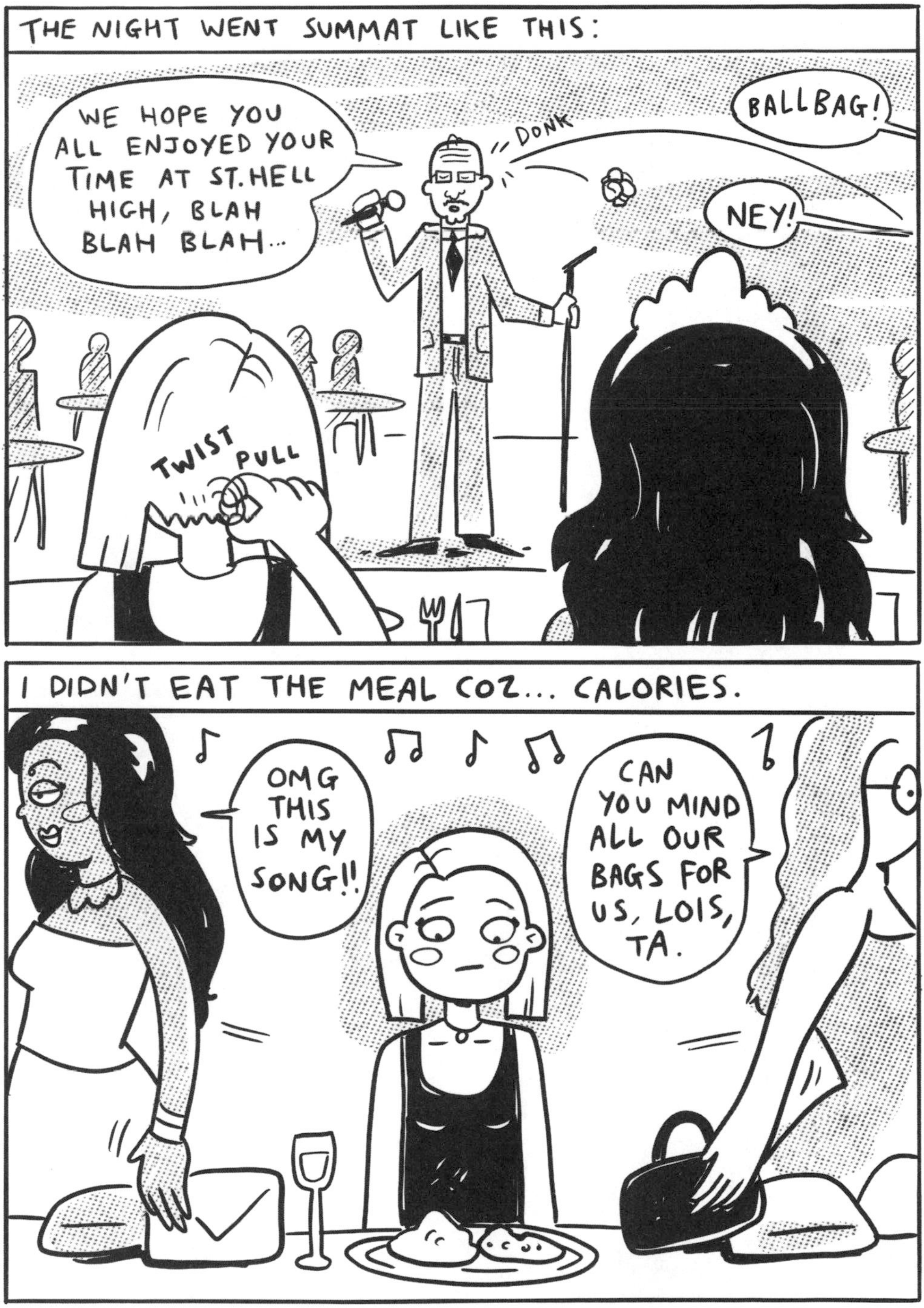
THE NIGHT WENT SUMMAT LIKE THIS:
WE HOPE YOU ALL ENJOYED YOUR TIME AT ST. HELL HIGH, BLAH BLAH BLAH...
DONK
BALLBAG!
NEY!
TWIST
PULL
I DIDN'T EAT THE MEAL COZ... CALORIES.
OMG THIS IS MY SONG!!
CAN YOU MIND ALL OUR BAGS FOR US, LOIS, TA.

EVERYONE DANCED TO POP SONGS I DIDN'T KNOW.

I'M BUSY TEXTING BACK ALL MY ADMIRERS, ANYWAY!

CLICK
CLICK
CLICK

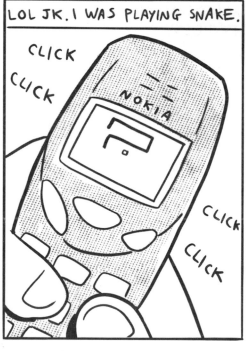

LOL JK. I WAS PLAYING SNAKE.

CLICK
CLICK

NOKIA

CLICK
CLICK

I MAY NOT HAVE KNOWN WHO I **WAS** BACK THEN...
BUT I WAS STARTING TO LEARN WHO I **WASN'T**.
A PROCESS OF ELIMINATION, I GUESS.
BUT IF I COULD REWIND...

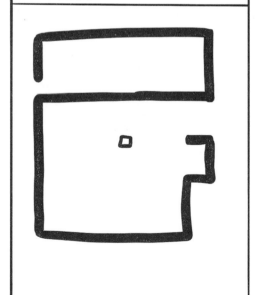

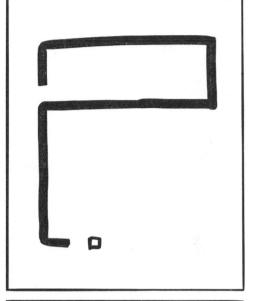

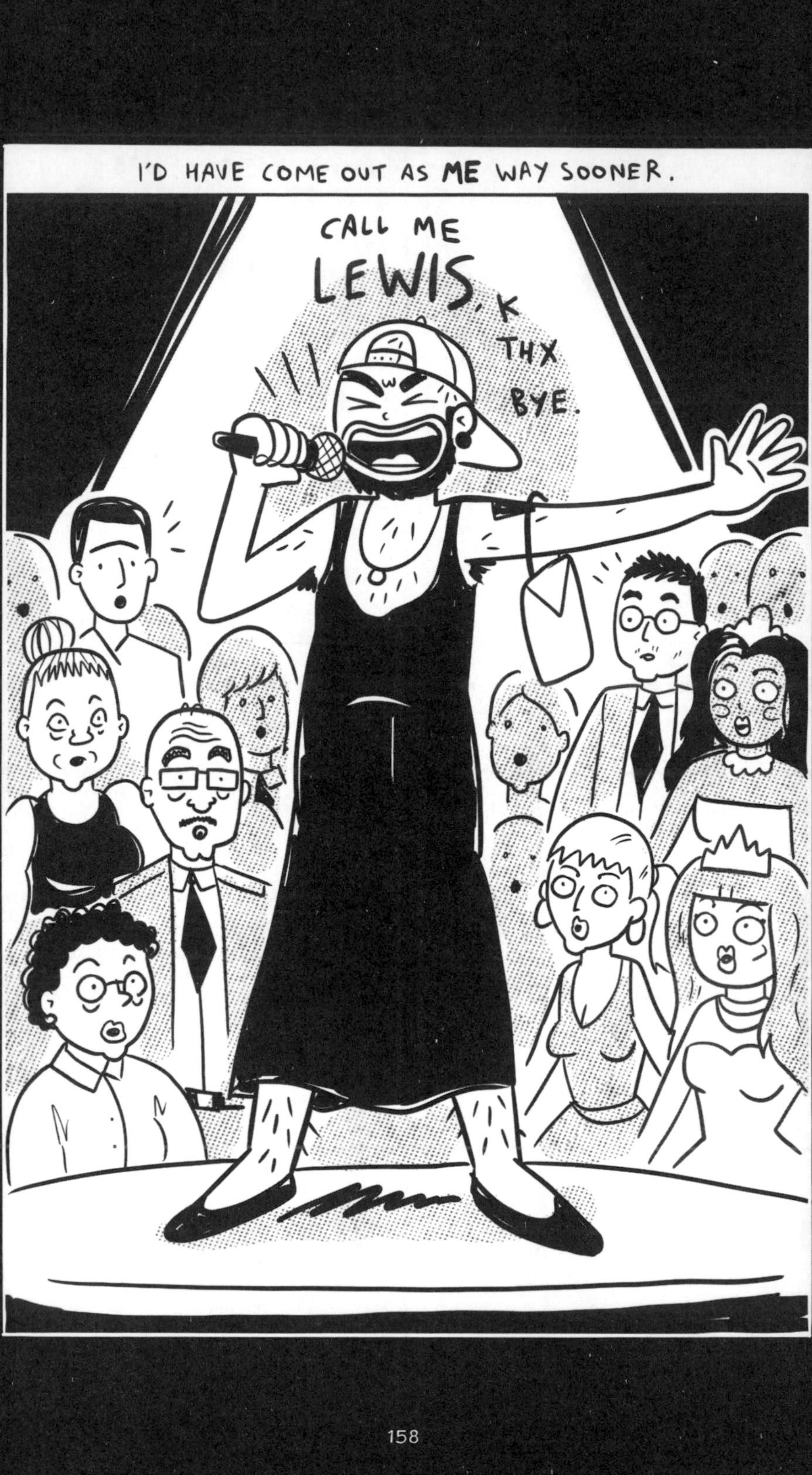
I'D HAVE COME OUT AS **ME** WAY SOONER.
CALL ME LEWIS, K THX BYE.

PART TWO:
LOIS TO LEWIS

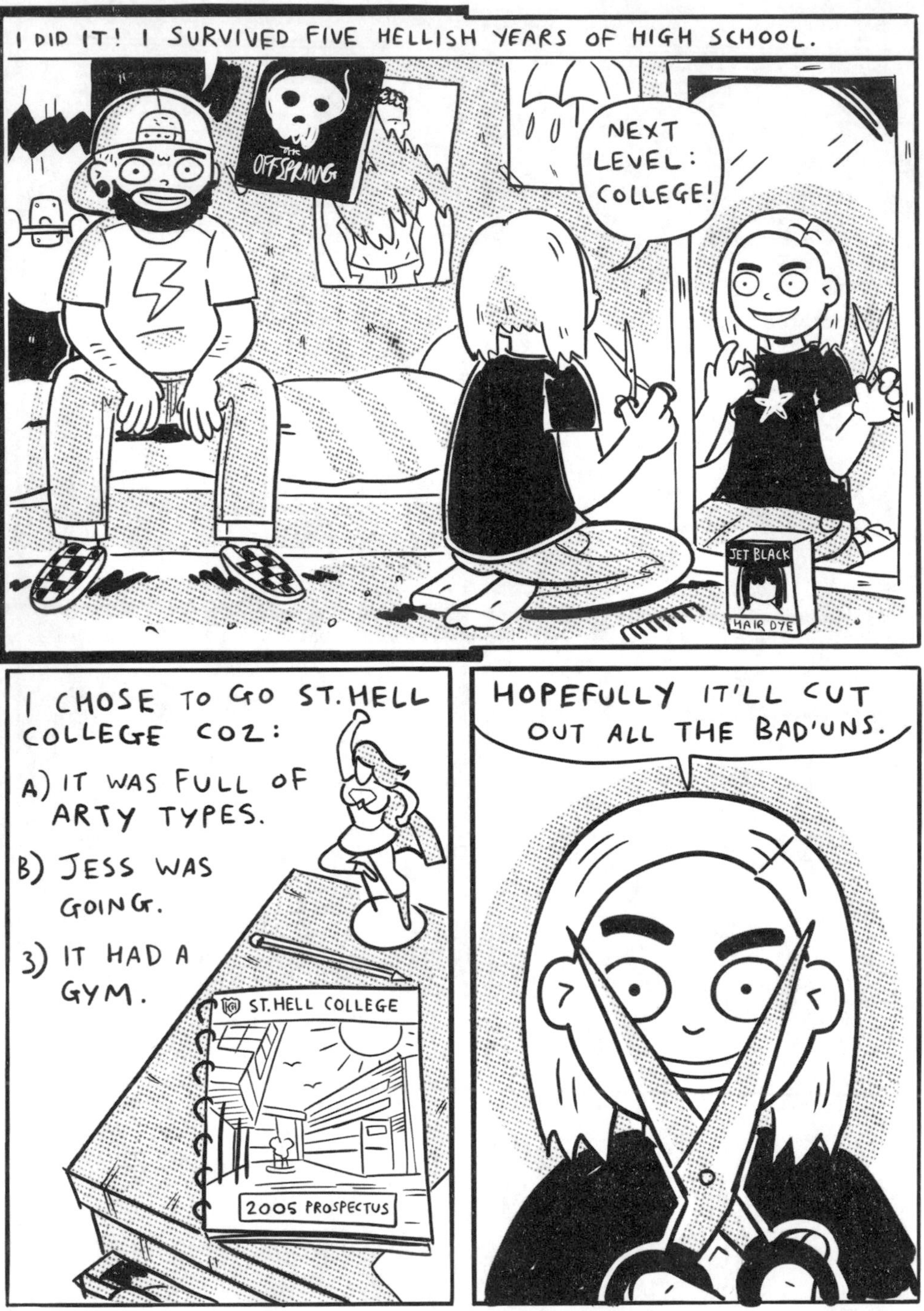
I DID IT! I SURVIVED FIVE HELLISH YEARS OF HIGH SCHOOL.
THE OFFSPRING
NEXT LEVEL: COLLEGE!
JET BLACK
HAIR DYE
I CHOSE TO GO ST. HELL COLLEGE COZ:
A) IT WAS FULL OF ARTY TYPES.
B) JESS WAS GOING.
3) IT HAD A GYM.
ST. HELL COLLEGE
2005 PROSPECTUS
HOPEFULLY IT'LL CUT OUT ALL THE BAD'UNS.

TIME TO SAY GOODBYE TO LITTLE **LOSER** LOIS.

I'M SICK OF ALWAYS TRYING TO FIT A MOULD!

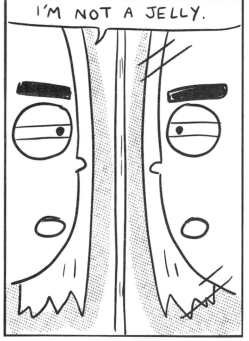

I'M NOT A JELLY.

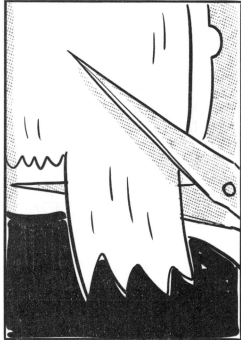

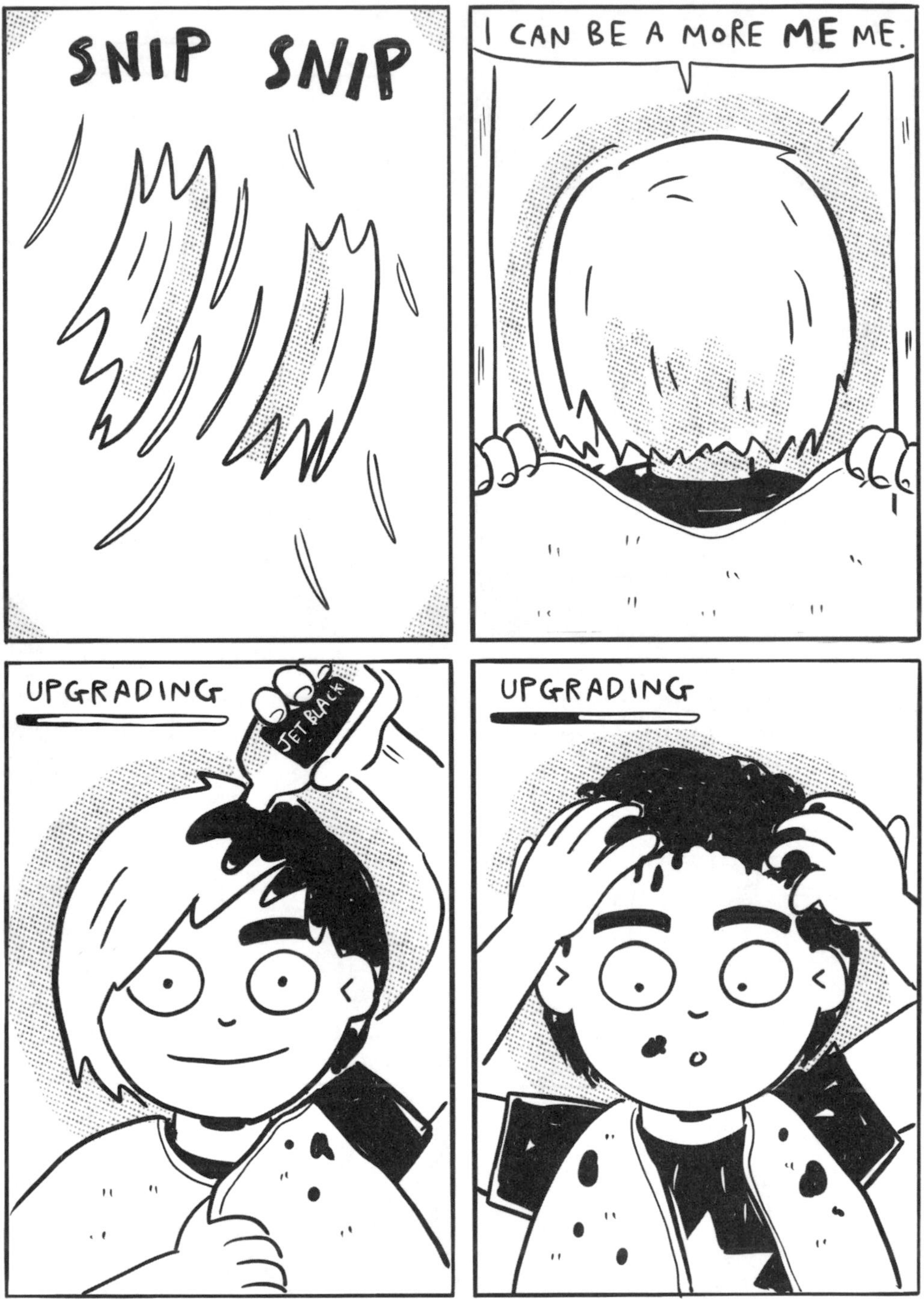
SNIP SNIP
I CAN BE A MORE ME ME.
UPGRADING
JET BLACK
UPGRADING

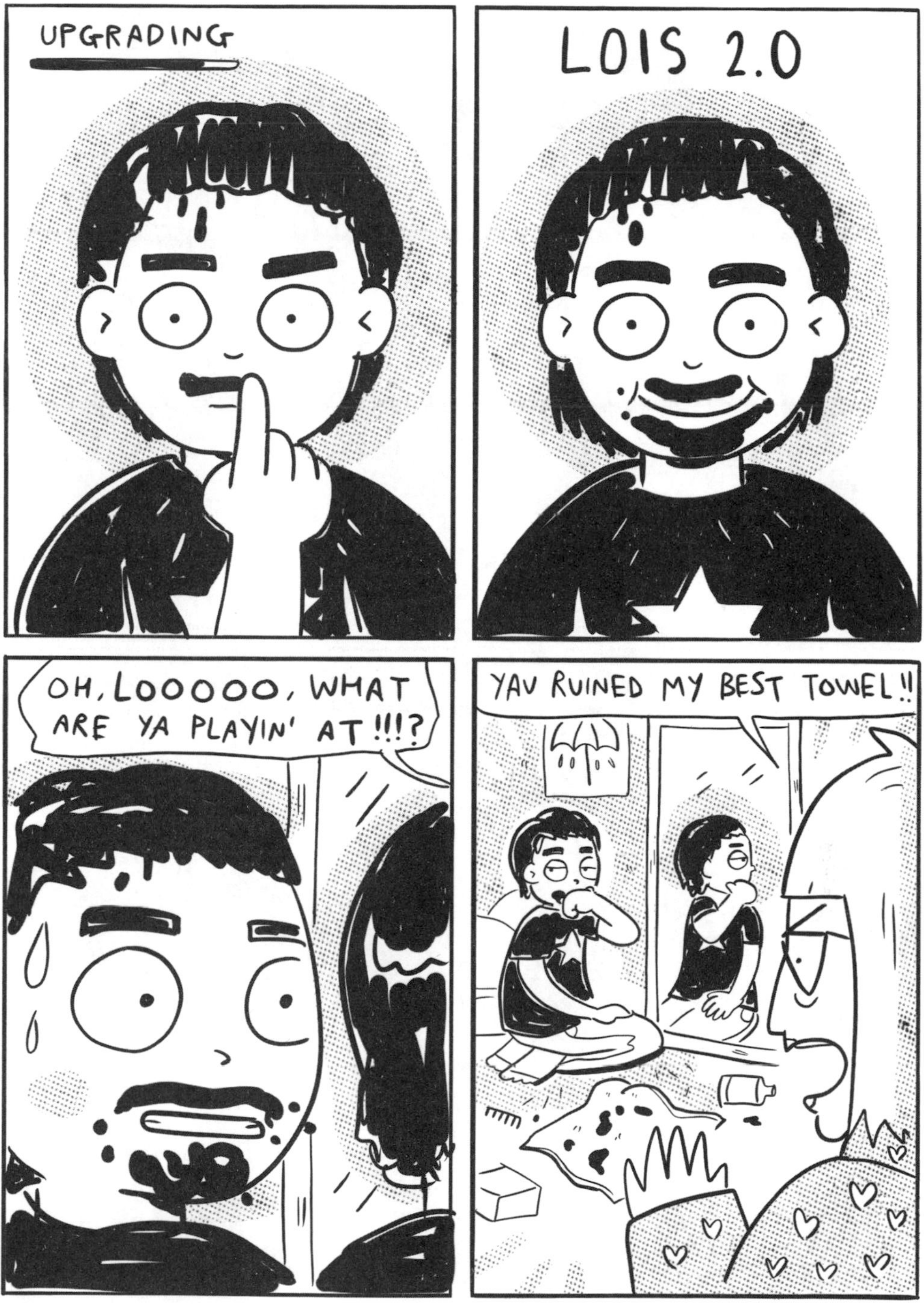
UPGRADING
LOIS 2.0
OH, LOOOOO, WHAT ARE YA PLAYIN' AT!!!?
YAU RUINED MY BEST TOWEL!!

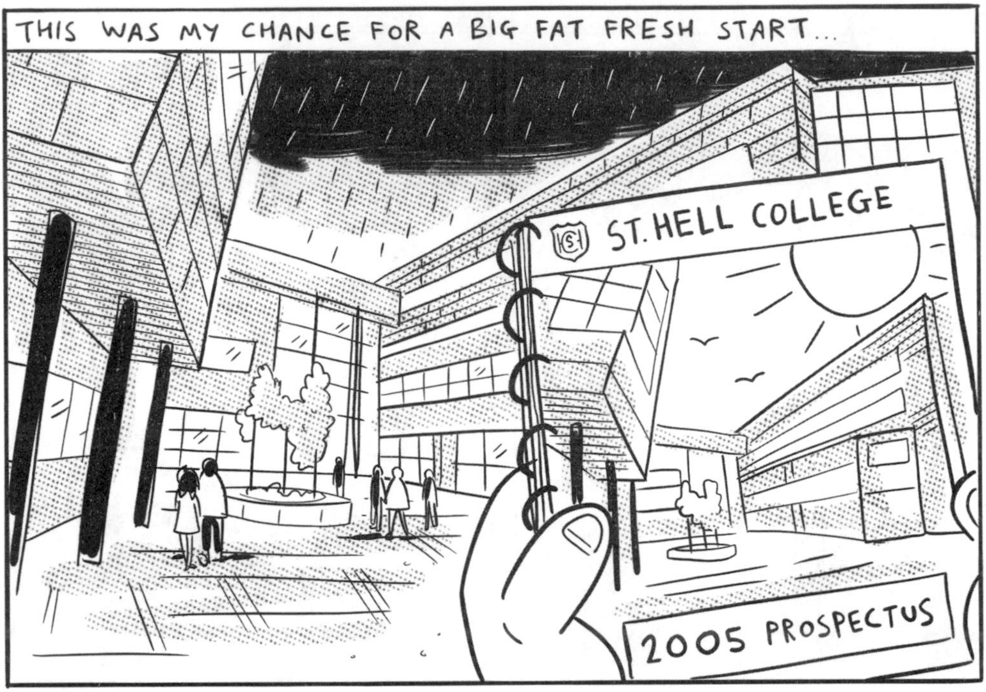
THIS WAS MY CHANCE FOR A BIG FAT FRESH START...
ST. HELL COLLEGE
2005 PROSPECTUS

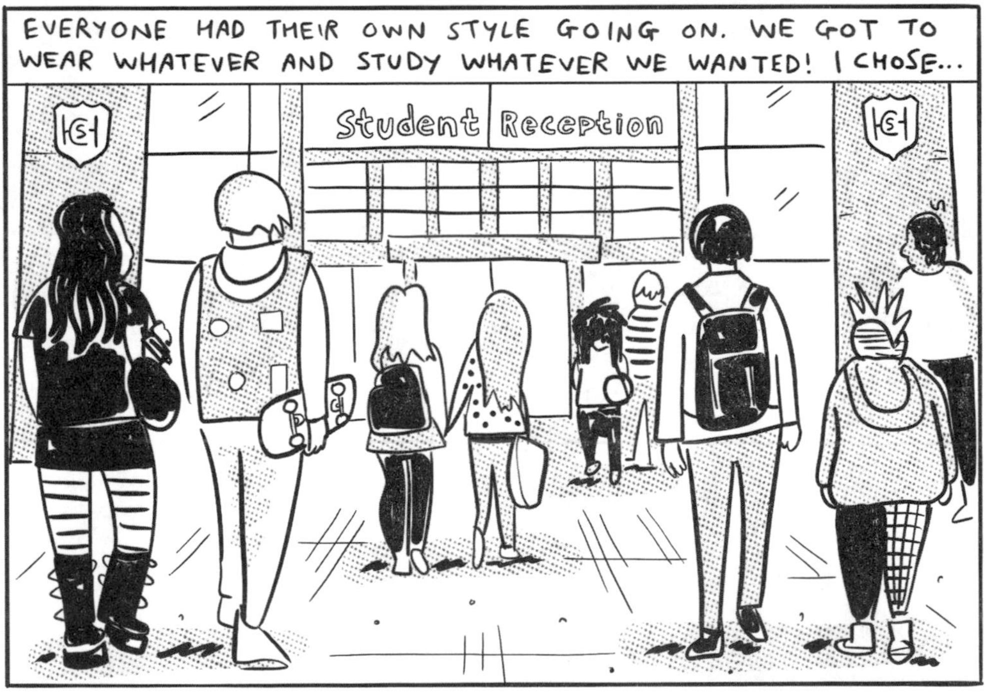
EVERYONE HAD THEIR OWN STYLE GOING ON. WE GOT TO WEAR WHATEVER AND STUDY WHATEVER WE WANTED! I CHOSE...
Student Reception

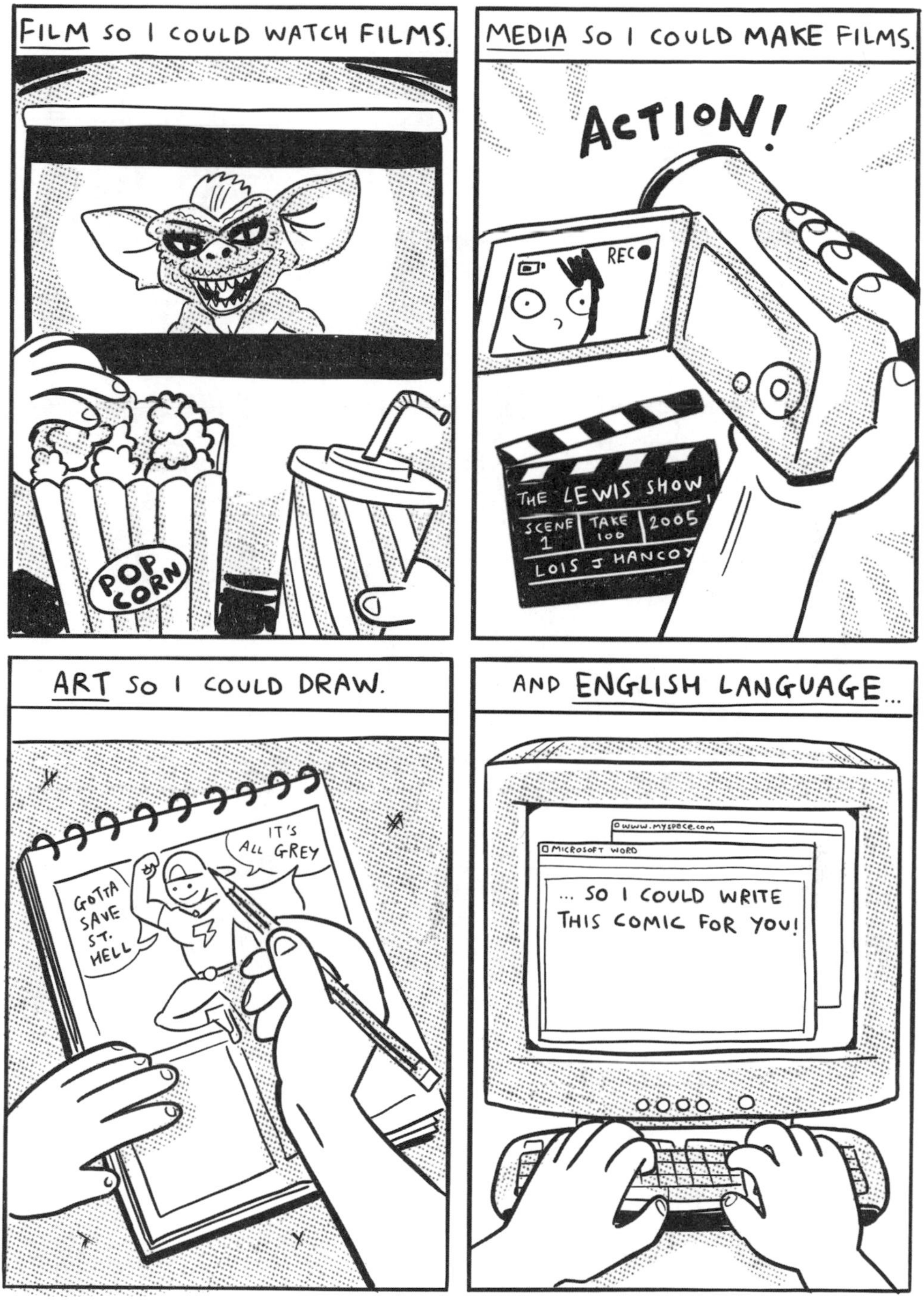
FILM SO I COULD WATCH FILMS.
POP CORN
MEDIA SO I COULD MAKE FILMS.
ACTION!
REC
THE LEWIS SHOW
SCENE 1
TAKE 100
2005
LOIS J HANCOX
ART SO I COULD DRAW.
GOTTA SAVE ST. HELL
IT'S ALL GREY
AND ENGLISH LANGUAGE...
www.myspace.com
MICROSOFT WORD
... SO I COULD WRITE THIS COMIC FOR YOU!

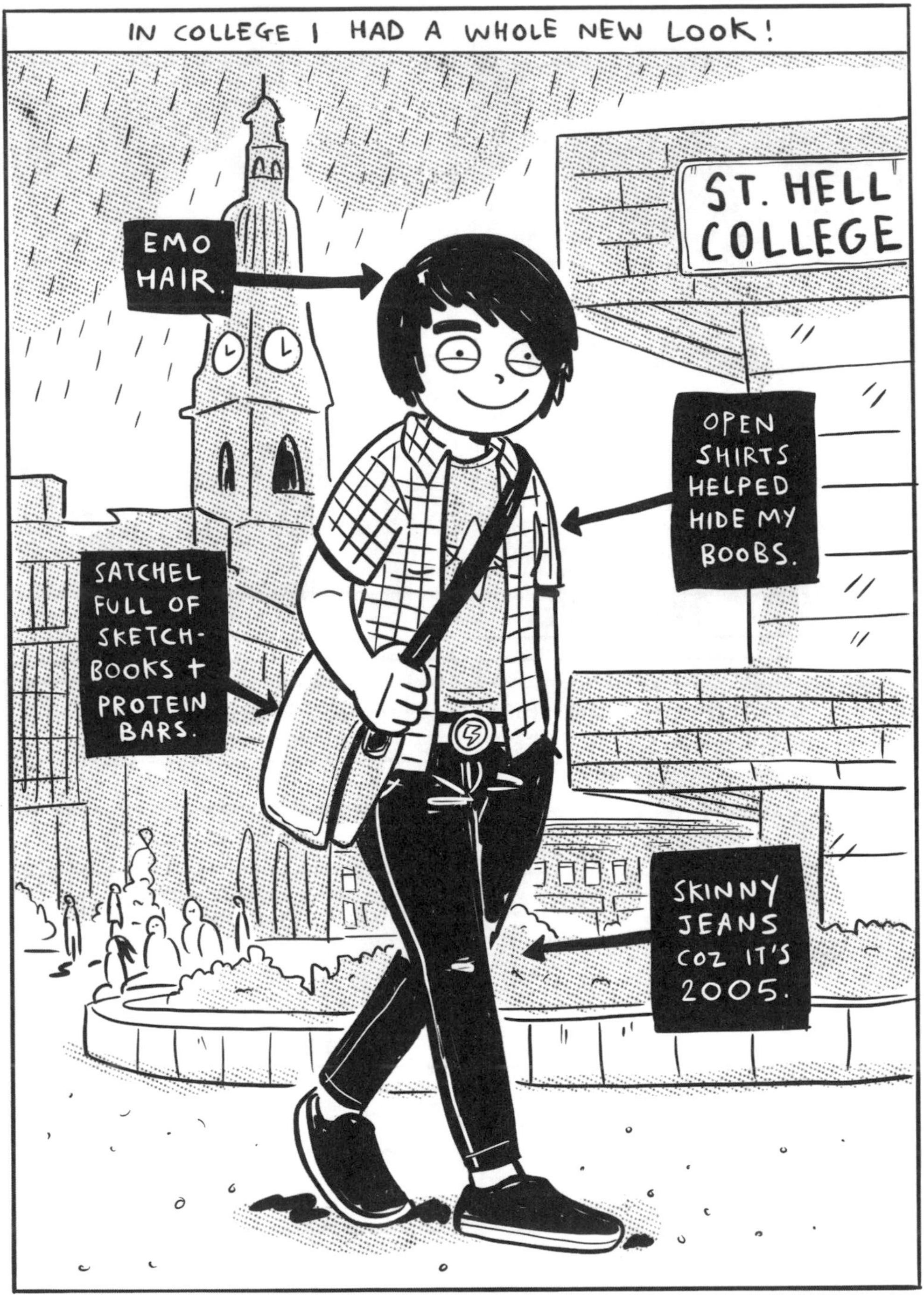
IN COLLEGE I HAD A WHOLE NEW LOOK!
ST. HELL COLLEGE
EMO HAIR.
OPEN SHIRTS HELPED HIDE MY BOOBS.
SATCHEL FULL OF SKETCH-BOOKS + PROTEIN BARS.
SKINNY JEANS COZ IT'S 2005.

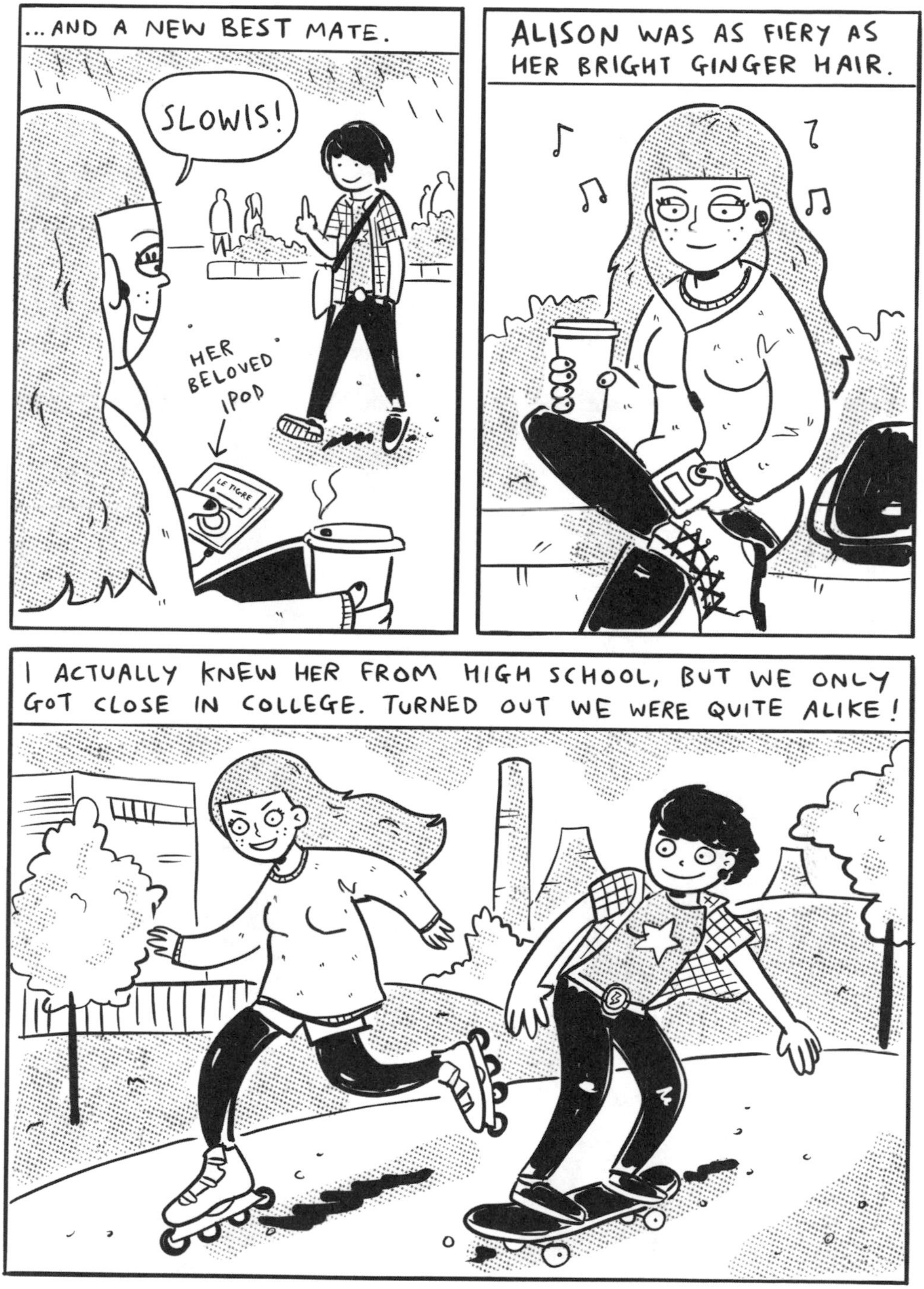
...AND A NEW BEST MATE.
SLOWIS!
HER BELOVED IPOD
LE TIGRE
ALISON WAS AS FIERY AS HER BRIGHT GINGER HAIR.
I ACTUALLY KNEW HER FROM HIGH SCHOOL, BUT WE ONLY GOT CLOSE IN COLLEGE. TURNED OUT WE WERE QUITE ALIKE!

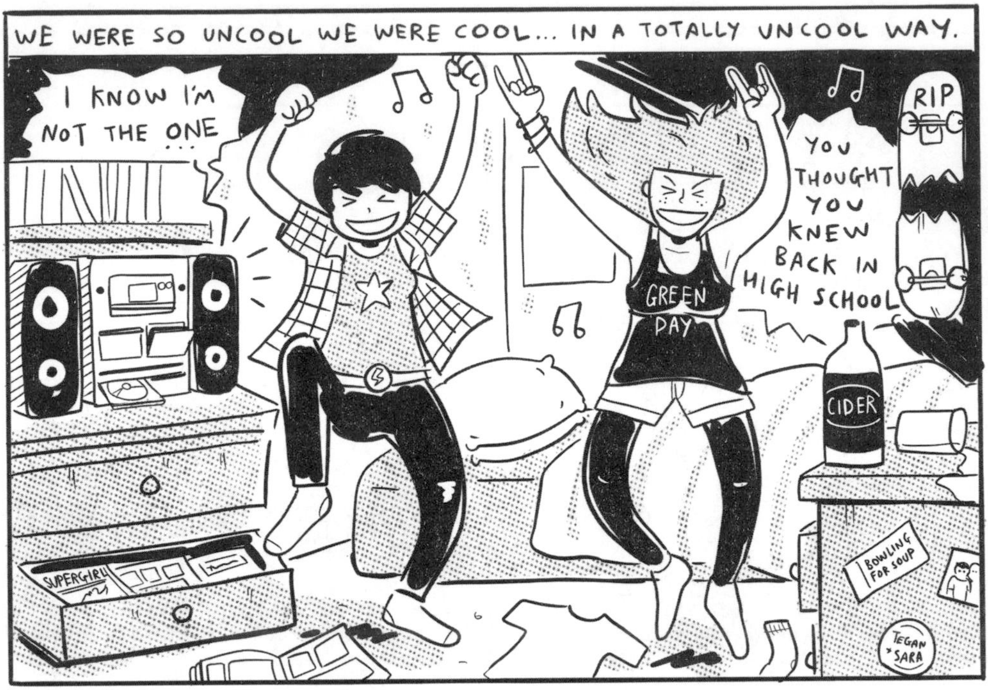
WE WERE SO UNCOOL WE WERE COOL... IN A TOTALLY UNCOOL WAY.
I KNOW I'M NOT THE ONE...
YOU THOUGHT YOU KNEW BACK IN HIGH SCHOOL
RIP
GREEN DAY
CIDER
SUPERGIRL
BOWLING FOR SOUP
TEGAN + SARA

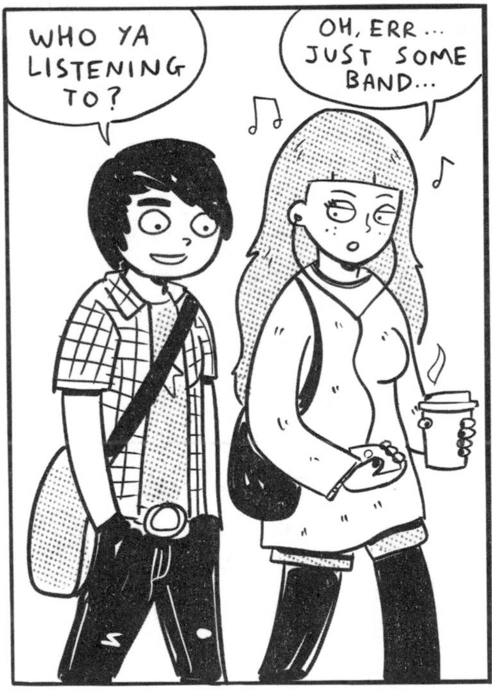
WHO YA LISTENING TO?
OH, ERR... JUST SOME BAND...

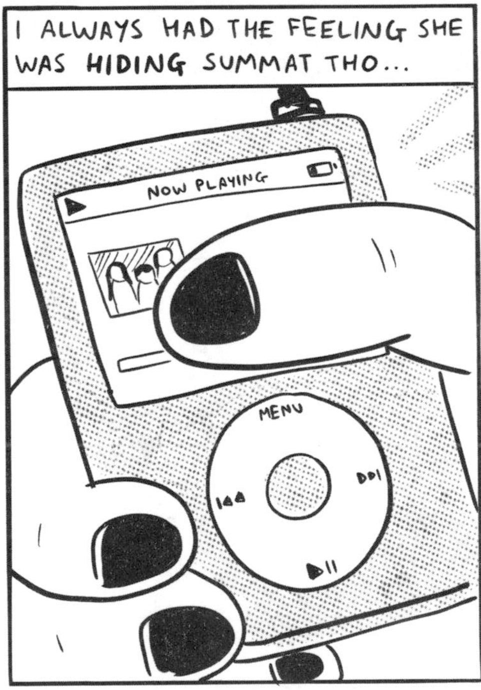
I ALWAYS HAD THE FEELING SHE WAS **HIDING** SUMMAT THO...
NOW PLAYING
MENU

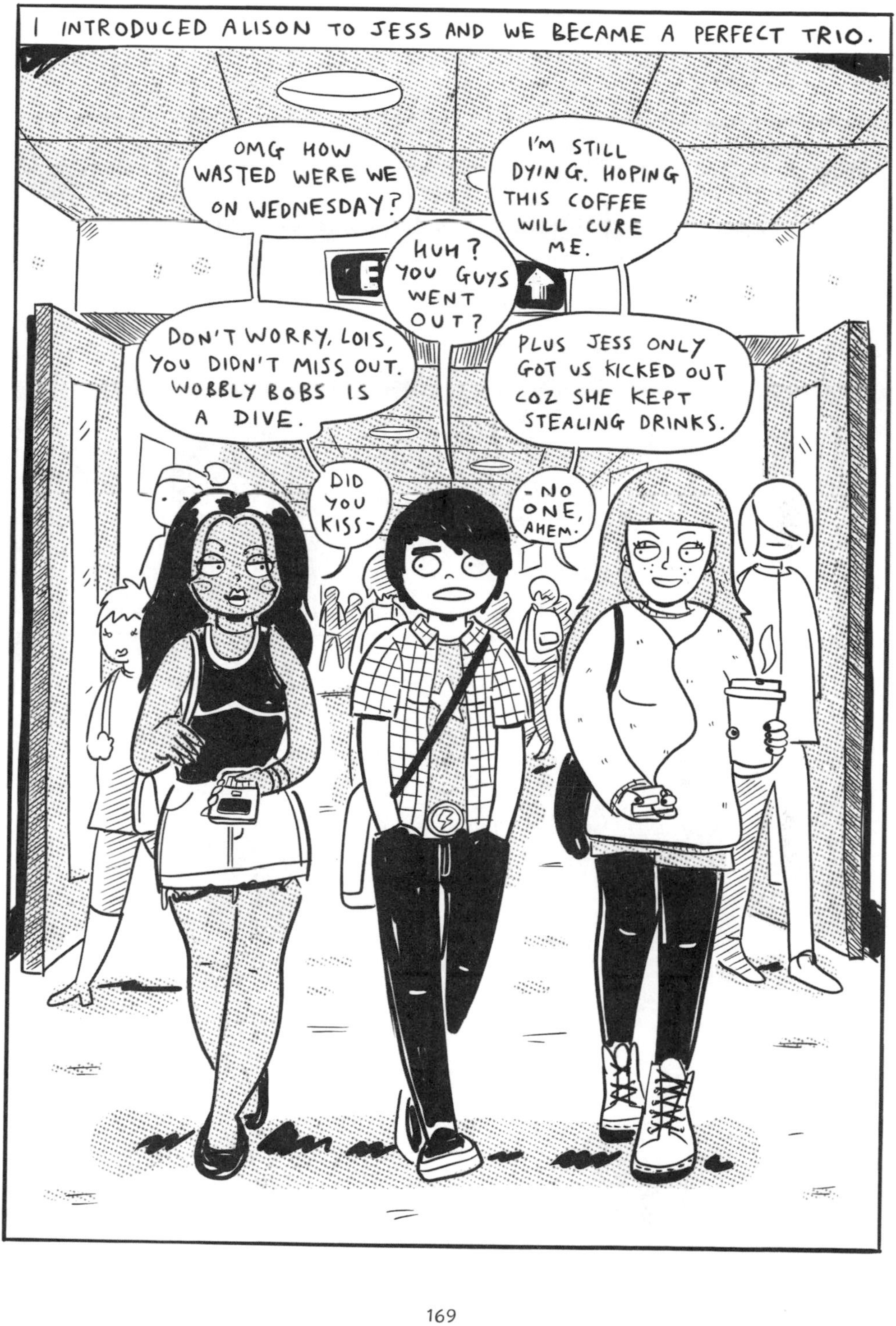
I INTRODUCED ALISON TO JESS AND WE BECAME A PERFECT TRIO.
OMG HOW WASTED WERE WE ON WEDNESDAY?
I'M STILL DYING. HOPING THIS COFFEE WILL CURE ME.
HUH? YOU GUYS WENT OUT?
DON'T WORRY, LOIS, YOU DIDN'T MISS OUT. WOBBLY BOBS IS A DIVE.
PLUS JESS ONLY GOT US KICKED OUT COZ SHE KEPT STEALING DRINKS.
DID YOU KISS-
-NO ONE, AHEM.

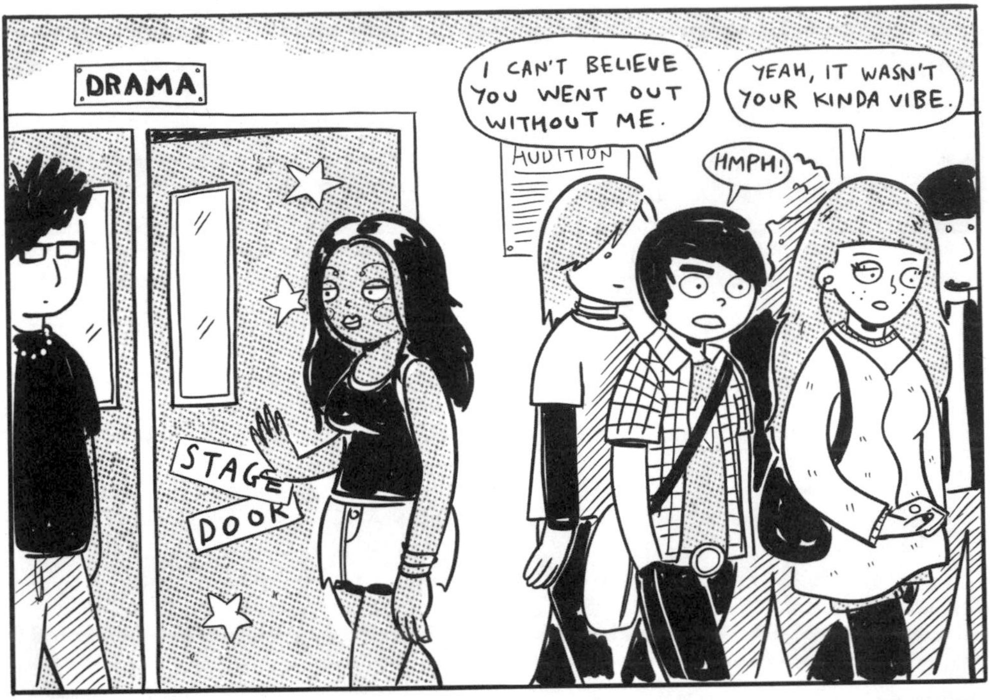
DRAMA
STAGE DOOR
AUDITION
I CAN'T BELIEVE YOU WENT OUT WITHOUT ME.
HMPH!
YEAH, IT WASN'T YOUR KINDA VIBE.

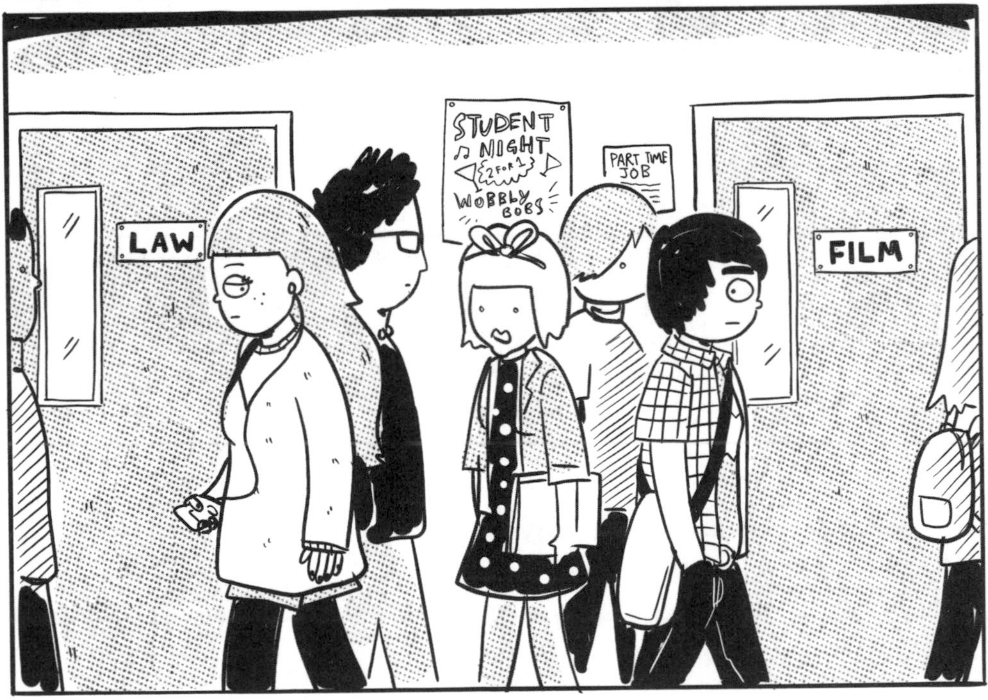
LAW
STUDENT NIGHT
2 FOR 1
WOBBLY BOBS
PART TIME JOB
FILM

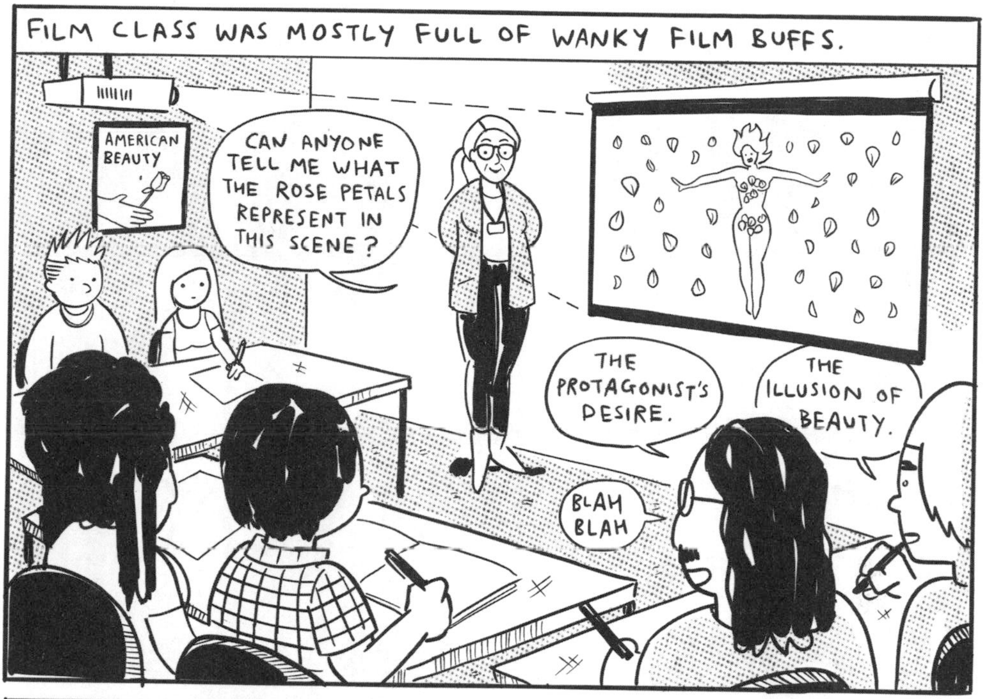
FILM CLASS WAS MOSTLY FULL OF WANKY FILM BUFFS.
AMERICAN BEAUTY
CAN ANYONE TELL ME WHAT THE ROSE PETALS REPRESENT IN THIS SCENE?
THE PROTAGONIST'S DESIRE.
THE ILLUSION OF BEAUTY.
BLAH BLAH

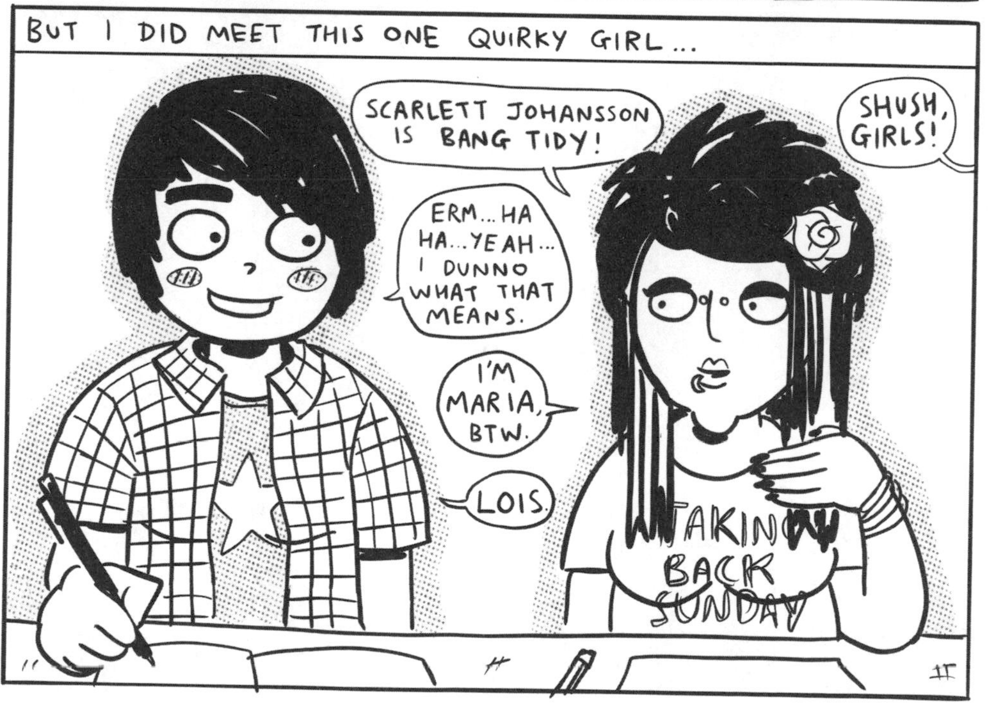
BUT I DID MEET THIS ONE QUIRKY GIRL...
SCARLETT JOHANSSON IS BANG TIDY!
SHUSH, GIRLS!
ERM... HA HA... YEAH... I DUNNO WHAT THAT MEANS.
I'M MARIA, BTW.
LOIS.
TAKING BACK SUNDAY

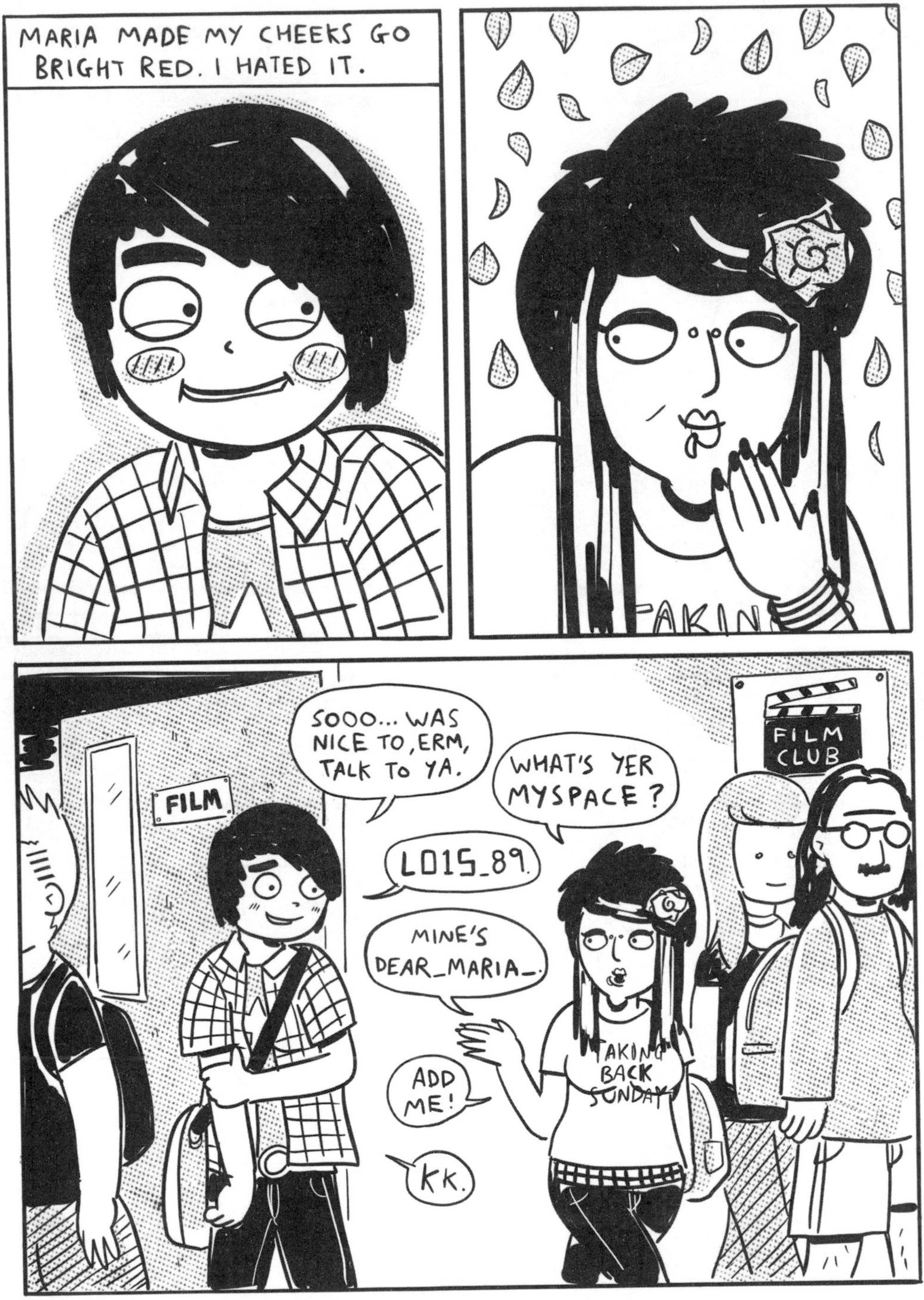
MARIA MADE MY CHEEKS GO BRIGHT RED. I HATED IT.
FAKING
FILM
FILM CLUB
SOOO... WAS NICE TO, ERM, TALK TO YA.
WHAT'S YER MYSPACE?
LO15_89.
MINE'S DEAR_MARIA_.
ADD ME!
KK.
TAKING BACK SUNDAY

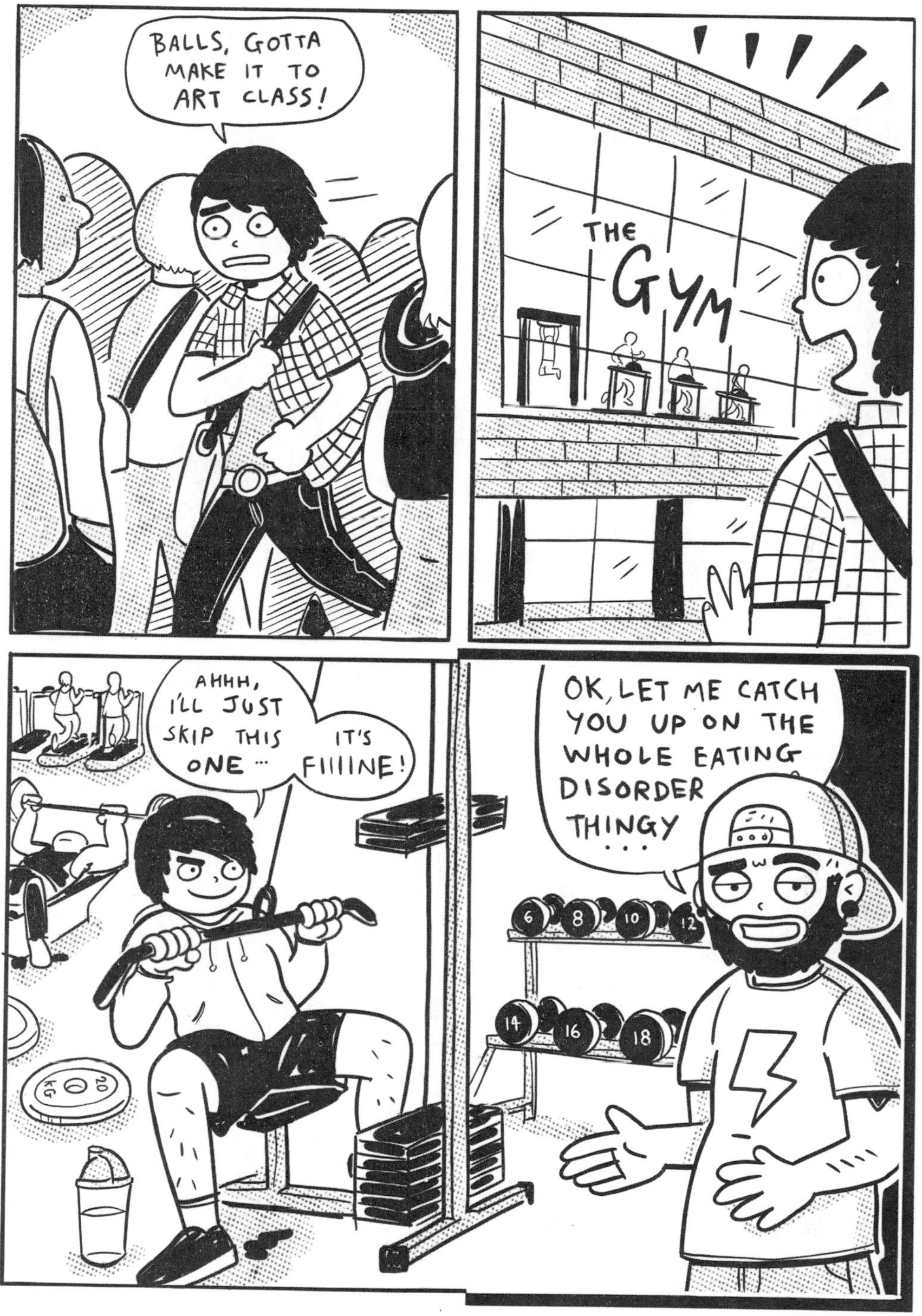
BALLS, GOTTA MAKE IT TO ART CLASS!
THE GYM
AHHH, I'LL JUST SKIP THIS ONE...
IT'S FIIIINE!
OK, LET ME CATCH YOU UP ON THE WHOLE EATING DISORDER THINGY...

I SPENT A FEW NIGHTS IN HOSPITAL AT THE START OF SUMMER, SO THEY COULD CHECK I HADN'T DAMAGED MY INSIDES...

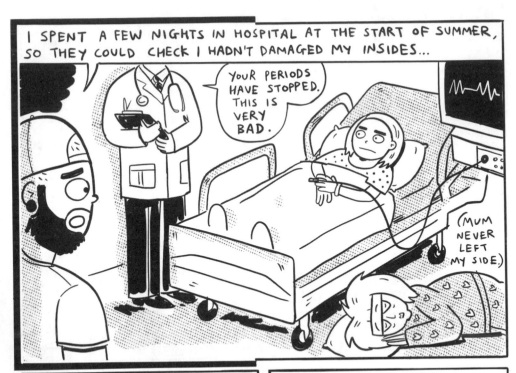

YOUR PERIODS HAVE STOPPED. THIS IS VERY BAD.

(MUM NEVER LEFT MY SIDE.)

I HAD WEEKLY WEIGH-INS...

WHAT'S IN YOUR POCKET?

AND TRIED SOME SNEAKY TRICKS.

OOPS... HOW'D THAT GET IN THERE?

2KG

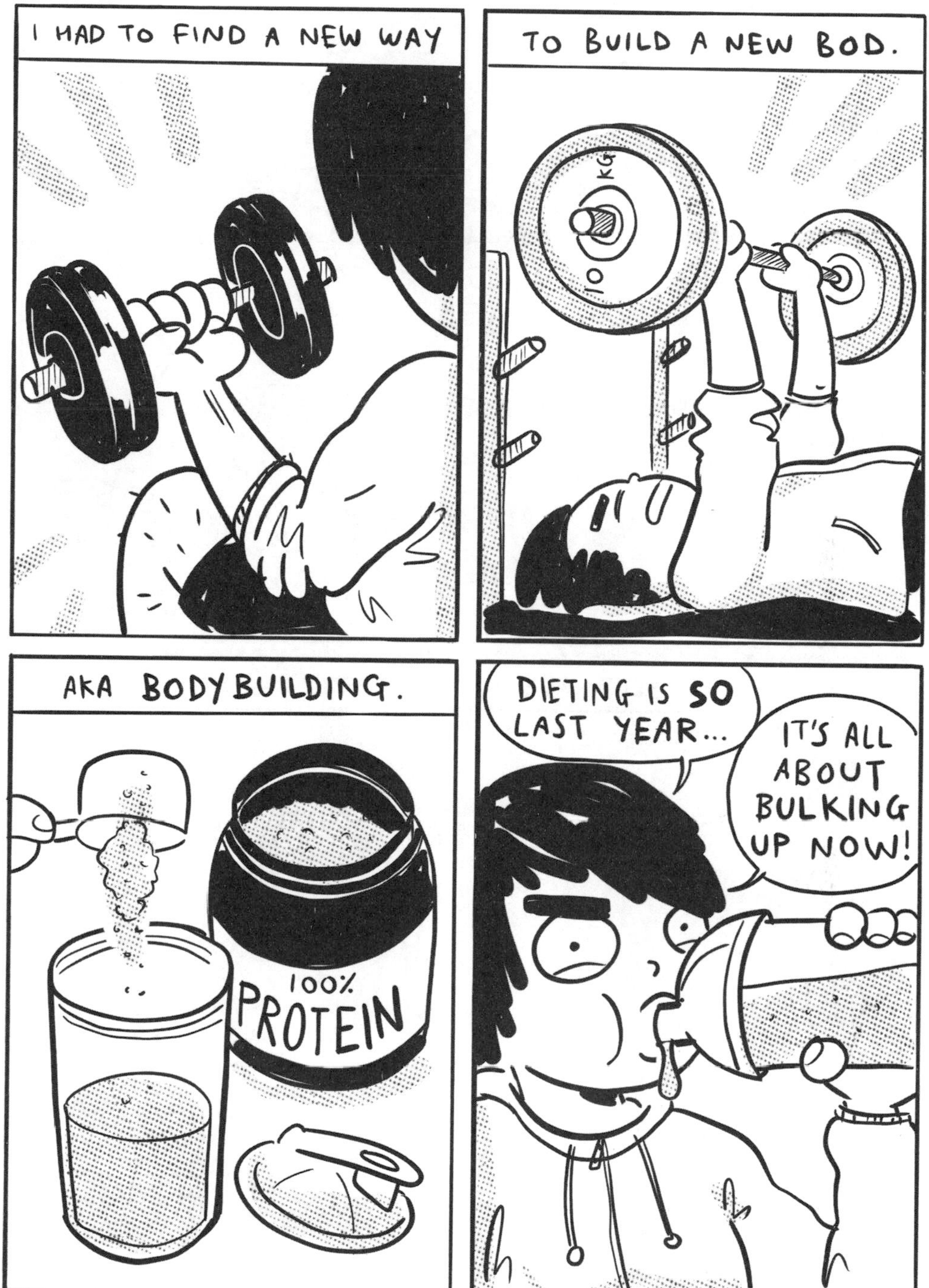
I HAD TO FIND A NEW WAY
TO BUILD A NEW BOD.
10 KG
10
AKA BODYBUILDING.
100%
PROTEIN
DIETING IS SO LAST YEAR...
IT'S ALL ABOUT BULKING UP NOW!

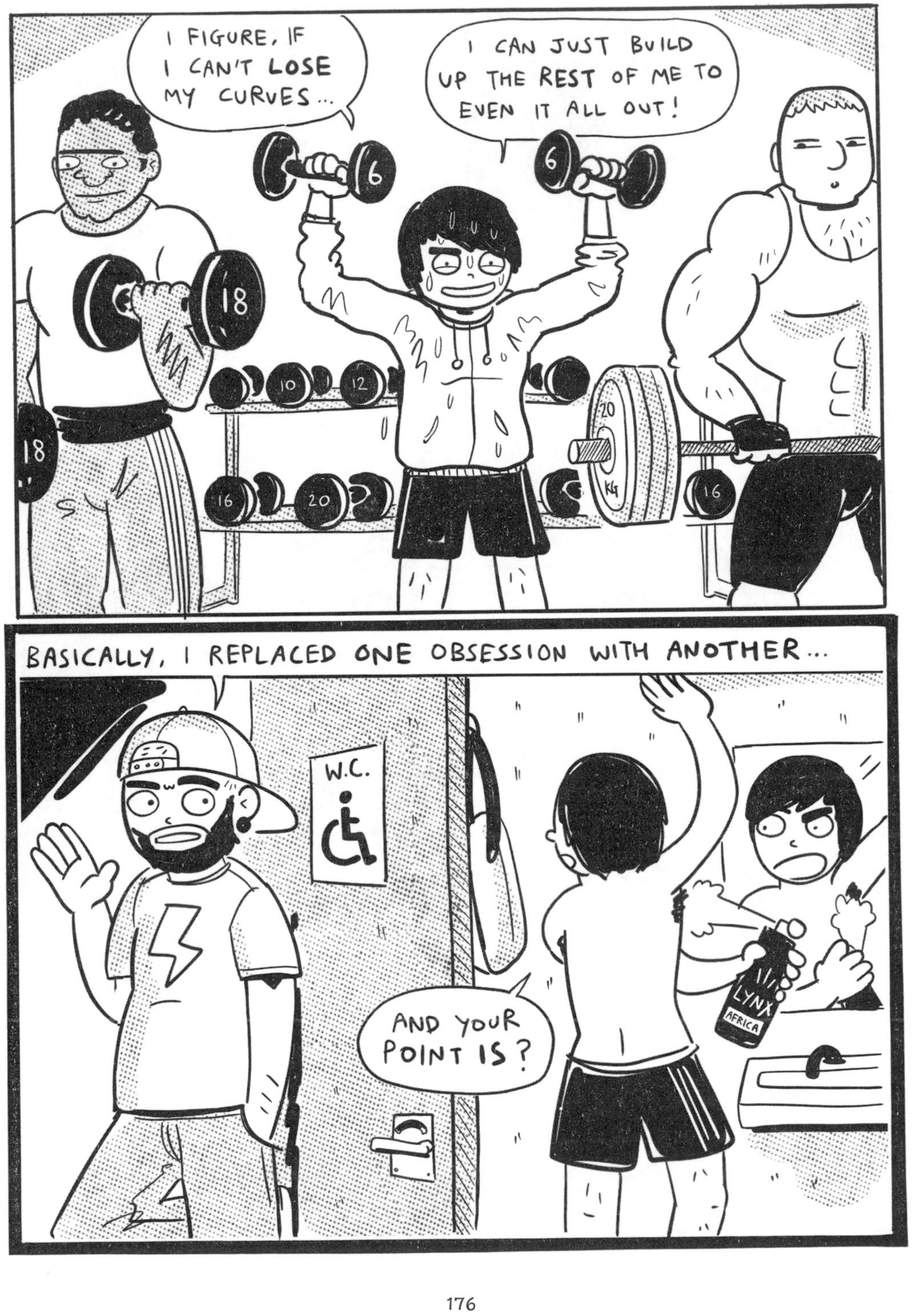
I FIGURE, IF I CAN'T **LOSE** MY CURVES...
I CAN JUST BUILD UP THE **REST** OF ME TO EVEN IT ALL OUT!
BASICALLY, I REPLACED **ONE** OBSESSION WITH **ANOTHER**...
W.C.
AND YOUR POINT **IS**?
LYNX
AFRICA

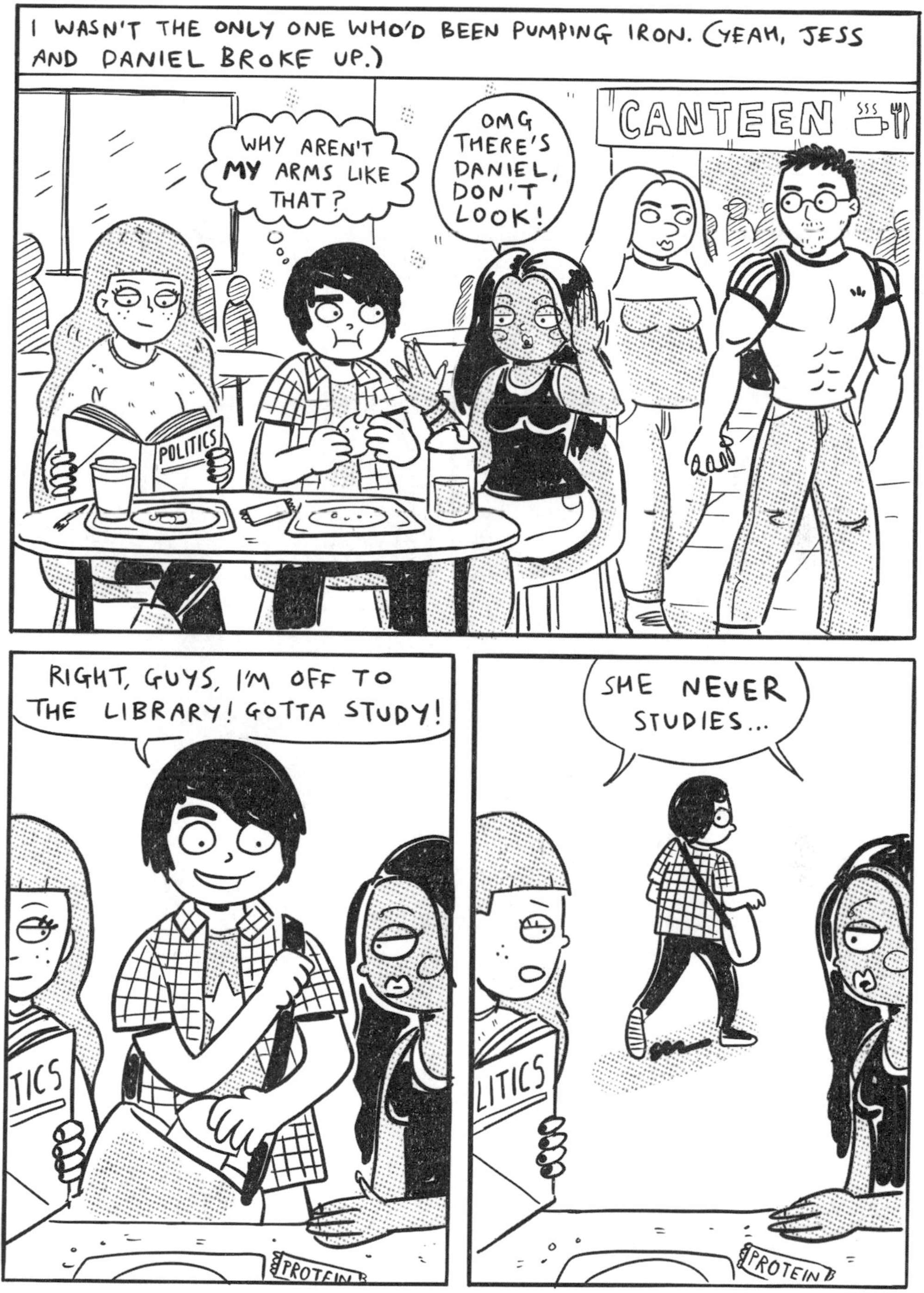
I WASN'T THE ONLY ONE WHO'D BEEN PUMPING IRON. (YEAH, JESS AND DANIEL BROKE UP.)
CANTEEN
WHY AREN'T MY ARMS LIKE THAT?
OMG THERE'S DANIEL, DON'T LOOK!
POLITICS
RIGHT, GUYS, I'M OFF TO THE LIBRARY! GOTTA STUDY!
TICS
PROTEIN
SHE NEVER STUDIES...
LITICS
PROTEIN

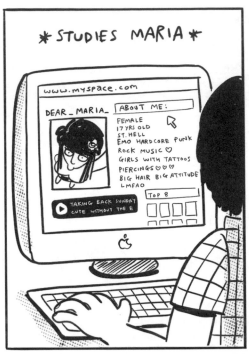

STUDIES MARIA
www.myspace.com
DEAR_MARIA_
ABOUT ME:
FEMALE
17 YRS OLD
ST. HELL
EMO HARDCORE PUNK
ROCK MUSIC ♡
GIRLS WITH TATTOOS
PIERCINGS ♡♡♡
BIG HAIR BIG ATTITUDE
LMFAO
TOP 8
TAKING BACK SUNDAY
CUTE WITHOUT THE E
DEAR_MARIA_ TOOK UP A LOT OF MY BRAIN SPACE.
LIBRARY
I'D SEE HER IN THE SMOKING SHELTER LOOKING ALL MOODY.
SNEAKY SNOOP
WITH HER BIG... PERSONALITY.
TAKING BACK SUNDAY

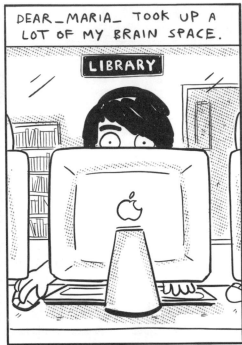

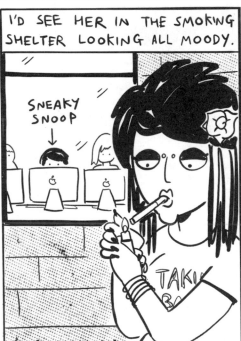

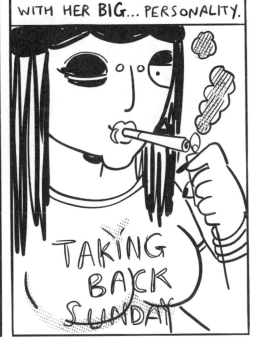

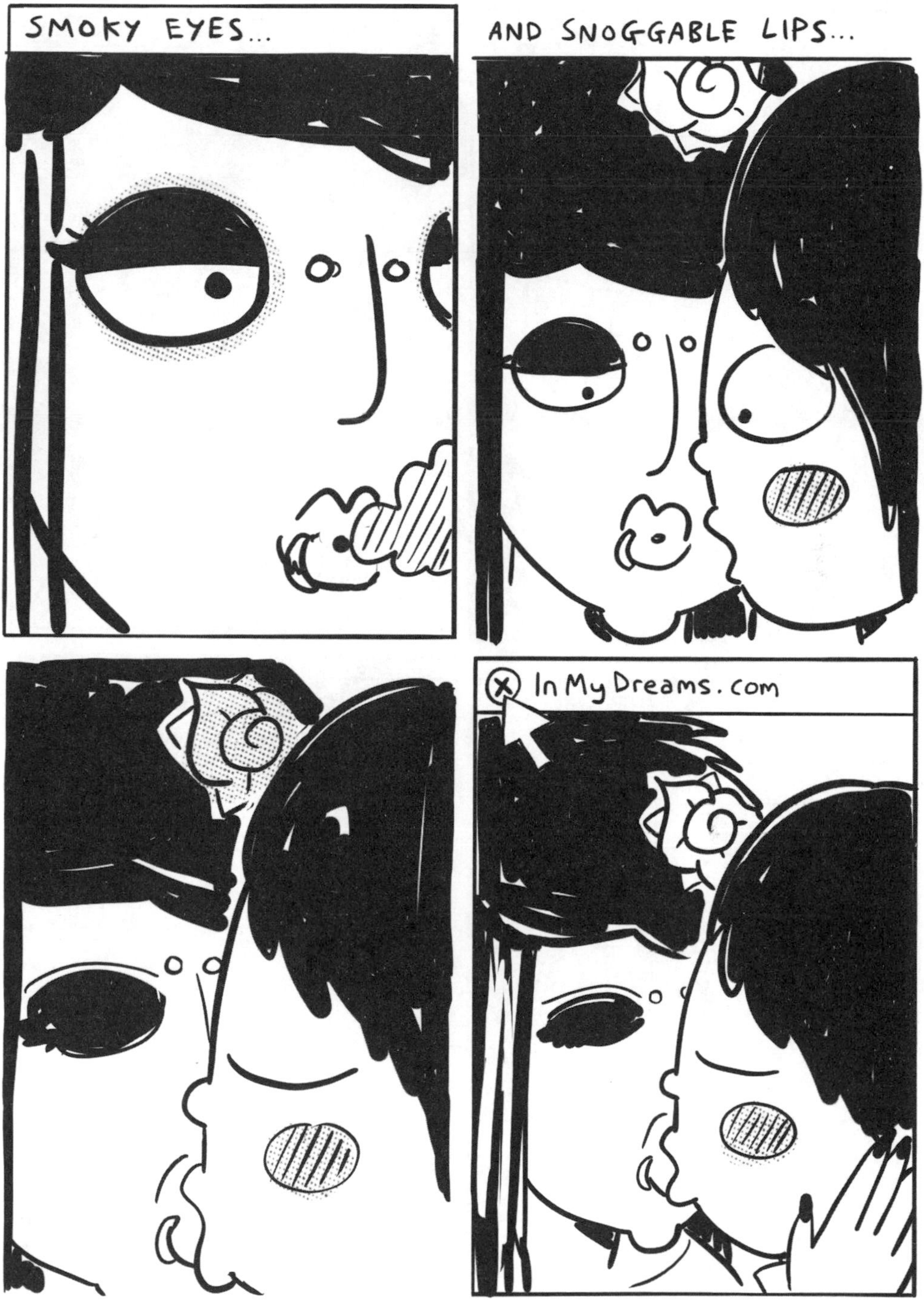
SMOKY EYES...
AND SNOGGABLE LIPS...
InMyDreams.com

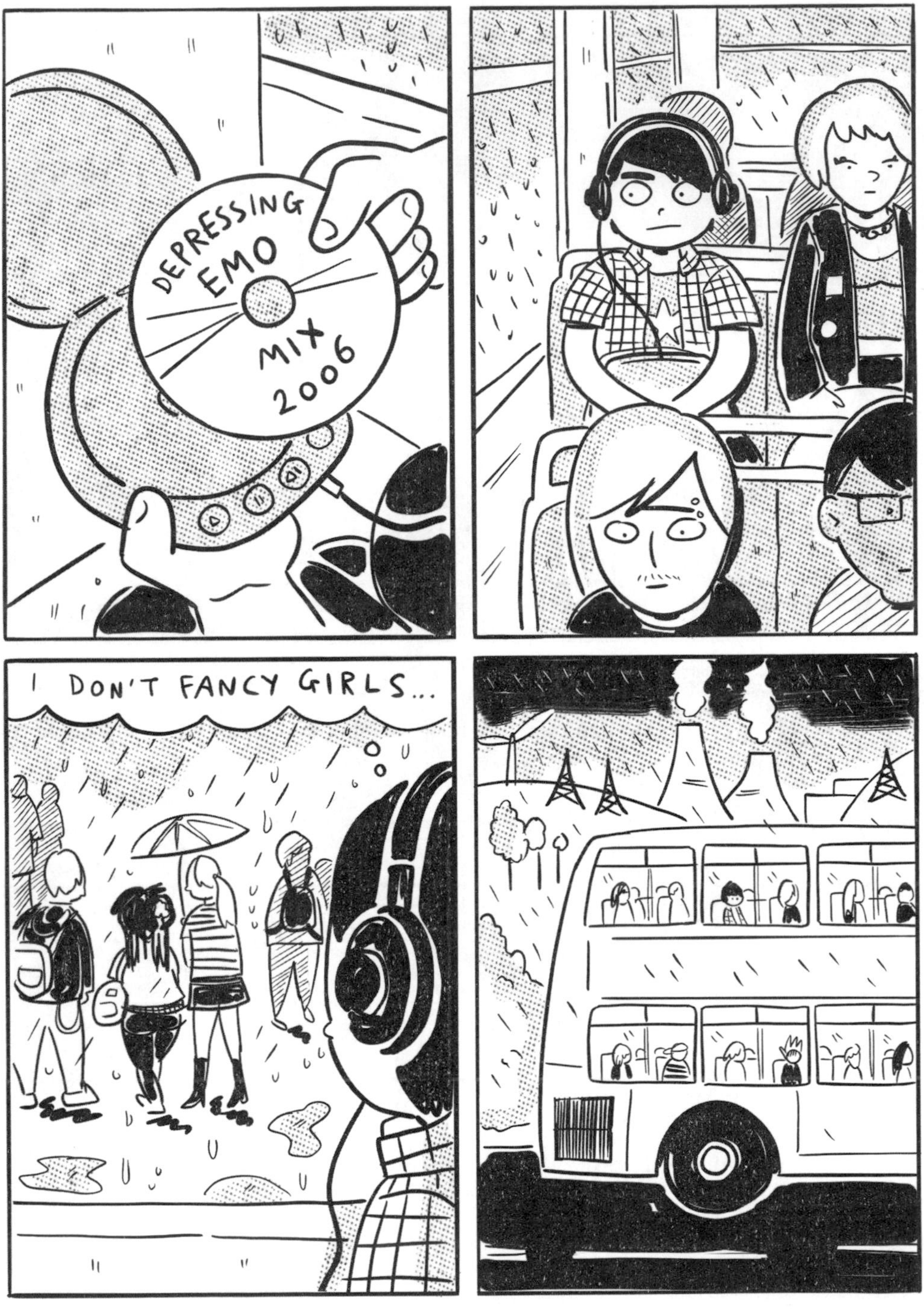
DEPRESSING EMO MIX 2006
I DON'T FANCY GIRLS...

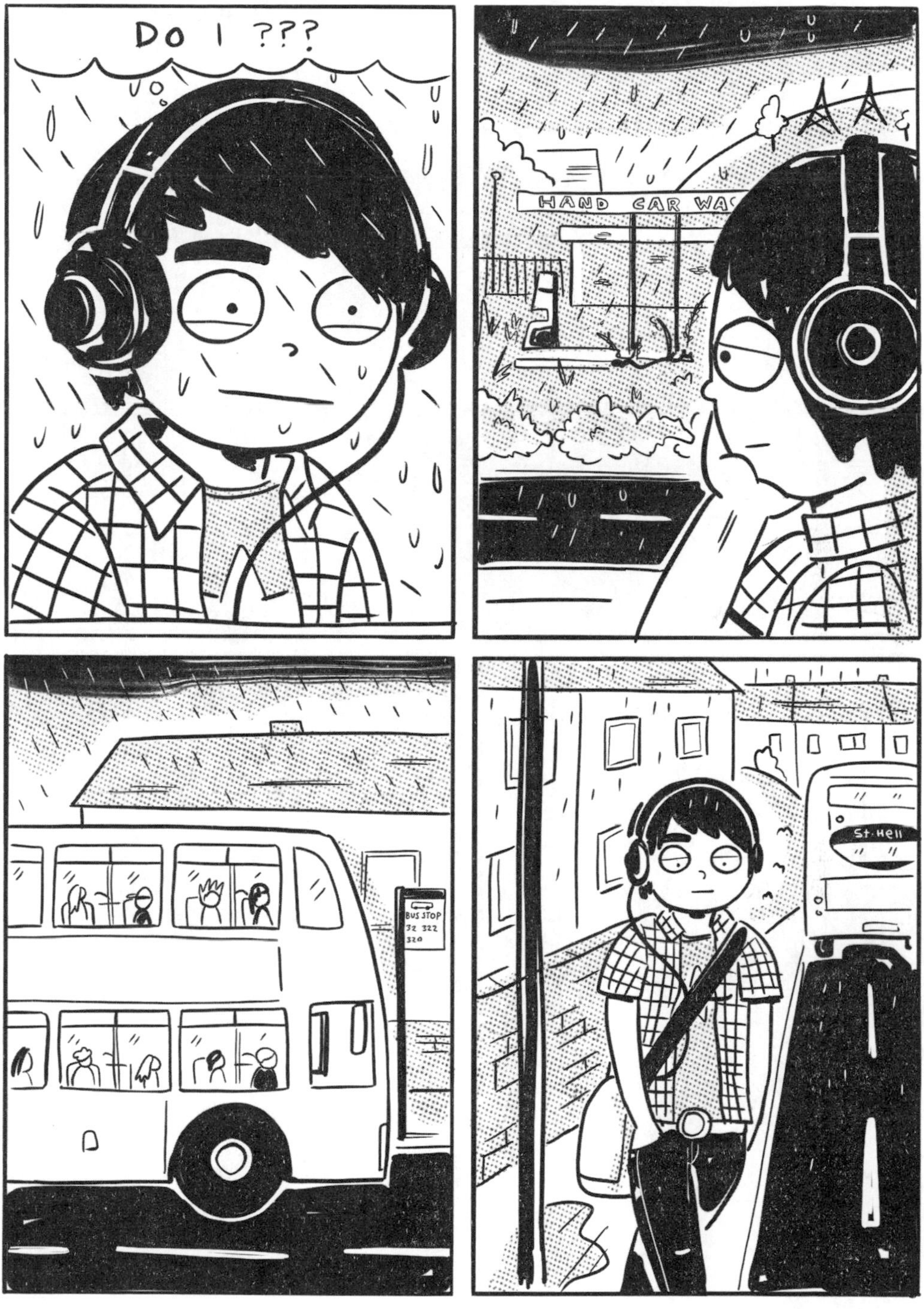
DO I ???
HAND CAR WA
BUS STOP
32 322
320
St. Hell

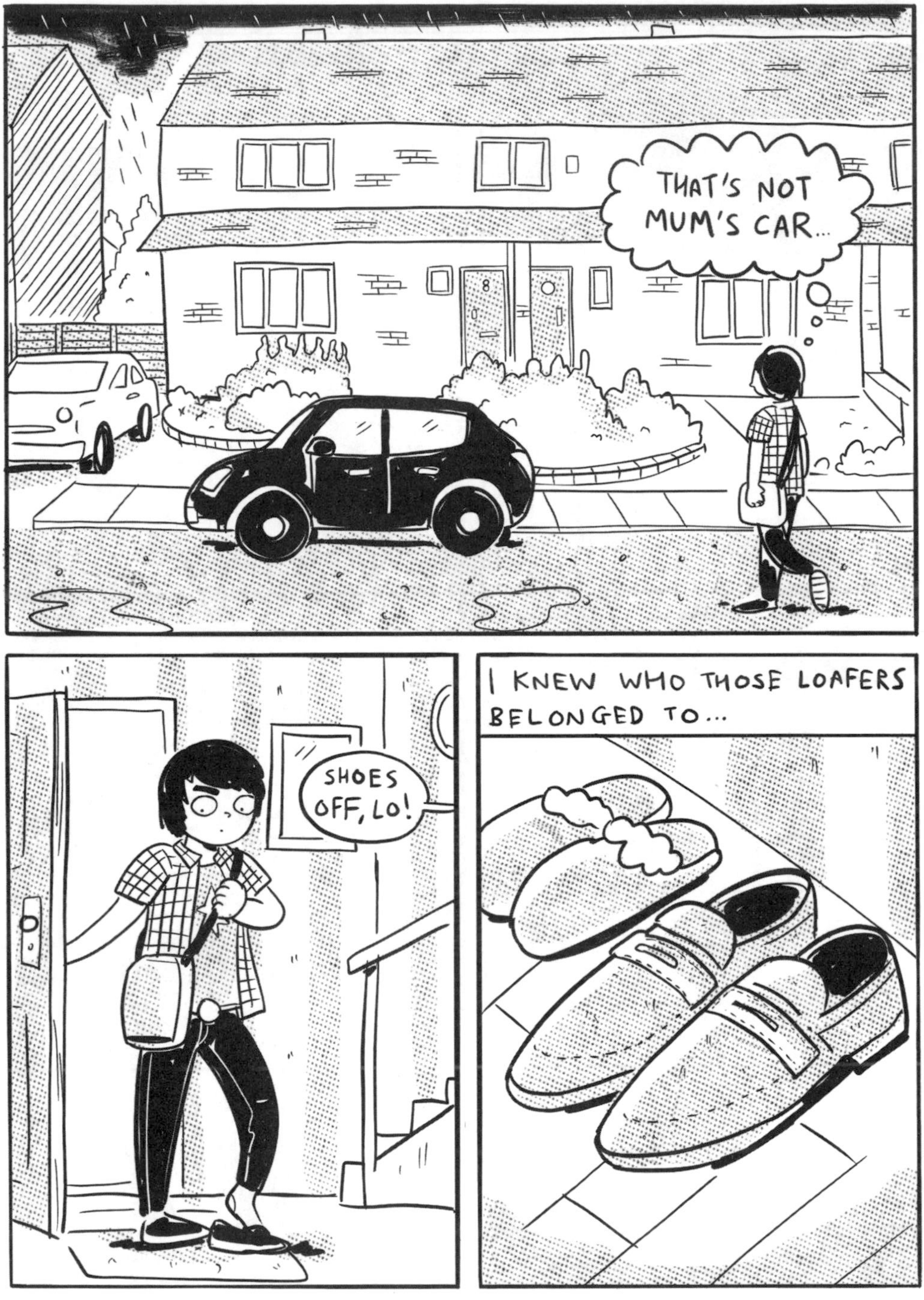
THAT'S NOT MUM'S CAR...
SHOES OFF, LO!
I KNEW WHO THOSE LOAFERS BELONGED TO...

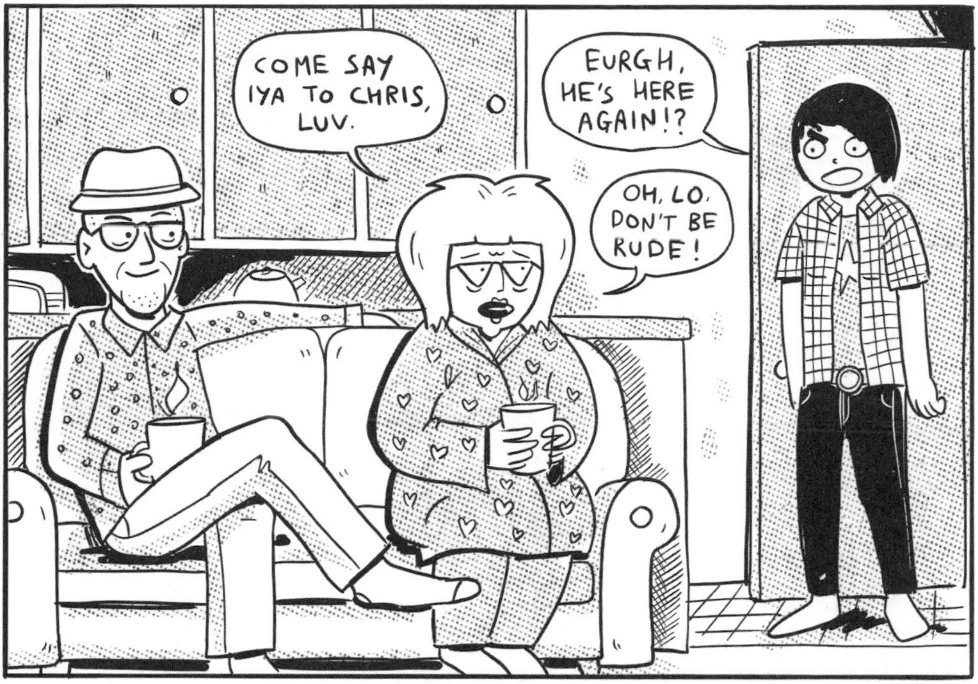
COME SAY IYA TO CHRIS, LUV.
EURGH, HE'S HERE AGAIN!?
OH, LO. DON'T BE RUDE!

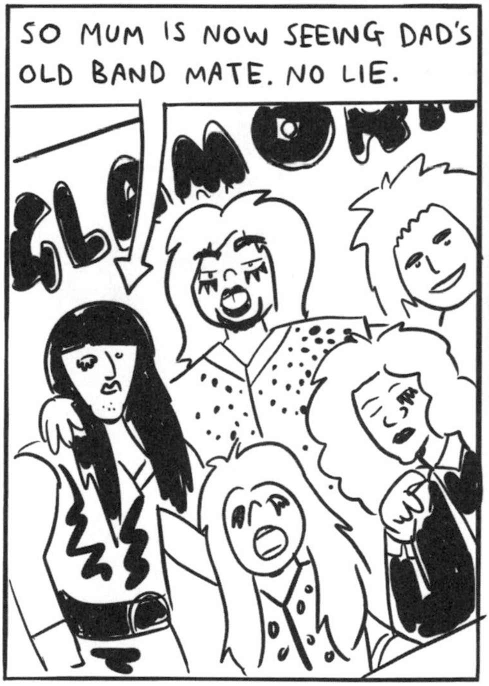
SO MUM IS NOW SEEING DAD'S OLD BAND MATE. NO LIE.

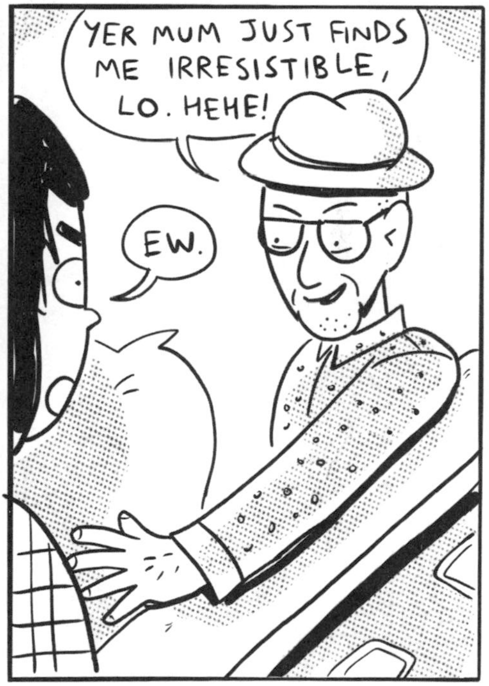
YER MUM JUST FINDS ME IRRESISTIBLE, LO. HEHE!
EW.

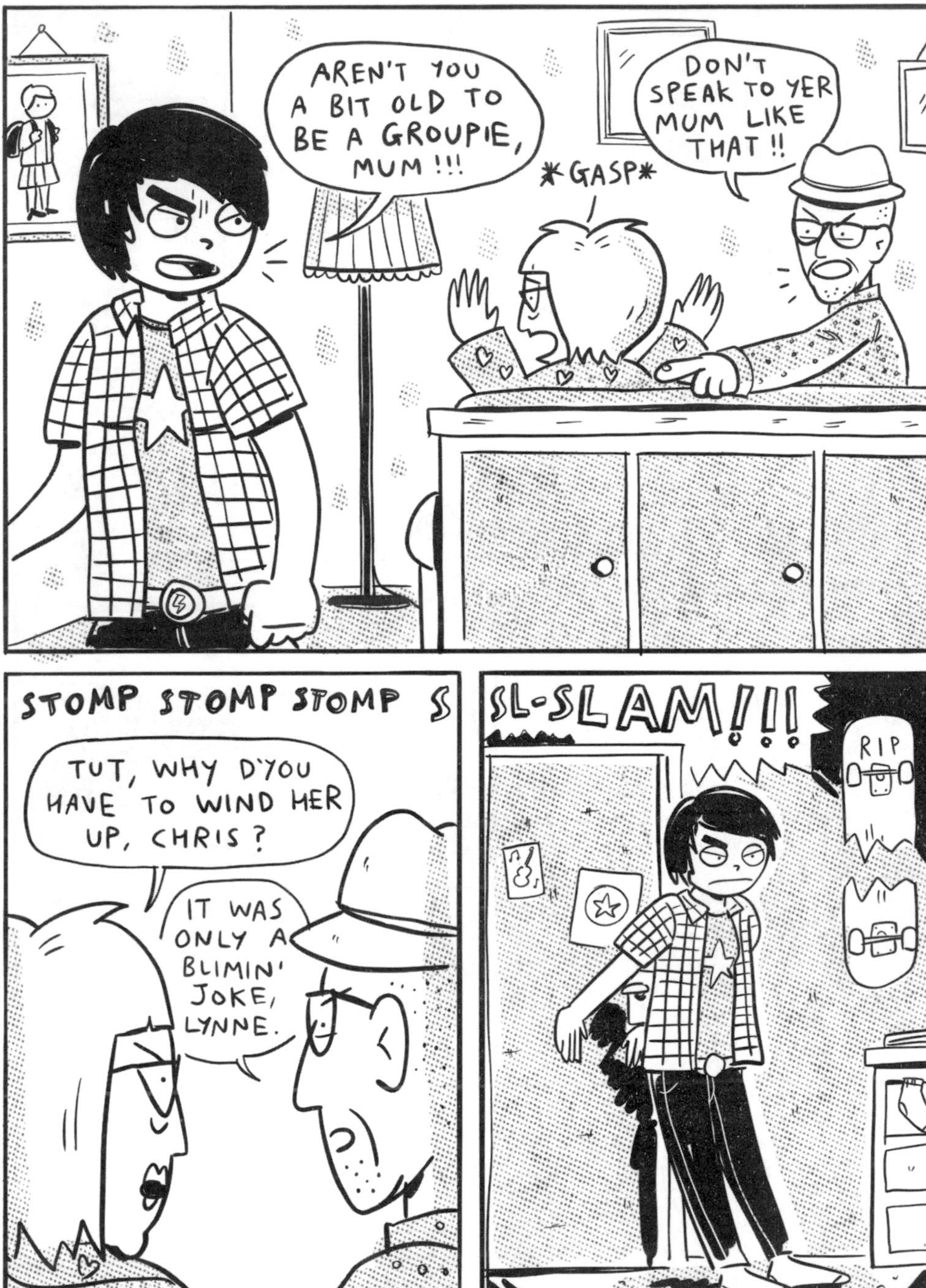
AREN'T YOU A BIT OLD TO BE A GROUPIE, MUM!!!
GASP
DON'T SPEAK TO YER MUM LIKE THAT!!
STOMP STOMP STOMP S
TUT, WHY D'YOU HAVE TO WIND HER UP, CHRIS?
IT WAS ONLY A BLIMIN' JOKE, LYNNE.
SL-SLAM!!!
RIP

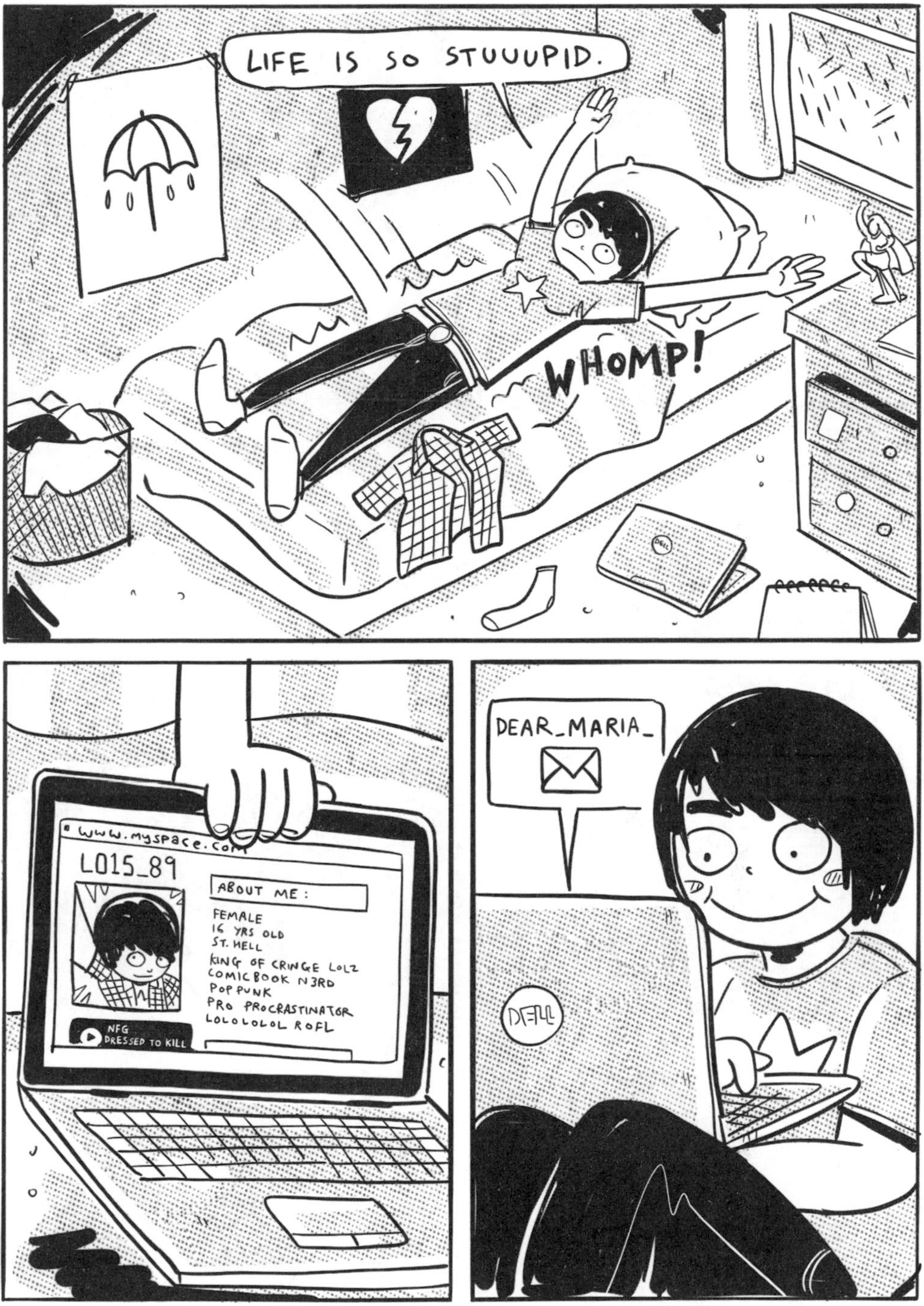
LIFE IS SO STUUUPID.
WHOMP!
DELL
www.myspace.com
LO15_89
ABOUT ME:
FEMALE
16 YRS OLD
ST. HELL
KING OF CRINGE LOLZ
COMICBOOK N3RD
POP PUNK
PRO PROCRASTINATOR
LOLOLOLOL ROFL
NFG
DRESSED TO KILL
DEAR_MARIA_
DELL

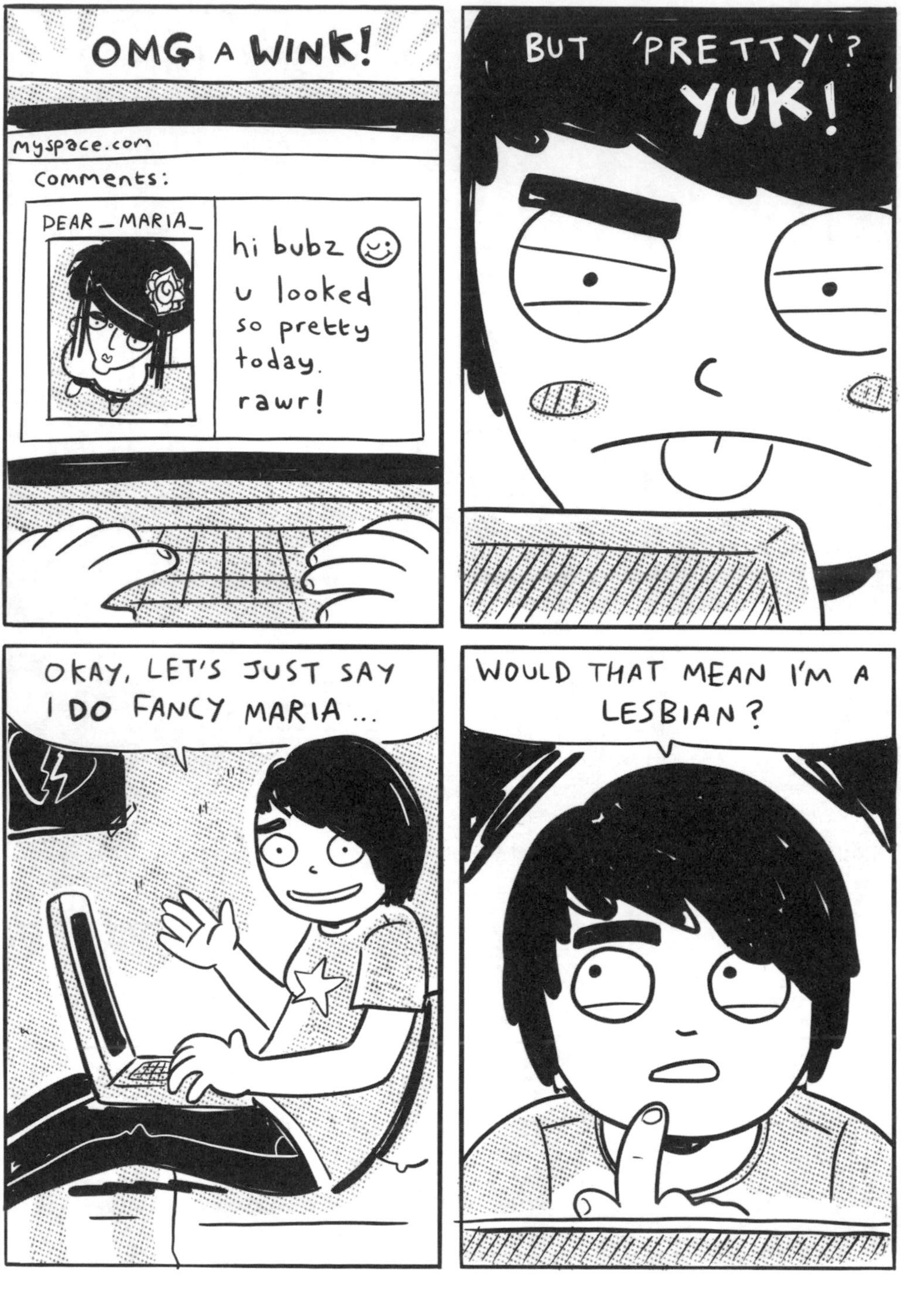
OMG A WINK!
myspace.com
comments:
DEAR_MARIA_
hi bubz
u looked so pretty today.
rawr!
BUT 'PRETTY'?
YUK!
OKAY, LET'S JUST SAY I DO FANCY MARIA ...
WOULD THAT MEAN I'M A LESBIAN?

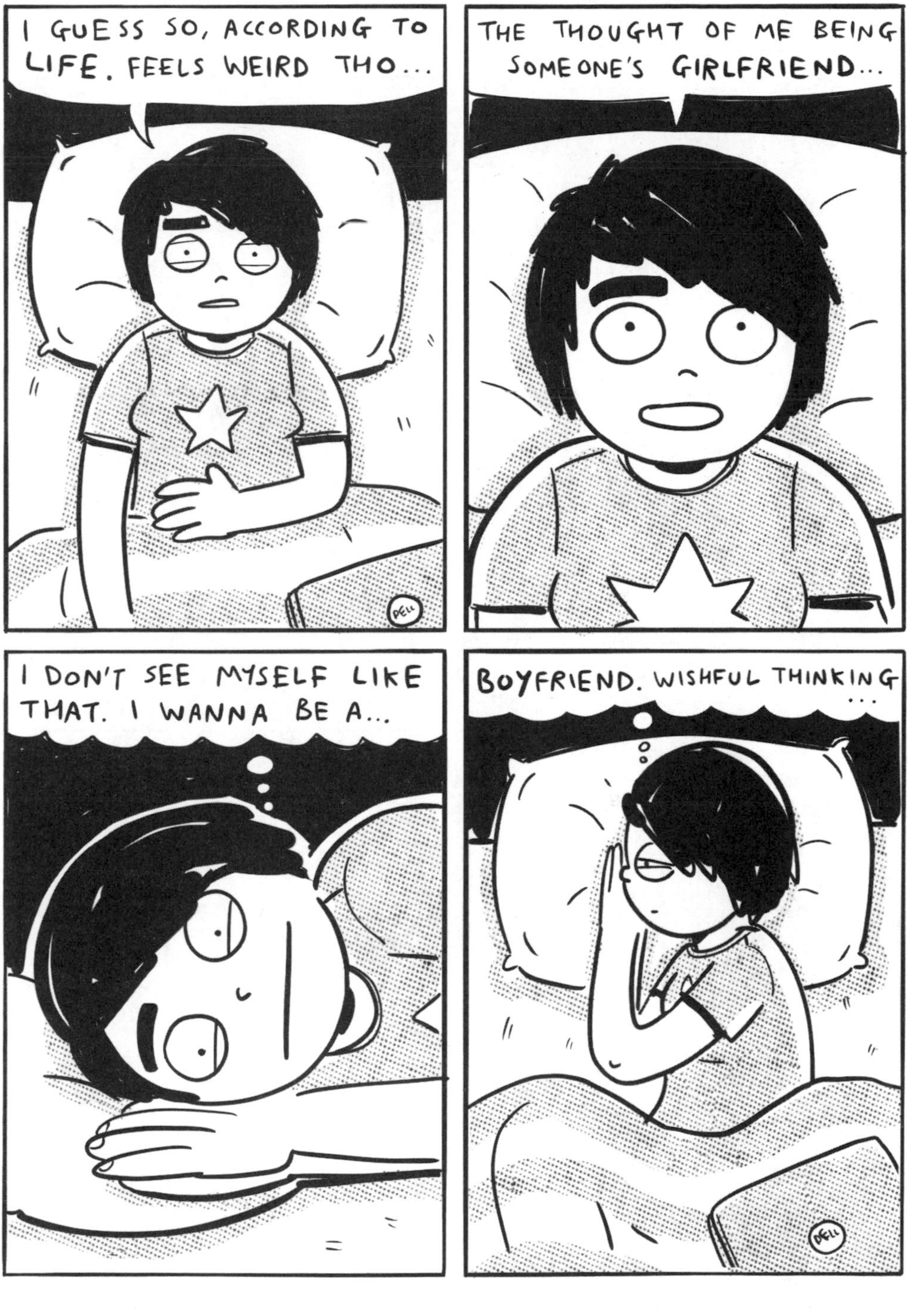

I GUESS SO, ACCORDING TO LIFE. FEELS WEIRD THO...
THE THOUGHT OF ME BEING SOMEONE'S GIRLFRIEND...
I DON'T SEE MYSELF LIKE THAT. I WANNA BE A...
BOYFRIEND. WISHFUL THINKING...

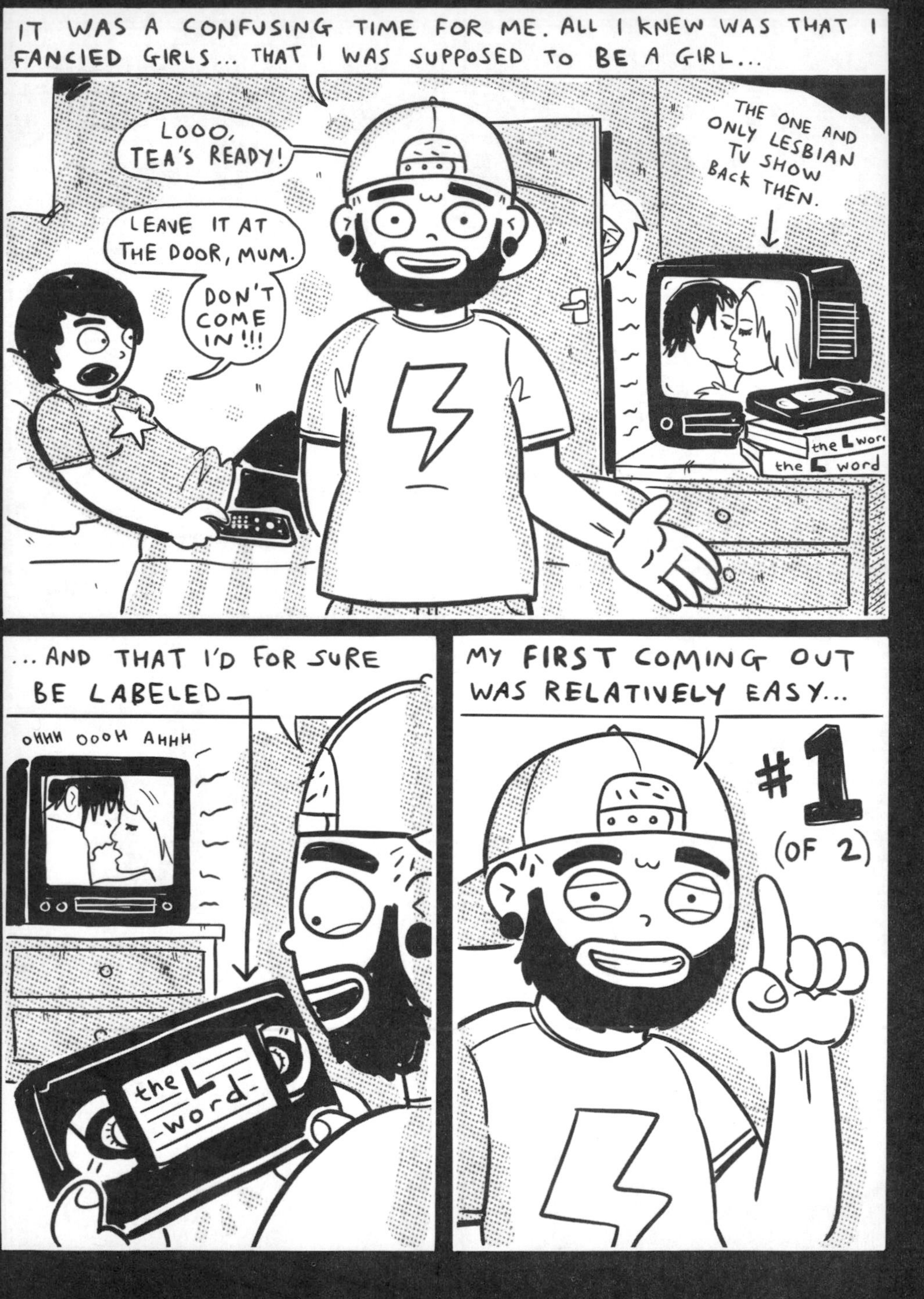
IT WAS A CONFUSING TIME FOR ME. ALL I KNEW WAS THAT I FANCIED GIRLS... THAT I WAS SUPPOSED TO BE A GIRL...
LOOO, TEA'S READY!
LEAVE IT AT THE DOOR, MUM.
DON'T COME IN!!!
THE ONE AND ONLY LESBIAN TV SHOW BACK THEN.
the L word
the L word
...AND THAT I'D FOR SURE BE LABELED
OHHH OOOH AHHH
the L word
MY FIRST COMING OUT WAS RELATIVELY EASY...
#1
(OF 2)

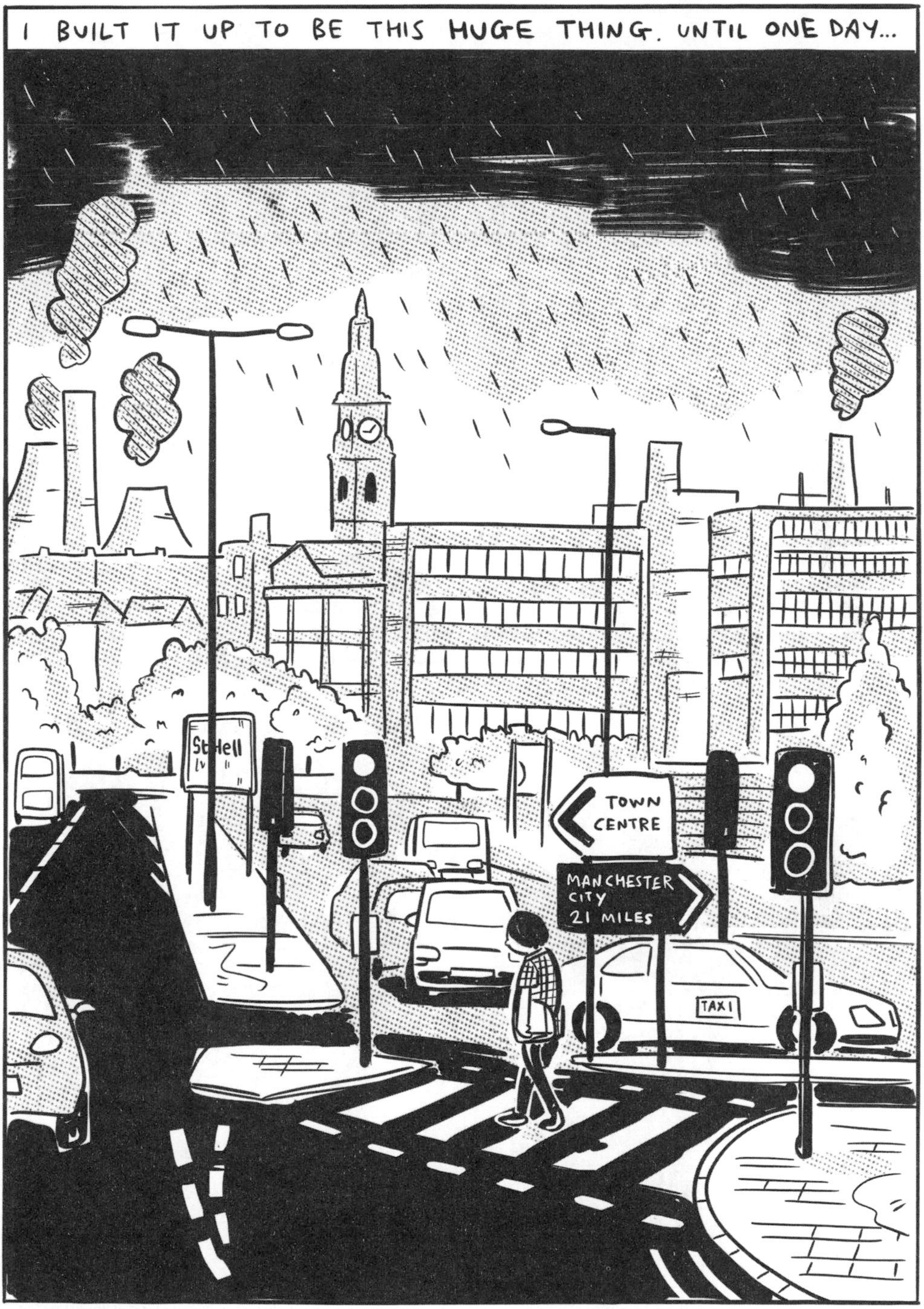
I BUILT IT UP TO BE THIS HUGE THING. UNTIL ONE DAY...
St Hell
TOWN CENTRE
MANCHESTER CITY 21 MILES
TAXI

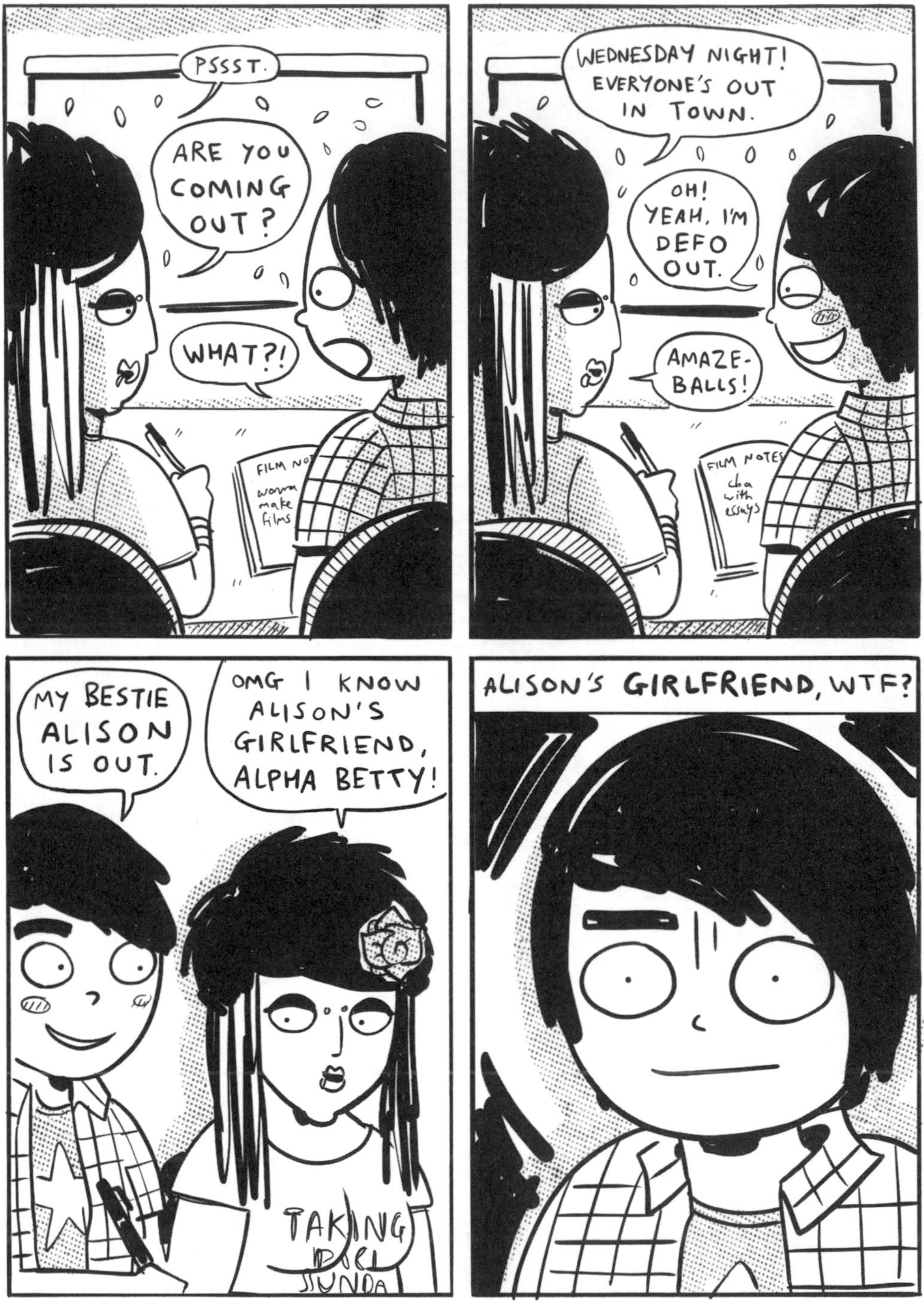
PSSST.
ARE YOU COMING OUT?
WHAT?!
wanna make films
WEDNESDAY NIGHT! EVERYONE'S OUT IN TOWN.
OH! YEAH, I'M DEFO OUT.
AMAZE-BALLS!
FILM NOTES
cba with essays
MY BESTIE ALISON IS OUT.
OMG I KNOW ALISON'S GIRLFRIEND, ALPHA BETTY!
ALISON'S GIRLFRIEND, WTF?

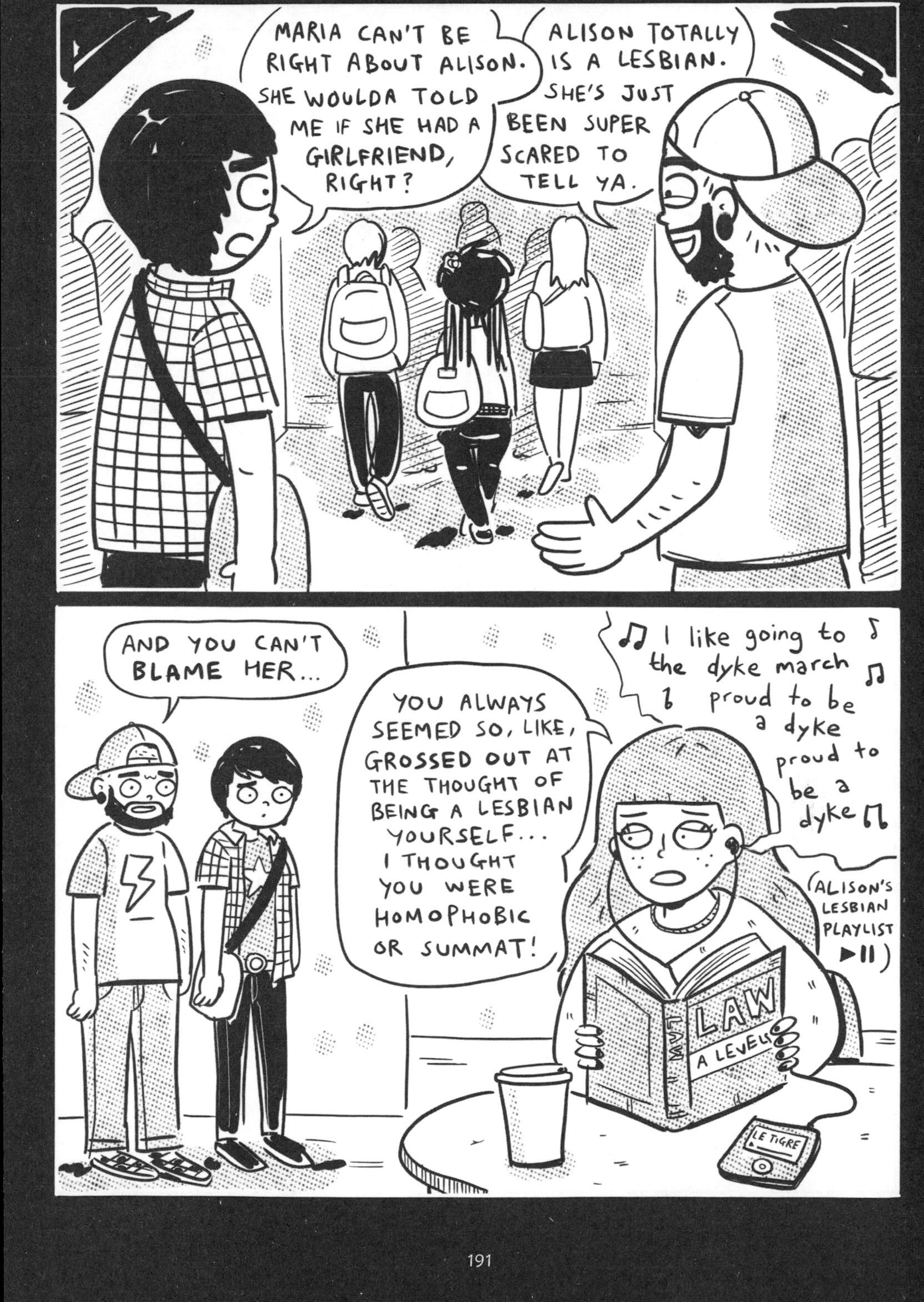

MARIA CAN'T BE RIGHT ABOUT ALISON. SHE WOULDA TOLD ME IF SHE HAD A GIRLFRIEND, RIGHT?
ALISON TOTALLY IS A LESBIAN. SHE'S JUST BEEN SUPER SCARED TO TELL YA.
AND YOU CAN'T BLAME HER...
YOU ALWAYS SEEMED SO, LIKE, GROSSED OUT AT THE THOUGHT OF BEING A LESBIAN YOURSELF... I THOUGHT YOU WERE HOMOPHOBIC OR SUMMAT!
I like going to the dyke march proud to be a dyke proud to be a dyke
(ALISON'S LESBIAN PLAYLIST ▶II)
LAW
LAW A LEVEL
LE TIGRE

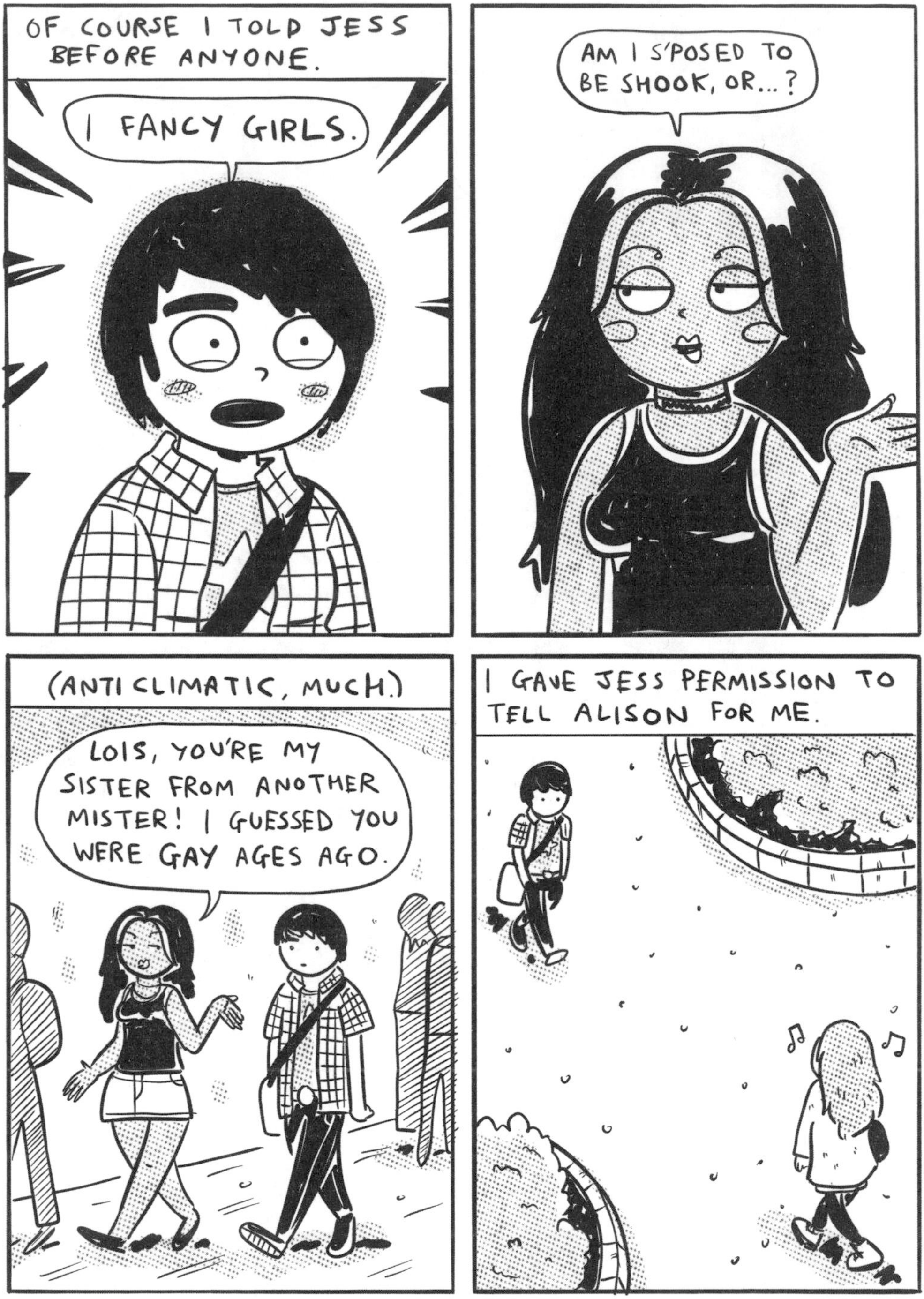
OF COURSE I TOLD JESS BEFORE ANYONE.
I FANCY GIRLS.
AM I S'POSED TO BE SHOOK, OR...?
(ANTICLIMATIC, MUCH.)
LOIS, YOU'RE MY SISTER FROM ANOTHER MISTER! I GUESSED YOU WERE GAY AGES AGO.
I GAVE JESS PERMISSION TO TELL ALISON FOR ME.

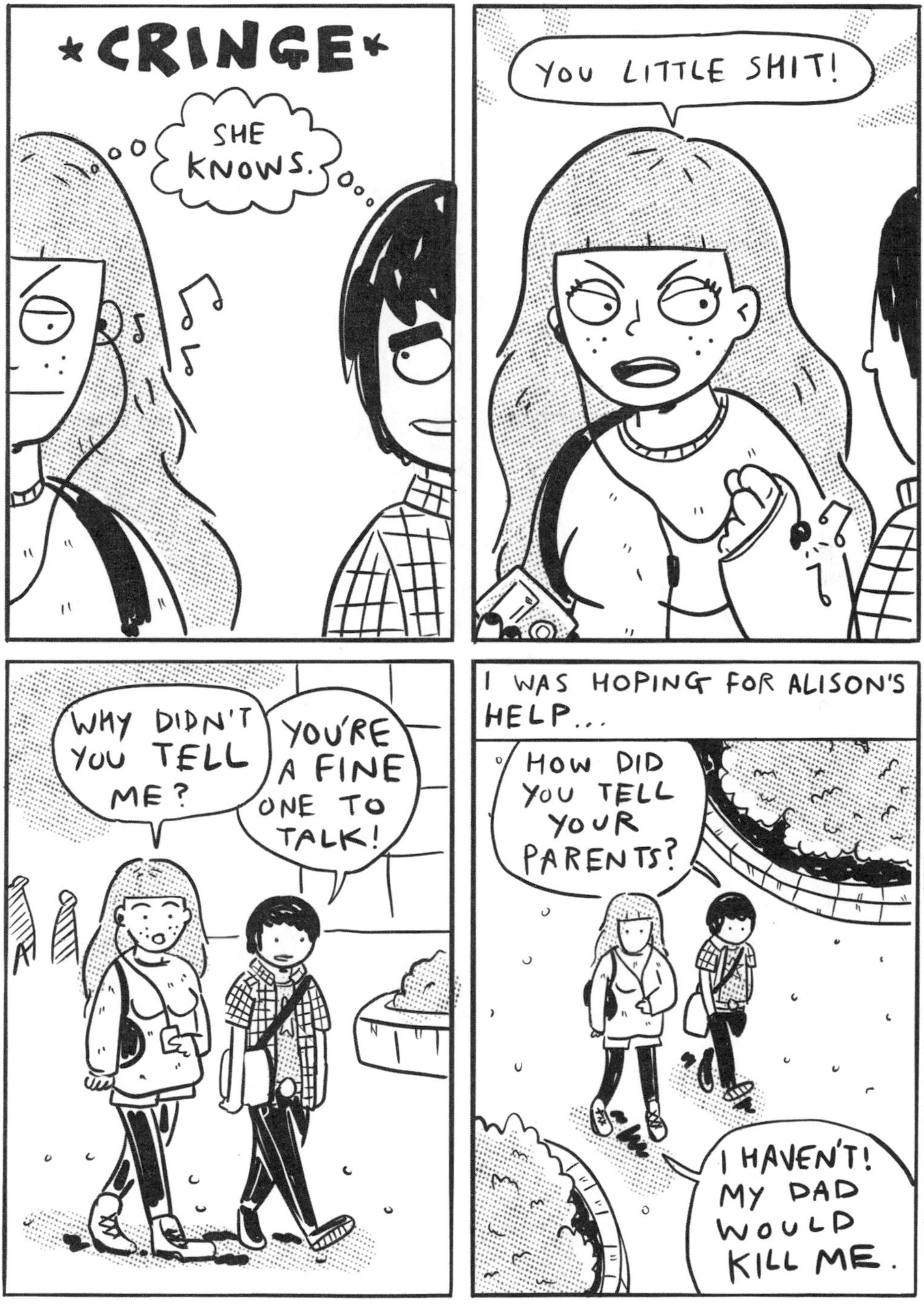
CRINGE
SHE KNOWS.
YOU LITTLE SHIT!
WHY DIDN'T YOU TELL ME?
YOU'RE A FINE ONE TO TALK!
I WAS HOPING FOR ALISON'S HELP...
HOW DID YOU TELL YOUR PARENTS?
I HAVEN'T! MY DAD WOULD KILL ME.

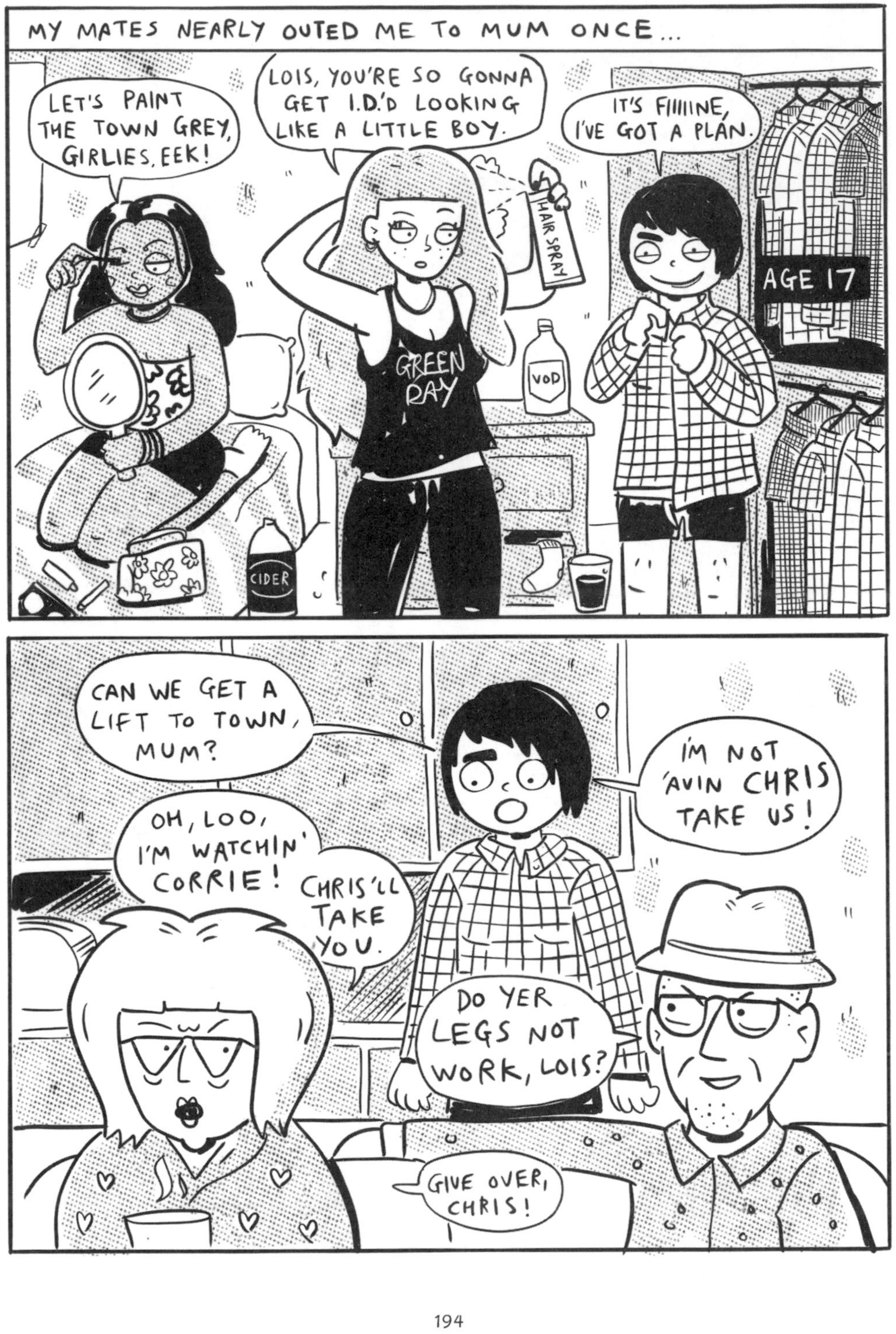
MY MATES NEARLY OUTED ME TO MUM ONCE...
LET'S PAINT THE TOWN GREY, GIRLIES, EEK!
LOIS, YOU'RE SO GONNA GET I.D.'D LOOKING LIKE A LITTLE BOY.
IT'S FIIIIINE, I'VE GOT A PLAN.
HAIR SPRAY
AGE 17
GREEN RAY
VOD
CIDER
CAN WE GET A LIFT TO TOWN, MUM?
I'M NOT 'AVIN CHRIS TAKE US!
OH, LOO, I'M WATCHIN' CORRIE!
CHRIS'LL TAKE YOU.
DO YER LEGS NOT WORK, LOIS?
GIVE OVER, CHRIS!

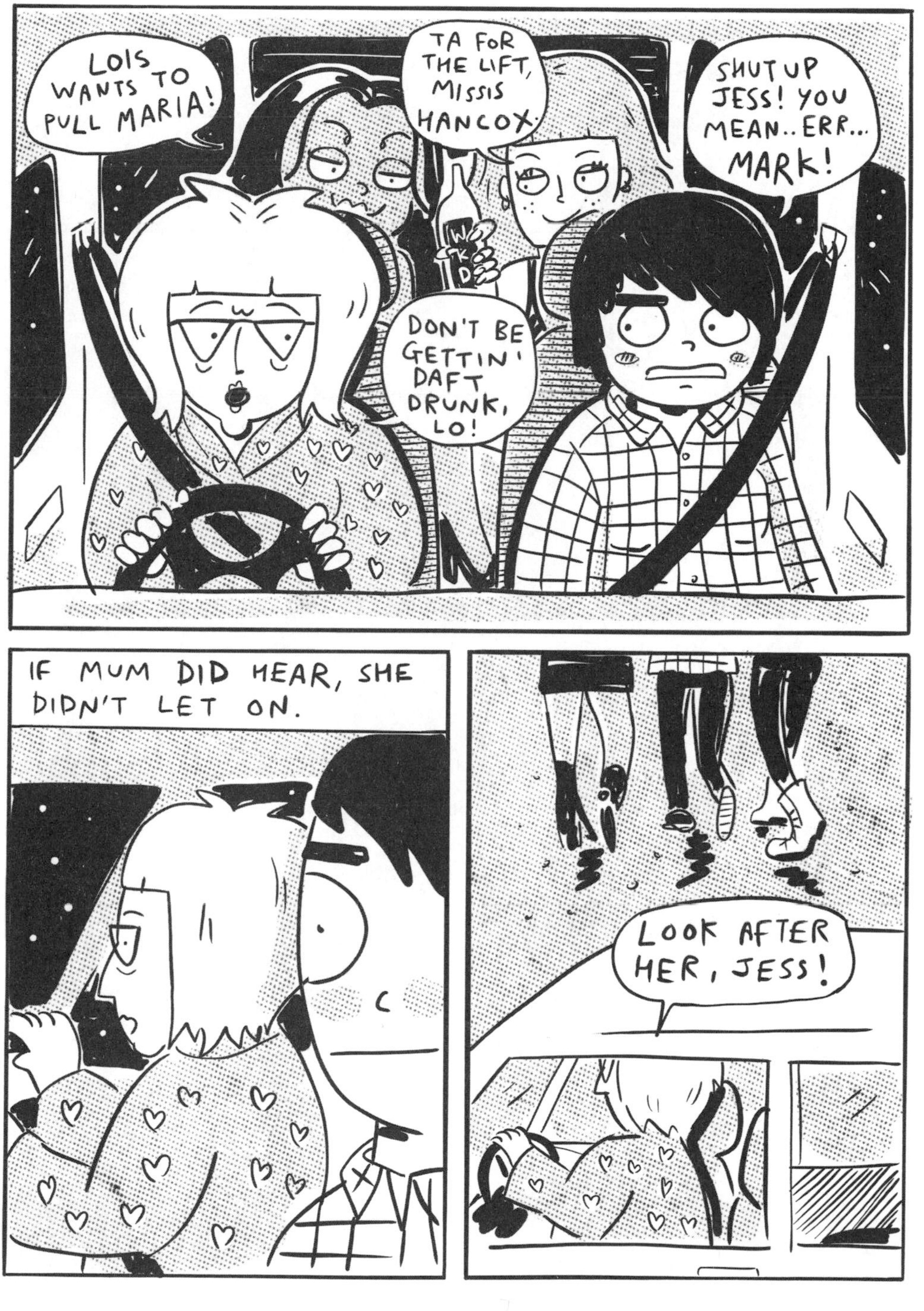
LOIS WANTS TO PULL MARIA!
TA FOR THE LIFT, MISSIS HANCOX.
SHUT UP JESS! YOU MEAN.. ERR... MARK!
W K D
DON'T BE GETTIN' DAFT DRUNK, LO!
IF MUM DID HEAR, SHE DIDN'T LET ON.
LOOK AFTER HER, JESS!

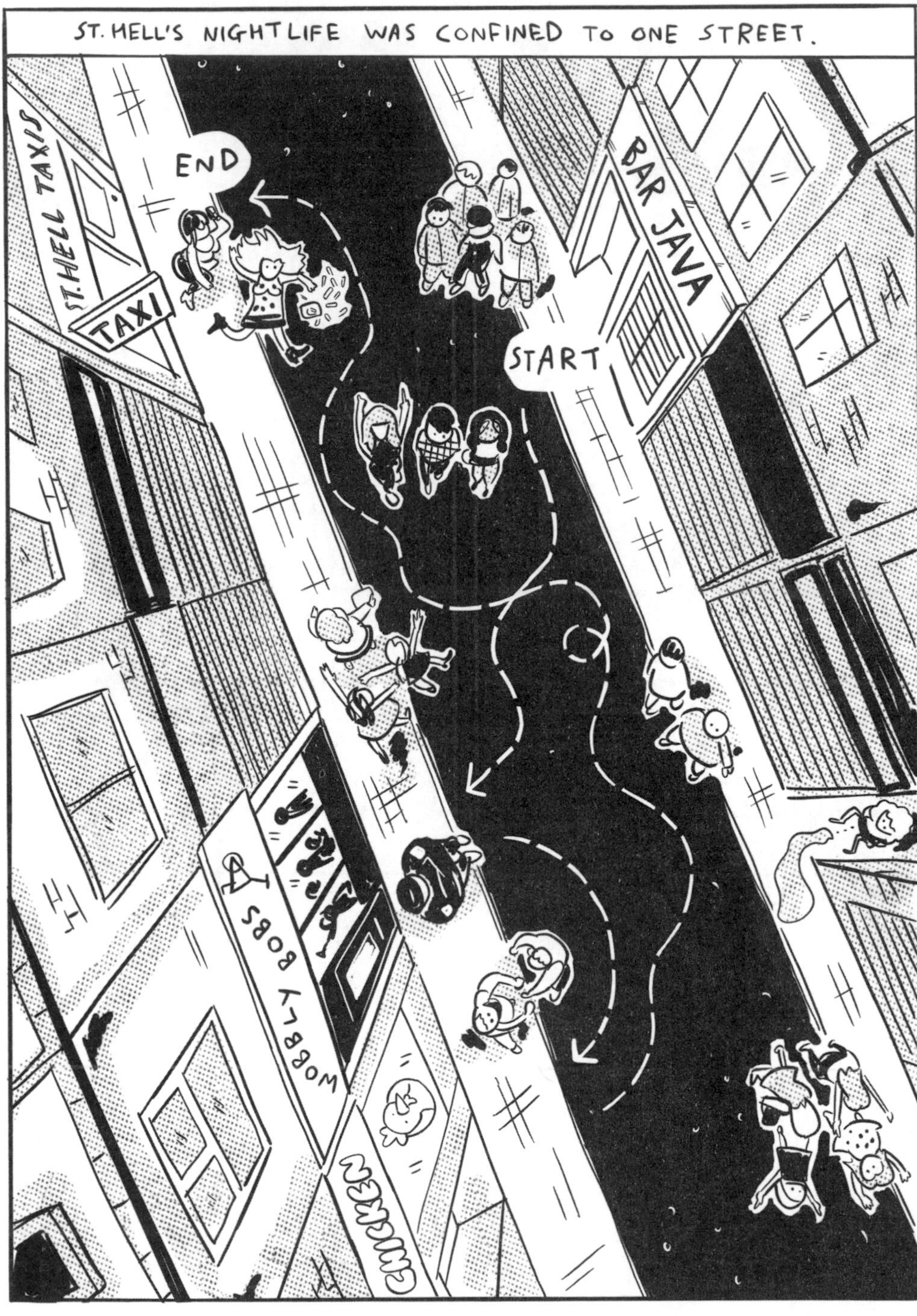
ST. HELL'S NIGHTLIFE WAS CONFINED TO ONE STREET.
ST. HELL TAXIS
TAXI
END
BAR JAVA
START
WOBBLY BOBS
CHICKEN

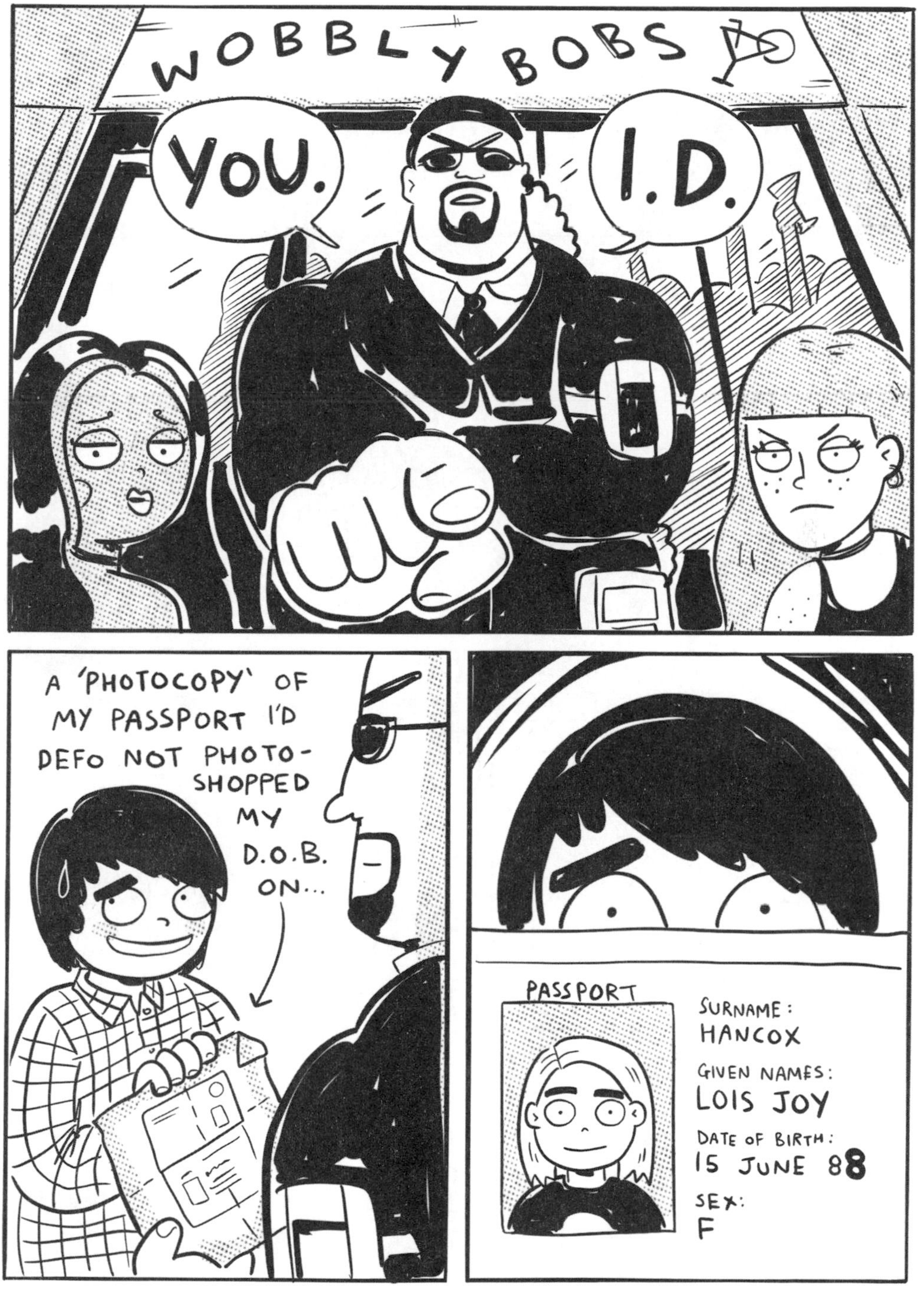
WOBBLY BOBS
YOU.
I.D.
A 'PHOTOCOPY' OF MY PASSPORT I'D DEFO NOT PHOTO-SHOPPED MY D.O.B. ON...
PASSPORT
SURNAME:
HANCOX
GIVEN NAMES:
LOIS JOY
DATE OF BIRTH:
15 JUNE 88
SEX:
F

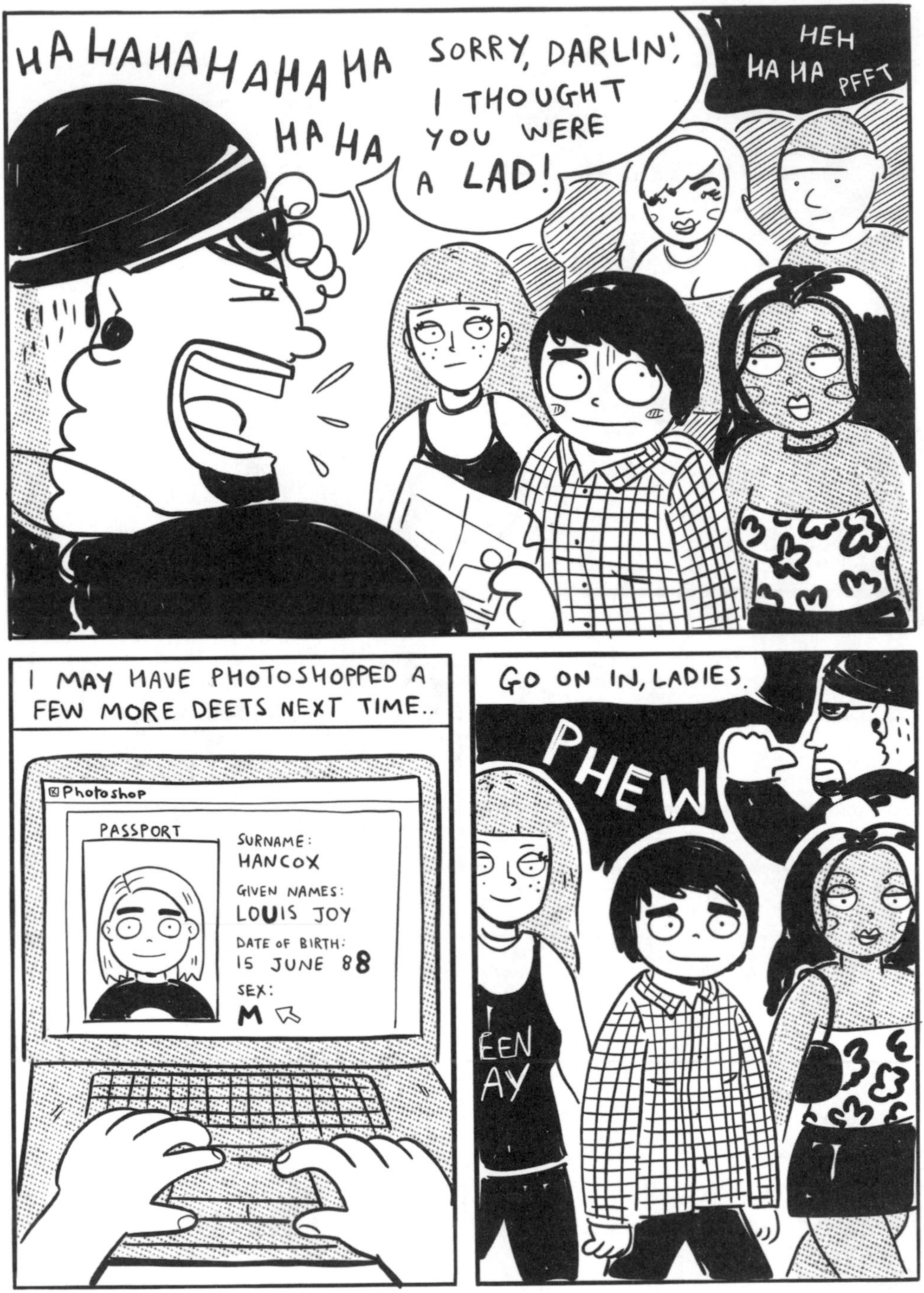

HA HAHAHAHAHA HA
HA HA
SORRY, DARLIN', I THOUGHT YOU WERE A LAD!
HEH HA HA PFFT
I MAY HAVE PHOTOSHOPPED A FEW MORE DEETS NEXT TIME..
Photoshop
PASSPORT
SURNAME: HANCOX
GIVEN NAMES: LOUIS JOY
DATE OF BIRTH: 15 JUNE 88
SEX: M
GO ON IN, LADIES.
PHEW

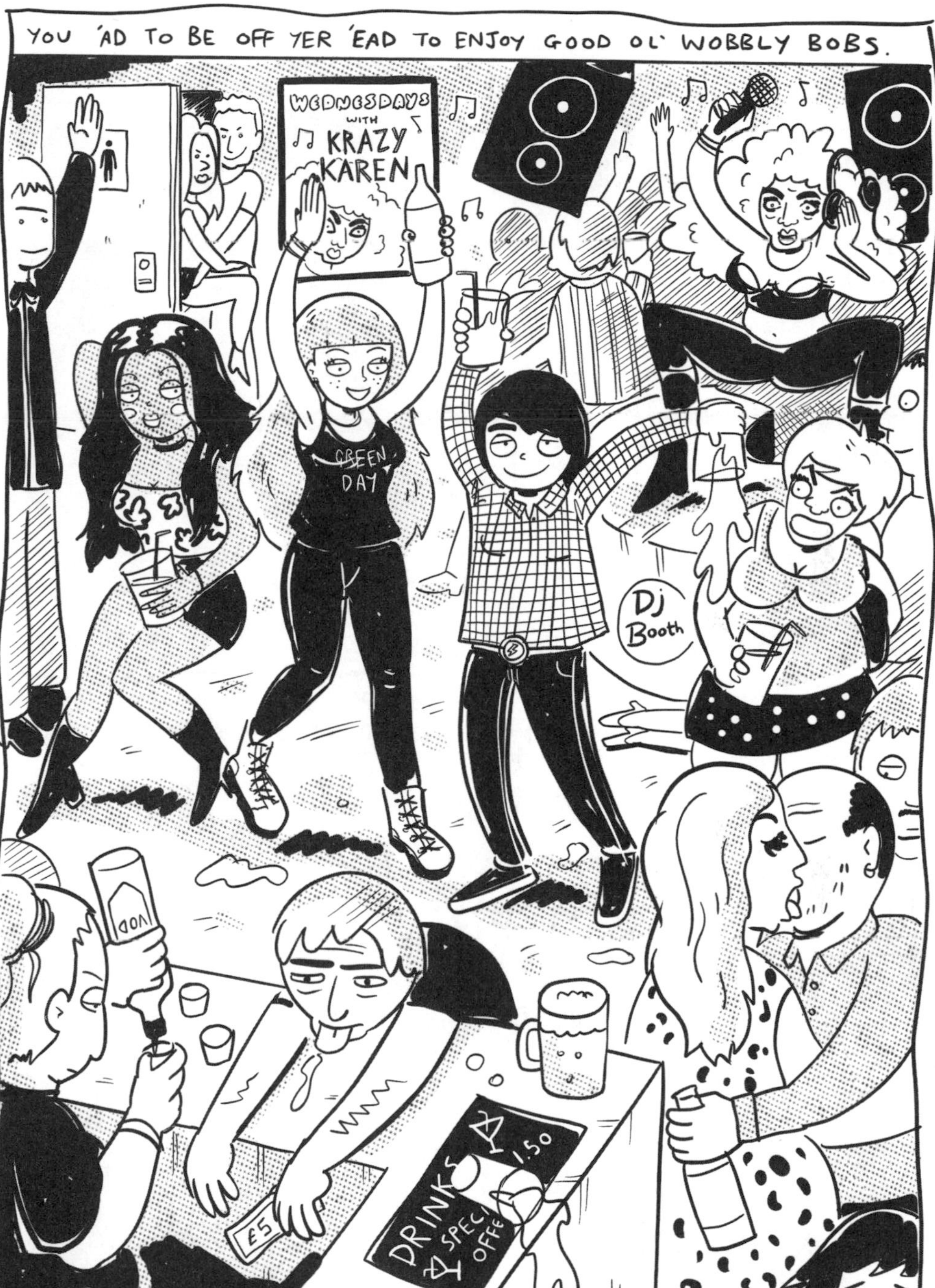
YOU 'AD TO BE OFF YER 'EAD TO ENJOY GOOD OL' WOBBLY BOBS.
WEDNESDAYS WITH KRAZY KAREN
GREEN DAY
DJ Booth
VOD
£5
DRINKS SPECI OFFE 1.50

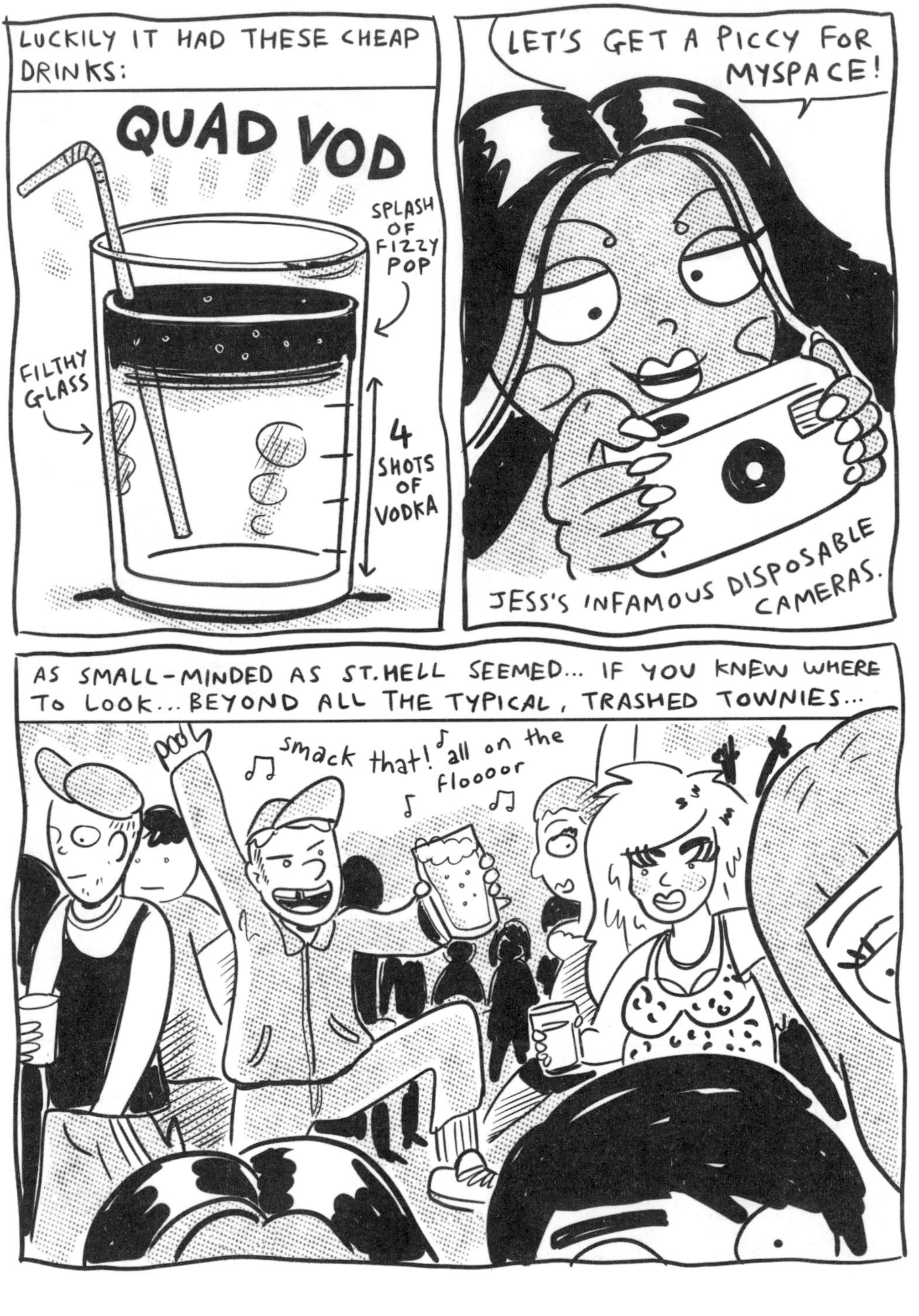
LUCKILY IT HAD THESE CHEAP DRINKS:
QUAD VOD
SPLASH OF FIZZY POP
FILTHY GLASS
4 SHOTS OF VODKA
LET'S GET A PICCY FOR MYSPACE!
JESS'S INFAMOUS DISPOSABLE CAMERAS.
AS SMALL-MINDED AS ST. HELL SEEMED... IF YOU KNEW WHERE TO LOOK... BEYOND ALL THE TYPICAL, TRASHED TOWNIES...
poo!
smack that! all on the floooor

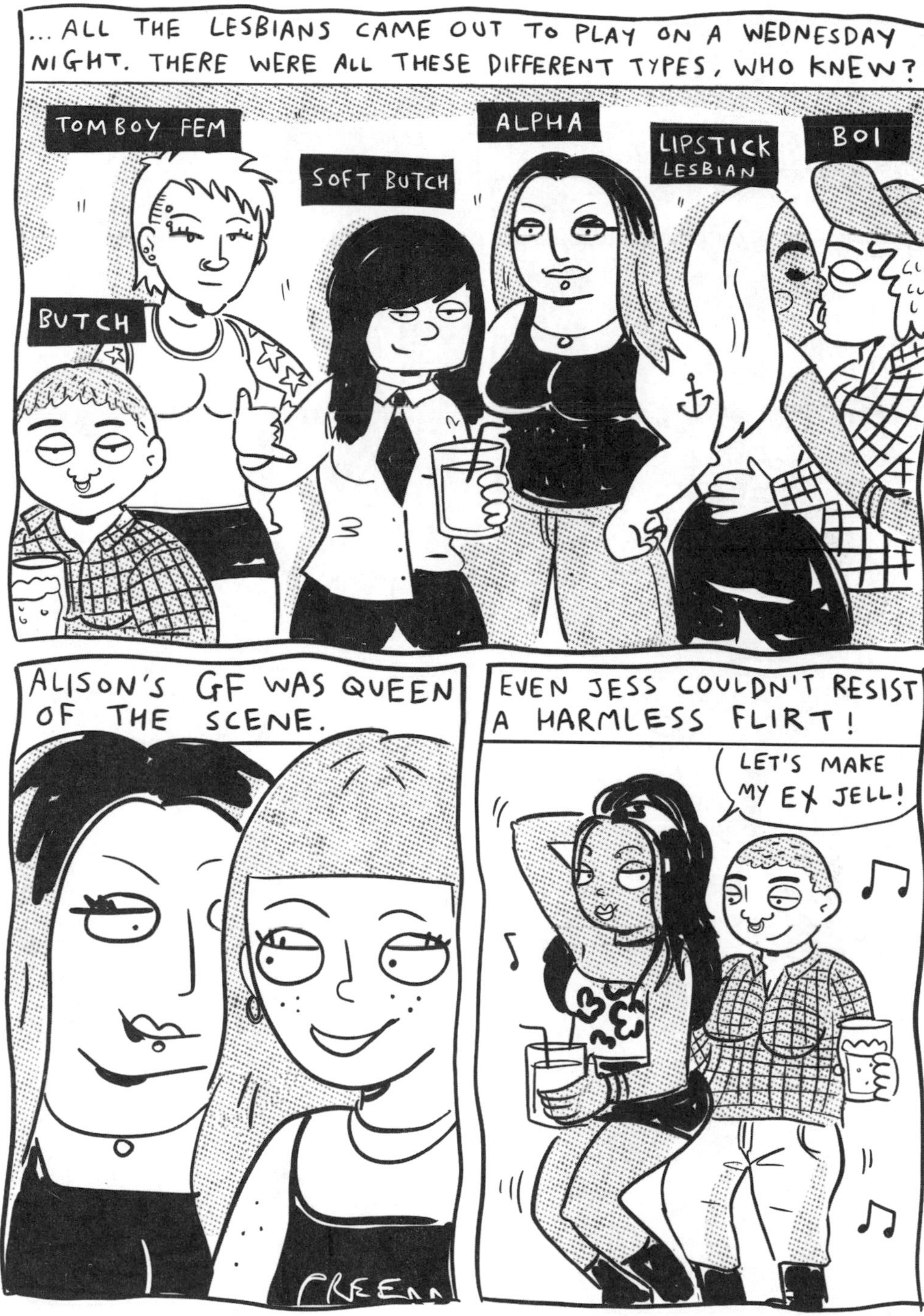
...ALL THE LESBIANS CAME OUT TO PLAY ON A WEDNESDAY NIGHT. THERE WERE ALL THESE DIFFERENT TYPES, WHO KNEW?
TOMBOY FEM
ALPHA
LIPSTICK LESBIAN
BOI
SOFT BUTCH
BUTCH
ALISON'S GF WAS QUEEN OF THE SCENE.
EVEN JESS COULDN'T RESIST A HARMLESS FLIRT!
LET'S MAKE MY EX JELL!

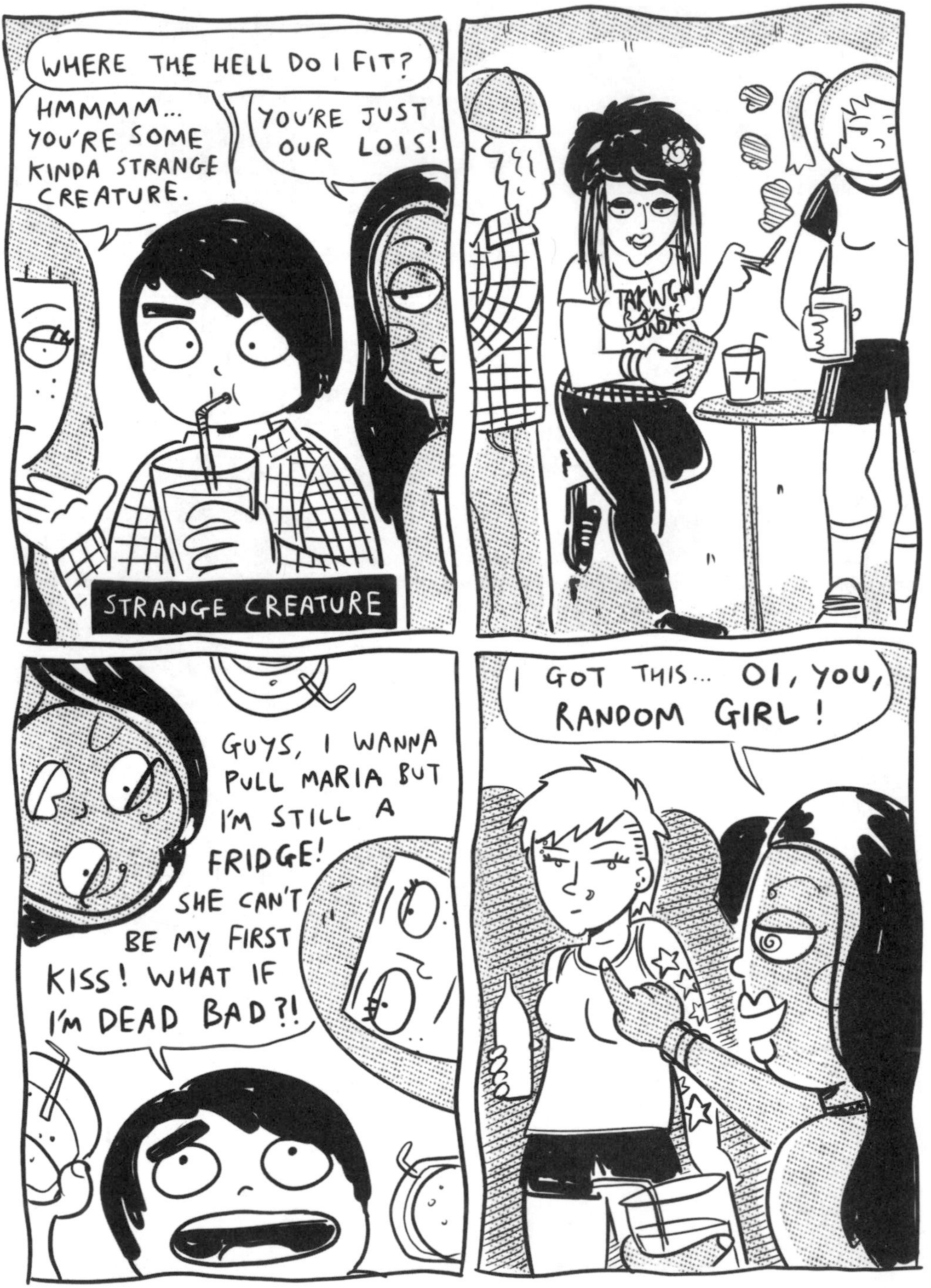
WHERE THE HELL DO I FIT?
HMMMM... YOU'RE SOME KINDA STRANGE CREATURE.
YOU'RE JUST OUR LOIS!
STRANGE CREATURE
GUYS, I WANNA PULL MARIA BUT I'M STILL A FRIDGE! SHE CAN'T BE MY FIRST KISS! WHAT IF I'M DEAD BAD?!
I GOT THIS... OI, YOU, RANDOM GIRL!

THE VALOROUS VIXEN USED HER PERSUASIVE POWERS.
KISS 'ERRRR!
SNOG
WAS THAT OKAY??
IT WAS GREAT.
GREAT. NOW I CAN GO KISS MARIA!

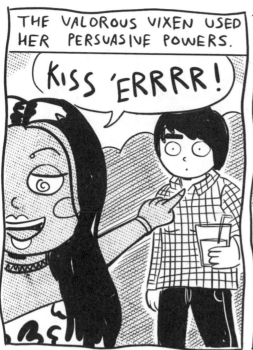

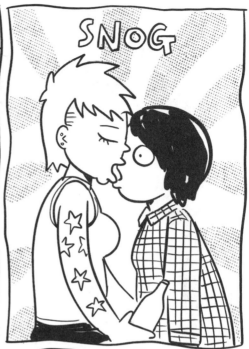

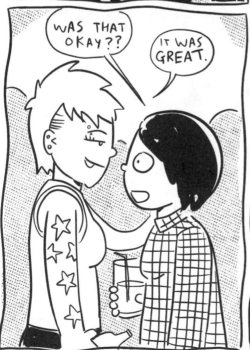

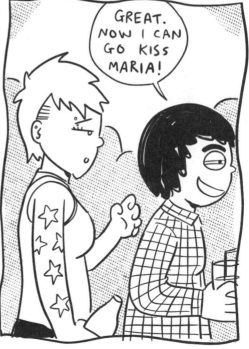

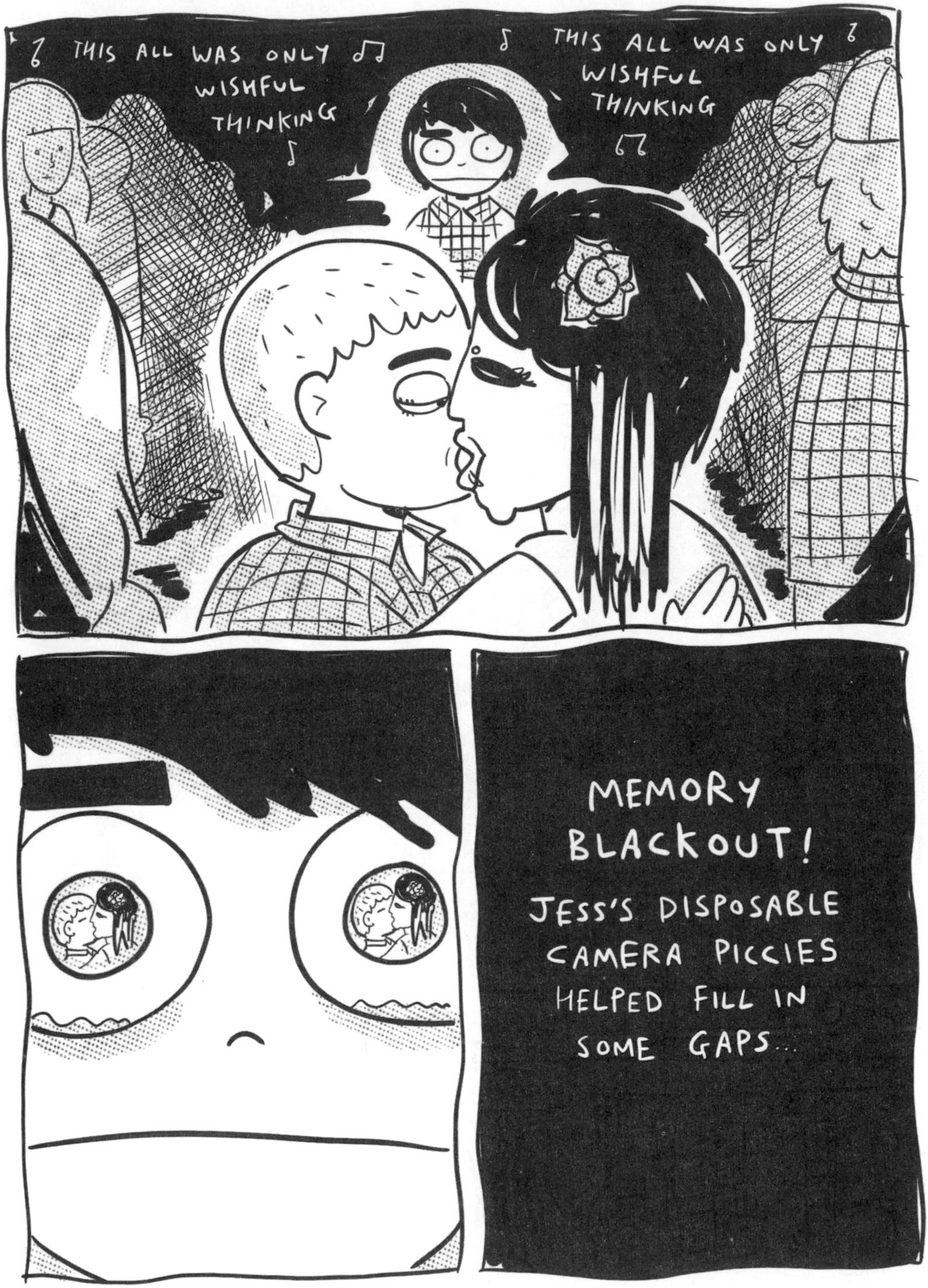
THIS ALL WAS ONLY WISHFUL THINKING
THIS ALL WAS ONLY WISHFUL THINKING
MEMORY BLACKOUT!
JESS'S DISPOSABLE CAMERA PICCIES HELPED FILL IN SOME GAPS...

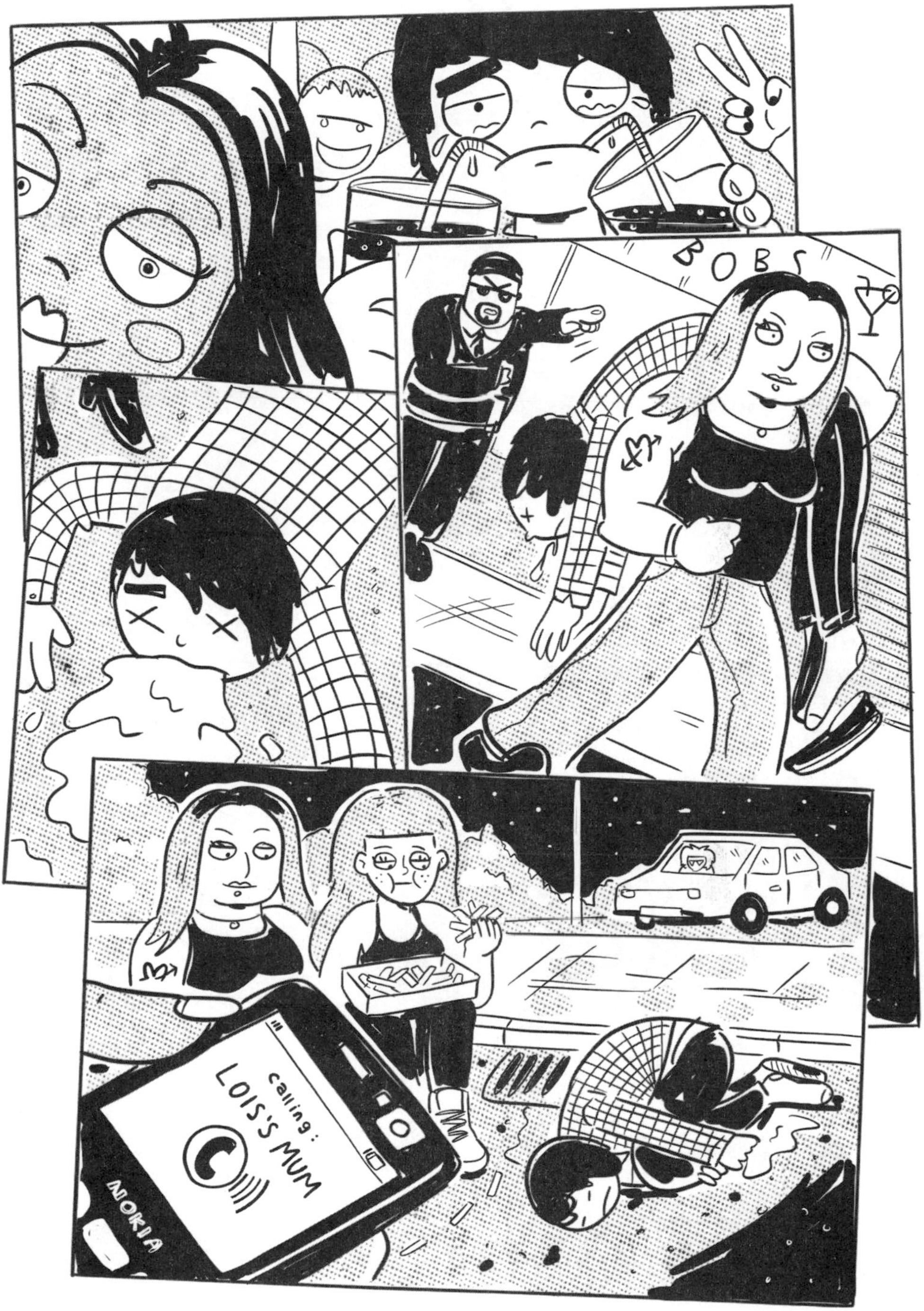
BOBS
calling:
LOIS'S MUM
NOKIA

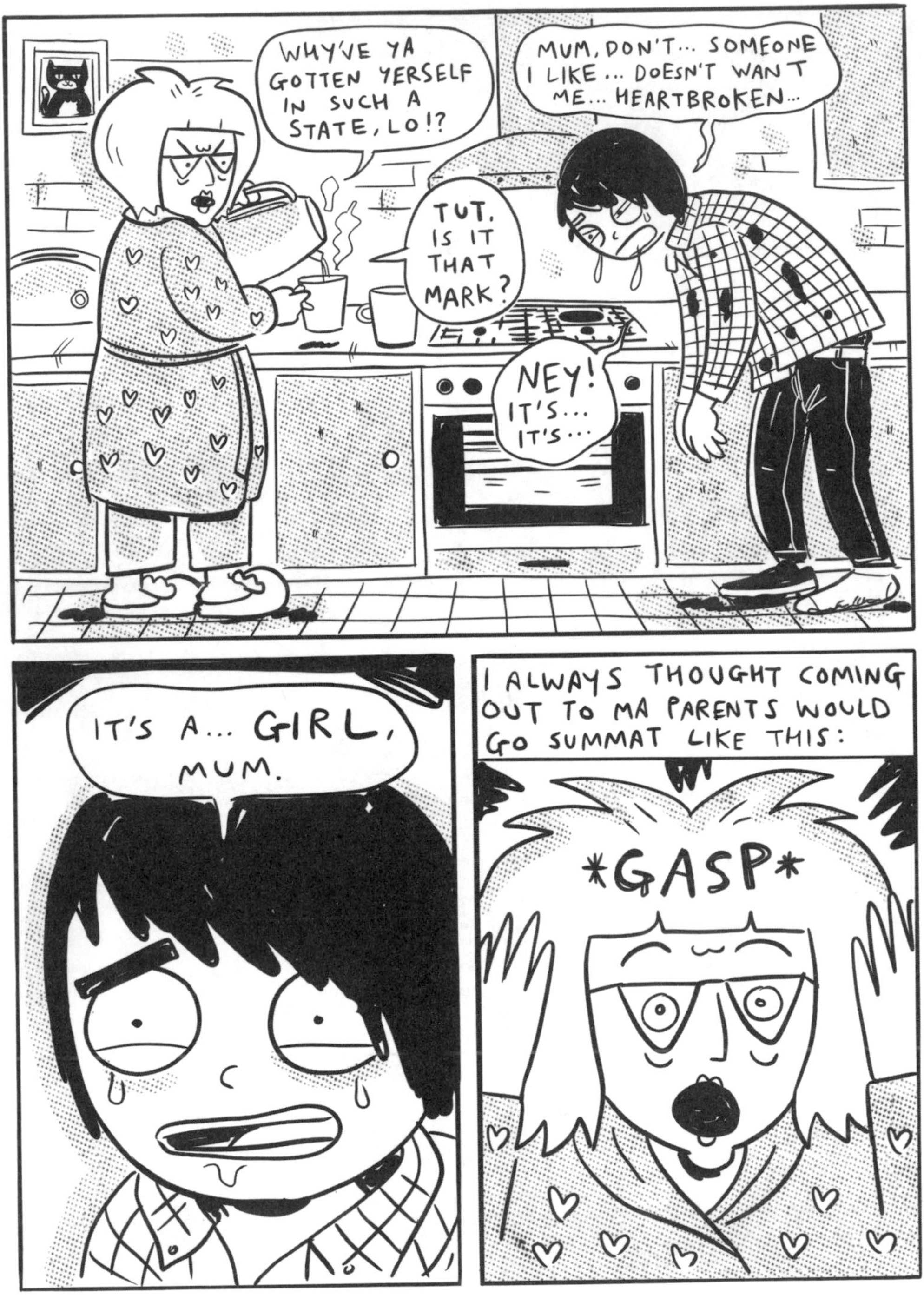
WHY'VE YA GOTTEN YERSELF IN SUCH A STATE, LO!?
MUM, DON'T... SOMEONE I LIKE... DOESN'T WAN T ME... HEARTBROKEN...
TUT. IS IT THAT MARK?
NEY! IT'S... IT'S...
IT'S A... GIRL, MUM.
I ALWAYS THOUGHT COMING OUT TO MA PARENTS WOULD GO SUMMAT LIKE THIS:
GASP

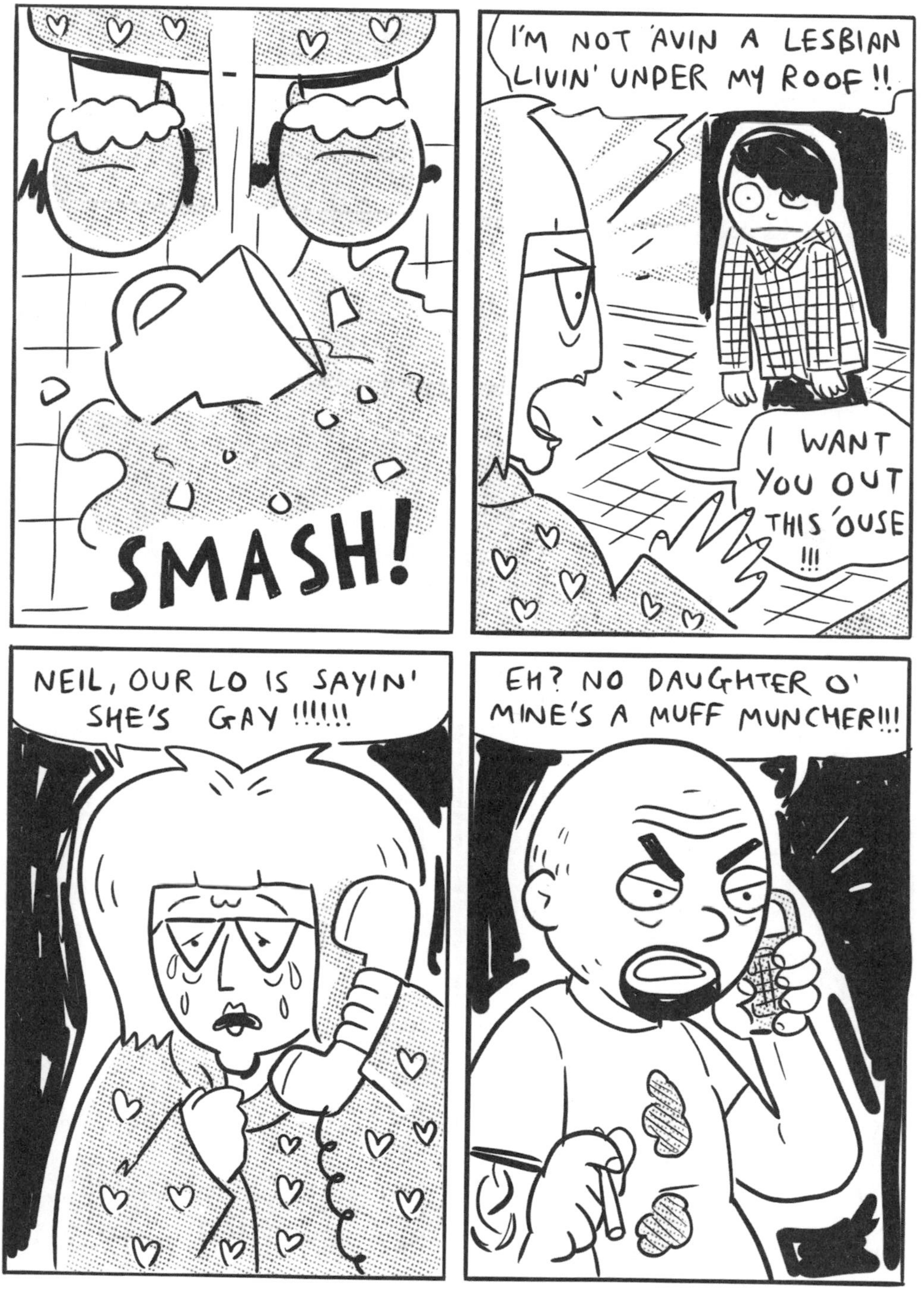
SMASH!
I'M NOT 'AVIN A LESBIAN LIVIN' UNDER MY ROOF!!
I WANT YOU OUT THIS 'OUSE !!!
NEIL, OUR LO IS SAYIN' SHE'S GAY !!!!!!
EH? NO DAUGHTER O' MINE'S A MUFF MUNCHER!!!

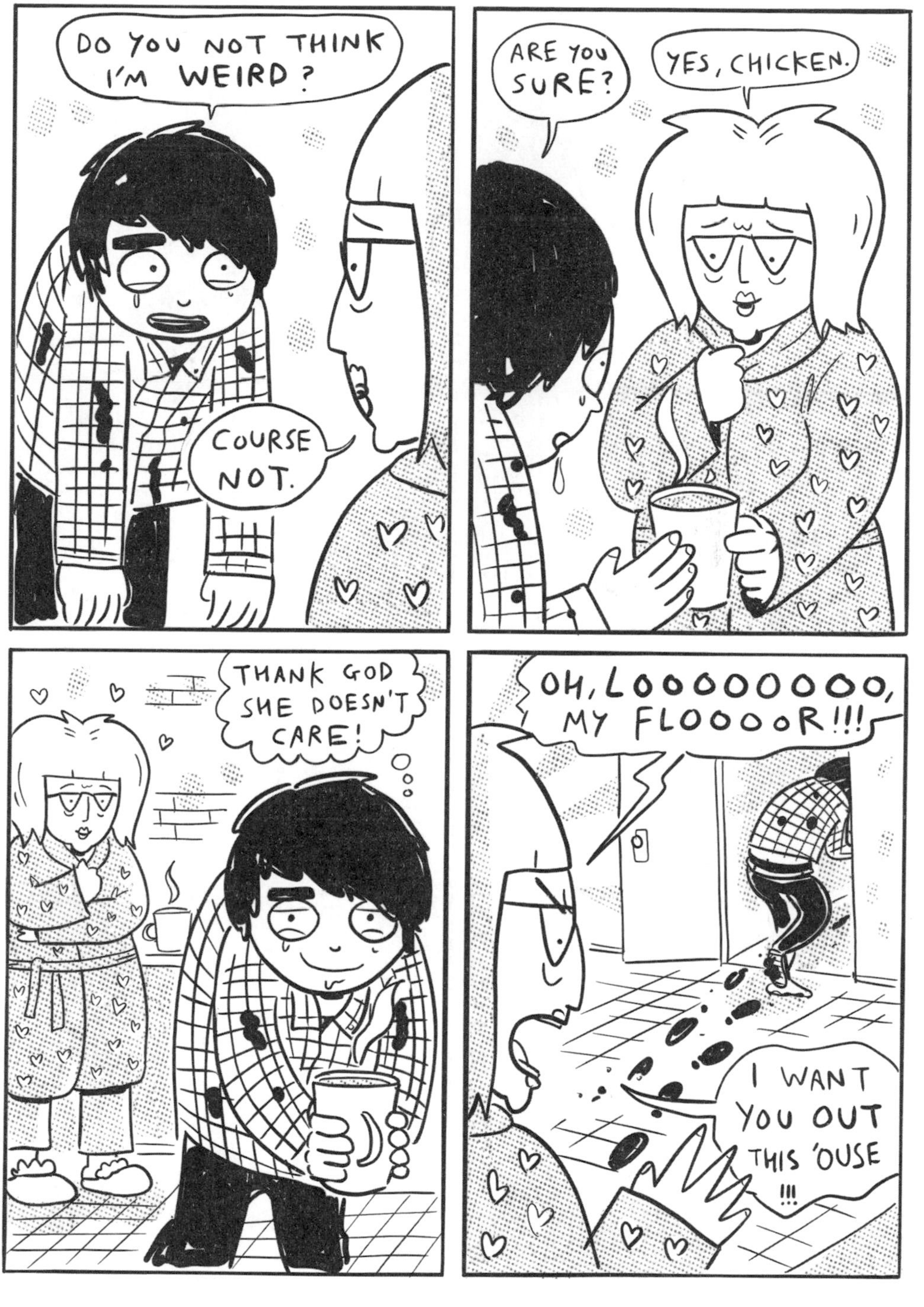
DO YOU NOT THINK I'M WEIRD?
COURSE NOT.
ARE YOU SURE?
YES, CHICKEN.
THANK GOD SHE DOESN'T CARE!
OH, LOOOOOOOO, MY FLOOOOR!!!
I WANT YOU OUT THIS 'OUSE !!!

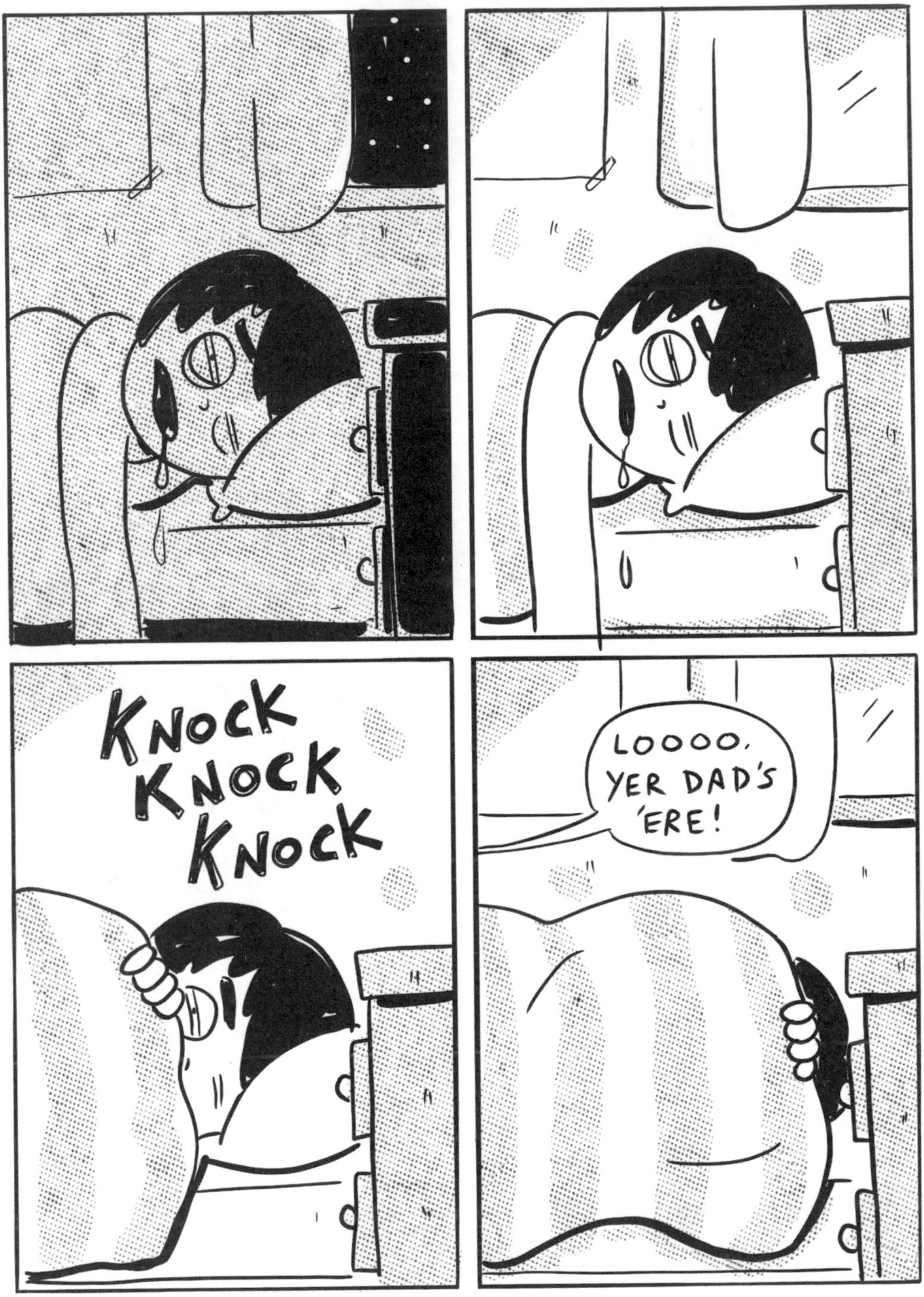
KNOCK
KNOCK
KNOCK
LOOOO, YER DAD'S 'ERE!

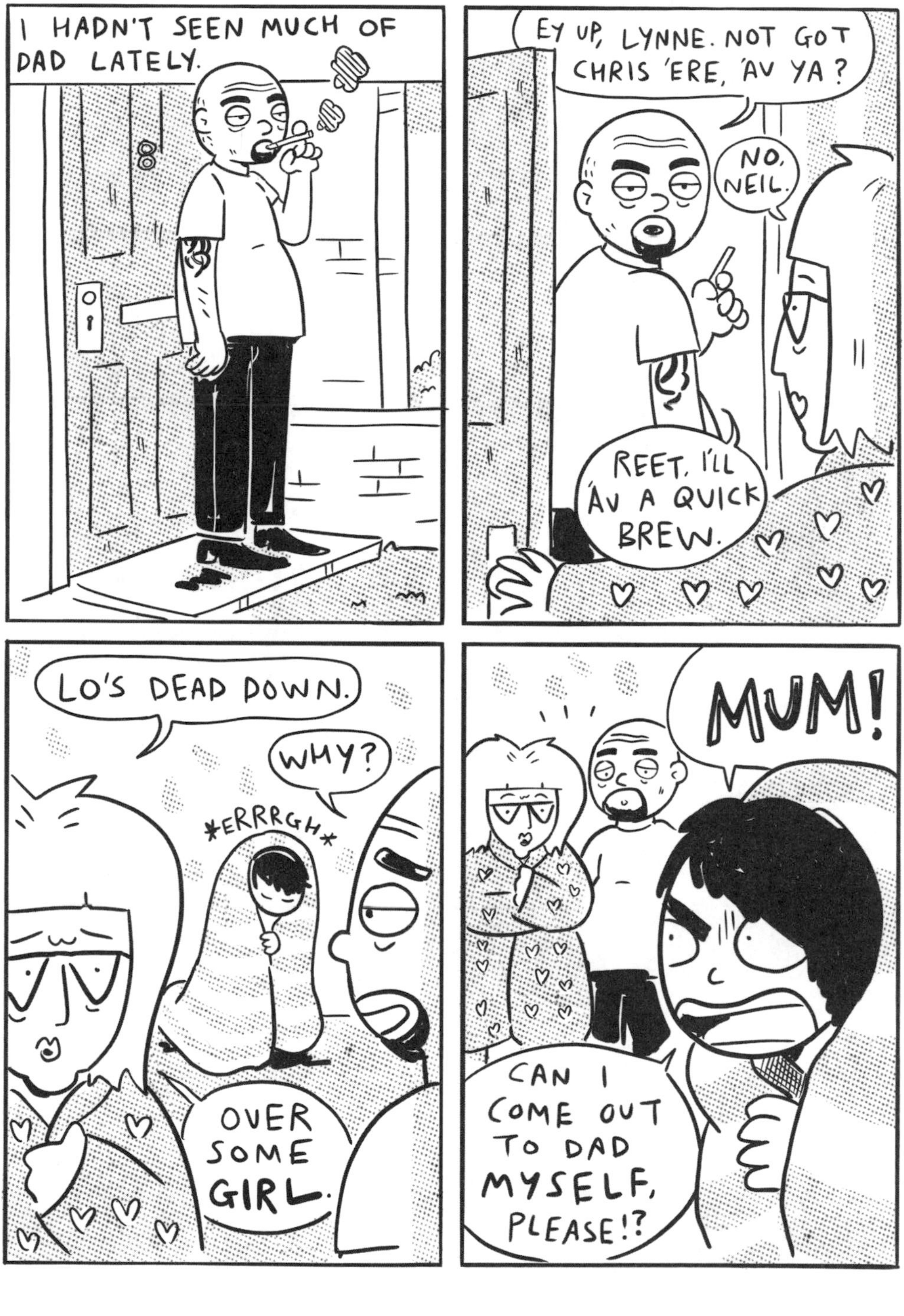

I HADN'T SEEN MUCH OF DAD LATELY.
EY UP, LYNNE. NOT GOT CHRIS 'ERE, 'AV YA?
NO, NEIL.
REET. I'LL 'AV A QUICK BREW.
LO'S DEAD DOWN.
WHY?
ERRRGH
OVER SOME GIRL.
MUM!
CAN I COME OUT TO DAD MYSELF, PLEASE!?

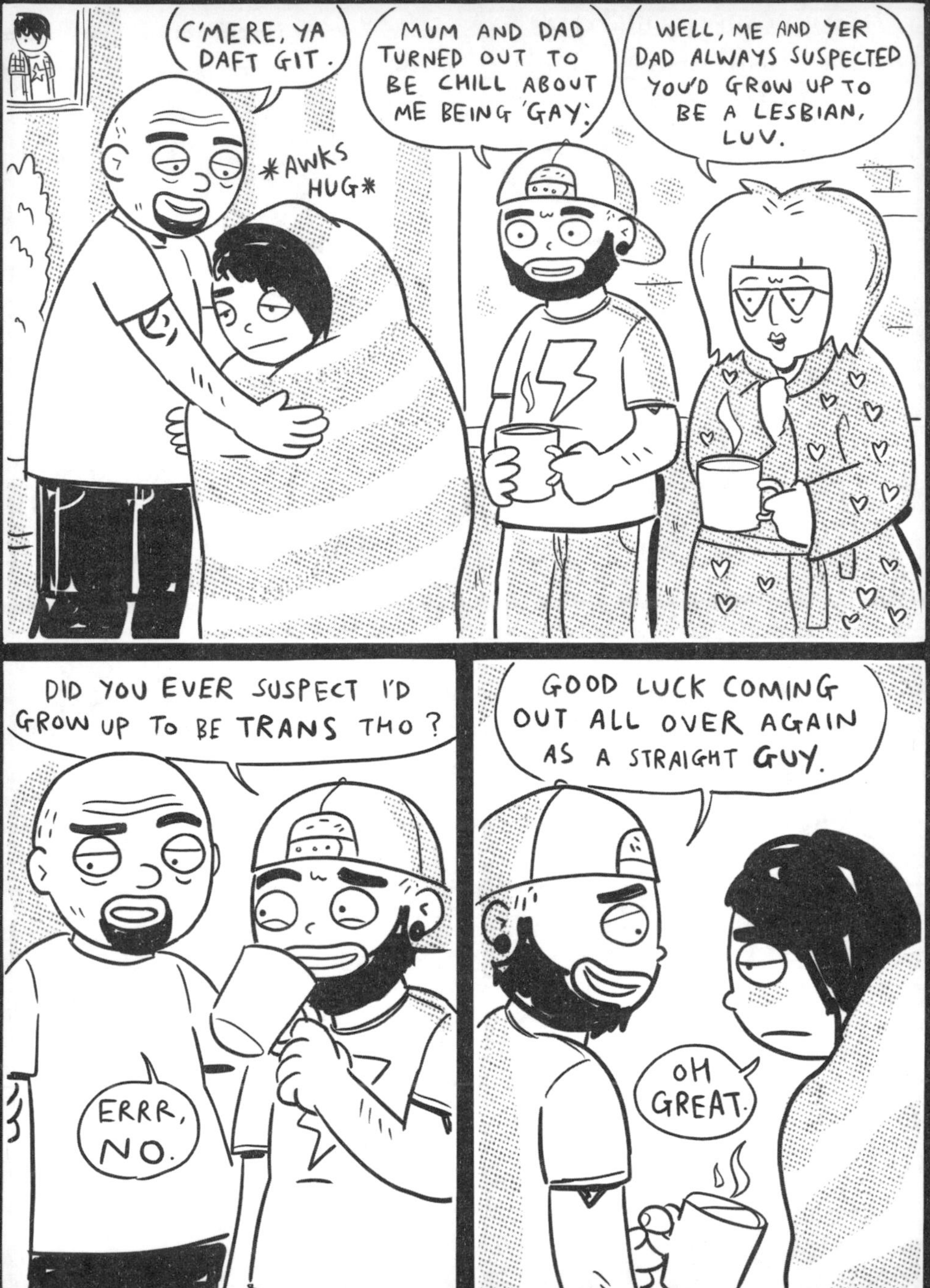
C'MERE, YA DAFT GIT.
AWKS HUG
MUM AND DAD TURNED OUT TO BE CHILL ABOUT ME BEING 'GAY'.
WELL, ME AND YER DAD ALWAYS SUSPECTED YOU'D GROW UP TO BE A LESBIAN, LUV.
DID YOU EVER SUSPECT I'D GROW UP TO BE TRANS THO?
ERRR, NO.
GOOD LUCK COMING OUT ALL OVER AGAIN AS A STRAIGHT GUY.
OH GREAT.

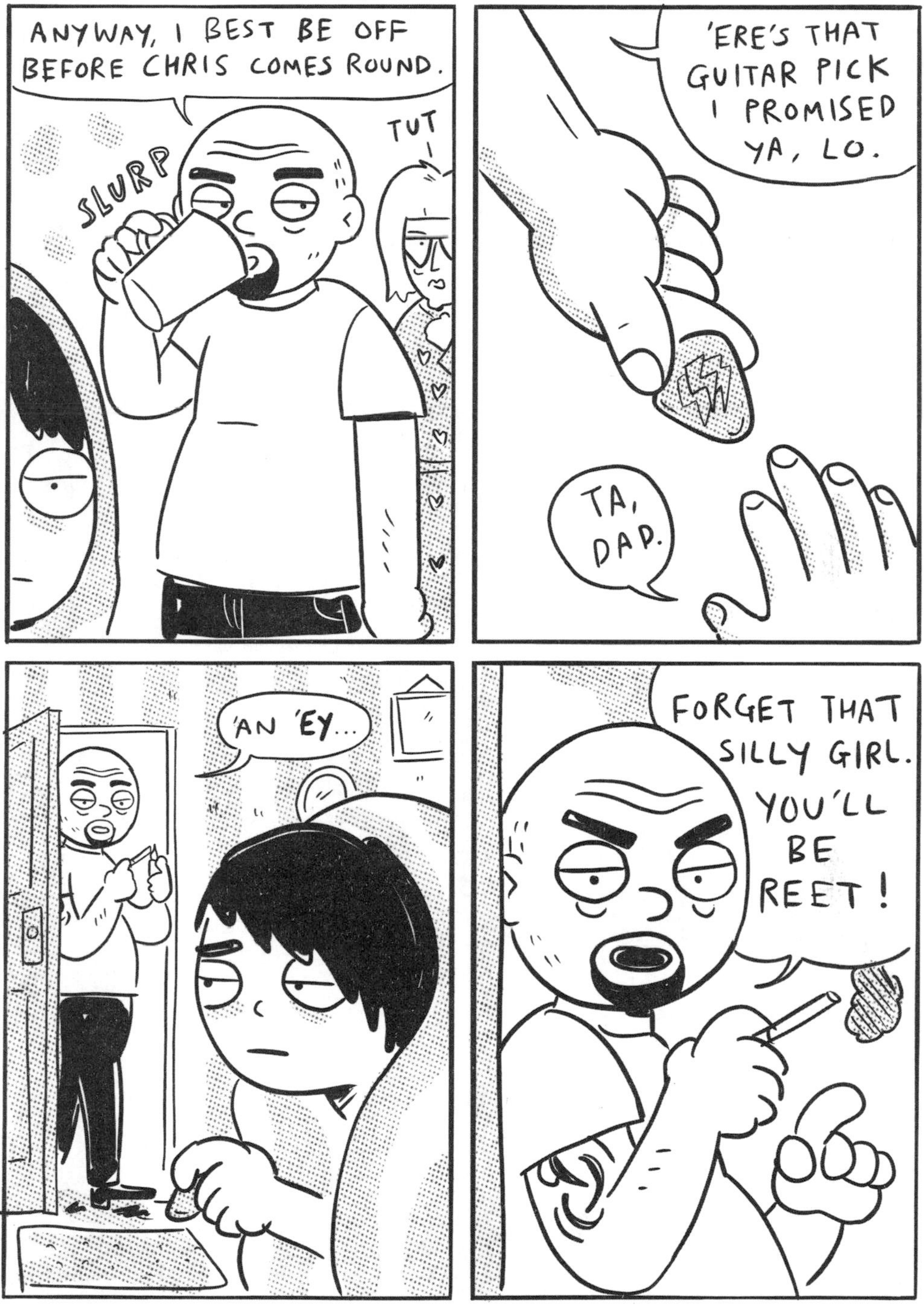
ANYWAY, I BEST BE OFF BEFORE CHRIS COMES ROUND.
SLURP
TUT
'ERE'S THAT GUITAR PICK I PROMISED YA, LO.
TA, DAD.
'AN 'EY...
FORGET THAT SILLY GIRL. YOU'LL BE REET!

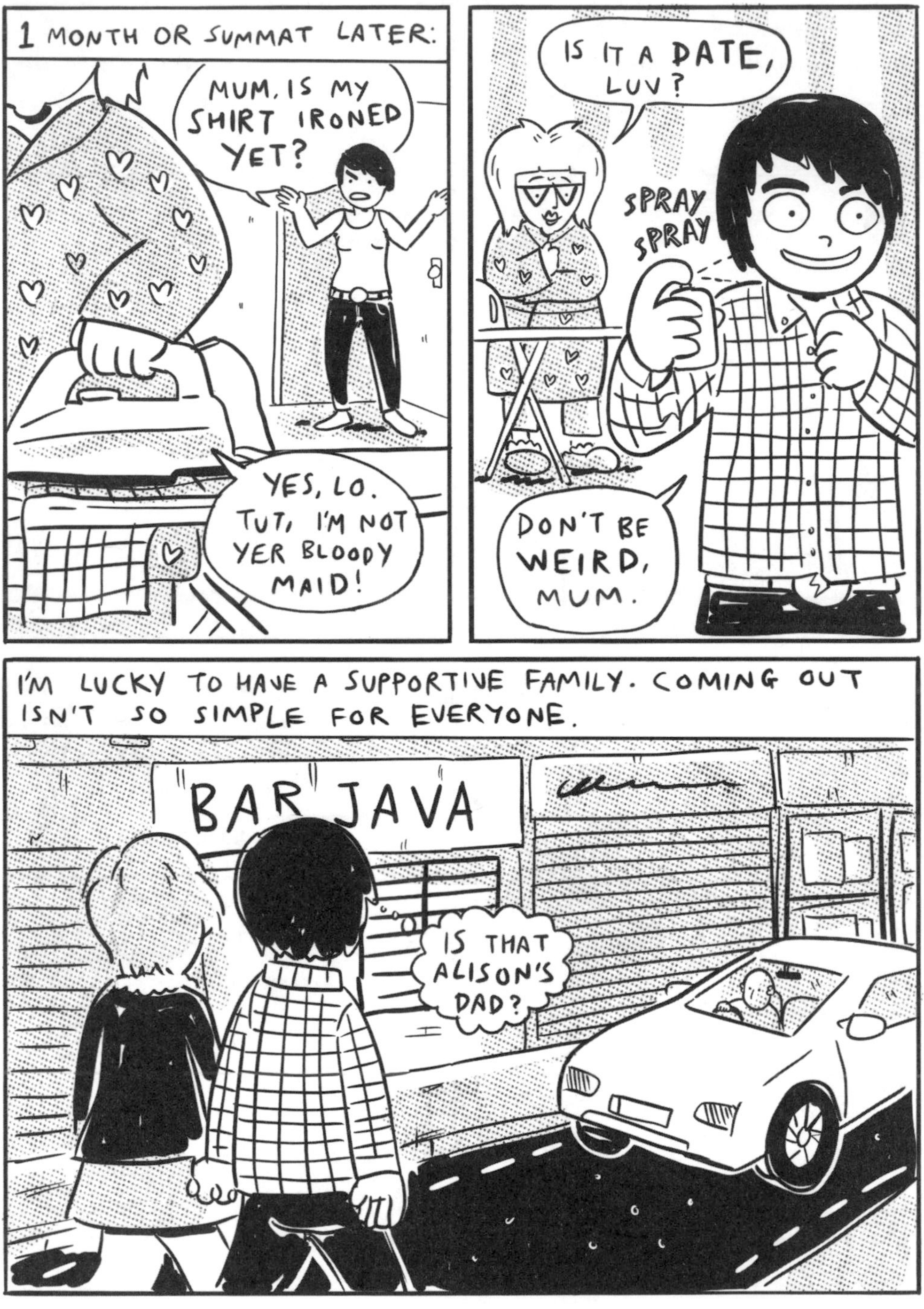
1 MONTH OR SUMMAT LATER:
MUM, IS MY SHIRT IRONED YET?
YES, LO. TUT, I'M NOT YER BLOODY MAID!
IS IT A DATE, LUV?
SPRAY SPRAY
DON'T BE WEIRD, MUM.
I'M LUCKY TO HAVE A SUPPORTIVE FAMILY. COMING OUT ISN'T SO SIMPLE FOR EVERYONE.
BAR JAVA
IS THAT ALISON'S DAD?

ALISON?
FUCKKK, DAD'S HOME.
GREEN DAY
I JUST DROVE PAST LOIS HOLDING A GIRL'S HAND! DID YOU KNOW SHE WAS-
I'M GONNA KILL LOIS.
NO, DAD!
I LIKE TO THINK PEOPLE CAN SUPRISE YOU THO.
HMMM. WELL, IT'S NICE TO SEE HER HAPPY.
G'NIGHT.
NIGHT, DAD.
COUGH
SHUTUP.

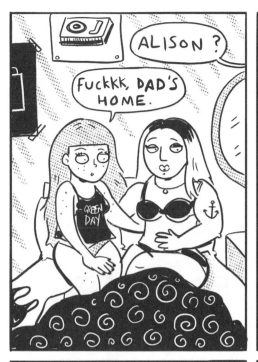

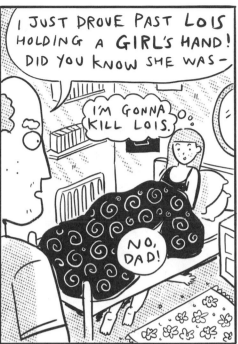

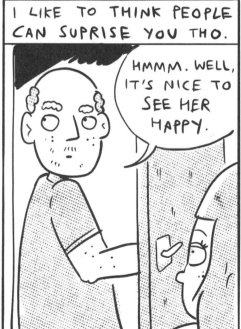

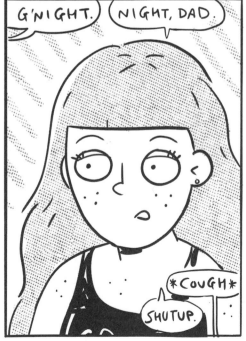

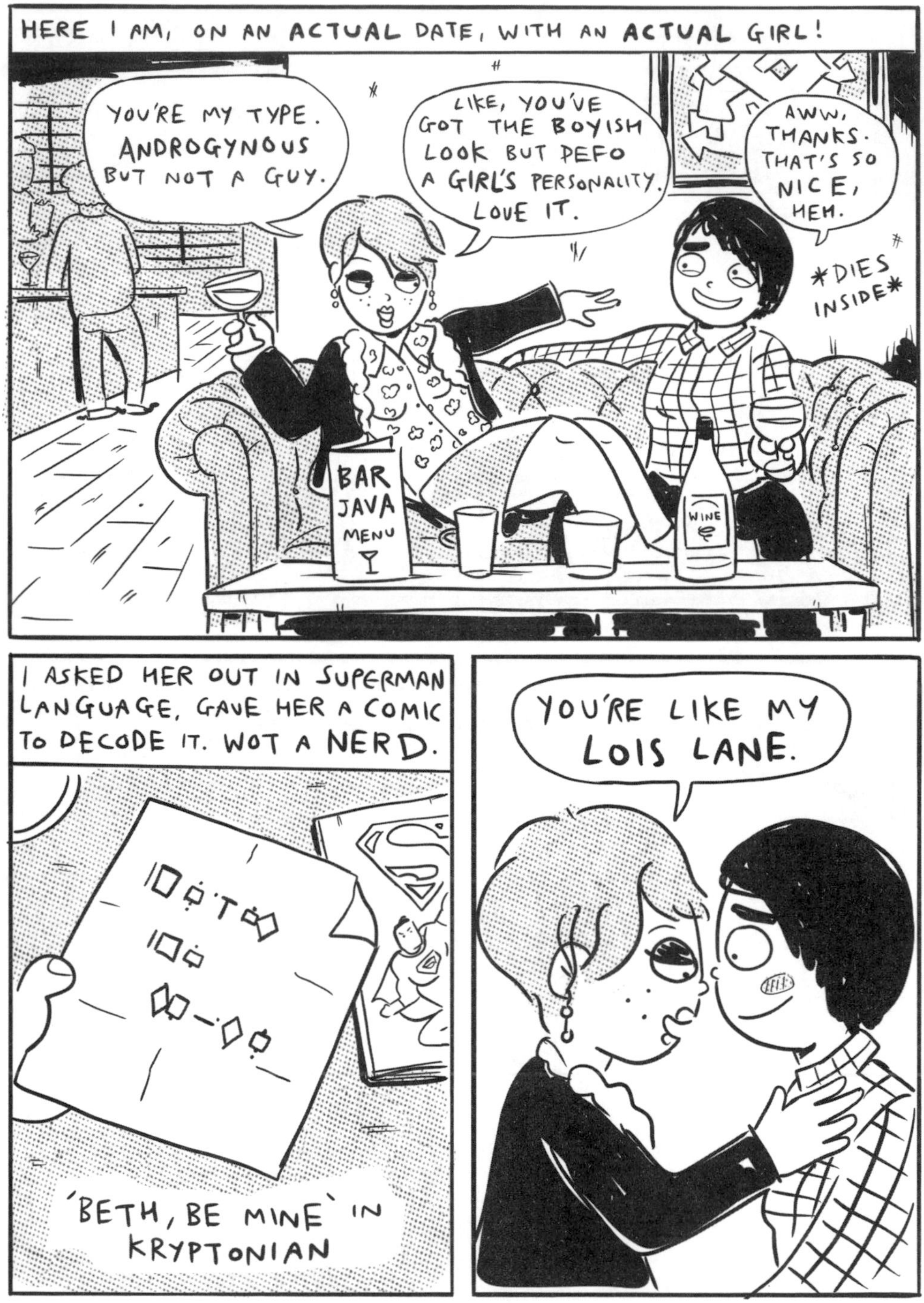
HERE I AM, ON AN ACTUAL DATE, WITH AN ACTUAL GIRL!
YOU'RE MY TYPE. ANDROGYNOUS BUT NOT A GUY.
LIKE, YOU'VE GOT THE BOYISH LOOK BUT DEFO A GIRL'S PERSONALITY. LOVE IT.
AWW, THANKS. THAT'S SO NICE, MEM.
DIES INSIDE
BAR JAVA MENU
WINE
I ASKED HER OUT IN SUPERMAN LANGUAGE, GAVE HER A COMIC TO DECODE IT. WOT A NERD.
'BETH, BE MINE' IN KRYPTONIAN
YOU'RE LIKE MY LOIS LANE.

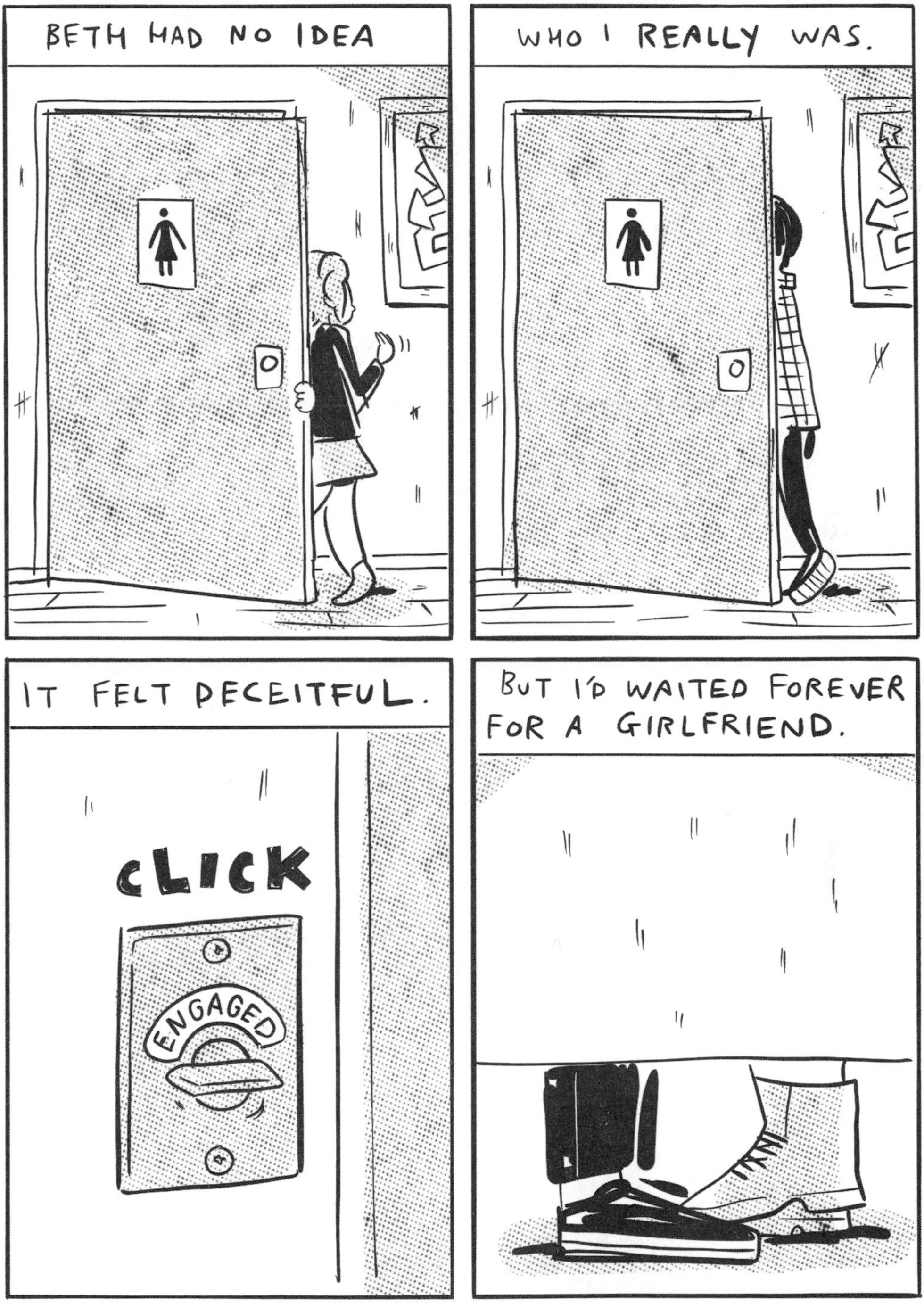
BETH HAD NO IDEA
WHO I REALLY WAS.
IT FELT DECEITFUL.
CLICK
ENGAGED
BUT I'D WAITED FOREVER FOR A GIRLFRIEND.

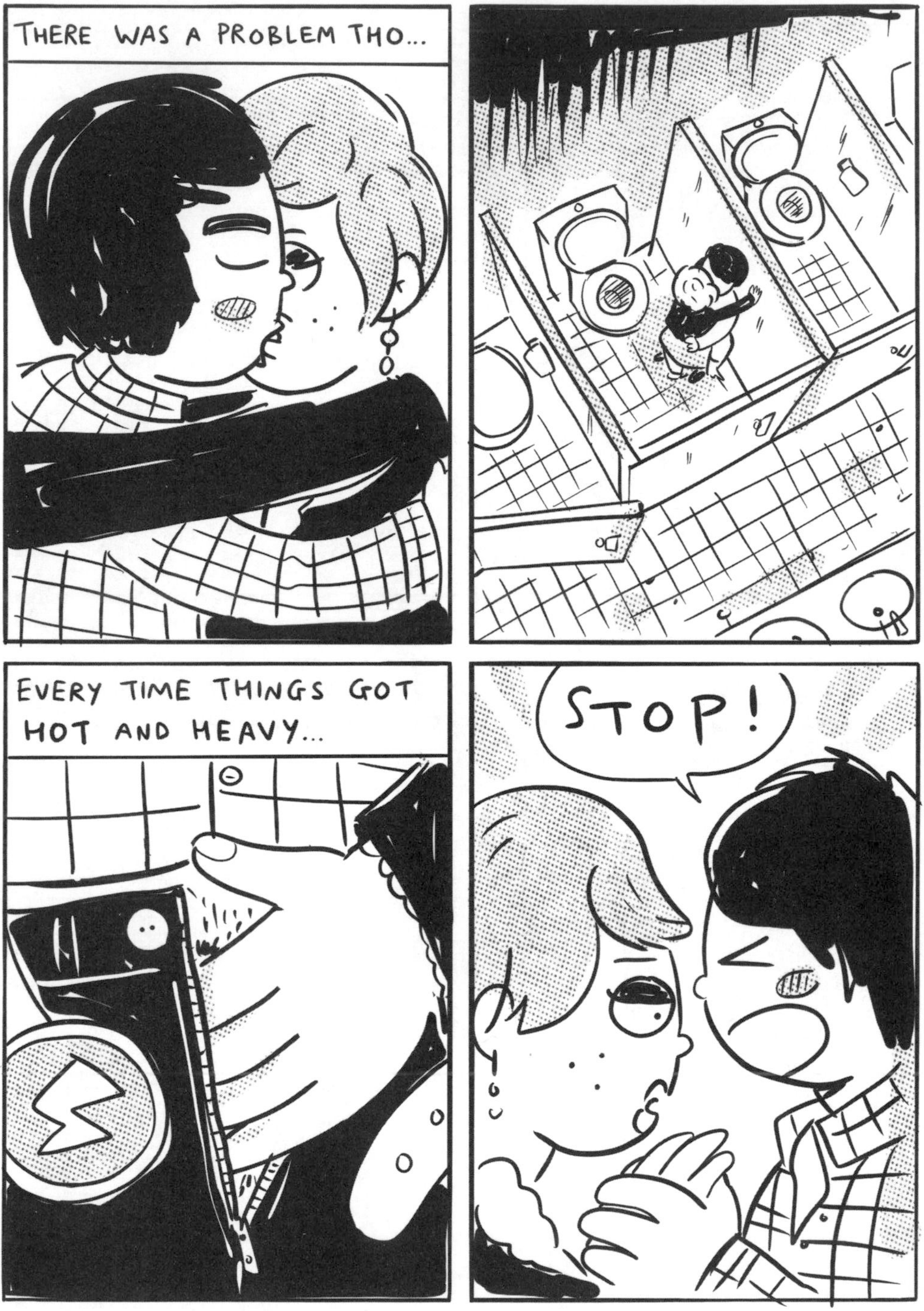
THERE WAS A PROBLEM THO...
EVERY TIME THINGS GOT HOT AND HEAVY...
STOP!

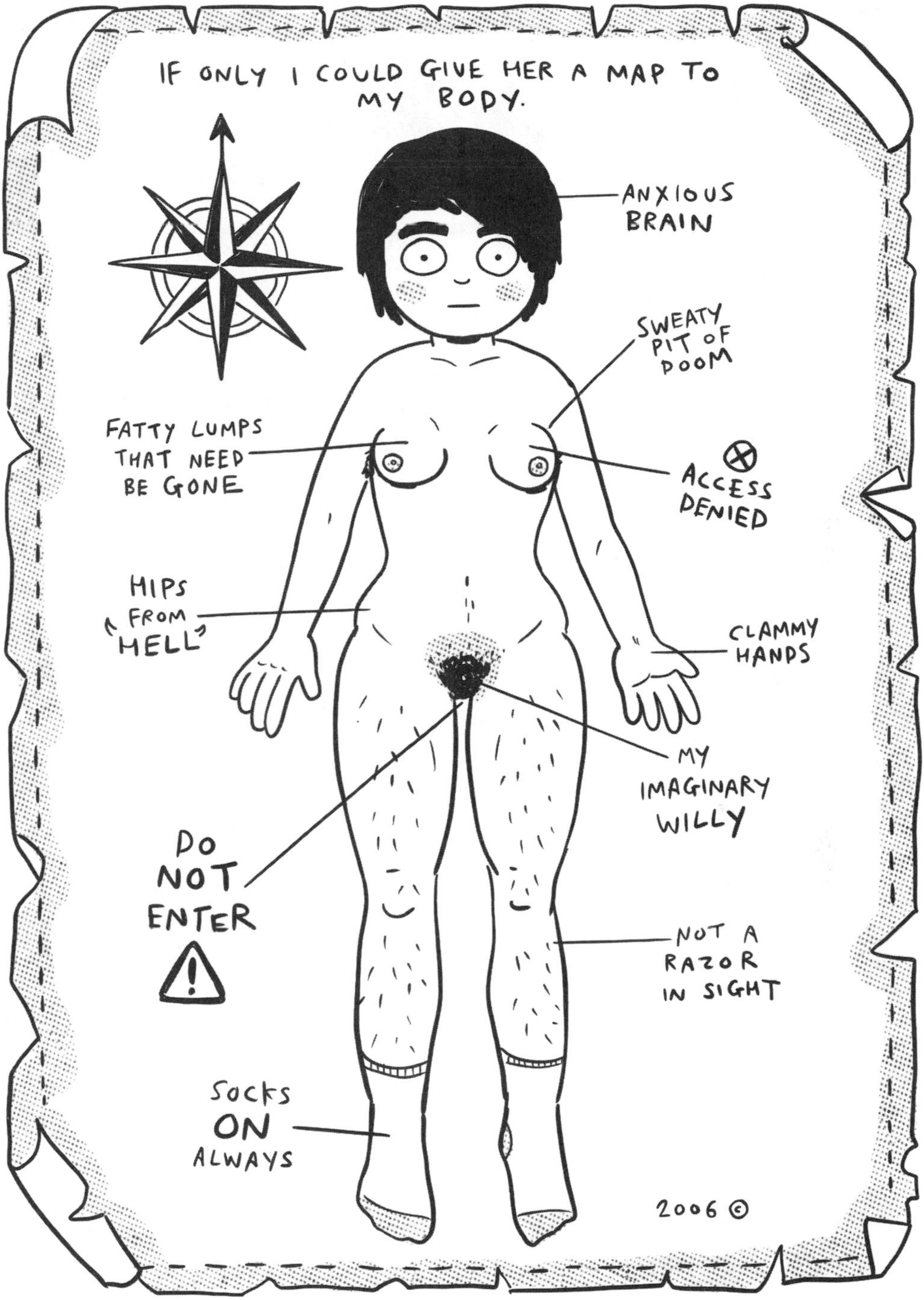
IF ONLY I COULD GIVE HER A MAP TO MY BODY.
ANXIOUS BRAIN
SWEATY PIT OF DOOM
FATTY LUMPS THAT NEED BE GONE
ACCESS DENIED
HIPS FROM HELL
CLAMMY HANDS
MY IMAGINARY WILLY
DO NOT ENTER
NOT A RAZOR IN SIGHT
SOCKS ON ALWAYS
2006 ©

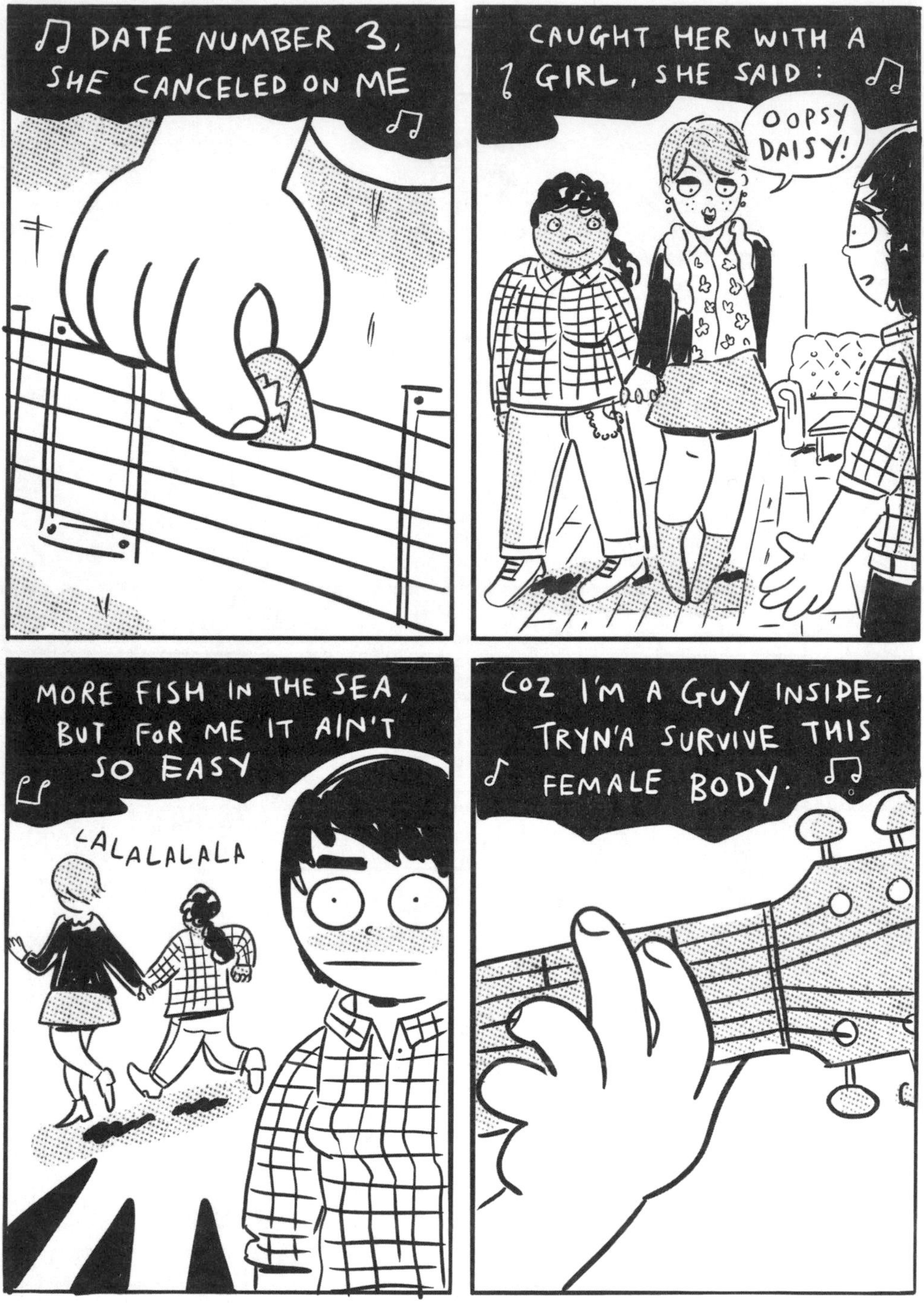
DATE NUMBER 3, SHE CANCELED ON ME
CAUGHT HER WITH A GIRL, SHE SAID:
OOPSY DAISY!
MORE FISH IN THE SEA, BUT FOR ME IT AIN'T SO EASY
LALALALALA
COZ I'M A GUY INSIDE, TRYN'A SURVIVE THIS FEMALE BODY.

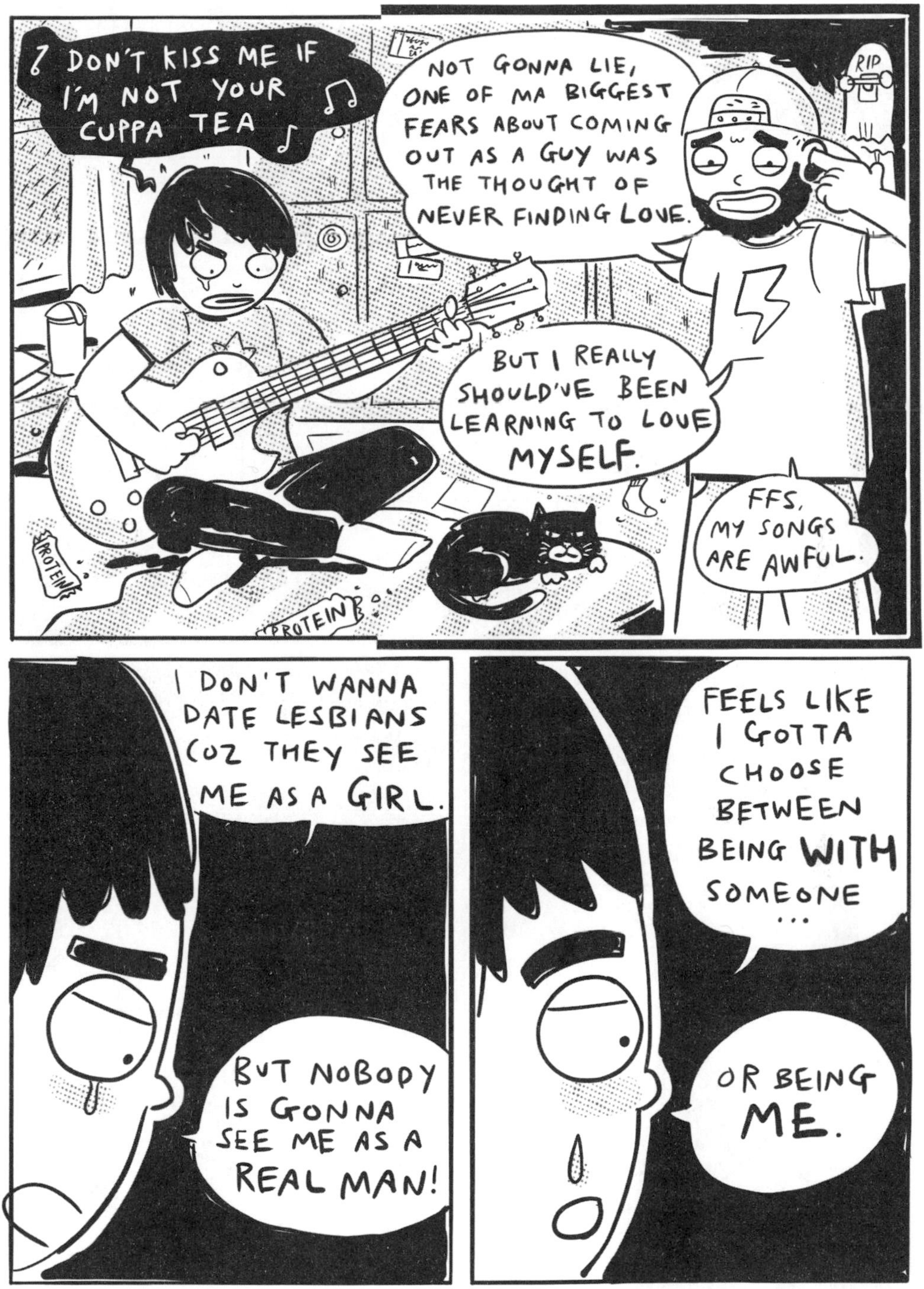
DON'T KISS ME IF I'M NOT YOUR CUPPA TEA
NOT GONNA LIE, ONE OF MA BIGGEST FEARS ABOUT COMING OUT AS A GUY WAS THE THOUGHT OF NEVER FINDING LOVE.
BUT I REALLY SHOULD'VE BEEN LEARNING TO LOVE MYSELF.
RIP
FFS, MY SONGS ARE AWFUL.
PROTEIN
PROTEIN
I DON'T WANNA DATE LESBIANS COZ THEY SEE ME AS A GIRL.
BUT NOBODY IS GONNA SEE ME AS A REAL MAN!
FEELS LIKE I GOTTA CHOOSE BETWEEN BEING WITH SOMEONE . . .
OR BEING ME.

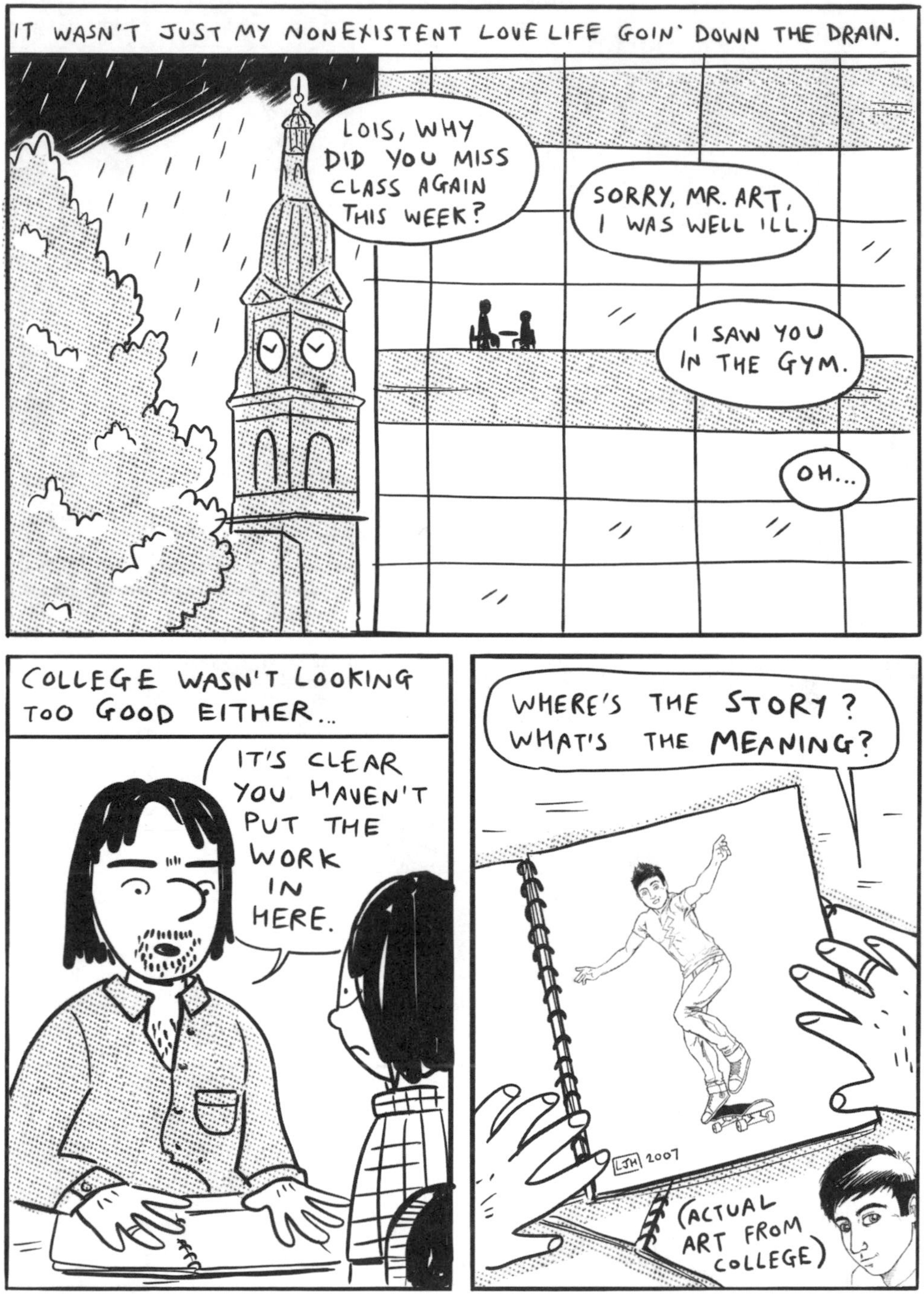
IT WASN'T JUST MY NONEXISTENT LOVE LIFE GOIN' DOWN THE DRAIN.
LOIS, WHY DID YOU MISS CLASS AGAIN THIS WEEK?
SORRY, MR. ART, I WAS WELL ILL.
I SAW YOU IN THE GYM.
OH...
COLLEGE WASN'T LOOKING TOO GOOD EITHER...
IT'S CLEAR YOU HAVEN'T PUT THE WORK IN HERE.
WHERE'S THE STORY? WHAT'S THE MEANING?
LJH 2007
(ACTUAL ART FROM COLLEGE)

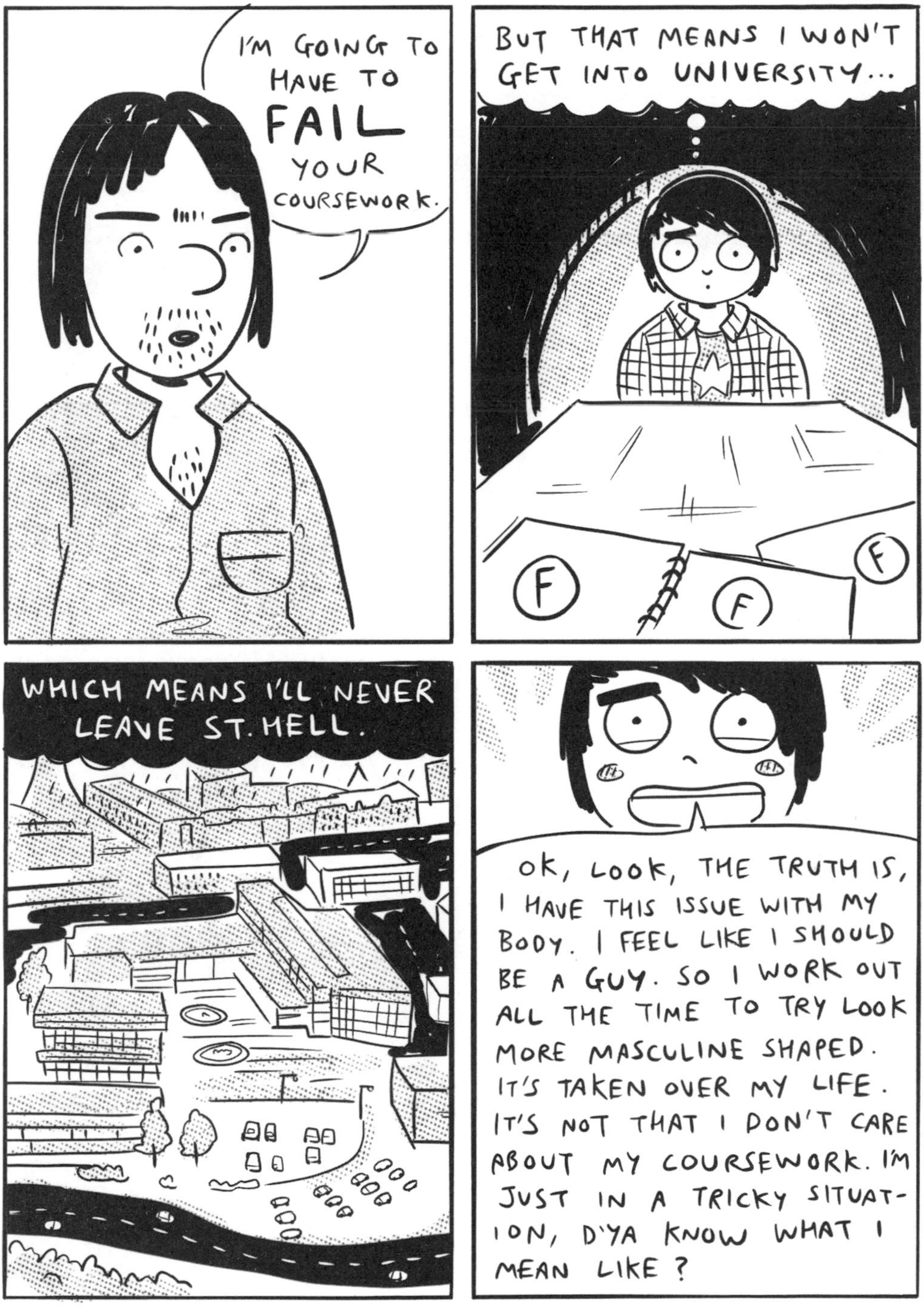

I'M GOING TO HAVE TO FAIL YOUR COURSEWORK.
BUT THAT MEANS I WON'T GET INTO UNIVERSITY...
WHICH MEANS I'LL NEVER LEAVE ST. HELL.
OK, LOOK, THE TRUTH IS, I HAVE THIS ISSUE WITH MY BODY. I FEEL LIKE I SHOULD BE A GUY. SO I WORK OUT ALL THE TIME TO TRY LOOK MORE MASCULINE SHAPED. IT'S TAKEN OVER MY LIFE. IT'S NOT THAT I DON'T CARE ABOUT MY COURSEWORK. I'M JUST IN A TRICKY SITUATION, D'YA KNOW WHAT I MEAN LIKE?

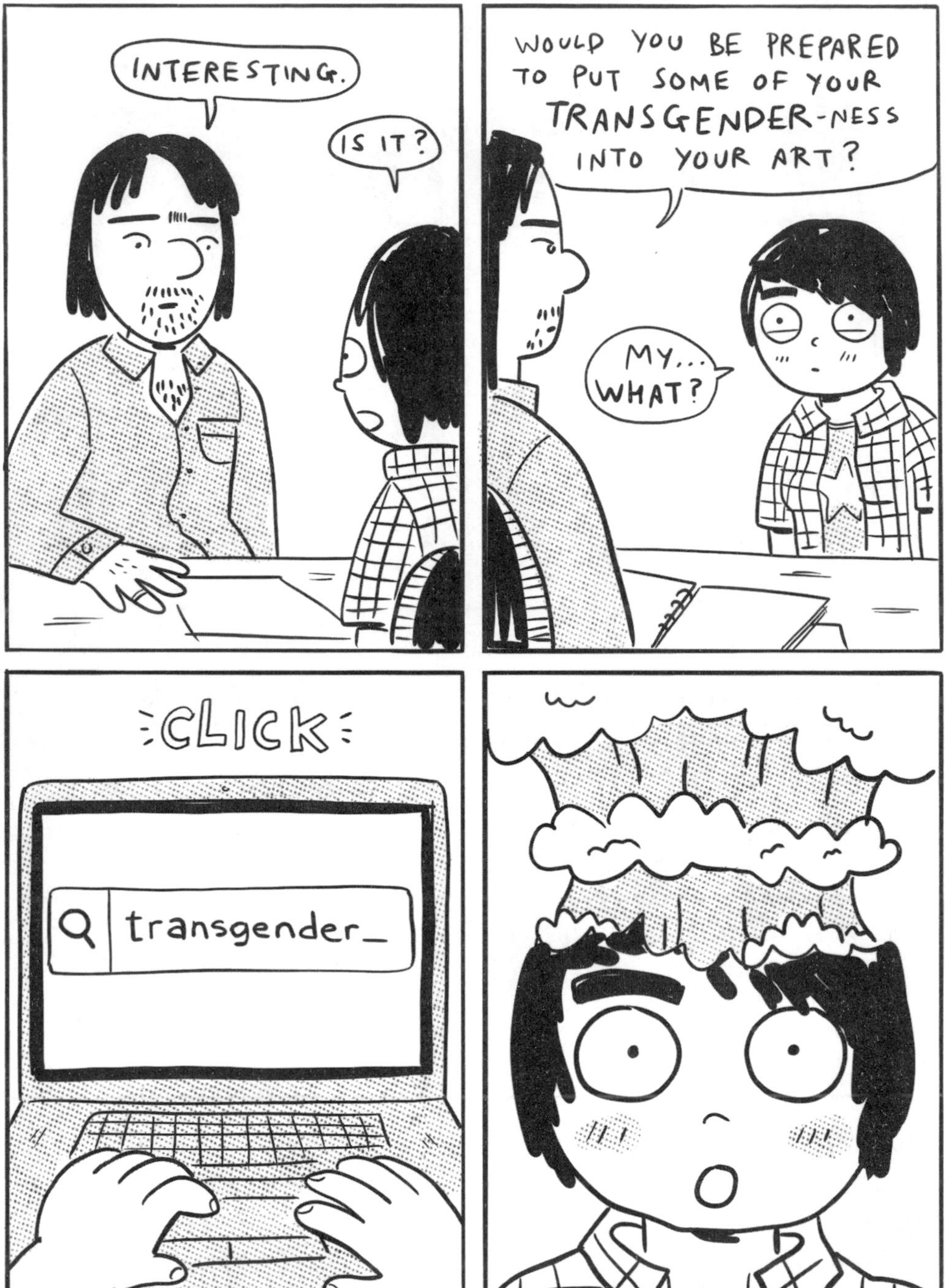
INTERESTING.
IS IT?
WOULD YOU BE PREPARED TO PUT SOME OF YOUR TRANSGENDER-NESS INTO YOUR ART?
MY... WHAT?
CLICK
transgender_

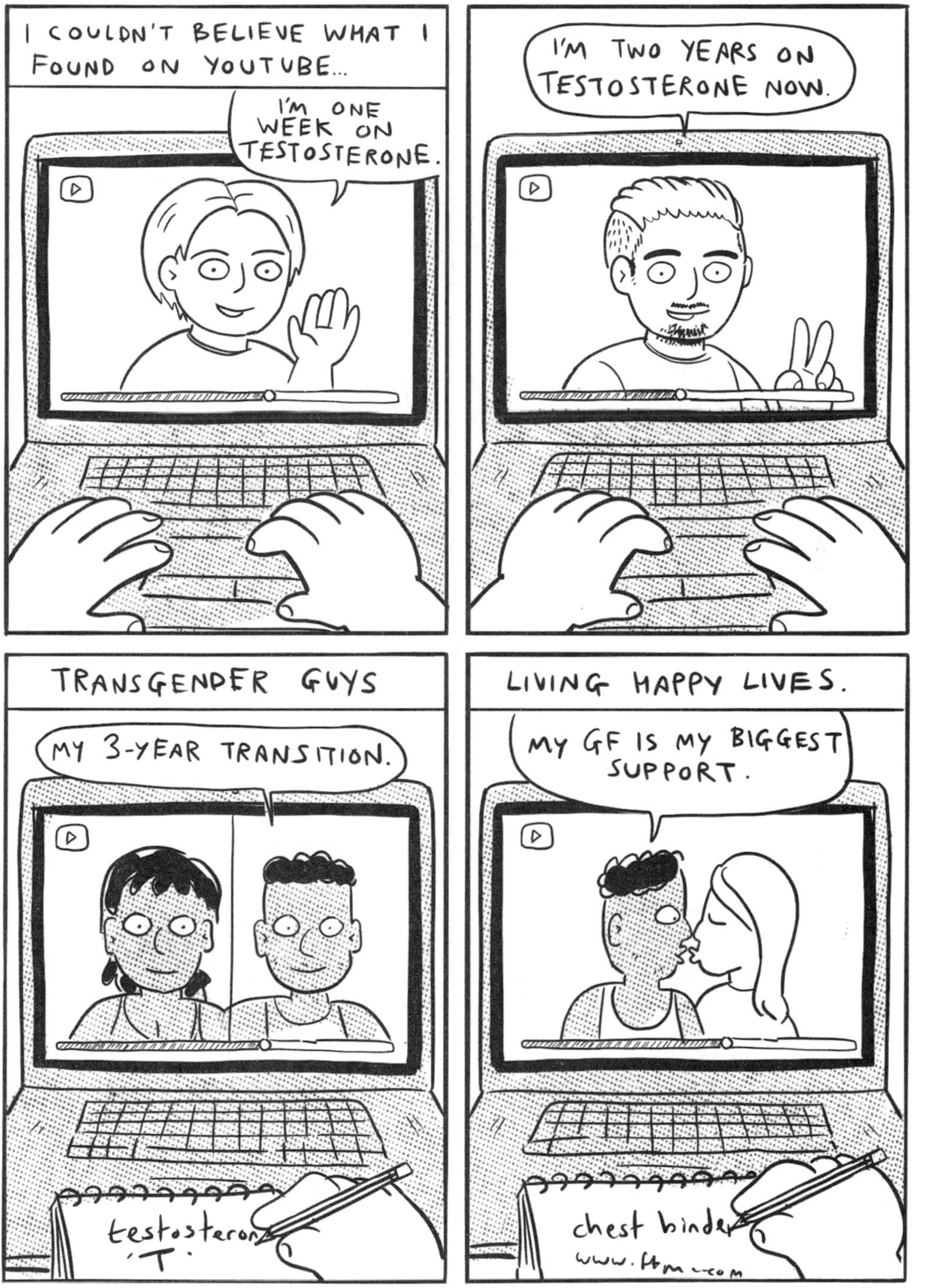
I COULDN'T BELIEVE WHAT I FOUND ON YOUTUBE...
I'M ONE WEEK ON TESTOSTERONE.
I'M TWO YEARS ON TESTOSTERONE NOW.
TRANSGENDER GUYS
MY 3-YEAR TRANSITION.
testosterone
'T'
LIVING HAPPY LIVES.
MY GF IS MY BIGGEST SUPPORT.
chest binder
www.ftm.com

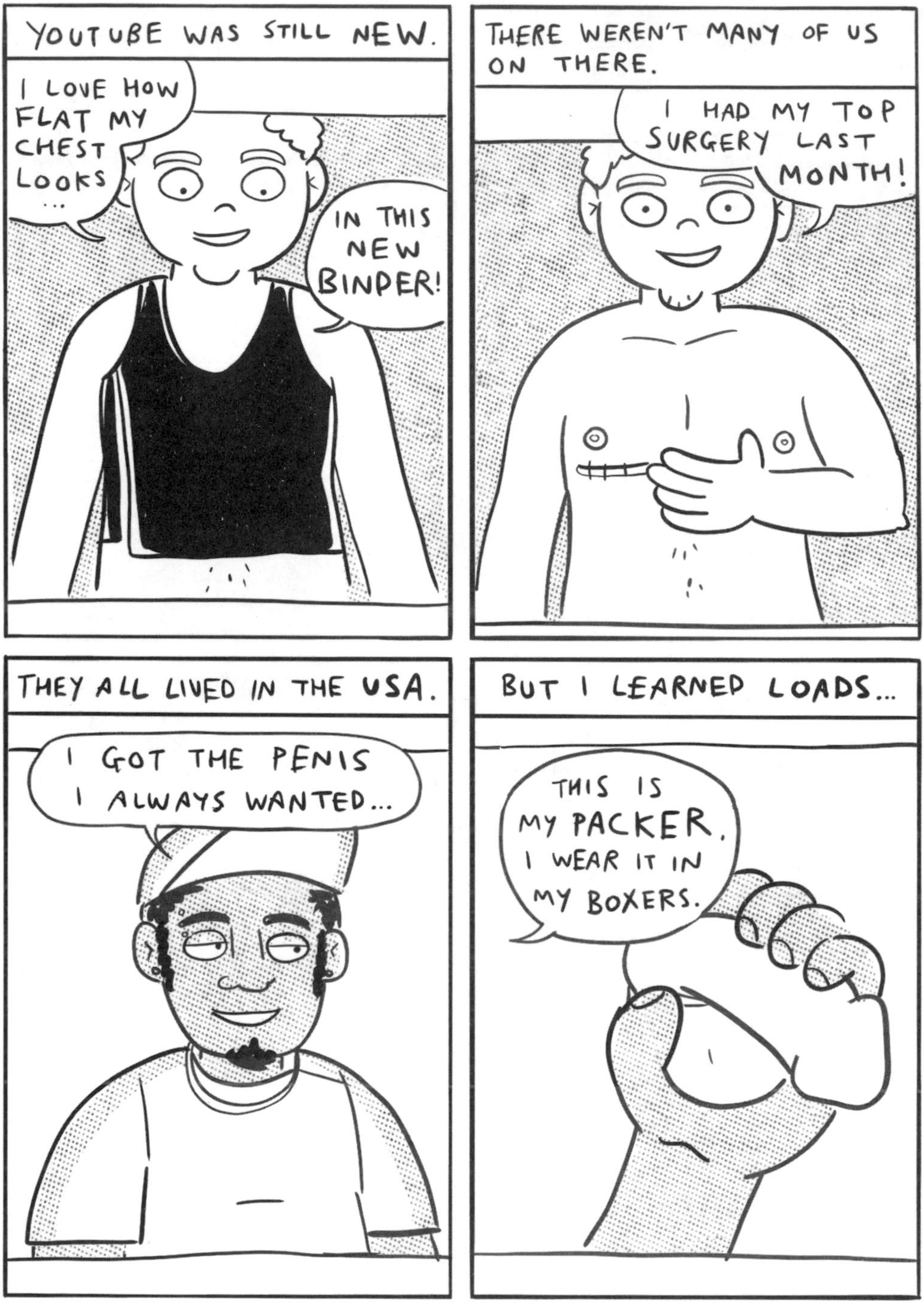
YOUTUBE WAS STILL NEW.
I LOVE HOW FLAT MY CHEST LOOKS ...
IN THIS NEW BINDER!
THERE WEREN'T MANY OF US ON THERE.
I HAD MY TOP SURGERY LAST MONTH!
THEY ALL LIVED IN THE USA.
I GOT THE PENIS I ALWAYS WANTED...
BUT I LEARNED LOADS...
THIS IS MY PACKER. I WEAR IT IN MY BOXERS.

THE EFFECTS OF HORMONE THERAPY, TESTOSTERONE.

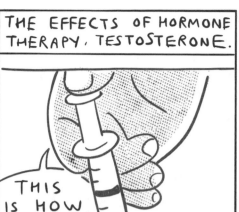

THIS IS HOW I INJECT MY OWN T.

INCREASED BODY HAIR.

VOICE DEEPENING.

CLITORIS GROWTH, AKA:

GROW YOUR OWN WILLY

WOW

CAN GROW UP TO 2"!

BODY FAT REDISTRIBUTION.

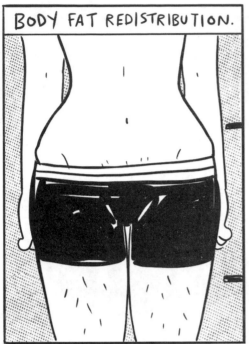

(LESS PEAR SHAPE, MORE APPLE.)

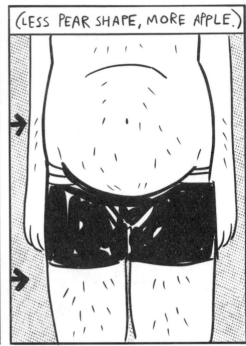

NO MORE PERIODS.

THIS IS BASICALLY THE PUBERTY I SHOULDA HAD!

OTHER POSSIBLE SIDE EFFECTS INC:
ACNE
INCREASED LIBIDO
WEIGHT GAIN

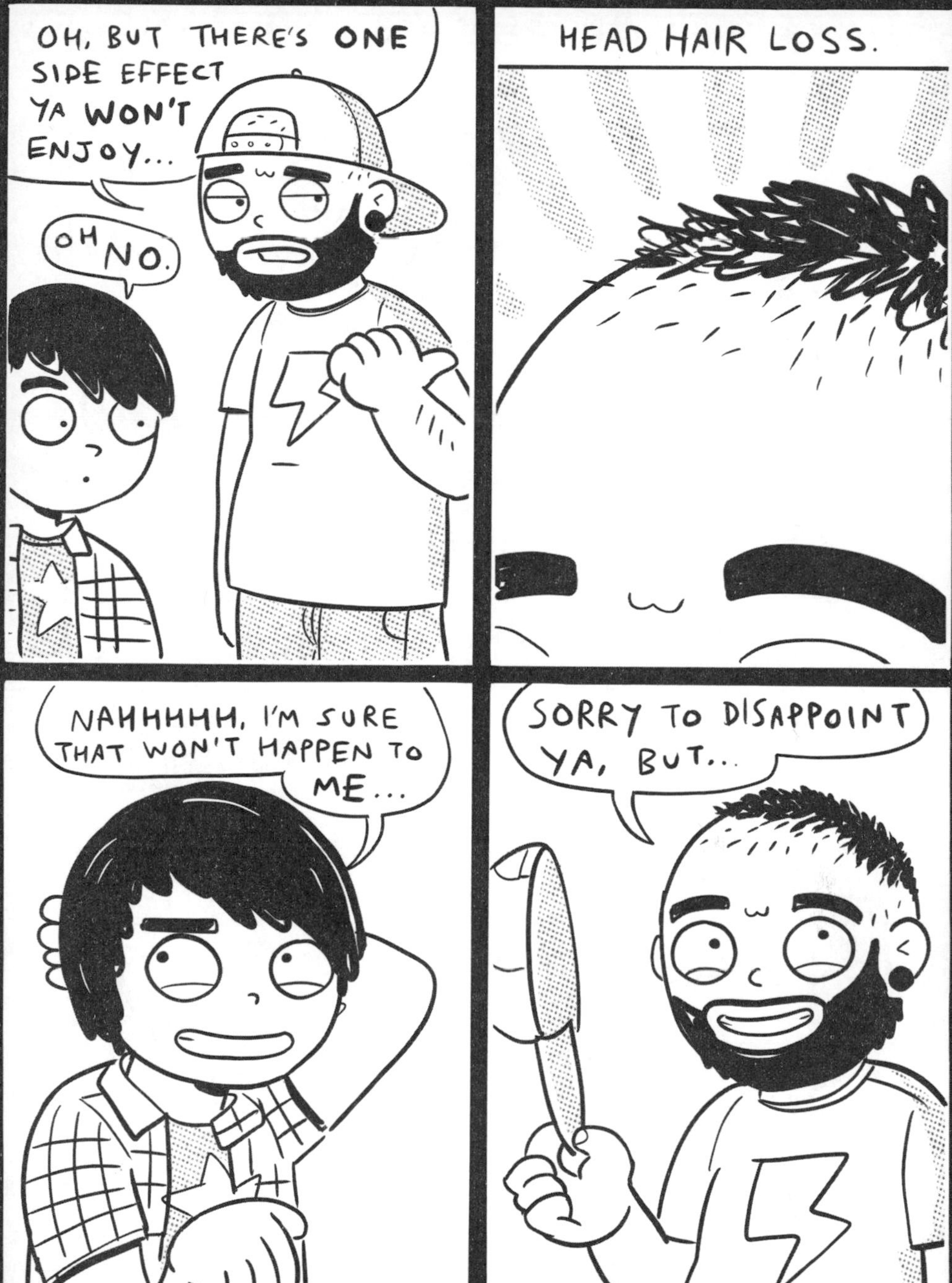
OH, BUT THERE'S ONE SIDE EFFECT YA WON'T ENJOY...
OH NO.
HEAD HAIR LOSS.
NAHHHHH, I'M SURE THAT WON'T HAPPEN TO ME...
SORRY TO DISAPPOINT YA, BUT...

IT WAS LIKE ALL THE PIECES OF THE PUZZLE FINALLY FIT.

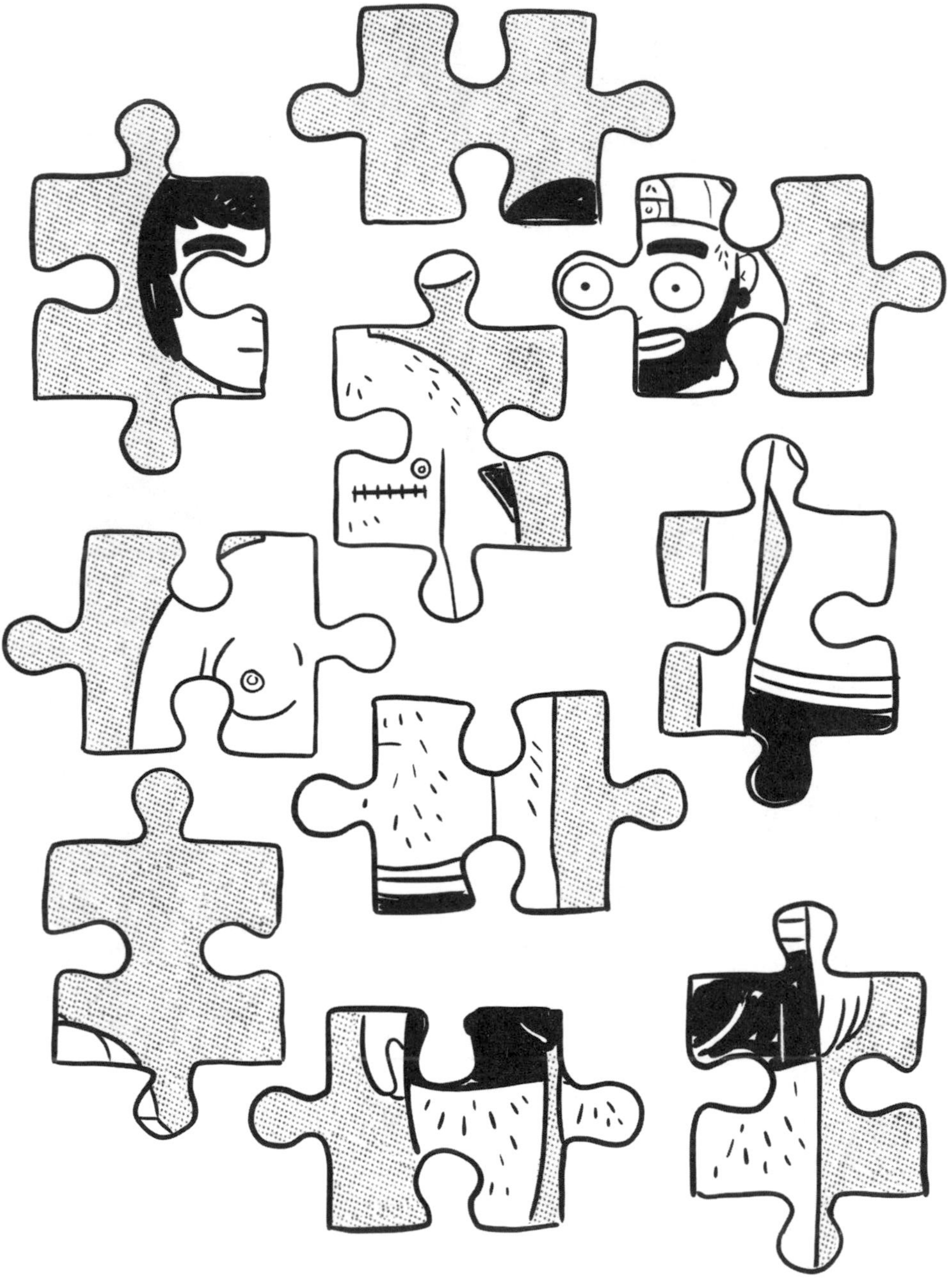

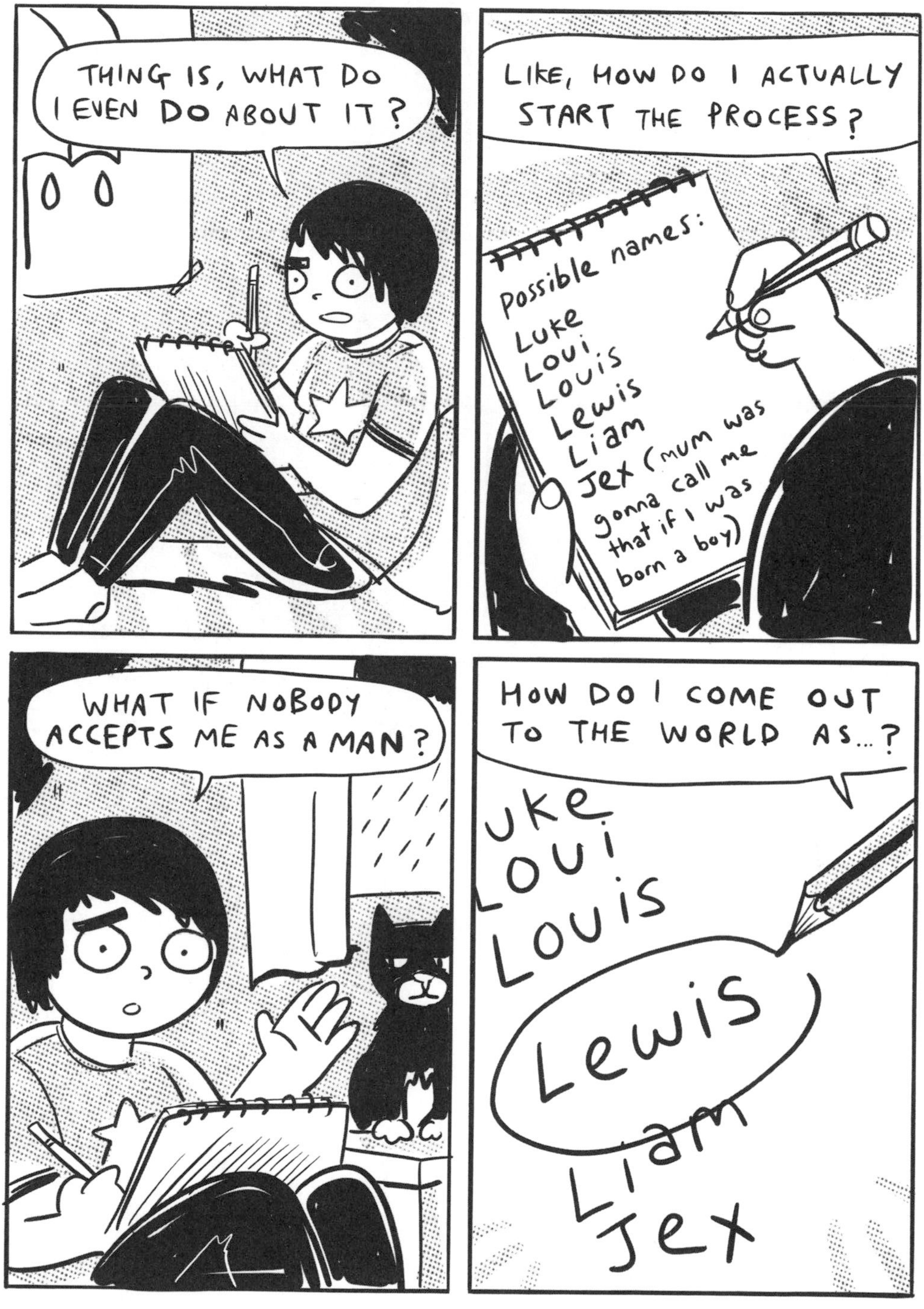
THING IS, WHAT DO I EVEN DO ABOUT IT?
LIKE, HOW DO I ACTUALLY START THE PROCESS?
Possible names:
Luke
Loui
Louis
Lewis
Liam
Jex (mum was gonna call me that if I was born a boy)
WHAT IF NOBODY ACCEPTS ME AS A MAN?
HOW DO I COME OUT TO THE WORLD AS...?
uke
Loui
Louis
Lewis
Liam
Jex

BLEEP
BLEEP
BLEEP

5:00 AM

AGE 18.

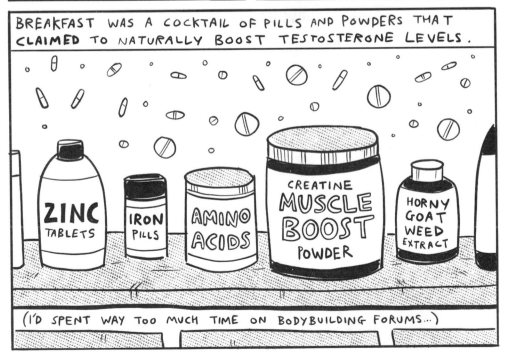

BREAKFAST WAS A COCKTAIL OF PILLS AND POWDERS THAT CLAIMED TO NATURALLY BOOST TESTOSTERONE LEVELS.

ZINC TABLETS

IRON PILLS

AMINO ACIDS

CREATINE MUSCLE BOOST POWDER

HORNY GOAT WEED EXTRACT

(I'D SPENT WAY TOO MUCH TIME ON BODYBUILDING FORUMS...)

I TRIED EVERYTHING POSSIBLE
GRRR UNT
TO GET THE BODY I WANTED.
Men's Health
TRUTH ABOUT SUPPLEMENTS
GET YOUR BEST BOD
PROTEIN PACKED PILLS
HOW TO MAKE A MOVE ON HER
BE A MAN
I STILL DON'T SEE MYSELF
IN THE MIRROR.
NOTHING WAS ENOUGH.
RIP

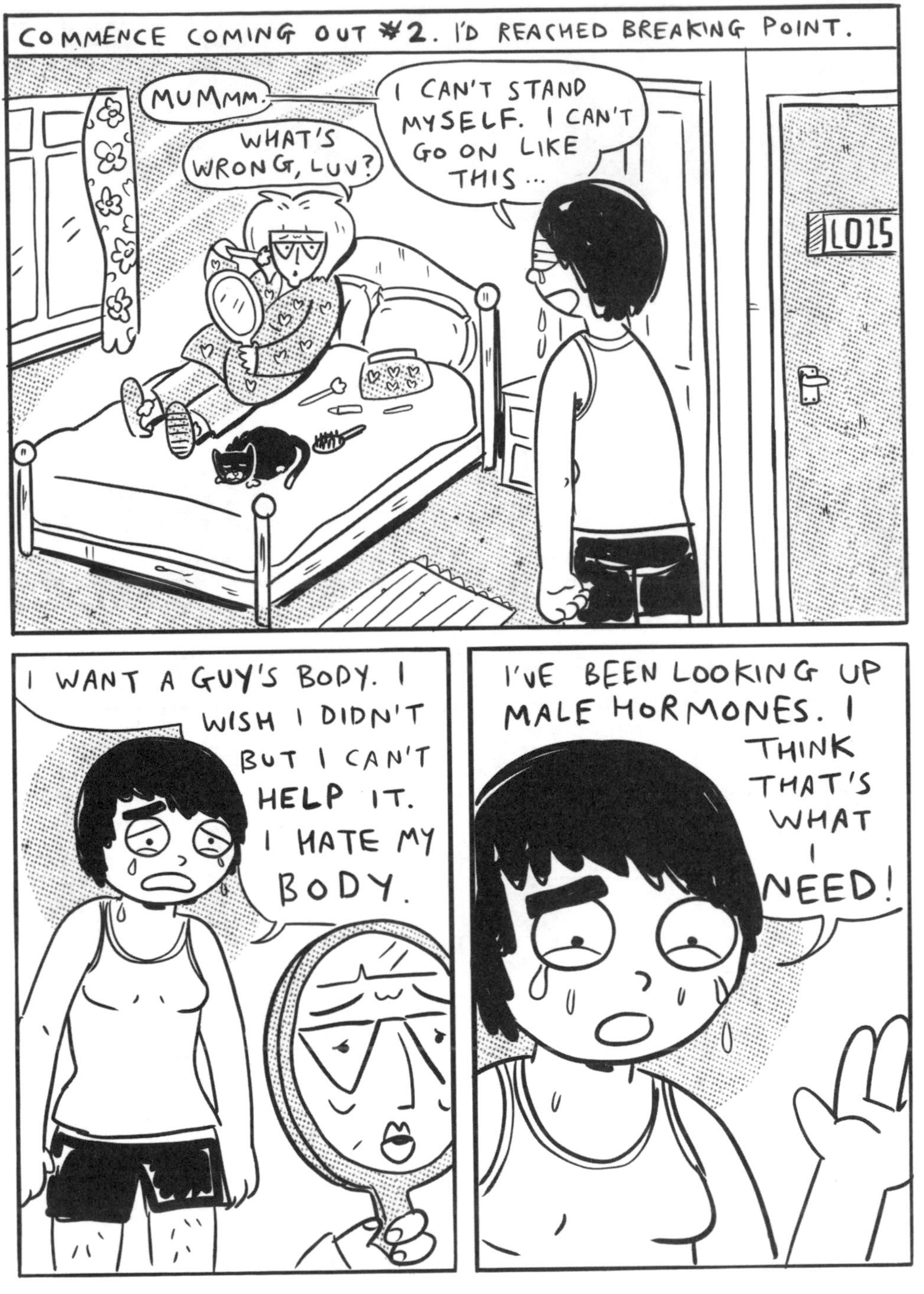
COMMENCE COMING OUT #2. I'D REACHED BREAKING POINT.
MUMMM.
WHAT'S WRONG, LUV?
I CAN'T STAND MYSELF. I CAN'T GO ON LIKE THIS...
L015
I WANT A GUY'S BODY. I WISH I DIDN'T BUT I CAN'T HELP IT. I HATE MY BODY.
I'VE BEEN LOOKING UP MALE HORMONES. I THINK THAT'S WHAT I NEED!

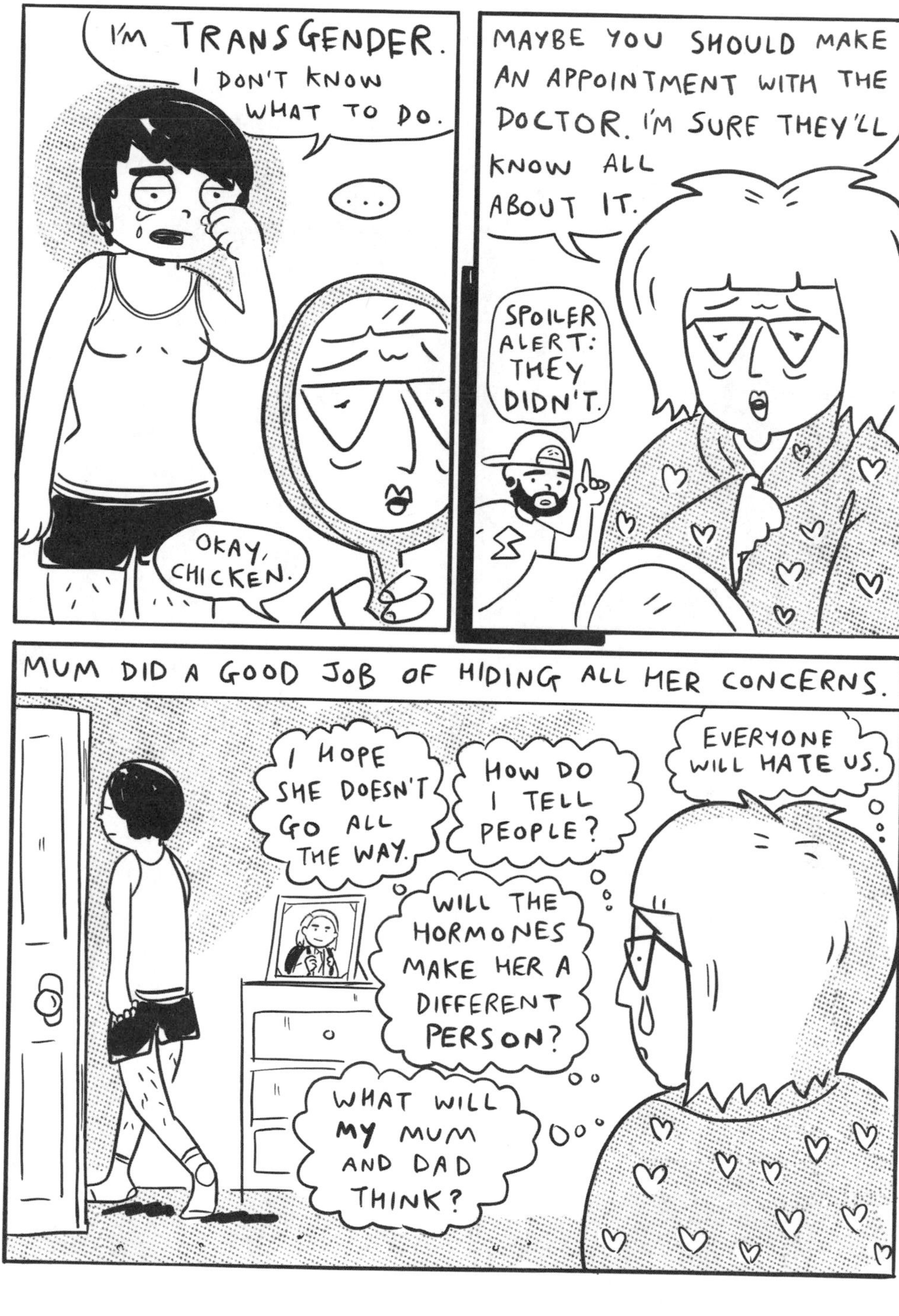
I'M TRANSGENDER.
I DON'T KNOW WHAT TO DO.
...
OKAY, CHICKEN.
MAYBE YOU SHOULD MAKE AN APPOINTMENT WITH THE DOCTOR. I'M SURE THEY'LL KNOW ALL ABOUT IT.
SPOILER ALERT: THEY DIDN'T.
MUM DID A GOOD JOB OF HIDING ALL HER CONCERNS.
I HOPE SHE DOESN'T GO ALL THE WAY.
HOW DO I TELL PEOPLE?
EVERYONE WILL HATE US.
WILL THE HORMONES MAKE HER A DIFFERENT PERSON?
WHAT WILL MY MUM AND DAD THINK?

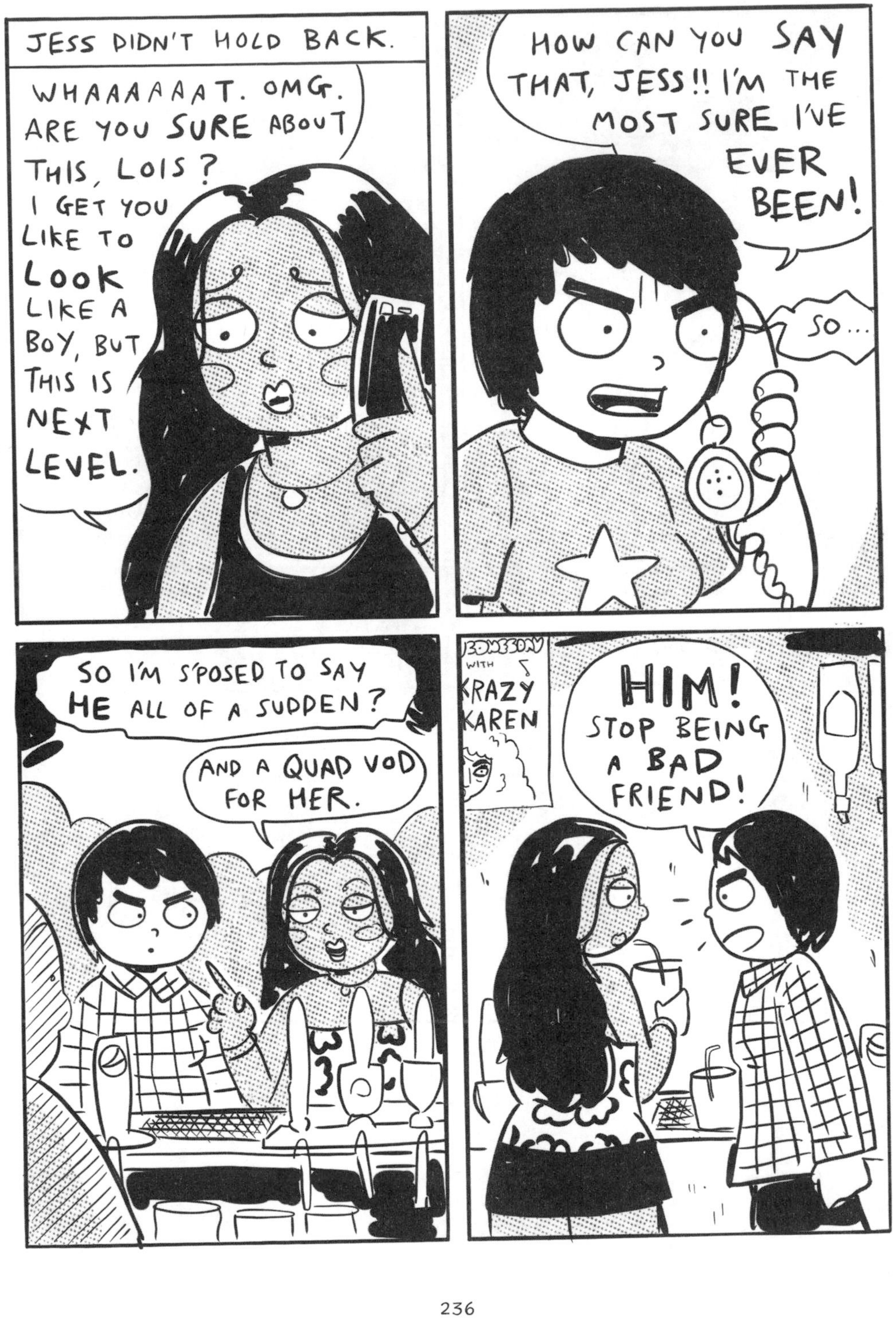
JESS DIDN'T HOLD BACK.
WHAAAAAAT. OMG. ARE YOU SURE ABOUT THIS, LOIS? I GET YOU LIKE TO LOOK LIKE A BOY, BUT THIS IS NEXT LEVEL.
HOW CAN YOU SAY THAT, JESS!! I'M THE MOST SURE I'VE EVER BEEN!
SO...
SO I'M S'POSED TO SAY HE ALL OF A SUDDEN?
AND A QUAD VOD FOR HER.
KRAZY KAREN
HIM! STOP BEING A BAD FRIEND!

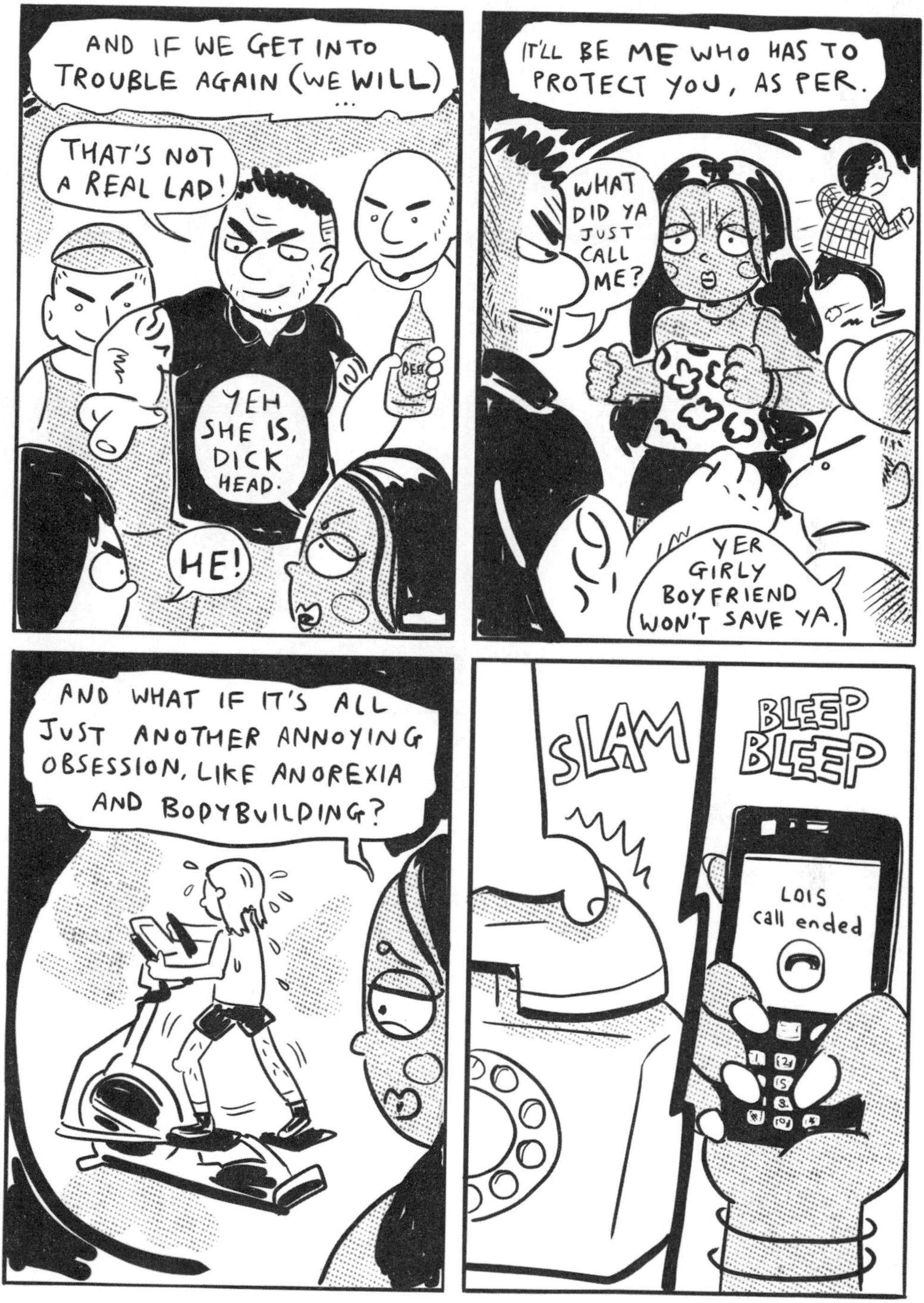

AND IF WE GET INTO TROUBLE AGAIN (WE WILL) ...
THAT'S NOT A REAL LAD!
YEH SHE IS, DICK HEAD.
HE!
IT'LL BE ME WHO HAS TO PROTECT YOU, AS PER.
WHAT DID YA JUST CALL ME?
YER GIRLY BOYFRIEND WON'T SAVE YA.
AND WHAT IF IT'S ALL JUST ANOTHER ANNOYING OBSESSION, LIKE ANOREXIA AND BODYBUILDING?
SLAM
BLEEP BLEEP
LOIS
call ended

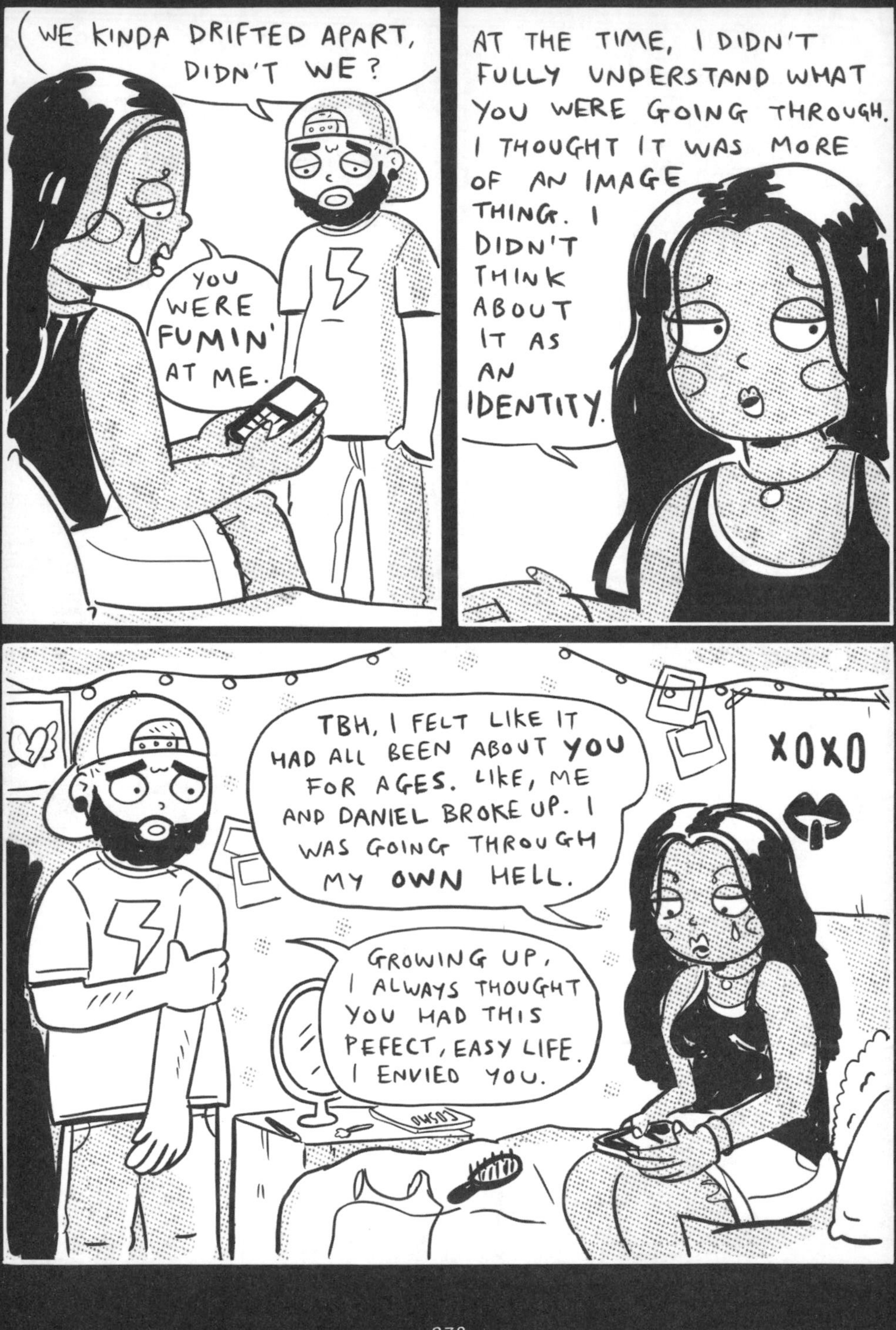
WE KINDA DRIFTED APART, DIDN'T WE?
YOU WERE FUMIN' AT ME.
AT THE TIME, I DIDN'T FULLY UNDERSTAND WHAT YOU WERE GOING THROUGH. I THOUGHT IT WAS MORE OF AN IMAGE THING. I DIDN'T THINK ABOUT IT AS AN IDENTITY.
XOXO
TBH, I FELT LIKE IT HAD ALL BEEN ABOUT YOU FOR AGES. LIKE, ME AND DANIEL BROKE UP. I WAS GOING THROUGH MY OWN HELL.
GROWING UP, I ALWAYS THOUGHT YOU HAD THIS PEFECT, EASY LIFE. I ENVIED YOU.

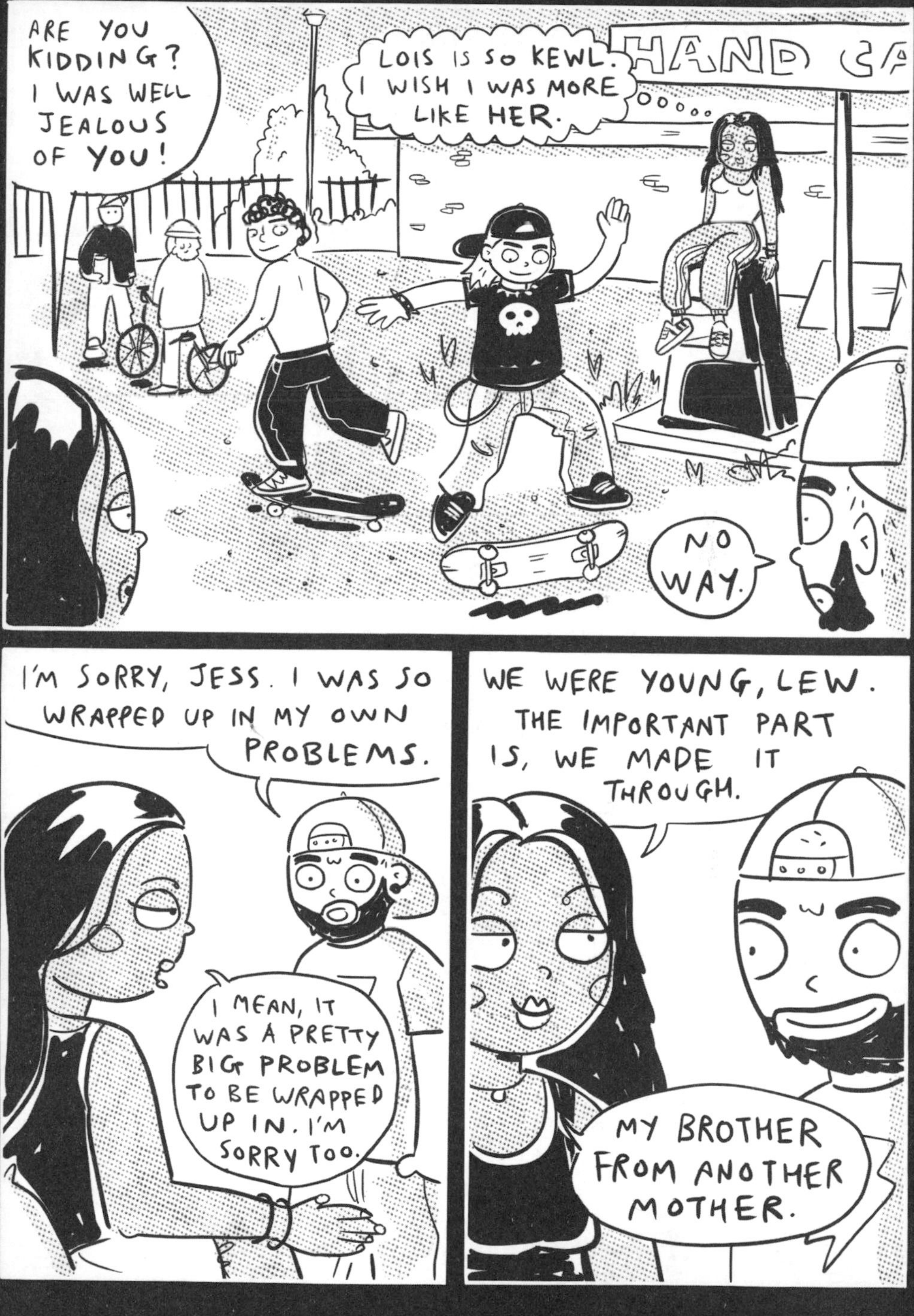
ARE YOU KIDDING? I WAS WELL JEALOUS OF YOU!
LOIS IS SO KEWL. I WISH I WAS MORE LIKE HER.
HAND CA
NO WAY.
I'M SORRY, JESS. I WAS SO WRAPPED UP IN MY OWN PROBLEMS.
I MEAN, IT WAS A PRETTY BIG PROBLEM TO BE WRAPPED UP IN. I'M SORRY TOO.
WE WERE YOUNG, LEW. THE IMPORTANT PART IS, WE MADE IT THROUGH.
MY BROTHER FROM ANOTHER MOTHER.

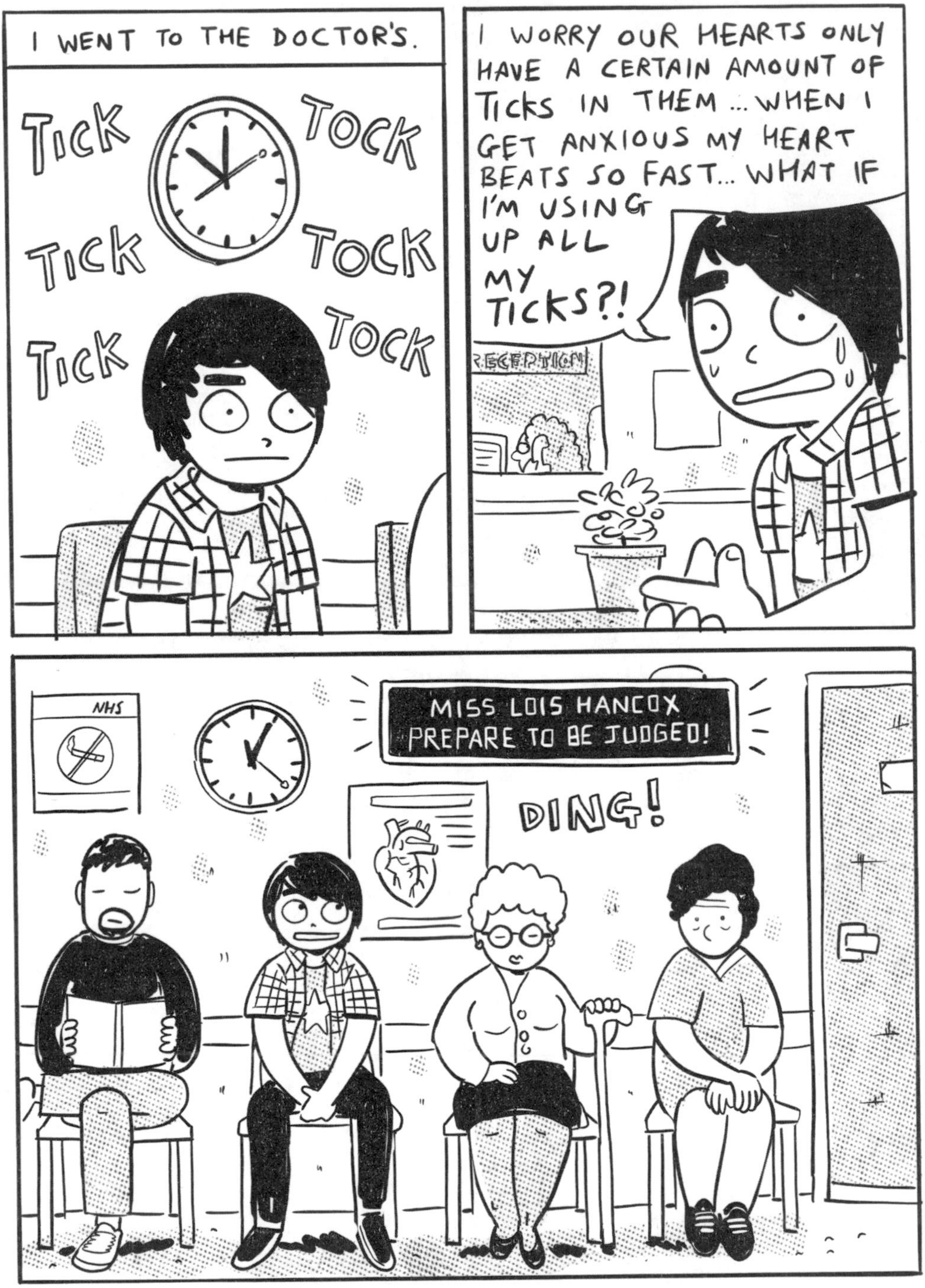
I WENT TO THE DOCTOR'S.
TICK TOCK
TICK TOCK
TICK TOCK
I WORRY OUR HEARTS ONLY HAVE A CERTAIN AMOUNT OF TICKS IN THEM... WHEN I GET ANXIOUS MY HEART BEATS SO FAST... WHAT IF I'M USING UP ALL MY TICKS?!
RECEPTION
NHS
MISS LOIS HANCOX PREPARE TO BE JUDGED!
DING!

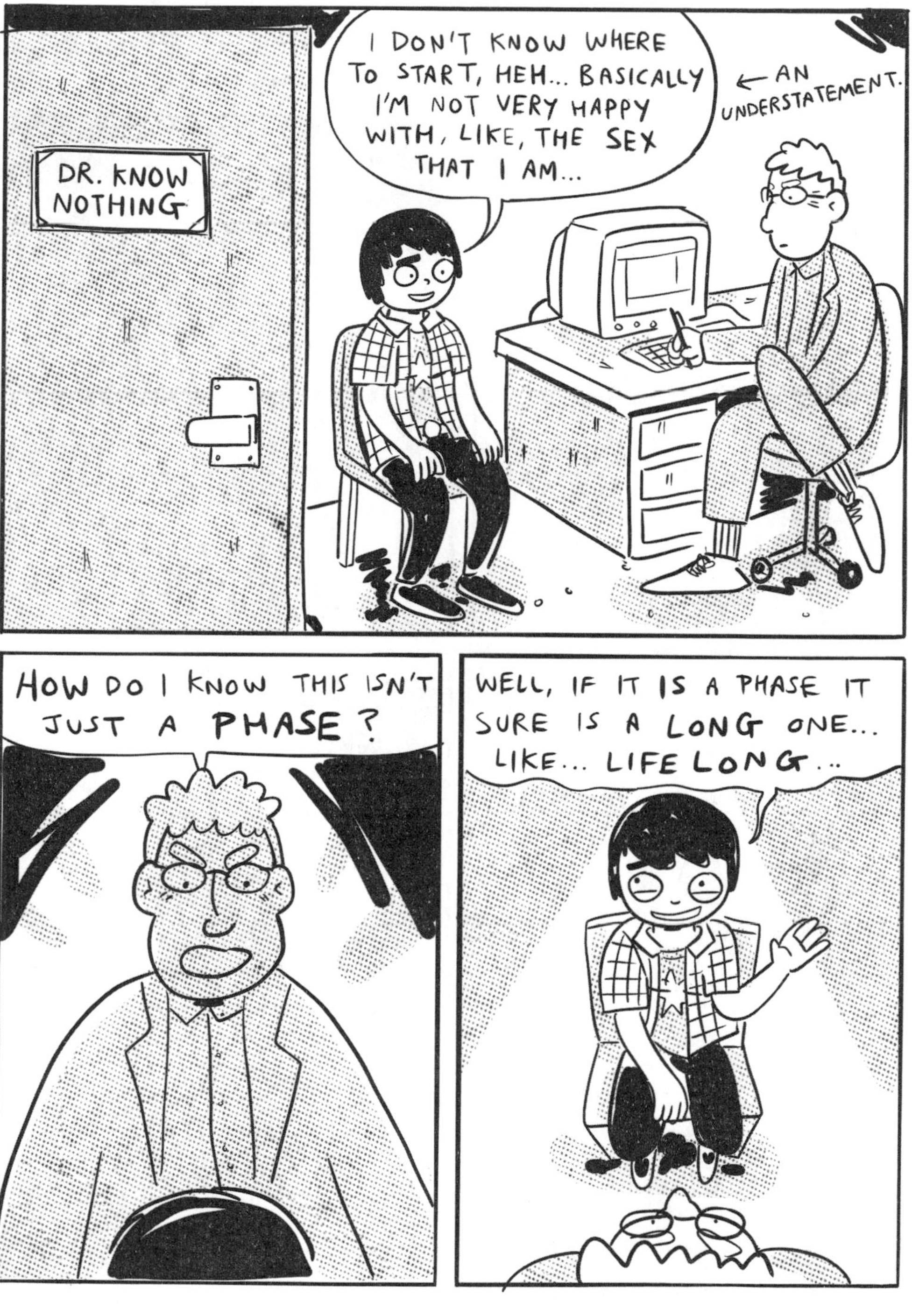
DR. KNOW NOTHING
I DON'T KNOW WHERE TO START, HEH... BASICALLY I'M NOT VERY HAPPY WITH, LIKE, THE SEX THAT I AM...
← AN UNDERSTATEMENT.
HOW DO I KNOW THIS ISN'T JUST A PHASE?
WELL, IF IT IS A PHASE IT SURE IS A LONG ONE... LIKE... LIFE LONG...

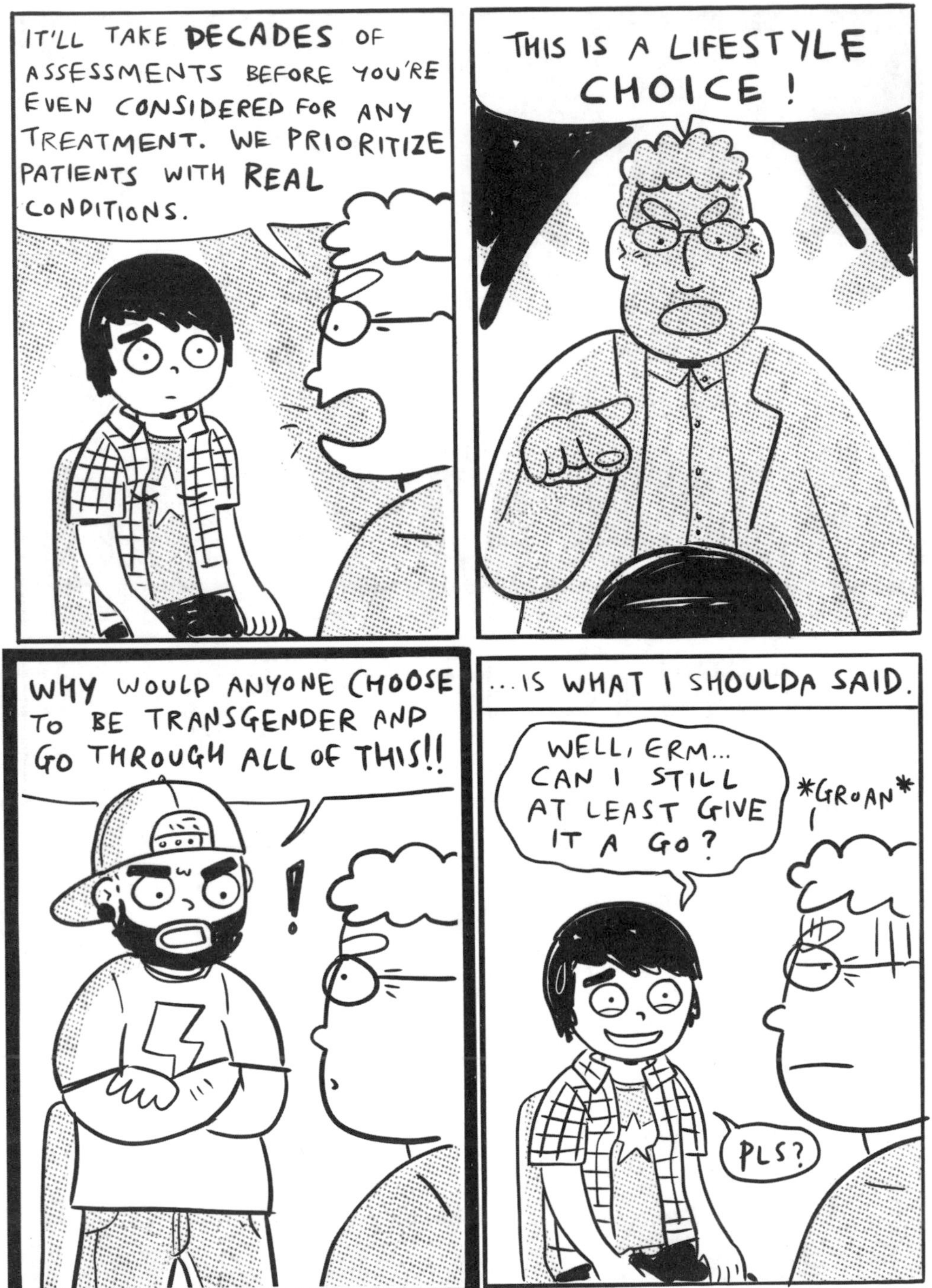
IT'LL TAKE DECADES OF ASSESSMENTS BEFORE YOU'RE EVEN CONSIDERED FOR ANY TREATMENT. WE PRIORITIZE PATIENTS WITH REAL CONDITIONS.
THIS IS A LIFESTYLE CHOICE!
WHY WOULD ANYONE CHOOSE TO BE TRANSGENDER AND GO THROUGH ALL OF THIS!!
!
...IS WHAT I SHOULDA SAID.
WELL, ERM... CAN I STILL AT LEAST GIVE IT A GO?
GROAN
PLS?

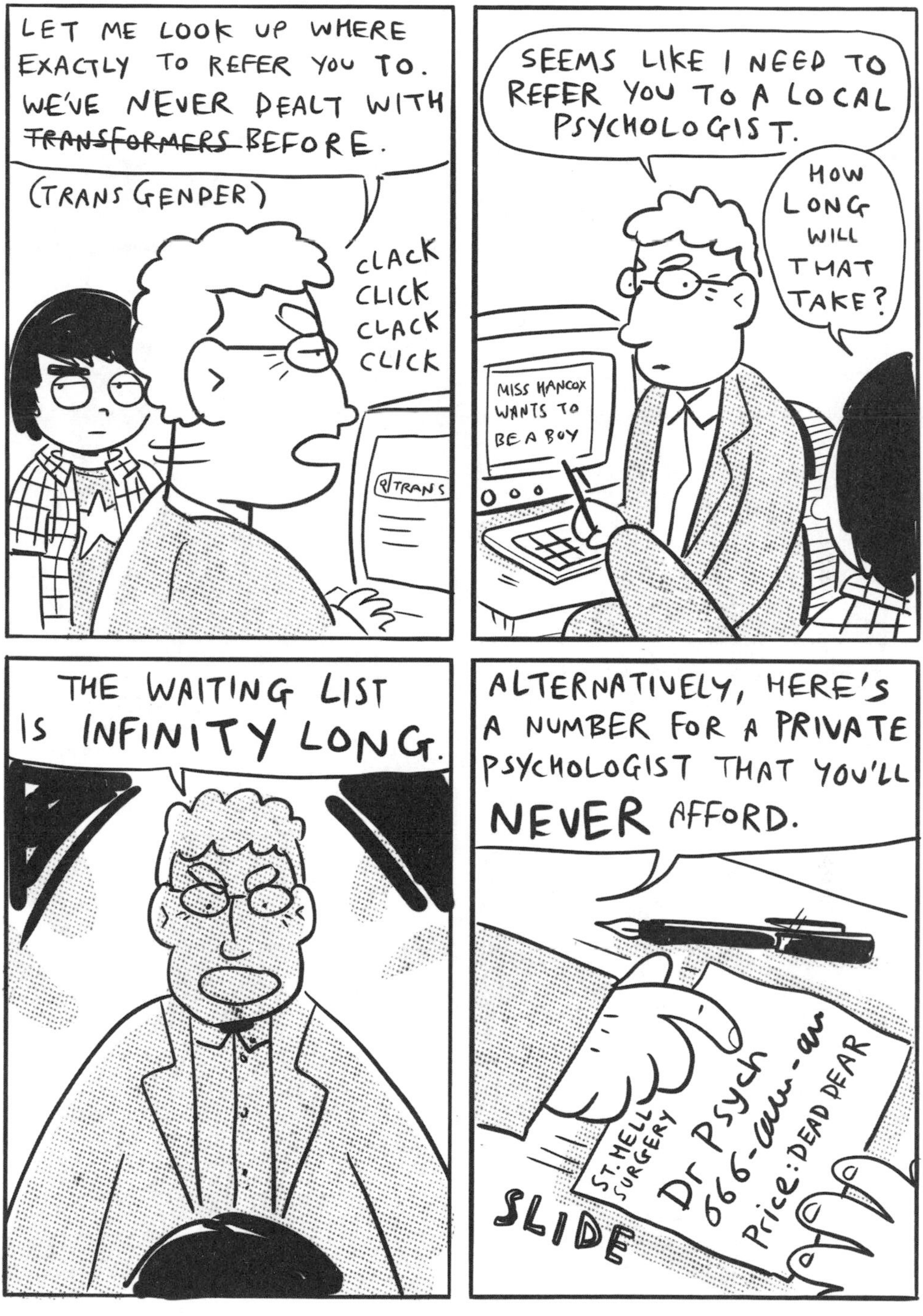
LET ME LOOK UP WHERE EXACTLY TO REFER YOU TO. WE'VE NEVER DEALT WITH ~~TRANSFORMERS~~ BEFORE.
(TRANS GENDER)
CLACK CLICK CLACK CLICK
TRANS
SEEMS LIKE I NEED TO REFER YOU TO A LOCAL PSYCHOLOGIST.
MISS HANCOX WANTS TO BE A BOY
HOW LONG WILL THAT TAKE?
THE WAITING LIST IS INFINITY LONG.
ALTERNATIVELY, HERE'S A NUMBER FOR A PRIVATE PSYCHOLOGIST THAT YOU'LL NEVER AFFORD.
ST. MELL SURGERY
Dr Psych
666-
Price: DEAD DEAR
SLIDE

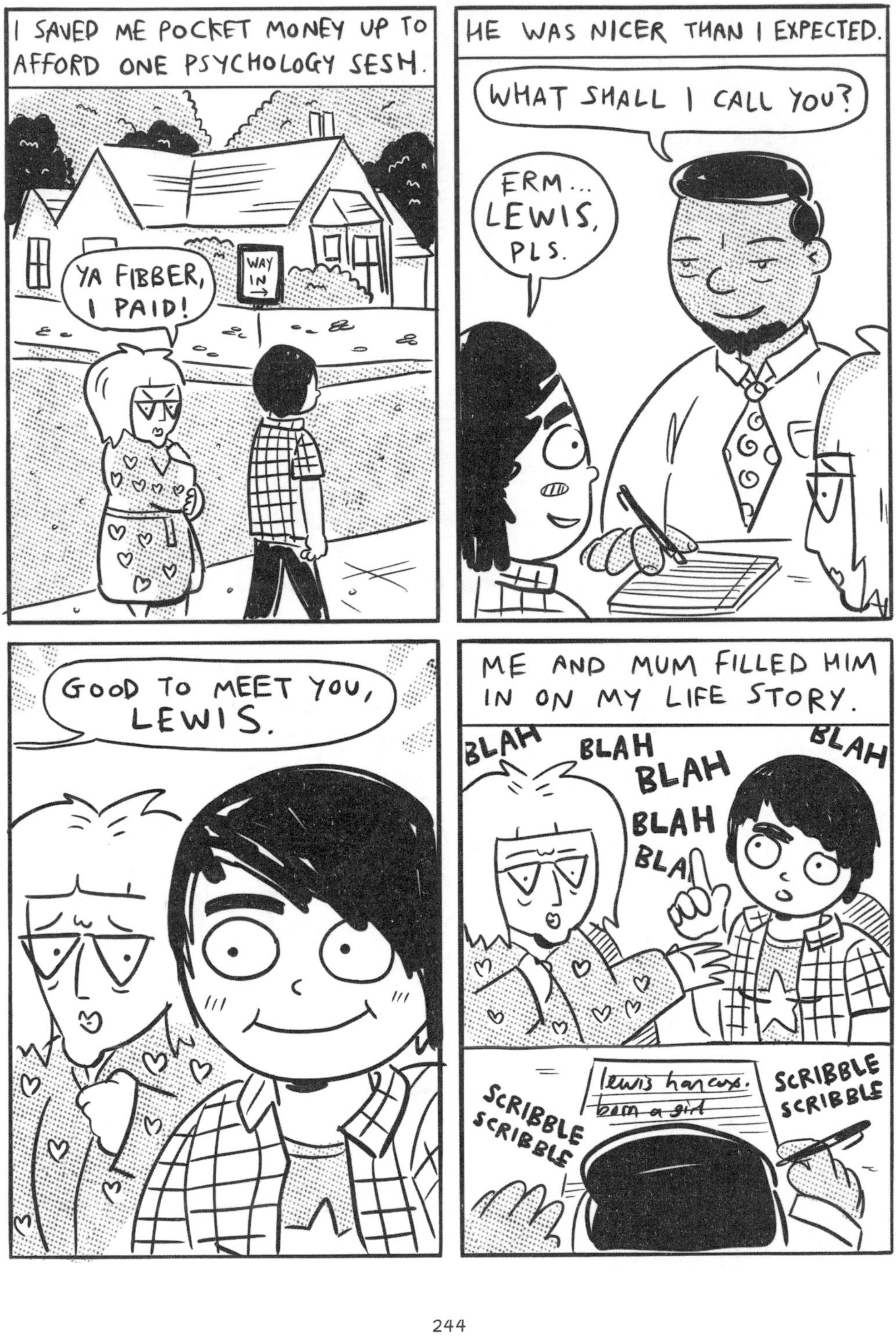
I SAVED ME POCKET MONEY UP TO AFFORD ONE PSYCHOLOGY SESH.
YA FIBBER, I PAID!
WAY IN →
HE WAS NICER THAN I EXPECTED.
WHAT SHALL I CALL YOU?
ERM... LEWIS, PLS.
GOOD TO MEET YOU, LEWIS.
ME AND MUM FILLED HIM IN ON MY LIFE STORY.
BLAH
BLAH
BLAH
BLAH
BLAH
BLA
born a girl
SCRIBBLE SCRIBBLE
SCRIBBLE SCRIBBLE

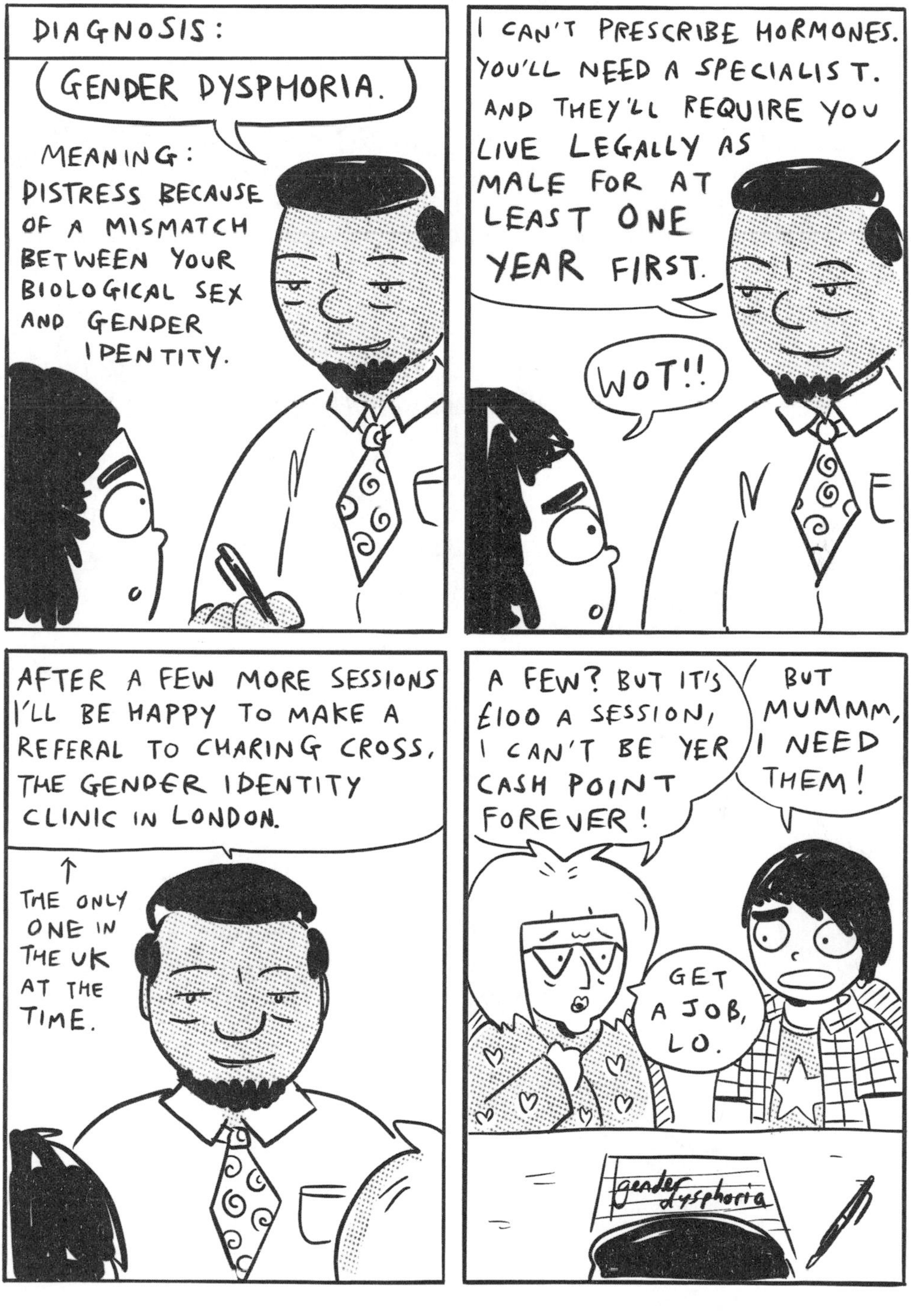
DIAGNOSIS:
GENDER DYSPHORIA.
MEANING: DISTRESS BECAUSE OF A MISMATCH BETWEEN YOUR BIOLOGICAL SEX AND GENDER IDENTITY.
I CAN'T PRESCRIBE HORMONES. YOU'LL NEED A SPECIALIST. AND THEY'LL REQUIRE YOU LIVE LEGALLY AS MALE FOR AT LEAST ONE YEAR FIRST.
WOT!!
AFTER A FEW MORE SESSIONS I'LL BE HAPPY TO MAKE A REFERAL TO CHARING CROSS, THE GENDER IDENTITY CLINIC IN LONDON.
THE ONLY ONE IN THE UK AT THE TIME.
A FEW? BUT IT'S £100 A SESSION, I CAN'T BE YER CASH POINT FOREVER!
BUT MUMMM, I NEED THEM!
GET A JOB, LO.
gender dysphoria

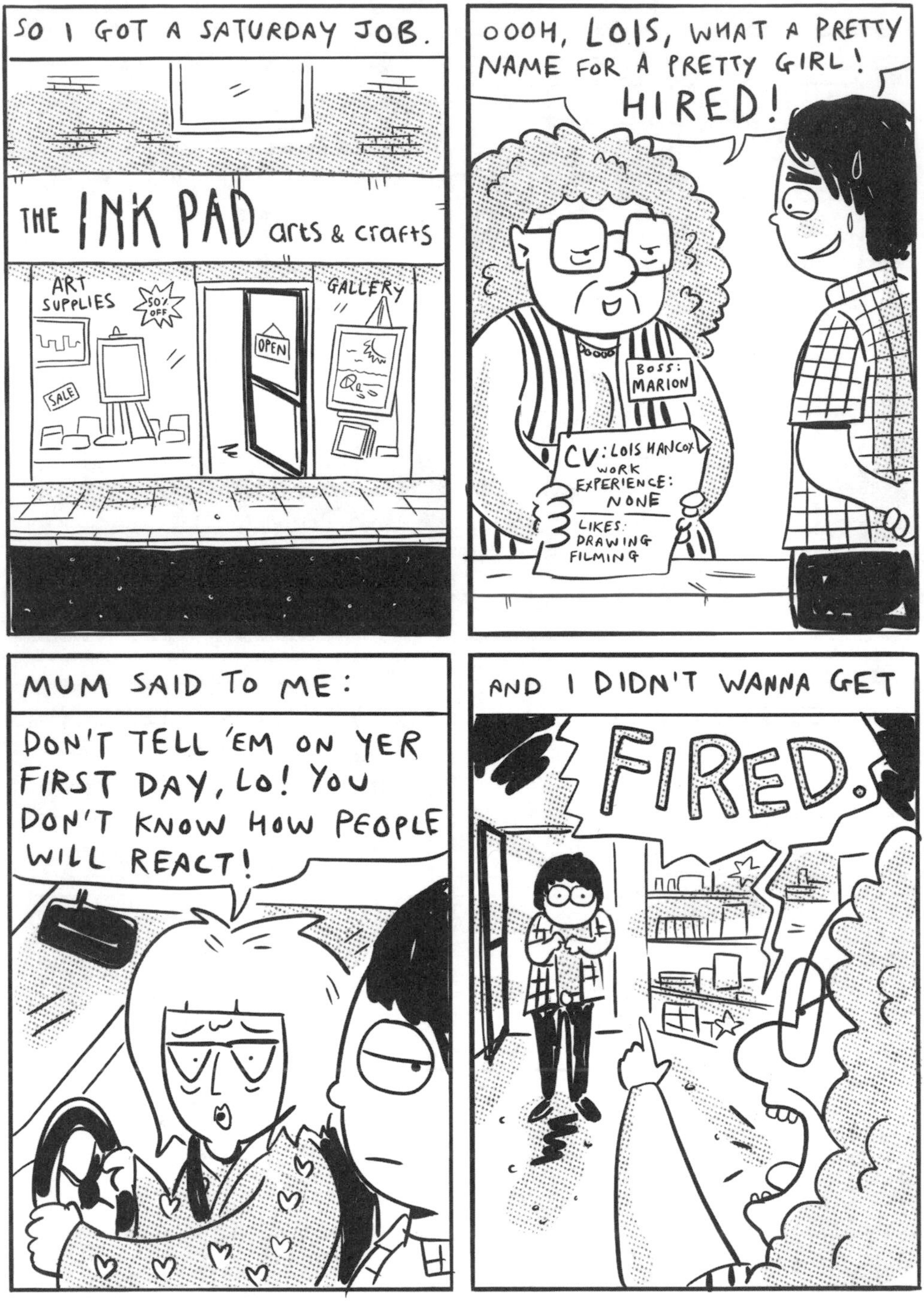
SO I GOT A SATURDAY JOB.
THE INK PAD arts & crafts
ART SUPPLIES
50% OFF
SALE
OPEN
GALLERY
OOOH, LOIS, WHAT A PRETTY NAME FOR A PRETTY GIRL! HIRED!
BOSS: MARION
CV: LOIS HANCOX
WORK EXPERIENCE: NONE
LIKES: DRAWING FILMING
MUM SAID TO ME:
DON'T TELL 'EM ON YER FIRST DAY, LO! YOU DON'T KNOW HOW PEOPLE WILL REACT!
AND I DIDN'T WANNA GET
FIRED.

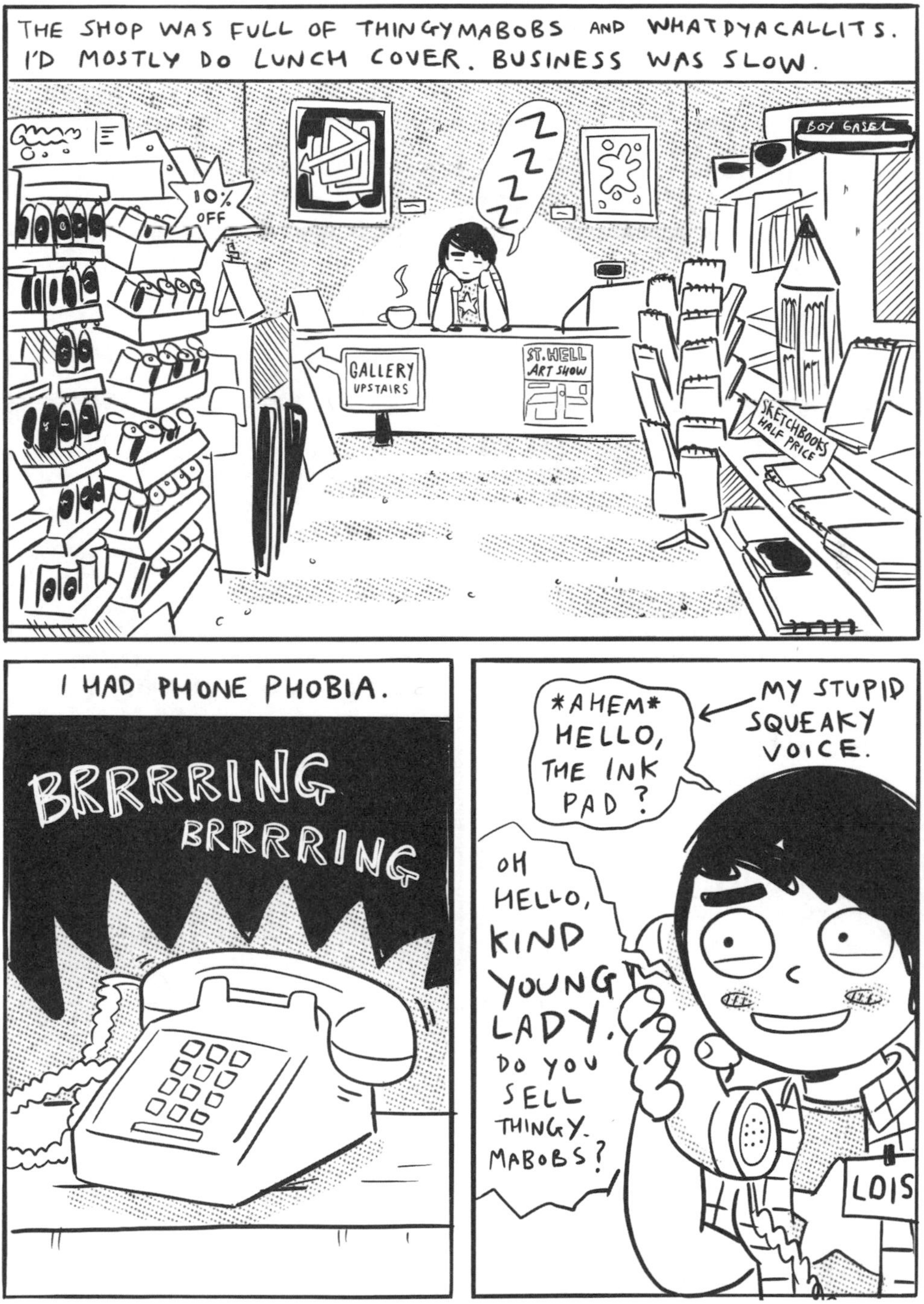
THE SHOP WAS FULL OF THINGYMABOBS AND WHATDYACALLITS. I'D MOSTLY DO LUNCH COVER. BUSINESS WAS SLOW.
10% OFF
ZZZ
GALLERY UPSTAIRS
ST. HELL ART SHOW
SKETCHBOOKS HALF PRICE
I HAD PHONE PHOBIA.
BRRRRING BRRRRRING
AHEM HELLO, THE INK PAD?
MY STUPID SQUEAKY VOICE.
OH HELLO, KIND YOUNG LADY. DO YOU SELL THINGY-MABOBS?
LOIS

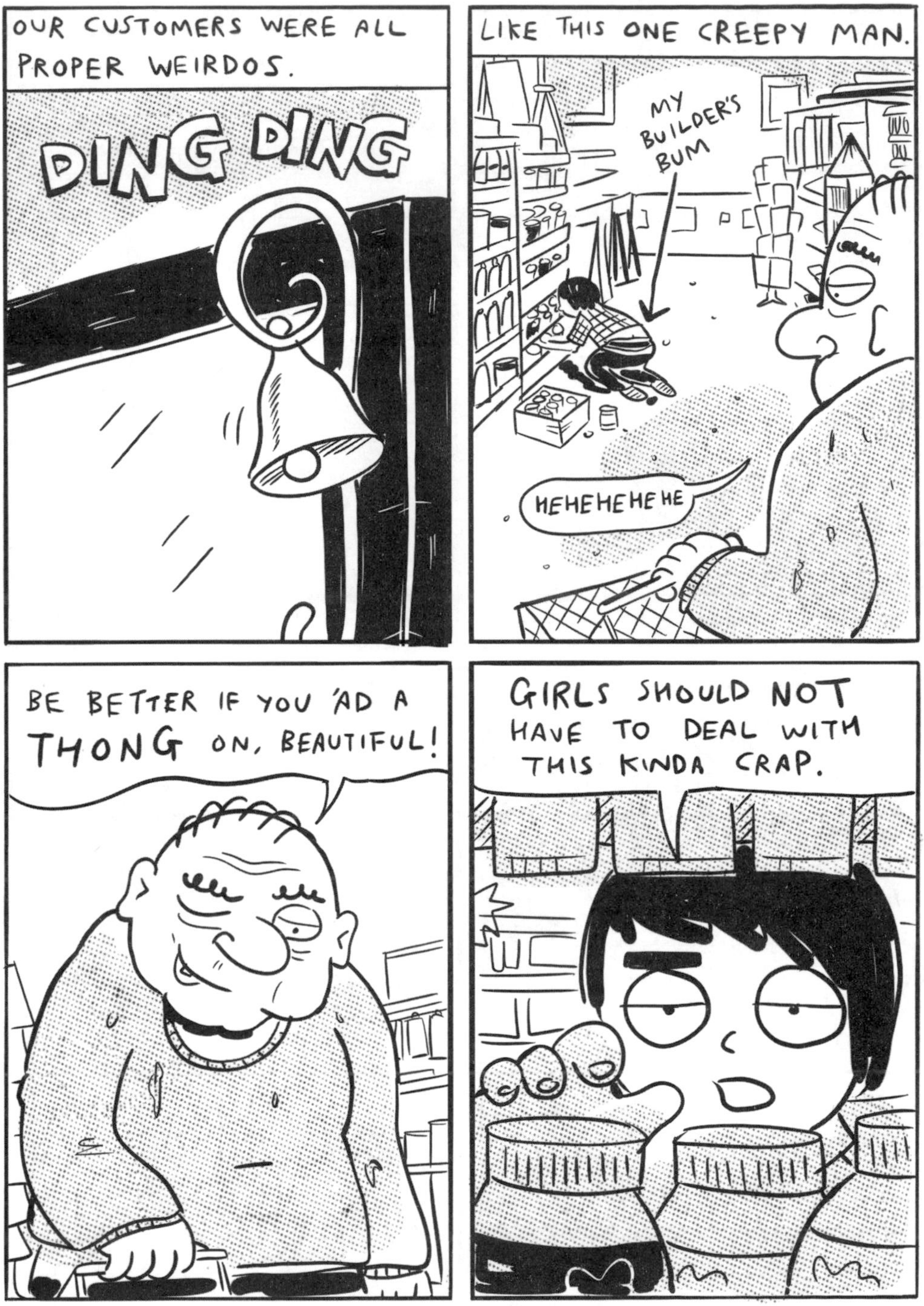
OUR CUSTOMERS WERE ALL PROPER WEIRDOS.
DING DING
LIKE THIS ONE CREEPY MAN.
MY BUILDER'S BUM
HEHEHEHEHEHE
BE BETTER IF YOU 'AD A THONG ON, BEAUTIFUL!
GIRLS SHOULD NOT HAVE TO DEAL WITH THIS KINDA CRAP.

TWO WEEKS IN, I DECIDED TO REVEAL THE REAL ME...

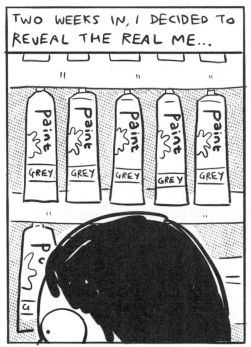

MARION... PLEASE DON'T JUDGE ME... BUT I'M TRANSITIONING!

OOOOH! WERE YOU BORN A BOY, DEAR?

ARE YOU BECOMING A WOMAN?

SO IT TOOK A BIT OF EXPLAINING, OBUS, BUT FROM THEN ON WORK MADE SURE ALL THE CUSTOMERS GOT IT RIGHT.

HAVE YOU MET LEWIS, OUR NEW MALE ASSISTANT?

LEW

SLURP

LEWIS

BOSS: MARION

BOSS

GALLERY

ST. HEL

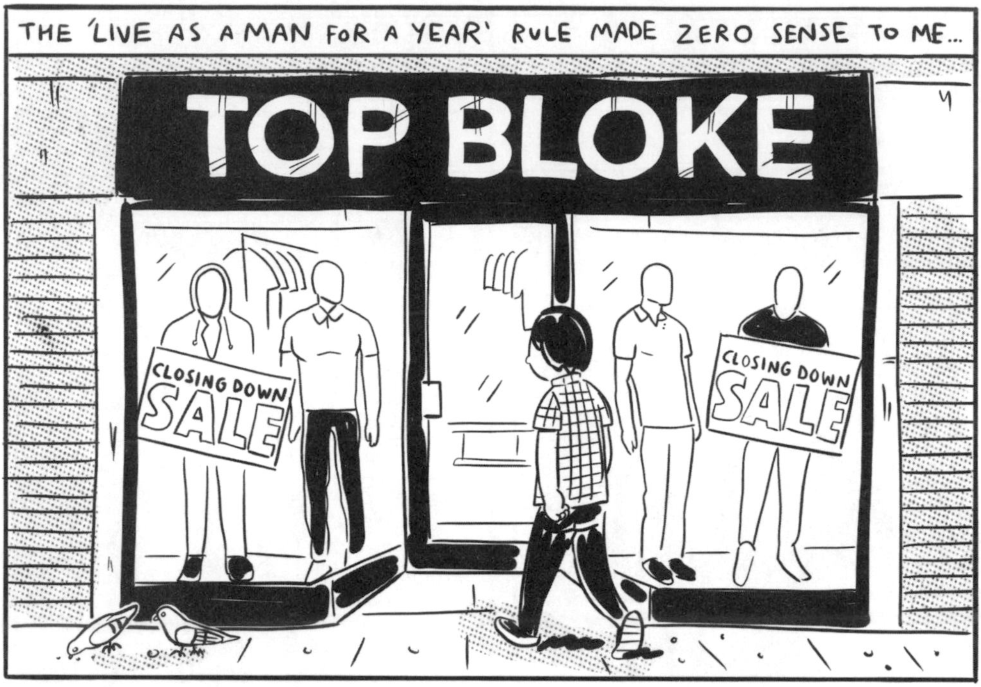
THE 'LIVE AS A MAN FOR A YEAR' RULE MADE ZERO SENSE TO ME...
TOP BLOKE
CLOSING DOWN SALE
CLOSING DOWN SALE

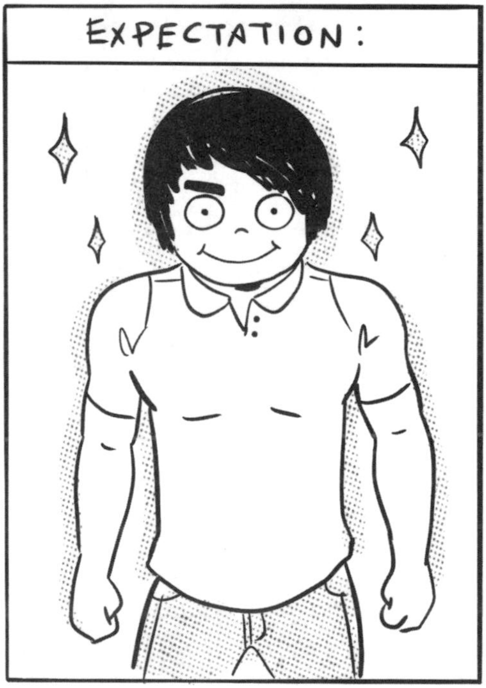
EXPECTATION:

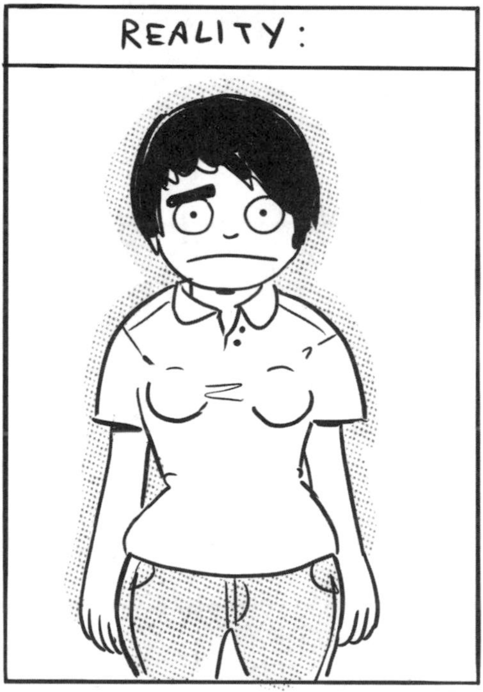
REALITY:

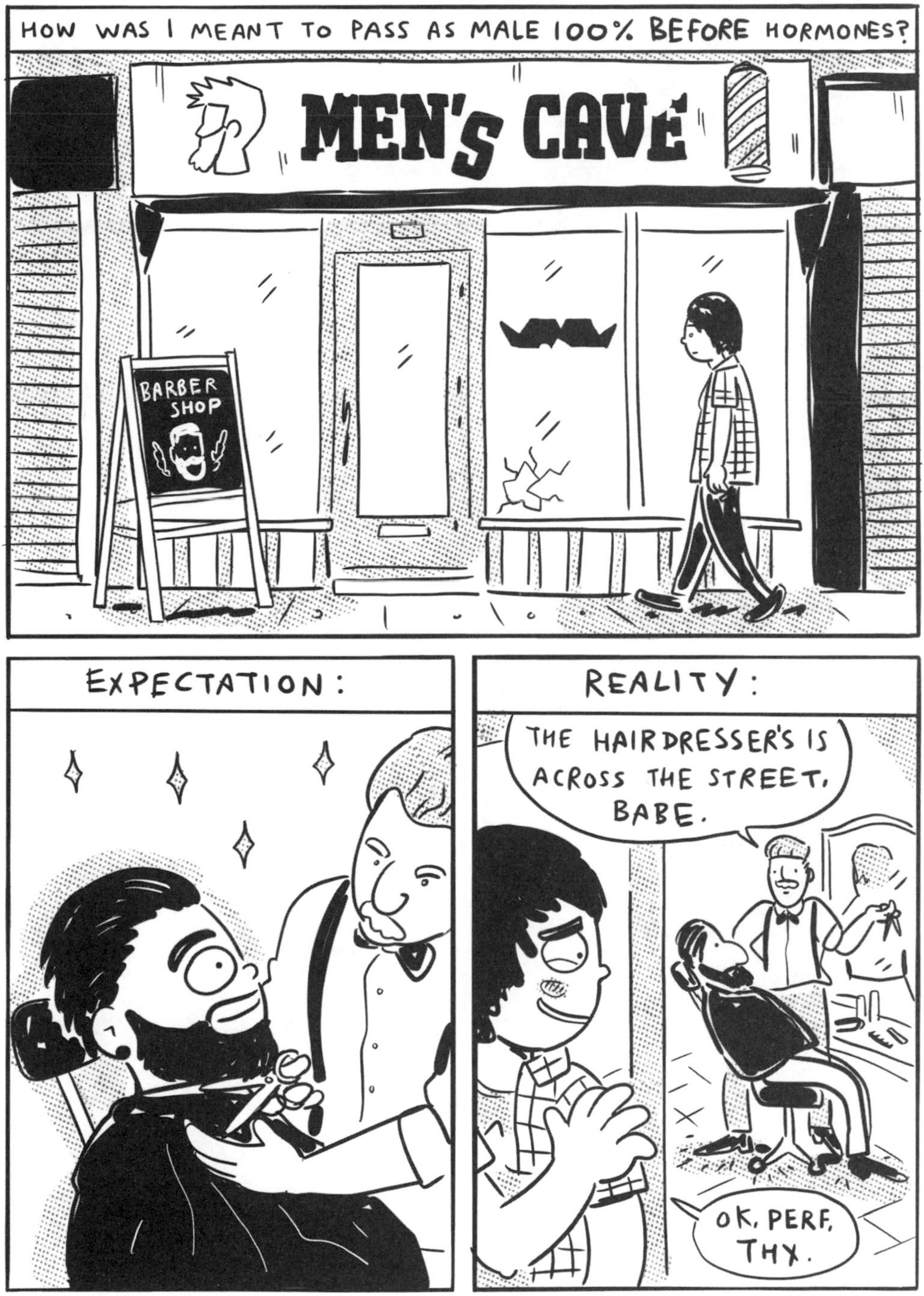
HOW WAS I MEANT TO PASS AS MALE 100% BEFORE HORMONES?
MEN'S CAVE
BARBER SHOP
EXPECTATION:
REALITY:
THE HAIRDRESSER'S IS ACROSS THE STREET, BABE.
OK, PERF, THX.

LIVE AS **MALE**™ CHECKLIST:

☑ NAME CHANGE

Deed-Poll-Office

Adult Name change £30

Lois → Lewis

(I KEPT MY MIDDLE NAME IN THE END, COZ IT'S AN EMOTION.)

Deed of Change of Name

Miss Lois Joy Hancox
to
Mr Lewis Joy Hancox

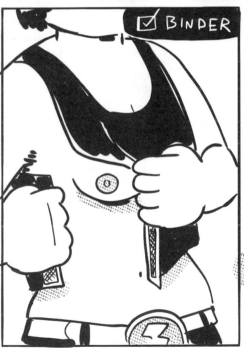

☑ BINDER

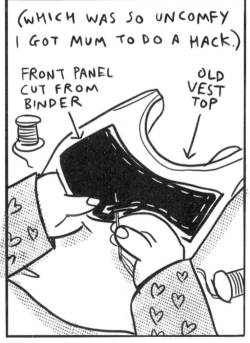

(WHICH WAS SO UNCOMFY I GOT MUM TO DO A HACK.)

FRONT PANEL CUT FROM BINDER

OLD VEST TOP

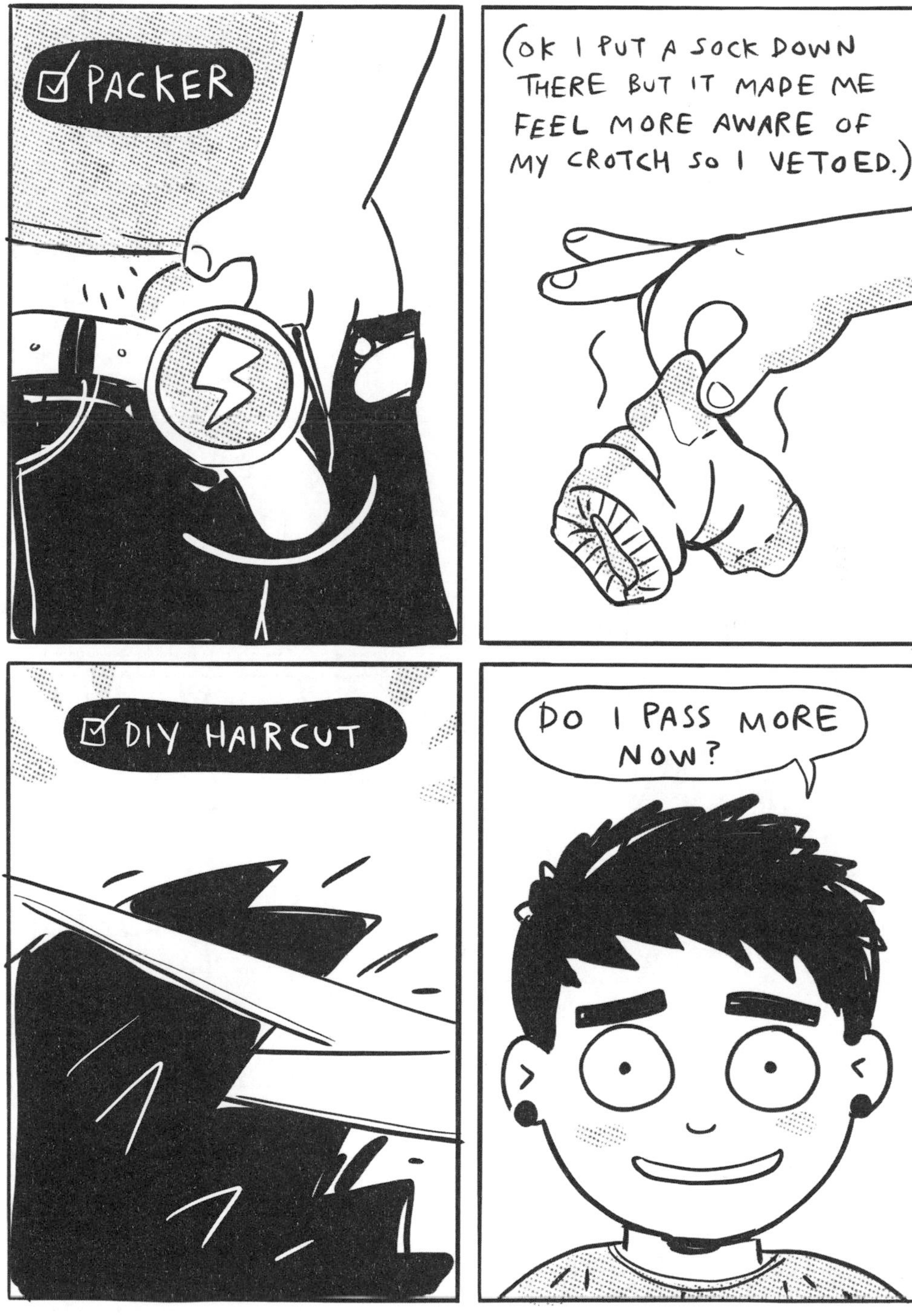
PACKER
(OK I PUT A SOCK DOWN THERE BUT IT MADE ME FEEL MORE AWARE OF MY CROTCH SO I VETOED.)
DIY HAIRCUT
DO I PASS MORE NOW?

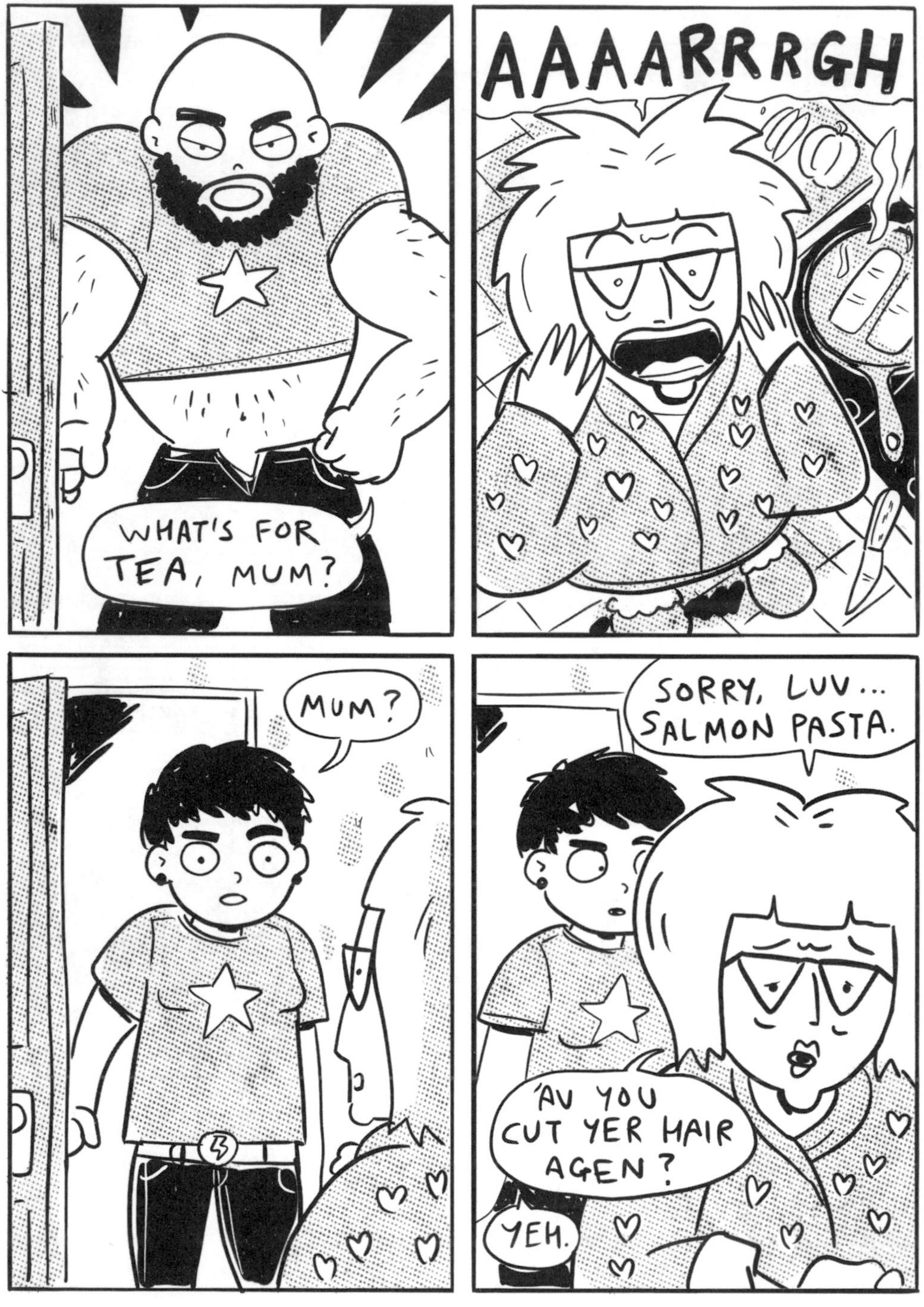
WHAT'S FOR TEA, MUM?
AAAARRRGH
MUM?
SORRY, LUV... SALMON PASTA.
'AV YOU CUT YER HAIR AGEN?
YEH.

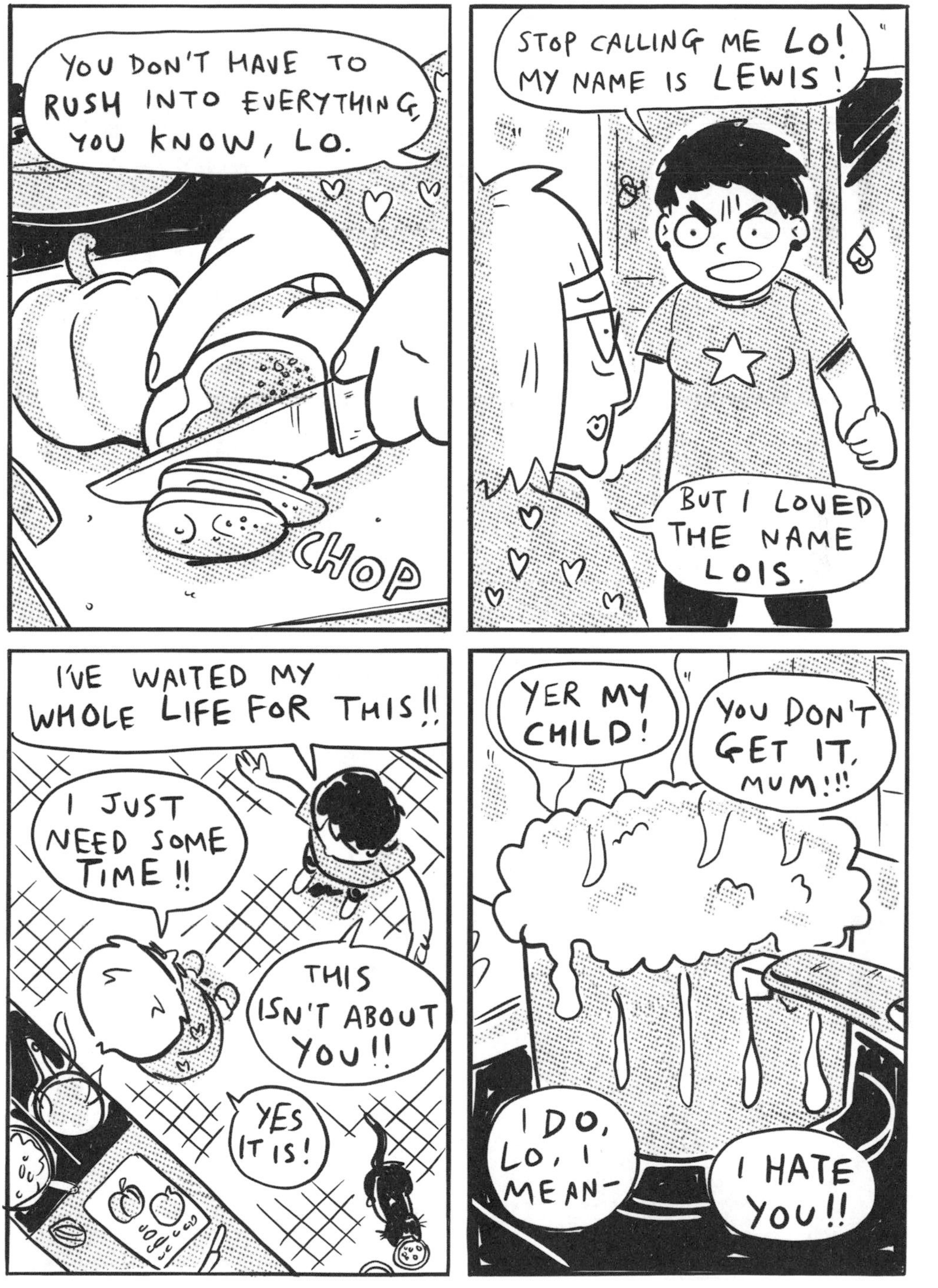
YOU DON'T HAVE TO RUSH INTO EVERYTHING, YOU KNOW, LO.
CHOP
STOP CALLING ME LO! MY NAME IS LEWIS!
BUT I LOVED THE NAME LOIS.
I'VE WAITED MY WHOLE LIFE FOR THIS!!
I JUST NEED SOME TIME!!
THIS ISN'T ABOUT YOU!!
YES IT IS!
YER MY CHILD!
YOU DON'T GET IT, MUM!!!
I DO, LO, I MEAN-
I HATE YOU!!

SMASH
I JUST WANTED TO BE UNDERSTOOD.
RIP
WHY COULDN'T I JUST'VE BEEN BORN A BOY?

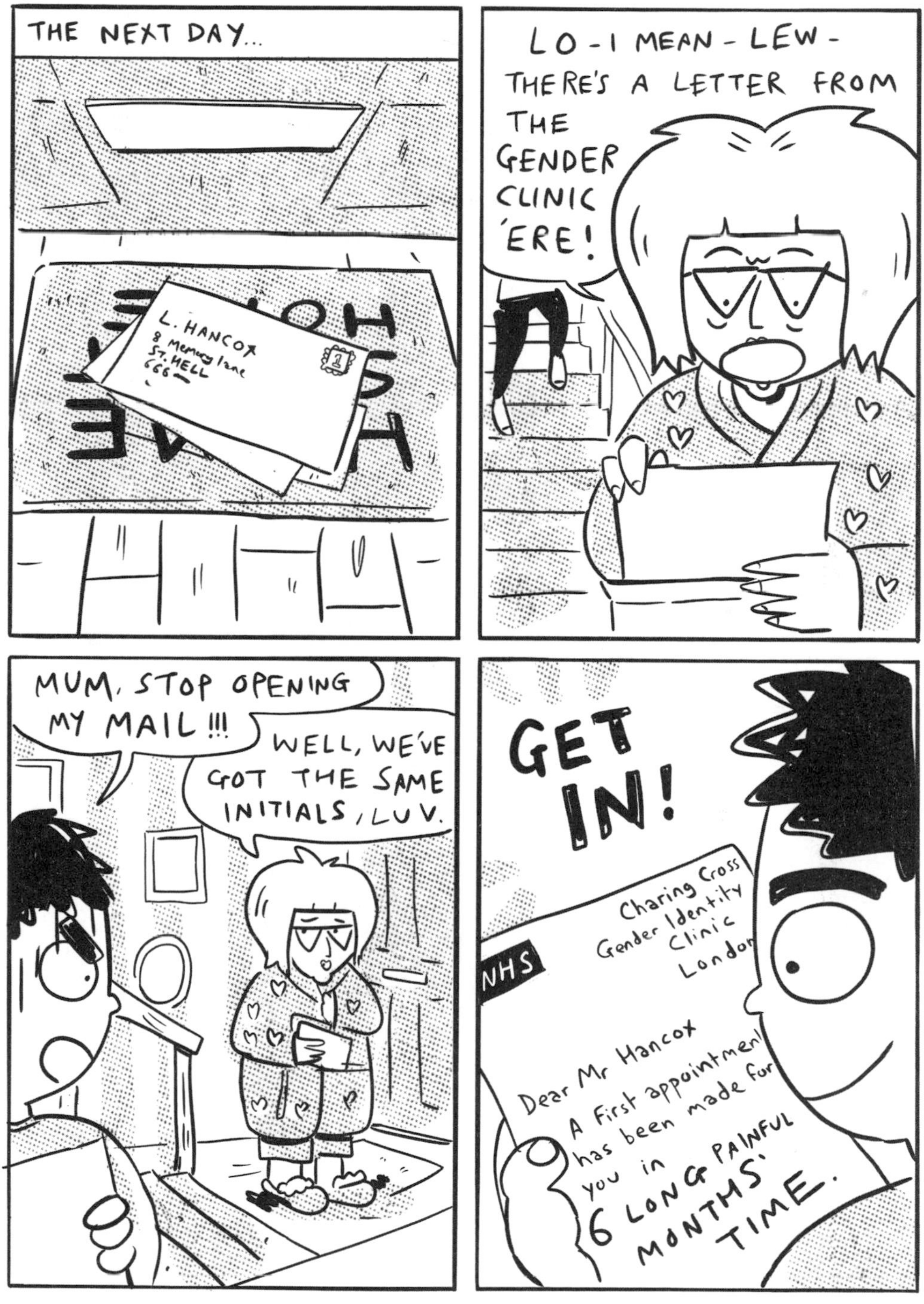
THE NEXT DAY...
L. HANCOX
8 Memory lane
ST. HELL
666
LO - I MEAN - LEW - THERE'S A LETTER FROM THE GENDER CLINIC 'ERE!
MUM, STOP OPENING MY MAIL!!!
WELL, WE'VE GOT THE SAME INITIALS, LUV.
GET IN!
NHS
Charing Cross
Gender Identity
Clinic
London
Dear Mr Hancox
A First appointment has been made for you in
6 LONG PAINFUL MONTHS' TIME.

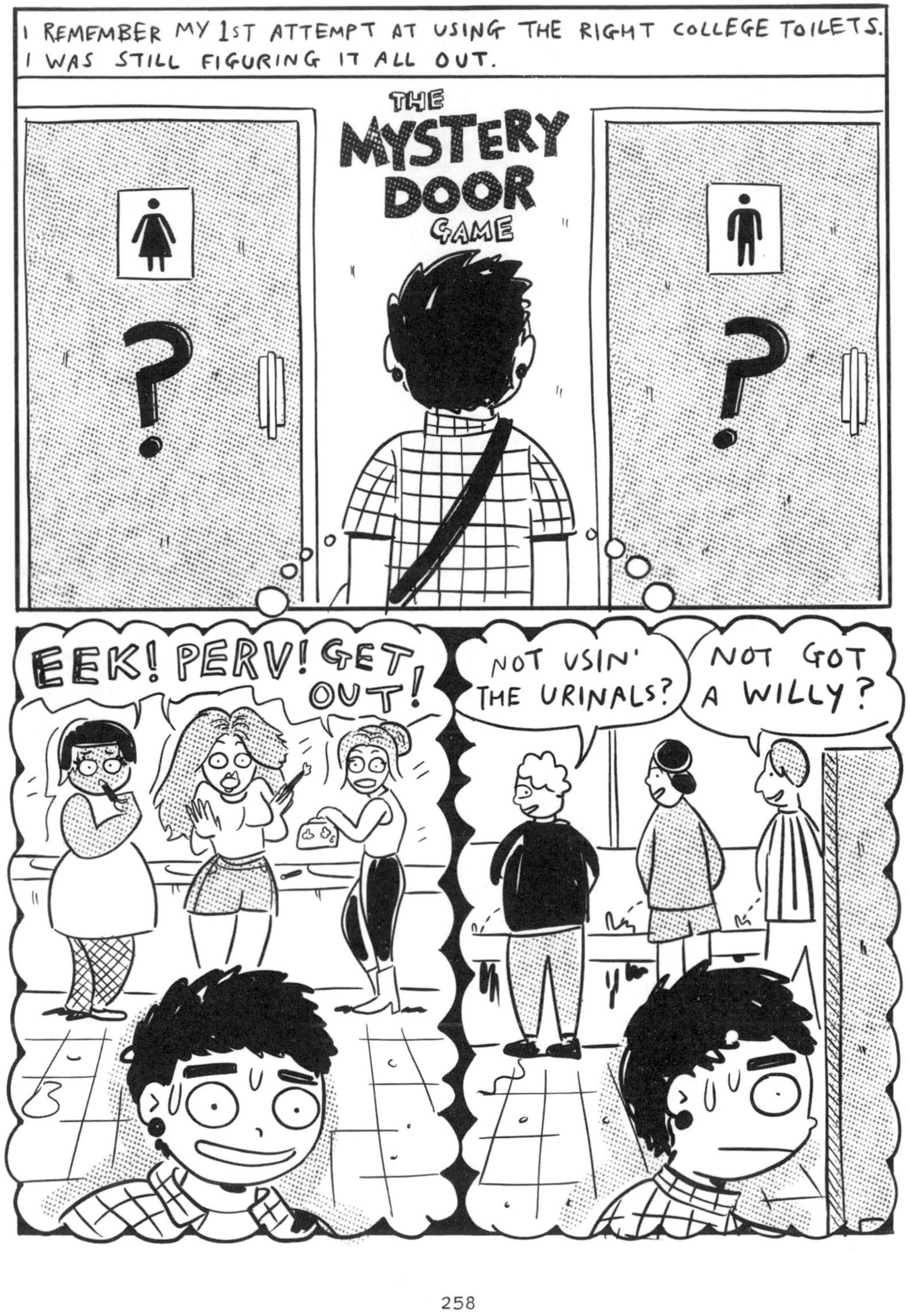
I REMEMBER MY 1ST ATTEMPT AT USING THE RIGHT COLLEGE TOILETS. I WAS STILL FIGURING IT ALL OUT.
THE MYSTERY DOOR GAME
?
?
EEK! PERV! GET OUT!
NOT USIN' THE URINALS?
NOT GOT A WILLY?

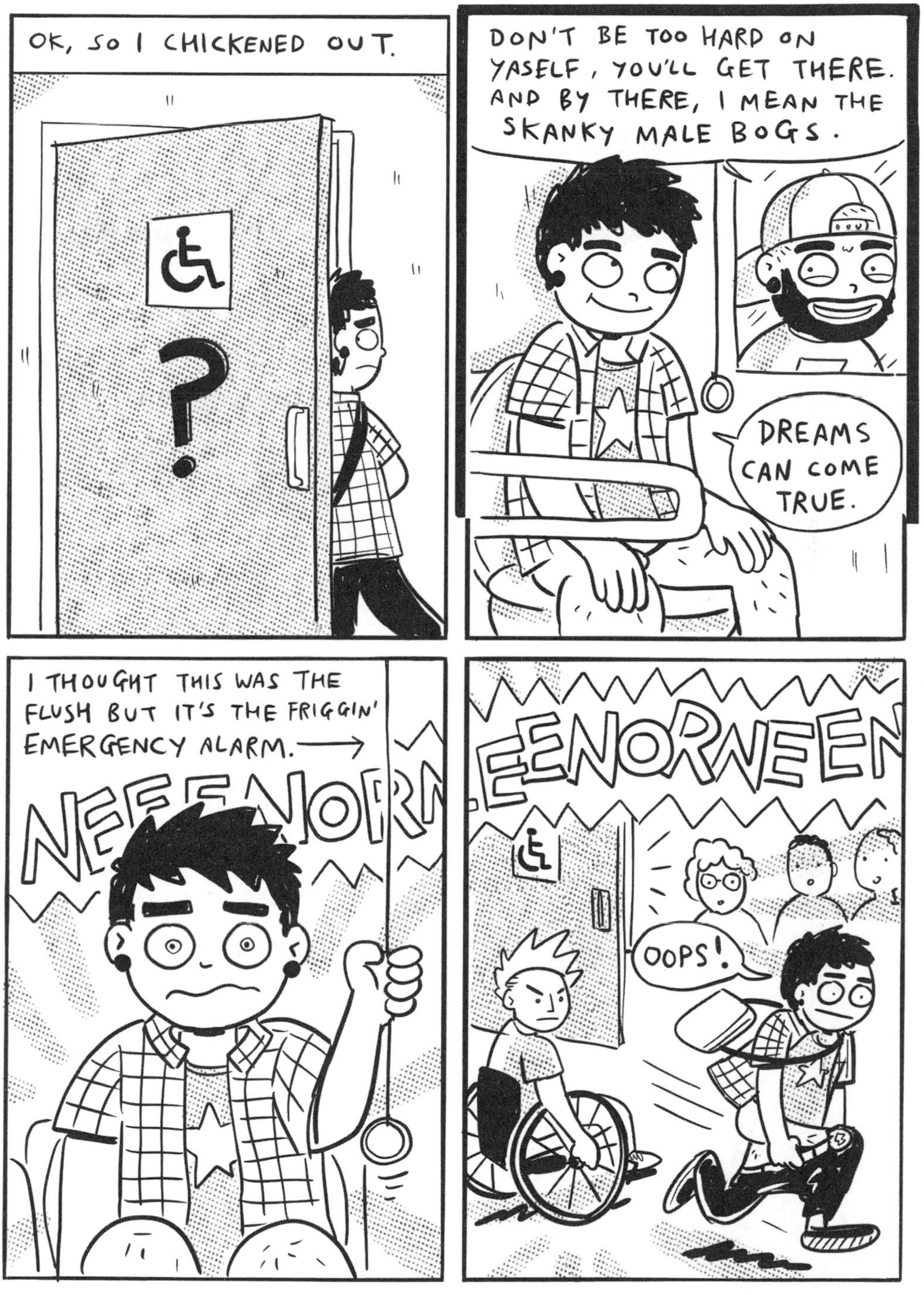
OK, SO I CHICKENED OUT.
DON'T BE TOO HARD ON YASELF, YOU'LL GET THERE. AND BY THERE, I MEAN THE SKANKY MALE BOGS.
DREAMS CAN COME TRUE.
I THOUGHT THIS WAS THE FLUSH BUT IT'S THE FRIGGIN' EMERGENCY ALARM. →
NEEENORN
EENORNEEEN
OOPS!

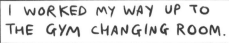
I WORKED MY WAY UP TO THE GYM CHANGING ROOM.

Male change Room

DO THEY NOTICE I NEVER TAKE MY HOODIE OFF?

OR THE LACK OF BULGE IN MY BOXERS?

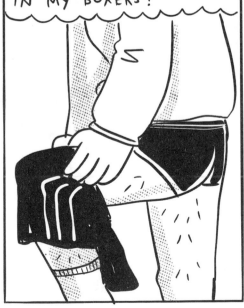

MY GIRLY AF VOICE?

ANY PLANS TONIGHT, MATE?

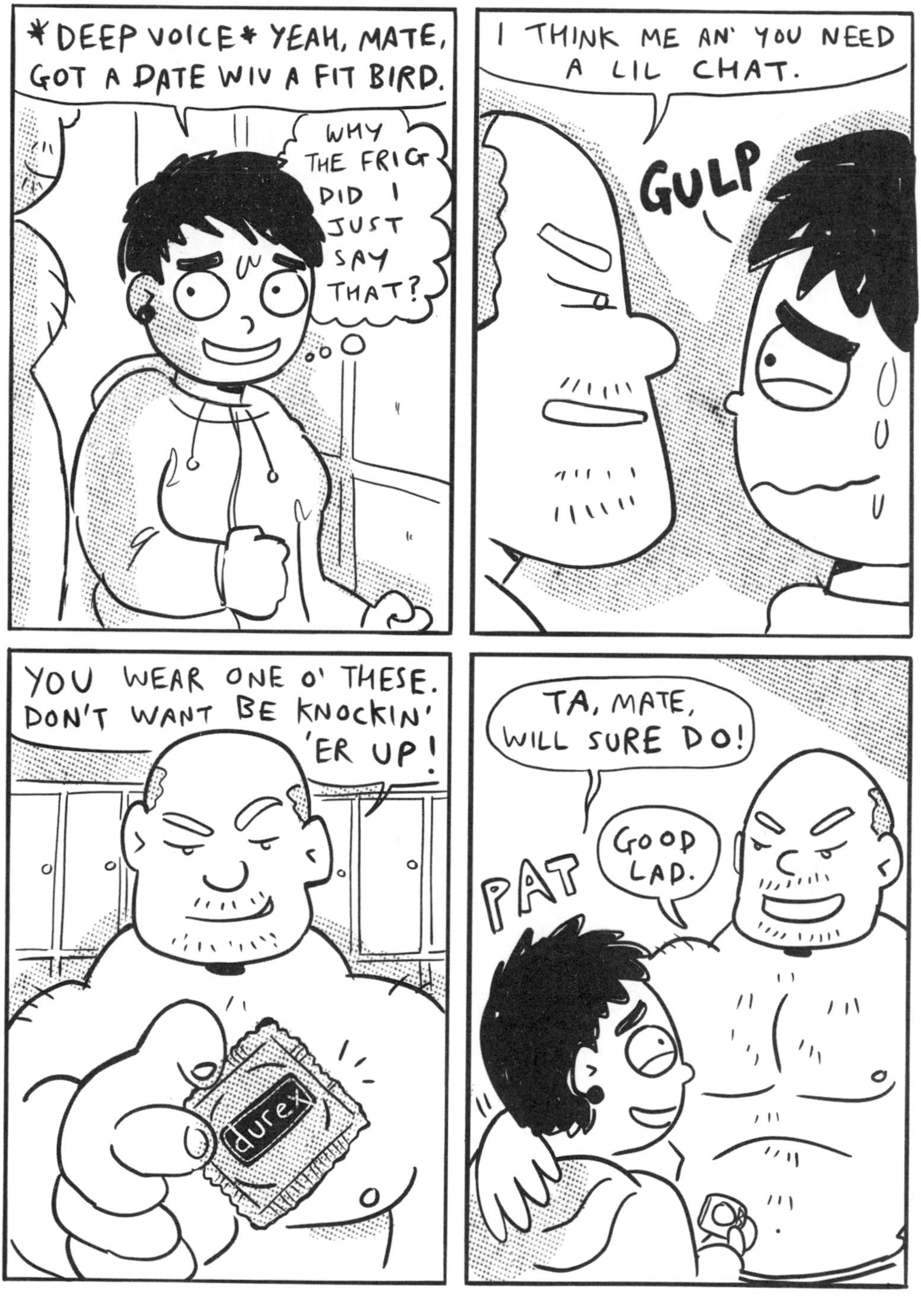
DEEP VOICE YEAH, MATE, GOT A DATE WIV A FIT BIRD.
WHY THE FRIG DID I JUST SAY THAT?
I THINK ME AN' YOU NEED A LIL CHAT.
GULP
YOU WEAR ONE O' THESE. DON'T WANT BE KNOCKIN' 'ER UP!
durex
TA, MATE, WILL SURE DO!
GOOD LAD.
PAT

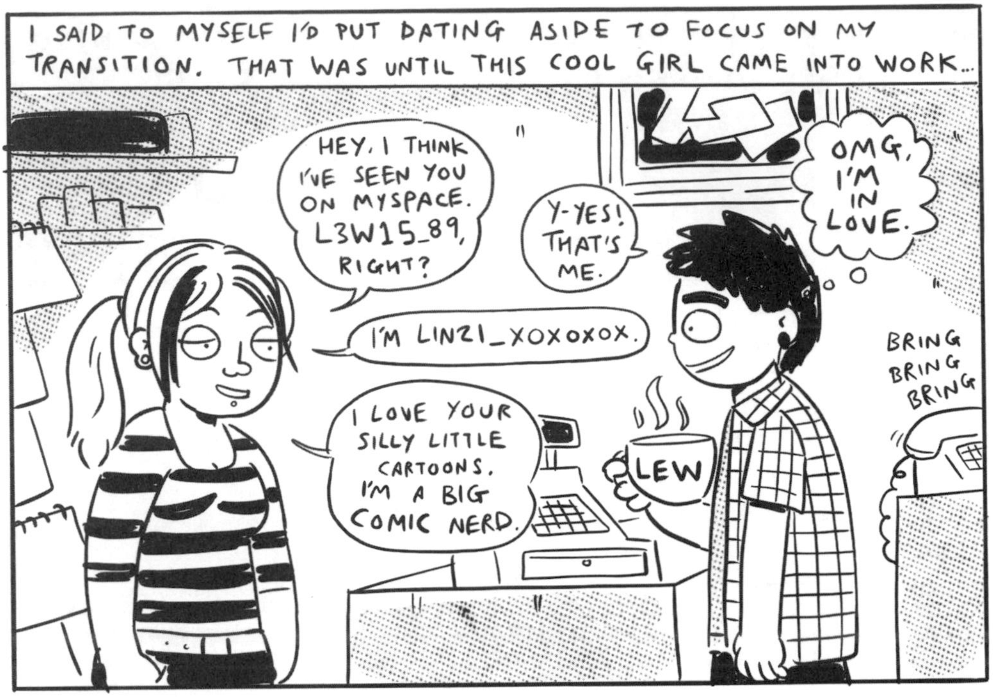
I SAID TO MYSELF I'D PUT DATING ASIDE TO FOCUS ON MY TRANSITION. THAT WAS UNTIL THIS COOL GIRL CAME INTO WORK...
HEY, I THINK I'VE SEEN YOU ON MYSPACE. L3W15_89, RIGHT?
Y-YES! THAT'S ME.
OMG, I'M IN LOVE.
I'M LINZI_XOXOXOX.
BRING BRING BRING
I LOVE YOUR SILLY LITTLE CARTOONS. I'M A BIG COMIC NERD.
LEW

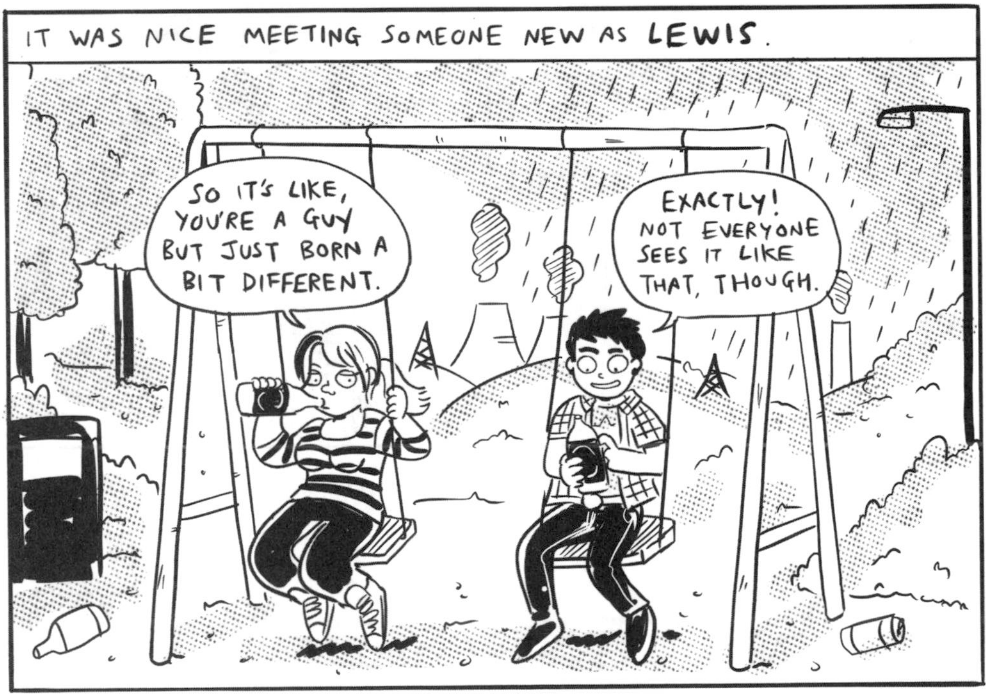
IT WAS NICE MEETING SOMEONE NEW AS **LEWIS**.
SO IT'S LIKE, YOU'RE A GUY BUT JUST BORN A BIT DIFFERENT.
EXACTLY! NOT EVERYONE SEES IT LIKE THAT, THOUGH.

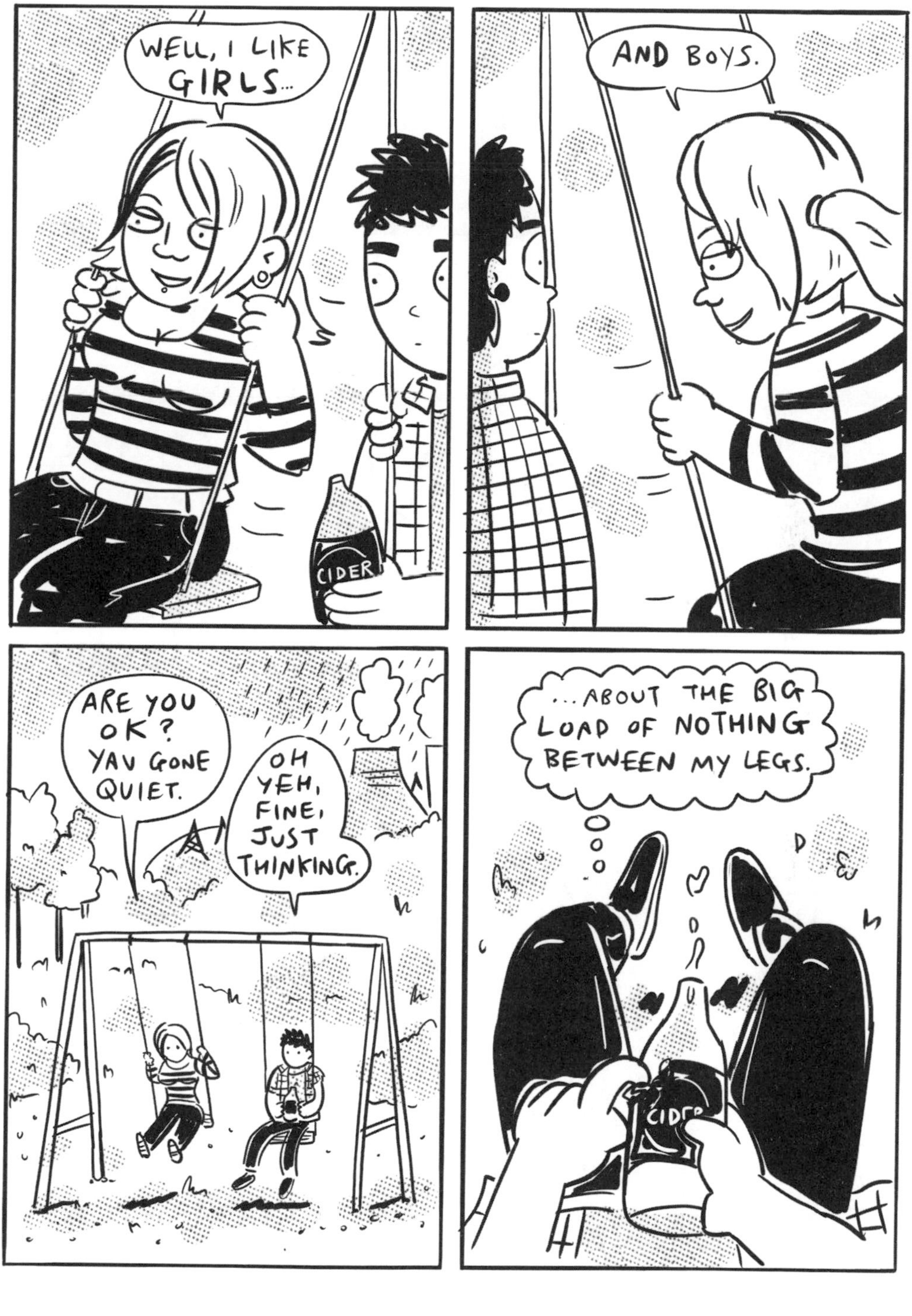

WELL, I LIKE GIRLS...
AND BOYS.
ARE YOU OK? YAU GONE QUIET.
OH YEH, FINE, JUST THINKING.
...ABOUT THE BIG LOAD OF NOTHING BETWEEN MY LEGS.
CIDER
CIDER
CIDER

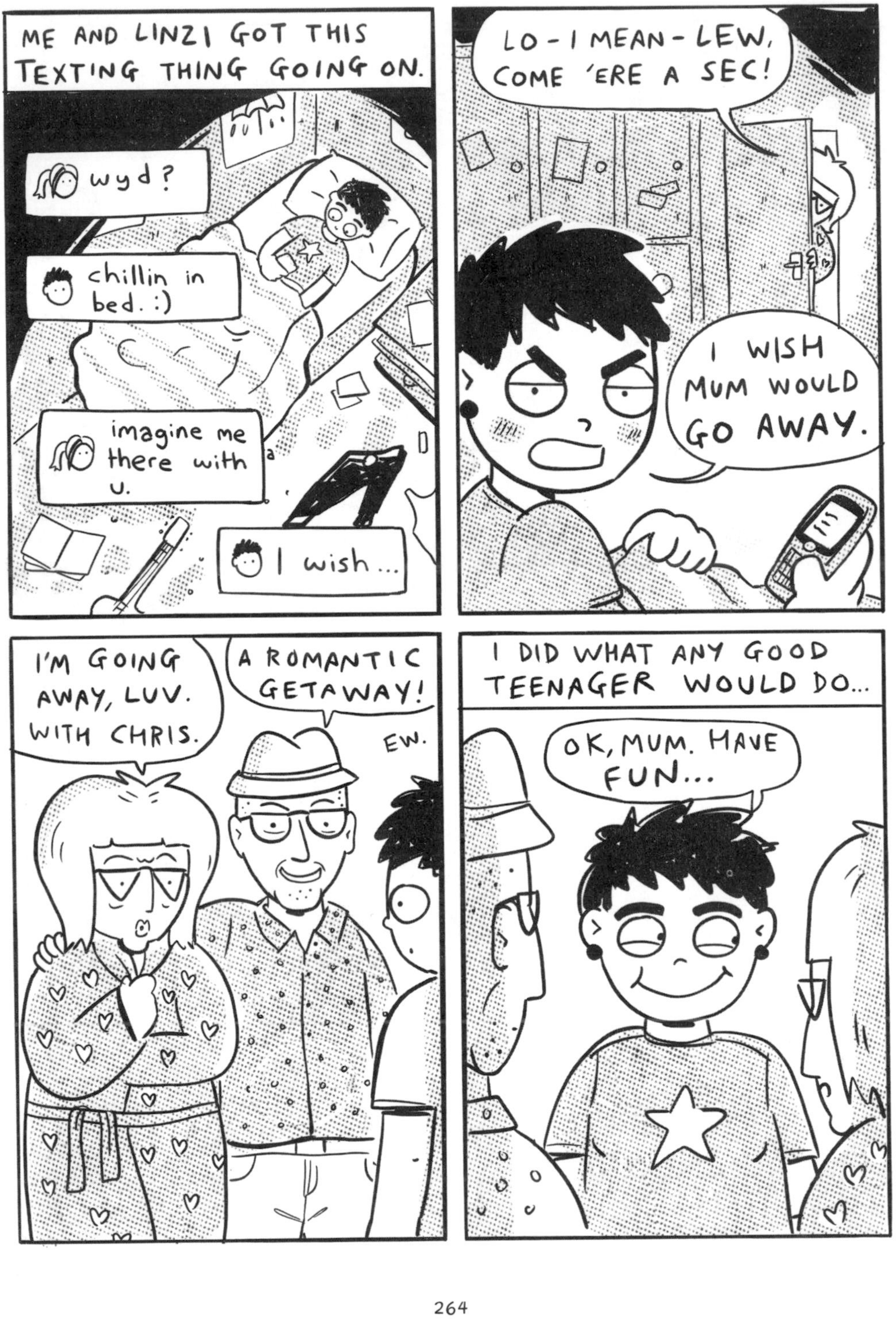
ME AND LINZI GOT THIS TEXTING THING GOING ON.
wyd?
chillin in bed. :)
imagine me there with u.
I wish...
LO-I MEAN-LEW, COME 'ERE A SEC!
I WISH MUM WOULD GO AWAY.
I'M GOING AWAY, LUV. WITH CHRIS.
A ROMANTIC GETAWAY!
EW.
I DID WHAT ANY GOOD TEENAGER WOULD DO...
OK, MUM. HAVE FUN...

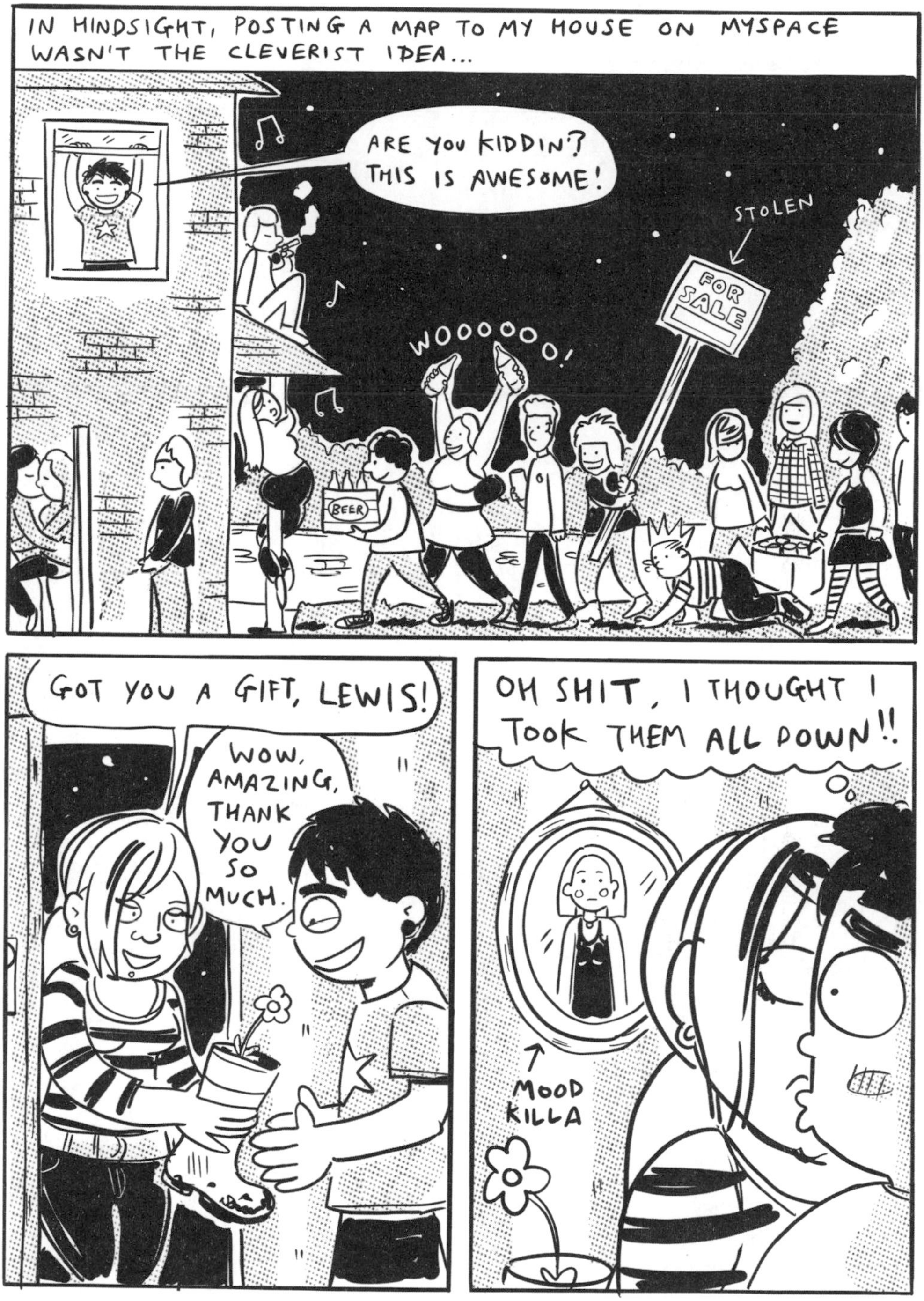
IN HINDSIGHT, POSTING A MAP TO MY HOUSE ON MYSPACE WASN'T THE CLEVERIST IDEA...
ARE YOU KIDDIN'? THIS IS AWESOME!
STOLEN
FOR SALE
WOOOOOO!
BEER
GOT YOU A GIFT, LEWIS!
WOW, AMAZING, THANK YOU SO MUCH.
OH SHIT, I THOUGHT I TOOK THEM ALL DOWN!!
MOOD KILLA

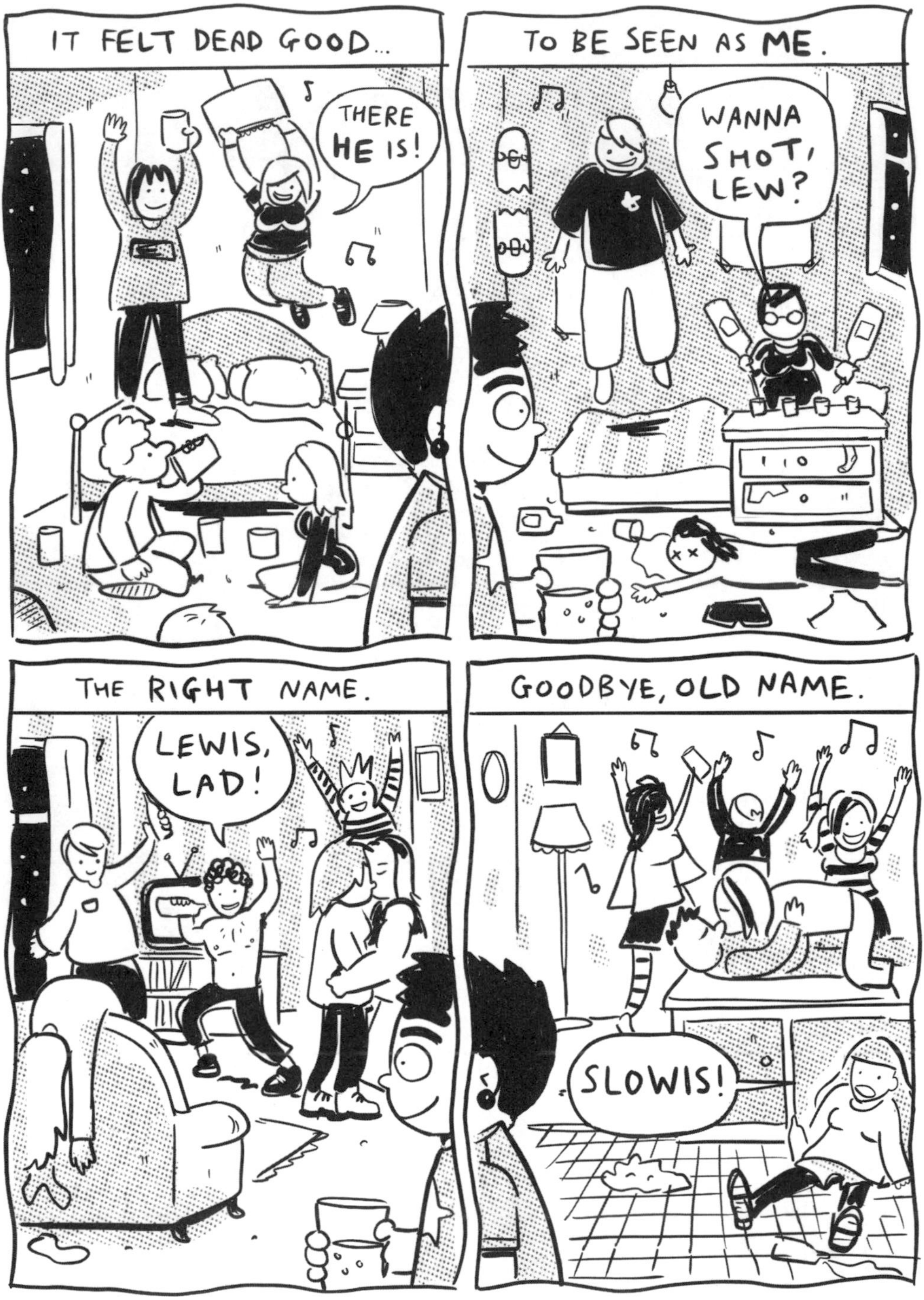
IT FELT DEAD GOOD...
THERE HE IS!
TO BE SEEN AS ME.
WANNA SHOT, LEW?
THE RIGHT NAME.
LEWIS, LAD!
GOODBYE, OLD NAME.
SLOWIS!

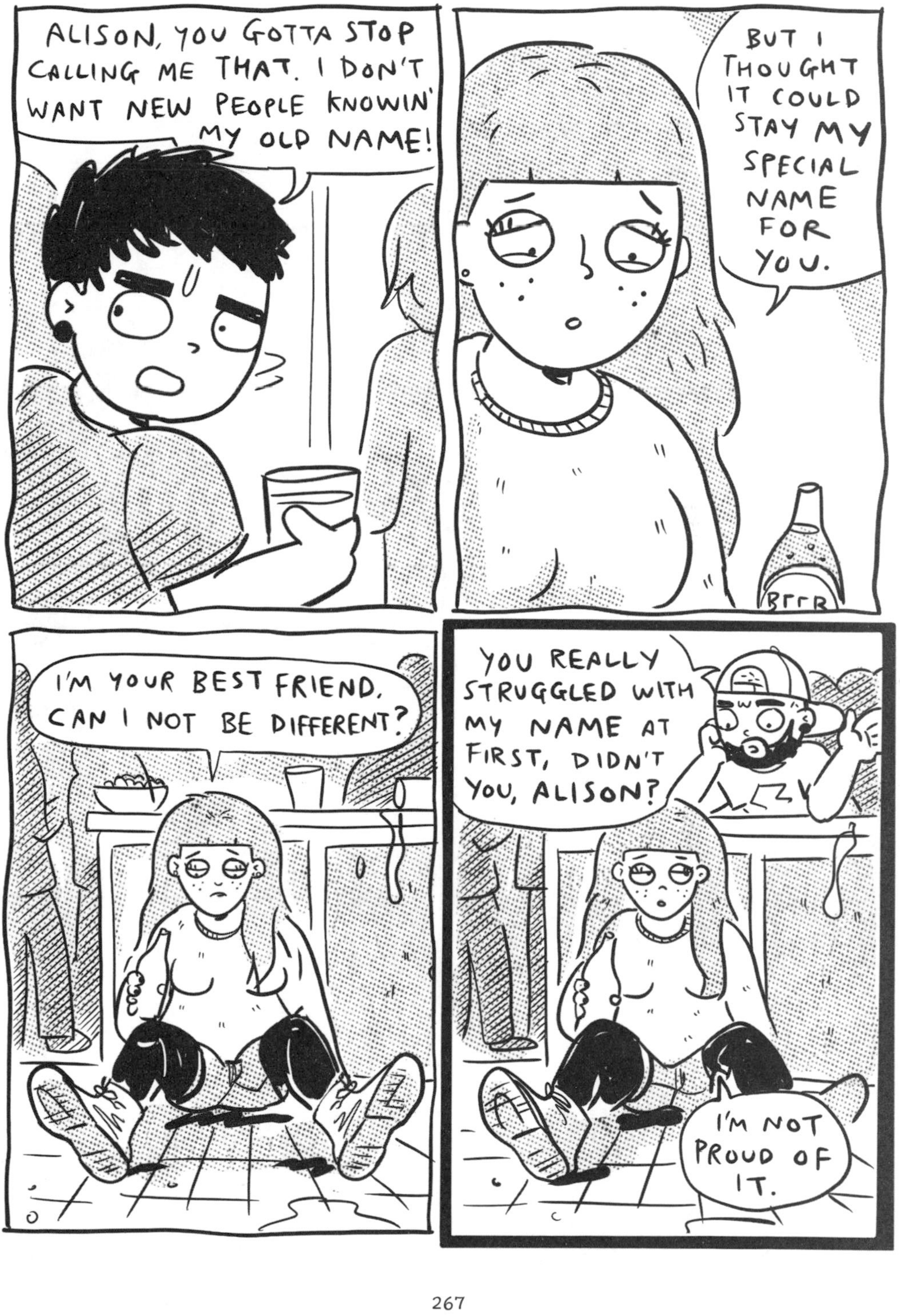

ALISON, YOU GOTTA STOP CALLING ME THAT. I DON'T WANT NEW PEOPLE KNOWIN' MY OLD NAME!
BUT I THOUGHT IT COULD STAY MY SPECIAL NAME FOR YOU.
I'M YOUR BEST FRIEND. CAN I NOT BE DIFFERENT?
YOU REALLY STRUGGLED WITH MY NAME AT FIRST, DIDN'T YOU, ALISON?
I'M NOT PROUD OF IT.

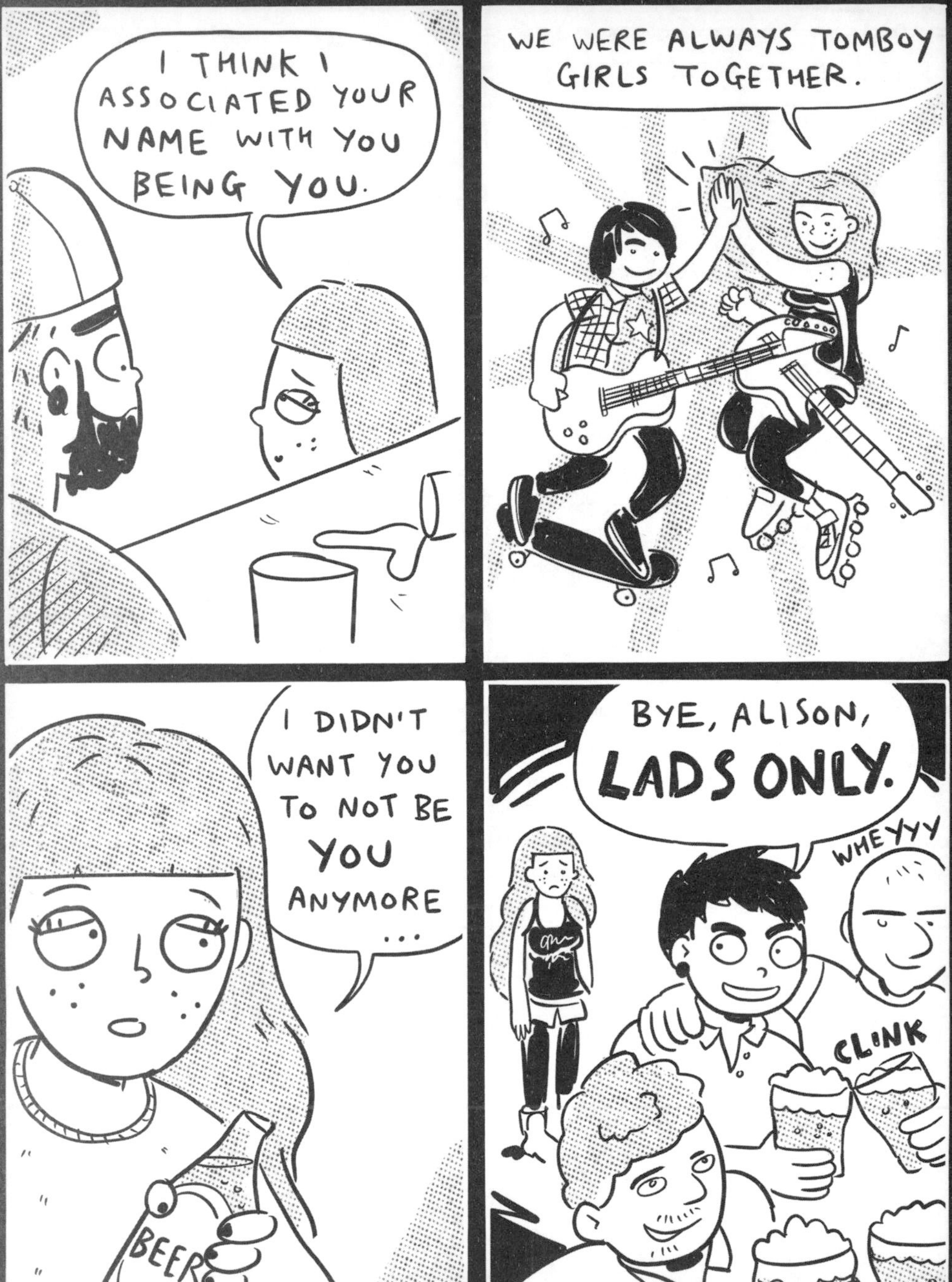

I THINK I ASSOCIATED YOUR NAME WITH YOU BEING YOU.
WE WERE ALWAYS TOMBOY GIRLS TOGETHER.
I DIDN'T WANT YOU TO NOT BE YOU ANYMORE ...
BEER
BYE, ALISON, LADS ONLY.
WHEYYY
CLINK

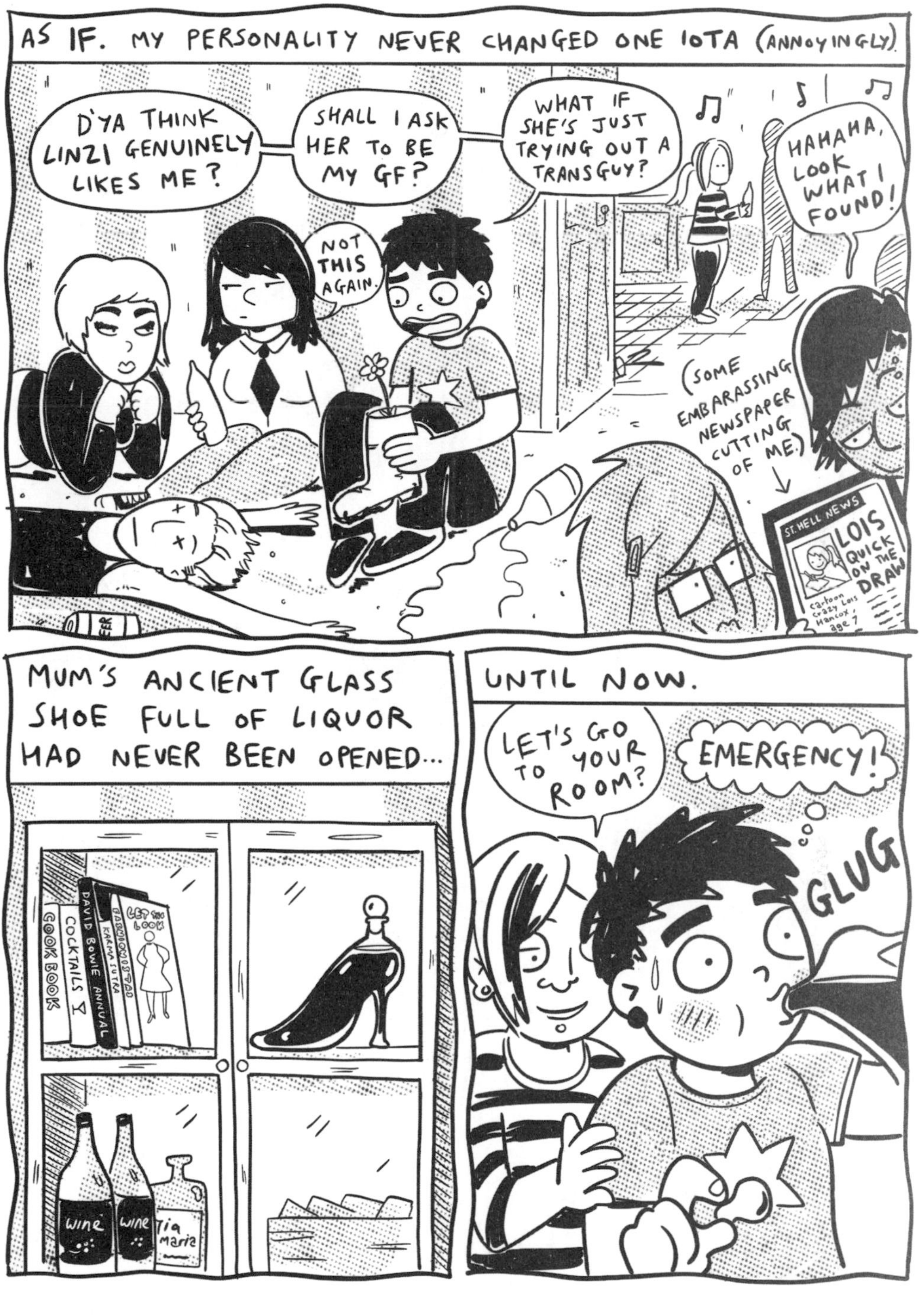

AS IF. MY PERSONALITY NEVER CHANGED ONE IOTA (ANNOYINGLY)
D'YA THINK LINZI GENUINELY LIKES ME?
SHALL I ASK HER TO BE MY GF?
WHAT IF SHE'S JUST TRYING OUT A TRANSGUY?
NOT THIS AGAIN.
HAHAHA, LOOK WHAT I FOUND!
(SOME EMBARASSING NEWSPAPER CUTTING OF ME.)
ST. HELL NEWS
LOIS QUICK ON THE DRAW
cartoon crazy Lois Hancox, age 7
MUM'S ANCIENT GLASS SHOE FULL OF LIQUOR HAD NEVER BEEN OPENED...
COOK BOOK
COCKTAILS
DAVID BOWIE ANNUAL
KARMA SUTRA
wine
wine
UNTIL NOW.
LET'S GO TO YOUR ROOM?
EMERGENCY!
GLUG

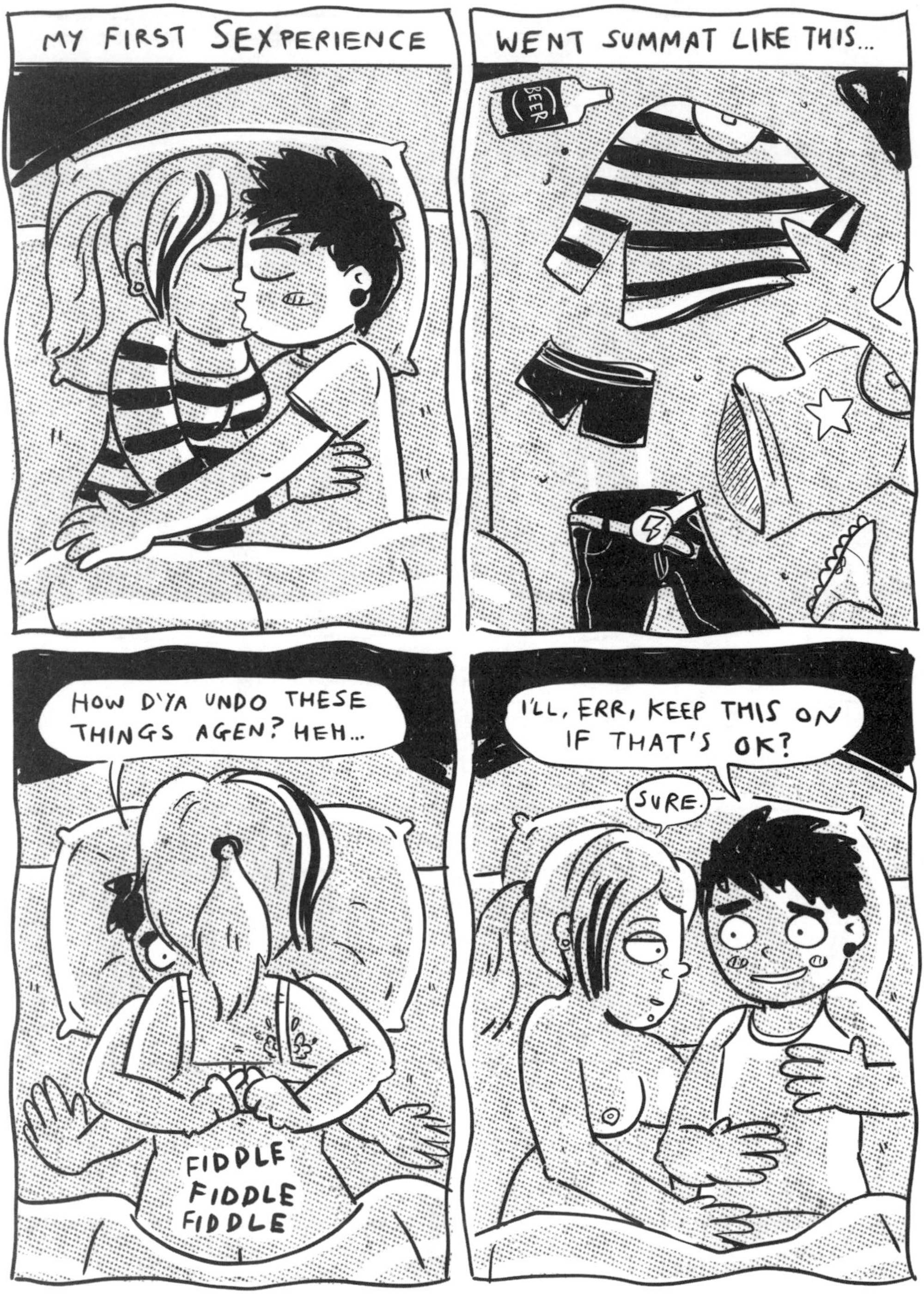
MY FIRST SEXPERIENCE
WENT SUMMAT LIKE THIS...
BEER
HOW D'YA UNDO THESE THINGS AGEN? HEH...
FIDDLE FIDDLE FIDDLE
I'LL, ERR, KEEP THIS ON IF THAT'S OK?
SURE.

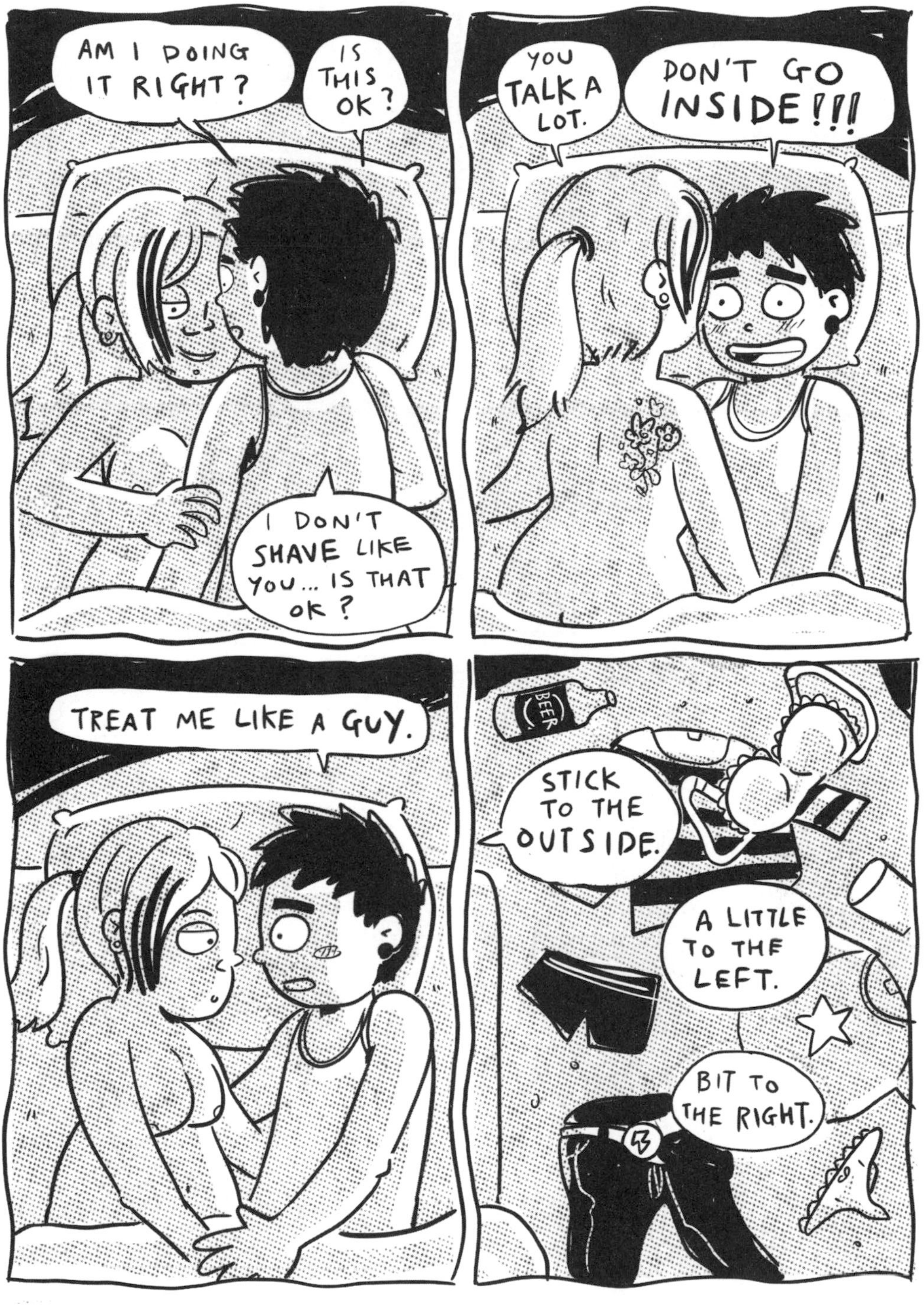
AM I DOING IT RIGHT?
IS THIS OK?
I DON'T SHAVE LIKE YOU... IS THAT OK?
YOU TALK A LOT.
DON'T GO INSIDE!!!
TREAT ME LIKE A GUY.
BEER
STICK TO THE OUTSIDE.
A LITTLE TO THE LEFT.
BIT TO THE RIGHT.

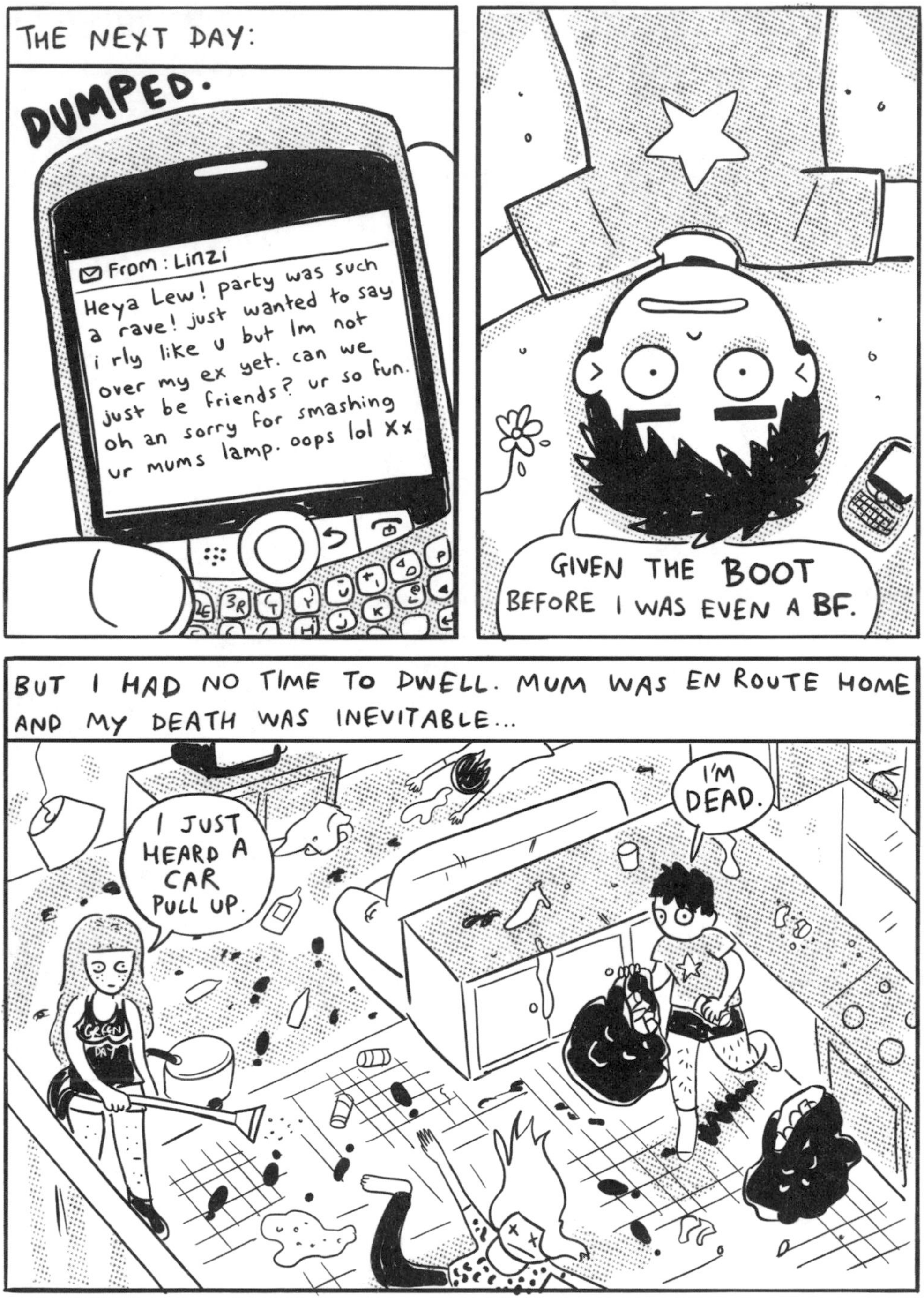
THE NEXT DAY:
DUMPED.
From: Linzi
Heya Lew! party was such a rave! just wanted to say i rly like u but Im not over my ex yet. can we just be friends? ur so fun. oh an sorry for smashing ur mums lamp. oops lol Xx
GIVEN THE BOOT BEFORE I WAS EVEN A BF.
BUT I HAD NO TIME TO DWELL. MUM WAS EN ROUTE HOME AND MY DEATH WAS INEVITABLE...
I JUST HEARD A CAR PULL UP.
I'M DEAD.
GREEN DAY

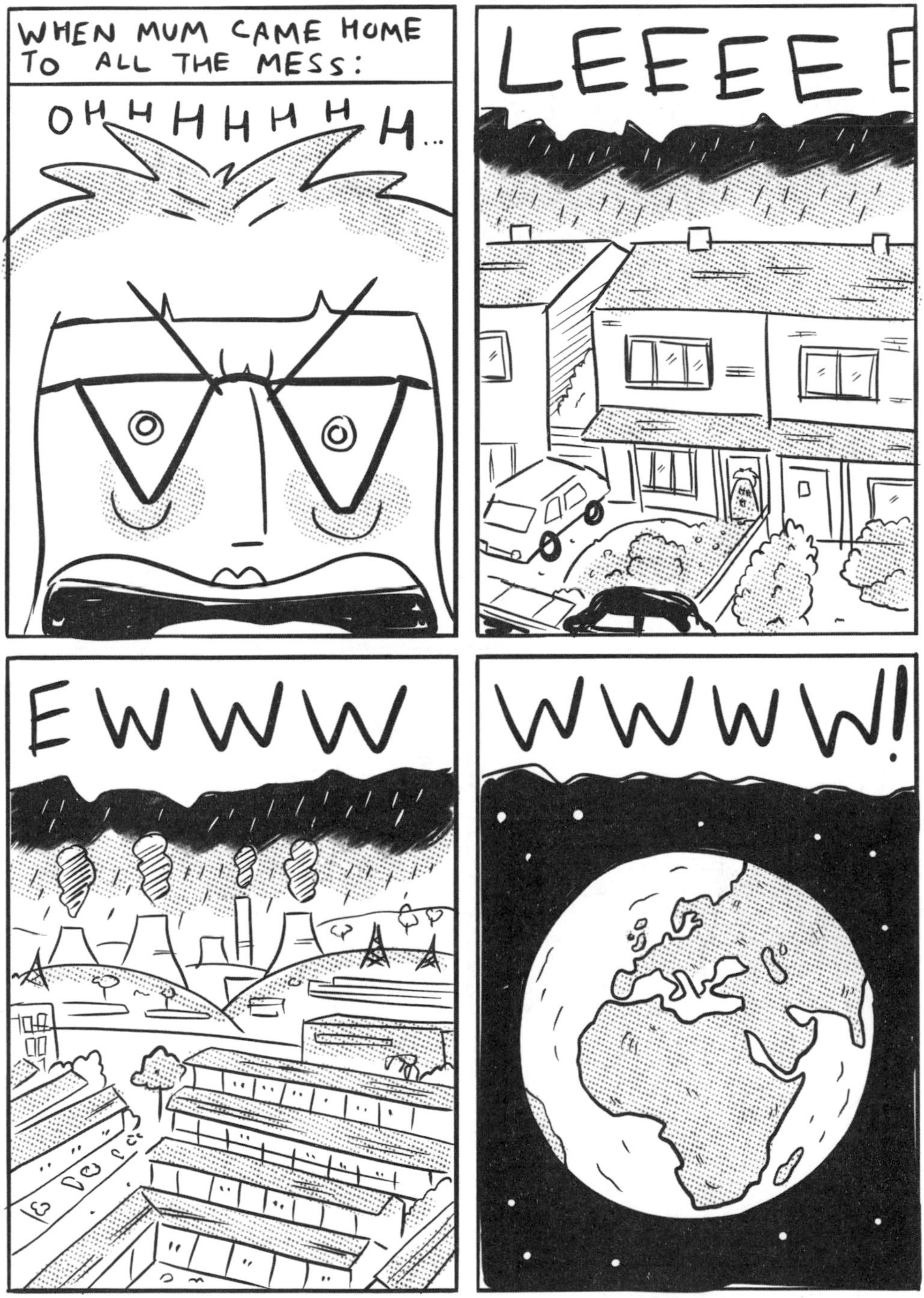
WHEN MUM CAME HOME TO ALL THE MESS:
OHHHHHHH...
LEEEEE
EWWW
WWWW!

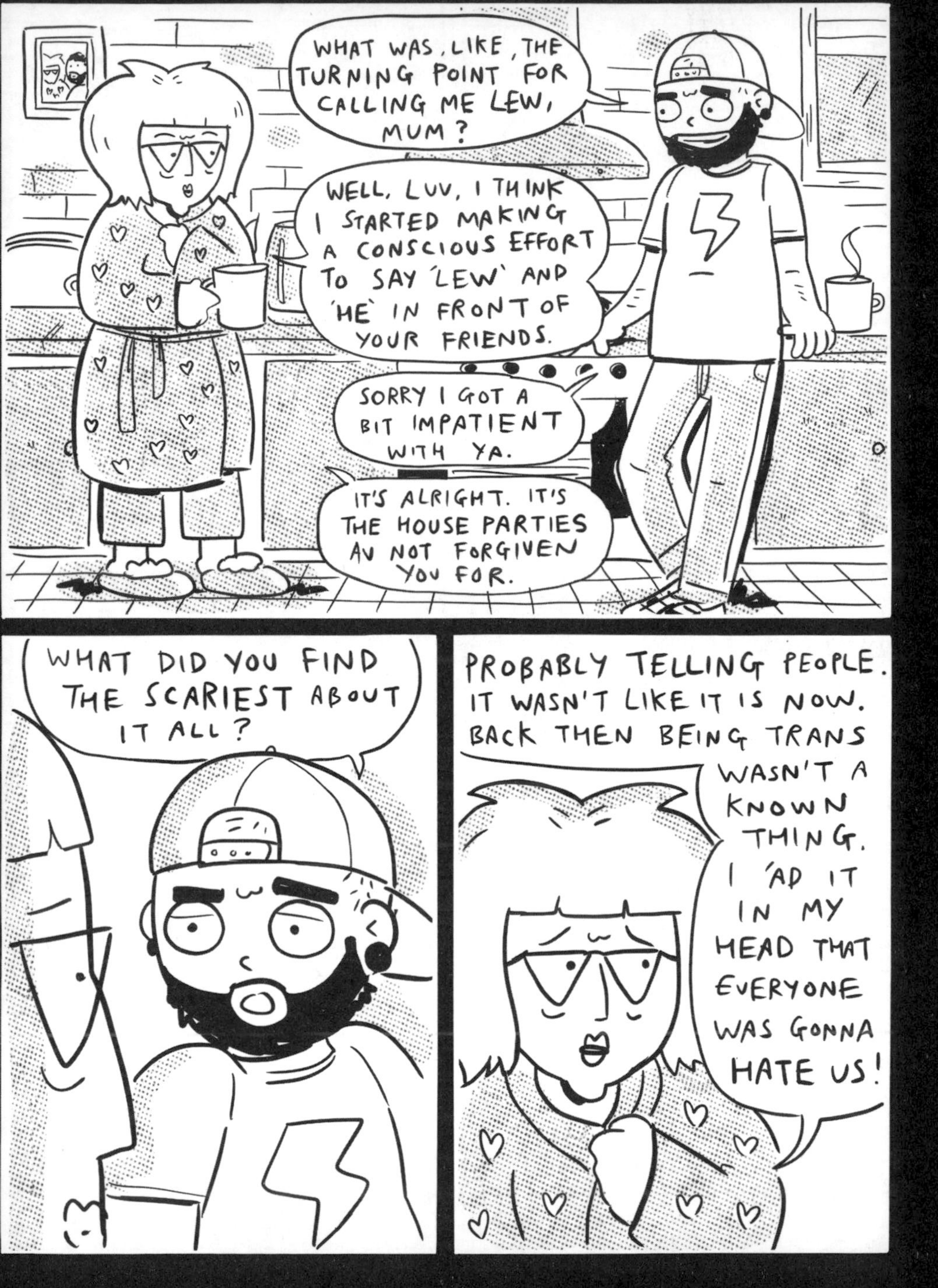
WHAT WAS, LIKE, THE TURNING POINT FOR CALLING ME LEW, MUM?
WELL, LUV, I THINK I STARTED MAKING A CONSCIOUS EFFORT TO SAY 'LEW' AND 'HE' IN FRONT OF YOUR FRIENDS.
SORRY I GOT A BIT IMPATIENT WITH YA.
IT'S ALRIGHT. IT'S THE HOUSE PARTIES AV NOT FORGIVEN YOU FOR.
WHAT DID YOU FIND THE SCARIEST ABOUT IT ALL?
PROBABLY TELLING PEOPLE. IT WASN'T LIKE IT IS NOW. BACK THEN BEING TRANS WASN'T A KNOWN THING. I 'AD IT IN MY HEAD THAT EVERYONE WAS GONNA HATE US!

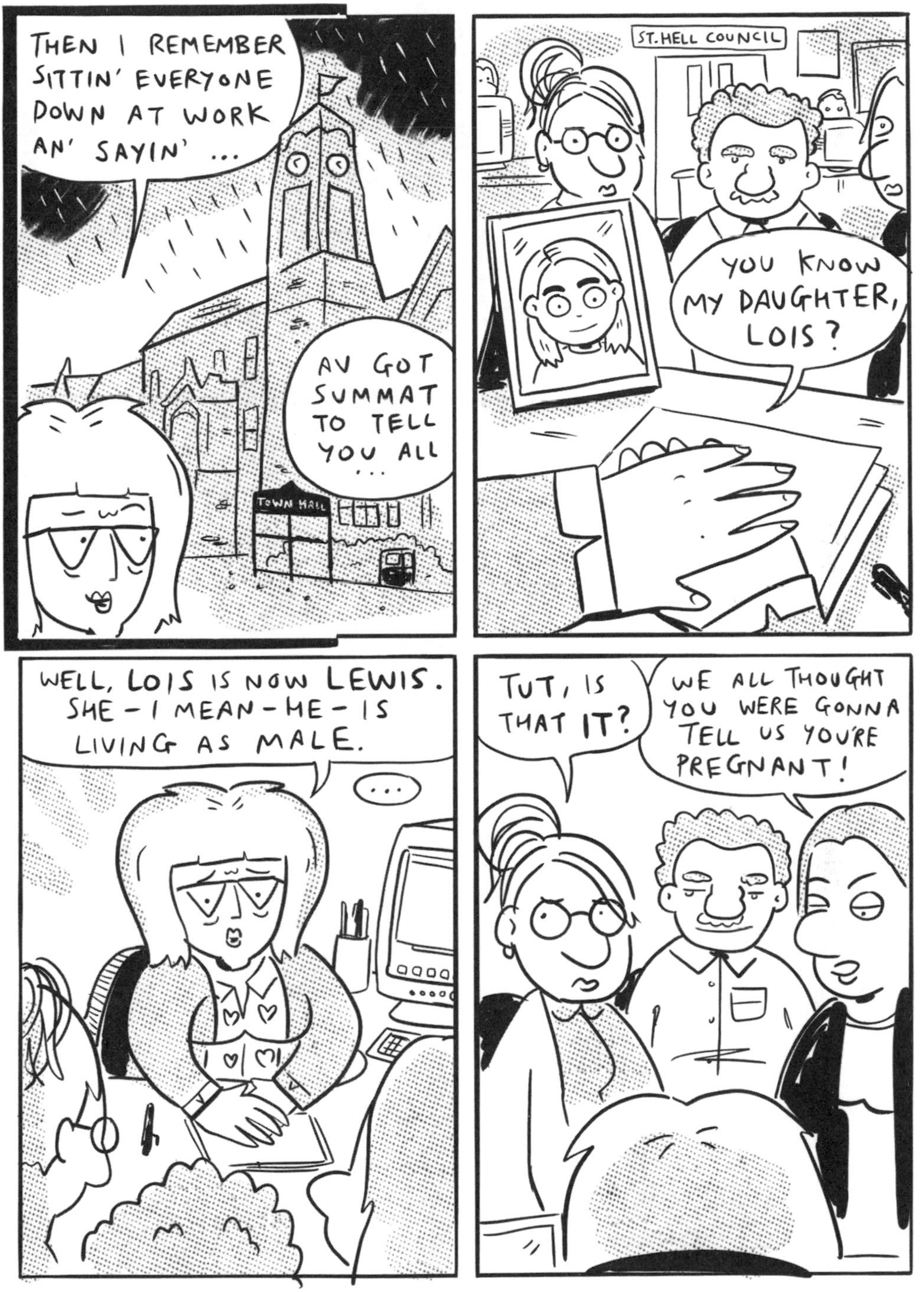
THEN I REMEMBER SITTIN' EVERYONE DOWN AT WORK AN' SAYIN' ...
AV GOT SUMMAT TO TELL YOU ALL ...
TOWN HALL
ST. HELL COUNCIL
YOU KNOW MY DAUGHTER, LOIS?
WELL, LOIS IS NOW LEWIS. SHE - I MEAN - HE - IS LIVING AS MALE.
...
TUT, IS THAT IT?
WE ALL THOUGHT YOU WERE GONNA TELL US YOU'RE PREGNANT!

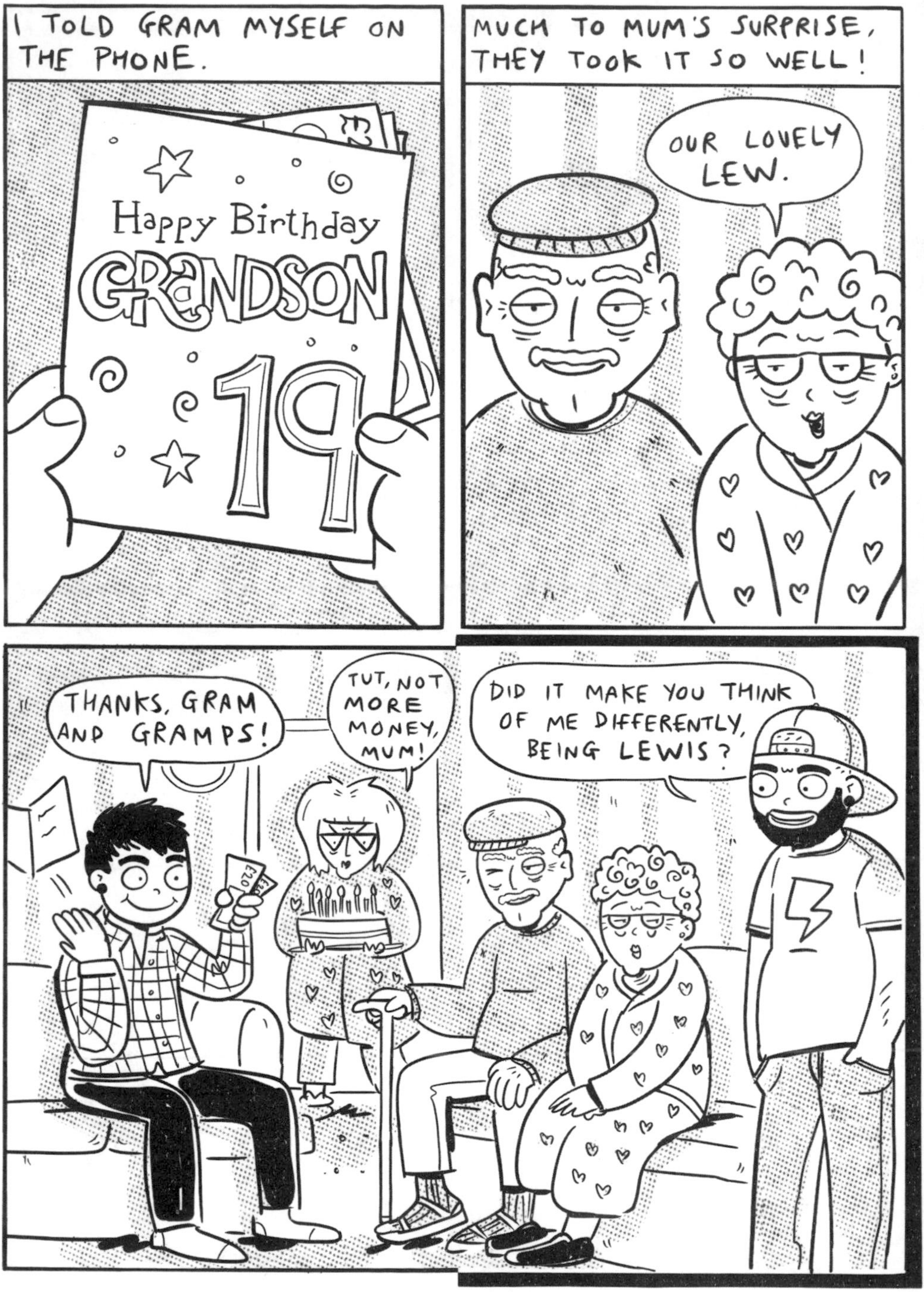
I TOLD GRAM MYSELF ON THE PHONE.
Happy Birthday GRANDSON 19
MUCH TO MUM'S SURPRISE, THEY TOOK IT SO WELL!
OUR LOVELY LEW.
THANKS, GRAM AND GRAMPS!
TUT, NOT MORE MONEY, MUM!
DID IT MAKE YOU THINK OF ME DIFFERENTLY, BEING LEWIS?

OOOH NO, LUV. MAKES US EVEN MORE PROTECTIVE. WE CAN'T IMAGINE YOU ANY DIFFERENT NOW. YOU'RE JUST LEWIS. WE ONLY WANT YOU TO BE HAPPY.

OH YES.

AND WE ALWAYS KNEW YOU WEREN'T HAPPY BEIN' A GIRL. EVER SINCE YOU WERE LITTLE AND YOU'D SNATCH THE CLOTHES OFF THE DOLL AND THROW IT DOWN THE STAIRS!

OH NO.

WHAT WOULD YOU SAY TO ANYONE HAVING A HARD TIME ACCEPTING THEIR TRANS GRANDCHILD?

THE SOONER THEY GET IN THE REAL WORLD, THE BETTER!

GRAMPS DROPPIN' TRUTH BOMBS.

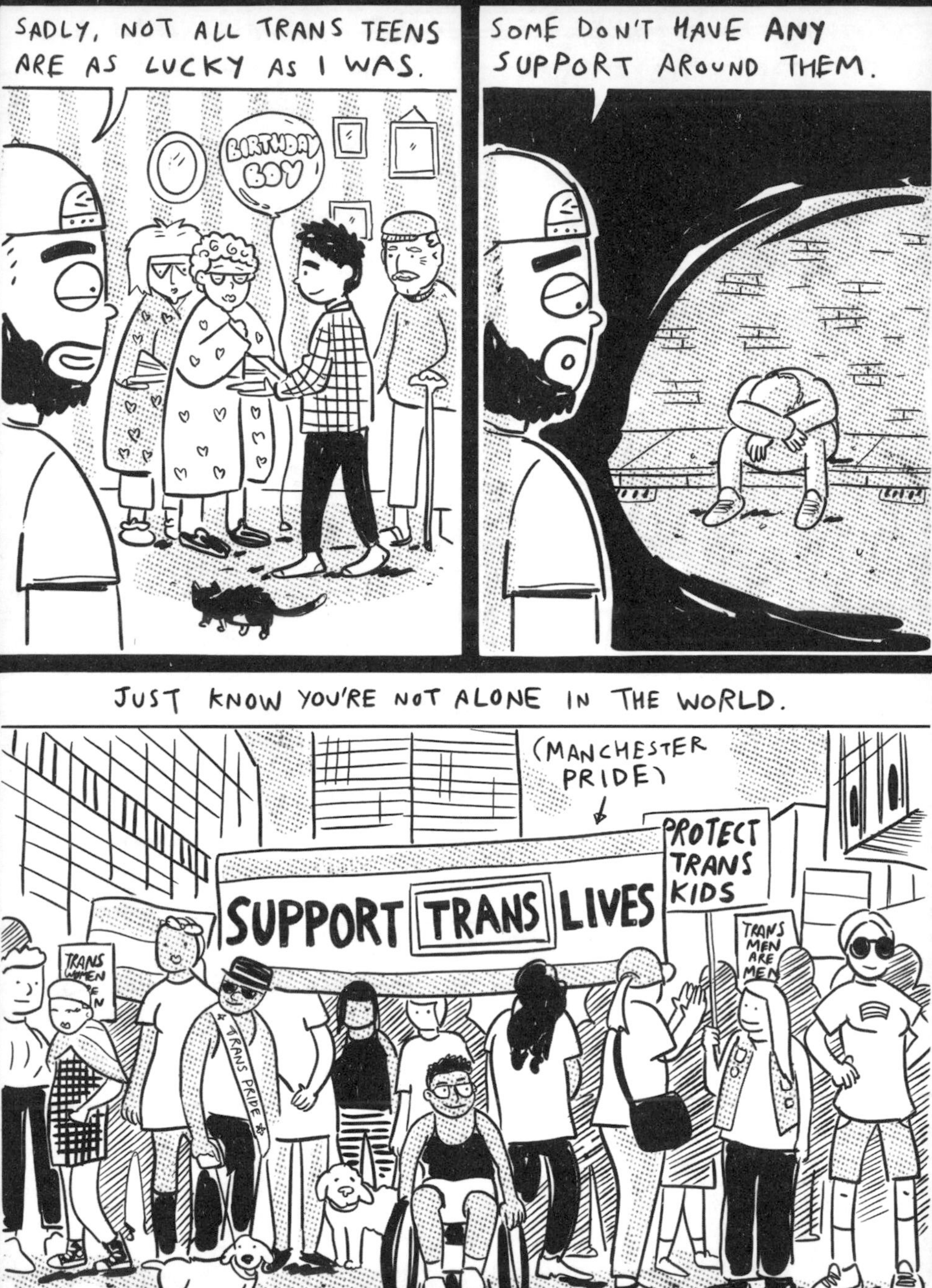
SADLY, NOT ALL TRANS TEENS ARE AS LUCKY AS I WAS.
BIRTHDAY BOY
SOME DON'T HAVE ANY SUPPORT AROUND THEM.
JUST KNOW YOU'RE NOT ALONE IN THE WORLD.
(MANCHESTER PRIDE)
SUPPORT TRANS LIVES
PROTECT TRANS KIDS
TRANS MEN ARE MEN
TRANS PRIDE

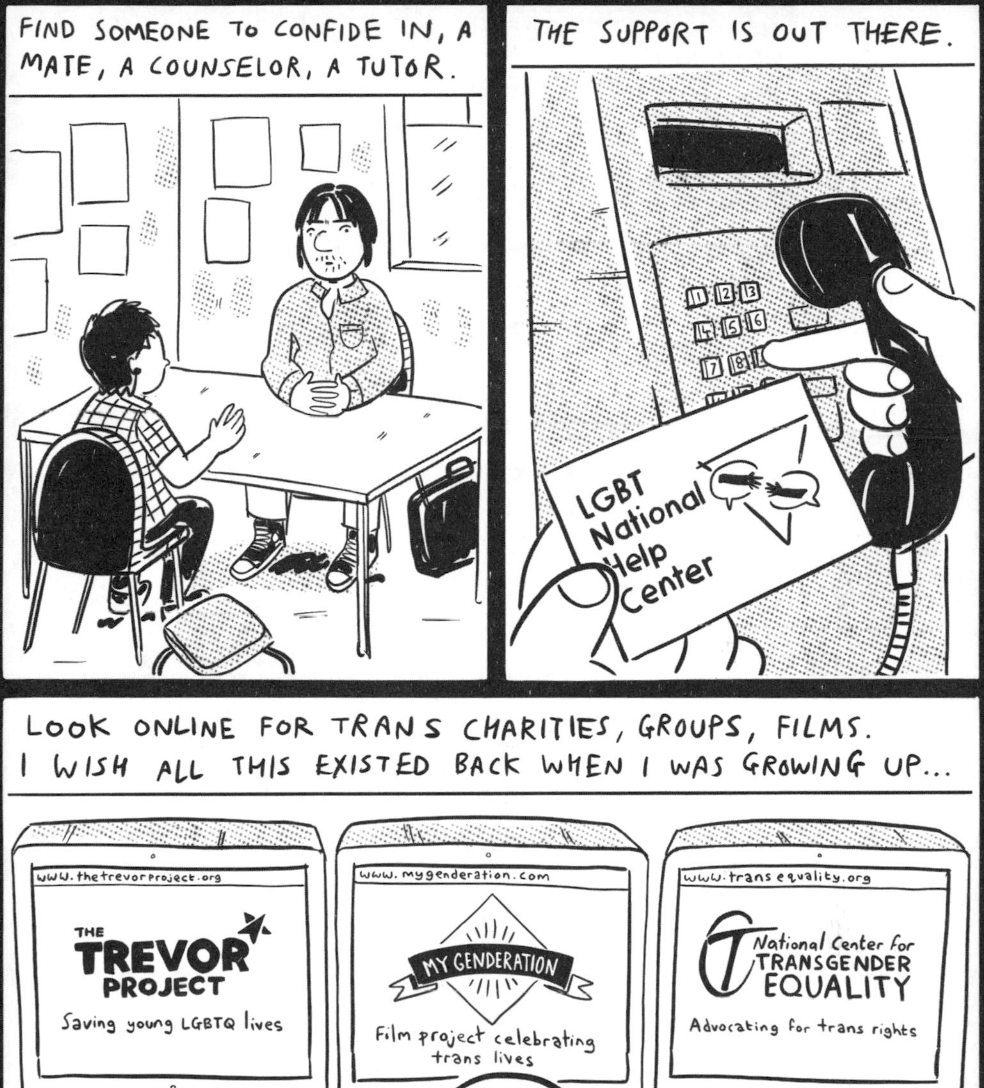
FIND SOMEONE TO CONFIDE IN, A MATE, A COUNSELOR, A TUTOR.
THE SUPPORT IS OUT THERE.
LGBT National Help Center
LOOK ONLINE FOR TRANS CHARITIES, GROUPS, FILMS. I WISH ALL THIS EXISTED BACK WHEN I WAS GROWING UP...
www.thetrevorproject.org
THE TREVOR PROJECT
Saving young LGBTQ lives
www.mygenderation.com
MY GENDERATION
Film project celebrating trans lives
www.transequality.org
National Center for TRANSGENDER EQUALITY
Advocating for trans rights

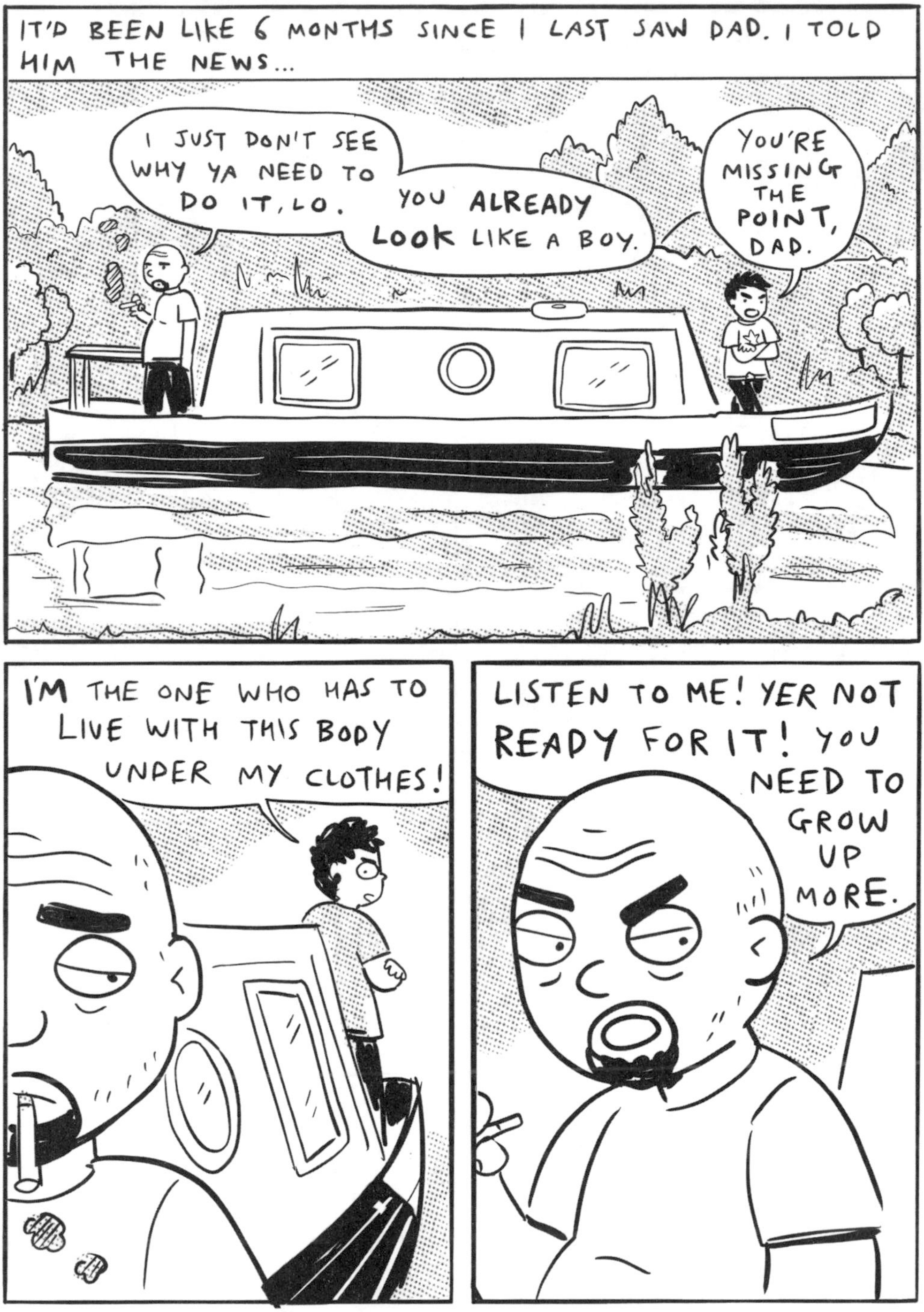
IT'D BEEN LIKE 6 MONTHS SINCE I LAST SAW DAD. I TOLD HIM THE NEWS...
I JUST DON'T SEE WHY YA NEED TO DO IT, LO.
YOU **ALREADY LOOK** LIKE A BOY.
YOU'RE MISSING THE POINT, DAD.
I'M THE ONE WHO HAS TO LIVE WITH THIS BODY UNDER MY CLOTHES!
LISTEN TO ME! YER NOT READY FOR IT! YOU NEED TO GROW UP MORE.

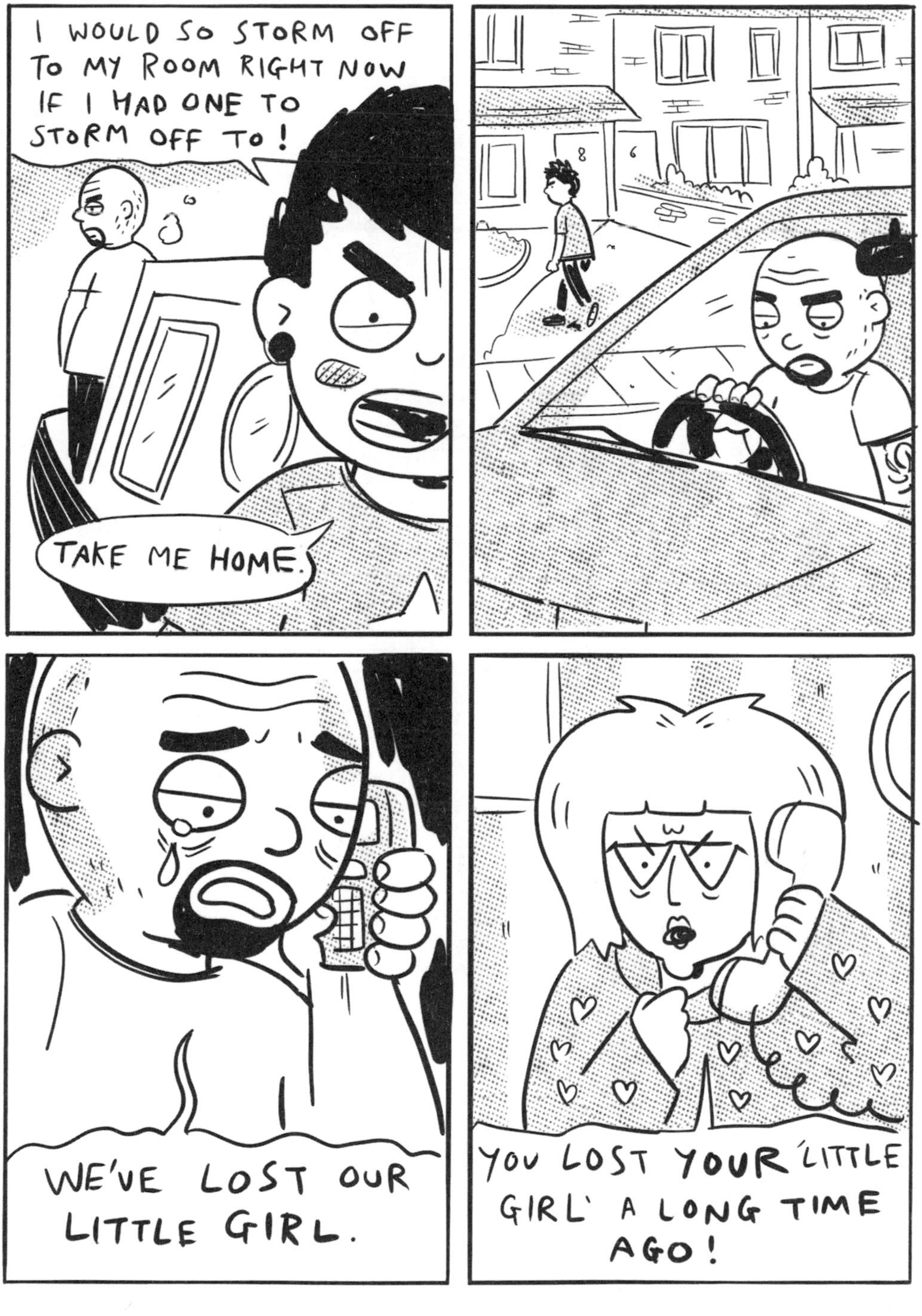
I WOULD SO STORM OFF TO MY ROOM RIGHT NOW IF I HAD ONE TO STORM OFF TO!
TAKE ME HOME.
WE'VE LOST OUR LITTLE GIRL.
YOU LOST YOUR 'LITTLE GIRL' A LONG TIME AGO!

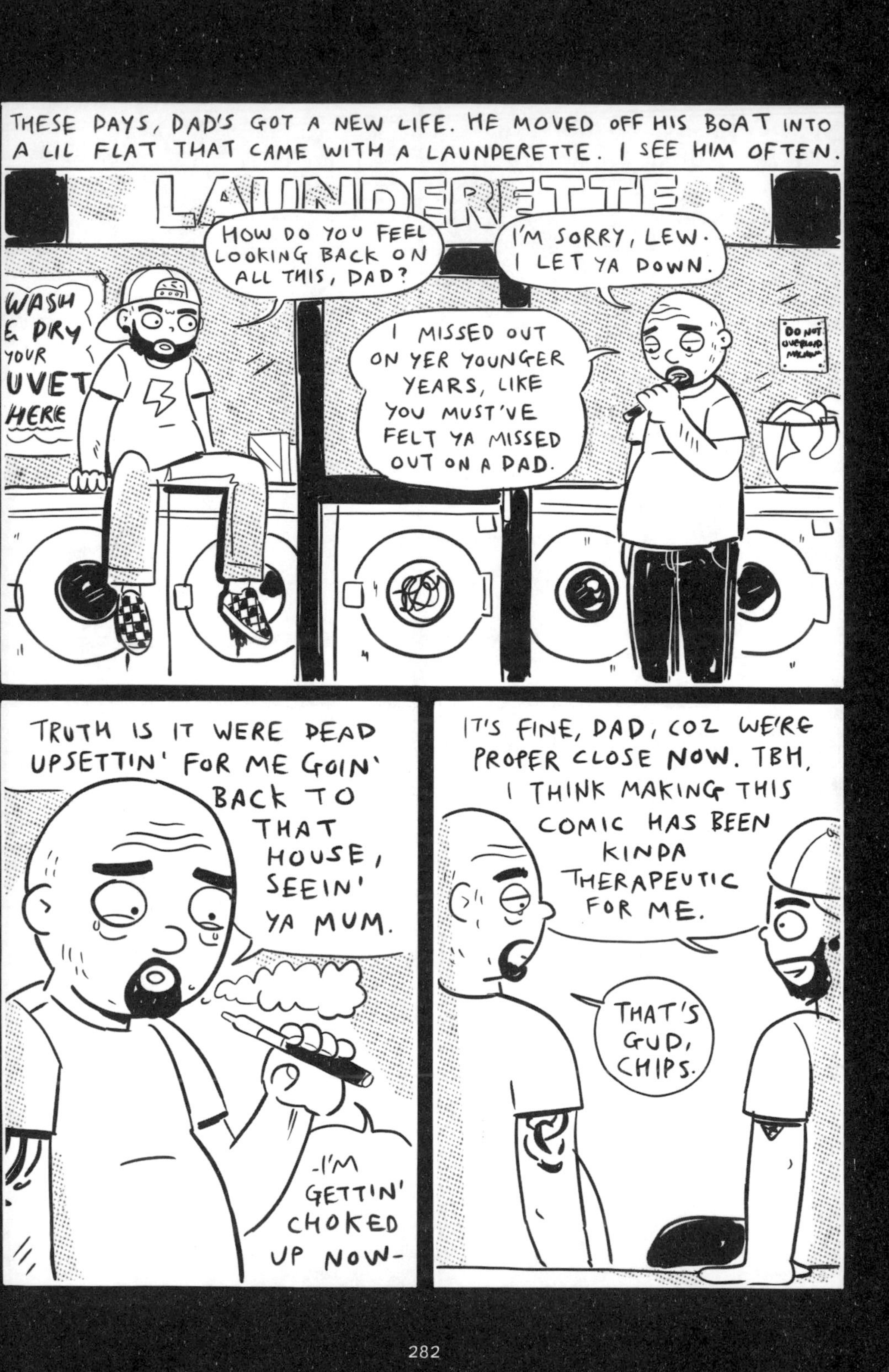
THESE DAYS, DAD'S GOT A NEW LIFE. HE MOVED OFF HIS BOAT INTO A LIL FLAT THAT CAME WITH A LAUNDERETTE. I SEE HIM OFTEN.
LAUNDERETTE
WASH & DRY YOUR UVET HERE
HOW DO YOU FEEL LOOKING BACK ON ALL THIS, DAD?
I'M SORRY, LEW. I LET YA DOWN.
I MISSED OUT ON YER YOUNGER YEARS, LIKE YOU MUST'VE FELT YA MISSED OUT ON A DAD.
TRUTH IS IT WERE DEAD UPSETTIN' FOR ME GOIN' BACK TO THAT HOUSE, SEEIN' YA MUM.
-I'M GETTIN' CHOKED UP NOW-
IT'S FINE, DAD, COZ WE'RE PROPER CLOSE NOW. TBH, I THINK MAKING THIS COMIC HAS BEEN KINDA THERAPEUTIC FOR ME.
THAT'S GUD, CHIPS.

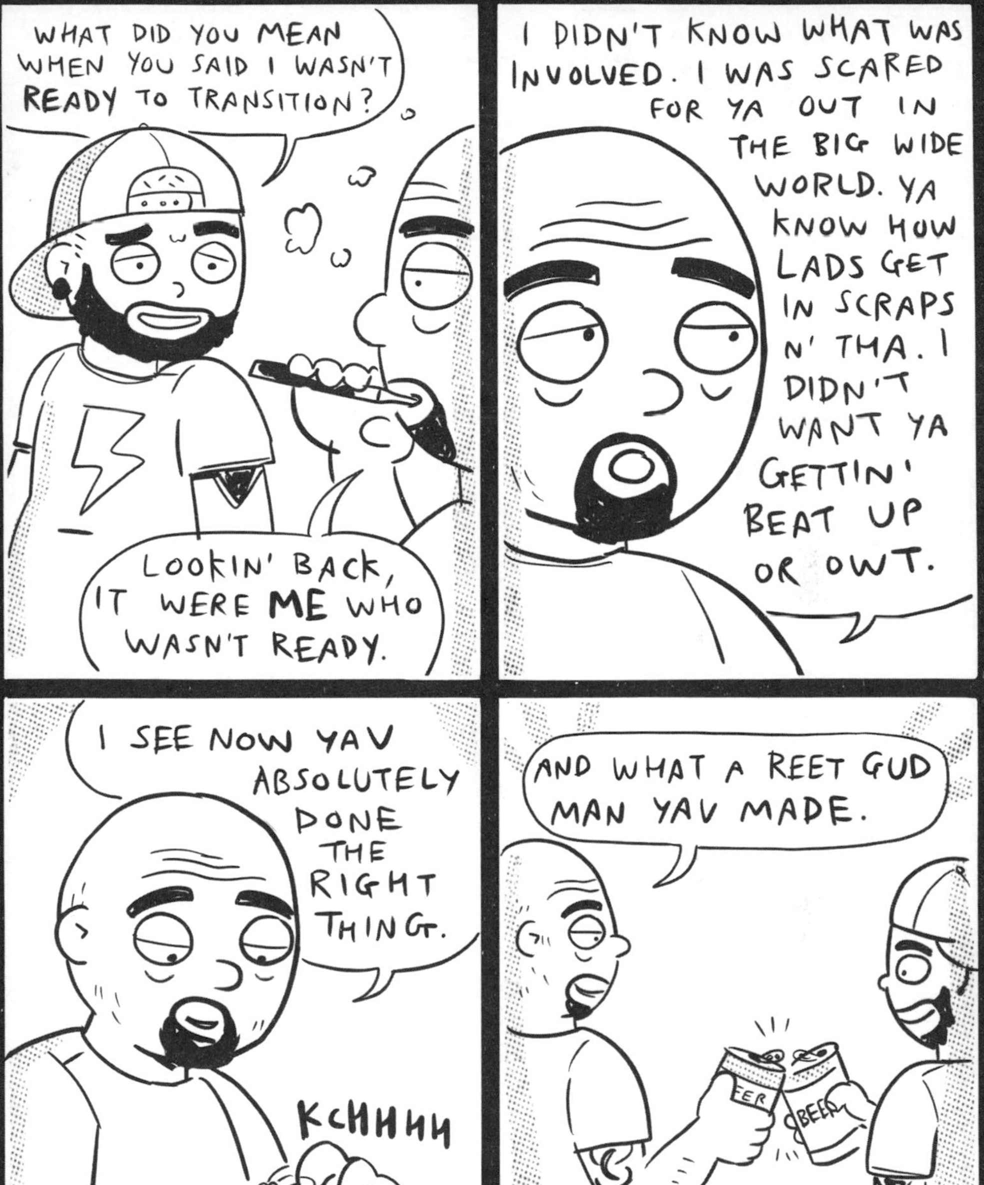
WHAT DID YOU MEAN WHEN YOU SAID I WASN'T READY TO TRANSITION?
LOOKIN' BACK, IT WERE ME WHO WASN'T READY.
I DIDN'T KNOW WHAT WAS INVOLVED. I WAS SCARED FOR YA OUT IN THE BIG WIDE WORLD. YA KNOW HOW LADS GET IN SCRAPS N' THA. I DIDN'T WANT YA GETTIN' BEAT UP OR OWT.
I SEE NOW YAV ABSOLUTELY DONE THE RIGHT THING.
KCHHHH
BEER
AND WHAT A REET GUD MAN YAV MADE.
BEER

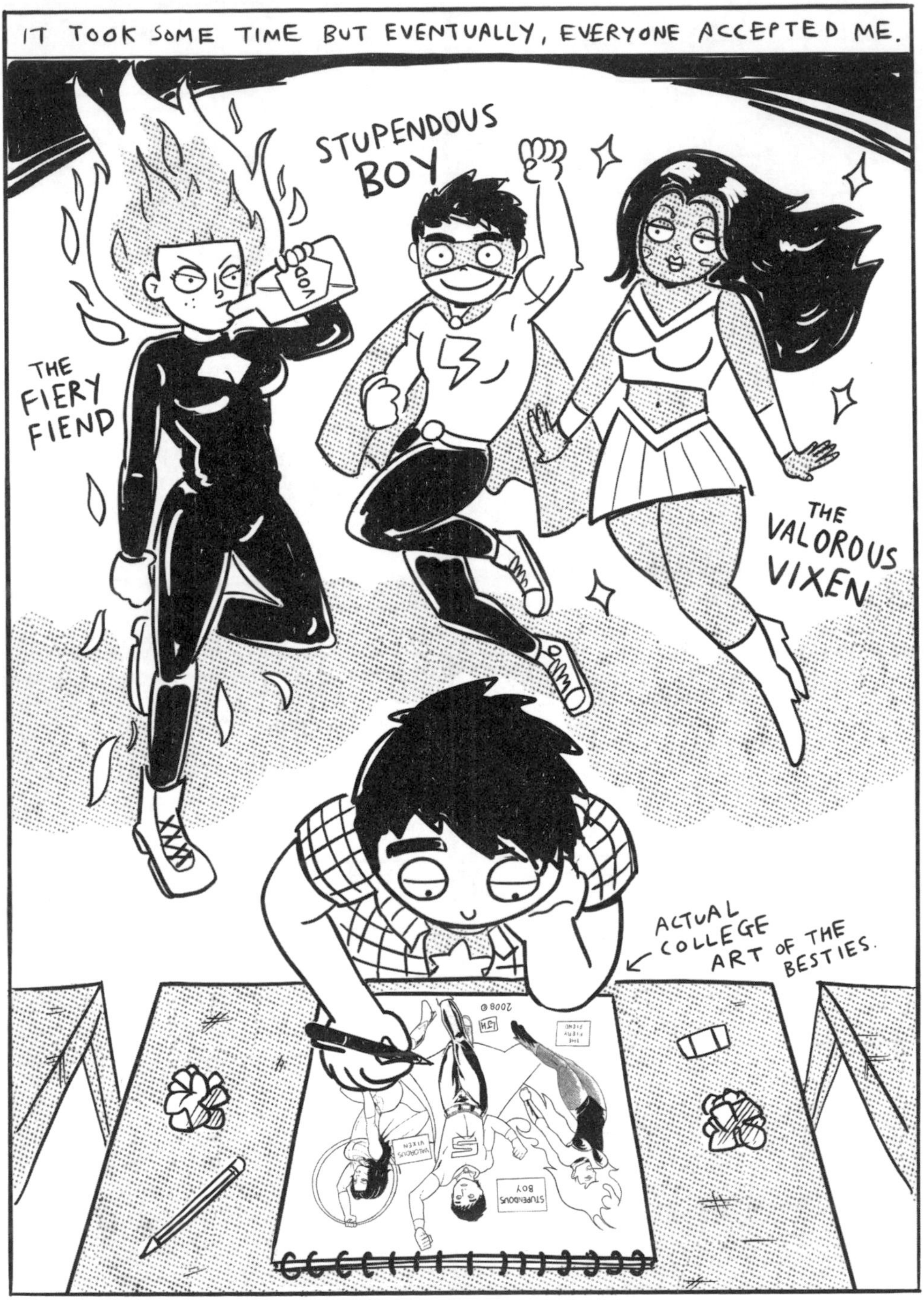
IT TOOK SOME TIME BUT EVENTUALLY, EVERYONE ACCEPTED ME.
STUPENDOUS BOY
THE FIERY FIEND
THE VALOROUS VIXEN
ACTUAL COLLEGE ART OF THE BESTIES.

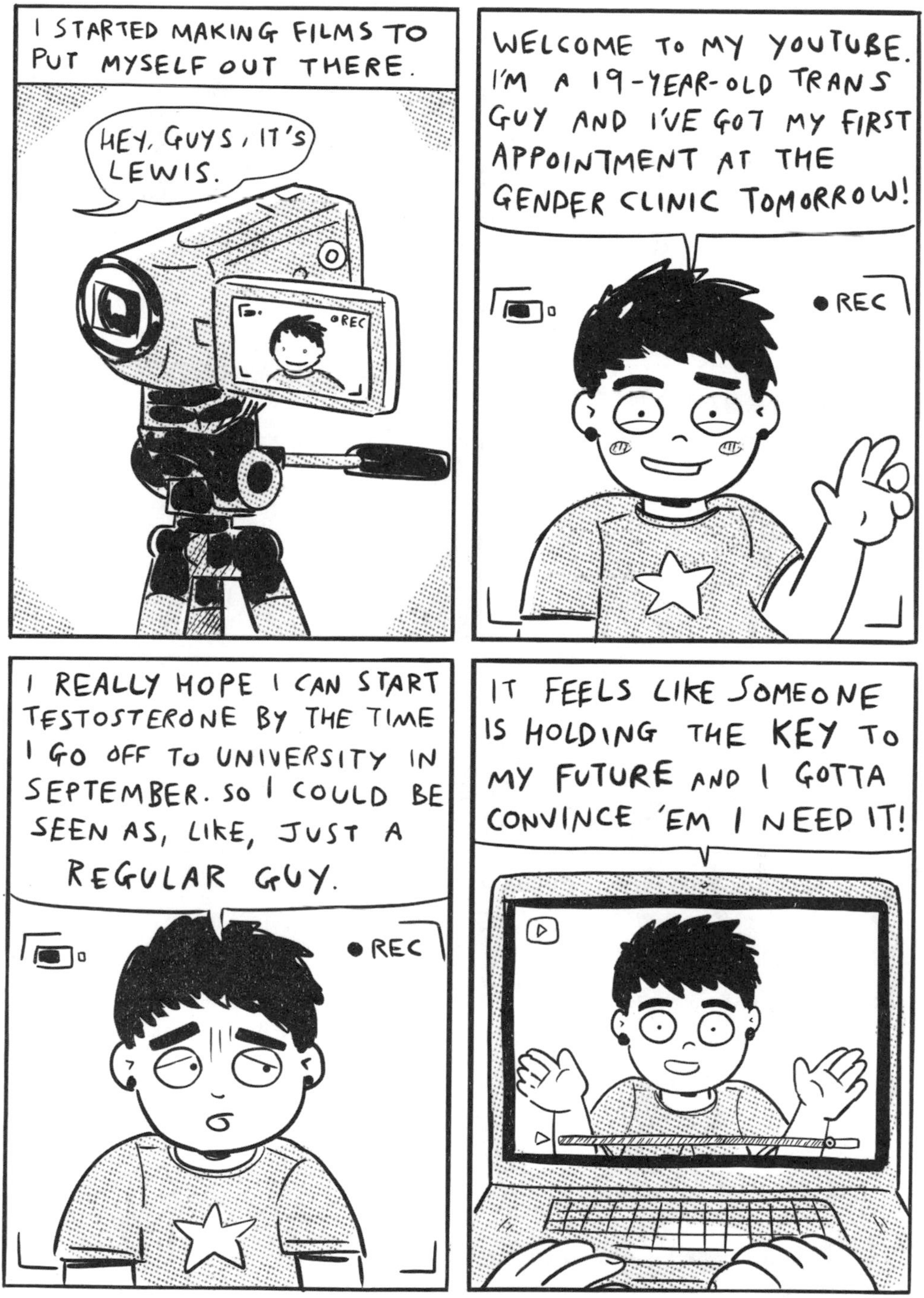
I STARTED MAKING FILMS TO PUT MYSELF OUT THERE.
HEY, GUYS, IT'S LEWIS.
REC
WELCOME TO MY YOUTUBE. I'M A 19-YEAR-OLD TRANS GUY AND I'VE GOT MY FIRST APPOINTMENT AT THE GENDER CLINIC TOMORROW!
REC
I REALLY HOPE I CAN START TESTOSTERONE BY THE TIME I GO OFF TO UNIVERSITY IN SEPTEMBER. SO I COULD BE SEEN AS, LIKE, JUST A REGULAR GUY.
REC
IT FEELS LIKE SOMEONE IS HOLDING THE KEY TO MY FUTURE AND I GOTTA CONVINCE 'EM I NEED IT!

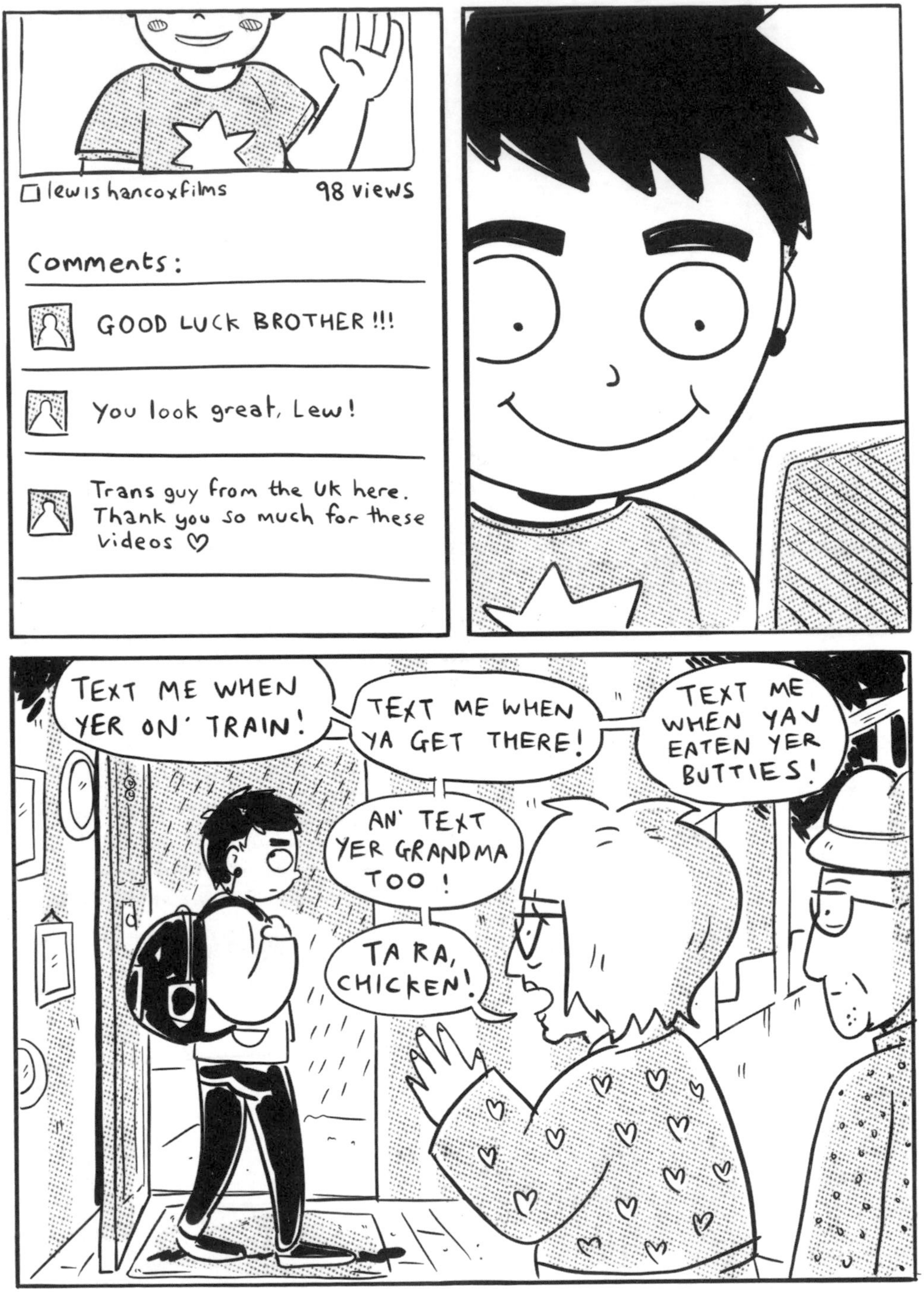
lewishancoxfilms
98 views
Comments:
GOOD LUCK BROTHER!!!
You look great, Lew!
Trans guy from the UK here. Thank you so much for these videos ♡
TEXT ME WHEN YER ON' TRAIN!
TEXT ME WHEN YA GET THERE!
TEXT ME WHEN YAV EATEN YER BUTTIES!
AN' TEXT YER GRANDMA TOO!
TA RA, CHICKEN!

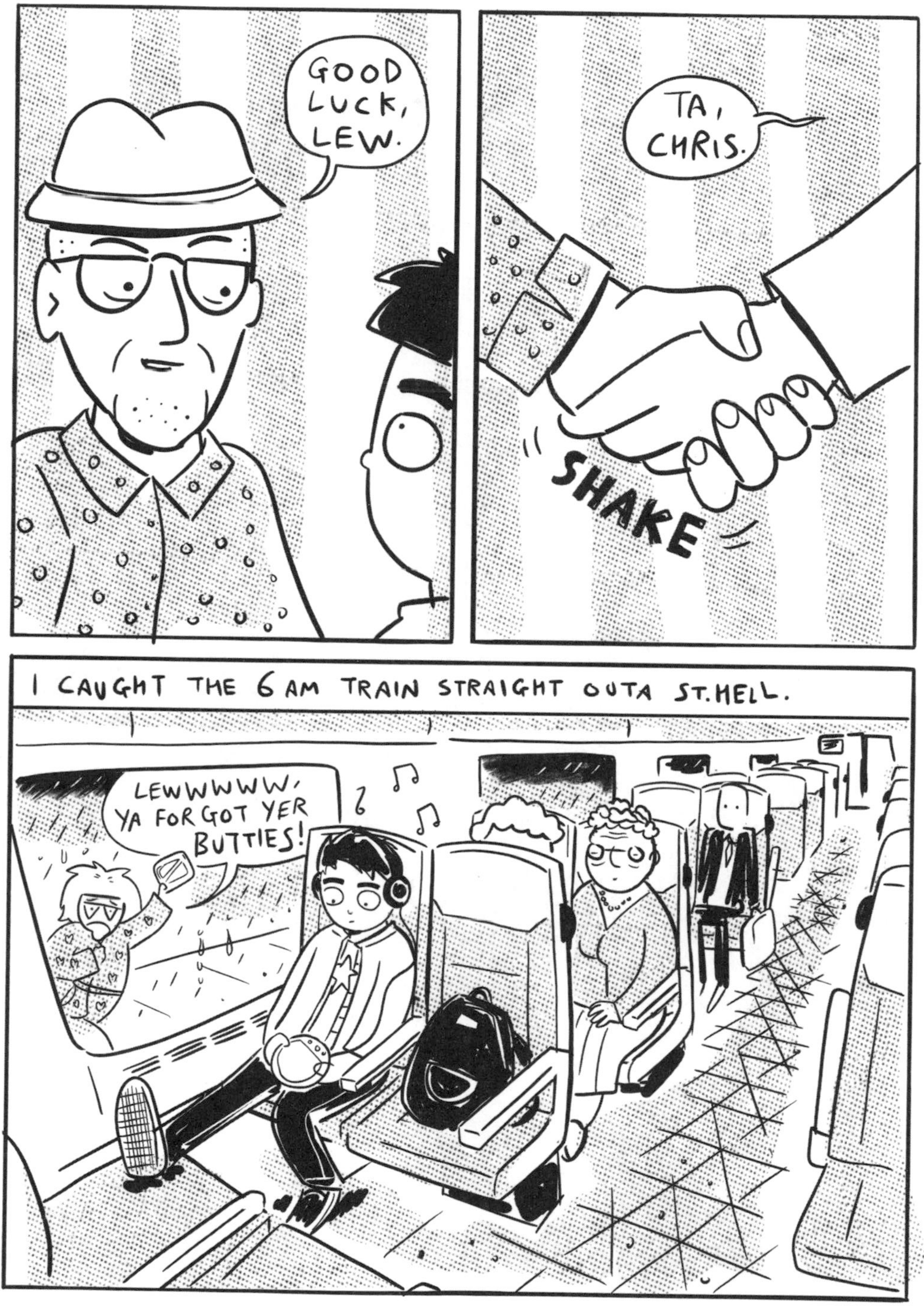
GOOD LUCK, LEW.
TA, CHRIS.
SHAKE
I CAUGHT THE 6 AM TRAIN STRAIGHT OUTA ST. HELL.
LEWWWWW, YA FORGOT YER BUTTIES!

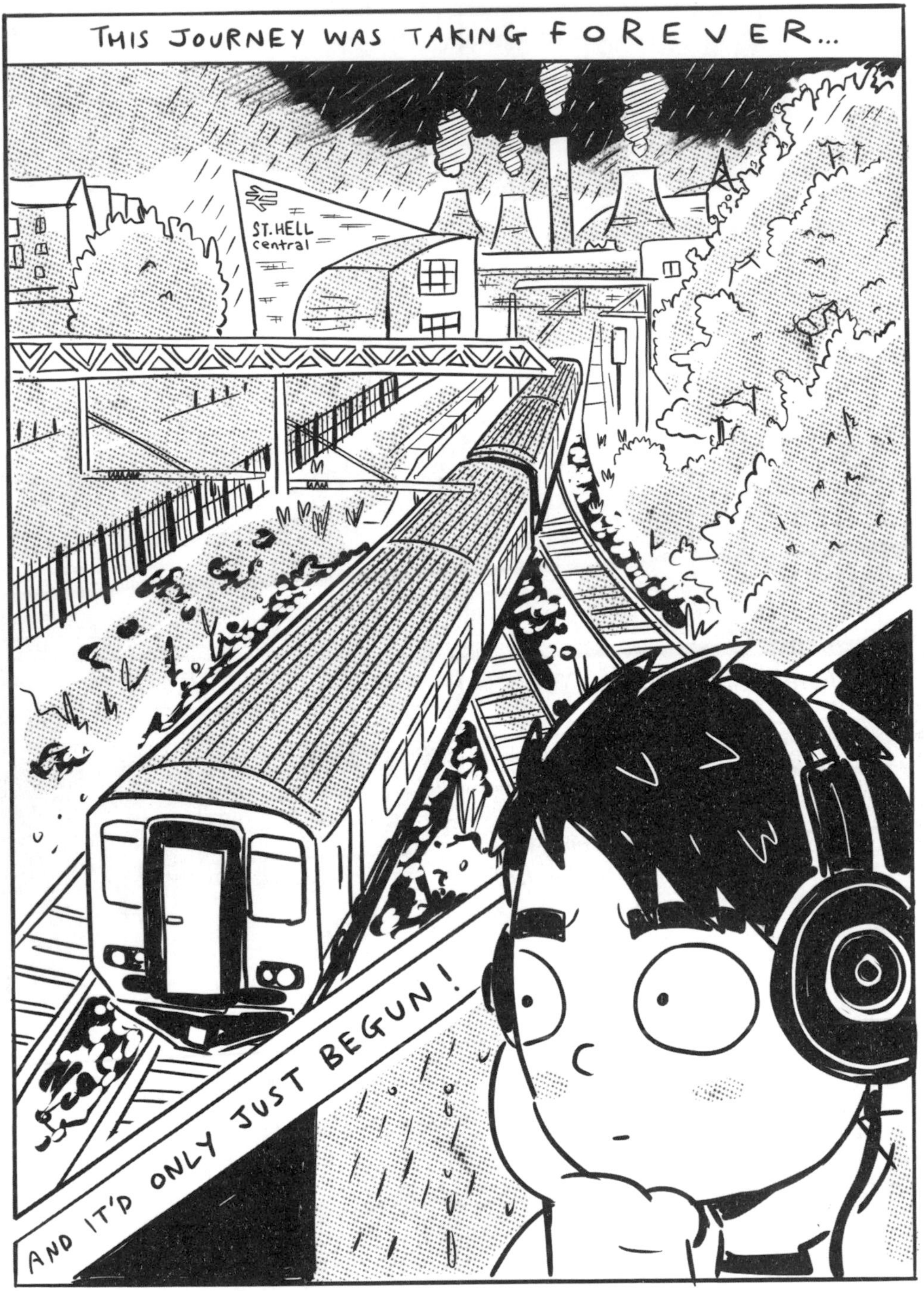
THIS JOURNEY WAS TAKING FOREVER...
ST. HELL central
AND IT'D ONLY JUST BEGUN!

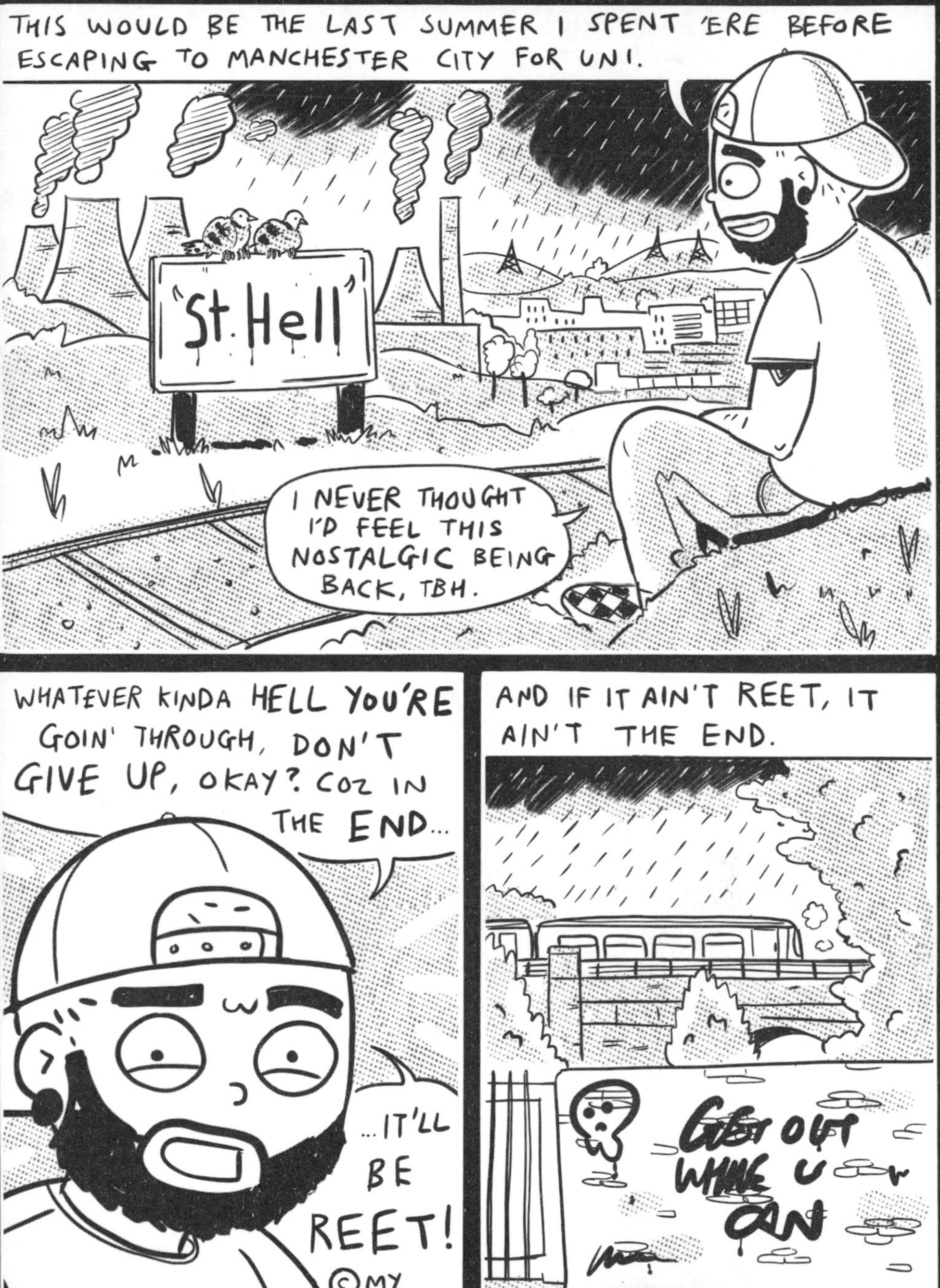
THIS WOULD BE THE LAST SUMMER I SPENT 'ERE BEFORE ESCAPING TO MANCHESTER CITY FOR UNI.
"St. Hell"
I NEVER THOUGHT I'D FEEL THIS NOSTALGIC BEING BACK, TBH.
WHATEVER KINDA HELL YOU'RE GOIN' THROUGH, DON'T GIVE UP, OKAY? COZ IN THE END...
...IT'LL BE REET!
© MY DAD
AND IF IT AIN'T REET, IT AIN'T THE END.
GET OUT WHILE U CAN

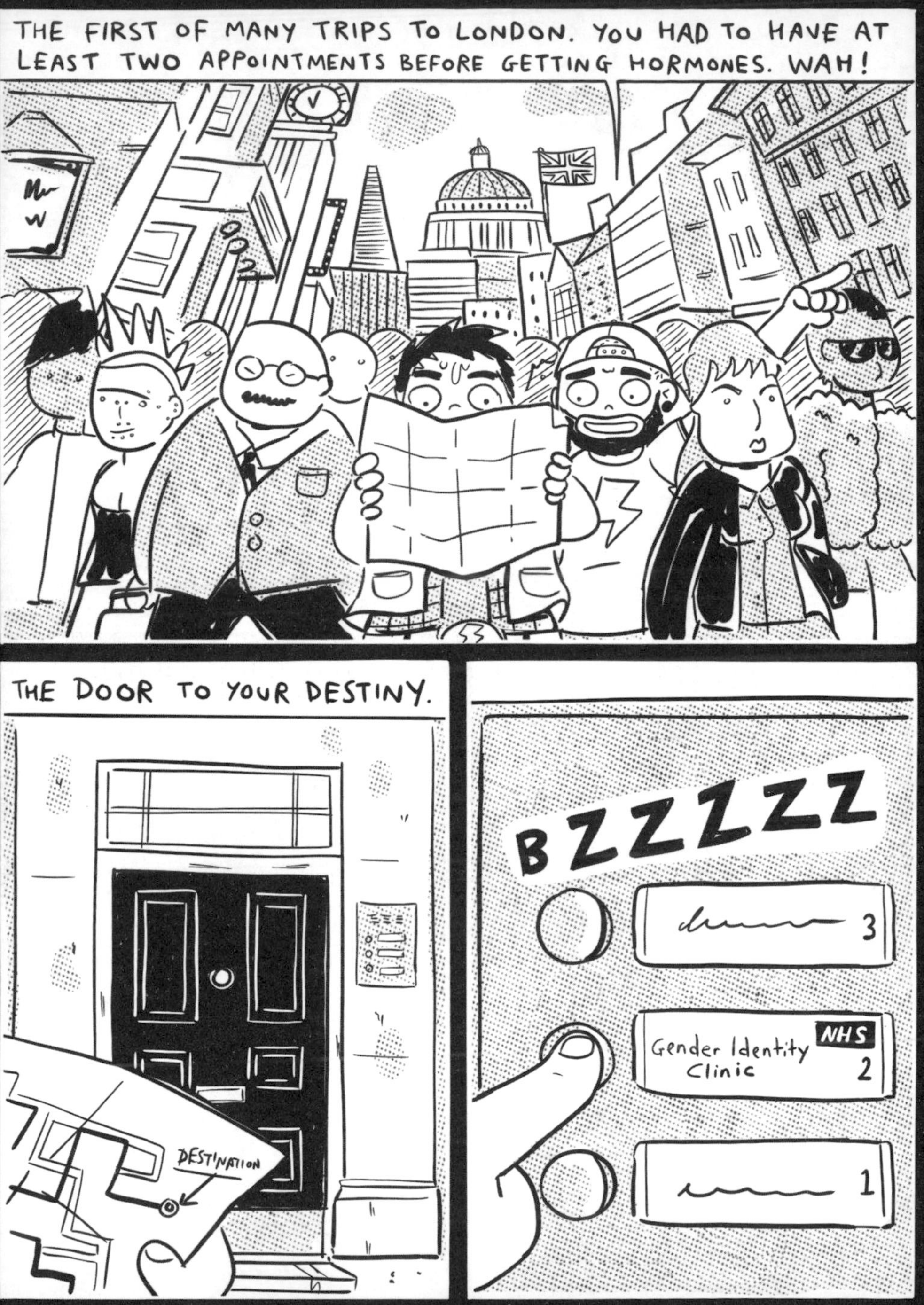
THE FIRST OF MANY TRIPS TO LONDON. YOU HAD TO HAVE AT LEAST TWO APPOINTMENTS BEFORE GETTING HORMONES. WAH!
THE DOOR TO YOUR DESTINY.
DESTINATION
BZZZZZ
3
Gender Identity Clinic
NHS
2
1

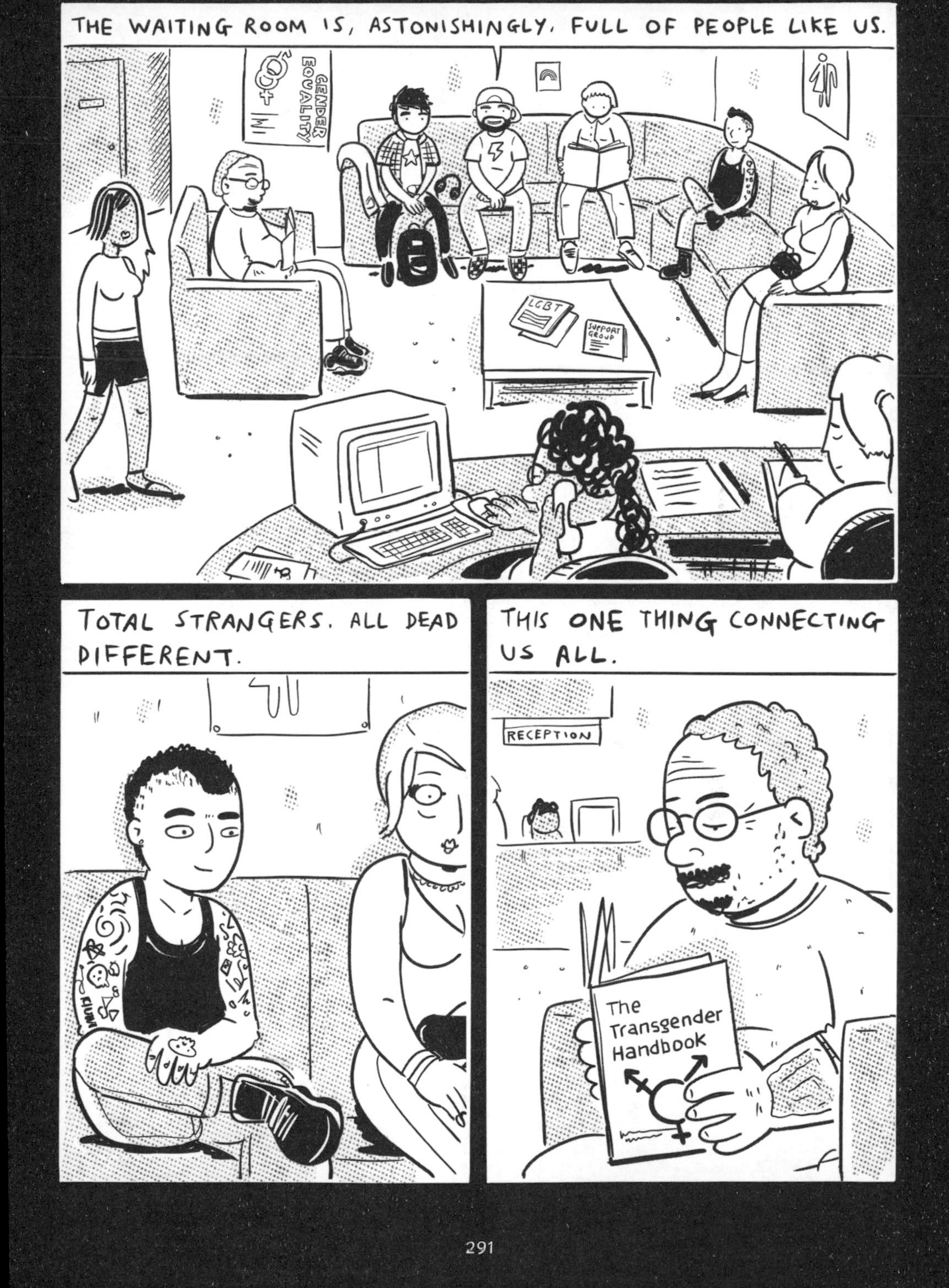
THE WAITING ROOM IS, ASTONISHINGLY, FULL OF PEOPLE LIKE US.
GENDER EQUALITY
LGBT
SUPPORT GROUP
TOTAL STRANGERS. ALL DEAD DIFFERENT.
THIS ONE THING CONNECTING US ALL.
RECEPTION
The Transgender Handbook

LEVEL 1 BOSS:

WHEN DID YOU FIRST SHOW SIGNS OF FEELING DISCOMFORT WITH YOUR GENDER?

WAAHHHH HHH HH HH

WHAT'S YOUR RELATIONSHIP LIKE WITH YOUR BODY?

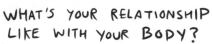

TOXIC.
WE WANNA BREAK UP

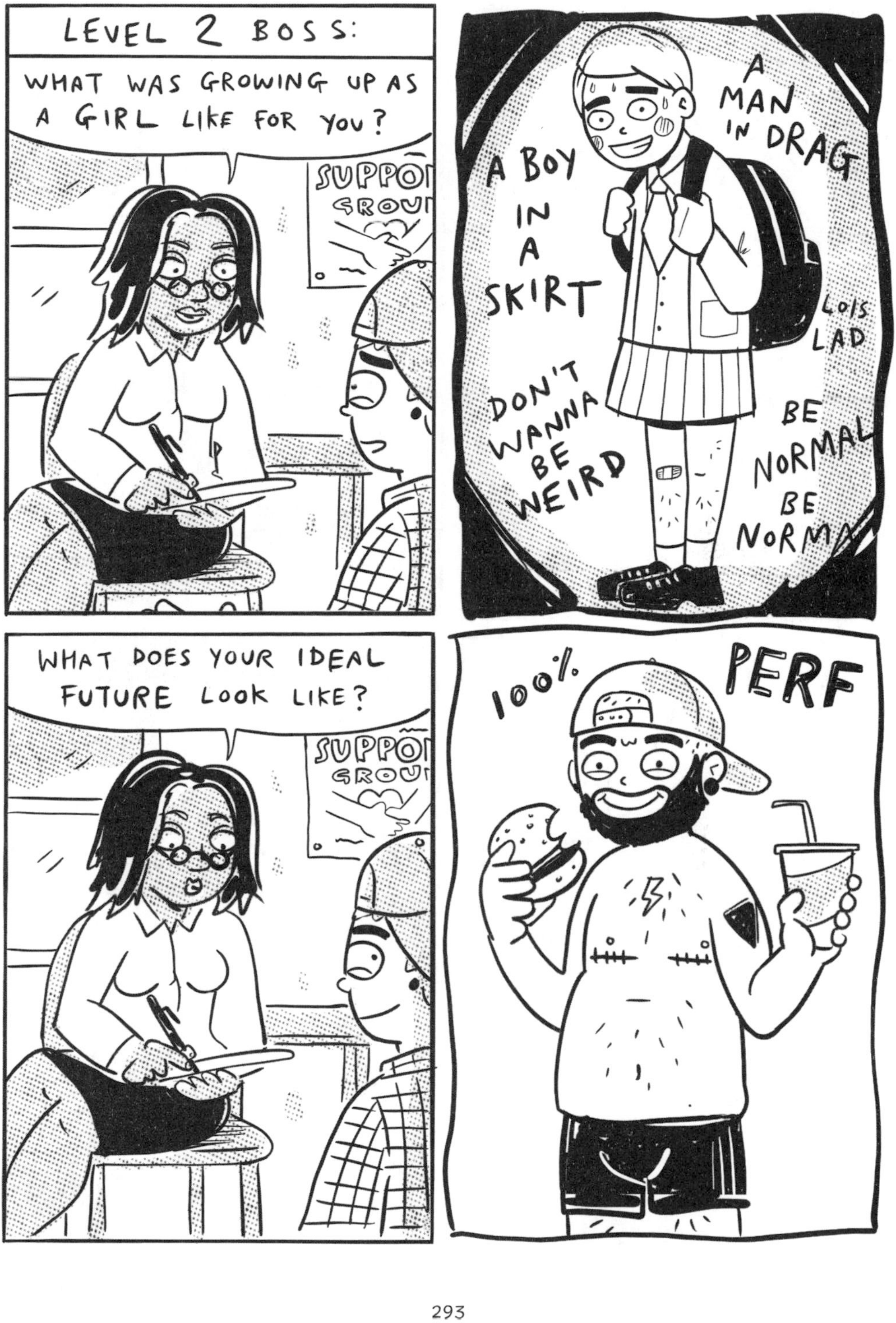
LEVEL 2 BOSS:
WHAT WAS GROWING UP AS A GIRL LIKE FOR YOU?
SUPPO
GROU
A BOY IN A SKIRT
A MAN IN DRAG
LOIS LAD
DON'T WANNA BE WEIRD
BE NORMAL
BE NORMA
WHAT DOES YOUR IDEAL FUTURE LOOK LIKE?
SUPPO
GROU
100%
PERF

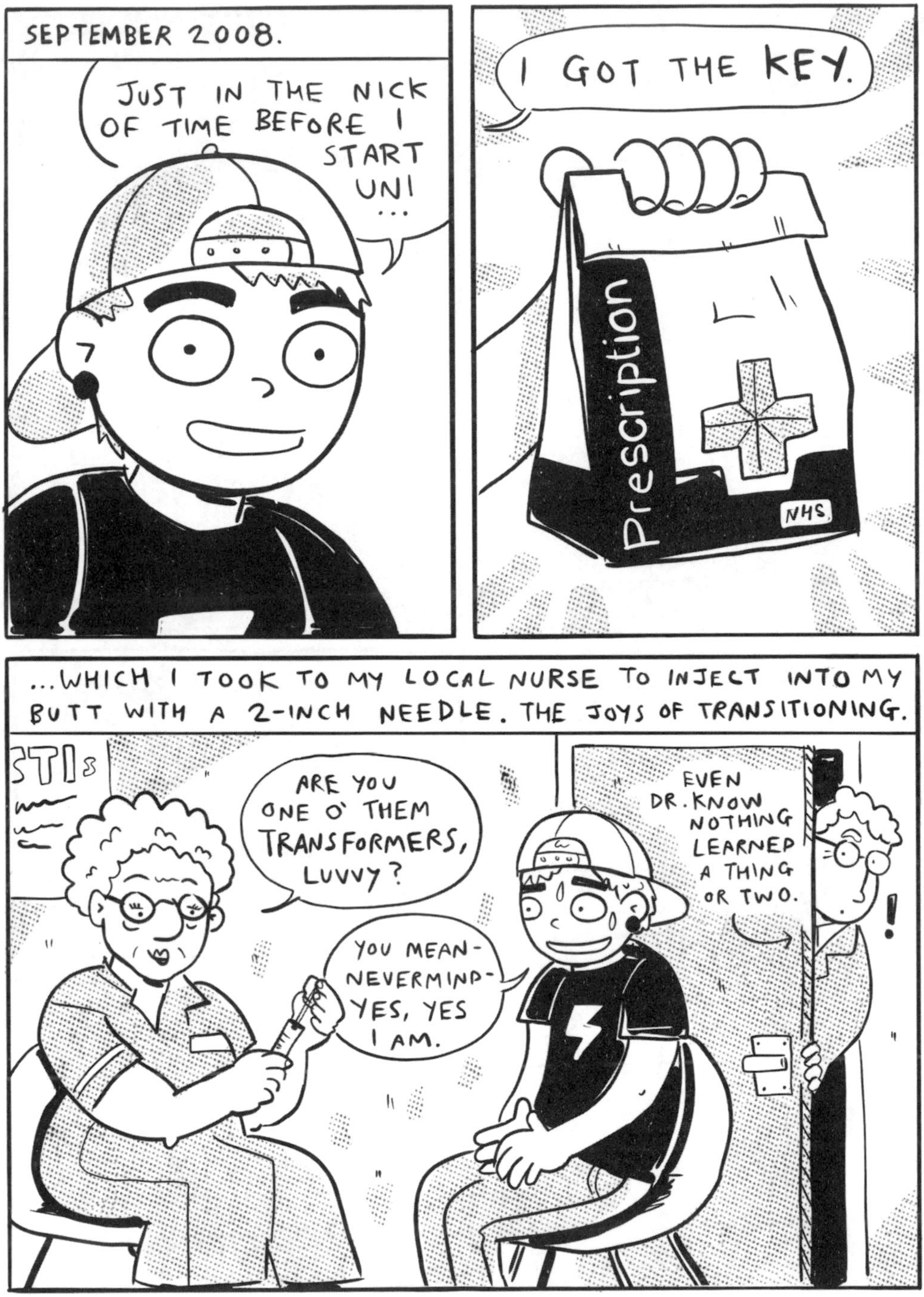
SEPTEMBER 2008.
JUST IN THE NICK OF TIME BEFORE I START UNI ...
I GOT THE KEY.
Prescription
NHS
...WHICH I TOOK TO MY LOCAL NURSE TO INJECT INTO MY BUTT WITH A 2-INCH NEEDLE. THE JOYS OF TRANSITIONING.
STIs
ARE YOU ONE O' THEM TRANSFORMERS, LUVVY?
YOU MEAN- NEVERMIND- YES, YES I AM.
EVEN DR. KNOW NOTHING LEARNED A THING OR TWO.
!

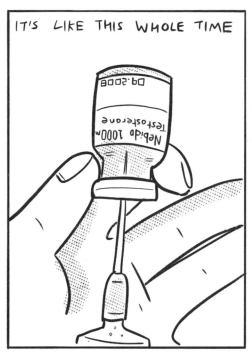

IT'S LIKE THIS WHOLE TIME

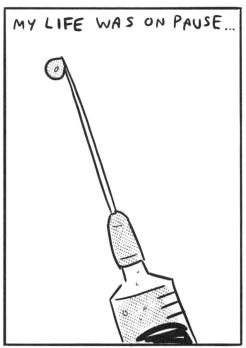

MY LIFE WAS ON PAUSE...

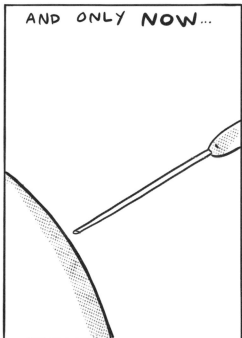

AND ONLY **NOW**...

WAS I ABOUT TO

Press Start

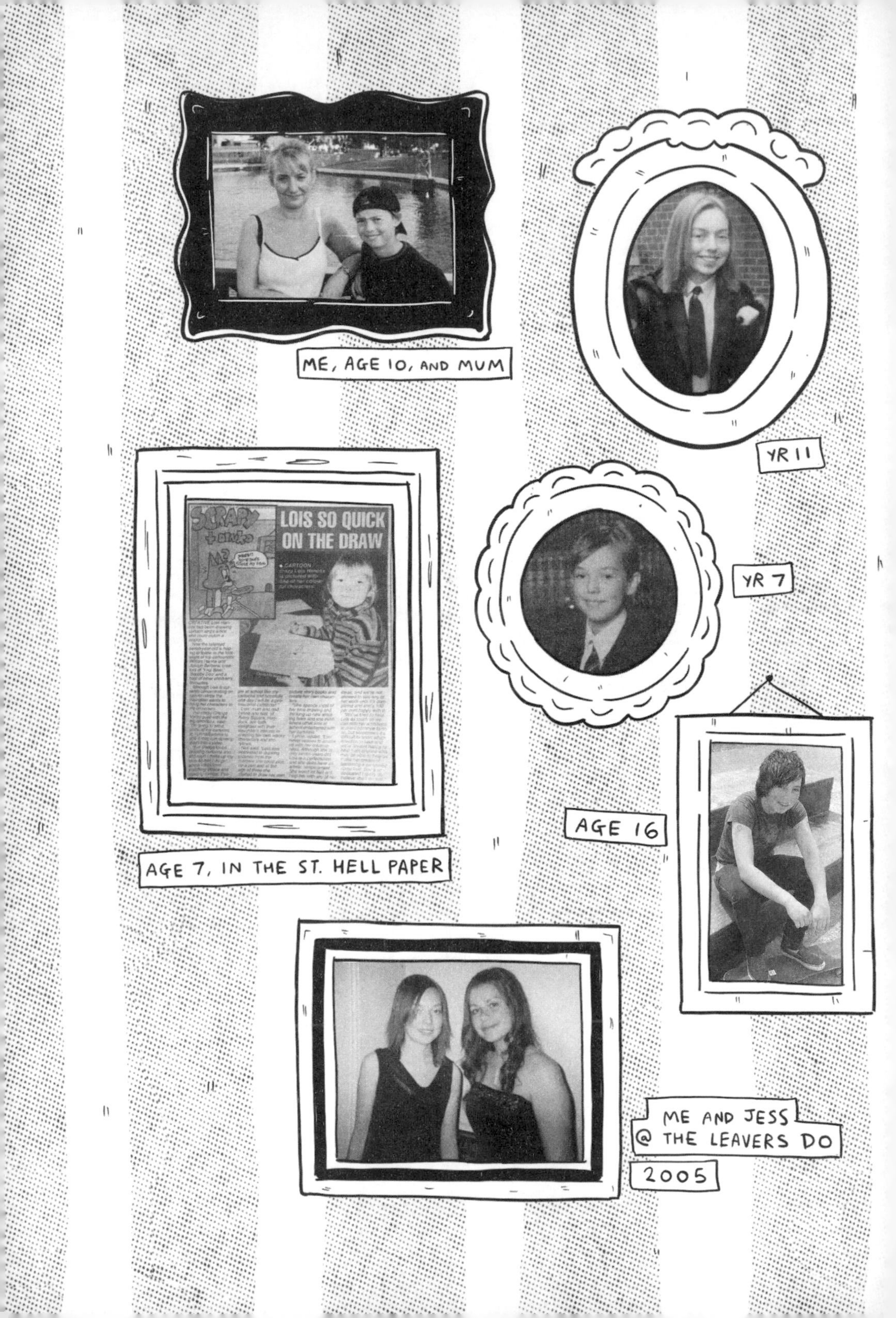
ME, AGE 10, AND MUM
YR 11
LOIS SO QUICK ON THE DRAW
YR 7
AGE 7, IN THE ST. HELL PAPER
AGE 16
ME AND JESS
@ THE LEAVERS DO
2005

ME, ALISON, AND JESS. 2007

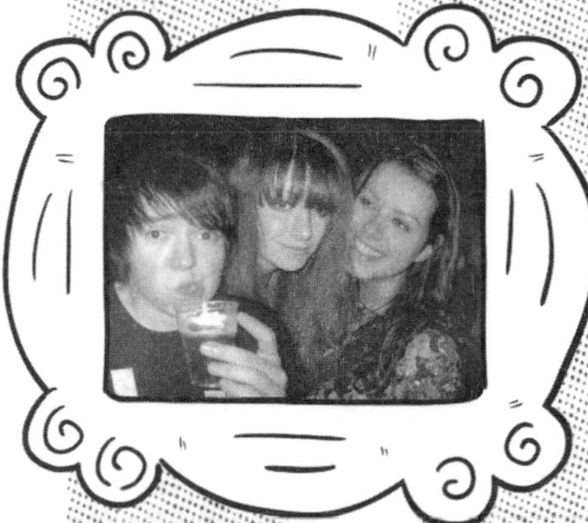

WEDNESDAYS @ WOBBLY BOBS

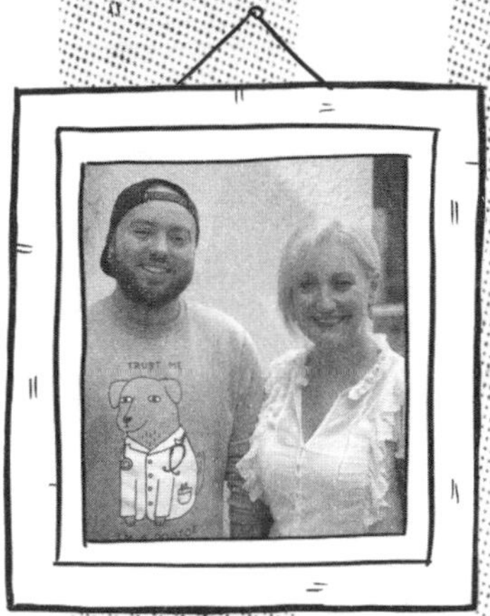

ME AND MUM. 2021

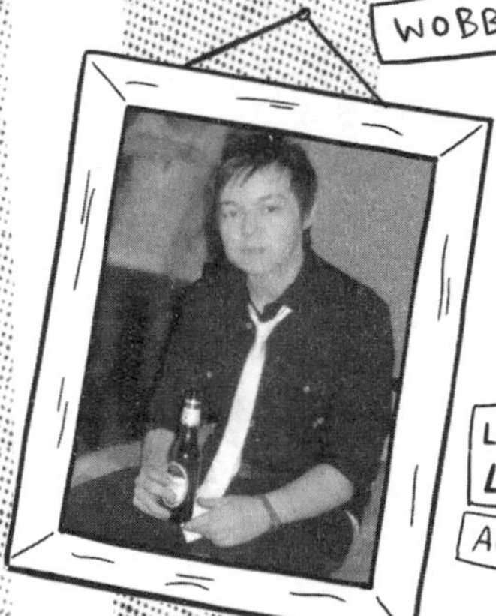

LIVIN' AS **LEWIS**
AGE 19

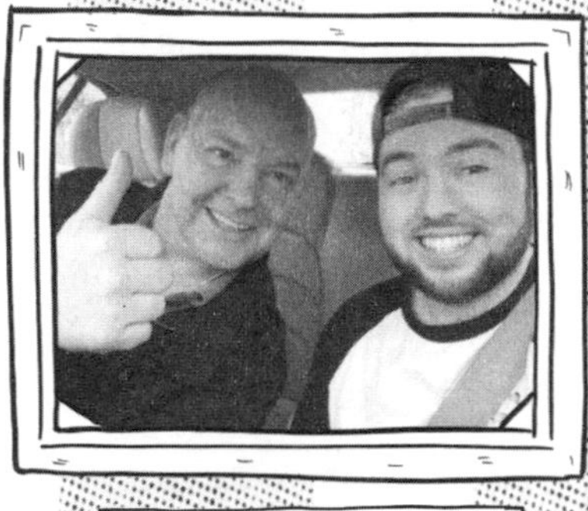

DAD AND ME. 2018

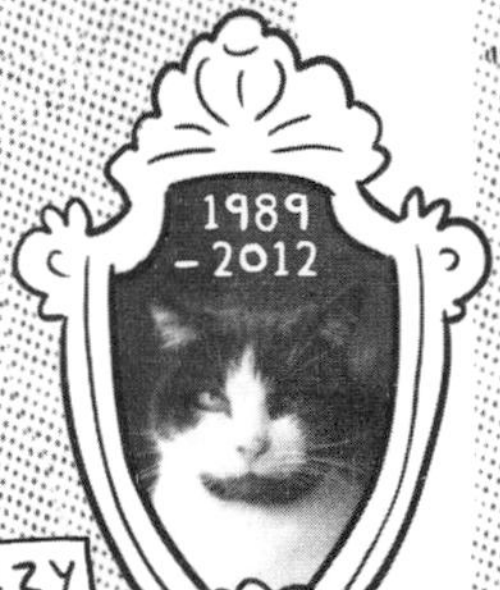
1989 - 2012

GIZZY

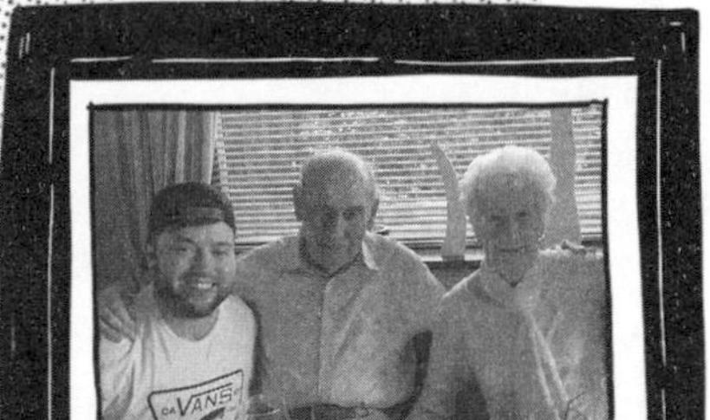

ME, GRAMPS, AND GRAM. 2017

ACKNOWLEDGMENTS

For anyone like me, I hope this book has brought you some cringey kind of comfort. If you're at the start of your transition and your doctor isn't giving you the information you need, or if you are feeling isolated and need someone to talk to, please reach out to local and online support groups like Trans Lifeline at translifeline.org. There is a loving community out there for you–don't give up!

I'd like to acknowledge my mum, my dad, and all my mates– especially Jess, the two Alisons, the two Mattys I grew up with, Melka, Laura, Fox, Jakki, Amei, and the rest of you– for all your support and for bringing different perspectives and meaning into my life. Without you, there would be no story to tell! Special thanks to Mum for reading every draft with her eagle eyes.

I'm forever grateful for my agent, Jenny Heller, who totally just "gets me" and pushed me to create something I'm actually proud of for once. My UK editor, Leah James; my US editor, David Levithan; and the whole Scholastic team. I've never known such encouragement and appreciation for what I do.

Finally, I'd like to thank my girlfriend, Jo–who is a constant, colourful source of inspiration. Along with our two cats, Evie and Emeress, she kept me going through the love/hate relationship with this book. Ta, luv!